The
Collected Papers
of
Sherlock
Holmes
Volume II - Records
Sherlock Holmes:
Tangled Skeins
and
Sherlock Holmes and
The Eye of Heka

New Sherlock Holmes

THE COLLECTED PAPERS

OF

SHERLOCK HOLMES

*A Florilegium of Sherlockian Adventures
in Multiple Volumes*

FROM THE NOTEBOOKS OF DR. JOHN H. WATSON, M.D.

VOLUME II — RECORDS
(5 SHORT STORIES AND A NOVEL)
SHERLOCK HOLMES — TANGLED SKEINS
AND
SHERLOCK HOLMES AND THE EYE OF HEKA

BY
DAVID
MARCUM

MX PUBLISHING

Published by MX PUBLISHING, 335 PRINCESS PARK MANOR, London, England.

ISBN Hardback 978-1-78705-903-0
ISBN Paperback 978-1-78705-904-7
AUK ePub ISBN 978-1-78705-905-4
AUK PDF ISBN 978-1-78705-906-1

Published by
MX Publishing
335 Princess Park Manor, Royal Drive,
London, N11 3GX
www.mxpublishing.com

David Marcum can be reached at:
thepapersofsherlockholmes@gmail.com

Cover design by Brian Belanger
www.belangerbooks.com and *www.redbubble.com/people/zhahadun*

Internal illustrations by Sidney Paget

CONTENTS

Forewords

Records

Sherlock Holmes – Tangled Skeins

Sherlock Holmes and The Eye of Heka

(Continued on the next page . . . .)

Sources

Sherlock Holmes – Tangled Skeins was originally published by MX Publishing in 2015

Sherlock Holmes and The Eye of Heka was originally published by MX Publishing in 2021

These additional adventures are contained in
Volume I – Tales
(9 Short Stories and a Novel)

Volume III – Accounts
(22 Holmes Adventures)

(Continued on the next page . . . .)

As always, this is for Rebecca and Dan, with all my love

"It's all one case."
by David Marcum

It's all about playing The Game.

That's the bottom-line reason behind these stories. And what is The Game? For those who don't know, it's reading the Sherlock Holmes stories with the firm belief that he and Watson were real historical figures. That Dr. Watson wrote the stories, and Sir Arthur Conan Doyle was his Literary Agent. That Our Heroes actually lived in Baker Street (for a couple of decades, off and on, and not forever) and solved real cases for real people, even if names and places and dates were changed and obfuscated to protect the innocent, or maybe because Watson's handwriting was bad, or because of some hidden agenda that the Literary Agent needed to fulfill.

By acknowledging that Holmes and Watson were real, living, breathing, functioning people, then it's a given that were born, lived, and died. (No magic immortal detectives need apply!) And if they were born and lived and died, then these lives occurred across a fixed period. These men aren't Time Lords who can be picked up and dropped into other eras, or supernaturally gifted monster hunters in a world where such things exist, and they cannot be remade into a plethora of completely different people to fit whatever agenda some current reader needs to project upon them.

No, the stories in these books are about the same Sherlock Holmes and Dr. Watson that one finds in the original Canon – those pitifully few sixty stories that were published from 1887 to 1927.

I've enjoyed the notion that Mr. Sherlock Holmes was real from nearly the same time that I discovered him – as a boy of ten in 1975. Before I'd even read many of the Canonical adventures, I found two other books that reinforced this idea: William S. Baring-Gould's biography *Sherlock Holmes of Baker Street* (1962), with its chronology of the events in Holmes's long and amazing life (1854-1957), and also Nicholas Meyer's *The Seven-Per-Cent Solution* (1974), in which Holmes meets historical figures such as Sigmund Freud. How could one read those books, especially at that age, and not be convinced that Holmes was real?

In the decades that have passed since then, my interest in Mr. Holmes has only grown. While I read and collect a great many volumes about my other "book friends", as my son called them when he was small – and there

1

are a great lot of them besides Holmes – I've always had a special interest in the consulting detective in Baker Street and his Boswell. Since obtaining my first Holmes book in 1975, I've managed to collect and read (and create a massively dense chronology for) literally thousands of traditional Canonical adventures. I've worn a deerstalker as my only hat, all year long and everywhere since age nineteen. I've been able to make three extensive Holmes Pilgrimages to England and Scotland (so far), wherein I pretty much visited only Holmes-related sites. So it was probably inevitable that, in 2008, I started writing Holmes adventures.

I'd always wanted to write, all the way back to when I was eight years old and intensely reading about The Three Investigators and The Hardy Boys. Not satisfied with just the official publications, I wanted more new stories too. I spent quite a few Saturdays of my young boyhood tapping away on my dad's typewriter to create new "books".

As I grew, I dabbled with writing little short pieces, mostly humorous, just intended to make family members laugh, because I loved to write, and it always came easily to me. By the late 1980's, I was a U.S. Federal Investigator employed by an obscure government agency, often sent away from home for long periods, conducting investigations that lasted anywhere from five weeks to three months. Once, when I was sent to Albuquerque for several months to conduct extensive field investigations, I impulsively stopped at a local Walmart and bought a hundred-dollar typewriter and a big pack of paper with some of my *per diem* money. (This was the early 1990's – a long time before personal computers or laptops.)

It was there that I sat down for my first real effort at being a writer – and before I departed I'd finished most of a 600-plus page Ludlumesque novel. (One can get a lot of writing done night after night in a bleak hotel room.) The book was coincidentally about a heroic federal investigator – not unlike myself – who stumbled into a vast Russian-led conspiracy in the American southeast where I'm from. I still have that book – *Civil Servants* – stored in my old federal investigator briefcase, pushed underneath my bed. Its plot is mired in the early 1990's when it was written, locked to the aftermath of the Cold War, but it isn't half bad, and it taught me the valuable lesson that other writers also know: *The secret to writing is to put your butt in the chair and do it.*

After that particular trip, I went back home, finished up what was left of my epic adventure novel, and then settled back into writing the occasional short piece for our private amusement – but it was inevitable that at some point I would write a Holmes adventure.

In the mid-1990's, the federal agency where I'd been employed was abruptly eliminated, a victim of the end of the Cold War and a move to reduce the size of government. (After all, the higher-up wise men thought, who needs security now? We won!) Over the next few years, I went back to school and obtained a second degree in Civil Engineering. Then, in 2008 at the start of the Great Recession, I was unexpectedly laid off from my engineering job. With time on my hands, and a desire to try my hand at Sherlockian pastichery, I began writing each morning after the daily job searching was finished.

I ended up with nine of Holmes pastiches, written over several weeks, and then . . . I did nothing with them. That's right. Simply satisfied that I'd written them and that they existed, I put them in a binder labeled *The Papers of Sherlock Holmes* and shelved them with the rest of my Holmes Collection, happy with my secret collector's item.

But eventually I began to wish for other Sherlockians to see them. I shared one with a Sherlockian friend here and another one there, and the response was very positive. Finally I became bolder and wanted more people to see them, asking myself: *Why not put them in a real book of my own?*

I communicated about it with a Sherlockian publisher from whom I'd bought books in the past. He immediately offered to publish *The Papers*, and after a great deal of back-and-forth, my first book eventually appeared. For those who have had that experience – Opening the newly delivered carton to see *your book!* – there is nothing like it. It's a satisfaction that cannot easily be described.

That was in 2011. Over the next couple of years, I became aware of MX Publishing. I saw that an acquaintance of mine who'd also had his first book published with the same original publisher as mine had switched to MX, and I reached out to him. He informed me that he was happy to have switched to MX. With that in mind, I sent an email to Steve Emecz, Sherlockian Publisher Extraordinaire – and that was truly life-changing and improving decision.

In 2013, Steve republished my first book, *The Papers of Sherlock Holmes*, and he made the whole experience so painless that I set about writing a Holmes novel, *Sherlock Holmes and A Quantity of Debt.* That same fall, I was making my long-planned first Holmes Pilgrimage to London, and Steve arranged for me to have a book-signing in The Sherlock Holmes Hotel in Baker Street, where I was staying (when not traveling about to Dartmoor, the Sussex Coast, Edinburgh, and other locations). I was able to meet Steve for the first time on that trip, and found him to be one of the nicest, most supportive, and most thoughtful people around – and that hasn't changed a bit.

Jump ahead a little bit: In early 2015, I woke up early from a dream in which I'd edited a Holmes anthology. Instead of rolling over and forgetting the idea, I arose and started thinking about authors whom I admired and that I might want to invite to write stories. I ran the idea by Steve, and he was willing to publish it, so I began sending invitations. I hoped that I might get a dozen stories (at best) for a modest paperback volume. Fearing a lack of response, I kept sending invitations to everyone that I could think of – and then, amazingly, people started signing up. New Sherlock Holmes stories started to arrive in my email in-box – which quickly becomes addictive. More and more authors heard about it – some that I didn't even know about yet – and before we knew it, the little idea had grown into a three-volume hardcover behemoth of over 60 new Holmes stories – *Parts I, II,* and *III* of *The MX Book of New Sherlock Holmes Stories,* the largest collection of its kind ever produced to that point.

Early on, Steve and I had decided that the royalties from the project would go to support the Stepping Stones School for special needs children, located at Undershaw, one of Sir Arthur Conan Doyle's former homes. The books were a smashing success and received a lot of attention, and I was able to go to London in the fall of 2015 for the release party – what turned out to be Holmes Pilgrimage No. 2. There I was able to meet a number of the contributing authors in person – and to my everlasting regret, I was so thrilled that I barely remembered to take any photos!

After I returned home, I began to receive more emails, now asking when the next book was planned – *Good grief! A next book?!?* – and also stating that many authors (both returning and new) wanted to contribute.

I'd had no plans to do any more books, thinking that the first three were lightning in a bottle that couldn't be recaptured . . . but then I realized that the heavy-lifting in terms of decision-making and set-up and formatting and process-building had already occurred, so Steve and I decided to keep going. (I think I said to him "Let's do one more . . . .")

Part IV came out in the spring of 2016 – and after that, more people kept sending stories for *the next books* and wanting to join the party. We came up with the plan to have yearly books. But we received so many stories that it grew to twice a year. We now have an un-themed spring collection – the yearly *Annual* – and also a fall collection with a specific theme, such as Christmas adventures, seemingly impossible crimes, Untold Cases, etc. As more and more stories kept rolling in, it became necessary for each season's particular set to grow to multiple simultaneously published volumes. That's how, in just a few short years, we're now up to *Parts XXVIII, XXIX,* and *XXX* (to be published in Fall 2021), and as I write this, I'm already receiving stories for the *Spring 2022 Annual, Part XXXI* (and *XXXII* and *XXXIII* too . . . ?)

4

So far the books have raised over $85,000 for the school, and it's my hope and expectation that they'll go over $100,000 within the next few months of writing this foreword.

As part of editing these books, I couldn't let them pass by without adding my own stories – editor's prerogative. Thus, that helped to motivate me to sit my butt in the chair and write more about Mr. Holmes. By way of these books, I've met some really incredible people, including the incomparable Belanger Brothers, Derrick and Brian. Derrick initially contributed short stories, while Brian – a truly gifted artist – became the MX cover artist after the original artist passed away.

At one point, the two Belangers wrote a series of Holmes books for children. Eventually they formed Belanger Books – another amazing Sherlockian publishing venture. Between MX and Belanger Books – both of which cooperate beautifully with one another – the Sherlockian publishing field is amazingly well covered, providing an opportunity for so many people to be Sherlockian pasticheurs when they would otherwise be excluded by those who happily and aggressively seek to squash that aspect of the Sherlockian experience.

In 2016, the Belangers asked me to assemble and edit a Holmes story collection for them. I did, and as it also consisted of traditional and Canonical adventures, and had many of the same authors as in the MX anthologies, I formatted it the same way. After that, I edited another one for them, and another, and those also grew to simultaneously published multiple volumes. This extra editing also served to motivate me to write more Holmes stories for each of those collections as well – because I didn't want those trains leaving without me being on them.

From there, I began to receive invitations to write still more stories for other editors' anthologies and magazines. Along the way I published a couple more of my own books – *Sherlock Holmes – Tangled Skeins* (2015) and *Sherlock Holmes and The Eye of Heka* (2021) – but most of my stories that I wrote over those years remained uncollected within the various anthologies and magazines in which they had originally appeared. All along, I stayed too busy with real life and family and my dream job (as a civil engineer working for my home town's public works department), along with writing more stories and editing various books, to take the time to properly collect them all into my own books.

But within the last few months, I looked up and saw that (as of right now) I've now written 86 Holmes pastiches, (along with 20 pastiches about Solar Pons, "The Sherlock Holmes of Baker Street" – but that's another story and another hero.) Thus, the idea of this collection was born.

5

These initial five books of *The Complete Papers* contain 77 of those 86 stories. The others are still in the pipeline to be published elsewhere. Right now (as of mid-September 2021), I also have five more Holmes stories promised to be written for various editors before the end of the year, and all of these, plus whatever I'm able to write in 2022 – with a plan to reach Pastiche No. 100 – will be published in Volume VI of this set in later 2022 . . . *Fingers crossed!*

Many people have sports figures or musicians or actors or (curiously) politicians as heroes. My heroes have always been my book friends and authors – all the way back to when I was eight or nine and wondering about why I couldn't track down satisfying biographical information concerning the brilliant and prolific and mysterious author Franklin W. Dixon. I've always admired writers for what they accomplish and create while spending great chunks of their lives self-imposed isolation – something which I now understand. And at least if I had to set aside all that time to put my butt in the chair, I've been very fortunate that all of these stories almost told themselves. I almost never outline or plan. Instead, when I write – when I find that it's time for another story – I simply open a blank Word document on the computer and then wait for Watson to begin whispering to me. It's scary, but I trust the process now, and when it works – and it always has so far – there's no feeling quite like it.

Through these stories, I've achieved two important personal goals: In my own small way, I've become a writer, and I've also added to *The Great Holmes Tapestry*, a phrase I coined several years ago to describe the massive collection of narratives about the true Holmes and Watson – novels, short stories, radio and television episodes, movies and scripts, comics and fan-fiction, and unpublished manuscripts – that tell the complete and entire course of their lives from beginning to end. The Canon serves as the supporting structure – the wire core of the rope, the heavy steel girders of the skyscraper – but the thousands of traditional post-Canonical pastiches provide essential depth and color, filling in all the spaces around The Canon, and adding important information about The Whole Lives of Our Heroes.

I've long described myself as a missionary for The Church of the Traditional Canonical Holmes, preaching that the bigger picture of both Canon and the traditional pastiches should be seen and supported. This means giving respect and value to additional Holmes adventures, and not just those original sixty because they were the ones that came across the first Literary Agent's desk.

Ross MacDonald – (Real Name: Kenneth Millar, another of my authorial heroes because of his incredible private eye, Lew Archer) – said

"It's all one case." In other words, a *Great Tapestry*. He meant that even though he'd written eighteen Archer novels and a number of short stories from the 1940's to the 1970's, they were never meant to stand alone. They were all part of one overall arching story – Lew Archer's story – spanning across multiple narratives.

It's the same with the Holmes adventures – *all* of them, Canon and traditional pastiche, mine and everyone else's. They fit together to tell the *entire* story of Sherlock Holmes, and with the stories in this collection, I'm incredibly proud to have added my own contribution.

* * * * *

"Of course, I could only stammer out my thanks."
– *The unhappy John Hector McFarlane,* "The Norwood Builder"

At some point during the foreword-writing for the various MX anthologies, I began to use the quote shown above from Mr. McFarlane in regard to Thank You's. It's fitting – I can only stammer out thanks, and never adequately express how grateful I am for all the help and encouragement I've received over the years in all aspects of my life – not just the writing and editing of Sherlock Holmes stories.

First and foremost, I am always overwhelmed at how incredibly fortunate I am to have my wife and son in my life. In all aspects, my wife – of 33 years as I write this – is the kindest and wisest and most beautiful person inside and out I know, and she has been there throughout with complete support and encouragement when we went through such things as some terrible jobs and the grind of my returning to school. We have pushed through together, and anything that I can ever accomplish I owe to her. And equally amazing is our son, so incredibly funny and smart, and truly an amazing person in every way. I enjoy every minute spent with him, and it only gets better. I love you both, and you are everything to me!

Then there are my parents and sister, who put up with me during those first couple of decades – I probably don't even realize how bad that was for them. My parents did everything to encourage me – music lessons leading to a piano scholarship in college, all the books that I could read, and generally anything to help me grow as a person, so that it never occurred to me that I couldn't do whatever I wanted. And my sister was my best friend then, patiently listening as I rambled about whatever interested me. Even then, she probably heard more about Sherlock Holmes than she'd ever bargained for!

There is a group that exchanges emails with me when we have the time – and time is a valuable commodity for all of us these days! As the years have gone by, we've gotten busier and busier, and I don't get to write as often as I'd like, but I really enjoy catching up whenever we get the chance. These people are all wonderful writers, and I recommend them highly as both friends and authors: Mark Mower, Denis Smith, Tom Turley, Dan Victor, and Marcia Wilson.

Next, I wish to send several huge Thank You's to the following:

- *Steve Emecz* – When I first emailed Steve from out of the blue back in 2013 – *Only eight years? So much in eight years!* – I was interested in MX re-publishing my first book. Even then, as a guy who works to accumulate *all* traditional Sherlockian pastiches, I could see that MX (under Steve's leadership) was *the* fast-rising superstar of the Sherlockian publishing world.

    The re-publication of my first book with MX was an amazing life-changing event for me, leading to writing many more stories and then editing books, along with unexpected Holmes Pilgrimages to England. By way of that first email with Steve, I've had the chance to make some incredible Sherlockian friends and play in the Holmesian Sandbox in ways that I'd never before dreamed possible.

    Through all of it, Steve has been one of the most positive and supportive people that I've ever known. He works far more than a full-time week at his day job, and he still finds time to take care of all aspects of MX Publishing, with the help of his wife Sharon Emecz, and cousin, Timi Emecz. (That's right – MX is just the three of them who get all of this done!)

    Many who just buy books and have a vague idea of how the publishing industry works now might not realize that MX, a non-profit which supports several important charities, consists of simply these three people. Between them, they take care of running the entire business, including the production, marketing, and shipping – all in their precious spare time, in and around their real lives.

    With incredible hard work, they have made MX into a world-wide Sherlockian publishing phenomenon, providing opportunities for authors who would never have them otherwise. There are some like me who return more than once to Watson's Tin Dispatch Box, and there are others who only find one or two stories there – but they get the chance to publish their books, and then they can point with pride at this accomplishment, and how they too have added to The Great Holmes Tapestry.

From the beginning, Steve has let me explore various Sherlockian projects and open up my own personal possibilities in ways that otherwise would have never happened. Thank you, Steve, for every opportunity!

- *Derrick Belanger* and *Brian Belanger* – I first "met" Derrick Belanger when he graciously reviewed one of my early books, and we quickly became friends. Then he interviewed me several times for his online blog, and when I had the idea for the first MX Holmes anthology in 2015, he quickly joined the party and contributed a fine pastiche. From there he's written a number of others, and then he formed Belanger Books with his brother, Brian. It's turned into a Sherlockian powerhouse, working in tandem with MX Publishing, supporting each other to produce more and more wonderful Holmes adventures. I've very grateful to have had this additional opportunity to further contribute to The Great Holmes Tapestry by editing and writing stories for their different anthologies. Derrick continues to write, but he also stays quite busy as a noted aware-winning teacher, husband, and father, as well as running Belanger Books with Brian.

Over the last few years, my amazement at Brian Belanger's ever-increasing talent has only grown. I initially became acquainted with him when he took over the duties of creating the covers for MX Books following the untimely death of their previous graphic artist. I found Brian to be a great collaborator, very easy-going and stress-free in his approach and willingness to work with authors, and wonderfully creative too. His skills became most apparent to me when he created the cover for my 2017 book, *The Papers of Solar Pons*, which was one of the most striking covers that I've ever seen. Later, when the Belangers and I began reissuing the original Pons books in new editions, and then new Pons anthologies, Brian's similarly themed covers continued to astound me. He truly deserves an award for these.

9

In the meantime, he has become busier and busier, continuing to provide covers for MX Books, and now for Belanger Books as well, along with editing and occasionally writing.

I finally met both Brian and Derrick in person in early (pre-pandemic) 2020 at the annual Sherlock Holmes Birthday Celebration in New York City, and they're just as great in person as they were by way of email. I immediately felt like I'd known them both forever. I cannot express to either one of you just how grateful I am.

- *Roger Johnson* – I had known of Roger for quite a while, having seen his name connected with the "District Messenger" newsletter of *The Sherlock Holmes Society of London Journal*. I could tell, even then, that he represented the finest kind of Sherlockian. When I wrote my first Holmes book, I sent him a copy – out of the blue, as he had no idea who I was – as a thank you, and with the timid and dim spark of a hope that he would review it, because having him do so would mean (to me) that what I had written was legitimized. He did write a wonderful review, and we began to correspond. When I was able to get to England for my first Holmes Pilgrimage in 2013, I made arrangements to meet with Roger and his wonderful wife, Jean Upton, in person, and I discovered that what I'd already known by email was true: They are both the very best people!

  Later, in 2015 on Holmes Pilgrimage No. 2, they invited me to stay with them for several days in their home, and that was one of the best parts of all the trips. They gave me tours, they showed me their incredible collection, they let me see life in a real British household and not just from a hotel room, and we had some wonderful conversations along the way. I was able to see them again in 2016, Holmes Pilgrimage No. 3, when we attended the Grand Opening of the Stepping Stones School at Undershaw.

  I'm more grateful than I can say that I know Roger. His Sherlockian knowledge is exceptional, as is the work that he does to further the cause of The Master. But even more than that, both Roger and his wonderful wife, Jean, are simply the finest and best, and I'm very lucky to know both of them – even though I don't get to see them nearly as often as I'd like, and especially in these crazy days! In so many ways, Roger, I can't thank you enough, and I can't imagine these books without you.

- *Nicholas Meyer* – I started reading Nick Meyer's Holmes books before I'd even read all of The Canon, and for that I'm eternally grateful. It was through his first two books, *The Seven-Per-Cent Solution* and *The West End Horror* (the latter of which is still one of my favorite pastiches to this very day) that I firmly understood that The Canon wasn't the be-all end-all of Sherlockian story-telling. I obtained Nick's first book as part of a free book give-away at school, and I found the second not long after when my mother took my sister and me to buy school clothes and I spotted it in the mall bookstore. (I sat cross-legged along an out-of-the-way wall in a Sears while my mother and sister shopped and started reading *The West End Horror* straight out of the bag.)

After those first two books, Nick went on to have a very successful career in film. (More about that in a minute.) But he has continued to dip in an out of Sherlockian pastichery with *The Canary Trainer* (1993), *The Adventure of the Peculiar Protocols* (2019), and *The Return of the Pharaoh* (2021). He is a Sherlockian legend, and it's an indisputable fact that the publication in 1974 of *The Seven-Per-Cent Solution* – a pastiche, mind you! – was the beginning of the Sherlockian Golden Age when has grown and grown, and has never stopped, all the way to today.

If it was just that, Sherlockians – and especially pasticheurs – would owe him an unpayable debt. But then there's *Star Trek*, which he also saved. As mentioned above, I have lots of interests besides Mr. Holmes, although he does demand more and more attention as my years pass. But I've been a Trekkie (or Trekker, or whatever the correct term is) since I was a wee lad in the late 1960's, when my babysitter happened to watch one of the original prime-time episodes. After that, I grew up seeing the original series in re-reruns, and then I was among those who saw the first Star Trek film in 1979 (and truthfully felt mightily disappointed. I do like it better now.) But it was Nick Meyer's *Star Trek:*

11

The Wrath of Khan (1982) which electrified the Trek Universe, jump-starting it into motion in a way that – like the Holmes Golden Age – has only grown. And how it's grown! Hundreds and hundreds of Star Trek novels and comic books, multiple films and television shows, with more in planning and production all the time, and fan interest around the world at an all-time high. As a nearly life-long Star Trek fan, who loves it nearly as much as The World of Sherlock Holmes, I credit the origin of this original escalation entirely to Nick Meyer.

I generally despise social media, but it's a very useful way for Sherlockians to connect. Imagine my thrill when I began to see occasional online posts from Nick Meyer – and when I dared to respond, sometimes he would respond back! I've learned that if you don't ask, you'll never know, so I connected with him a bit more often, and eventually I boldly asked him to write a foreword to one of the MX anthologies that I edit, and he most-generously agreed. After that, we've stayed in touch off-and-on, and that still never ceases to amaze me.

I met him in person at the 2011 *From Gillette to Brett* conference in Bloominton, Indiana, where he was the featured guest. I took my Holmes book, asked him to autograph them, and asked – like everyone does – when he'd write his next Holmes book. He certainly doesn't remember that, but he was the main reason I chose to attend that event.

One of my greatest regrets is that, while attending the 2020 Sherlock Holmes Birthday Celebration in New York, I was almost able to meet him in person again – and this time he'd know who I was – but I didn't get to speak with him, and it was my own fault. We had emailed ahead of time, planning to meet, and that day I entered the famed dealer's room and saw him seated at a table near the door, surrounded by many fans. I wandered away, intending to return in a just a very few minutes and dive into the crowd, hoping that it might have thinned a bit. But when I got back over there, he'd already left! Hopefully I'll get another chance, sooner rather than later, where I can thank him in person for so many things . . .

. . . including generously writing a foreword for these volumes. When I was considering who could write a foreword, I couldn't think of anyone more fitting. Through Nicholas Meyer I found pastiches, which have been so important to me over the years. Nick, thanks from the bottom of my heart for taking the time to be part of these books!

And finally, last but certainly *not* least, thanks to **Sir Arthur Conan Doyle**: Author, doctor, adventurer, and the Founder of the Sherlockian Feast. Honored, and present in spirit.

As I always note when putting together an anthology of Holmes stories, the effort has been a labor of love. This time the labor and love have been mine. These adventures are more tiny threads woven into the ongoing *Great Holmes Tapestry*, continuing to grow and grow, for there can *never* be enough stories about the man whom Watson described as *"the best and wisest . . . whom I have ever known."*

David Marcum
September 8th, 2021
A most important day,
for all kinds of reasons

Questions, comments, or story submissions
may be addressed to David Marcum at

thepapersofsherlockholmes@gmail.com

A Note on the
Modern Publishing Paradigm

For the longest time, publishing something was mostly impossible for most people. The Great Publishing Houses – which sounds like something from *Dune* – are giant machines, with carefully calculated formulas to know just how many books they need to sell to make a profit. It's no different than selling cereal: Many of the boxes of cereal on grocery store shelves won't be sold, and they were never meant to be sold, and the manufacturers are okay with that, because they've calculated the amount that they do need to actually sell in order to stay profitable while figuring in just how much can be discarded.

It used to be the same with books. Publishers would create a print run of a certain number of copies, sending out so many of them to bookstores across the country. Some would be sold – enough, hopefully, to cover costs – while many copies would just sit there, unsold, forever. Then, after a certain amount of time, they would be removed – either destroyed, or "remaindered", to be sold at rock-bottom prices in bargain bins.

It's an investment by the publishers to go to the trouble and expense to create all of those physical books, hoping to make their money back on enough of them to justify the waste of the others. That's why they're so restrictive about what they publish: They must meet the razor-thin edge of profit. But that makes the path to being published a very narrow needle's eye.

Several years ago, the paradigm began to shift. Online sales began to disrupt the physical bookstore model. And as people ordered online, some publishers figured out that they didn't have to have back rooms and warehouses jammed full of physical books sitting around waiting for a physical customer to enter a store or a dealer's room, examine it, and possibly buy it. Instead, when an online order arrived, the manufacturing of the book could commence right then, only as needed, and not months or years earlier.

This print-on-demand idea had been around for a while. (When I was going back to school for my second degree in civil engineering, the campus print shop did the same thing for certain locally produced text-books, printing them as they were purchased on fancy copying machines.) Publishers and authors began to take advantage of technological advances to produce their own books – straight from author to reader, happily eliminating the giant publishing middlemen.

Steve Emecz of MX Publishing brilliantly took advantage of this, building his business and allowing authors who would have never had a chance otherwise – like me – to create and connect.

But there are certain legitimate complaints.

In the olden days, the giant publishers slow-walked books through the process, so that it sometimes took literally years for a book to actually be published. Authors could actually die before ever seeing their work excreted at the far end of the giant publisher's process. The print-on-demand process, by comparison, is nearly immediate. As part of the large publishers' slow walk, there were battalions of editors who went through books forwards, backwards, and upside down. With the new technology, where a file can be loaded with the book manufacturer with very little effort and time spent, there is clearly less editing . . . and mistakes slip through.

Some readers continue to expect flawless and perfect works, as if legions of editors were behind the curtain as in days of old, still involved in the process. For this type of reader/consumer, the new format of publishing will always be pain they just can't ease. That's why, with this set of my stories, I want to apologize up front to those who will find typos – *because in spite of every effort, there will be some typos.*

In my own case, I love to write and edit, and I spend a sizeable amount of time doing both, but I also have a very busy and rich life doing other things. I spend time with my family, and I work more-than-full time as a civil engineer, fitting in these Sherlockian writing and editing projects during lunch hours, evenings, and weekends. It's a high wire act with no safety net. I'm the writer and sole editor of the stories in this collection. My wife, with a Bachelor's Degree in Journalism and two Master's Degrees in English Literature and Library Science, and with a first job as a copy editor, used to go through my stories and catch what I missed – because you never *ever* see your own mistakes – but she works way more than full time at her own job, and she just doesn't have any extra time to spare for playing uncredited editor on these projects. So they're all on me.

It's the same with the anthologies that I edit – any mistake that slips through in the end is my fault, because there are no other editors. When assembling a Holmes anthology, I receive the stories, format them to the "house style", print them on 8½ x 11-inch paper, edit and revise, go back and forth with emails to the author – sometimes a lot of emails – and then plug them into a giant Word document for more editing and revision. But from the time I get the story until I send the final file to the publisher, there isn't anyone else to edit, and no time to work one into the process. It's the new publishing paradigm.

16

As a print-on-demand publisher, MX does not have squadrons of editors. The business consists of three part-time people who also have busy lives elsewhere – so the editing effort largely falls on the contributors. Some readers and consumers out there in the world absolutely despise this – apparently forgetting about all those self-produced Holmes stories and volumes from decades ago with awkward self-published formatting and loads of errors that are now prized as collector's items.

These critics should recall that every one of these new volumes by various authors – even those that have typographic and formatting errors – are the very best efforts that can be produced by very sincere people who don't have professional full-time editors to help, and who would never ever have had the opportunity to publish otherwise, and because of these authors, there is thankfully more Sherlockian content in the world.

I'm personally mortified when errors slip through – ironically, there will probably be errors in this essay – and I apologize now, but without a regiment of editors looking over my shoulder, this is as good as it gets. Real life is more important than writing and editing, and only so much time can be spent preparing these books before they are released into the wild. I hope that you can look past any errors, small or huge, and simply enjoy these stories, and appreciate the effort involved, and the sincere desire to add to The Great Holmes Tapestry.

And in spite of any errors here, there are more Sherlock Holmes stories than there were before, and that's a good thing.

David Marcum

Watson's Descendants
by Nicholas Meyer

It is generally felt that the short story was Sherlock Holmes's best venue. The novellas, by contrast, are judged to be . . . lesser. Even the fabled *The Hound of the Baskervilles* suffers from the detective's absence for many pages. Though *A Study in Scarlet*, *The Sign of the Four*, and *The Valley of Fear* remain deliciously absorbing, it is in the short stories that Holmes and Watson truly flourish.

As Michael Chabon has observed, all fiction is fan fiction. Almost from the beginning, Sherlock Holmes has prompted imitators of his creator's creation. Arthur Conan Doyle wrote sixty Holmes cases in all – fifty-six short stories and four novellas. When they ended, boys and girls, men and women of all ages mourned Watson's silence and the series' cessation. But it wasn't long before others took up – or attempted to take up – Sir Arthur's pen.

Writing a full-length Holmes novel has always posed a challenge, even for Doyle himself, to say nothing of generations of later writers and filmmakers. Short stories, on the other hand, pose problems of their own. A good short story must compress action and character. It must – obviously – be short. The gift of writing compelling short fiction remains in a class by itself. Poe, Doyle of course, Twain, Saki, and Hawthorne are among the masters of the form from the Victorian and Edwardian eras, but over the years, the short story has produced many masters.

I alas am not among them. Even as a kid in art class, my paintings were so huge the murals I attempted had to be unfurled in the hall, not the studio. And so it comes as no surprise that writing a short Holmes story does not come easily to me. In fact, it does not come at all.

I retain nothing but admiration for those writers who *can* create short fiction, and a special respect for those who can bring off simulacra of Doyle's charming and distinctive Holmes tales. There many practitioners, including some whose efforts, unfortunately, resemble nothing so much as taxidermy. But among the best I must number David Marcum, who, by this point has written more Holmes stories than Doyle himself. Characterized by unflagging imagination and ceaseless ingenuity, along with felicitous prose, these tales continue to provide what we all crave: More Sherlock.

All Sherlock Holmes stories, (except Doyle's), are of course forgeries. And it's the rare forger who can resist signing his own work. See if you can spot David Marcum's fine Italian hand.

Enjoy.

Nicholas Meyer
Los Angeles, 2021

Sherlock Holmes (1854-1957) was born in Yorkshire, England, on 6 January, 1854. In the mid-1870's, he moved to 24 Montague Street, London, where he established himself as the world's first Consulting Detective. After meeting Dr. John H. Watson in early 1881, he and Watson moved to rooms at 221b Baker Street, where his reputation as the world's greatest detective grew for several decades. He was presumed to have died battling noted criminal Professor James Moriarty on 4 May, 1891, but he returned to London on 5 April, 1894, resuming his consulting practice in Baker Street. Retiring to the Sussex coast near Beachy Head in October 1903, he continued to be associated in various private and government investigations while giving the impression of being a reclusive apiarist. He was very involved in the events encompassing World War I, and to a lesser degree those of World War II. He passed away peacefully upon the cliffs above his Sussex home on his 103rd birthday, 6 January, 1957.

Dr. John Hamish Watson (1852-1929) was born in Stranraer, Scotland on 7 August, 1852. In 1878, he took his Doctor of Medicine Degree from the University of London, and later joined the army as a surgeon. Wounded at the Battle of Maiwand in Afghanistan (27 July, 1880), he returned to London late that same year. On New Year's Day, 1881, he was introduced to Sherlock Holmes in the chemical laboratory at Barts. Agreeing to share rooms with Holmes in Baker Street, Watson became invaluable to Holmes's consulting detective practice. Watson was married and widowed three times, and from the late 1880's onward, in addition to his participation in Holmes's investigations and his medical practice, he chronicled Holmes's adventures, with the assistance of his literary agent, Sir Arthur Conan Doyle, in a series of popular narratives, most of which were first published in *The Strand* magazine. Watson's later years were spent preparing a vast number of his notes of Holmes's cases for future publication. Following a final important investigation with Holmes, Watson contracted pneumonia and passed away on 24 July, 1929.

Photos of Sherlock Holmes and Dr. John H. Watson courtesy of Roger Johnson

The
Collected Papers
of
Sherlock
Holmes

Volume II - Records
Sherlock Holmes:
Tangled Skeins
and
Sherlock Holmes and
The Eye of Heka

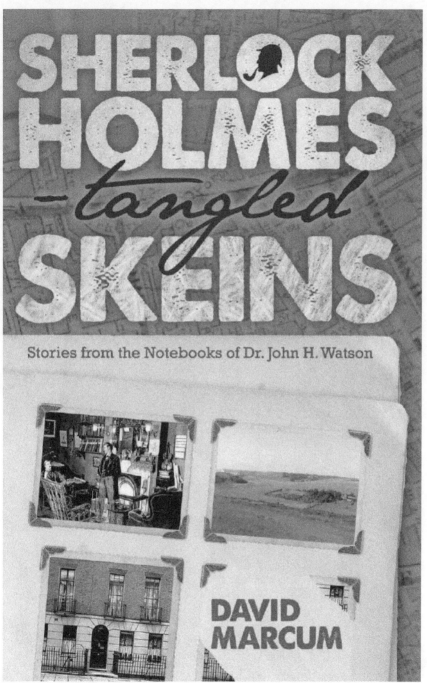

2015 Cover

Introduction:
In Praise of the Deerstalker, *and*
A Truly *Great* Hiatus, *and*
How This Book Came To Be

Part I: In Praise of the Deerstalker

As I've related elsewhere, I started reading about Holmes and Watson when I was ten years old. Not long after, my parents gave me a copy of William S. Baring-Gould's *Sherlock Holmes of Baker Street*, and it greatly influenced my future enjoyment of the World of Holmes, so much so that I have been collecting and reading stories about him ever since. I was amazed at all of the sources that Baring-Gould referred to in the back of the book, and I wanted to *be* one of those people who actually *knew* about Holmes, rather than just a casual visitor to Baker Street.

One cannot think about Holmes without seeing the iconic, universally recognized, and archetypal figure of *The Man in the Deerstalker*. It can be argued that Holmes never actually wore such a hat in the original Canon (although his "ear-flapped traveling-cap" was mentioned in "Silver Blaze") and that the use of that type of hat was simply a touch added by that incredible illustrator, Sidney Paget.

But when one becomes acquainted with Holmes at an early age, and when he is wearing a deerstalker during that initial introduction, as he was on the cover of the first Holmes book that I acquired, one comes to associate it with him, whether it is strictly accurate or not. And from an early age, I wanted a deerstalker of my own.

I can still see it clearly, the very first deerstalker that I constructed from a plain blue cap of my father's. It had no logos, insignias, or advertisements. It was simply blue. I didn't permanently damage it, although I *did* destroy a different cap with a red bill, in order to sew the red bill onto the back side of the blue cap. Thus, one deerstalker, rather odd looking, and without ear flaps. I don't know why I thought that the red attachment on the back was acceptable, but I did. And I wore it proudly in connection with the detective agency that I opened in the basement of our house. (We actually made a little money, performing chores for a neighbor that took pity on us, but those cases are *not* resting in a tin dispatch box somewhere, and they will never be written or read about.)

At some point I lost track of that first deerstalker, and my father snipped the threads holding it together, removing and discarding the red bill and reclaiming his blue cap. But even as I grew up, I wanted a *real* deerstalker.

When I was nineteen and a sophomore in college, I went home on my birthday, where my parents proudly presented me with the real thing, a true and authentic deerstalker. It was a houndstooth pattern, heavy tweed, and the earflaps were tied up with thin leather thongs. It had actually been made in England, and my parents had ordered it from somewhere quite expensive in New York. I was thrilled and amazed.

So I was back at college the next day with my deerstalker, and it was time to make a decision. Did I keep this thing as a treasured souvenir to sit in dust on a shelf, or did I wear my Sherlockian Pride on my head, proclaiming my beliefs and walking the walk? I decided to live up to my convictions and *put on the hat!* And then I walked to the dining hall for lunch. No looking back.

The hat caused some initial comment around campus and amongst my friends, but amazingly not as much as I'd feared. It became *my* hat and look for the remainder of my time there until graduation. I wore it to and from class, and for walks in the college woods, and to the mall or out to eat or to the movies, and wherever else that I went. I wore it in yearbook photos. I'm sure it attracted some stares, since one did not and does not see that type of hat where I live. I've had a few comments from passers-by over the years, but they are rare. One person pronounced that I must be a Robert Downey, Jr. fan. (No.) One wag cleverly called me Inspector Clouseau. Even when I've worn my hat during trips to New York or Washington, D.C. and walked the streets, no one has really said anything. And in the last thirty years, since I received and started wearing that very first hat, I've never yet encountered anyone else who was simply wearing a deerstalker in his or her everyday life as an everyday hat.

A few years ago, some of my family got together and bought for me the ultimate Christmas gift, a real Inverness and matching Deerstalker, custom made for me in Scotland. While I'm used to wearing a deerstalker everywhere, I must admit that it is more difficult to find excuses to go out in full Inverness and Fore-and-Aft, but I have occasionally done so, and even then I did not attract the excessive attention that one would expect. Possibly I carry it off with such swagger that it elicits no curiosity. Or perhaps I look eccentric or even dangerous, and people are giving me a wide berth. In deference to my wife, and the point when I would definitely cross her mortification line, I don't go out often in full regalia, but I still wear a deerstalker on a daily basis for most of the year.

32

So I've always worn a deerstalker as my only hat, from the time that the weather cools off in the fall until it becomes too warm to wear it in the spring. And it goes without saying that I wore a deerstalker when I was finally able to make my trip-of-a-lifetime Holmes Pilgrimage to England.

Part II: A Truly *Great* Hiatus *or* The Holmes Pilgrimage

I had wanted to go to England for most of my life. It called to me. I couldn't watch any movie or television program about the place without wanting to put my feet there. In most directions back, my family tree is English or Scottish. (My mother was a Rathbone, and my great-grandmother was a Watson.) And most of all, I wanted to visit all of those places that I had only imagined when reading the Holmes Canon. Finally, after making exhaustive lists, giving my employer plenty of notice, and consulting my collection of over a dozen Holmes travel books, I was ready. This trip was just me and the places that I wanted to go. And my sole companion on the journey was my deerstalker.

I wore that hat everywhere while I was over there. For a few weeks in September 2013, a man in a deerstalker roamed Baker Street once again. Of course, I went to the Sherlock Holmes Museum in Baker Street multiple times, and tried to visit the sites of all the other possible theorized locations for 221b up and down Baker Street as well. I stayed in the Sherlock Holmes Hotel on Baker Street on every night that I was in London, and it was there that MX Publishing held a book-signing for me. (To be honest, I didn't actually *wear* the deerstalker during that event, but I had it with me, and it sat on my lap while I did a reading from a previous book.)

I went to as many Holmes-related sites as I could while I was there. If it wasn't connected to The Master one way or another, I pretty much didn't do it. I didn't go up on the London Eye, for example, because it wasn't something that was there in the good old days. (The few exceptions to my Holmes-only rule included visits to Poirot's lodgings, James Bond's house in Chelsea, and most of all, 7B Praed Street, the residence of Solar Pons and Dr. Parker. It certainly doesn't look the same now as it did in the old pictures – what a loss!)

My deerstalker and I ate well at Simpson's. I went to the Sherlock Holmes Pub with it – and through the courtesy of a kind Sherlockian friend, was actually able to go *into* the exhibit room/museum and touch many of the Sacred Objects, and then this same noted Sherlockian gave me a personal "Empty House" walking tour through various streets and mews to the back of Camden House. I went to Montague Street and visited the exact building that Michael Harrison identified (in *The London of*

Sherlock Holmes – 1973) as the one where Holmes lived in the 1870's, when he first came up to London. I roamed Pall Mall, identifying The Diogenes Club and Mycroft Holmes's residence across the street to my own satisfaction. I went to both of the old Scotland Yards. I went to the front door of each of Watson's identified residences – Paddington, Kensington, Queen Anne Street – based on information culled from the Holmes travel books in my collection. I journeyed up to Hampstead to visit Milverton's house. I explored up and down the river and around "Upper Swandam Lane," The Tower (the location of many pastiches), and sites in the City. I went to Paddington and King's Cross and Charing Cross and Victoria.

Since Holmes has been in so many pastiche encounters with Jack the Ripper, and I have over two dozen in my collection so far, I went through Whitechapel twice – the first time on a drizzly night with *the* Ripper expert Donald Rumbelow, who added some extra Holmesian content to his tour because I was wearing my deerstalker. The second time was by myself on a quiet Sunday morning, when the deerstalker and I went to each murder site in order, as well as other related locations, such as the Juwes doorway, and the Ten Bells pub, where I had lunch. Possibly the man in the deerstalker making his way up and down those streets caught someone's attention.

The deerstalker and I made our way into the lab at Barts, where I pulled out my Complete Sherlock Holmes and re-read about the first meeting there between Our Heroes. I went west by train to Dartmoor, where I explored the Moor and read "The Man on the Tor" and the "Second Report of Dr. Watson" from *The Hound* while sitting atop Hound Tor. I went to Edinburgh, because I wanted to go to Scotland while I was there, and where better than to visit the Holmes statue and the Conan Doyle pub? (Some excellent pastiches are set in Edinburgh, too.) Back in London, I took a river tour, trying to imagine chasing Jonathan Small and Tonga after departing from the very same dock that Holmes and Watson and Athelney Jones used, below Scotland Yard.

I also spent a couple of days in and around East Dean, Birling Gap, and Beachy Head in Sussex, because Holmes actually lived the majority of his lifetime in his retirement cottage there on the South Downs. (If you believe Baring-Gould – and I do – Holmes resided there from the fall of 1903 until his death in 1957, having lived to the ripe old age of 103 years, thanks to Royal Jelly!)

In East Dean, I stayed at the Tiger Inn, a smuggler's inn from hundreds of years back, where I encountered a ghost – one of the few events of the trip that wasn't strictly Sherlockian. The inn is across the village green from a building that has a historical plaque, supposedly identifying it as Holmes's retirement villa. I don't agree with that location, as my research led me to decide that my personal choice for Holmes's retirement villa is nearby Hodcombe Farm. I went all around there as well.

While in that area, I found a seat on the ground at the top of the cliffs of Beachy Head, directly across from Hodcombe Farm, and re-read "The Lion's Mane," while looking down at the farm and "Fulworth" (Birling Gap) and Maud Bellamy's house, The Haven, in the distance. (It's actually there, just as described in the story! You can see it if you go to Birling Gap. It's the house at the top of the hill and the end of the lane, "the one with the corner tower and slate roof," as Holmes describes it in "The Lion's Mane"). While there, I also re-read the final chapter of Baring-Gould's *Sherlock Holmes of Baker Street* describing Holmes's death there on that spot on January 6th, 1957. Very moving, I assure you.

Throughout my travels, I kept my eyes open for fitting souvenirs. I wasn't buying the usual tourist items. I purchased some Holmes trinkets, and a bust of Our Hero, and Holmes-related books that I couldn't find in the U.S. But mostly I bought some more deerstalkers. A lifetime supply of them. Eighteen more of them, as a matter of fact – added to the six that I already owned – from various spots in London (the Sherlock Holmes Museum, the Sherlock Holmes Pub, a shop on Baker Street, a shop in Whitehall, a shop across from the British Museum around the corner from Montague Street) and even a really nice one in Edinburgh. Some were obviously souvenir quality, but others are definitely the real thing, solid and heavy. In each case, the vendors where I shopped looked oddly at me, a man already wearing a deerstalker, as I would take mine off in order to try on one of theirs. What could I possibly need with *another deerstalker*? (I'm sure that my wife has asked herself that question many times over by this point.)

On my Great Hiatus, I crammed in more Holmes-related sites than I can possibly list here. But one of the places on my list – which was actually four places – directly led to the existence of this book.

Part III: How This Book Came To Be

In "The Problem of Thor Bridge", Watson states:

> *Somewhere in the vaults of the bank of Cox and Co., at Charing Cross, there is a travel-worn and battered tin dispatch box with my name, John H. Watson, M. D., Late Indian Army, painted upon the lid.*

I had specifically wanted to visit the site of Cox & Co. of Charing Cross. My research in the various Holmes travel books revealed that there were at least four past Cox & Company locations, so I visited all four. There was one on the Strand that is now a Lloyd's bank. I went inside and used my card to get some money while I was there. Another was in Craig's Court, off Whitehall. (That location is also the site of the office of Cyrus Barker, Holmes's "hated rival upon the Surrey shore," mentioned in "The Retired Colourman," and as chronicled in an excellent series of books presented by Will Thomas.) A third former location of the bank is at Whitehall Place, where there is currently a business occupying the old site, its stylized sign covering the still-visible "Cox & Co." carved in the stone over the door.

The final location of one of the old Cox & Co.'s is at 16 Charing Cross Road. This narrow shop, still involved one way or another in the matter of money, was one of the places that I visited on September 25th, 2013. Little did I realize that my deerstalker and I were being watched.

As I mentioned in the introductions to *Sherlock Holmes in Montague Street, Volumes I, II,* and *III,* I had been at that particular Cox & Co., taking pictures, before making my way down Charing Cross Road for a nearby appointment with Catherine Cooke, keeper of the Sherlock Holmes Collection at the Westminster Reference Library. As expected, visiting the collection was incredible, and I'm very thankful for the chance to see it.

When I departed the library, it was still mid-afternoon, and I was trying to decide where to go next. I had returned back to London from Dartmoor the day before, and I was due to journey home in just a few days. I had been successfully crossing Sherlockian locations off my list, but there were still so many places to find and visit. I turned down the hill, zigzagging my way toward Trafalgar Square. I had only gone a few steps before I sensed that I was not alone.

That is a strange statement to make in one of the world's busiest cities, but a traveler hopefully develops and cultivates some survival skills along the way, and sensing that I was being followed was one of them.

As I stopped and looked around me, a small man approached. He had probably always been short, and now that he was quite elderly, the years had only robbed him of whatever height he'd once had, as he inevitably collapsed in upon himself. There was nothing unusual about his clothing. It was his manner that was odd, as he approached slowly, almost fearfully, holding a package and darting glances between the ground and my hat, without meeting my eyes.

His story was hard to follow, especially due to my awkwardness in deciphering his rather thick accent. Essentially, he had seen me earlier in my deerstalker, taking photographs while standing outside of the old Cox

36

& Co. in Charing Cross Road. He was one of a series of people who had been told, many years ago, to deliver the package that he was pressing into my hands to a man in a deerstalker. (At least that was what I understood. Some parts were not clear, and it was possible that he said that the original delivery instructions had been given to *his father*. This made sense after I read what was in the package. If he himself had been the man who had first received the package, he was a *very* old man indeed.)

While I was still trying to puzzle out what he was telling me, and looking at the package in my hands, he finished what he was saying, gave a great sigh of relief at a job finally finished, and turned away. In a few steps, he had vanished into the crowds.

I made my way to a small shop selling juice and snacks on the south side of Leicester Square. Purchasing something to drink, I sat down and carefully opened the package. And then I quickly rewrapped it, terrified that someone was going to come and take it away from me.

I considered, just for a moment, returning to the Westminster Reference Library, just to show what I had found. But selfishness overtook me. I wanted to keep this for myself, at least until it could be prepared to share with the world.

As I've mentioned elsewhere, part of the package consisted of the documents that were later edited and published as the three volumes of *Sherlock Holmes in Montague Street*. But there were other documents, including a collection of additional adventures already prepared by Watson for publication. As he explains in his "Foreword," he chose to leave them with someone, intending to pick them up later. There is no explanation given for this decision, or why he never came back to get them. Based on the date of Watson's comments, it is apparent that events overtook Our Heroes.

I have prepared this volume for publication by correcting – when necessary – the places where the manuscript has faded or blurred. In addition, I have also Americanized the spellings in the manuscript. Any dissatisfaction about the spelling choices, as well as any identified errors or discrepancies, are completely *my* fault, and should not be laid at Watson's feet.

As in previous volumes, I wish to dedicate my efforts involved in preparing this manuscript for publication to both my wife Rebecca and my son Dan. They continually put up with my ever-increasing interest in Holmes and Watson, and the exponentially rising number of Holmes-related volumes that keep finding their way to our house. They helped me prepare for my trip to England in September 2013, realizing that it was an almost religious experience for me. And they are still willing to go places in public with me while I continue to wear a deerstalker. My wife knew what she was getting into when we became a couple and later married, now over a quarter-of-a-century ago, but my son had no choice in the matter, having been born into this Holmesian Household. I am exceedingly blessed to have both of them!

David Marcum
January 6, 2015
The 161st Anniversary of the Birth of Mr. Sherlock Holmes

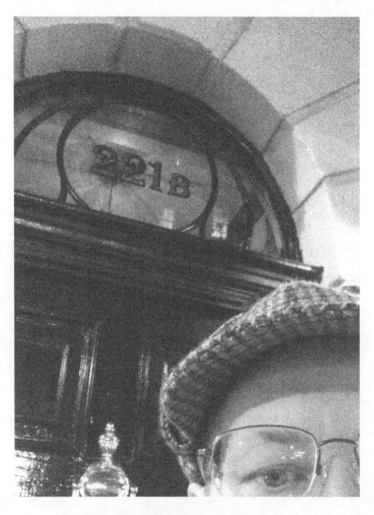

*The Editor and his Deerstalker
in Baker Street
September 17th, 2013*

Foreword
by Dr. John H. Watson

If I have given the impression, while recording certain examples of the adventures of my friend Sherlock Holmes, that he suffered from long spells of inactivity between cases, then I must apologize, and explain that, except for those early years when he was first establishing his practice as what was then the world's only consulting detective, my friend's plate was usually very full indeed, and the cases frequently overlapped one into another. It was during the times in the mid- to late-eighties, when I first attempted to arrange some of my notes into published narratives, initially with *A Study in Scarlet,* and subsequently with *The Sign of the Four,* that I realized I must be carefully selective regarding which threads I chose to weave into my tapestry, or else I would find the resulting tangled skein simply overwhelming, and unpleasant to look upon as well. And if I were to feel that way about it, I can only imagine how distasteful the finished mess would appear to the casual reader.

Often, one case did not have a clear and definite finish before bleeding into the next. For example, this became most obvious to me when trying to recreate the events of the Sholto murder, and the subsequent pursuit of the Great Agra Treasure, which I recounted in the aforementioned *Sign of the Four.* That particular investigation, only the second that I had prepared for publication, took place in September 1888, which was no doubt part of the busiest and most complex period of time that I can ever recall facing Holmes, and only to a slightly lesser degree, myself.

That fall was crowded with events, and my notes for the months of September through November alone fill five thick volumes. Our involvement with the steeply escalating problem of the Whitechapel Murders, as well as taking care of the many other calls upon Holmes's attention – including one notable and lengthy trip to Dartmoor – are narratives that I have either already presented for publication, or that I may record elsewhere at another time. Suffice it to say that when it came time to write up *The Sign of the Four* two years later, at the request of an American publisher in 1890, I was faced with the considerable dilemma of deciding how to record *only* the events of the Sholto murder, while leaving out any references to the other matters which were occurring concurrently.

I believe that I accomplished my mission, and that the final published narrative appears to be self-contained, with no indication in the least that between and woven throughout the events surrounding our pursuit of Jonathan Small, we also visited Whitechapel on a number of occasions, including one grim trip to view the murder site of one of the Ripper's victims, on that very same early morning following our ill-fated trip to the Thames with that amazing dog, Toby, detouring by way of a creosote barrel.

Later, in the spring of 1891 when I believed that Holmes had died at the Reichenbach Falls while locked in mortal combat with Professor Moriarty (of evil memory), I again set out to record some of Holmes's cases, both to preserve his reputation for posterity, as well as to protect it from the malicious aspersions of the Professor's brother, the Colonel. Reaching an agreement with a periodical that had only recently gone into business a few months earlier, an arrangement that I believe has been beneficial to both of us over the years, I began to write about my friend Holmes. And I was faced with an overwhelming amount of material from which to choose.

I have always tended to favor those cases which showed various aspects of my friend's gifts, rather than selecting the most exciting tales simply for the sake of titillating the reading audience. Thus, in 1891 I was again forced to narrate specific and isolated pieces of each day involved, stitching them together to make single self-contained tales while carefully leaving out references to many other cases that were occurring simultaneously.

As Holmes's practice developed over the years, so did his abilities, and he was able to juggle successfully a number of cases at the same time. Careful reading of my narratives might reveal that a breakfast conversation, for instance, is the only recorded action that occurs on an identified day that is related to that specific case, without alluding to what else happened with some other completely unconnected investigation occurring at the same time. Hopefully I may be forgiven for writing in such a way as to imply that this was the sole occurrence that actually took place on that day, and that Holmes then spent the rest of those hours on just that one solitary matter. I also plead for mercy for giving the impression that Holmes spent a great deal of his time simply waiting around the sitting room at 221b without purpose, ill-tempered or worse, as he wished for cases and clients to appear. This device, making each case into an isolated island on its own, was used – against my better judgment, perhaps – to increase interest at the dramatic start of a published narrative, and was suggested to me by my literary agent. It was not a device that I always favored, but it had its uses.

In fact, Holmes's cases overlapped one another considerably, often with the next beginning while the current was still in motion. Some moved linearly from start to finish without interruption, while others stretched, a piece here and a piece there, across weeks, months, or even years and decades. There are cases from the past that resonated into the present, or times when Holmes's path was detoured from the middle of one case into a completely different matter without warning. A few never reached any conclusion at all. Sometimes, as in the matter of the stolen Dickens letter which I propose to include in this collection, Holmes would find himself surrounded by the returning ripples of a matter that he had believed to be concluded years earlier, with the guilty miscreant supposedly far behind him. I have chosen the other cases in this portfolio to reflect these same aspects.

I trust that this collection will meet with approval, as have others in the past. I am gratified with the continuing interest in narratives related to Holmes's methods, and I plan to continue providing them to the public for as long as I am able. In the days which lie ahead of us, I believe that reminders of my friend's skill, as well as his unflagging patriotism and chivalry, will be of value to us all.

I go now to join Holmes in another investigation, this time on the Continent. I shall depart as soon as I complete this introductory material, only stopping on the way to drop off the manuscript with my friend Lomax for his review and amusement, where it will be held until such time as either Holmes or myself can retrieve it and take it on to the publisher. I trust that, barring any unforeseen circumstances, it will soon be in your hands, dear reader, and that you find as much joy in the reading of Holmes's adventures as I have had recalling them.

John H. Watson
2 July, 1929*

* Editor's Note: Sadly, Watson passed away on July 24th, 1929. Obviously, he never retrieved these notes from his friend, Lomax, who, along with Lomax's heirs, waited a long time for someone in a deerstalker to show up and take possession of them. I don't know why Holmes never retrieved them, but I'm glad that I was able to receive them.

The Mystery at Kerrett's Rood

M r. Sherlock Holmes finished lighting his pipe, and concluded by stating, ". . . and I cannot say that it is likely to weigh very heavily upon my conscience." With that, he flipped his spent match out the window and into the warm April air of the English countryside.

Holmes was referring to his own recent actions, which had resulted just hours before in the death of a particularly evil man, and I could not disagree with him at all. We had only met the dead man once during his lifetime, but that was all that had been needed to size up the black-hearted villain. We had just spent a horrifying night, hiding in silence while waiting for a diabolical murder attempt to take place. The murderer's scheme had been turned back on him, and he had fallen in the same agony and terror that he had caused for his first victim, and had attempted to impose on his second. The killer, one of the most grim and immoral men that Holmes and I had ever faced, was now dead himself, no doubt because of Holmes's frantic and successful efforts to repel the lethal creature that had been sent to kill the dead man's poor stepdaughter.

I had been grateful the previous night for the warm and dry spring weather, as we made our way in darkness from the local inn at Stoke Moran, and through the dense undergrowth of the neglected estate to the manor house. Now, however, the balmy air, along with the relaxation that inevitably arrives at the end of a tense adventure, threatened to put me to sleep.

We were returning from Harrow, where we had taken the unfortunate surviving stepdaughter to stay with her aunt, following the previous night's events. The train was unusually crowded that morning with travelers going up to London. As we pulled into some small station in the vicinity of Sudbury Hill, I could see the press of humanity stepping toward the great resting beast, anxious to board before it renewed its relentless journey to the capital. I sighed and shifted. Holmes and I had been unable to get a private carriage, and I knew that we were about to have fellow sojourners joining us.

I was soon proved correct. The door opened to reveal a small middle-aged woman, who began to carefully step up into the compartment. Behind her was a large man with a case, wearing a slightly-too-small billy-cock which accentuated his red meaty face and great untrimmed moustache. He was quite impatient for the woman to get out of his way so that he could entrain as well.

I was amused to see that the woman paused for the smallest of instants, glancing back and forth from myself to Holmes. Her eyes narrowed when she observed his pipe. This helped to make her decision, as she turned to her left and sat down beside me. The large man took the opposite seat, settling in by Holmes, who glanced at me in wry amusement. The man put his oversized case on the floor behind his feet, and began to pat around his coat before pulling out the makings of a cigarette.

Beside me, the woman gave a small disapproving cough, as only the ladies can do, spurring the large man to glance up. She glared at the tobacco pouch in his hands with fierce yet concentrated subtlety, causing him to deflate somewhat and return it to whence it came. I knew that there was no prohibition on smoking in this compartment, and I wondered what Holmes would do when the lady inevitably turned her gaze upon him, and his recently-lit pipe.

As I expected, he ruefully smiled, nodded to her, and reached over to the window, knocking out the ashes and still-unburned tobacco onto the ground below. I hoped that gallantly surrendering to the woman's wishes would not cause a track fire. As the door slammed shut and the guards' whistles signaled our departure, Holmes returned the offending implement to its resting place underneath his Inverness.

Our strong-willed feminine companion did not feel the need to gloat over her victories. She simply turned and looked out the door to her right as the train resumed its movement towards London.

The large man, deprived of his stimulant, chose a different path and settled into an immediate doze, his face appearing to collapse around the fixed constant of its wild moustache. I envied him.

We rode in silence for some moments, and my feelings of drowsiness, due to the warm weather and the complete lack of sleep the night before, began to overtake me. Only the fear of appearing to be like the softly snoring bear across from me kept me awake at all, although I have no doubt that my struggles were visible to my other companions. Finally, as though taking pity on me, Holmes began a conversation that was certain to revive me.

"Do you believe in Providence, madam?" he asked the woman to my right.

She looked up sharply from whatever inner thoughts she had been pursuing, and frowned as might be expected, possibly fearing that she had stumbled into a nest of proselytizing zealots.

Holmes smiled, as if to dispense with her concern. Finally, as if deciding that he was harmless, or if not, that she was worthy to stand against him, she replied in a slight Scottish accent, "I do, but I also believe that the Good Lord expects us to help ourselves along the path of life when we are able."

"Then," replied Holmes, "you will be happy to learn that your efforts to assist the Divine Plan come to fruition have been successful, and you have been delivered to what, or rather whom, you seek. I am Sherlock Holmes."

This odd statement made no sense to me at all, and the woman seemed as surprised as well for just a moment, before a look of comprehension led to a smile on her face. I would have been surprised that such a grim visage as she had first presented could warm so quickly and pleasantly. "I see that what I have been told about you is true, Mr. Holmes."

"By your sister, no doubt."

"Why, yes. How did you know? I have not been to visit her in a good five years."

"But obviously you must regularly communicate with her, to have some knowledge of me," replied Holmes.

"Certainly," said the woman. "We are constant correspondents, and tales of your activities make up a substantial portion of her letters."

"Yet you did not tell her that you were coming up today?"

"No, for I believed that she might discourage me. Again, how did you know?"

"Because Dr. Watson and I have obviously been away, and if you had notified your sister that you were coming to see us, she would have told you that we were not at home and had not let her know when we might be returning."

"Wait," I said, struggling to catch the discussion which had left me far behind. "Sister?" I looked more closely at our companion. "I think that I see it now. Are you *Mrs. Hudson's* sister?"

"Yes, I am," said the woman, a friendly smile now fully lighting her face, such a sharp contrast to the closed expression that she had previously assumed, one that all travelers wear during a journey at one time or another.

"The resemblance is obvious," said Holmes, "the shape of the ears and eyes, and the skull, if you will forgive me for saying so, madam. The unique ways of speaking certain words, indicating a distinct northern regional dialect, only confirmed the matter once our conversation began. I'm sure if your hands were ungloved, there would be similarities there as well."

"But how did you know to begin with?" asked the lady again. "That it was *you* that I was journeying to see?"

"It was no great feat, I assure you, and I'm rather loath to spoil the effect from such simple reasons. I had observed one of the papers protruding from your book," said Holmes. "I can see from here that, along with your railway ticket, you have written in precise and artificially neat letters, '221 Baker Street' on that long slip of yellow paper, no doubt to have at the ready, should you find a non-English-speaking cabbie at the train station. That, in itself, might indicate that you were simply going to visit your sister. However, below the address, and still partially tucked into the book, is what appears to be the top of a capital letter 'S', followed shortly by a capital "H" as well. As both these letters are also followed by what appears to be the tops of the other lower-case letters in my name, the conclusion was inescapable. And in addition, if you were simply going to visit your sister, you would not have needed to write out my name along with the address for the benefit of a cabbie.

"I must confess," he added, "that modesty prevents me from elaborating on the fact that the particular address you have inscribed is generally known to many of the London cabbies who transport people needing my special skills and abilities.

"Thus, seeing that you had taken care to write it all out ahead of time, including what appeared to be my name, before departing on your journey, I made the conclusion that you were coming to consult me about some problem. I then made a closer examination of you, and was startled to see your quite notable resemblance to our good landlady. A rather circular series of confirmations, as one led to another, confirming it, and returning again to the first.

"You see, Watson," he said, glancing my way, "there really is a place in the world for coincidence."

"Or Providence, as you so recently pointed out," I said, my earlier sleepiness entirely dispelled.

"Exactly," said Holmes. "And now, Mrs. – ?"

"Grimshaw," said the woman. "The widow of Mr. J.A. Grimshaw."

"Mrs. Grimshaw. How may the doctor and I help you? As I said, it is obvious that you did not consult with your sister before departing for London, or you would have realized that we were not at home, and had not indicated when we would return."

"That is correct, Mr. Holmes. Martha has always been the most sensible sister of us all, in every sense of the word, and she might have tried to talk me out of relating my story to you. After all, she would say that it was a just a ghost story, but I know what I've seen. Therefore, I decided to journey up to London, as if I were simply a client, and then listen to my sister's sharp criticism on the matter after the fact."

Holmes glanced out the window as the train slowed for the next station. "Perhaps, if you do not wish for your sister to know about the reason for your trip, it might be better for us to leave the train here, at the next stop, and discuss the matter, instead of traveling on up to town. That would also have the benefit of putting us closer to your home, should we decide to return there, rather than going all the way up to London, simply to come back again."

"That would suit me admirably, Mr. Holmes. There is a small tea shop near this station where we may talk, and you can tell me whether my fears have any merit, or are simply caused from living alone for too long. Although I will tell you," she added, "I am not a woman given to fancy!"

As the train huffed to a stop, we gathered our things and departed, moving awkwardly around the sleeping behemoth sprawled by the door. He sputtered and blew out his moustache several times, but never awakened. I hoped that he roused himself in time to disembark at his destination.

"Do not worry about our friend, the salesman," said Holmes softly, reading my thoughts. "He is obviously from London, and is returning after a successful week or two roaming the Midlands and the West Country. He will awaken at the end of the line and make his way home to his wife and three young children, the youngest being the only boy, who will all be glad to see both him and the small trinkets that he is bringing to them."

Before I could ask how Holmes had determined these facts about the man, he had left me, hurrying to catch up with Mrs. Grimshaw as she turned in her ticket and walked out of the station, never looking back, and rightly assuming that we would be following smartly behind her.

After a short left turn, and then a right into a quiet lane, we found ourselves seated in one of those little tea shops that occur with great regularity throughout the country, crowded with dainty furniture and tea-related appurtenances. It was not too heavily occupied at that time of the morning, and we made our way to a quiet table along a side wall, not quite in the back, but close enough to the front to have the benefit of the morning light without being too visible from the street outside.

We ordered a strong pot of tea and a selection of cakes, although something more substantial, such as coffee and sandwiches, would have been more to my liking, following the night that Holmes and I had just faced. After the comestibles were placed on the table by the shop's apparent owner, a scrubbed-looking and doughy woman in her sixties, Mrs. Grimshaw began her tale.

"As I said, my sister Martha has always been the sensible one of us girls, and I do not doubt that she would have tried to discourage me from asking your advice. However, while I don't like to think of myself as any less sensible, I know what I've seen, and I finally decided that I must speak to you.

47

"I'm fortunate to know so much about you already from Martha's letters, and also from what I hear from time to time from one of our other sisters, Mrs. Turner, who lives nearby, and who I understand occasionally helps Martha when needed."

I nodded. "We think a great deal of both of your sisters."

"The others are just as sensible as well," said Mrs. Grimshaw, taking my comment to refer to their Scottish pragmatism.

"As we grew, we all went our different ways. I married Mr. Grimshaw, who was a soldier at the time, but he was soon invalided out, which suited us both just fine. He had good reference from one of the officers for whom he had done a turn once, and we found positions at a house and grounds north of Sudbury, him as the handyman and groundskeeper, and me as housekeeper.

"I need to describe things so you'll understand me when I tell what I've seen. When we went to work there, over twenty years ago, the house was already mostly empty and closed off, and owned by a retired broker named Mr. Felton."

Holmes's eyebrows slightly lifted. "Clifton Felton?" he asked.

Mrs. Grimshaw smiled. "I see that you remember him. I'm not surprised."

"Well, I'm not ashamed to admit that I have not made his acquaintance," I interrupted.

"All in good time, Watson," said Holmes. "Let Mrs. Grimshaw continue with her narrative, and I'm sure Mr. Felton's relevance will become obvious as we go along."

With a smile, Mrs. Grimshaw continued. "At the time that my husband and I went to work for the man, he was a widower, living a very quiet life amongst his papers and books. He had a young son, still a boy, Theodore, or Ted as he was called. After about ten years or so, Ted grew up and moved away, only visiting on occasion. I believe that he held a job somewhere around Oxford. The two seemed to get along well enough with one another, on the occasions when Ted came to visit.

"My husband and I never had very difficult duties. Mr. Felton did not entertain, and great portions of the house were permanently shut up. The grounds, which consisted of several acres enclosed by a wall, did not require a great deal of work, as Mr. Felton did not have formal gardens. Rather, he simply wished for the natural intrusion of the trees and other plants to be kept at bay, instead of completely tamed. Therefore, my husband usually had his work well in hand each day, and did not require any assistance from other employees, unless he had to bring in an occasional day helper, if a tree fell, for instance, or something else along those lines, that was too much for him.

48

"In the main house, we had a cook and a maid that came in by day, but left in the evenings. My husband and I did not live in the big house – in fact, no one lived there but Mr. Felton. He allowed us to live in a small cottage on the western side of the grounds and its surrounding quarter-acre at that corner of the property, which has come to be known locally as the Kerrett's Rood. The overall property has always been known as Kerrett House, in reference to the rich shipping agent who first built it early in the century. Although there have been several owners since that time, the original name has stuck.

"We existed in the same routine for many years. Cooks and maids would come and go, but naturally, without any great drama. Day in and day out, I would make my way up to the house in the morning and my husband would carry out his tasks outdoors, and we would return to our little cottage at night, leaving Mr. Felton in the house.

"All until September of 1878," said Holmes, with a knowing look.

"Exactly," said Mrs. Grimshaw. "Suddenly, Mr. Felton's quiet life was exposed as a lie, and as it all tumbled down, it shook what my husband and I had with it for a while, despite our complete ignorance of what had happened."

I struggled to remember what had occurred during that time, before quickly realizing that I had not been in England then at all, and could not be expected to know. Earlier that year, I had taken my degree as a Doctor of Medicine at the University of London, and had left London to begin a series of events that eventually took me to the other side of the world and back, before depositing me again in that great metropolitan cesspool, where I would have probably foundered and died if not washing up on the friendly steps leading up to 221b Baker Street.

Holmes noticed my chain of thought, and interrupted. "You would not have known anything about what happened, my friend, although you might have heard me mention it once or twice in passing. Perhaps you recall a reference here or there to the Reckless Goings-on at the Suicide Club?"

I did remember hearing of it, but no details of this case had ever been provided to me. Mrs. Grimshaw nodded in agreement. "That was it. That's what the papers called them. That all took place about the same time that Martha's husband was killed in a railway accident, and she decided to take in boarders. Is that when you first moved there?"

Holmes shook his head, and I added, "Holmes and I met on the first day of January, 1881, when he had learned of the available rooms, and was introduced to me afterwards upon realizing that he needed a fellow lodger to share expenses."

Holmes smiled. "By that point in time, your sister had already been renting the rooms for a year or so, and believed that she understood what was involved with being a landlady." His eyes took on a mischievous glint, and he added, "That was before I moved my little practice there."

We laughed, Mrs. Grimshaw included, and the owner of the shop used the opportunity to approach our table. Mrs. Grimshaw indicated that another pot of tea would be welcome, while I expressed a desire to switch to a cup of strong black coffee instead. The owner quickly returned, and after our cups were filled, Holmes indicated that Mrs. Grimshaw should continue her story. She glanced at me, and then back at Holmes, who said, "Tell us why you have decided to seek me out in London, braving possible discouragement from your sister, whom to my knowledge you have not visited since Watson and I became tenants."

"Because I have seen Mr. Ted Felton, the son, in the window of the big house at night, staring down the hill toward my cottage."

I could see that the statement meant something to Holmes. "And why should that be unusual?" I asked, feeling that I was still very much in the dark.

Holmes answered. "After the events of 1878 were concluded, and Clifton Felton, the father, died, Ted Felton did away with himself."

Mrs. Grimshaw nodded. "I see that you still remember it, Mr. Holmes. After Mr. Clifton's death, and what followed, it was said that Mr. Ted couldn't bear the shame, and that he drowned himself in the Thames."

"Where his body was never found," added Holmes. "And his 'ghost' has contented itself with a peaceful rest for over four years until recently, when suddenly it has returned to haunt his father's former home. I can see why you believed that your sister might discourage you from bringing this story to my attention."

His statement seemed to rub Mrs. Grimshaw the wrong way for a moment, as I could see her eyes tighten, resembling more the grim woman who had first entered our train compartment that morning. But then she seemed to sense what I already knew: Holmes was not dismissing her story outright, and was in fact interested in what circumstances could have led her to believe that a young man had returned from the dead.

"How," said Holmes, "has this manifestation of Ted Felton made itself known?"

"By showing himself in the great window of the big house, that is centered in the very front of the building. It was two weeks or so ago that I first looked up and saw him. I was out in the small garden behind my cottage, seeing what needed to be done for the spring planting, when I glanced up and there he was, framed in the window. As you might recall from before, Mr. Holmes, the land slopes up to the east from the back of my cottage, toward the big house. That main west-facing window looks down toward me. It is several hundred feet away, but I could see him as plain as day, as the evening sun was shining full on the front of the big house. He was always a lanky lad, and he had a unique way of standing, leaning back on one leg as if he were propped on a shooting stick. That first night, I admit, I was so shocked that I just stood and looked. He was there for another minute or so, and then he seemed to vanish."

"How many other times has he appeared?

"Oh, five or six, I suppose. The next night, after I first saw him, I stood around outside at sunset, waiting to see if he appeared again, but he did not. I haven't been out every night since then, but I've tried to see if he reappeared. A few nights he has."

"And did you only watch from the back of your cottage, or did you investigate further?"

"I must admit that I did not want to know anything about why he was there. At least not at first. But last night, when I saw him again, I finally got up my nerve and took the old key and made my way up there."

"And the house has stood empty since the tragedy to which you have referred took place in 1878?" I interrupted. "Who is the current owner of the property? Are you the caretaker?"

"After Mr. Clifton Felton died, and then Mr. Ted followed soon after, I was visited by the old family solicitor, Benjamin Weekes. His office is located in the village, in the High Street. He had known the Felton family for many years, and I believe there was some gossip that, when they were all young, Mr. Weekes had set his cap for the woman who later became Mr. Clifton's wife. Of course, this was long before I knew any of them."

"I heard something of it at the time, during that day or so when I was in the village," said Holmes.

"Mr. Weekes explained that, while Mr. Clifton's affairs were tangled because of the events that led to his death, Mr. Ted had inherited his own separate income from his mother, and that the father's will had indicated that after his death, my husband and I were to inherit Kerrett's Rood, which would be sectioned off as its own property, and that the residue of the money would go to pay the taxes on the remaining estate for as long as it would last. Mr. Weekes told me that the amount of money left by Mr. Ted would last a long time.

"My husband, while he was still alive, worked out an arrangement with Mr. Weekes to continue to keep up the estate. He would maintain the grounds in a limited way, and check the house on a regular basis. After my husband passed last year, I've hired some day jobbers to work in the grounds as needed, but the house has stood empty this entire time, although I do walk through it once a quarter or so to see that everything remains the same. It is a solid old place, and may sit there for many years as it is, dark and quiet and still inside. I take in work as a seamstress now, and Mr. Weekes still sends me something each month for keeping an eye on the place, but I don't have the time or the authorization to keep the house clean inside. So there it stands, and will continue to do so, I suppose. Which is why I was so surprised to see Mr. Ted's spirit come back."

"And you've only seen it manifest itself at sunset?" said Holmes. "It is a curious spirit indeed that eschews the haunted midnight hour to reveal itself during daylight. You say that he only first appeared a couple of weeks ago. Around the twenty-first day of March?"

Mrs. Grimshaw nodded, and Holmes continued, "Around the first of spring, then. Had you been outside much before that in the evenings, or was that an activity that you had only recently resumed, upon the return of warm weather, and the need to begin preparations for this year's garden?"

"Just about then, I should say," replied Mrs. Grimshaw. "Everything was all tucked away tidily enough last fall for the winter, and there was no need to go out back until recently."

"Just so," said Holmes. "And the big windows where you saw this spirit face toward the west, so they are directly looking at the setting sun, whose path across the earth is progressing northwards this time of year. Our ancients understood where to look for the rising and setting of the sun against the horizon on different dates, and it still has an effect on our activities as well."

"Do you mean," I said, "that the springtime sunset was in such a location as to fully highlight the large windows where the figure was seen, whereas in the winter it might have lit the house from a different direction?"

"Exactly," said Holmes. "The spirit, or whatever it is, might have been standing there in that location for weeks or even months before Mrs. Grimshaw first spotted it – or him – but it was only the combination of her desire to examine the area behind her house, along with the exact angle of the sun on those windows upon those dates, that made him visible. In fact, I would wager that the figure, man or spirit, who was standing in those windows looking down the hill, did not see you at all, Mrs. Grimshaw."

"But how could that be?" she asked. "It is only a few hundred yards away, and I was right there in front of him. The lawn slopes between the two buildings, and there are no trees or bushes between to block his view."

"Yes, but he was facing into the setting sun," said Holmes, "and you were in the shadow cast by your cottage, as the sun was setting behind it. That is why he probably felt free to return to the window on subsequent nights. He did not believe that he had been observed."

"You sound as if you already have a theory, Holmes," I said.

"And so I do," he replied. "Let us make our way back to the station, and we will journey with Mrs. Grimshaw to Kerrett's Rood. I'm afraid that your visit to your sister will have to be postponed," said Holmes. He then lifted his teacup, which had been mostly ignored during the conversation, and swallowed the entire contents in two gulps.

I could see that that owner of the shop had been watching us with some impatience as we continued to occupy space, although there did not seem to be any great influx of patrons as the morning progressed. Happy to accommodate, we paid our bill and stepped out into the quiet street.

We made our way to the station, and only had to wait a few minutes for a down train to arrive. While Mrs. Grimshaw and I stood about, Holmes sent several wires, without revealing their destination or contents. There were far fewer passengers waiting to travel away from London, and we quickly found a private compartment. I noticed with a suppressed grin that Holmes, always the gentleman when circumstances allowed, made an effort to lead us to one that did not accommodate smoking.

After we had seated ourselves, Holmes said, "While we make our way, perhaps we can elaborate for Doctor Watson the tragic events of 1878, so he will have some context of what I expect to discover when we arrive."

Mrs. Grimshaw nodded and began. "As you mentioned earlier, it was late September, 1878, just another month in just another year. Mr. Felton's son, Ted, was away at the time, as he usually was, probably in Oxford, but I couldn't say for sure.

"I need to further explain how the estate around Kerrett House is laid out, for the doctor's benefit. It is a walled enclosure of about five acres. As I have said, the grounds were managed by my husband, but not strictly controlled and landscaped, if you understand my meaning. The house itself sits in the middle of the property, on a slight rise that drops off in all directions. There are a few small outbuildings at the back toward the eastern wall, but they are still quite a distance from the walls.

"The only building that is adjacent to the wall is the cottage in which I live, on the West Road. In fact, the front of the cottage is part of the wall, so that my front door opens directly into the street, and the first floor windows look down into it. There is only one door in that whole wall, front or back, other then the front door to my house, and it is the great gate that also opens onto the West Road. This is located some little distance from my house, in the same side.

"This gate is probably twenty feet wide, in two ten-foot sections that swing wide when something big goes in or out. Set into one of these sections is a smaller door for regular in-and-out foot traffic. That is what we used when we needed to enter or leave on any normal day."

"We?" interrupted Holmes. "Who would have used that gate, or visited the Felton house?"

"Why, the cook and maid would come in by the regular door in the gate, as would my husband or myself if we had business in that direction. That was where Mr. Felton's son would enter as well, when he was home. Tradesmen would use it when they brought supplies to the big house, although sometimes they would deliver in a wagon. If that was the case, arrangements would be made for my husband to unlock and open the big gate."

"So the large gate was normally kept locked, but the regular door there was not?"

"During the day only. And at night, the smaller door was locked as well, by my husband. Of course," she added, "my husband and I used the front door in our own house, which opened through the wall into the street, to go in and out as we felt like."

"Did Mr. Felton leave specific standing instructions that the gate be locked?"

"He did," replied Mrs. Grimshaw. "He greatly valued his privacy, and did not really see anyone during the day but me or my husband. The cook and the maid stayed out of his way, and he kept to himself. At night, when the small staff would leave, he wanted the gate locked. He told me that, living as he did in that big house, he did not like the idea of people getting in at night and roaming the grounds, and him up there alone. It did not seem to be unusual to either me or my husband, and locking the gate was simply one of the few duties in my husband's day."

"Thank you," said Holmes. "I quite understand."

Mrs. Grimshaw smiled and continued. "September 1878 was like any other month, until that early morning when the police knocked us up, showing us papers and demanding to be let into the grounds. For it turned out that Mr. Felton, the man that we had believed was asleep in the big house, was dead in the cellar of a London warehouse. And as if that were not enough, it turned out that he was the leader of a criminal gang that had been in existence for years."

Holmes nodded, and Mrs. Grimshaw said, "I believe at this point, Mr. Holmes, you might be able to tell us more than I can of what was behind Mr. Felton's mysterious past. Even after nearly five years, come this September, I'm not sure that I understand it all."

As Holmes gathered his thoughts for a moment, and then said, "At the time these events were going on, I was living in Montague Street, beside the British Museum, dividing my efforts unevenly between investigations and my unique studies. When I became involved in this investigation, I had no idea that it would lead to exposure of the Suicide Club as well, of which we have recently spoken."

"But not explained," I said. "I am anxious to hear about this grim-sounding group. Did it have anything to do with Stevenson's story, first published about that same time, if I recall correctly?"*

"I believe that around the time these events first came to light, some clever member of the press remembered the title of Stevenson's book and appropriated it. Otherwise, there were no connections.

"Without taking too much of our time with this tale, I was approached in early September of that year by the banker, Sir Wilton Cole, whose house in Surrey had been burglarized a week or so before.

"Most of the silver plate, as well as some minor artworks, had been taken. It was not a substantial loss to Sir Wilton, but he was nevertheless quite angry, and did not enjoy being taken advantage of without making some effort to fight back.

"He informed me that it was the opinion of the authorities that the crime seemed to be the latest to have been perpetrated by a group known as the Bracknell Gang. They had come to be given that colorful title throughout Surrey, and areas to the north and west, not because of any known fact about them that would affix the name to them, but rather because Bracknell was the first location that one of their robberies had seemingly taken place.

"The crimes were all very similar in method, location, and what was stolen. They had been occurring for several years at that point on a sporadic but predictable basis. The loot would eventually turn up in London, having been sold and resold, untraceable, and long after the actual robberies. I must admit that, in my more-than-adequate time to study London crime during those periods between clients in my Montague Street rooms, I had found several occasions to look into the activities of the supposed Bracknell Gang and ponder their methodologies. Since this is another story for another time, and without elaborating too much, which I am sure is a disappointment to the doctor," he said, smiling in my direction, "I will simply say that I had been able to form a theory or two, and I was glad of this opportunity to test them first hand."

* Editor's Note: See *The Suicide Club* (1878) a collection of three related stories by Robert Louis Stevenson.

"I traveled to Sir Wilton's Surrey home, with a letter in my pocket informing his staff to provide all cooperation that I would need. In short, I saw evidence, underneath the trampling of the police, that three men had been involved in the crime. I tracked them across the grounds to where a wagon had been secured in a nearby copse at the rear of the estate, alongside a small and little-used farm road. The wagon had a crooked left rear wheel, and the footmarks of the horse had their own unique characteristics, especially in the poor way in which the right rear shoe had been attached. The wagon had been there for an hour or so, unattended but with the horse tied, based on the evidence on the ground. Also, the wagon was heavier leaving than it had been when it had arrived. If Sir Wilton had waited one more day to seek me out, the clues would have faded away.

"I managed to follow the trail to a nearby village, where I located both the wagon and the horse at a stable. They had been rented on the day of the robbery. I obtained a very accurate description of the three men, since it was quite unusual that the wagon had been returned so late at night. With this description in hand, I also discovered that these same three men had been at the local railway station an hour or so before returning the wagon, where they had arranged to ship a number of sealed wooden crates on the last train of the night, the very same train that they themselves used. It was relatively easy from that point, based on the descriptions and carelessness of the burglars, to track them back to an area north of Sudbury. The crates were to be delivered to that station, where they would be held until retrieved.

"They had become rather arrogant after several years of successful robberies, and had not bothered to take the time to adequately cover their trail. An hour or two of asking questions identified the three men, two of whom were locals who had taken delivery of the crates, Amos Sykes and Steven Wells. The third, as you will have determined, my dear Watson, was our reclusive Mr. Clifton Felton.

"I made my way to the local constabulary, well aware that my youth and small reputation at the time would require some little extra effort on my part in order to convince them that the three men were in fact the Bracknell Gang. In particular, from what I had learned, this Mr. Felton, a retired broker who seemed to live a quiet and reclusive life within his walled estate, would seem a most unlikely villain.

"I made my initial explanations, and was soon passed along to an Inspector Ross, since deceased, who tolerantly allowed me to explain my reasoning. He listened with increasing interest as I made my case.

"Finally, he said, 'I am convinced, Mr. Holmes. At least enough to follow up on what you have brought to me. But there is one thing, one small factor that you should know. Perhaps, being away from London for

56

a day or so as you trailed these three men, you have been prevented from hearing the latest news.'

"He handed me a wire from London sent that very day, revealing the death of Mr. Clifton Felton, just the night before. He had killed himself in the basement of a London warehouse. Although we did not know it yet, not having any idea of the true nature of the crime, Felton's would turn out to be the last of the deaths connected to the reckless 'Suicide Club'."

Mrs. Grimshaw nodded, while I sat up straighter, interested in learning more of this sinister and intriguing organization.

Holmes, however, veered away from it, instead stating, "Inspector Ross explained that he was expecting a representative from Scotland Yard on the next train, whereupon they would go to the house to break the news to the staff. My information relating to the robbery added a new layer to the problem. By the time the London man had arrived, Ross had a warrant to examine the property, looking for stolen goods. He had also sent out men to take Amos Sykes and Steven Wells into custody for further questioning.

"And so I set out for Kerrett House with Inspector Ross, along with Inspector Plummer from London, whom I previously knew." He turned to Mrs. Grimshaw, "I do not know if you recall that I was accompanying the police when we searched Mr. Felton's house."

"You'll forgive me, I'm sure, that I did not notice you. I was understandably not very observant that morning," she said. Turning to me, she explained, "The day had started like any other. My husband and I were up very early, eating our own breakfast before he was to leave, in order to unlock the small gate for the cook and maid, and I to go on up to the big house. The cook and maid were never required to arrive particularly early, as Mr. Felton always slept until mid-morning. Only later did we realize that he was probably sleeping so late because he was often out far into the night, and he was not home in bed as we had always believed.

"We did not know that the police had arrived and had been pounding on the main gate for quite some time before one of them got the idea to knock on our door."

"Actually, I was the one who knocked on your door," said Holmes. "However, Inspector Ross had followed me down the wall to your house, and by the time you opened it, it was he who took charge, with great authority."

"As I said, I'm afraid that I don't recall you," said Mrs. Grimshaw. "In any event, we were told that there was evidence indicating Mr. Felton was the leader of a long-standing burglary ring, and there was a warrant to search the house and grounds. In addition, the inspector mentioned, almost as an afterthought, that Mr. Felton was dead by his own hand."

"You can imagine, gentlemen, that this news fairly astounded me and my poor husband. Mr. Felton, who never left home – or so we thought then – was accused of being a criminal, and he had been found dead as well, on the far side of London. And there was every indication that the police believed that we were somehow involved in his crimes along with him."

"The police mind," said Holmes, "first looks at everyone with suspicion, assuming that all involved are initially guilty, and then sorts out the wheat from the chaff later, so to speak, hopefully successfully. When I first presented my theories to Inspector Ross, I could tell that he was even weighing my own possible involvement and guilt in the matter, as if my accusations were part of some too-clever plan to implicate one of my fellow gang-members and thus take over the operation for myself. As you know, it was soon established that neither you nor your husband had any knowledge of Mr. Felton's night-time activities."

Mrs. Grimshaw nodded. "And for that I'm grateful, Mr. Holmes. After the police were let in, the house was searched, and a great deal of the stolen materials were found hidden in a locked room in the basement of the big house. But one great mystery was that there was never any explanation as to how they had actually come to be there. My husband always locked the only gate every night, and surely we would have noticed something suspicious during the years that the gang was going about its business. We never saw any signs of anyone leaving or entering at night, let along carrying in heaps of stolen property. We truly believed that Mr. Felton stayed inside and had no visitors."

"And you may not have been aware that no key for the gate was ever found in the big house, or on Mr. Felton's person. The only key that we could locate was your husband's, which had remained with him the entire time. How the loot came to be in the basement of the house, as well as the other indications that the two other gang members were frequent visitors down there, remains a mystery to this day. Inspector Ross theorized that somehow they came and went over the back wall, but I remain unconvinced, as the estate is surrounded by fairly well-traveled roads on all sides, and moving that amount of material back and forth over the walls, even in the dead of night, in order to carry it across the grounds and hide it in the house, seems unlikely and would have left some trace. And there was no indication anywhere that the walls had been climbed or breached, and no paths in the grounds leading from the walls to the house. Sykes and Wells were certainly never forthcoming with any useful information. They went to Dartmoor with the secret sealed within them."

"But surely," I said, "you must have theorized some other explanation."

"Ah, Watson, you must remember that I was younger then, only twenty-four years old. I was still learning my craft, and not as confident as I am now. Besides, Inspector Ross was not interested in finding out specifics. He had captured the Bracknell Gang, he had recovered some, if not all, of the booty, and he did not yet know the deeper connection to the sensational events of the Suicide Club, as it came to be called afterwards in the London papers. He was more than full with the meal that I had brought to him. He did not need to seek anything else."

"And this 'Suicide Club'?" I asked. "What was it? How did it fit in to this odd business?"

"Again, that should be another story for another time. Nevertheless – "

"But Holmes!" I interrupted, refusing to be denied the details of this intriguing story. "Surely it is relevant to Mrs. Grimshaw's problem."

"As I started to say," Holmes continued, "I will give a short précis of the events, so that Mr. Felton's death, and the subsequent suicide of his son Ted, may be better understood."

He glanced out the window and said, "I see by the slow progression of the quarter-mile posts that I should have time to tell you what happened next.

"Following the exposure of the robbery gang, and the arrest of the surviving members, I returned to Montague Street. I was not completely satisfied with the case, as there were several questions left unexplained. How had the loot made its way to the big house without any signs being left of its passage? What had prompted Clifton Felton to take his own life, on the very night before his long-standing criminal activities were about to be exposed? Was there a connection, or was it merely coincidence, which does happen more than I would like. I intended to see what could be discovered in London, at the other end of the matter, on my own time and for my own edification. Before I could begin, however, I was visited by Mr. Ted Felton, who had come up to London to hire me to answer the very same questions that I had been asking myself.

"Even then, I was learning to recognize the various approaches that a client might make as they made their way to my lodgings. Whether they forcefully approached the door and pulled the bell with great vehemence, or possibly stepped close to the doorway in a timid fashion several times, before veering off and then returning, finally overcoming great reluctance to meekly climb the stairs to state their business, each client was a great study for an up-and-coming consulting detective. I had observed Ted Felton from my first-floor window. He came straight on, with the look of a man walking with grim purpose to the gallows.

"When he was shown in, he took a few moments to get to the reason for his visit, a reason that I had already divined: He wished to know what lay behind his father's participation in the robbery ring, and more importantly, why had had killed himself.

"I could see that something else was on his mind, until he finally could not hold it in any longer. 'Mr. Holmes, do you think that word of your trailing my father from the robbery site in Surrey could have reached him, and he therefore chose to end his life before he was to be arrested?'

"I had been asking myself the same question, but I had already decided that I had been quite careful not to reveal any information during my travels, nor had I given my questions too much importance as I tracked the robbers. Clifton Felton could not have known that I was on his trail, and his suicide must have come about from some other cause. So I said to Ted Felton, and I think that he believed me. I agreed to examine the matter further.

"After he departed, I made my way from Montague Street down to Scotland Yard, where I found Inspector Plummer, now long since retired. I questioned him about several aspects of the matter, including the whereabouts of Sykes and Wells on the night of the suicide. He had established without a doubt that both men were in the local pub near their homes, and had not been in London when Felton's suicide occurred.

"Inspector Plummer also revealed other specific circumstances related to the events of Clifton Felton's death. He told me that the body had been found in the basement of a warehouse, one of those brooding and dangerous buildings between Cannon Street and the Thames. The building had been standing empty for nearly a year, as the heirs to the previous owner squabbled amongst themselves, choosing to make no income in the meantime in order to spite one another. There had been no reason to believe that Felton would have been found anytime soon, perhaps not for weeks, except that a message had been left at the nearby police station, stating that a man, named specifically in the note as Clifton Felton, had hanged himself at that particular warehouse. A couple of constables had been dispatched to the scene, whereupon they confirmed the contents of the short note.

"Inspector Plummer had the note with him, in his file relating to the case, and he gladly let me examine it. I could see right away that it was not written by some civic-minded vagrant who had trespassed into the warehouse and discovered the body. It was on good quality paper, with better ink than one might expect from that area, and there were no instances in the note of either misspellings or punctuation errors. I asked Plummer if the quality of the note did not seem unusual to him, but he commented that he had not found it to be so. He expected that it was

60

probably left by one of the children of the former owner, who had been inspecting the property and found the body. Rather than become involved in the matter, an anonymous note had been written. When asked how the writer had known that the dead man was Clifton Felton, and could thus name him in the note, Plummer dismissed my query by saying that the discoverer of the body no doubt knew Felton when he was a broker, before his retirement.

"I was filled with objections, as this theory assumed too much without proving anything, but to Plummer the case was closed. Thanking him, I departed and wondered what to do next. More to fill up my time than having any expectation of discovering a new fact, I made my way to the warehouse, in order to inspect the scene of the death. Something was preventing me, even at that point, of thinking of it as a suicide.

"Although the building was sealed, I had no difficulty in gaining entrance. I quickly saw that there was very little to be learned, as the building truly had been closed and empty for quite some time. There were no signs of any vagrants having obtained access, and the movements of the various policemen at the time of the body's discovery were quite obvious. The remains of the rope were still tied around a rafter, but it had been cut, certainly when the body was removed. I realized that I would have to return to Scotland Yard to ask if the knotted section from around the dead man's neck had been retained. It was something that I should have thought to ask about when I was there, showing that at that point in my career, I still had much to learn. If I had examined the knot on my first trip, the second would not have been necessary. I retraced my steps westward. I left Scotland Yard later that afternoon, having determined that the rope was knotted in a perfectly ordinary fashion, and not showing any signs of exotic origin, such as might have been tied by a one-armed Siamese sailor."

I could see that Holmes made the last statement with a twinkle in his eye, and Mrs. Grimshaw, who did not know him as well, appeared to believe that he was speaking in jest and that such an obscure clue could not exist. The irony was that, in spite of Holmes's subtle ridicule of such a thing, just such a knot had been relevant not three weeks before, although the matter had related to a complicated and grotesque fraud case, rather than a murder.

"Not knowing where to turn next," Holmes continued, "I decided to start over and look for a pattern, a system that has been of use to me in the past. Returning to Montague Street, I began to examine my scrapbooks, which even then were proving to be quite useful. It was there that I found the loose thread. I had been reminded of something while I was examining

61

the warehouse, and I was sure that there was information about it back in my rooms.

"And I was correct. Over the past eight months, there had been six seemingly unconnected suicides, all men of Clifton Felton's approximate age and station in life. Each was an older man, retired from a professional career. Each was a widower who, if he did have children, did not live with him. In fact, each of the men lived alone, with a minimal housekeeping staff. Each was believed to be the sort of man who stayed in at night, and each had been found in remote London locations, dead by their own hands, although by a variety of methods, including a couple of hangings, one who left the gas on in a rented room, two self-inflicted gunshot wounds, and one fellow who was suffocated by shutting himself up in a servant's bedroom in an empty house while burning a brazier full of charcoal. In each case, an anonymous note had been left for the authorities, telling where the men might be found, and specifically naming them to speed their identification.

"Those were the stories of the six men that I found, based on clippings that I had kept for my scrapbooks. It was my habit to docket news stories related to odd or unusual deaths, but I was not yet experienced enough to have noticed the pattern when I first clipped the stories, spread out as they were over a number of months. And even after identifying those six, I did not realize then how many others there were. However, surely six was enough to indicate further investigation was required.

"Even in those days, I was making connections within the police force, and no one was more obligated to me than our old friend, Inspector Lestrade. He was able to allow me access to the files regarding these various and seemingly unrelated suicides. As they had been spread out over a period of months, had occurred in different parts of London and the surrounding Home Counties, and had involved victims who lived in all the compass points around the capital, no one had associated any connection between them. I started with a list of six names, and by the time I had combed through the Yard's files, I had identified thirteen other probable and similar victims, going back for a period of several years.

"I shared my findings with Lestrade, who agreed that there was indeed a pattern. He also held my belief that this needed to be investigated quietly, so as not to spook whoever was involved in what was seemingly a large number of similarly suspicious suicides.

"I spent the better part of a week traveling here and there, cautiously interviewing servants, family members, train station employees, and cabbies, who might have remembered taking any of the men in question to any common locations. Eventually, one recurring factor became clear. At some time before their deaths, the men in question had been spending an evening or two a week at a pub in Hampstead, unknown to their servants.

"I had determined this by querying various railway employees in the stations near each man's home, determining through further questioning along the line that their destinations had been Hampstead. Once there, I was able to find one or two people who remembered the destination of this or that man. I assure you that what I have boiled down to a sentence or two was rigorous and painstaking work, and for every successful thread that I isolated and followed to its conclusion, I had to drop a hundred others. It was an excellent educational experience for a young consulting detective, I can assure you.

"By the end of my investigations, I had identified a common locality as 'The Dog and Wolf' in Hampstead. It will do you no good to look for it the next time you are up that way. It is out of business and gone, and both of the owners, a pair of brothers named Will and Edward Duval, are no longer there either, or with us among the quick at all, for that matter.

"Edward actually ran the pub. Will, who went by the more formal 'William' when he was in the City every day, worked for several life insurance companies over the course of his last few years. It was there that he managed to keep track of the various insurance policies that he and his brother had taken out in the names of the numerous dead men, naming fictitious individuals of their own invention as beneficiaries.

"It was never clear exactly how their scheme started, and obviously they were not very forthcoming in revealing how many men had fallen into their trap, beyond the number that we confirmed. Their scheme was simple. They had gained a reputation for running an establishment that seemed to attract older, retiring men of like backgrounds and disposition. By providing several less-than-salubrious activities to their hand-picked customers, they managed to keep these men returning on a semi regular basis. And every once in a while, when they had found out enough about this or that man to know personal information and forge signatures, they would apply for a life insurance policy, with a fictitious person as the beneficiary. Usually, Will would open an account at an out-of-the way bank in this fictitious person's name, so there would be a place for the insurance payments to be deposited. Then, once the funds were there, the account would be quietly closed and the money funneled back to the two brothers.

"Ordinarily, this scheme could not succeed. However, Will Duval had worked for a number of years as a trusted employee of some of the larger insurance firms in the City, and he was able to slip the policies through the cracks in the system at each of his employers. Then, after each of the victims died, he would process the claim himself, while making sure that any mention of suicide did not show on the official books, as that would invalidate the policy. However, when the Duvals killed their victims, they had to make it *appear* as a suicide so that there would be no ongoing murder investigations. And it was the two of them who left the anonymous notes, so that the bodies could be discovered quickly, speeding along the death payment from the insurance companies.

"None of the policies were ever very large, and therefore did not attract attention from anyone higher up at any of the firms. During the course of their activities, Will changed employers three times, always welcome at his new location, and always careful to leave the previous employer before anything unusual was noticed.

"It seems likely that they were working this system for a while before eventually attempting to take a big prize, one that would perhaps allow them to leave the country. However, their last victim, Clifton Felton, was, to their misfortune, also identified at the same time as the leader of a burglary ring. It was, as it turned out, a coincidence that Felton had been murdered while he was being scrutinized and pursued for his crimes.

"The arrest of the two brothers was surprisingly a quiet affair. The police, led by Lestrade, closed upon the pub, catching both brothers unaware. Their records were easily found, as they had become quite careless due to the ongoing success of their schemes. A few other names of victims were revealed as well, bringing the total number of murdered men to nearly two dozen. It was believed at the time that there may have been even more, before they began to document their records in such a helpfully systematic way.

"Lestrade received a commendation of some sort that turned out to be of value to him, and I subsequently received his gratitude. The insurance companies were both embarrassed at the way the two brothers had used the weaknesses within their system in order to hide their activities, and they were also grateful that these same weaknesses had at last been exposed. They have since tightened up many aspects of the way they do business. And the press, once it learned of the activities promoted at 'The Dog and Wolf' that had been used to attract the lonely old men and start them on the path to their early deaths, was happy to have a story with all the seamy aspects ready made that sell newspapers. The fact that Stevenson's story, 'The Suicide Club,' had appeared just months earlier, only helped to give them a peg to hang their hat upon.

"However, neither of us, Lestrade nor myself, could ever figure the complete story behind Clifton Felton's relationship to the events. No doubt he had heard about the place from someone or other, by word of mouth. He may have been leaving his home at night for years. His visits to the pub were verified as having started a month or so preceding his death. His movements were traced from the station near his home to Hampstead, and then back again in the early hours. But after all was said and done relating to the matter of his murder, we never learned how he departed from his property to either go out at night or to commit the robberies, any more than we could determine how the burglary ring was able to enter or depart the premises, leaving a mound of stolen loot in the basement.

"But there was one final chapter left in the story, or so I thought until today. The part about Ted Felton, and his death following the revelations regarding his father."

There would be no time to hear this part of the story now. The train was pulling into the station. We stepped down to the platform, but instead of moving toward the exit, Holmes walked over to a man standing off to one side, wearing a stiff-looking glove on his left hand and a noticeable red scarf around his throat. The fellow handed Holmes a packet of documents which turned out to be a collection of telegrams. Holmes and the man in the scarf shook hands, and the fellow turned and left without another word.

"That was Sacker," said Holmes. "He sometimes acts as my unofficial agent up in these parts. Lost most of the fingers on his left hand, back in '79, during a gelignite accident while trying to blow one of the Cox & Company safes. If I hadn't arrived there in time, his compatriots might have blown up the rest of him, as well." He started reading through the telegrams.

"And the scarf?" I asked.

Holmes shook his head, almost testily. "Do I have to explain everything, Watson?" Then, realizing his tone, he lifted his head and smiled. "It was so I could spot him easily in the station and save a few moments."

As if Sacker wouldn't be able to spot Holmes first, I thought, looking at him, reading the telegrams in his Inverness and fore-and-aft.

Finally, Holmes completed his perusal of the messages and said, "Let us be off." He led us outside, whereupon Mrs. Grimshaw gestured to the left. "The West Road is this way, Mr. Holmes."

"We are not going to your cottage, or to Kerrett House," said Holmes. "At least not immediately. Our way first leads us to the offices of Mr. Weekes." He tapped his pocket, where the telegrams now rested. "He is expecting us."

Five minutes later, we had traversed the typical village high street to arrive at the door of Mr. Weekes's small but well-kept law office. Holmes turned to us and said quietly, "Perhaps it might be best to allow me to do the talking." Then he led us inside.

Mr. Weekes's law office was on the first floor above a sweet shop. The incongruity of this made me smile, but only to myself. I sensed that there was a grim purpose to this visit, and that Holmes was not simply stopping here to ask a few questions, or from a feeling of good fellowship.

Upstairs, the clerk appeared to have been expecting us, and appeared to be nervous in Holmes's presence. As he led us into Weeke's office, he kept glancing anxiously toward Holmes.

Weeke's office was a room that must have taken up most of the space on that floor. There were a number of old legal tomes filling fine-looking shelves around three of the walls, while the fourth wall was a large window overlooking the street. Weekes's desk was centered before this window, and at a different time of day, the sun would have been behind his back. Holmes had used this trick before, placing his chair in the Baker Street sitting room with its back to his chemical corner and the window behind, allowing him to watch visitors in the basket chair while he appeared to them to be shadowed.

Fortunately, the sun had not yet crossed to the point where it would shine in our faces, and I could see that Weekes was a wiry fellow, probably in his fifties. He stood and came from behind the desk, offering us his hand. While we found chairs, he stood beside the desk, and I was shocked to see that as he waited there before resuming his seat, he leaned back on one leg, as if – one might say – sitting on a shooting stick. It is not often that I can anticipate Holmes's thoughts move for move, but on this occasion, I saw that Holmes had noticed it as well, and I began to have some inkling or intuition about at least one thing that might be discussed or revealed in this room very soon.

Weekes settled himself behind the desk and moved some papers away from him. He seemed to be rather fidgety, but I did not know if this was his usual manner of existence, or if it was related to our visit.

"I received your wire, Mr. Holmes, and I've had my clerk pull the files relating to the unfortunate Felton family." He clucked his tongue and pulled the papers back in his direction. He looked down and turned over the top two or three sheets. "Most unfortunate."

"I have been relating some of the history of the events of 1878 for the doctor, who was not previously aware of any of it," said Holmes. "Mrs. Grimshaw knows about some aspects of the matter, as you are aware." Weekes nodded but did not speak. "Perhaps," said Holmes, "you recall our conversation in these rooms some four-and-a-half years ago, following the suicide of Ted Felton." Weekes nodded again. "Would you care to relate the details of that suicide for Doctor Watson and Mrs. Grimshaw?"

"Certainly, certainly," said Weekes, again glancing at his papers. Then he pushed them aside again, laced his fingers, and began to speak.

66

"It was a few weeks after the facts regarding his father's murder, as well as the separate incident of his implication in the burglary ring, first came to light in the press. As you may recall, it was a nine days' wonder. The group of men who had been murdered, those who came to be known as 'The Suicide Club,' were all considered together as a group, and as such were simply names that were quickly forgotten. But Clifton Felton came under a special and intense scrutiny, as his story was augmented and made more interesting due to the related account of the burglaries. This too was soon forgotten, at least by many, although it was obviously still a subject of talk for a longer time around these parts.

"Ted shouldn't have let himself be bothered by it. He had inherited a substantial income from his mother, who was a fine woman, if I may say so. A fine woman indeed. Her money was set aside in her will for Ted, and had been kept separate from Clifton Felton's finances. Young Ted could have chosen to return to Oxford, or anywhere else, with no difficulty at all. But he was always a sensitive lad, very intelligent. Much too sensitive for the burdens that the discovery of Felton's crimes placed upon him. He took after his mother in that respect, poor woman. Finally, when it all became too much for him, Ted left a note in his Oxford lodgings saying as much and threw himself into the Thames. The river isn't very intimidating at that point, but if a man is set on ending his life, he won't let that stop him."

"I understood at the time that he was working in town there, and attempting to carry out studies as well," said Holmes.

"That's right," said Weekes. "However, he never seemed to be able to settle on exactly what field of study would suit him best. He was always interested in the sciences, and particularly physics and astronomy, but he just did not have the mathematical aptitude to get started. Time and again he would plunge off in some new direction, only to be disappointed. I had hoped he might return to this part of England and read for the law, but he wanted to remain in Oxford. He only returned here to visit Clifton Felton on a very irregular basis. I believe that they did not get along all that well with one another, and that living in this area pained him somehow."

"Not true," interrupted Mrs. Grimshaw, speaking for the first time in a while, and forgetting Holmes's injunction to allow him to carry the conversation. "Mr. Clifton and Ted were warm enough to each other. In all the years I dealt with them, I never saw any signs of disagreement. And if he didn't have any feelings for his father, why then would he feel the need to do away with himself upon his father's death?"

Weekes seemed nonplussed at Mrs. Grimshaw's argument. "I, um, well, based on my experience, I – "

"I believe that we have had enough of this charade," said Holmes impatiently, reaching into his pocket for the telegrams that he had received at the station. "Were you aware, Mr. Weekes, that Ted Felton is back at Kerrett House? That he has been back for at least several weeks, if not longer?"

Weekes's jaw dropped in surprise before he recovered himself. He straightened in his chair, and his gaze shot to the right as he stared into the distance for a few seconds and collected his thoughts. He cleared his throat several times, and then said, rather weakly I thought, "Not possible. Ted committed suicide. That is an established fact."

"Nonsense," said Holmes. "After the full truth about his father was revealed in 1878, it was obvious that the young man was under a great deal of stress. That much is true – I observed it myself. As obvious as it was that he was a rather weak young man – like his father – who might break as you have suggested." Weekes bristled at this statement, but Holmes continued. "When he disappeared, I could not believe that he would actually kill himself because of what had happened. You are correct when you state that the matter was quickly forgotten, even in Oxford. I made some inquiries of my own at the time, and determined that a man closely matching Ted's description left Oxford on the night of his supposed death and made his way to Belgium. I was satisfied then that he had *not* killed himself, but had simply chosen to escape from the attention he was receiving related to his father's crimes and subsequent death.

"I had a few quiet words with the police, and they tended to agree with me, although with no hard evidence to the contrary, such as tracking the young man down and dragging him home, the suicide verdict still stood. No one, myself included, felt that it was worthwhile to go and find the young man on the Continent, since he had committed no crime. I was content to let the matter rest, and wish Ted Felton good luck with his decision to begin a new life elsewhere, even if that new life began with a faked suicide.

"Today, Mrs. Grimshaw came to me with the story that she has seen Ted Felton staring down from the windows of the great house for the last couple of weeks. She truly believed that he had died over four years ago, but I knew that in all likelihood he still lived, and had simply returned home, although choosing to do so in secret, without telling his father about his decision. That is, without telling *you, Mr. Weekes*, he had done so, as it is highly unlikely that he knows you are his real father."

Weekes was folding and unfolding his fingers, shaking his head. "I don't understand. I simply don't understand."

"It's time to come clean, Weekes," said Holmes. "You aided Ted Felton when he left the country after Clifton Felton's death, because he is

68

your son, whether he knew it or not. I heard something of the matter in '78, about how you had first loved Ted's mother years ago, before she eventually chose another and married the much older and wealthier Clifton Felton. As it wasn't relevant at the time, I saw no need to pursue it, but I did not forget it. Perhaps, if I had questioned you then, I would have learned that you had helped Ted in his quest to leave the country. But I had moved on to other matters.

"While supposedly carrying out the terms of settling Ted's estate, you arranged for the small cottage, Kerrett's Rood, to be transferred to the Grimshaws, and for the rest of the estate to continue to be kept up as well, should Ted ever decide to return. Using his money that he inherited from his mother, you paid the bills, and you provided funds as necessary to Ted, who I presume was still in Belgium until recently."

"But why would he come back? Why now? And why wouldn't he tell me?"

Holmes slapped another telegram onto the desk. "I believe this is why. Steven Wells, one of Clifton Felton's partners in the robbery ring, died while in Dartmoor, but the other, Albert Sykes, was released from prison two months ago, early as it turns out, for good behavior. Tell me," he said, "how much of Ted Felton's current *vitae* is contained in that file?" He pointed to the papers by Weekes's trembling fingers.

"Nothing too specific," he replied. "But enough to find him if I need him. His current address. The name that he is using on the Continent. There is nothing specifically saying that the alias is Ted's but the fact that it is in the file would be . . . suggestive, as there is no other clarifying context with it, should anyone happen to look with the idea that Ted is still alive and living elsewhere under another name."

"Have you had any signs of a break-in in the last month or so?" asked Holmes. "Has there been any reason to believe that the information in that file has been compromised?"

Weekes shook his head with some confusion. "No, no, nothing like that."

"And what of your clerk? Is he completely trustworthy?"

"Who? Sykes? Why, he is – Oh, my God."

"A relative?"

"Albert Sykes's cousin, I believe. We are a small village here, Mr. Holmes."

"I believe that we should call him in."

It was only the work of a moment to break down the story of the nervous young clerk. He was, in fact, the cousin of Albert Sykes, who had been released from prison in February of that year. Sykes had not returned to the village, but had arranged to meet the clerk, Josiah Sykes, in a

69

neighboring town, where he had revealed that he believed Ted Felton to still be alive, and that if he was, Weekes would know how to find him. Albert Sykes had then pressured the clerk into finding out Ted's true location. Josiah was surprised, as he had, like everyone else in the village, believed that Ted had committed suicide years before. However, Albert Sykes seemed convinced, and would not take no for an answer. All that Josiah had been able to discover was an unconnected name and address in the Ted Felton file. That had been enough, however, to please Albert Sykes, and he had gone on his way.

While I kept an eye on the clerk, Holmes stepped out and summoned a constable. After identifying himself, the constable snapped to with a smart, "Yes, sir!" Holmes explained that Josiah Sykes had vital information in a case and needed to be kept incommunicado for the time being. It was a tribute to Holmes's increasing fame and notoriety that his wishes were carried out without question.

"There is no doubt," added Holmes, "that Albert Sykes contacted young Ted, and did something to convince him to return to this country, where he has taken up residence in Kerrett Hall."

"But why?" asked Weekes.

"I believe that if Sykes is involved, it must relate somehow to the old burglary ring. Perhaps Sykes knows something that he is using to blackmail Ted. We will only find out by asking him."

"But what do you suggest, Mr. Holmes," said Weekes. "We cannot just go up and knock on the front door."

"I still have the key," interrupted Mrs. Grimshaw.

"It does not matter," replied Weekes. "If he is in there and does not want to be found, he will bolt, and we won't find him."

"By way of the house's secret?" asked Holmes. "How much did he reveal to you before he left the country."

Weekes swallowed once or twice, and then said, "Not everything. Just that he had found how Felton was able to leave and return without detection, and how the stolen items had been moved the same way into the basement. It seemed to add to his shame, as if, by discovering it, the facts of the matter became more real to him somehow. But he never told me what it was. He said . . . he said that it would die with him. I was sure that he meant that the secret would go with him when he faked his death. Could he mean . . . ?"

"Mr. Weekes, that unfortunate young man, who was so shamed by the one that he believes to be his father – he *does* still believe that Clifton Felton is still his father, doesn't he?"

Weekes nodded. "I could not harm my precious Emily's reputation by revealing the true facts of the matter, and the . . . bargain that she made with Felton when she chose him over me at the end of it all."

Holmes continued, "Then Ted Felton, who was somehow pressured by the criminal Sykes to return from his exile, has been living alone in that house for weeks, caught in what he perceives to be a trap. I am certain that Sykes is somehow trying to force him to either restart the burglary ring, or give him access to something that is still hidden in the house. In any case, we have to speak to Ted Felton immediately."

"But I repeat, Mr. Holmes, that if we approach it, he will simply hide or bolt."

"Then we will have to gain entrance from the other side, from his escape tunnel."

"Escape tunnel? What do you propose? Do you know where this tunnel is located?"

"I believe so." Holmes laid the final telegram on the desk. "I know a great number of people who owe me a great number of favors. It was relatively easy to get a line on exactly what is involved in the property owned by Ted Felton. Or should I say, properties. Mr. Weekes, doesn't Ted Felton also own an empty house, located some little distance to the east of the property, on a dead end lane running away from the eastern perimeter of the Kerrett House estate?"

"Why, yes. Yes, he does! Is that it? Is that where the secret entrance is?"

"I believe so," said Holmes. "Mrs. Grimshaw!"

With a start, the sister of our landlady sat up straighter and turned toward Holmes. "Yes?"

"Will you serve as our beater? Will you, at the appointed time, enter the great house and begin to call for Ted Felton, explaining that you know he is there? It may be that he will come out and speak to you. But if not, we three will be approaching silently from the other end, through the tunnel that surely begins in the empty house, and will bottle him up somewhere between us. Then we can learn what hold Albert Sykes was able to exert over him, and let him know that he has nothing to fear with our assistance."

"Certainly," said Mrs. Grimshaw.

"And we can count on you as well, Weekes?"

"Of course, of course."

The rest is quickly told. With a time agreed upon, we separated, Mrs. Grimshaw to return to her cottage, and Holmes, Weekes, and I to the empty house. Weekes had a key for the place, but before he could use it, Holmes examined the outer premises. He called us over to a window on the south side, shaded by overgrown bushes, and opening into the dining room. "This has been forced open, fairly recently," he said. "This is how Ted gained access when he returned from the Continent."

Weekes quietly opened the door, and we crept in, pausing a moment to listen for any sounds. Holmes had previously warned us to move softly, watching where we stepped in case Ted had left anything rigged to make a loud noise if disturbed. However, in the afternoon light, we saw nothing.

It did not take a Sherlock Holmes to find the entrance to the secret tunnel. Making our way through the house had revealed nothing, but in the cellar, there was a different story. By the light of several candles that we had appropriated upstairs, Holmes silently indicated the dust on the floor, previously disturbed by numerous footprints leading both ways between the stairs and a seemingly blank wall on the western side. It was but the work of a moment for Holmes to find an unusual knot in a board. We heard a small click, and a wide segment of the wall swung noiselessly open. I realized that the cellar was particularly and unusually clear in front of the path of this door, while the rest of the room was cluttered with old and broken furniture.

There was another candle in a sconce, just inside the secret door. Holmes lit it, and we could see an arched stone passage leading off into the darkness. It was at least eight feet wide, and nearly as tall. There was no need to stoop at all as we started down the tunnel.

As Weekes later explained to us, these houses had been built outside the estate wall by the original Kerrett, long before the road which lay atop the tunnel had been constructed. No doubt there had been some reason, possibly illegal, for the two to be connected, back in the early part of the century. It was never known how Clifton Felton had learned the secret, although Weekes was able to confirm that it was a good five years after he bought Kerrett House that Felton suddenly felt moved to buy the empty house at the other end of the tunnel, indicating that perhaps it was only then that he learned of the terminus of the passage leading from his own home, and he wanted to own both ends, for whatever reason.

The floor of the tunnel remained level as we progressed, and the stones lining the arched walls appeared quite solid. However, there were a number of roots hanging from the ceiling, indicating to me that the structure was perhaps not quite as stable as it might appear. I, for one, would be quite happy to reach the other end.

As we progressed, we occasionally came across other sconces hanging on the walls, all with fairly new candles within them. As we would pass each one, Holmes would pause to light it, increasing the visibility in the gloomy tunnel. With each candle, I could perceive that the air in the tunnel had more dust, or perhaps vapor, hanging in it than I had first noticed. I began to be aware that my breathing was rather labored, and as there was no climb associated with our traverse of the tunnel, I concluded that it must be from breathing the poor-quality air. Beside me, I could hear Weekes begin to wheeze, and as I glanced at him, I could see that he was breathing through a cloth clenched to his nose and mouth.

None too soon, we reached the end of the tunnel. We could all perceive a greater degree of brightness ahead. There was no door or separation. The walls simply widened out into a greater area, lit by a lantern standing on a rough deal table off to the side. A cot was located beside it, and there were several empty crates along the opposite wall. Across from us, as we stood quietly in the entrance to the tunnel, was a young man, ignorant of our approach, his face and hands pressed against a wooden partition that had been built across the width of the stone chamber.

He was listening intently to the sound of Mrs. Grimshaw's muffled voice, calling in the distance, asking him, for I assumed that this was indeed Ted Felton, to come out, as all was known, and he would be safe. He listened for another moment, and then with a small sob turned away from the wall, only to discover the three of us in the tunnel entrance.

"Mr. Felton," said Holmes, only to be interrupted by Weekes.

"Ted," said the man gently, stepping forward, his hand stretched forth. "It's all right. We now know that you are here. There is no need to keep it secret any longer. Everything will be all right."

Mrs. Grimshaw continued to call from the other side of the wall, in the cellar of the great house, where Holmes had sent her. Ted looked over his shoulder at the wall, and then back toward Weekes. He seemed to vibrate, as if he were a string that had been stretched too tight for too long.

"Ted," said Weekes again, and the string broke.

Ted sank to the ground, saying to himself, "I couldn't find it. God help me, I couldn't find it."

Weeks and I rushed toward him, while Holmes moved to the wall, only taking another moment to discover the method to open the connecting door. While Mrs. Grimshaw stepped through, I knelt by the bed, pushing Weekes away as I commenced an examination.

"He is malnourished, and has suffered a great deal of mental anguish, but he will make a full recovery," I said. "However, we need to remove him from this place. May we take him to your cottage, Mrs. Grimshaw?"

"Certainly," she replied.

We managed to get the young man to his feet and through the connecting door into the larger cellar. Holmes stopped me for a moment to indicate how the hidden door appeared on the tunnel side, nearly invisible once the door was shut. He quickly found how to open it on the side of the great house cellar. "I was not able to discover this door when I looked several years ago," he said. "It is no self-flattery to state that my skills have improved, and I would have been able to find it, if I had been given the task today. Do you need any help taking him down to the cottage?"

I indicated that between us, we should manage all right. Holmes nodded, and said he would go back through the tunnel to blow out the candles, and then join us in a few minutes.

We managed to get Ted to his feet, and he climbed upstairs on his own, although he paused once or twice going up. I stood behind him, ready to catch him should he collapse. Outside, the sun was just starting its descent toward the cottage, and was shining full in our faces as we walked down the slope. Looking beside me, I could see how pale Ted was, while Weekes's shown with tears at the condition of his son.

In the cottage, Mrs. Grimshaw made a place for Ted on the settee, and then bustled out of the room, only to return in an unbelievably short amount of time, carrying a hot drink that appeared to be heavily laced with spirits. Ted coughed at the first sip, and then cautiously took another. Mrs. Grimshaw nodded, and then left, muttering about warming up some of the beef soup.

Holmes had entered during all this, and I saw that he was not wearing his Inverness or hat. Rather, the Inverness was rolled over, and he placed it on a nearby chair before centering the hat on top. "How is he?"

"He will be fine," I said. "He has simply used himself up much too freely by living in that dark, foul-aired cellar, with insufficient food for too long. I imagine that his expeditions to look at the setting sun were the greatest joys that he had during that time."

Ted cleared his throat, took another sip of the drink, and said, "You are right, sir. I tried to stay hidden, but sometimes it was just too difficult to remain in that dungeon. I wanted to get in and get out, but day after day I looked and couldn't find it, and I knew what would happen if I didn't. Sometimes I went up in the morning as well, but the evening sun was best. I could feel the warmth upon my face before I went back downstairs to resume my search. Was that how I was discovered?"

"It was," said Holmes. "Mrs. Grimshaw noticed you. She thought that you were a ghost."

"Not really?" said Ted, with a glimmer of unexpected but welcome amusement.

Mrs. Grimshaw returned with a bowl of savory-smelling soup. "Yes, I did." She handed him the bowl. "You were thought to be dead. Eat that, young man."

Holmes pulled a chair closer and sat down, facing Ted. I realized that Ted and Holmes were about the same age, each in their late twenties, but two men could not be more different. Holmes was hawk-like and alert, while Ted seemed uncertain and hesitant. I knew that it was not just the recent deprivations that gave this impression.

"We understand from Mr. Weekes how you came to flee to the Continent, leaving the impression that you had thrown yourself to your death in the Thames. But why have you come back, and put yourself through all of this misery? Is there a connection to the recent release of Albert Sykes from prison?"

"He had never believed that I truly died," agreed Ted with a nod. "He thought that I got away with his treasure, and went to start a new life. A month or so ago, he found out my address from his cousin, who works for you, Mr. Weekes." Weekes hung his head, but did not interrupt.

"Sykes showed up at my home in Ostend over a month ago. I wouldn't let him in, but made him stay on the doorstep. That only made him angry. But how could I let my wife and son – "

"You are married?" said Weekes with wonderment. "I have a grand – That is to say, you have a son?"

Ted nodded, unaware of Weekes's near slip. "I met Sykes at a place by the water. There he told me what he wanted. He told me a great many things. He said that if I did not help him, he would rake up the whole scandal once again. He would reveal that I was still alive, and make sure that I paid for my father's crimes." He closed his eyes. "And he threatened my family."

"What exactly was it that he wanted?" said Holmes.

"He said that during the course of their last robbery, he, James Stevens, and my father had inadvertently found, along with their other loot, a chest full of gold coins. They had brought it with them, and my father had hidden it in a secret place somewhere in the great house, with the idea that it would be split in a few days. However, before this could take place, Sykes and Wells were arrested, and my father was found dead in London.

"Sykes and Wells did not mention this gold, and he was greatly surprised that the man from whom it had been stolen did not mention it either."

"Sir Wilton Cole," said Holmes. "I wondered why he was not very grateful at all when his stolen property was recovered from the cellars of the great house. Now I understand. He was most interested in the recovery of the gold coins. I would expect that he had himself gained them in some illicit or illegal manner, and could not report them stolen without implicating himself. He must have believed that they were still hidden, as

75

it turned out, or that I had found them myself and chosen to keep them. But he could say nothing."

Ted nodded. "Sykes told me that Sir Wilton visited him in prison, trying to get Sykes to admit that he had taken the coins. He offered to assist Sykes in getting a reduced sentence, but Sykes told him nothing. Sykes knew that the coins were still in the house, and after his release, he went there on numerous occasions, searching for them himself. He came in through the tunnel which leads to the empty house on the other side of the road. When he couldn't find them, he became convinced that I knew where they were. He sought me out, told me about the tunnel, and forced me to come and search." He swallowed. "What choice did I have?"

"But you could not find the coins."

"No."

"How did you search?"

"The same way that Sykes did, I suppose. I knocked on walls, and looked up and down the tunnel. I went through my father's papers in his desk, seeking a clue, but to no avail."

"I believe that your weeks of effort, combined with those of Sykes, who was just as desperate as you, indicates that there was a good chance that the coins were not in the house after all. My quick examination while you were being brought to the cottage proved that as well."

"So . . . so this was all a waste?" said Ted. "Sykes will not believe me. He will reveal the truth to my wife, and to everyone else. It was all a waste."

"Not so," said Holmes, standing and retrieving his folded Inverness. "When we found you, you said that you had been unable to find 'it,' whatever that was. I decided that you must have spent the last few weeks looking in the wrong place.

Unfolding the coat, he revealed a wooden chest, about the size of a large family bible, its dark wood bound by ironwork at the corners. There was a broken lock in the hasp. "Instead of looking in the cellar of the great house, I examined the empty house at the other end of the tunnel. It was only a few minutes work to find a sliding panel in the woodwork near the tunnel entrance."

He raised the lid of the box to reveal a small fortune in gold coins. They seemed to shine in the afternoon light penetrating Mrs. Grimshaw's front window.

Holmes plucked out one of the coins, looking at it front and back, before turning it on its edge. "Look here, Watson. At the inscription on the side of the coin, showing a mint mark. That was a new thing that was tried back in the mid-70's, but soon rejected. A box of them was stolen and never recovered." He shut the lid. "Until now. I anticipate some interesting questions for Sir Wilton Cole before the week is out."

He set the box aside. "How were you to reach Albert Sykes, once you had found the box?"

"He has come in the night on several occasions, but not lately. I have an address where I'm to send a letter. It was too risky to send a wire. Someone might recognize me. Instead, I was to write, and slip the letter into a local box. He will come within a day."

"Then we must send him an invitation to join us."

And so we did. Holmes dropped the short letter, written by Ted, into the village postal box, arranging a meeting for the very next night. We were there, Holmes, Inspector Lestrade, and myself, when Albert Sykes made his way in through the empty house and found us in the chamber under the great house. His attempt to turn and flee was blocked by the two burly constables who had silently followed him down the tunnel. His return to Dartmoor was swift and uncomplicated. Lestrade was quite pleased to return the missing coins to London.

The afternoon of the discovery of Ted Felton and the missing gold coins, we still sat in Mrs. Grimshaw's parlor, waiting for Holmes to return from his postal errand. Ted had progressed to eating some cold slices of ham, but not too many, as Mrs. Grimshaw felt that any more might put a strain on his digestive system. Weekes sat by Ted's side, asking and repeating questions about Ted's wife and child. At one point, Weekes looked up and caught my eye. I glanced meaningfully at the weakened young man lying on the sofa beside him, as if to say that it was time to tell him the truth. Then I stood up and excused myself, taking Mrs. Grimshaw with me into the kitchen.

We did not hear their conversation, but in a few moments we perceived the sounds of both men breaking down, and by the time Holmes returned, the truth was known to Ted, to his great amazement and happiness. Mr. Weekes was overcome, planning a visit to Ostend in order to meet his new family, while Ted promised to return to Kerrett House and reopen it, making it a showplace once again, as it must have been early in the century. It turned out that Mrs. Grimshaw had been wrong, and Mr. Weekes right. Young Ted and his supposed father, Clifton Felton, had not been very close after all. Mr. Clifton, as Mrs. Grimshaw called him, had long felt a certain resentment toward his wife that he passed on to the boy, although they had maintained civil relations. Following the revelations about Clifton Felton's secret life, Ted was more than happy to have found his real father.

Holmes cautioned that Ted Felton should remain hidden until the capture of Albert Sykes, and it was arranged that he would stay with Mrs.

Grimshaw. Weekes agreed to tell no one. Holmes indicated that, while he had been out to mail the letter to Sykes, he had also conferred with the police, revealing something of the story to them, and making sure that Josiah Sykes could not notify his cousin of the fact that his activities were discovered before he could step into the trap on the next night.

As we stood at the door to Mrs. Grimshaw's cottage, on the stoop leading to the West Road, Holmes said, "We must be getting back to London. Mrs. Hudson will be looking for us soon. And we did tell the inspector this morning at Stoke Moran that we would be available later today in Baker Street for any questions that he might have. He probably believes that we have fled the country.

"Might we expect, Mrs. Grimshaw," he continued, "to be formally introduced to you by your sister sometime in the next week or so?"

"I believe that would be likely," she said. "I would enjoy seeing Martha again, and this time it would be without any criticism that might come from bothering her lodgers with a ghost story."

"Mrs. Grimshaw," said Holmes, "feel free to bring us any little problem that might cross your path at any time, with no fear of recriminations from your sister. If your next visit provides something as interesting as this one, it will be most welcome, and if you have no story to tell us at all, that will be fine as well. However," he added, "I suspect that soon you will be too busy to visit very often, as Kerrett House, and Kerrett's Rood beside it, will soon welcome a new family and the new vitality that comes with it."

And so it proved. The next week, Mrs. Grimshaw was "introduced" to us by Mrs. Hudson, who never suspected that her sister had been a client. If Mrs. Hudson wondered why we got on so well so quickly with her sister, she was too canny to say so. Mrs. Grimshaw visited off and on over the years, but on a rare basis indeed, as Kerrett House became a vibrant home for Ted Felton, that is, Ted *Weekes*, along with his wife and – eventually – his eight children as well.

Sir Wilton Cole's future after the clearing-up of the affair of the stolen gold coins was not so bright. But that is another story entirely.

The Curious Incident
of the
Goat-Cart Man

It is sometimes easier to believe a man from Bedlam than in coincidence. In the case of the following narrative, my friend Sherlock Holmes and I believed both.

Like his older brother Mycroft, whose great mind served as something of a great clearinghouse for the various departments of Her Majesty's Government, Sherlock Holmes had created a special and unique niche for himself, acting as a resource for those in need, while forever seeking to improve and increase his knowledge and awareness of crime in the great tapestry that is London. He liked to believe in the order of his system, as reflected by the hard work that he put into it. It is certain that without his specialized knowledge, allowing him to make connections from one disparate set of events to another, the curious incident of the Goat-Cart Man of Meadcroft might have gone forever unresolved, or at least it might have concluded in a more tragic manner. And yet, it was only through coincidence, which Holmes was always loathe to credit, that the matter was placed before him at all.

In recording these varied sketches, I have attempted to balance the fantastic with the prosaic, relying neither upon the involvement of important and well-known figures, nor upon the rehashing of events that are already familiar to readers of the daily press. Rather, I have tried to present those matters that best illustrate the gifts and skills of my friend. This particular adventure occurred as something of a pause or detour in the midst of a larger investigation, taking only an hour or so. However, no record of my friend's activities would be complete without it.

It was on the last Saturday in September of 1890, only a day or so after Holmes and I had returned from Dartmoor, and specifically King's Pyland. We had journeyed there regarding the matter of a missing race horse and its murdered trainer, whose body had been found on the Moor. Our return to London had followed Holmes's confident assurance to the horse's owner, Colonel Ross, that the great beast would be found in time to participate in the Wessex Cup, to be run on the subsequent Tuesday. Colonel Ross had seemed less than confident in Holmes's assurances as we departed, but had reluctantly agreed not to withdraw the horse's name from competition. Although I had been privy to Holmes's masterful

79

discovery of the horse's true location, and his reluctance to share it with Colonel Ross, I did not as yet know the murderer's identity. However, I was certain that the matter would be resolved to everyone's satisfaction, having seen Mr. Sherlock Holmes do this sort of thing before.

Early in the afternoon of that particular day, I had been finishing my lunch with my wife, following a light morning of rounds and seeing patients. I think that neither of us was surprised when the abrupt ringing of our bell led to the maid's announcement that Holmes was calling.

He refused anything to eat, as was to be expected, but he did agree to a hurried cup of black coffee. He was there to request my assistance on what he described as a "long shot." After a concise explanation, I made to get my coat and hat. Holmes graciously and sincerely thanked Mary for sharing me in this way, to which she simply smiled and laid an affectionate hand on his shoulder.

The matter which required my participation that afternoon is neither here nor there in relation to the events that I propose to recount. They simply served to place us where the current narrative began. At that time, Holmes was engaged in following the series of steps that would culminate the next spring at the top of Reichenbach Falls. Holmes had finally managed to find a narrow crack in the armor of that master criminal, Professor Moriarty, and had slowly been wedging it wider as the weeks and months progressed. That day, he had learned of a diary that was supposed to contain incriminating information of an explosive nature, and was to be carried back to London from Exeter by one of the Professor's lieutenants, whereupon it would be delivered to the Professor himself. Holmes and I, along with Inspector Patterson and a number of plain-clothed detectives and constables, had made every effort to track the diary and arrest the courier, but alas, on this day, it was not meant to be. The identified courier was successfully followed and detained, but when the trap was sprung, on one of the platforms in Paddington Station, no diary was to be found.

After it was clear that there would be no victory on this occasion, most of the Yarders had dispersed from the station, while Holmes and Patterson remained in quiet conversation to one side of the great and noisy waiting room. I was standing beside them, watching the ebb and flow of the crowds as trains arrived and departed. It was then that I noticed one of the porters talking to two men and pointing them in Holmes's direction. They nodded to him and then began to walk our way.

Interrupting Holmes's conversation, I spoke in a low voice and made him aware of the approaching men. He and Patterson turned, and we all separated slightly, almost instinctively, in case either of the strangers should pose some threat.

It was quickly obvious that neither man presented any sort of danger. The man to my left was tall and fit, wearing a fine overcoat, perhaps a little heavy for the unseasonable warmth of the evening. He kept one arm protectively about the other, a smaller fellow, draped in clothing that was more worn than that of his companion, but still thoroughly respectable.

I could see that the second man had recently been ill, and possibly ill-used as well. His face was pale, with bruised-looking smudges under his deep-set eyes. An unsuccessful effort had been made to comb his hair, and there were stains upon the knees of his trousers. His shirt was pulled to, but a few of the buttons were missing. I could see the outline, barely visible underneath his hair, of a contusion above his left temple. He carried himself with that pulled-in and self-aware look that illness brings to a man, when he evaluates every movement to see if it will be tolerated, or if it will worsen whatever condition is being suffered.

"Mr. Holmes?" asked the stronger of the two men, instinctively facing my friend. Holmes nodded his head, and the other continued. "My name is Walter Forsythe, and this is my brother, Henry. We were walking down the street outside just now, arguing whether to continue onward to my home or instead seek medical attention for my brother nearby at St. Mary's, when we heard a group of departing constables mention your name. I was for continuing on, but my brother, as weak as he is, insisted that we come inside to see if we could find you in the station."

Patterson had looked surprised, and then angry, when he heard that Holmes's name was being discussed by his men out in the street. "This was supposed to remain confidential," he muttered, before turning to Holmes. "If I may, I will call upon you later in your rooms to discuss our strategy, Mr. Holmes." Then, without waiting for Holmes's response, he turned and made for the exit, in that peculiar gait when a man wants to run but is forcing himself to remain at a dignified, although accelerated, walking speed instead.

"Really, Henry," said Walter Forsythe, turning to the other man as Patterson departed, "we should not bother Mr. Holmes. After all, you've been ill. What you recall may not have really happened at all!"

Henry Forsythe flashed an angry glance toward his brother.

"I am a doctor," I interrupted. "Perhaps I can be of some assistance."

"We will be fine," replied Walter. "My brother simply had a fit last night. I just need to see him home. Please excuse our imposition."

"Hearing your name mentioned outside seemed like a sign, Mr. Holmes," said Henry, in a weak voice. "You are just the man to get to the bottom of this situation. But we must be quick about it. The old man may already be dead!"

Holmes glanced at me with a flash in his eyes, as if to cry, *"The Game is afoot!"* Then he turned toward Patterson, who was just disappearing out of the station and into the sunlit afternoon. "Perhaps," said Holmes, "you would be more comfortable relating your story while we sit. With a cup of tea? Or would you rather return with us to my rooms in Baker Street, to share the details of your recent travails?"

"Let us be on our way!" cried Henry, a shrill tone rising in his voice and attracting the judgmental notice of a pinch-faced matron passing by.

Holmes nodded, and spoke to me. "I will get a four-wheeler. Can you help our new acquaintances outside?" And then he was off in that way of his that never seemed hurried but covered ground at an incredible pace when he wished.

As Holmes walked away, Walter continued to insist that none of this was necessary, and that he should not have indulged his brother's whim to enter the station after hearing Holmes's name. Nevertheless, Walter Forsythe assisted me as we maneuvered his brother out of the station to the street. Henry seemed quite weak from whatever he had experienced. I began to ask a few general questions, in order to ascertain the nature of his condition, but Henry stopped me, explaining that it would become known what had happened to him when he could tell his story to Holmes.

Outside, there was no sign of Patterson or the loose-lipped Yarders. Holmes was standing with his hand upon the door of a four-wheeler. Up top, I could see the grinning face of our old friend, Bert Deacon, the former Houndsditch ramper who had been falsely accused of a particularly brutal murder, back in '82. Holmes had proven his innocence, based on the reversed obverse of a shilling found clutched in the dead man's hand, as well as the inward twist of Deacon's left foot. Holmes had then found him steady work as a cab driver, much to the relief of Deacon's wife and six children. His former line of work had not paid nearly as steadily as driving a cab.

I nodded at Deacon, and we boarded the growler. I noticed an odd alertness had come into Holmes's eyes, but I did not presume to question him about it in front of the two brothers. We all settled back as the cab lurched into motion without any instructions having been given as to our destination, and I realized that Holmes must have already told Deacon to take us to Baker Street.

"Where are we going?" cried Henry Forsythe, sitting up abruptly, looking from side to side. I could tell that his nerves were stretched to the limit, and I was concerned that the mere effort of telling his story might propel him into brain fever. "We must go back to Meadcroft! The old man may already be dead!"

"Calm yourself, sir, and you may tell us of the danger to this old man," said Holmes, in the soothing tone that worked so well in situations of this type. I was amazed yet again to see the hypnotic affect that Holmes's voice could have on someone. While he often insisted that the problem itself was his only interest, and that people were simply factors in the equation, he had an amazing ability to empathize with their troubles when needed. "We are going to my rooms in Baker Street," he said softly, "where you can tell your story. Then we shall decide upon a course of action."

"We should get you home, Henry," said Walter, but in a resigned way, as he realized that his brother was set on relating his story.

"My tale is easily told right now, here in this cab," Henry replied. "Once you hear it you will agree that we should make our way to Meadcroft at once."

"Henry," interrupted Walter, "all of this may have just been the result of your fit last night. There is no need to take any more of Mr. Holmes's time."

Ignoring him, Holmes said, "My knowledge of London is fairly exact. Is that the Meadcroft that is located by Kennington Park, on the South Side?"

"It is," said Henry. Holmes's display of omniscience seemed to calm him further. "It is where I have leased a house since early this year, attempting to improve my craft."

"You are a writer, then?" asked Holmes. I glanced at the man's hands and sleeves, and could see, from the collection of unique callosities and shiny right cuff, the source of Holmes's deduction.

"Yes," he said. "My stories are in the manner of Sir Walter Scott's, although I have not yet duplicated his mastery of the form, or believability. I must admit, I'm afraid, that I have also yet to duplicate his ability to have anything published. Perhaps, if I went out and experienced life, rather than simply trying to write about it – "

"Now, now," said Walter Forsythe, "you will achieve your goal! I am certain of it. But you do not have to live apart from your brother to do so."

We were traveling down Praed Street, nearing the Edgware Road crossing. I glanced up and to my right. I did not know if Mary would be watching as we passed, but I looked forward, as always, to telling her of the day's events. Hopefully this new and unexpected adventure would have a better and more successful conclusion than that upon which Holmes had initially summoned me.

"In January," said Henry, shifting in his seat to a more upright position, "I had resolved, with the turning of the new year, to move out of my brother's home, where I had lived for the past two years, and find a place of my own."

"You were no bother to me at all, Henry," interjected Walter. "You are my brother." He glanced at me, and whispered, for no reason, "I have a position in the City."

Henry continued as if he had not been interrupted. "I intended to give myself a year in which either to master my craft, or abandon it. My brother and I have both inherited money, and I could afford to indulge in this quest – or folly – for a little while. I found a small house of rather new construction in Meadcroft, arranged terms with the landlord, and settled in to my routine.

"In case you don't know it, doctor," said Henry, shifting to address me, "Meadcroft is a new set of houses by Kennington Park, east of The Oval. It was once part of a larger estate of several acres, but eight or ten years ago, the owner, Sir Giles Gidley-Hall, was forced to sell everything but the main house to cover some long-standing debts, after some mysterious circumstances depleted his funds."

"The Threadneedle Scandal," interrupted Holmes. "I was able to satisfy myself at the time that Sir Giles had no part in the matter, although his own personal honor compelled him to make restitution." Turning to me, he said, "It was before your time, Watson."

Holmes looked back at Henry, and said, "You were telling us about the construction of Meadcroft? I assume that it is relevant to your story?"

Henry Forsythe nodded. "New houses were built in rows stretching out to the left and right from the front of the main house, and a large open area in the front center was left as something of a park for the residents.

"It was into one of these houses, near the main house, that I moved last winter. And it was not long before I became aware of Sir Giles's strange eccentricity, which has become a source of great amusement – and sometimes irritation – to the entire neighborhood.

"You must know then that Sir Giles, after being forced to sell the land adjacent to his house, became something of an eccentric recluse. It is rumored that he has still managed to retain quite a bit of money, but he released all of his staff, and lives alone in the big house, making do for himself. At night, one can see that the entire building remains dark, but for one room on the front right corner of the ground floor.

"Although the grounds stretching in front of the house serve as the common park for the new houses, Sir Giles still seems to feel some attachment for them. During the daylight hours, when people make use of this open area, Sir Giles ventures forth from the house on a regular basis, approaching his neighbors in a manner stopping just short of harassment. What makes this situation almost comical, rather than criminal, is that Sir

Giles's defense of the common green is done from atop a small wagon, pulled by a large goat."

Holmes's eyes twinkled at this revelation, and I felt a smile tug at my mouth at this ludicrous image. Even Walter Forsythe, concerned for his brother as he was, smiled as well.

"If just hearing about him makes you smile, imagine actually seeing him as he charges his way across the green, with a thin cane rod held high overhead, serving to encourage the goat if it slows down. I must admit that the first time I saw him, I thought I was dreaming, or going mad." He paused, and the humor which had lightened his face for a moment and seemed to chase away his illness drained away. "After last night, however, I should never joke about my sanity again."

He fell silent for a moment. Traffic was thick during that time of the afternoon, and our progress was slow, even with Bert Deacon's best efforts. Still, I wondered if Henry's tale would be completed before we reached Baker Street.

As if reading my thought, Henry continued. "Sir Giles is a small, withered old fellow, and the burly beast does not seem to strain at the burden, although it certainly displays no enthusiasm for it, either. Sir Giles harnesses it each morning, leaving it tied by the front door with something to eat and drink. As the day progresses, he will burst out of his front door and sally forth whenever he sees someone enter the park, riding toward them as fast as he can go, before suddenly reining in the goat and then pausing to examine the trespassers critically. Then he will circle away, before returning again, sometimes approaching three or four times before he is satisfied. I do not know if he is trying to intimidate them, or simply to examine them for some unknown reason at close range. He doesn't speak, and the residents are tolerant of him, even the mothers with their young children.

"I cannot tell you the number of days when I have been distracted from my writing as I would look up and see Sir Giles go flying this way and that across the green. And I myself have not been ignored by him, either, during my times outside. Perhaps this is what led to my unfortunate experience. If I had not repeatedly encountered him, then he and I might not have formed a wary friendship, if I may call it that, and his disappearance would not have mattered to me one way or the other. Certainly, I would never have ended up here today, or where I found myself this morning after the events of last night.

"Sir Giles and I met in this way. One day a month or so ago, in the hottest part of summer, I had taken myself outside to walk and think my way through a point in my plot. It was then that I became aware of the unsurprising approach of Sir Giles. He circled me once, and again, when finally I impertinently asked him the name of his goat.

"I cannot believe that no one had asked him that before, but he seemed surprised that anyone would speak to him. Not as surprised as I, however, when he replied back to me that the goat's name was Tommy.

" 'Not Billy?' I returned with a smile.

"He started to scowl, and then chose to reply instead. 'Tommy after my dead brother,' he said. 'He was my only family. He's gone now, and he looked like the goat.' And then he laughed, a harsh bark of a laugh, and I could not help but join him.

"After that, we would talk sometimes when I was taking a stroll. It was not every day, by any means, and it never progressed to the point where we socialized in each other's homes. I suppose that I cannot even say that we were any more than passing acquaintances, rather than friends. But I think that he enjoyed the experience of our occasional conversations, as did I, and when I would appear on the green, his charge toward me on the goat-cart did not seem as aggressive as it must have appeared to others who were his targets.

"I have never spoken to any of my other neighbors during the entire time that I have lived there, and have in fact never revealed any of my reasons for choosing to live in the neighborhood to Sir Giles. I did not explain about my labors to become a better writer, and I never mentioned any of my family to him. From small things that he said, as we stood and talked for odd random moments on the green, I believe that Sir Giles was alone in the world, and certainly he must have believed that of me as well.

"Several days ago, when I went out for my afternoon constitutional, I was mildly surprised when Sir Giles did not appear. This led me to observe that, over the next day or so, he and the goat did not make their usual inspections whenever anyone else walked the green. I did notice, however, that the usual light was showing in the front corner room of his house at night. Unusually, however, there were also lights burning in other parts of the building, something that had never happened during the time that I have lived there.

"Finally, the day before yesterday, my concern grew, and at dusk, I hesitantly made my way over to Sir Giles's front door, with the intent of checking to see if he was all right. I knocked, and after long quiet moments, hearing nothing but the wind sighing in the great trees behind me surrounding the green, I knocked again.

"As I was looking back toward the green, and thinking how abandoned it was at that time of night, I heard footsteps within, and then the door opened. Two men faced me, one tall and heavy-set, about forty years of age, and the other a decade or so older, with a pointed beard and a sharp expression.

" 'Well?' said the younger man.

"I explained my concern for Sir Giles, as he had not been seen in the last few days. The younger man gruffly replied, 'I'm his brother. He's been ill, and I've come to take care of him. This other man here is a doctor. Now clear off!' And he slammed the door in my face!

"I made my way back home, puzzled by this encounter, and trying to reconcile the idea that the man, clearly much younger than Sir Giles, could be his brother, when Sir Giles had intimated to me that his only brother, Tommy (who had looked like the goat) was dead. I continued to brood over the matter, and by the next evening, yesterday, I had decided to go back and inquire more forcefully as to Sir Giles's condition. We were not truly friends, you understand, but I felt some responsibility for him, as I was obviously the only person in the neighborhood that ever had any true interaction with him.

"Knocking as I had during my previous visit, I realized that it was later in the evening than when I had been here the day before. In the distance toward the Park, the gaslights were already lit, but they had always been markedly absent around the green, having been left out by the builders when the place was constructed. My surroundings were quite dark.

"When the door unexpectedly opened, this time without the necessity of me knocking a second time, the light from the inside hall momentarily blinded me. I had the impression that the same two men were standing there. Events subsequently proved this to be true. This time, however, there was no conversation between us whatsoever. The younger man simply reached forward, grabbing my arm and pulling me inside.

"The door slammed shut behind me, and there was a muffled thud as my head was hit with a hard object. That is how I received this." He lifted a hand to his left temple, gingerly brushing back his hair to reveal the contusion that I had noticed earlier.

"This served to further obscure my vision, as my eyes had not yet adjusted to the bright lights in the entrance hall. Still trying to regain my balance, I was shocked when my coat was roughly pulled down from behind, thus trapping my arms at my sides. Then, as I was completely pinned from behind by the younger man, the older man stepped forward into the blurred field of my vision and pulled open my shirt, baring my shoulder. He stepped back for a moment, fumbling with something on a side table, as I uselessly struggled against my larger captor. Then the older man returned into my line of sight, holding a hypodermic needle before him, reflecting the lamplight.

" 'Are you sure,' asked the man who had been identified the previous night as the doctor, 'that he is alone and has no family?' His accent was unusual. It was American, but in a flat way that I have never heard before. 'This could be a mistake, and we're not ready to move on yet.'

" 'That's what the old man said,' replied the younger man. 'He lives alone across the green, and never has any visitors.'

" 'Then,' said the older man, 'let the doctor take care of this.' And he plunged the hypodermic needle into my arm.''

We crossed Upper Montagu Street, and Henry Forsythe took a moment as he breathed deeply and recalled the next portion of his story.

"I cannot say for certain what happened next. I recall the impression of swirling colored lights, and having difficulties breathing, and hearing loud noises that seemed as if they almost made sense as words, but were beyond my comprehension. I sometimes felt that I was hanging suspended above the earth, with a weightless sensation that I have never experienced before. I also had the sense of motion, and long periods of darkness when all that I could hear were the sounds of my own pulse in my head. It would get louder and louder until it sounded like the roar of a cataract, before I would suddenly be plunged into stretches of stark silence, the loneliest emptiness I have ever experienced.

"I had no idea how long this went on. I could not have told you anything about myself if you had asked me. The next thing that I knew for certain was when I awoke this morning and was being examined by a stranger who subsequently identified himself as a doctor, asking me if I knew my name.

"I did not know the time or even the day or year when I first recovered. It was only when my senses had cleared that I finally realized I had only suffered from my breakdown for only a single night.

" 'Where am I?' I asked, ignoring the doctor's question.

" 'You're in Bethlem Royal Hospital,' " he replied.

"His response puzzled me for a moment, as I attempted to reconcile the pieces of my memory that were trying to stitch themselves back into a whole cloth. Finally, the meaning of his answer seemed to resonate somehow with more meaning.

" 'Bedlam,' I whispered.

" 'We don't like to call it that,' the doctor said. 'You were brought here last night by two men after you went mad in the street and became a danger to passers-by. You continued to exhibit the symptoms that your rescuers reported for several hours after your arrival here. You broke an orderly's arm, and ruined the night director's coat in a way that I do not wish to describe. This evaluation is to determine if you are any further danger to yourself or others.

" 'Now,' he asked again, 'what is your name?'

"I told him, and he began to question me more closely. I could tell that he did not believe my story at first, of the attack and the use of the hypodermic syringe, thinking instead that I was suffering from a delusional episode. As my mind cleared, however, and I was able to consistently provide further details that matched my basic story, he admitted the possibility that what I was saying was true.

"The doctor indicated to me that my admission by the two strangers from off the street was unofficial, and that there was no reason that he could keep me here without further orders. He finally decided that, except for my disheveled condition, I appeared to be functionally sane, and he agreed to send a message to my brother, who obtained my release."

"The least I could do," murmured Walter. "We should get you home, Henry."

"The doctor offered to summon the police to hear my story," continued Henry, ignoring Walter's latest interruption, "but Walter refused. We were making our way to Walter's home when we heard your name mentioned outside the railway station. Having heard of you before, and your ability to bring light where there has been only darkness, I insisted that we find you inside the station and relate my story, in the hopes that you will return with us and help rescue Sir Giles, should he still be alive.

"I believe," said Holmes, "that he was probably still alive as late as yesterday, at least. Otherwise, how would the younger man have known from him that you had no family, as he mentioned when you were attacked? Obviously, they had questioned Sir Giles after your first visit to obtain information as to your identity."

Henry nodded, and Holmes continued, "Did you happen to ask the doctor at Bethlem if the two men who brought you in for admission matched the descriptions of your attackers?"

"I did," replied Henry. "He did not know, but he asked an orderly at the front and confirmed, at least superficially, that they were in fact the same men. They did not leave their names, simply saying that they were concerned citizens who had discovered me nearby in the street."

"Describe these two men in Sir Giles's house in more detail, if you please."

As Henry closed his eyes for a moment, the growler lurched, turning into Baker Street. Finally, Henry looked up and said, "The younger man was wearing a plaid waistcoat, which seemed rather gaudy. He has a long head, wide at the bottom as if he habitually clenches his jaws, and rather narrow at the top. His hair, what there is of it, is cut quite short and parted in the middle."

89

"Did he have a mole on his right temple?" asked Holmes.

Henry stared straight ahead for a moment, and then looked surprised. "Why, yes he did! I recall being surprised by it on that first night, when he turned his head while shutting the door and the light caught it just so."

"And the second man," said Holmes. "Was he rather short and narrow, with thin legs, and an unnaturally substantial paunch that stretches his waistcoat? And does he have sandy hair that is combed straight forward onto his forehead, and trimmed across in a straight line an inch or so above his eyes?"

"Why, Mr. Holmes, it is as if you know them already! But how could you describe them so well?"

"Because I have been expecting them to arrive back in London for some time," Holmes replied. "I just did not know exactly when or where they would wash up."

"Two-twenty-one, Mr. Holmes," growled Bert Deacon from atop the four-wheeler.

"Wait here, Bert," said Holmes, jumping down. He leaned back into the vehicle and said, "I will only be a moment." Then he dashed inside, leaving the door ajar as he went.

After a moment, Mrs. Hudson leaned out, looking left and right before spotting our cab. I waved from within, and she wearily smiled and shook her head knowingly. As she started to close the door, I could hear Holmes return as he descended the seventeen steps from the sitting room, crashing down two at a time. He danced around Mrs. Hudson, said something to her that I could not hear, and climbed back into the cab.

"Scotland Yard, Bert, if you don't mind."

"Right, Mr. Holmes," Bert replied, and we made a lurch into motion, heading south.

"Is this really necessary?" asked Walter, only to receive a glare from Henry.

Holmes did not reply to Walter's question. He was holding a small clutch of papers, which he proceeded to sort on his lap, keeping some of them carefully hidden. I could see that it was a mixture of cables and photographs, as well as a large envelope holding additional sheets. Finally, he held up two of the sheets, both photographs, and asked, "Are these your attackers, Mr. Forsythe?"

I could see that the images were of the two men that Holmes had previously described while questioning Henry, who simply nodded wordlessly as the memory of the attack was obviously replaying itself in his mind.

"The younger of the two," said Holmes, glancing at one of the cables in his other hand, "is named Jack Gables, a career criminal and most recently a bank robber, originally from Manchester. The other is known as Layton Carr, which may or may not be his real name. He is an American, and originally from Chicago, which may explain the flat American accent which seemed unfamiliar to you. Carr is often a crony of Gables, and he fancies himself a doctor. I believe that he did have a form of medical training at one time in his life, but not to any meaningful completion. This has not prevented him from making dangerous use of the little knowledge that he has.

"I received a notification regarding Gables and Carr several months ago from my friend Wilson Hargreaves, of the New York Police Bureau, following a violent bank robbery that the two men had pulled off there. Both of them managed to gain illegal entrance to one of the larger New York banks, and using a chemical devised by Carr, overpower the guards. Things were touch-and-go, as they were discovered during the robbery, but they managed to escape, and haven't been seen in the United States, or anywhere else for that matter, since. Hargreave believed that they would make their way to England, and his initial message notifying me to keep my ear to the ground, as they say in America, was followed by this more extensive packet of information including these photographs. Hargreaves has also notified Scotland Yard, in case the two fugitives are spotted here, but he also wanted me to be on the lookout, as he put it."

"These men did make their way to England, as Hargreaves suspected they might, and for some reason have gone to ground in Sir Giles's home. Gables may be related to Sir Giles in some way, in spite of your impression that the old gentleman had no family. There may be some other connection of which we are as yet unaware. In any case, they must have decided to hide out there, thinking that Sir Giles had no friends or family to inquire after him. Your return on the second night must have prompted them to take action."

"I'm lucky that I was not killed, then, I suppose," said Henry.

Holmes shook his head. "They are not killers, at least so far. Even during the American bank robbery, when it would have been far easier for them to kill the bank guards who interfered with them, they took great effort simply to bind them, in spite of the fact their identification was assured, and also that it delayed and nearly ruined their escape. But," he added, "you have been lucky, nonetheless. Their decision to place you in Bedlam is unique in my experience, and could have been disastrous for you, if a different doctor there had decided to keep you for further evaluation, believing that your story was part of some greater delusion. No doubt Carr, the amateur doctor, assumed that the effects of the drug that he administered to you would last much longer, and that your incarceration in the asylum would be of an indefinite duration, rather than just for one night."

Traffic had thinned as the afternoon waned, and we were soon rounding Trafalgar Square and approaching Scotland Yard. Upon our arrival, Holmes decided that we should wait in the four-wheeler while he went inside, rather than waste the time it would take for all of us to go in and explain our purpose. With a bound, he carried his documents within.

It was less than ten minutes later, as I was wishing that we had all chosen to evacuate the hot cab and wait inside the imposing building, that Holmes returned to the pavement with Inspector Youghal and three burly constables. Youghal nodded toward me, and then raised his arm, summoning a second four-wheeler from a short way up the street. When everyone was aboard both cabs, we set out.

Crossing Westminster Bridge, we turned along the south side of the river, before making a series of turns, working our way ever closer to Kennington Park. "It is fortunate that Youghal was at the Yard this afternoon. He has a particular interest in renewing his acquaintance with Gables. Watson, have you ever noticed that reddish scar across the back of Youghal's left hand?"

"From an old knife wound, I think he said," I replied. "Did he get that from Gables?"

Holmes nodded. "Years ago, back when Gables was just beginning his illustrious criminal career. Gables escaped, and he has since risen to greater heights, within certain circles. Youghal is anxious to congratulate him."

The distance to our destination shortened rapidly, Holmes changed the subject entirely, discussing our planned excursion to the Wessex Cup on the following Tuesday. Without mentioning specifics about either the missing race horse or our client, he speculated as to what set of circumstances during a horse race could cause an owner to be permanently warned off the turf for life. Neither Walter nor Henry Forsythe felt the need to contribute to this conversation.

Soon we were pulling up at one of the outer boundaries of the Park. Henry indicated with a gesture that Meadcroft was not far away, but our current location was not in direct sight of Sir Giles's home. The Scotland Yard men emptied from their four-wheeler, and Youghal dispersed his troops in different directions to surround the house.

There was still an hour or so of sunshine left in the sky, so our approach could not be entirely hidden. Walter and Henry stayed with the cabs, while Holmes, Youghal, another plain-clothed detective named Benton, and I walked down the side of the green, showing no interest in the great house that stretched across one end of the common.

The old house was a big and double-fronted affair, gone to seed. However, it had been built in a time when workmanship was solid, and it might still remain standing when the newer houses around it have fallen into decay.

As we neared the old house, having been walking in an oblique and indirect way toward it, we abruptly changed direction and mounted the steps. Standing to one side, in case someone fired a weapon through it, Youghal pounded upon the door with all the authority of the Yard behind him, demanding that the occupants open in the name of the law. After a few seconds of silence, he pounded again with a bellow. In a moment, we heard scrabbling sounds from the right side of the house, followed by a blow and a cry. Leaving Benton at the front door, we ran to the side to find both Gables and Carr, struggling in the hands of some of Youghal's men after their unsuccessful and awkward attempt to exit a side window.

The matter was quickly sorted out. A search of the house found the bulk of the New York bank robbery loot, still packed in the men's cases. More importantly, we discovered Sir Giles Gidley-Hall, gagged and bound hand and foot on a sofa in one of the interior ground floor rooms. I ordered that he be carried out into the fresh air, where I began to administer what aid that I thought necessary. He was a tough old man, and was soon on his feet, as mad as blazes, although he seemed to calm himself when one of Youghal's men reported that Tommy, the goat, had been discovered well-fed and watered in his shed behind the house.

While I was assisting Sir Giles, I was unable to hear the exact exchange between Youghal and Gables, but I did see that Youghal was holding his scarred hand in front of Gables's face and explaining something in a very precise manner. Gables, who had attempted a belligerent attitude up to that point, seemed to collapse when he realized that his story was completely known, and that there would be no escape this time.

Holmes asked a few questions of Gables and Carr, chiefly to confirm his explanation of the events. It was revealed that Gables was a distant cousin of Sir Giles, and he had long been aware of the old man's hermit-like existence. Upon his and Carr's return to England, the house in Meadcroft had seemed like a good place in which to hide. They had initially been left alone there, waiting until they deemed it safe to move on, but then Henry Forsythe's concerns had led him to check on his neighbor, thus causing the fugitives to become irrationally fearful of discovery.

Neither man had wanted to kill Henry Forsythe, but they had not wanted to have him remain as a captive in Sir Giles's house either. They believed that if someone had arrived and had insisted on examining Sir

Giles, they could have drugged the old man and explained that he was under a doctor's care. But a persistent neighbor was another matter. He might talk, and then more people might investigate. It was decided to do something about Henry Forsythe, sooner rather than later. Keeping Henry there in the house, along with Sir Giles, was deemed too great a risk, as Henry might escape, or someone might have seen him visiting the house on two successive nights and suggest that as a location to examine if someone noticed that he was missing as well.

It was Carr who decided that they should drug Henry and have him hospitalized in the Bethlem Asylum. He had mistakenly believed that his concoction would last for much longer than it had, and that Henry would be held incommunicado at the hospital until long after Gables and Carr were gone. It was much better, in their opinion, than drugging him and simply leaving him to be found in the street. After Henry's capture, they had made sure that Sir Giles was adequately bound, and then they had taken Henry to Bedlam, telling the cab driver that they were transporting a sick friend.

After Gables and Carr had been taken away, Walter and Henry were brought up to the house, where Henry and Sir Giles were able to speak to one another. It was difficult for the old hermit, but he managed to express his thanks to Henry in a gruff way. Henry then introduced the old man to his brother, Walter, who seemed relieved that the whole matter was at an end.

As Youghal was making motions that he was prepared to depart, Holmes spoke. "By, the way, Youghal, there is one other little matter that should be taken care of while we have the opportunity."

"And that would be?" asked Youghal, in a jovial tone.

"Would you mind having a couple of your men take Mr. Walter Forsythe into custody?"

A shocked silence fell upon the group for just a moment, before Walter bolted. Youghal's men were not close enough to make any sort of attempt to stop him, although there is no doubt that they could have soon run him down. Walter made as if to dash toward the open green, in a perpendicular path away from the front of the great house where we stood. As no one else was in a position to intervene, I stuck out my right leg into Walter's path. He tumbled and fell hard, skidding into a pile of autumn leaves. Youghal's men were on him in an instant, dragging him to his feet.

"Well done, Watson," murmured Holmes

Gone was the mild older brother. Instead, a raging, foul-mouthed beast stood between the two officers, cursing Holmes in every way imaginable. Henry Forsythe seemed to shrink within himself, and took a step backward. Sir Giles, without thought, put a fatherly hand on Henry's shoulder to calm him.

"Well, we've got him," said Youghal. "Now can you tell me why?"

"Certainly," said Holmes, reaching into his coat and pulling out the sheaf of papers that he had brought from Baker Street. As he thumbed through them, pulling previously hidden sheets from the envelope, he said to Benton, who was one of the men holding Walter, "Would you mind pulling back his left sleeve to expose the inside of his wrist?"

Walter began to struggle all the harder, but to no avail. Benton roughly pulled back the sleeve and turned Walter's hand to reveal a tattoo. It was about two inches long, blue, and rough-looking and faded. It was a short, segmented serpent, and each of the three segments contained a number: 7, 4, and 2. The number seven was crossed in the Continental manner.

Holmes plucked out two sheets from his bundle and held them out for Youghal. I stepped over so as to observe them as well. The first was a document, dated nearly a decade before, from the Manchester police, describing the activities of a sophisticated gang of thieves. A sketch of the same tattoo was included on the sheet.

"It is a gang symbol," said Holmes. "An amateur tattoo. It is the house number on the street in Manchester where they were initiated. This other sheet from my scrapbooks," he said, holding out the second piece of paper, "is more specific."

It was written in Holmes's close script, describing one Walter Forsythe, late of Manchester, and now a mid-level cog in the machine of Professor James Moriarty. "I noticed the tattoo when Walter's sleeve pulled up, as he was helping Henry into the cab. I verified it when I went into my rooms to retrieve Hargreave's information about Gables and Carr.

Holmes faced Walter, who had slightly calmed himself as the evidence against him was revealed. He kept looking toward Henry, whose head was down and would not look back.

"Did you come to London after the Portland Street robbery in Manchester turned into a hanging job?"

Youghal looked up from the paper. "He was involved in that one? Then we're very glad to find him, and make no mistake about that!"

"I do not know if Moriarty planned the Portland Street business, and made a place for Walter Forsythe and the others after they had to flee Manchester when it went wrong, or if he came to the Professor's attention after he arrived in London. Nevertheless, he has been an important and rising part of the Professor's organization since then. From his position in the City, obtained for him by the Professor, he has been able to carry out all sorts of interesting chores." Holmes tapped the second sheet of paper.

"This is a partial list of some of Walter's activities since he came to London, on behalf of his employer. I was not planning to try to land him yet, as I was waiting to net all the fish in one great haul, but as Walter has placed himself unavoidably on my hook this afternoon, the opportunity was too great to ignore, and I reeled him in."

"Well, to extend your metaphor, we'll fillet him and learn all about what he's been up to, and more, I assure you," said Youghal. "Take him away."

Walter kept trying to turn back and look at his brother as he was walked down the green and out toward the cabs. Henry would never glance his way. Sir Giles's hand had remained on Henry's shoulder throughout, and finally I heard him say, "Come inside with me, son. We'll have a little something." They turned and went into the great house.

Holmes and I were left standing alone on the green. The sun was finally dropping behind the surrounding houses, and shadows were rapidly lengthening from west to east.

"You know," I said, as we began to stroll back toward Bert Deacons's four-wheeler, "I have often heard you deride coincidence, but today had several of them. If you had not noticed Walter's tattoo – "

"That was not coincidence," interrupted Holmes. "That was observation."

"All right then," I countered. "If circumstances had not conspired to place Walter's tattoo before you, where it could be observed, and if the Forsythes had not been walking down Praed Street, and if Henry had not heard your name mentioned indiscreetly by one of Patterson's men outside the station, they would have never come inside and involved you, the one man in England with knowledge of these varied and wide-spread crimes at his fingertips, in these events. It is undeniably coincidence."

"Coincidence, Watson?" said Holmes. "Perhaps. But is it possible that it was simply an adjustment on the great scale of life in order to keep things in balance? We, on the side of good, were denied a victory today with Patterson and the matter of the diary. Score one for Moriarty. But perhaps it was only fitting that we then be allowed to achieve something on our side in order to keep things in equilibrium."

"It is a chess game, and you have taken one of Moriarty's pieces!" I cried.

"A pawn, possibly. But this is not a chess game where one player takes his turn, and then sits and waits patiently for his opponent to plan strategy before responding in kind. One does not wait for the other side to take its turn in this game. You can be sure that Moriarty will already be thinking of his next move, and the next. So it is up to me to plan my next move as well, and the next, and for three moves past that, and so on, until the end of the game."

"A game you will win," I said.

"That is my plan, Watson," said Holmes. "But I must have time – I must have time!"

We strolled together in silence back to the cab as the sun set and the wind picked up.

The Matter of Boz's Last Letter

Part I: The Client

"Make a long arm, if you would, Watson, and hand me my index for the letter 'R'."

I had been standing behind my chair, near the fireplace, when Holmes made his request, and it required no great effort to retrieve the volume in question. It was a large black thing, roughly matching its brothers lining the wall shelves to the left of the mantel, and it required careful handling, as numerous loose scraps of paper protruded from various pages, some newspaper clippings, and some of more obscure origin. Here and there across the slips were various notations in Holmes's careful fist. One caught my eye as I passed Holmes the book: *The most vilified man in Marylebone.* I had my own ideas as to whom that might refer, and I resolved to look it up at some later date, when the scrapbook had been returned to its resting place.

I turned toward the door, when Holmes stopped me. "Are you going out?"

"I had not planned to do so."

"That is fortunate, then. I have had a note from a prospective client, and I would value your opinion. He is due to arrive at the hour."

I glanced at the mantel clock and noted that it was nearly a quarter of nine. I informed Holmes that I would return momentarily, and continued on toward my room, one flight above.

I returned to the sitting room moments later, having retrieved the book which I sought, as Holmes laid aside his "collection of R's," as he often referred to that particular volume. He maintained that it was a fine one, but not so fine as his "M's." I saw that he had tossed a note into my chair. Lifting it, I sat and read the contents:

Mr. Holmes,

I propose to call upon you this morning at nine o'clock to discuss a matter of great importance to both myself and my business. It concerns the auction planned for the ninth of this month, less than a week away. As the affair is of extreme importance, I trust that you will make yourself available, and devote your full attention to this affair, in spite of any other matters which are currently engaging you.

Regards,

Leonard Rathham

"Rathham?" I said. "Of New Bond Street?"

"The same," replied Holmes, gesturing toward the index. "You are welcome to see for yourself, but my information on the man is limited. He is in his early fifties, has never married, is the sole proprietor of Sefton's, which he purchased from the Sefton family some fifteen years ago after working his way up from the bottom. It is a story that would be inspiring if not for the tedious and workmanlike way in which he accomplished it. The man is capable, wealthy, and most uninterestingly honest."

I laughed. "He also seems to feel that he can assume your complete willingness to set aside whatever you are working upon at the present time in favor of his own case." I paused, and then asked, "What do you have on hand at the present time?"

"Some ten or twelve other little matters, none of which present any points of interest. Let us hope that Mr. Rathham can remedy that."

We spent the next few minutes in desultory conversation, speculating on the origin of our prospective client's unusual surname. I was not aware of ever having encountered it before. Holmes felt that in spite of this, it seemed somehow fundamentally British. Soon, we were interrupted by the sound of footsteps on the stairs, followed by a pause on the landing as the man, presumably Rathham, paused for a moment to catch his breath.

"He is in poor condition indeed," said Holmes softly, "if seventeen steps can conspire to defeat him so easily. Perhaps, when he has settled, a drop of medicinal brandy?"

I nodded as there was a knock on the door.

Holmes called and invited him in, and a more English looking fellow we had yet to encounter. He was short, not much over five feet in height, and not heavy at all. In fact, if not for the grayish pallor of his skin, I would have expected him to show a great deal of boundless energy, and not the breathless weakness that presented itself. His clothing was well-made and expensive, but not ostentatiously so.

Shepherding him to the basket chair in front of the fireplace, between Holmes's chair and my own, I offered him some medical spirits.

"No, thank you, Doctor," he replied. "I am a lifelong teetotaler. I have no doubts that, were I to sample something right now, I would be asleep before I could convey to you the seriousness of my problem."

I acknowledged his refusal and made my way to my own chair. Holmes began by asking him to state his business.

Taking a deep breath, Rathham began "No doubt you gentlemen are aware of the auction to be held on the ninth, featuring a great number of fine pieces, a mixture of artworks and various examples of fine furniture with historical interest."

Holmes glanced my way. I shook my head, and he turned back to Rathham. "I am afraid that, while I try to stay aware of notable upcoming auctions, especially those related to works of art, I have not acquired any previous knowledge of this particular event."

"I suppose that is no surprise, after all," said Rathham. "It is not one of our more important auctions. At least, it did not start out that way. The offerings are certainly of fine quality, but the seller is not, shall we say, *first tier*. The furnishings and artwork have been in storage for ten years, prevented by a legal dispute from being sold. Only recently was it determined that the owner has true legal title to them, allowing him to offer them for sale. In all honesty, the auction would have merited no special interest, since it is only to provide needed funds for the current owner of the properties. Rather, what has elevated this auction to a position of rather more interest than it would have ordinarily generated is the item that was discovered by my staff, hidden in one of the pieces of furniture to be sold."

"And that would be . . . ?"

"Many of the furnishings, as I previously stated, are of historical interest. For example, there is a chair, collected by the owner more than ten years ago, and before his legal troubles began, that belonged to King George III, the Queen's grandfather. It is rather worn, but its provenance is unquestioned. And the bureau that came down from – "

"Are any of these furnishings that you have mentioned relevant to your problem?" asked Holmes, trying with great courtesy to keep Rathham on the track.

"No, they are not," replied the auctioneer. "I apologize. To stay on the point, I will tell you that one of the items is a desk that belonged to the late author, Charles Dickens, at the time of his death."

"In 1870, as I recall."

"Quite right, Mr. Holmes. The ninth of June, as a matter of fact. It was because of the interest in that particular desk that we chose to schedule the auction on the same day as that of the anniversary."

"But," I interrupted, "surely Dickens's desk, while interesting in and of itself, is not any more interesting or worthy of note than some of the other furniture, such as that which once belonged to a king."

"Dr. Watson, it was the item that was found *within* that desk that generated a greater interest in the sale. While the desk is now more of a curiosity than it was before the discovery, it is the item itself which is now the featured property in the auction."

"And that would be . . . ?" asked Holmes, with a small amount of vexation that only his closest friends might perceive.

"Dickens's lost ending to his final unfinished novel, *The Mystery of Edwin Drood.*"

Holmes and I were silent for a second or two, each pondering the implications of such a statement. I personally had more of an appreciation of one of the country's greatest writers, much more than Holmes. However, we both recognized the value of such a document.

"Such a thing might be worth a fortune," I said. "How is it that the discovery was not immediately announced in the press?"

"Perhaps I overstated the exact nature of the discovery," said Rathham. "The document is not the *definitive* lost ending. As far as we know, Dickens died without completing the book, and the version that is published ends where he stopped. What was discovered in the desk, pushed back behind one of the drawers, was not the legitimate answer to the mystery presented in the novel. It was not even an outline indicating what his planned ending would have been. Dickens was still working on the book up to nearly the hour that he died, and whatever solution he planned for the mystery that he had devised is still a secret that he took with him. Rather, this discovery is a letter that he wrote on the day of his death, outlining a 'false' solution, for the purposes of amusing, or perhaps appeasing, his correspondent."

"So," said Holmes, "the document would have some interest to a Dickens scholar, but that is the limit of its importance."

"If that were all it was, then you would be correct, Mr. Holmes. However, the nature of Dickens's false solution is quite . . . well, one would have to say that it is *incendiary* at best." Rathham fell silent then, pondering his own thoughts.

"Would you care to elaborate?" Holmes finally said, interrupting Rathham's reverie.

"Um? Oh, certainly, certainly. At the time of Dickens's death, he had been estranged from one of his greatest friends, fellow author Wilkie Collins, for a number of years. It seems that by June 1870, both men were making attempts to restore their friendship. In the letter, Dickens refers to other missives that had passed between the two in recent weeks, and it is clear that Collins was informed of the nature of Dickens's latest novel. Dickens, with almost a whimsical tone, replies that the murderer – and this is what gives the document such an explosive power – was the Queen herself, carrying out first-hand crimes with the assistance of her ministers, family, and other associates, all of whom are identified by name. Various outrageous motivations are also given as well.

101

"After the document was found in the desk, it was brought to me for examination. Frankly, my astonishment at the discovery was balanced with my feelings of revulsion that one of our greatest writers could have made such offensive statements, even in jest. It goes beyond satire. Dickens mentions one or two events from the later completed parts of *Drood*, and then he spins a web from that point consisting of all sorts of depravity, laying the whole matter at the foot of the Crown.

"I called on several men of letters who have assisted me in the past, and they felt that the work was certainly written by Dickens. One of these men tried to dilute the importance or influence of the document, indicating that Dickens was simply being *whimsical* in order to amuse Collins, as well as to play up to Collins's strong feelings regarding social injustice, which had been increasing over the years."

"Dickens had a concern regarding society's ills, as well," I said. "It is revealed all through his books. But I'm not aware of him ever putting anything such as you have described to paper before."

"So said my experts," replied Rathham. "They felt that it was an ill-conceived impulse on his part, and either the letter would have been sent to Collins and kept between the two of them, at least until Collins's death, when it would have been discovered, or possibly Dickens would have chosen to destroy it before it was sent. However, neither outcome occurred, as Dickens's death took place that same day, and the letter was somehow lost in the desk until its discovery a few weeks ago."

"And yet, despite your obvious revulsion at the document, it was decided to proceed with the plan to auction it?" said Holmes.

"It was. After all, Mr. Holmes, I have an auction house. If I did not do it, someone else would. In my own way, I have directed matters so that only scholars who will be discreet with the document are even aware of it, or will be bidding on it. The current owner of the desk simply wants to accumulate funds, and does not care to whom the letter is offered, as long as he makes a profit. There have been certain scholars as well who have encouraged suppression of the document, or at least a temporary loan to various seats of learning for further study, but the owner insisted on an immediate sale, and the impending date of Dickens's death, as well as the anniversary of when the letter was written, was chosen as the day of the auction.

"And there the matter stood, with the letter being revealed to a limited number of buyers, all learned men or collectors of Dickens ephemera, every one. The seller had at least agreed to that much, that is, to keeping the matter out of the press. Then, this morning, events conspired to send me here, to plead for your help, Mr. Holmes."

"Then the logical conclusion," said my friend, "is that the letter has disappeared."

"Stolen!" cried Rathham. "I'm certain of it. It was kept in my own safe, to which only I have the combination. When I opened it this morning, the letter was gone."

"Are you certain? Might it not have simply become mixed with some of the other papers in the safe? Such things have happened once or twice before, in my experience."

"I assure you that I would not be here now in such a state if that were so," replied the little auction master. "There are very few papers in that safe, and the letter, a fairly thick packet of nineteen heavy-bond and folded sheets, was not there."

Holmes was silent for a moment, and then surged to his feet, peeling off his dressing gown as he made for the doorway to his room. "Then we must examine the scene for ourselves, Mr. Rathham. I assume that the safe to which you refer is located at the auction house?"

"It is. My carriage is outside."

"Excellent." Holmes left the room for a moment, and returned fully clothed, having exchanged dressing gown for acceptable outer wear. "Have you informed the owner of the desk that his property is missing?"

"Not yet," said our client. "After my initial shock, I wrote to you, and soon after made my way here. I am hoping that the matter can be resolved before I need take such action. I can assure you that the owner, who had hoped to realize some profit on the original items in the sale, has speedily become accustomed to the idea that he will receive a much greater amount of money with the inclusion of the discovered letter."

"And who is this man?" said Holmes, swinging into the Inverness that he insisted on wearing year-round, in city or country.

Rathham sniffed. "Not my usual clientele, I can assure you," he said. "Truth be told, if some of the items that he wishes to sell had not been of such fine quality, I would not have involved myself with him. I understand that he collected them all a number of years ago, before his imprisonment. Between ourselves, gentleman, I have heard more than one whisper that he is not really a Baron at all."

Holmes paused, reaching for his fore-and-aft cap, hanging on the peg behind the door. "And you say that this Baron's possessions were legally tied up for ten years?" he said. "May I inquire as to the Baron's name?"

"Maupertuis," replied Rathham. "You may have read of him. He was released from prison a month or so ago, after serving ten years at Princetown. Some financial scandal, as I recall."

Part II: The Auction House

We settled into Rathham's elaborately decorated four-wheeler, and set off south for New Bond Street. Rathham kept up a running chatter about his work, veering toward the current matter, but following conversational tangents without providing any further insight to the present affair. He told tales and gave sly hints regarding other scandals related to auctions over the years, both relating to his clients and those of his competitors. I politely nodded as necessary, but I kept my eye on Sherlock Holmes, who sat quietly and peered unseeing out the carriage window at the passing street. I knew that he was thinking of the name that he had just heard, and the events of the spring of 1887, just over ten years earlier, during his first meeting with Baron Maupertuis, and the resulting crisis that had overtaken him then.

I had reason for concern, as the events of the past few months had mirrored in some crucial ways those that had taken place in 1887. In that current spring of 1897, ten years after Holmes had defeated the Baron and resolved the dreadful scandal associated with the Netherland-Sumatra Company, I had been more aware than perhaps ever before of Holmes's high-strung nature, as he raced pell-mell towards a collapse of the sort that I had already seen once or twice in the years of our friendship. During the early years of our association, when I first met him and shared rooms in Baker Street, I had gradually become aware of Holmes's habit of dosing himself with weakened solutions of cocaine or morphine whenever he was bored, between cases, and, as he liked to put it, when he was "like a racing engine, tearing itself to pieces because it is not connected up with the work for which it was built."

Gradually, his chosen methods of making use of the substances, particularly cocaine, changed so that he was using it in order to provide himself with extra bursts of stamina and clarity of thought during particularly difficult cases. This was rare and infrequent, to the best of my knowledge, until early 1887, when he was taxed for several months during his successful investigation into the Netherland-Sumatra business, and the Baron's machinations. At the conclusion of that affair, Holmes's health was shattered, and I was called to Lyons to bring him back to England and help return him to his former strength.

But the devil that was Holmes's addiction was only sleeping, and not dead. After the death of my first wife, Constance in late 1887*, I moved back to Baker Street, and my presence, I believe, helped keep Holmes's attentions focused on his affairs and not on the siren call of the syringe. However, 1888 turned out to be a year necessitating massive efforts from my friend. That fall, while involved in one of Holmes's investigations, I met the woman who would be my second wife, Mary Morstan.

Following our courtship, I remarried in mid-1889, and my absence from Baker Street allowed the reliance on the evil drug to return, as Holmes required more and more stamina during his ever-increasing battles with Professor Moriarty. Fortunately, I realized in time what was happening, and intervened by seeking help from an expert physician in Vienna during the fall of 1890. Holmes and I traveled there, and when we departed, I believed that he had found a path, albeit a shaky one, toward what he needed to do.

The following spring, Holmes was believed to have died at the hands of Professor Moriarty at the Reichenbach Falls. After his miraculous return to Baker Street three years later, in 1894, he seemed to have no need for the drug, having learned several calming techniques during his travels in the East. My second wife, Mary, had died during the years that Holmes was missing and presumed dead, and following his return to London, I again began to share rooms with him. I must confess that it was several years after that before I began to see, once again, evidence of the dark intrusive tentacles of the opiate that Holmes seemed to need, at first just a little here or there, winding their way into his very existence.

As the carriage crossed Oxford Street, I watched my friend, even as he looked at the passing street views, and tried to see if the return of the Baron was causing any unhealthy reaction, as I
did not want a relapse of his recent condition. For he had only recently fought his addiction, yet again, and at that time I was uncertain as to the complete reliability of his recovery.

By late 1896, it had become dreadfully obvious that, if somehow he were not stopped, Holmes would be unable to shake the grip of the drug, progressing to a steady and steep decline that would almost certainly lead to his death. Eventually, in a long and painful process that need not be recounted here, Holmes was finally persuaded to abandon London for a time and travel with me to the furthest stretches of Cornwall, where he and I obtained a house at the sea, and he set about bravely purging the drug from his system. It was not an easy thing for him, or for me, but as his friend and physician, I knew that we had to see it through or his life was forfeit.

---

* Editor's Note: See Chapters 7-10 of William S. Baring-Gould's *Sherlock Holmes of Baker Street* for further information regarding Constance Watson.

After our return to London, a month or so before the events of the present narrative, he had some difficult moments, and he often fell into deep brown studies. But he had finally found the strength and understanding to rouse himself from them without the need to seek the drug. As I write this, now some thirty years on from the events of that June, I can affirm that he has never made use of the drug – or any other substance of a similar nature – again.

But I did not know on that day whether or not Holmes had truly defeated the demon. I had seen him slide back too many times before. So I kept a sharp watch, knowing well that a shock, such as learning of the involvement of his old enemy, Baron Maupertuis, might be the very thing that would bring about some new disastrous craving for the drug.

Rathham's carriage had turned into Brook Street, and so on until we reached New Bond Street. Not long after we turned the corner, we stopped in front of that austere building which had become noted in recent years for the nature of its auctions and for its discreet conduct. Rathham's man in livery at the door ushered us inside. We passed through an ornate lobby, and on through to the auction rooms themselves. Tapestries hung from the walls, and heavy chairs with golden trim lined the room from side to side, facing the short dais at the front. The great space was fairly well lit, and I knew that a closer examination of the room's various *accoutrements* that adorned the surroundings would show that they were indeed as fine as they looked. There would be nothing of a theater about this place, where the magic and illusion of the darkened room are revealed to be shabby and threadbare once the lights are turned up.

But after passing through the finely decorated public space, where nothing was too good for Rathham's patrons, it was something of a shock, although not altogether unexpected, when we went through a tasteful and heavy white door, and thus into the inner chambers of the great auction house. For here there was no decoration, and no need to impress anyone. The place resembled nothing so much as a warehouse, or perhaps more appropriately fitted to my earlier metaphor, the well managed backstage area of a theater.

Deep shelves were stacked far above our heads with all sorts of items, including works of art and furniture. Smaller cabinets, many appearing to be locked, held finer objects, each cluttered together so that it was impossible to tell at a glance exactly what one was seeing. However, I was certain that Rathham had everything organized, and could walk immediately to this or that location and lay his hands on any specific item that he wanted without a moment's delay

Our host led us past numerous bustling workmen and supervisors, all of whom continued to carry out their tasks, but gave us surreptitious

106

glances along the way. We reached a plain door at the rear of the building and passed into Rathham's office.

It was a working space, with no signs of luxury. I felt that Rathham would reserve meeting the public, or clients or buyers, in more luxurious spaces near the front of the building. This was the man's inner sanctum, as evidenced by stacks of documents and materials waiting for his attention. In some ways the room looked like what happened when Holmes was allowed to pile objects and papers related to his investigations around our sitting room in Baker Street, following some obscure filing system that he kept to himself. It was only by the stern intervention of Mrs. Hudson or myself that we were not eventually overrun by Holmes's archives.

Holmes immediately made his way across the room to the rather modest safe, standing alone beside a chair stacked with catalogs.

"A Victor safe," said Holmes, softly. "Combination lock only, no key." Slightly louder, he said, "Would you mind opening it, Mr. Rathham?"

"Certainly, certainly," said the small man, stepping forward. The safe was quickly opened, and Rathham showed no hesitation at revealing the contents. It was as he had said earlier: the Dickens letter was not there.

"When was the last time that you saw it?" questioned Holmes.

"About five o'clock last night. I always keep the safe closed and locked unless I am specifically taking or replacing some of the contents. I never walk away, even for an instant, with the door open. As you can see from the remaining contents, these items are highly confidential. Yesterday afternoon, I opened the safe to replace an estimate that was being consulted by one of my trusted employees. I laid the estimate on top of the Dickens letter. I specifically recall doing so because the letter itself is an unusual color, brought about by the discoloration that has occurred within the paper, and also because the estimate was slightly smaller than the folded letter, and I was able to center it exactly on top of the larger document."

"Who else has the combination?"

"No one."

"You are sure?"

"Absolutely."

"Do you have it written down somewhere that could have been discovered, in case you forget it?"

"No, Mr. Holmes. It is a number that has personal significance to me from a time in my youth. No one could guess it, and I would have no need to write it down, as it is something that I will not forget, at least as long as I retain my faculties."

Holmes was silent for a moment, before saying, "How many employees do you have?"

"Nearly thirty," replied Rathham. "Of course, many are laborers, or delivery people. About ten who work with the clients, and have knowledge of the business side of things."

"And how many of them knew about the letter?"

"Internally, just two. Angus Menzies, my chief assistant, and my secretary, Mr. Addison."

"I will need to speak with them, and possibly other members of your staff as well," said Holmes, looking around. "Will it be possible to make use of your office?"

"Certainly, certainly. I will just – "

Rathham was interrupted before he could finish by a knock at his office door, followed by the entrance of an average-looking man in a brown suit. "Mr. Holmes?" he said, looking toward my friend.

Holmes nodded, and the fellow stepped forward, holding an envelope in front of him. "No reply is expected," he said, stepping back, turning smartly, and departing the way that he came.

Holmes opened the envelope and removed the simple folded note. Opening it, he quickly read the short handwritten message, and then seemed to read it again, more slowly this time.

Shoving it into the pocket of his Inverness, he barked a short, "Ha!" and turned to our client. "It will not be necessary to interview your staff at the present time," he said. "New information has come to light that will require our presence elsewhere."

"But . . . " said Rathham, with confusion, "but how could there be any new information if you have only learned of the letter's theft just a short time ago in your rooms, from my very lips?"

"Nevertheless," said Holmes, nodding toward the door. "We must seek answers elsewhere. We shall be in touch, never fear!"

With that, we left the small man and made our way outside. My last view of Rathham was a study between puzzlement and anger, with the latter winning.

Outside, a smart-looking private hansom was waiting, its driver looking toward us expectantly. Without hesitation, Holmes entered, and I followed. As I sat back, he handed me the note.

Sherlock,

Your time will be better spent joining me for lunch to discuss the matter of the Dickens letter. Questions will be answered. A carriage awaits.

Mycroft

Part III: The Diogenes Club

The vehicle gained momentum, rolling through the crowded throngs of New Bond Street. I said, "Your brother? What could he know about this? And why should he care?"

"Possibly there is some government interest in this document that smears the Royal Family, written by such a noted author. That is the only theory that I can advance at the present time without more data. Data, it would seem, that we shall have in a very short period of time."

Indeed, the skillful maneuvering of the driver brought us along to Piccadilly quick enough, where a sharp right and then a left had us rolling down St. James and thence into Pall Mall. Halfway down that illustrious avenue, we drew to a stop between the Diogenes Club on one side of the street, and Mycroft Holmes's lodgings on the other. Holmes cast an interrogatory glance toward the driver, who nodded his head toward the Club. We went up the short flight of steps and inside.

In spite of what I knew to expect every time I entered that curious place, the vast silence still seemed overwhelming. The rustle of cloth as we removed our coats and handed them off seemed deafening and almost embarrassing, feeling as if it were something for which I should apologize, akin to bursting into laughter at a funeral. Holmes did not appear to suffer such concerns – he never did – as he turned and briskly moved deeper into the place, making for the Stranger's Room, the only place in the building where conversation was allowed or tolerated.

We found Mycroft, standing in front of one of the tall windows, resembling a great lion on its hind legs as he looked down at the street. It was the same stance that he had been making when I had first met him, back in the fall of '88, just hours before we were so deeply involved in the affair of Mr. Melas's problem.

"You were followed," said Mycroft. It was a statement, not a question.

"I was aware of it," replied his brother, joining him at the window. "The man across the street, two doors down."

I looked to see him. He was leaning in a doorway, looking up and down the street in every direction but towards us.

"He is an Australian by birth," said Holmes, "wounded in the left leg at some point in the past. In his early-to-mid-forties. He has recently had his unusually pale hair cut, and is wearing a false moustache."

I peered at the man, feeling safe to do so since he was conspicuously not looking our way. "I believe I can see the evidence of the hair cut, since the skin at his hairline and above his ears is noticeably paler than that of his face and hands. And he stands awkwardly on one leg, which reveals his injury."

"Very good, Watson. And his Australian background?"

After a moment's silence, with no answer from myself forthcoming, Holmes said softly, "His tie bar, Watson, although you might be excused for not being able to see it clearly now. As I circled behind the hansom after we arrived, I was able to glance at it. Although he is a street's width away, it is still visible, illuminated as it is by the sun. Although you may not have recognized it, it is definitely a stylized symbol of a kangaroo."

"Indeed," said Mycroft, "you are correct, Sherlock. But you would do well not to forget the tattoo of a kangaroo in the bend of his right forearm as well."

Holmes straightened slightly and smiled with a look of enlightenment, but I was confused. "Ah," said Holmes.

"This is surely too much," I said. "How can you know of any tattoo, hidden beneath his shirt cuff and coat sleeve?"

"Simply because," replied Mycroft Holmes, "he is one of *my* agents."

"Was, perhaps you mean?" asked his brother. "If he was following me on your orders, perhaps for my protection, or possibly to see where I have been and will be going, you would not have felt the need to point him out to us. That fact, coupled with that ridiculous false moustache, makes me think that for some reason, this agent is no longer under your control."

Mycroft sighed and turned away from the window, moving toward a table at the rear of the room, set for luncheon. "You are right, Sherlock. I fear that this man, one of my most trusted, for a while at least, has gone rogue."

"But why the obviously false moustache?" said Holmes. "Surely your agents are not so careless as to display such patent amateurism."

"I believe that he is sending me a message, although its meaning escapes me. Perhaps a taunt that, even with such poor protective coloring, he still believes that he is now beyond my reach."

Holmes nodded toward the window. "Why don't you simply send word to block up the street and catch him, then? I have half a mind to go do it myself, and I don't even know the full story yet."

"It is not that easy," replied Mycroft, dropping heavily into a chair. "Join me, please," he gestured to the seats beside him. "I am not certain of his plans, and until I have a better understanding, I must let him play his own game, though time grows short."

"From the fact that you knew how to find Watson and me at Rathham's auction house, I must believe that this rogue agent of yours has something to do with the stolen Dickens letter, and the auction in just a few days."

"He has everything to do with it," sighed Mycroft. "For he is the man that stole the blasted letter in the first place."

"That simplifies matters," said Holmes. He sniffed. "Curry?"

Mycroft nodded, and indicated that we should help ourselves. "I, for one," said Holmes, ignoring the offer as I lifted the lid of the serving dish with pleasure, "was not looking forward to tediously interviewing Rathham's employees, one by one, to eliminate the innocent and terrify the guilty. To the expert, there is a strong family resemblance about crimes, and if you have assembled for questioning a thousand witnesses at your finger ends, the thousand-and-first is very much like the first thousand."

"Perhaps, brother, when you hear more about this matter, you will admit that this is a little different than your usual inquiries."

I could tell that there was something about this situation that amused Holmes. Mycroft could see it as well, but he did not choose to let it rile him. "The fellow out on the street," said the elder Holmes, "who probably got onto your trail at the auction house, is named Julius Shipton. As you observed, he is Australian. He was raised without a father, and I gather that he ran rather wild during his youth. He managed to obtain passage to this country in his early twenties, and after his arrival, he pursued higher learning in a rather haphazard fashion, first at Oxford, and then at a few of the lesser establishments. At some point he drifted north into Edinburgh, where he fell into an acquaintance with a reporter who had chosen over time to make personal use of the facts that he uncovered while gathering information for his stories, rather than providing this information to his newspaper.

"Between the two, this reporter and Shipton, there evolved a rather systematic way of achieving payment from the subjects of their inquiries."

"Victims, you mean," said Holmes, finally deigning to take a serving of curry. "He was a blackmailer."

"Yes," said Mycroft, "and I am aware of your feelings regarding such creatures, and I am in complete agreement as well. But Shipton showed great finesse, and when one of the victims finally shot and killed the reporter, there were enough indications about what had truly been going on that my local representative in the Scottish capital was able to identify Shipton, and more specifically his skill and finesse at carrying out his chosen activity, albeit a dark one. I could make use of these skills, as well as the man himself, and I recruited him as an agent. I must say that it has generally been a satisfactory arrangement, at least up until now. While he certainly has not been the most patriotic chap to ever carry out an order, he has shown great initiative with a certain measure of luck in the bargain, and had earned a degree of trust."

"Until this matter of the Dickens letter," said Holmes.

"Yes. We first became aware of it a few weeks ago, never mind how. There was obviously some concern about such a thing possibly becoming common knowledge, just a short time before the Queen's Diamond Jubilee is to take place. There is already enough criticism in the press regarding the costs associated with the celebration, and so on. If it became known that Dickens himself had written such a volatile and critical letter regarding the monarchy, and about the Queen in particular, it could ruin the celebration, and have long-lasting consequences."

"Old Boz's last letter could never cause that much of a sensation, and you know it," countered Holmes.

"You should know better than that," said Mycroft. "It was you who prevented the same sort of scandal from occurring in August of '89, with the matter of 'The Bridal Night'."

I did not immediately recall the matter, and said so, asking if Holmes had investigated the case without me, due to my marriage.

"Yes, Watson," said Holmes, who seemed to recall the matter with some distaste. "Just another instance where the monarchy was saved from embarrassment."

"She was quite grateful, and you know it," said Mycroft. "That case could have been the making of you."

"As you said at the time. I have been 'made' quite well on my own, thank you."

"What was this matter of 'The Bridal Night'?" I asked.*

When Holmes made no effort to explain, Mycroft said, "In short, 'The Bridal Night' was a pen-and-ink illustration drawn and distributed by an American, Charles Leslie, in 1840, the year of the Queen's marriage. It consists of a man and woman in night clothing, standing in a bedchamber, and quite obviously the young Queen and Prince Albert on their wedding night. Nothing overtly distasteful, you understand. Husband and wife, perfectly legal. This drawing has resurfaced several times over the years, including a period during the last Jubilee."

"I do seem to recall something of the matter now," I said. "You were summoned on several occasions during the course of events to meet the Queen."

"And I managed to fulfill my commission regarding the suppression of the illustration. Now it is all water under the bridge."

* Editor's Note: The events of "The Bridal Night" are recounted in Chapter 17 "At the Queen's Command" from *I, Sherlock Holmes* (1977), by Sherlock Holmes, and edited by Michael Harrison.

"But," said Mycroft, "it illustrates my point that such things are a very real threat to the Crown. This newly discovered letter, indicting the Royals for all sorts of social ills, could gain real traction in spite of its outrageous nature, especially with its threatened revelation so close to the current Jubilee, now only a few days away."

"And what was your initial response to the perceived threat of the letter?"

"We initially sent Shipton to surreptitiously retrieve it during the night so that it could be examined. Obviously, Rathham's safe proved to be no difficulty at all, no matter how secure he believes it to be. I'm sure you made the same observation for yourself.

"After Shipton took the letter, he carried it a short distance to a rented room nearby, where it was carefully photographed. He then replaced the letter in the safe, and Rathham never knew that it had been taken.

"Upon reading the document, it was quite obvious that it was much more incendiary than you are willing to concede, brother. It was also obvious, but only to certain experts, that it was a clever forgery as well."

"A forgery? By the Baron?" asked Holmes with a wry smile. "Imagine that. Salting the mine with a gold nugget?"

"Quite."

"So this letter was never real at all," I said. "Dickens never wrote a document on his last day that would end up threatening the crown."

"That is correct," said Mycroft.

"Well, I must admit that I am relieved," I said. "This letter has the possibility of besmirching the Queen and soiling the reputation of one of our greatest writers."

"It still can, doctor, if we do not retrieve it," said Mycroft. "This scheme must have been in preparation for some time. I do not know if a subsidiary part of the Baron's goal was primarily to inflame the public against the Crown with the contents as it became more widely known, or if the shocking content of the letter was simply to increase its interest and notoriety, thus raising the asking price at the auction. Any damage to Dickens's reputation is probably only a secondary effect. One thing that is certain is that the Baron had assistance from someone or some organization. This scheme must have been started long before he left prison a few weeks ago. The forgery would have taken longer than that to accomplish."

"I would assume, then, that he has been working for Colonel Moriarty since his release, performing such deeds as he did for the Colonel's brother, the Professor, before his arrest and conviction in '87."

"Indeed. As you have been aware, the Colonel has been working to rebuild his brother's criminal network for several years now, although

114

without the total success that he craves. The conflicting actions of the youngest Moriarty brother, the former station master, to also declare himself the heir to the throne and take over the organization have served to stifle both their efforts. However, the Baron is *not* doing the same tasks for the Colonel that he did for the Professor. As you will recall, in '87 he fronted an incredibly complex scheme devised by the Professor that defrauded countless people of their money, some fatally so. Now, since his release from prison, the Baron is working as a simple collector, dealing with the riff-raff milling at the bottom of the Colonel's ladder. Still, he puts up a good front, dressing and living as well as the Colonel will allow him."

"And the false letter? What did you decide after you had examined it?"

"I did not want to steal or destroy it outright, as Rathham's outcry would give it too much attention – as has almost happened, as a matter of fact. We didn't want to bring Rathham into the circle of knowledge at that point in time, because he might have refused to cooperate and balked at participating in our scheme. Rather, I conceived the rather unique solution of forging a copy of the original forgery, but of such obvious clumsiness and false quality that it would be more easily denounced as a fraud, thus preventing a protracted debate about its authenticity, stopping it from ever being auctioned, and leaving it quickly forgotten without giving it any undue emphasis or importance. Plans are in place to make sure that the fraud reflects back upon the Baron, having the added benefit of embarrassing or ruining him as well. After all, he forged the letter to begin with. This simply made the identification of such a forgery that much easier.

"The new forgery was carried out by one of our experts. After its substitution, Shipton was to be finished with his involvement in the matter, and one of my more polished agents would have approached Rathham and explained the situation, attempting to enlist his participation. If that did not work, I would have then made an effort as well, and I must admit that Rathham's agreement would have been guaranteed."

"All of this forgery and counter-forgery, and burglaries and more burglaries, seems a little complex, even for you, Mycroft," said Holmes. "Couldn't you have just burned the initial forged letter, and let its disappearance remain a mystery?"

"You know better than that, brother," said Mycroft. "We create contingencies here, and who knows what possibilities we could have tied to various loose threads that we picked out of this cloak. For instance, at some point in the future, we might have used the existence of the letter to bring pressure in a certain quarter, in ways that I cannot yet imagine."

115

"I have to agree," I said, "that the whole thing seems unnecessarily complex."

Holmes turned to me. "I am reminded of a time when I was seven years old, I believe, and thus Mycroft was fourteen. Our father asked him to locate Sherrinford in the north field and have the sheep driven toward the ford for shearing. Mycroft – "

"You were only six at the time," interrupted Mycroft.

"It makes no difference to the main thrust of the story. As I was saying, after delivery of the message, Mycroft was nowhere to be found. He was eventually discovered in the village, talking with men there about setting up a series of telegraph lines across the farm in each direction in order to relay messages to various communication stations he intended to construct, dotted here and there in the fields. When he was found by our father, he had exhausted the inexact knowledge of the locals, and was planning on catching the next train to Thirsk to discuss it with someone there."

"It would have worked," replied Mycroft. "I understand that something along those lines was used by the Americans during their Civil War, which took place soon after."

"At least it was better than your initial scheme of having the sons of local crofters remain huddled in sheds spread out in lines stretching in each direction, waiting until they were needed to run messages up or down to the next lad as needed."

"The system had many advantages, especially in certain seasons."

"You simply did not like going to the fields to find Sherrinford."

"What I did not like was – " At that point, Mycroft stopped, and noticed my amused countenance as I listened to the bickering of the two brothers. With a cough, he returned himself to the matter at hand.

"Whatever our future plans were and still are regarding the forged letter, we must not lose sight of the fact that Shipton has stolen it for his own ends *now*. Last night Shipton was to make the swap, before Rathham was to be approached this morning by another agent. However, instead of carrying out his orders, Shipton stole the original and kept the copy as well. And then he wrote me a letter, delivered by messenger this morning, announcing that he intends to address his grievances against Her Majesty by releasing the blasted thing to the press on the day before the Jubilee Celebration. Apparently he has had several points of contention with our government that have festered for too long in secret, and have reached the lancing point."

"And also apparently," replied Holmes, "you should have made a better investigation into the background of your agent. Or perhaps you should have avoided recruitment of a blackmailer in the first place."

"As you said a moment ago, it is water under the bridge, brother," said Mycroft. "What remains now is to get the letter back. Shipton will know that you are involved, since he followed you here. It is possible that he had already expected you to take an interest one way or another. It will work out well, as your movements will serve as a distraction for him while my men work in the shadows to trap him."

"So I am to understand that I will simply be a decoy? Or a staked goat? Do you have no faith that I can resolve the matter satisfactorily?"

"I am sure that you could do it," replied Mycroft. "However, Lord Salisbury has been consulted, since he is expected to resume his post as Prime Minister any day now, and it is customary to begin briefing the new man in order to make for a smoother transition. At present, he is down in one of his troughs where his opinion of you is reflective of the events of late '88, when you pointed out his passive complicity in that vile matter which so occupied our attention at the time."

"I care not a farthing's worth about Salisbury's opinion of me. Ask him next week what he thinks about me and his comments will be glowing. The man is – "

" – still very influential," interrupted Mycroft. "And in any case, he has raised a valid point or two. Word of your . . . illness last March has reached his ears, and he has expressed concern whether you are now fighting fit, especially against an old foe such as the Baron, no matter how diminished are the man's current circumstances."

"I can assure you – "

"Additionally, he pointed out – and he was not the first to think of this, although he was the first to say it aloud – that you might not be willing to put forth your best effort to restore a piece of property to a former enemy, when that recovery would only seem to benefit him."

"Now see here," I interjected. "Holmes would never take a chance on endangering the Crown simply to vex the likes of Baron Maupertuis!"

"I agree, doctor, but there are other considerations, and at certain rarefied levels, one must go lightly. Therefore – "

"Therefore," said Holmes, rising from the table, his finely decorated china plate still holding the small serving of pristine and untouched curry, "we will go and serve as the distraction, while the pincers close on Mr. Shipton."

As he turned away, Mycroft added, "Brother, should you happen to find yourself in such a position as to effect a successful conclusion to this matter, to the satisfaction of *all* concerned parties, I am sure that no one, including our once and future P.M., would have any objections."

Holmes did not look back, but I saw the shadow of a smile cross his face. He understood the rules of the game, as did I.

Expressing my thanks for the meal to Mycroft Holmes, I took my leave in Holmes's wake, joining him outside in the early afternoon sunshine illuminating Pall Mall.

Down the street, about halfway between where we stood and Waterloo Place, I could see Julius Shipton, standing without a hat, his pale hair shining. Holmes tipped his fore-and-aft at the man, who returned the gesture by making a small bow. Then, he turned toward the Atheneum on the corner and in a moment was gone.

"I'm not sure but that we shouldn't follow him, Mycroft's wishes be d---ed!" I said.

"Not yet," said Holmes. "We need leverage. I must make a few inquiries." He turned from the east, where he had been gazing toward the site of Shipton's disappearance, and faced me. "Do you make your way back to Baker Street, there's a good fellow. I have an idea or two where to find the answers to my questions, and possibly start a few wheels turning in motion as well. I shall return in a few short hours."

And with that, he set off in the direction that Shipton had taken. I stood and watched for a few moments, but he did not turn right, as had the former blackmailer-turned-government-agent-turned-criminal. Rather, he continued onward, heading toward Trafalgar Square.

As he disappeared into the June haze, I turned and saw Mycroft Holmes, standing in the same window where we had found him upon our arrival. He nodded to me, and did not seem surprised at all to have been caught observing us. I nodded in return and set off walking, until shortly I found a hansom and returned to Baker Street.

Part IV: An Unpleasant Encounter

Fortunately, Mrs. Hudson had not prepared anything for lunch, as I was comfortably filled by the simple fare at the Diogenes Club. I settled into my chair by the fireplace to await Holmes's return, intending to catch up on my medical journals.

I had spent a fairly profitable three hours and a quarter when I heard the arrival of a cab outside our open windows. Surprisingly, there came the sound of a second vehicle stopping almost immediately after the first, and then the sound of Holmes's voice. Although I could not make out the words, the tone was sharp. I was rising from my chair to have a look when Holmes called, "Watson! Can you join me on the street? And bring your Afghan friend!"

I knew that Holmes meant my old service revolver, which I had left on my desk following my earlier return. I had learned long ago not to cross

118

the threshold without it. Holmes had many enemies, and by association I did as well. Several hard lessons had taught me the advisability of carrying that grim souvenir of my Army days.

Without bothering to look out the window in order to see what I was getting myself into, I dashed across the sitting room, down the seventeen steps, and out through the front door to find Holmes standing on the walk, in seemingly harmless conversation with a short, well-dressed man. There were two cabs beside them, as I had heard, but one was pulling away from the curb while the other, which had brought our visitor, paused as the path before him cleared. I looked more closely at the short man, and then recognized him with a shock. It was Baron Maupertuis.

Holmes was obviously tense, while the Baron seemed amused. I did not perceive any overt threat, but I kept my hand in my pocket and on the butt of my revolver.

The second cab was free to navigate, but Holmes held up a hand. "Wait," he said. "This man will not be staying."

"What?" said the Baron in a friendly tone. "Not inviting me in to reminisce about old times? The last time we met was in Lyons, when the British and French police took me in charge. You did not even appear at the trial. I was hurt."

"There was no need for you to mark my absence. The case was complete without my assistance."

"Oh, is that why? I had heard that you were ill."

"State your business," said Holmes shortly.

"My business," said the Baron, "is to make sure that you fulfill the task which you have taken upon yourself. Namely, to retrieve my Dickens letter that has been stolen from Rathham's auction house."

"So Mr. Rathham felt the need to inform you of its disappearance, then?"

"Rather, I stopped in this morning, and when I wanted to see it, he was forced to admit that it had been stolen last night. But he was quite enthusiastic in telling me that he had taken the initiative to hire you, Holmes. England's greatest detective. I know you are proud of your honor, so I wanted to make sure that the investigation would be carried out in an honorable way. After all, I have paid my debt to society."

"As you were only released a few weeks ago, you must have been required to pay every single day of your debt," said Holmes. "I must admit that I lost track of how you were progressing through your sentence. I had heard that the authorities had to keep you separated from Colonel Moran, and that the mere threat of putting you in the same cell – nay, the same wing of the prison – with him was enough to make you a model prisoner."

This statement seemed to break through the Baron's contrived good humor, and he frowned for an instant before his face devolved back into a bland, amused mask.

"That is all past now," said the Baron. "I am simply another one of your beloved Londoners, appealing to you for assistance. I am even in a position to provide a little something extra to whatever you expect to get from Rathham. As you might imagine, the sale of that letter will mean a great deal to me, and my continued rehabilitation into society."

"Your rehabilitation might seem more genuine if you had not, upon your release from prison, immediately found employment within Colonel Moriarty's organization."

"Surely you are mistaken," said the Baron. "I have a small establishment set up near Mayfair, where I counsel a select group of individuals on various financial speculations. I did have a gift for that type of work, you might recall."

"Do you wear your gloves throughout these appointments?" asked Holmes, gesturing toward the man's hands. "In order to hide the permanent darkening of your fingertips from picking oakum in Dartmoor?"

The Baron's pretense fell away. With a snarl, he turned back to the waiting cab. His sudden move caused the horse to shy before it was quickly taken in hand by the hansom driver.

At the cab, the Baron turned back and said, "I expect the return of that letter, Holmes. I have as much right to protection under the law as the next man. If I don't get it, Rathham's reputation, and yours as well, will be ridiculed from here to the sea."

"I will handle the matter according to my own lights, the way that I always do, Monsieur Petit."

I glanced at Holmes in puzzlement. The Baron seemed nonplussed as well, before asking, "What? What did you say?"

"I used your correct name," said Holmes, finally moving, taking a step forward as some of the tension fell away from his tall frame. He seemed to have attained the upper hand. "After your arrest in '87, I was ill for some time. Unraveling your scheme took two long months. It was only later that I realized that you had been backed by Professor Moriarty himself. I should have known – you were never intelligent enough to have constructed that unholy spider's web known as the Netherland-Sumatra Company.

"Although I did not need to attend your trial, I did keep an eye on you from afar, especially as the battle of wits with the Professor escalated over the next few years. And part of that was to delve into your background for

120

additional information, should your piece ever be returned to the chess board."

"You know nothing," said the man, now named by Holmes to be Petit. "Lies."

"You think that because so much time has passed, that the truth cannot be discovered. Just because you are on the books at Princetown Prison in the 'M's' for Maupertuis does not mean the truth won't eventually come out. Your real name is Rémi Petit, and the closest you've ever been to legitimately being a Maupertuis was when the circus that employed your mother stopped near Saint-Malo nine months before your birth."

This last statement seemed to enrage the small man. He threw his cane into the cab and moved his hand toward the pocket of his waistcoat. Holmes, indifferent now and having said his piece, turned toward our front door, while I removed my trusted service revolver from my own pocket and held it low to my side, while still quite visible to Monsieur Petit. "Time to go," I said.

Petit stayed still for a moment as the anger held on. Eventually, however, it began to settle away as he realized that this encounter was over. While he climbed into the cab, I asked the driver, "Do you work for Colonel Moriarty as well?"

"I really couldn't say, sir."

"I see. Well, it would be a good idea to keep this man away from here from now on. He will only cause the same problems and embarrassment for the Colonel that he did for the Professor. Do you understand?"

The driver nodded, and when Petit, formerly Baron Maupertuis, had closed the doors, he gigged the horse into motion. They headed towards Regents Park and soon turned out of site.

Inside our front door, I found Holmes laughing silently to himself. "That was enjoyable," he said. "I've held onto that little nugget for some time. Spending it just now gave me every bit of its worth in return. Did you realize that the Baron – which I will continue to name him, as it amuses me! – the Baron must not realize that we know the Dickens letter to be a fraud? If he thought it was discovered, I do not think that he would still urge its recovery. He might just write off the whole thing as a bad investment. Mrs. Hudson!" he suddenly and abruptly called without warning.

She quickly appeared from her rooms at the rear of the house, while Holmes fished a piece of paper from his wallet. While he scratched a note onto it, he said, "Things are working out rather splendidly, and I find that I am in the mood for a bit extra with tea today, if it would not be too much trouble."

"Not at all," she said, with a twinkle in her eye. Holmes handed her the note and a couple of coins, instructing her to have the message sent from the Post Office as soon as possible. She took it, with an amused smile on her face. And as Holmes started up the steps, she even had the audacity to give me a wink!

Upstairs, as we settled into our chairs, I remarked, "You certainly seem to be in good spirits."

"I should think so. I believe that this matter will be wrapped up by this time tomorrow."

"That soon? What were you able to accomplish after we separated at the Diogenes Club?"

"Oh, a great deal," he replied. "As I previously indicated, we needed some sort of leverage. It seemed to me the quickest way was to see if Shipton has anyone that he cares about. With his recent actions, he has cut the lines to the dock and drifted quite a ways out from shore, so to speak. However, if he has anyone for whom he feels affection, he might be approached from that direction.

"I stopped and wired Mycroft, asking him a few questions that should have occurred to me while we were there in the Strangers Room, such as when Shipton first came to this country, what boat he came in on, and the like. With this information in hand, I went to the shipping offices and managed to find someone who had been on that ship. I was fortunate that this company frequently breaks up its crews, so the likelihood of finding someone from that sailing was not too small.

"At first the man didn't remember anything. However, careful questioning eventually helped him to recall Shipton, and more importantly, the other person who had traveled with him in an adjacent cabin, a young Australian woman with a unique feature. A return to the shipping office revealed that her name is Emily Smith."

"Smith, eh?" I said. "It might as well have been Jones, I suppose. And the unique feature about this woman?"

"Although she is quite attractive otherwise, she has the sad affliction of having a *talipes equinovarus*."

"A club foot."

"Quite. With this information, I then went to the area around Shipton's residence near Cannon Street Station, as related to me by Mycroft. It did not take long to determine that a Miss Smith of matching description worked in a nearby pub, and lived 'round the corner."

"And did you approach her?"

"No, I did not, although I did observe her for a bit, while having a pint of rather mediocre quality. After identifying her, I went to the Yard, where I spent a productive quarter-hour with friend Lestrade, going over recent unsolved murders in the Cannon Street area."

"Murders?" I asked. "Is there a murder mixed up in this affair?"

"Not until I did the mixing," replied Holmes. "Going over the records, we found where the owner of a stable on Garrick Street had been found early yesterday morning, his head crushed in by a piece of stove wood discovered on the ground near him in one of the stalls. Lestrade and I went there, and it was quickly apparent to me that the murder had been committed by the dead man's brother, who is a half-owner in the business. So after this was established, confidentially between Lestrade and myself, you understand, we promptly went to 'The Crown and Garter' on Cloak Lane where Shipton's sister was working and arrested her for the murder."

"You . . . you arrested this poor girl for the murder, when you knew that it was committed by the dead man's brother? I don't understand."

"It is obvious, my dear Watson," said Holmes. "Lestrade will make sure that the arrest is trumpeted in the papers. 'Emily Smith Accused of Murder by Sherlock Holmes.' The press is such a useful institution, if one only has the knowledge of how to use it."

"But your reputation, Holmes," I said. "It will be trumpeted that you have identified this killer, only to subsequently admit that you made a mistake."

"I care not about my reputation," said Holmes. "And this won't be the first time that I have done something like this. I have to say that Lestrade had your same misgivings, but he quickly saw the wisdom of the plan, which seems like the quickest way to settle the matter.

"If Shipton doesn't find out at the pub about her arrest, he cannot fail to see it in the newspapers. He knows of my involvement. I'm sure he knows that his sister did not commit this murder. He will realize that this is a maneuver to flush him out, but he will have no choice but to come to me, knowing that I am essentially offering his sister as a trade for the documents. It was the leverage I needed."

"But the girl, Holmes! Put in cells for a crime that she did not commit!"

"Do not fear, Watson," said Holmes, as Mrs. Hudson arrived with our tea, along with all the delicious things that went with it. "She was placed on a train and smuggled discreetly out of town. She is now residing at a very pleasant inn near Eastbourne. She is under guard, and cannot be held for long, but she has been given to understand that she is helping us in a matter of national security – which she is! – and she was quite willing to assist us. She does not seem to hold her brother's anti-government beliefs in the least."

After she set down the tray of food, Mrs. Hudson stepped across the room, fishing a telegram out of her pocket. Holmes reached for it and tore it open. He read it quickly and smiled before tossing it toward me. It was from Mycroft, and simply said:

No.

- M

I knew that he would explain it when he was ready. "So now we wait?" I asked, rising and moving toward the food.

Holmes remained in his chair. "We wait. And I do not believe that we shall have to wait for very long at all."

He settled back and reached for a pipe. Clearly he meant to think for a while, and more importantly, he seemed to have forgotten about the tea that he requested. Mrs. Hudson's good humor slowly neutralized and then evaporated, and she looked at the ignored food, then shook her head and departed. Did the door perhaps close with a little more force than usual? If so, it did not intrude whatsoever on Holmes's three-pipe cogitations.

Part V: At the Old Roman Wall

We did not have long to wait. It was not more than an hour later that a boy arrived with a handwritten message. Holmes asked Mrs. Hudson to bring the lad up, and he waited by the door, looking as if he might bolt at any second, while the message was read.

"Are you empowered to deliver a reply?" Holmes asked. The boy simply looked confused, so Holmes tried again. "Tell him we will be there. And tell him to bring the letters."

The boy nodded and slipped through the door. I heard his feet land solidly on approximately four of the seventeen steps before he was gone. "He wishes to meet in an hour, just north of the Tower, at that segment of the old Roman wall where one can cross through into the City."

"I know the place. Are you going to notify Lestrade?"

"No, we will go alone. He has no reason to harm us. After all, we all know that there is no case against his sister, but he must surely think that without me to free her from the spider's web, she might be convicted. He won't risk harming or angering me before she is free. The letters cannot be that important to him, certainly not worth the girl's freedom."

We left soon after, walking for a bit until we hired the third cab that we encountered. There was a late spring fog rising, and it was turning out to be a cool evening for June. I pulled my coat tighter.

We wound our way east and south through the thickening mist, and I began to think that an hour was not enough time to reach our goal. However, traffic thinned as we neared our destination, and visibility was not yet bad enough to substantially slow our cabbie.

We left the cab and went on foot from the north side of the Tower. I glanced at the ancient pile, thinking of other occasions that we had been there. The times – and there were more than one – when Holmes and I had prevented the thefts of the Crown Jewels. The instances when we had gone there to question men suspected of high treason. That terrifying period in '88 when we had hidden Mary there, as the men involved in the terrible crimes occurring nearby in the City had tried to find her for a different kind of leverage. And they *had* found her, leading to the shedding of their blood on the Tower grounds. But that is another tale.

Holmes led me north for a few blocks, before turning right. My eyes had adjusted to the ambient light, and I could see that we were approaching the ancient Roman wall, a part of the original enclosure of Londinium centuries before. Holmes veered slightly to the left, and we came to the opening in the wall that led through and into the City proper. There he stopped and said, "We are here."

A small, hatless man stepped out of the doorway to face us. His very pale hair seemed to glow in the near darkness, as well as making him instantly identifiable. It was Shipton. He was only about halfway between five and six feet, and couldn't have been more than ten or eleven stone. His coat was buttoned, outlining his slim and wiry frame. He seemed to bounce with a barely-suppressed energy.

"You know Emily didn't kill that man," he began. "Well, you got me where you want me, Mr. Holmes. I brought the letters. But surely you can see that what I'm trying to do here isn't all bad?"

"Exposure of evil is not a bad thing, Mr. Shipton. I have spent my whole life pursuing that purpose. But what you have chosen to do, your initial foray into this type of reform, is not the way to go about it. You have picked the wrong ammunition for the wrong target. You may think that the Crown is evil, although Watson and I will disagree with you. Each man is entitled to his opinion. But embarrassing the Queen for no reason will do nothing but rile her loyal men as if you had kicked over a bee's nest."

"But she represents what is wrong," said Shipton. "Surely you know how England has treated Scotland, and Ireland, and Wales over the years.

125

And what about India? Why, even my home country has seen its share of abuse."

"Some of that was a long time ago," I said. "We are more enlightened now."

"Really, doctor? You can say that, after what you have seen?" He gestured behind him, to the east. "Would you care to walk with me for a quarter-hour in that direction? You've seen it all before, when the Ripper was there. I've seen some of the files. I know what went on then, and how some of the high and mighty were either the responsible parties, or else they stood by and let it happen. All under the skirts of this Queen.

"And I know what I myself have been ordered to do on occasion, Mr. Holmes, by your very own brother. He tries to justify it, saying that sometimes Britain needs a blunt instrument. I never wanted to be that, Mr. Holmes. But I never really had a choice."

"I, too, have occasionally had to be the 'blunt instrument,' Mr. Shipton. But I always tried to make sure that I was working for the greater good. Perhaps you did not have that option. You have been like a soldier, however much you were recruited against your will, and as such, you were expected to follow orders without question. It was the price you paid for an implied pardon to your crimes. But the fact that you were carrying out orders should also give you comfort in knowing that you were only doing your duty, and that the responsibility, or even guilt, lies on other men's shoulders."

"But what makes them any better to decide what is right or wrong? Who watches them? Do they justify it by simply passing the guilt on up to the next set of men?" He gave a weary little laugh and shook his head. "Well, it doesn't matter, and it's no use trying to explain it to you. It has always been that way, and it always will be. Right now it comes down to you and me, standing by this old wall, debating about the details of releasing my sister. For you know that I will give you the letters, and I believe that you will let her go. But then what? I trust you, Mr. Holmes, for it is known that you are an honorable man. Therefore, I know that there are no police here waiting to arrest me when you have the letters in hand. But what about tomorrow? What then?"

"My only brief is to recover the letters, both the original and the fake that you were supposed to plant in Rathham's office. After that, my work is done. I cannot offer you any assistance, but perhaps I could give you some advice. It might be prudent for both you and your sister to make your way to the Continent and leave England behind. Possibly to one of the neutral countries?"

Shipton nodded, and reached into his coat pocket. I tensed in spite of myself, although I did not believe that he was reaching for a weapon. In fact, he pulled out two folded packets and handed them to Holmes. "These are both of the letters," he said. "I would get them in your coat fairly quickly and examine them later, due to the dampness from the fog. You will see that they are what you are looking for. I wouldn't take a chance on risking my sister. You knew that. When will she be released?"

"Once I can look these over," said Holmes, slipping the documents under his Inverness, "I will send word to Lestrade to have her moved back to her lodgings. She is currently out of the city. Would you prefer her to be awakened and moved immediately, or in the morning?"

"The morning is fine. It will give me an opportunity to finalize my plans."

"I assume that you have funds squirreled away for such an eventuality?"

"Some. Also, I must admit that I came into another bit of money that gives me feelings of unease, but I suppose it's too late to worry about that now."

"Unease? And why is that?"

"Earlier this afternoon, before I saw that my sister had been arrested and I realized how this had to play out, I was not quite certain of my plans, including the disposition of the letter. In order to have another possible option, I sent a message to the owner of the letter, Baron Maupertuis, offering to sell it back to him. We met soon after, and I was careful that he wasn't able to identify me. Working for your brother has taught me several useful skills.

"The Baron gave me a substantial amount of money for the letter's return. I honestly told him that I did not have it with me at that time, but that I would let him know. I never intended that he should have the original, since I was going to have that published, but I was going to give him the forgery. Then he could auction it if he wanted, or not.

"He was not happy that he couldn't have the letter right then, as he had wanted to take possession of it immediately. I gathered that he had 'borrowed' the funds that he used to pay me from his employer without that man's knowledge, and he was understandably anxious to conclude our business. Having read some in the files about this Baron Maupertuis and his current employer, I could understand why he was nervous."

"Yes," said Holmes, "it does not pay to embezzle from one of the Moriartys."

"I feel no compunction to return the Baron's money, since it was dishonestly acquired by him to begin with, but if word gets to Colonel Moriarty about my having it, in spite of my efforts to hide my identity, I could be in for quite a bit of trouble. So that's an additional reason that I'm glad to be getting out of England."

"When you establish yourself in your destination and have time to ponder such things," said Holmes, "remember that there are better ways to accomplish what you tried to do here. A good government needs a balance of sensible limits and also to be able to take care of threats when necessary. We have seen when things are handled badly. Find a legitimate and helpful way to encourage things to be handled better."

Shipton nodded, and then to me as well. Turning, he slipped back through the passage through the wall and disappeared in the darkness.

Part VI: Conclusions

What remains is quickly summarized through a series of short epilogues:

A few days later, the auction of the Baron's furniture was held at Sefton's. The event was poorly attended, and the various bidders were quite unenthusiastic. Items of established historical significance went to people who would certainly appreciate them, but for very little money. Other lots with a set reserve amount were sold for that price and no more, and non-reserved items went for mere pounds.

At the side of the gallery, Baron Maupertuis, once known as Rémi Petit, watched with an increasing escalation of impatience, disbelief, and finally anger, as the possessions that he accumulated during his periods of affluence in the 1880's, those same items that he had managed to retain through legal twisting all during the years of his imprisonment, were sold for nearly nothing. And then, when it was announced at the end of the auction, that the Dickens letter had been withdrawn, there was no surprise in the room at all, except on the part of the apoplectic Baron.

For the whole matter had been explained to Rathham, who was more than grateful that the theft of the document had led to the revelation that it was a forgery. He had contacted those men who had been interested in purchasing the supposed Dickens letter, and they were quite happy to divest themselves of any connection to the matter as well. Somewhere in the whole process, no one had remembered to tell the Baron that the jewel of his crown was paste, and that not only was he not going to make a small fortune from the sale, but he wasn't going to make enough to return the money that he had stolen from Colonel Moriarty before it was discovered that it was missing.

As the auction concluded, the Baron surged to his feet, his rage directed toward Holmes, who sat beside me on the other side of the room. We were in shadows, watching the carefully contrived auction take place,

128

but I had known from the time of our arrival that the Baron had been observing us. Now, he moved toward us, with murder written on his face.

Before he had taken more than three steps, two nondescript men that had been seated near him throughout the auction rose and took his arms, one on either side. They wore matching plain dark suits, and each had anonymous faces with small military moustaches. They were Mycroft's men, and they held the Baron motionless as if he were chained to the wall of a tomb.

Holmes and I approached him. "I was unable to find a genuine letter by Dickens that had been written on the day of his death," said Holmes, "although I did come across another document during my investigation. However, it turned out to be a forgery, and as a valuable and rehabilitated member of society, you certainly would not have wanted any association with anything like that, would you, Monsieur Petit?"

The man hissed a string of offensive words, until one of Mycroft's men shook him as if he were a rat in a terrier's mouth. "Here now, none of that." When the Baron had fallen silent, the same man said to him, "We've got orders to assist you home, or back to your place of business in Mayfair. What's it to be then?"

At the mention of the business location, the man's eyes widened with terror. He looked back at Holmes, as if he were going to ask him for help, before he realized that such a thing was outrageous. Finally, he swallowed once or twice and whispered, "Home." As the two minders led him out, he stumbled once, but they still had his arms and continued to propel him forward, his short legs working until they found the ground again. It was the last we saw of him.

Later than night, we had a visit from one of Holmes's agents, Shinwell Johnson. He had been given the task of keeping an eye on the Baron after the auction. His report was short and to the point. "If I hadn't known who he was, and hadn't been watching him right up until it happened, I wouldn't've been able to swear that it was the same man. But it was, all right. After he left the auction house, the government men took him home and left him there. He went in, and came out a quarter-hour later with a trunk. I heard him tell the cabbie to get to Victoria as fast as possible. I managed to get on the back of the cab, which is a skill from my boyhood that I continue to whet, as its usefulness never diminishes. I hopped off right before we got there, and found a place from which to watch.

"He was still opening his coin purse to pay the cabbie when the shot struck him, dead center. There wasn't any noise at all. He just went down, and at first I thought that a rock had hit him. But it took him centered on the bridge of his nose, and ruined most of his face. The bullet must have spread out something awful."

"A soft-nosed revolver bullet," said Holmes, "fired from an air gun. It's good to know, I suppose, that there was more than one of the cursed things built by von Herder. And now we know that Colonel Moriarty has it. It certainly didn't take him very long, did it?"

"Not long at all," said Johnson. Then he glanced at our open windows, and beyond to the other side of the street, toward Camden House. He had heard the story about another one of the air guns, and the time that it had been fired from there and into our sitting room. He stood up and took a step to shift himself between the windows. "I'll be off, then."

Holmes nodded. "Thank you, Johnson. I'll be in touch." The man touched his forehead and was gone. His feet made no sound on the steps, but I could hear his labored breathing as it faded away nonetheless.

The next morning, we met Mycroft at the Diogenes Club. Luckily Holmes had not expected any effusive gratitude, as there was none forthcoming.

"I suppose it was the best solution for quickly resolving the matter," said Mycroft. "I have just one question. Why did you cable me to ask if Shipton knew that the document in the safe, which he was supposed to take, was also a forgery?"

"Ah," I said. "the laconic 'No' telegram."

"I simply wished to determine if he knew the value – or lack of value – of what he had taken. If he knew that he was simply replacing one forged document for another, he would not place any value on it, and he would know that *we* did not really place any on it, either. But if he thought that he was holding a real letter by Dickens, with the power to shake the crown, he would believe that he held something that was valuable enough to use in order to redeem his sister from the police."

Mycroft nodded. "I do wish, however, that you hadn't taken it upon yourself to allow Shipton to go free. Not – " he said quickly, as Holmes attempted to disagree, " – that your solution isn't what I would have ended up doing myself. It was rather tidy, actually, with a simple elegance. After all, he had only made the *threat* of releasing the letter to spoil the Jubilee, he hadn't actually done it yet. His only real crime was stealing the document from the safe, and that was done under orders. He disobeyed me in that he didn't leave the false replacement where he was told, or bring the supposed authentic letter from the safe back to me, but that is more of an internal administrative issue, rather than breaking a law."

"So my solution, and letting the man escape, is not going to result in *my* arrest, then?" said Holmes with a smile.

"No, no. It had a certain *finesse*. Baron Maupertuis is no longer a problem. Shipton and his sister 'escaped' the morning after you met with him, without any hindrance. And you did resolve the whole thing rather quickly. I think that we may consider this matter successfully concluded.

"Now, is it too early for a sip of Tokay? The quality has been off the last few years, but I managed to acquire a certain amount back in '74, in gratitude for a little matter in which I played a helpful part. I highly recommend it – only twelve bottles remain from this vintage, and nine of them are downstairs in the cellar. Let me ring to have one brought up, and then you can tell me how you plan to avoid the Jubilee celebrations. If any of your ideas have merit, I may join you."

The Tangled Skein at
Birling Gap

On the southbound train from London that Saturday morning, I had been fortunate enough to glance up from my newspaper in time to spot the ancient chalk man carved into the hillside, westward towards Wilmington. I was closer to my destination than I had realized, and began to ready myself for arrival.

In no time at all, I was standing in the Eastbourne station, waiting for the inevitable confusion that follows an arrival to clear. I was surprised that there had been so many other people making their way down from London and in this direction, but that September had produced some quite pleasant days, and I supposed there was no better time for taking a holiday, as most of my fellow travelers were. I was not averse to spending some time at the coast as well, but in my case, I had been summoned to provide assistance to my friend, Sherlock Holmes, now living in supposed retirement on the Downs, only a couple of miles west of where I now stood.

A man wearing a driving hat, with goggles pushed up, was leaning against the wall near the open exit to the station. As he spotted me, he straightened and walked my way. "Dr. Watson?" he asked.

I acknowledged the fact, and he identified himself as Hipkins, down from London to act as Holmes's factotum during the upcoming matter, which had attracted interest from the highest quarter. His voice was odd, both flat and a little too loud. I deduced that he had type of damage to his hearing, either congenital or resulting from a later cause.

We stepped out to the street, where Hipkins had parked a disreputable-looking Rover, at least two or three years old. He reached to load my luggage, in this case a single worn portmanteau of black, dull leather. My travel kit is never elaborate due to my former military background, but in this case I was journeying with somewhat more than usual. Hipkins pulled on a pair of driving gloves, and we set off slowly down the crowded street, picking up speed as we reached the road out of town toward Friston and East Dean.

I had a chance to study my driver as he fought with the automobile. He was a tall, thin man, with sallow skin and the look of a malnourished youth that gave me to believe he had grown up in one of the rawer quarters of London. Except for the fairly new-looking goggles, his clothing was worn and well-used, but clean. Before he had pulled on his gloves, I had noticed that his hands looked as if they had done their share of past work.

When we reached the first road that angled to the south, toward Beachy Head, I was surprised that we did not make the turn toward Holmes's residence, situated as it was on the road running parallel to the great chalk cliffs. It was there that he maintained the reclusive illusion of keeping bees. Oh, to be sure, there was an apiary there, and Holmes was quite interested in studying it. But his retirement had served multiple purposes besides watching the wee creatures (as Mrs. Hudson called them,) some of which I do not propose to relate at this time.*

One of the reasons for his move to this part of Sussex, back in October 1903, was to be able to surreptitiously increase the level of his assistance in the work of his brother Mycroft, who has been described broadly but accurately as sometimes being *the* British Government.

In those days, it had been feared by some, but not all, at the highest levels in government that a massive European war was inevitable, if not in a few years then certainly in a decade or so. Therefore, it had become imperative that someone of Holmes's intelligence and skill be available and at the forefront of the preparations, providing his own special abilities toward those matters that absolutely needed him – and only him. And that was

partially why I had traveled to Sussex that late summer morning in 1905. For a child had been taken, and even though no threats other than a ransom demand to the family had been made, it was postulated that the kidnapping might be used to pressure the child's father, a man of some influence, to make some move that would aid a future enemy.

Hipkins was not a talkative driver, possibly self-conscious about his speaking voice, and he simply gestured ahead of us along the Friston Road when he perceived my confusion when we did not turn directly toward Holmes's villa. I call it a *villa* because that is how Holmes refers to it, when he is not calling it a farm, but in truth it is a serviceable stone home, with a couple of acres of walled gardens, surrounded by the Downs and located just north and downhill from the highest of the chalk cliffs looking out over the channel. It is a site with a long history in that area, known locally as "H------- Farm." The house, consisting of a ground floor and cozy first floor as well, is surrounded by trees, and there is a barn of sorts on the eastern side of the property.

---

* Editor's Note: See "The Adventure of the Missing Missing Link" in *The Papers of Sherlock Holmes* Volume I (2013).

Toward the southwest, the Downs slope gradually toward Birling Gap (which both Holmes and I have at times referred to by the less-identifying and anonymously British *nom* of "Fulworth.") Holmes had been given the property years before, following the successful conclusion to an investigation that we had conducted in the area*, and had joked in the years following, when the Capital had proved particularly vexatious, that one day he would retire there and keep bees. Little did I realize that when it was necessary for Holmes to leave both London and his practice at the unlikely age of forty-nine, he would ensconce himself in the beautiful southern Sussex countryside.

Hipkins's car traveled past the East Dean turn as well, with the small village on the left, and Friston rising above us on the right. I began to wonder exactly where we were going. The answer was obvious in mere moments, as we topped the hill, and the vehicle slowed and then stopped outside the stone wall of the ancient St. Mary the Virgin Church. Through the greenery growing over the stones, I could see Holmes walking in the graveyard, reading the markers, and pushing back the grass where it was long with his stick.

After I had retrieved my single bag, Hipkins dismissed himself, turning and driving back down the hill toward Eastbourne. I did not question this, trusting that he understood his own purpose and role in the matter. But I did realize that I was now a mile or two from Holmes's villa, and still in possession of my bag. I foresaw an uncomfortable job of carrying it.

"Not to worry, Watson," said Holmes as I entered the graveyard. "We will make a stop or two on the way back, and I will do my share of acting as a pack mule if the need arises."

I suppose that my thoughts must have been visible on my face, as had been the case so many times before. I was not surprised at all, only happy to see my friend, since I had not set eyes on him for several weeks. On that last occasion, he had been in London carrying out more of his secret business, and had stopped at its conclusion to share a meal with my wife and me in our Queen Anne Street lodgings. It frequently seemed to amuse him that my home and practice were located in the same building that in times past had been a residence of Boswell.

I looked back and forth around the peaceful graveyard. "A fine place to spend eternity," I said.

* Editor's Note: For more information regarding Holmes's acquisition in 1900 of his retirement cottage in Sussex, listen to "The Adventure of the Out-Of-Date Murder" from *The New Adventures of Sherlock Holmes* Radio Show (September 17, 1945), or read about it in *The Lost Adventures of Sherlock Holmes* (1989), transcribed by Ken Greenwald.

"I doubt," replied Holmes, "that this hillside will outlast eternity."

"Well, certainly, everything will fade away. That is the nature of things. One only has to look at some of these stones to see that even they cannot resist time. In terms of how long the church has stood here, in one form or another, they have barely been here for any time at all."

"In this instance, I was referring to the very land upon which we stand. At some point, this spot will crumble into the sea."

"It will be some time before that happens," I said. "We are surely a mile back from the edges of the cliffs."

"Yes, but a few feet gone, year after year, century after century, and eventually our descendants will have to redraw their maps. As our friend, Hatherley, the hydraulic engineer, told us when he made that unexpected visit four years ago to introduce his latest child, water is the great leveler. Given time, it will dissolve or wear away everything, even the very land that pokes its way above the oceans."

With this cheery thought, Holmes led me over to a wooden bench, one of several scattered about the graveyard. Some were tucked under the trees along the bordering stone walls, but this one was in the open, with a magnificent view of the Downs. Behind us was the church, parts of it nearing a thousand years in age. A hill rose to the south, and in the distance we could see a couple walking on one of the footpaths that crisscrossed the grass. The birds were flying to and fro, catching the late-season insects. It was hard to believe that somewhere, probably near by, a small boy was being held captive. I refused to believe that he might already be dead.

Holmes and I spent a good three-quarters of an hour seated there in the graveyard, going over his plans for that day and night. It was warm and peaceful, and there was nothing fearful about the place in that bright morning, although I must confess that it might have had a different atmosphere on a windy autumn night.

I listened as Holmes complained that his involvement in the matter, at the specific request of Lord Holdhurst himself, had seriously interrupted his observations of his bees. I smiled to myself, knowing that Holmes would never have refused his assistance in such an affair. I also wondered if he was starting to begin to believe more in the fictional picture of a hermit that he had so carefully created, primarily a solitary and dedicated beekeeper, and only rarely a specially-skilled consultant, currently put out to pasture.

Lord Holdhurst, now quite ancient, was a close friend of the boy's father, the Earl of H-----, and it was he who had involved Holmes in the matter. The boy had been taken undetected two nights earlier from his own bedroom. A note had arrived with the post the next morning, before the boy was even discovered to be missing, asking for a substantial amount of money, with terms of delivery to be arranged later. The note read that police involvement was forbidden, upon threat of the boy's life. However, Lord Holdhurst, when advising his old friend, had pointed out that there was no injunction against involving Holmes, who now lived in Sussex, not far from the Earl's estate.

Holmes had spent less than a day, in disguise, tracing the man who had sent the letter through the local countryside. "It was mere child's play, Watson," he had told me. "The letter was mailed from the local post office. I must admit that I had a bit of luck. A man had come in on the afternoon before the child was found to be missing, and dropped a letter into the outgoing basket just as the post office was shutting up for the day. This was before the child had even been taken. The postmistress started to tell the man that she had already gathered the outgoing letters, and that he was too late, but the man was gone. Then she looked and saw that it was a local letter, being sent to the Earl's home, which is very unusual in these parts, as the locals do *not* send letters to the Earl. She recognized the man as someone she had recently seen going occasionally into the local pub down the street. Upon further questioning, the woman's husband had seen the man there a few times over the last few days as well, but did not know him."

Holmes had not wasted time trying to determine how the kidnapper had entered the estate undetected, or had managed to get away with the boy. Rather, he asked around the villages until he found other people who had seen the man who sent the random letter. By working backwards along this fellow's route, Holmes had identified where he was staying, in a lonely and recently rented cottage a few miles to the north, and subsequently his identity, one Les Chetwood. Holmes had set quiet inquiries in motion, quickly learning what he could. But there was no immediate sign of accomplices, if any, or of the boy, and he did not want to take the fellow into custody without knowing where the child was being held, or if there were other confederates involved. The Earl was adamant that the ransom must be paid as demanded, to ensure the boy's safety.

Holmes had sent to London to request the assistance of Hipkins, whom he had used in the past for various matters. A second note then arrived from the kidnappers, also mailed locally, arranging for the daylight exchange of the money in a nearby inn, which was described as a "neutral location." At that point, Holmes had sent a wire with specific instructions, requesting my presence as well.

I glanced at my watch. The ransom exchange was scheduled to take place within the hour. It was to be in the open, where we would pass over the money, and then, after the man receiving it – presumably Chetwood – safely took it away, the child would be released. Holmes was not happy with the situation, and some aspects about it still puzzled him, but he agreed that retrieving the child safely was the most important consideration, and that it would be fairly easy to pull in his net with the kidnapper – or kidnappers – caught in it later.

Thus, it was due to this ransomed child that I came to be in Sussex on that beautiful morning. But very quickly, unrelated events intruded upon us after our graveyard meeting, unraveling the proposal to deliver the payment, as well as doing much to tangle Holmes's other plans.

I knew that Holmes was not telling me everything, but he had shared what he felt that I needed to know. Having come to the logical conclusion of our discussion, Holmes stood abruptly. "Now," he said, "let us make our way down to East Dean, where your arrival will be noted with interest by at least one individual."

I lifted my bag, and we started down the path, separated by a thick hedge from the road which I had so recently traveled upon. I noticed that, even this late in the year, bees were working with great energy all around us. Leaning in, I looked more closely at an industrious little fellow and joked, "One of yours?"

"Hardly," Holmes replied. "You will notice the slightly tapered abdomen. This is a type of hornet, with remnants perhaps of the European honeybee in its makeup. I hope that they do not encounter my bees, as I fear the outcome." I leaned back slowly in order not to alarm the hornet or to seem too concerned in front of my friend. Over the last year or so, I had become used to Holmes's hives, and had come to an uneasy truce with, and even appreciation of, their residents. I certainly appreciated the honey that they provided on those regular visits that I made to Holmes's villa. Once or twice he had sent jars with me back to London. But I had no wish to have any closer associations with these hornet-like chaps, here in this enclosed hedged path leading down toward the village inn.

We walked for a few minutes in silence, each appreciating the wide views through gaps in the foliage, and anticipating the meeting that we expected upon our arrival. As we approached the village green and the buildings surrounding it, I wondered how many other people on strange missions had met over the years at that inn, which had been standing there now at that location for hundreds of years, and had frequently been the haunt in times past of coastal smugglers. Our appointment today was just the latest in a long list of quiet arrangements there, and no doubt there would be many others to come in the future.

Stepping onto the green, Holmes indicated for me to wait a moment as he went into a nearby stone building. I knew that he had use of some space in the structure, as well as an arrangement to receive messages there, along with what little mail that might find its way to him from individuals who had worked out that he lived in this part of Sussex, while not specifically knowing where. Although he cultivated, with my assistance, the impression of being a reclusive hermit, he did still take on the occasional private consulting job, in addition to those affairs which were assigned to him by his brother. I had the impression that Mycroft did not discourage the private investigations, as they managed to give the impression that Holmes was in Sussex on a full-time basis, being . . . Holmes.

My friend stepped out of the house, holding an unfolded note. He informed me that the members of his household, including Mrs. Hudson, were still in London, staying in Baker Street, and that we would be making do for ourselves, at least for a few days. After Holmes's retirement, Mrs. Hudson had joined him in Sussex, but had retained the lease on 221. When Holmes went back to the Capital on one of his activities for his brother, he regularly used it as a staging area, rather like one of his other London hidey-holes, and often in secret. During the periods when it stood unoccupied, Mycroft made sure that the place was well-kept and cared for.

We reached the door of the inn, ducking our heads as we went inside. I am a fairly big man, having played rugby in my youth, and my friend is very tall. Neither was the common size centuries earlier when the Tiger Inn's doorway was constructed.

The room was cozy and clean, with a bar across from us, and sunlit rooms opening to either the right or left. Standing and sipping a cold beer was my driver and Holmes's agent, Hipkins, now missing his driving hat and goggles. He ignored us, and Holmes led me to a nearby corner table in the shadows along the front wall, opposite the bar.

I looked around the taproom, representative of the finest aspects of so many similar inns and gathering places throughout Britain. The great hooded fireplace across the room from our table would make the place very snug indeed on those cold winter nights so close to the sea.

We sat down, and I pulled my case back behind my feet under the table. It made a rough sound as I dragged it along the floor, and Holmes said softly, "Did you pack too many extra collars along with your toothbrush?"

"No," I replied quietly, "just too much ammunition to go with the service revolver in my pocket."

At that moment, a small man appeared from one of the back rooms, to the left of the door. Holmes gave a small nod. This, then, was our man, Les Chetwood, the kidnapper that Holmes had managed to identify. He had a pint of something dark gripped in his right hand, and he squinted as he came into the darker room. As he paused for a moment in the low doorway, I had a chance to examine him. He was dressed in wool from head-to-toe, buttoned up and looking too warm for this late summer heat. He had a pale face, with some color on his cheeks that did not seem normal for him. He had thin, sandy hair, brushed straight forward and down toward his eyes. A soft mouth gave an initial impression of weakness, but there was an animal cunning that brightened his gaze as he finally recognized us. As he was taking a step toward us, the front door flew open with a crash, and a tall man in a Coast Guard uniform stepped in.

As the new fellow stopped to let his eyes adjust, Chetwood froze, looking back and forth from the newcomer to our table. No doubt to him, the man just entering appeared to be dressed in some variation of a police uniform.

His eyes having adjusted, the man in uniform saw us and his eyes lit up. "Mr. Holmes!" he cried. "It is so fortunate that you are here! I don't doubt that you would have been summoned at some point."

Chetwood, frozen in the door to the side room, our only link to pay the ransom and retrieve the boy, quickly set his glass on the bar and moved toward the door like an animal escaping a trap. Sliding around the man in uniform, he pushed open the door and was gone.

Under his breath, Holmes said, "Blast!" He tensed, as if starting to rise, before changing his mind. Realizing that to pursue Chetwood might make things worse, he settled back toward his seat and said with a sigh, "What is the problem, Commander?"

"Murder, Mr. Holmes! Down at the Coast Guard residences atop the cliffs. I came up to find Constable Anderson. He is getting ready to join me now in his house across the road – he was out working in his garden, you see, it being a Saturday. He told me to wait for him here, and then we would go down together." The fellow was obviously overwrought, his words tumbling out, one atop another.

Holmes caught Hipkins's eye, nodding toward the door. Hipkins nodded and slipped out of the inn. "Hipkins will follow him," Holmes whispered to me. The sound of the Commander's voice had attracted attention in the back, and a girl appeared through a doorway behind the bar. "Something for Commander Teague," said Holmes in a normal tone.

"Thank you, sir," said Teague, as the girl pulled a tall cider for him, already knowing exactly what he would request. "This has made me all rattled, and that's for sure." As he took a long draw from the glass, I had a chance to examine him. Middle-aged, soft-looking, no wedding ring. A career man in a backwater post. "We would have called you in, sir, I'm sure of it," said the commander. "What with someone of your reputation living amongst us now, so close, we would have been fools not to. Old Mr. Emerson would expect it."

139

"Mr. Emerson?" questioned Holmes, still irritated at the interruption of our other business, but becoming intrigued by this matter as well. "And he would be – "

"He is the grandfather of the murdered man," said Teague. "Ebersole Emerson, of Manchester."

"Ah," replied Holmes, "the celebrated and self-made industrialist."

"That's right, sir," said Teague. "It is his grandson, Lieutenant Andrew Warren, who has died not half-an-hour ago in his bed in the guard houses, and not a mark on him."

"You said 'murder'," I interrupted. "Was it poison?"

"Well, to be honest, I don't know. I wasn't there when he died, although two of the other lieutenants currently on station were. I was summoned in just after, being in command, you see. From how it was described to me, I would have thought it might be some type of seizure, except that Warren was able to gasp out 'murder' to his two mates before he went.

"The duty roster is rather light, today being Saturday you understand, and it's never very demanding there at the worst of times. There are never many of us assigned here anymore, even during the season. As I mentioned, I am in charge, and as soon as I heard, I put my second to watch the two men who were with Warren when he died, and set out as fast as I could to find the constable."

I could see that Holmes was about to ask another question, but the door opened, interrupting him. It was Anderson, the constable for that area. He was a large man with a strong touch of Scandinavia somewhere in his background. I had met him several times before, while visiting Holmes on other occasions.

He seemed as pleased as Teague had been at finding Holmes in the inn. A quick recap of what Teague had told us was enough to get him moving. He led us outside and down the narrow lane, away from the green and onto the small road that wound south toward the sea. His wagon was already hitched and waiting, and we climbed aboard and set forth. Personally I was glad to be pulled by a horse, and not conveyed by another automobile.

The way was not far, but there would have been enough time to talk. However, Holmes pointedly did not ask any further questions, preferring to wait until we reached the scene of the murder so that he could form his own impressions, instead of those that were filtered through the eyes of Commander Teague. Seeing that Holmes did not want to overhear Anderson asking anything either, the constable instead talked to me.

"I've been reading your stories to my boy," he said. "He's five now, so he doesn't understand it all, but he's bright, and he follows most of it."

140

We passed wide grassy fields on the left, and sloping up toward stands of trees on the right. Both fields were filled with sheep that paused in their grazing to watch us, with one or two trotting curiously toward the fences for a few steps before stopping to watch us pass.

"After one of the stories," continued Anderson, "I asked him if he wanted to be a detective like Mr. Holmes. Do you know what he said, doctor?" he asked enthusiastically. I smiled politely and said that I did not. "He said that he wanted to be a 'p'liceman' like his da." Anderson beamed with pride.

I murmured that he was fortunate indeed, and wondered privately how many other professions the boy might choose between now and when he reached his majority.

Within a few minutes, the land on either side of the road opened, and I could see the abrupt edge of the horizon that indicated the cliffs were rising before us. The road aimed toward a lower spot, where a cluster of buildings had been constructed. I knew that even here, the land did not open directly onto the beach. Rather, the cliff line dipped, and was simply lower than what was on either side. This was Birling Gap, where the Coast Guard cottages were located, as well as some other newer homes stretching up the hill to the west.

"The road here used to go all the way down to the beach, long ago," said Anderson, nodding ahead. "As the cliffs have fallen away over the years, the gap there that sloped gently down to the sea and gave the old smuggler's wagons access to it in dark of night has cracked away and been lost. I fear that eventually the cliffs will keep falling, a bit at a time, until they take the whole village." I thought of Holmes's earlier comments regarding the little church and graveyard with sadness.

At Birling Gap, the road upon which we traveled turned sharply east, back toward Eastbourne. Holmes's villa was less than a mile in that direction, but that was not where we were going. Our destination was that grim set of buildings on our immediate left as we faced the sea, perched back from the cliff top, where the Coast Guard kept a few men stationed. According to what Teague had told us, there weren't many men there right now, but I was unsure whether this was a seasonal choice, or simply because the place was slowly being abandoned. I didn't see any men in uniform standing outside, although there were certainly clusters here and there of civilians, residents of the nearby cottages, no doubt, pointing and whispering. Some, having spotted our wagon, began to gesture in our direction. Was it because of the arrival of the constable, I wondered, or perhaps at the unexpected appearance of the famed and celebrated local personality, that retired consulting detective down from London only a couple of years earlier, and still not here long enough to be considered a true resident?

We stopped in front of one of the central buildings, a two-storied affair that did not seem to be too unpleasant, compared to some military-type residences where I have been quartered. We climbed to the ground, and I struggled as I lifted my heavy travel case. "You can leave that in the wagon, doctor," said Anderson, but I simply shook my head.

Teague led us inside and upstairs to the room of the dead man, Warren. It was a dark and windowless room, reached by a single door from the hall. The hallway itself had a window, which allowed a small amount of light into what was little more than a cell. Warren was laid out on his bed, his limbs contorted and wound in the twisted sheets. He was in his uniform. There was only a strong lantern lighting the room, which was very close indeed. In addition to Holmes and myself, Anderson, and Teague, the room also contained two uniformed men sitting upright on chairs just inside the door, and another small and grim-looking fellow, also in uniform, standing over them. From the way that he was addressed by Teague, he was obviously the second-in-command left in charge.

"You didn't have to keep them in here with the body, Fellows!" he cried.

"You did not specify, sir," said Fellows with grim authority. "I thought that facing the victim might force the guilty party to confess."

Teague turned away, muttering, "Idiot," under his breath. Then, as an afterthought, he turned back to his second. "Did it work?" he asked.

"No, sir," replied Fellows. "The only one that said anything was Lester, here, who begged that we might shut Warren's eyes." Fellows glanced at the man on the right, apparently Lester, as if he had admitted his guilt then and there by such an action. Lester was slumped in his chair, his hand to his face, shielding his view of the unfortunate on the bed. "I knew better," continued Fellows, "than to tamper with the body, sir."

"Quite right, quite right," said Teague, turning back to Holmes, who was already leaning over the bed. He was muttering to himself, patting the man's clothing, examining his hands, and finally leaning in to smell the dead man's mouth.

"Fresh uniform," said Holmes. "He had not slept in it. He had arisen and prepared for the day. He is freshly shaved, as confirmed by the used razor, and also the ewer and bowl of soapy water on the table there. Rough going by lantern light."

We looked toward the wall where the plain table stood. It held the shaving implements, as well as a tall mirror, the previously mentioned lantern, and a few other objects of interest. Holmes moved in the direction of the table, saying as he went, "Watson, would you mind examining the body?"

I bent to my task as Holmes made his inspection of the table. Anderson did not say a word, having completely given the matter over to Holmes. The four guardsmen clustered along their wall, with Fellows giving frequent glances to the two seated men, as if one or both were about to bolt.

I examined the victim, who looked back at me with the filmy gaze of the dead. "Shutting his eyes now," I said softly, doing so. I saw no evidence of rigor, although I would not have expected it to have manifested so quickly, unless Warren had been diabetic. His hands were smooth, with no roughening indicating any laborious activities. Finally, I copied Holmes's actions and smelled the man's mouth. Then I arose and joined Holmes at the table.

He was kneeling, so that his eyes were at a level with items on the table top. Besides those that were related to shaving, there was a fairly new and open bottle of peach brandy with its top lying beside it, some plain brown wrapping paper, wrinkled and torn, and a single glass with dregs of liquid within it, presumably a portion of the brandy.

"Pray," said Holmes, "take special care not to touch the bottle or the glass."

I nodded, and then leaned over carefully and sniffed first the glass, and then the open bottle top.

"Cyanide," I said softly, so that only Holmes could hear me. "The same odor still lingers on his lips."

"Quite," he said. Straightening himself, he pivoted and took a couple of steps across the small room, placing himself in front of the seated guardsmen.

"I understand that Lieutenant Warren said the word 'murder' during his final struggles. Is that correct?"

Both of the seated men nodded. "Did he say anything else? Anything at all?"

The fellow on the left shook his head, while the man Lester said, "He seemed to be in too much pain to say much of anything."

"Show them," said Fellows, abruptly. Both seated men looked blankly at him. The one on the left revealed, upon slightly turning his head, a set of finger-spaced scratches, still raw, down the right side of his face.

"Show them, Lester," said Fellows again. "Show them your coat."

Lester rolled his eyes in disgust. Then he plucked out the coat in question and revealed that there was a missing button, the loose threads still prominently attached and quite obvious.

143

Fellows took a step toward us and held out his hand. Resting on it was a matching button. "This rolled out of Warren's right hand after he died," he said with little-disguised triumph. Clearly, he thought that he had the evidence that solved the case.

Lester snorted in disgust. "When we heard him having his attack, we ran in to see what was the matter with him. Gates and I leaned over the bunk, trying to hold him steady. He must have grabbed the button then as he grasped at me."

"No doubt," said Holmes, reaching to take it from Fellows. "Is that when Lieutenant Warren scratched your face as well, Lieutenant Gates?"

Gates, the man on our left, involuntarily moved his hand toward his face. "Don't touch it," I said. "We don't want that to get infected. I will clean it momentarily."

Gates nodded, and answered Holmes. "Yes, sir. He was bent backwards, almost double at one point, with his teeth clenched in agony. His hand got loose and swiped at my face. I didn't even know it had happened until later, when things settled down."

"There is evidence of the tissue scratched from your face under the nails of his left hand. You stood on that side," he said, pointing to the side of the bed corresponding with the victim's left hand. Gates nodded. Turning back to Fellows, Holmes said, "Why did you assume the button to be of significance? Wouldn't the scratches have also been an indication of possible guilt, according to your way of thinking?"

Fellows was at a loss, finally saying something about a detective story that he had once read as a boy, wherein a button found in the dead man's hand had been of the greatest significance. Holmes turned away from him in disgust. To me, he said quietly, "I do not have time for this, Watson. We must wrap this thing up and return our attention to more important matters."

"A murder is also important, Holmes," I murmured.

"In this case we can only avenge a death. In the other we can perhaps prevent one." Then, to the larger group, he asked, "Who is the woman that Warren has been seeing?"

There was silence for just a moment, and then Teague said, "Why, that would be Miss Collins, from one of the cottages up the hill. But how did you know about her?"

Holmes waved an impatient hand. "I must speak with her. These are not exactly appropriate surroundings, although I suppose that we could . . . ." He seemed to lose himself in his own thoughts for a moment, before returning. "No," he said. "I had thought that it might be of some benefit to question her here, in the presence of the victim, but perhaps it would be better to do so at her own home. Do you think that she is there now?"

144

"She should be," said Teague, glancing inexplicably toward Lester of the missing button. Lester did not notice, as his gaze was directed toward the floor.

"Then let us be off," said Holmes. Then, to Teague and Anderson he said, "Get these men out of here, and lock this room up tight. Make sure that no one touches anything in here. And Anderson, in that group of villagers standing around outside, is there someone that you trust?"

"Yes, sir," replied the constable.

"Excellent. Put him in a chair in front of this door. I want no one to enter it until we get back."

"Right away," said Anderson, hurrying out of the room.

By the time we had moved to the hallway, and Teague had locked the door, Anderson was back with a gnarled man, old before his time, a former soldier from the look of him. "Brown, here, will do," said Anderson. Holmes nodded and quietly gave the man his instructions before putting him in a chair before the door. The man crossed his arms, planted his feet firmly on the weathered floorboards, and looked as if the Devil himself would not get by.

I requested some medical supplies, and quickly treated the scratches on Gates's face. While I did so, Holmes took possession of the room key from Teague and slipped it into his pocket. Holmes, Anderson, Teague, and I then exited the building and started walking west toward a line of cottages stretching up to the end of a lane that terminated at the top of the hill. I shifted my heavy travel bag from side to side as we ascended.

Teague chatted at Holmes as we walked, pointing out this and that as we went, and toward the last house at the top, known as "The Haven." It had a corner tower and a slate roof, and had recently been taken by the Bellamys, a local family that owned all the boats and bathing cots there in Birling Gap. "The daughter, Maud, is quite a beauty," said Teague. "She's going to be the cause of trouble around here someday, mark my words."

"Is she relevant to today's affair?" snapped Holmes shortly. "Does this Miss Bellamy have any association with the dead man or the other lieutenants?"

"No," replied Teague, in a more subdued voice. "No, I don't suppose she does. It is Miss Collins that we go to see. Although I can tell you that, in my experience, if two beauties such as Miss Bellamy and Miss Collins are living in such a small village as this over too long a time, there will be fireworks, and that's for sure!"

"Tell me of this Miss Collins," said Holmes, turning away from Teague and toward Anderson, who gathered his thoughts for a moment. We were nearing our destination, and as the man needed more time to answer, he stopped in the lane, really little more than a rutted path. We turned to face him.

"She is an American girl, probably not more than twenty years old. She and her father leased one of the houses back in the early summer. They only have a local woman that they hired for cooking and housekeeping. They don't have visitors, and there has been idle speculation as to why they would shut themselves up in this little corner of the world.

"Of course, a girl like her is bound to attract some attention. She's a dainty thing, with fine blonde hair and blue eyes. Some of the ladies here do not care for her. The landlord at the Tiger, for one, told me that his wife believes the Collins girl is going to cause some strife, but perhaps I am just being unfair and repeating gossip."

At this point, Teague interrupted. "In any case, it was not long after she and her father arrived that she took up with Lieutenant Lester, whom you just met. We've had a difficult time keeping his mind on his duties, and he used to make any excuse that he could make to slip away and see his Edith. That is, Miss Collins.

"Then, inexplicably, a couple of weeks ago, she turned her attentions to the dead man, Lieutenant Warren, Lester's cousin."

"What?" exclaimed Holmes. "There is a family connection between the two of them?"

"That's right," said Teague. "First cousins."

"I thought that he seemed rather more shaken about the death than Gates," I said.

"So is Lester also a grandson of the industrialist, Emerson?"

"That I would not know," said Teague. "I try not to delve too closely into any of the lads' backgrounds."

He was finished speaking, and Holmes did not ask any further questions. We turned and resumed walking until we reached a plain-looking house about halfway up the slope. The grounds were tidy without being immaculate. Somehow, the place did not seem to have any personality, having gained nothing from its residents.

Anderson knocked on the door, with no response. He tried again, with more force, and in a few minutes the door was thrown open by a short, solid man, his face red with anger.

"What is it?" he asked in an abrasive American accent. "We don't want any!"

"I am Constable Anderson," said the man patiently. "There has been a murder at the guard houses, and we need to speak to you and your daughter about it."

"A murder?" cried the man. "Well, it has nothing to do with us!" He began to shut the door, but the constable's large boot had edged in to block the way.

"Police business," Anderson said in a flat tone, pushing the door steadily open. He took a step forward and said, after he was inside, "May we come in?"

The man, presumably Mr. Collins and the father of the girl in question, gave up with sullen acceptance and allowed us to pass. We found ourselves in a plainly furnished front room, with a large window looking out and down the hill, toward the small cluster of buildings. One could easily see the groups of people still standing and discussing amongst themselves. There would have been no way to spend any time in this room and not see that something was happening there.

Mr. Collins walked ahead of us, and then turned and planted his feet. The light from the window showed a network of fine lines across his choleric face, a visage that was marked with foul passions and ill tempers.

On a chair near the window was a girl, as opposite from her father as could be in every way, the late-morning sunshine reflecting from her blonde hair. With the light behind her, she appeared angelic. However, when she stood and took a step toward us, there was something wrong in some subtle way, almost too insignificant to be noticed. Perhaps it was just a smile behind her eyes, even as her face showed horror as she asked in a throaty whisper, "There has been a murder?"

No one immediately answered as the girl resumed her seat. Anderson remained standing near the front door, while the rest of us found chairs. Then, Holmes faced her and began to speak.

"That is correct, Miss Collins. Lieutenant Warren of the guards was poisoned this morning, and is dead. We understand that you and he had been seeing something of each other in recent weeks."

"No!" she said. "Not Andrew!"

"Now, wait a minute," said her father, standing near his daughter. "What are you trying to do? We barely knew any of those people."

"Nevertheless," said Holmes, "this is a very small community, and it is known that your daughter had been associated with the dead man. We would not be doing our duty if we did not at least ask her a question or two." Turning back to face the girl, he said, "Clearly, this has upset you." He reached into his pocket, fishing out a silver case. "Would you care for a cigarette?"

Mr. Collins bellowed, and Anderson muttered something about the inappropriateness of offering something like that to a delicate lady. Teague simply looked scandalized. Holmes raised his eyebrows in innocence and returned the case to his pocket.

"My apologies. I have often found the use of tobacco to be relaxing, and thought that Miss Collins might benefit from it as well." Turning back to her, he said, "Is there any information whatsoever that you can provide for us that might help to clear up this matter?"

"No," she said, softly. "Nothing at all. Andrew, that is to say, Lieutenant Warren and I were simply acquaintances, that's all. I enjoyed talking with him, and sometimes walking along the shingle at the base of the steps. He had traveled some in his youth, and was full of such interesting stories. It is so lonely here, ever since father chose to come to this place. I was just – " She stopped, dropping her head with a small sob.

We were all silent for a moment, embarrassed and not sure what to say. Then Holmes reached into another pocket and pulled out his small memorandum book, a gift from a grateful former client. It was small, only three inches tall, and about two inches wide. The book consisted of a mirrored metal case, enclosing minute sheets of notepaper inside, and it had been useful to Holmes on at least two occasions, not for making notes, but for signaling by turning the mirrored surface this way and that into the sun. I myself had fond memories of that memorandum book, as once it had helped to save our lives.

Holmes fished the stub of a pencil out of his pocket, opened the book, and wrote quickly for a moment or two on one of the tiny pages. Then he closed the book and rested its metal surface on one knee as he spoke to Miss Collins, who had raised her head in curiosity in the meantime, to see what Holmes was doing.

"I have prepared a statement, just a sentence really, indicating that you know nothing of this matter. Would you care to read and sign it?"

She nodded, and he handed her the case. She opened it, and read aloud, repeating what Holmes had essentially just said. " 'I, Edith Collins, know nothing about the murder of Lieutenant Andrew Warren.' "

"Here now," said her father. "Why do you want her to sign that, anyway? My daughter isn't signing anything." He began to reach for the notebook, but Holmes was quicker, retrieving it from her hand.

"Oh well," he said, taking it back. I noticed that he held the shiny case by the edges, and did not return it to his pocket. "It is not necessary, and perhaps you are right, sir. I apologize if I have overstepped my welcome."

"Quite right, you have," muttered Collins.

Holmes rose abruptly. "Gentlemen, our business is elsewhere, then. Thank you both for your time."

I could tell that both Anderson and Teague were surprised that we had made the effort to climb the hill and take the time to see the lady, only to leave almost immediately. Anderson, having worked with Holmes on a few occasions in the past, probably had an inkling that Holmes was

148

working toward some goal. I, who knew Holmes much better, was certain of it, and besides that, I was fairly sure that he must have managed to accomplish it.

Before I knew it, we were back outside and on the lane, walking down toward the low area that was Birling Gap. Anderson and Teague were out in front of us, speaking about the murder, and more specifically, about how someone like Miss Collins could not help but to be a motivation for a passionate crime. Holmes and I fell back, and then stopped altogether. I set my travel bag on the ground by my feet. Anderson and Teague noticed our absence and turned, but Holmes waved them on, and they continued their walk down the hill. I nodded toward Holmes's hand, which still carefully held the metallic memorandum book by its edges.

"Did you get what you needed?" I asked.

"I believe so," he said. "I want just a moment to examine this when we return to the guard houses." He held it up, turning it this way and that in the light. "It is likely that our first arrow hit the bulls-eye. If it had not, we might have found it necessary to repeat the same subterfuge with Miss Maud Bellamy.

"I would like to finish this distraction up quickly and get back to our real business. I'm taking something of a short-cut through this murder, although perhaps a leap would be a better metaphor, as we are so close to the cliffs. But if it works out, we can quickly put this distraction behind us."

He glanced back toward the house, and his eyes narrowed. Following his gaze, I saw Miss Collins, standing framed in the large window, watching us intently. Holmes glanced toward his memorandum book, still held prominently by the edges. Then he seemed to relax, saying, "That may have been an unfortunate mistake, but it cannot be helped now." Then, mysteriously he added, "Perhaps it will even provoke her into doing something to our advantage. Now, let us rejoin our companions."

Back at the guard houses, we were met by Hipkins, who was standing outside waiting for us. He handed Holmes a note, and said something to him softly in that odd voice of his. Holmes nodded and thanked him. "Do you want me to take your bag on to Mr. Holmes's farm?" asked Hipkins, reaching for the portmanteau in my hand. I shook my head, saying that I would keep it with me. Hipkins touched a finger to his forehead, and turned to go.

Holmes followed him for a moment, giving him some whispered instructions. Hipkins nodded and continued on his way.

Holmes then returned and faced me, while Anderson and Teague waited by the door to the building. "Hipkins followed Chetwood when he left the inn," said Holmes. "The man hung about until he saw us depart

149

with Anderson, and then went back inside. He wrote a note and asked that the innkeeper make sure that it was delivered to me. He then went back to his hiding place off the Eastbourne road, which I located yesterday. Hipkins saw no sign of any associates along the way, or of the boy. He returned to the inn, managed to convince them that he was working for me, and retrieved the note for personal delivery, as you saw.

"According to his message, Chetwood realized that the interruption of the ransom exchange was not my fault, and he has rescheduled for tonight, with certain conditions."

"And those would be . . . ."

"Later, Watson. Let us proceed with this business while it is still fresh."

Holmes walked to the building, where he asked Anderson and Teague to continue to wait. Then he led me back inside and upstairs to the dead man's room. Dismissing the man, Brown, guarding the room, after ascertaining that there had been no attempts by anyone to enter, Holmes pulled the key from his pocket and unlocked the door. We went in, and Holmes motioned toward the table.

The lantern was still lit, but otherwise the room was very dark, as it had been during our first visit. However, this worked to Holmes's advantage.

"Lean over and look at the brandy glass with the light behind it."

I did so, and saw that there were several finger marks on it, obviously from a man's hand, based upon their size. "Do you see anything significant?" Holmes asked.

I pointed to a place on the glass without touching it. "This mark in front is the thumb, and the other prints, four of them, closer together on the opposite side of the glass, are clearly the fingers."

"And?" prodded my friend.

"There is only one set. He must have only picked it up once, when he took it up to drink the brandy, and set it back down again."

"What else can you determine?"

"It was his left hand that lifted it, based on the angle and direction of the marks." I added.

"The victim is left-handed," said Holmes. "It is obvious from an examination of his muscular development."

"That is the hand that he used to scratch Gates's face," I said. "It was the hand that had some of Gates's tissue under the nails."

"That is of no significance," said Holmes. "The man was in his death throes. If he had been mysteriously attacked and strangled, for instance, and then found to have tissue under his nails, it would have been damning for the suspect that was found with such corresponding marks on his face.

150

But we believe that this man was poisoned. The scratches mean nothing. What is of significance," Holmes said, "is that the dead man's left thumb, the thumb that held the glass, has a scar across the large pad, as shown in the finger mark on the glass."

I bent to look at the glass again, and saw that indeed the evidence of the scar was there. "What of it?" I asked. "We are going on the assumption that the brandy in the glass is poisoned, since we can smell the bitter almond scent of cyanide wafting up from the dregs. We have smelled it from the bottle, and from Warren's own mouth. We can also assume that he poured the drink for himself, probably just after he finished his morning toilet and got into his uniform, as he was preparing to leave and start his day."

"Correct," said my friend. "Now look at the brandy bottle with the light behind it as well."

I bent again, and with a bit more difficulty, saw a similar-sized set of male finger marks on it, some from a left hand and some from a right. This time I was careful to note that on the left-hand thumb there was indeed a scar across the thumb pad.

"Again, I do not see the significance," I said. "Obviously, Warren used his right hand to hold the brandy bottle as he took off the cap with the left. Setting the cap down, he shifted the bottle to his left hand, his dominant hand, and then poured some of the brandy into the glass on the table. He left his finger marks as he did so, and then set down the brandy bottle to pick up the glass, again with his left hand. Holmes, what does this accomplish, other than to confirm that the man poured the poisoned brandy for himself? The question is, who put the poison *in* the brandy?"

"Look at the bottle once more. And look *past* the victim's finger marks this time."

I peered at the bottle with the oily marks illuminated by the lamp behind them. At first I was ready to admit defeat. And then, suddenly, I saw it. It was as if I were a child again, lying on a hillside looking at clouds with my brother. He would point at one and tell me that it looked like a horse or a dragon or some such shape. I would look and look, seeing nothing, and then suddenly it would lock into shape, as it did this time.

"Exactly," said Holmes, seeing my enlightened expression. He brought around the memorandum book, and, still holding it by the edges, positioned it beside the brandy bottle.

"The other finger marks – "

"The ones partially underneath those of the victim?" he said.

"Yes. Warren's marks overlay a set of smaller ones, superimposed on top of them."

"Because the smaller fingers held the bottle at some time *before* the victim."

"And the finger marks on your notebook case there – "

"Indeed. They match exactly. You will notice the three slight grooves or wrinkles, running parallel on the pad of the right index fingers as seen on the polished memorandum case cover when she held it to read what I had written."

I nodded "These three parallel marks are also on the brandy bottle."

"As I said, it was a long shot. I had seen these finger marks during my initial examination, and read from them that a woman, based on their size, had initially handled the bottle. Mind you, the marks belonging to Warren and the woman are the only ones on the otherwise clean bottle. I already knew from an examination of Warren's hand that the thumb mark with the scar on the larger set of marks belonged to him, placed there when he poured his final, fatal, drink, which took place sometime *after* the smaller marks were applied.

"One can also make a small leap, when considering the paper there on the table that was no doubt wrapped around the brandy bottle. Perhaps it was a gift? If so, then obviously the victim had not touched the bottle until *after* he unwrapped it. *Quod erat demonstrandum*, the person who *had* wrapped it was the last person to touch the bottle before giving it to the victim. And is it not reasonable to assume that this was the same person who poisoned the brandy?

"Having decided a woman was the poisoner, we then learned that a specific woman was involved with the victim. As you recall, we do not have a lot of time to waste trying to break down her story. I therefore devised a quick and crude stratagem to get the girl's finger marks."

He thought for a moment, and then said, "I know that you are aware of the theory that every man, woman, and child has unique markings on their fingers, and that efforts are being made to devise some way to classify them through various points of congruence.

I nodded, and he continued. "Before my departure from London, I had worked some on the problem, and I later passed on my findings to the Yard. Just a few years ago, they started making use of this finger mark classification system, but we certainly did not have the time to go through the whole process today, especially when this short-cut has essentially told us what we wanted to know. Why bother to collect and record the lady's finger patterns to match established classifications, when the three parallel lines on that one fingertip tell us all that we need to know?"

He glanced toward the dead man. "And here we are."

"But what is her motive?" I said. "Was her honor violated in some way? Was it revenge?"

152

"I cannot say for sure, but I have one or two ideas that I intend to explore. I suspect that she was simply running out of time."

Holmes turned toward the door, but stopped when I asked, "Do you think that her father could be involved in some way? I've rarely met someone who resembles a more likely criminal."

Holmes shook his head and laughed, that peculiar silent laugh of his. "I have already done some research on Mr. Collins. I make it my business to keep track of any new neighbors that arrive in this little community. He was the sole witness in the Grantham Trials earlier this year, in Chicago. He bravely testified, despite numerous threats against both himself and his daughter, and as a result, nearly two dozen evil men were convicted, with seven terminating their journeys at the end of ropes. Afterwards, it was certain that he would be safer elsewhere, and he made his way to this sleepy little corner of the world, where he and his daughter have tried to live quietly ever since. Unfortunately, his daughter has rashly ruined his plans."

Holmes led me out into the empty hallway, where he relocked the door. Downstairs, Holmes asked Teague for the private use of a telephone, and he was led into one of the adjacent houses. He was back in ten minutes or so, informing us that he had arranged for one of his agents in London to verify some information. He did not expand on what that information might be. In the meantime, all that we could do was to wait.

Teague made a cup of tea for me, but Holmes refused the offer. Instead, he paced back and forth, sometimes stepping outside to smoke his pipe. As we passed the hour mark after Holmes's telephone call, the enthused conversation that had been going on between Anderson and Teague seemed to reach a lull. Teague had been explaining that for the last few weeks, it had only been the five guards who were occupying the post, which was never considered important, even at the best of times. Holmes roused himself to ask whether it was planned for the men to depart from the station completely. "Why, yes, Mr. Holmes," said Teague. "We are entering a political climate where manning of this post is considered unnecessary, and we are closing it down for now. This, however, has happened often in the past, and will again. Soon, purse-strings will loosen, and someone else will be back here, staying until such time as the politicians once more become parsimonious."

Both Anderson and Teague resumed speculating on which of the two men, Lester or Gates, seemed the most likely to have poisoned Warren's brandy, with Lester being the obvious candidate. It was generally assumed that in any case, it must be due to some tangled connection to Miss Collins, and the competition for her affections. Teague idly pronounced that perhaps it was Fellows who had poisoned the brandy, but he had no real reason for this assertion, as it turned out. It was just wishful thinking.

After sitting in silence for a while, we were suddenly roused by the sound of Fellows's voice, calling to Holmes, who had stepped outside. A man was on the telephone, reporting to Holmes from London. We heard Holmes acknowledge the information, as he went to speak to his agent.

Knowing that Holmes did not want us listening over his shoulder, I encouraged my two companions to wait with me. It did not take long before Holmes came in and told us the summary of his conversation.

"The dead man, Lieutenant Warren," he began, "was the sole heir of his grandfather, Ebersole Emerson. The next in line is the dead man's first cousin and fellow guard, Lieutenant Lester."

"I knew it!" cried Teague, rising to his feet. "I knew that he was the killer!"

Anderson shook his head. "If so, how could he have been so stupid? Surely there would have been a more discreet way to go about it, and to avoid being so immediately and closely connected with the crime. He could have done it somewhere else, at some other time – any other time! Is this Lester an impulsive or stupid man, commander?"

Teague shook his head. "No. No, he is not. But you can be sure that it was because of that girl's involvement. After all, just a few weeks ago, she threw him over for his cousin, Warren. Perhaps Lester was jealous. A man bent on murder does not think clearly." Turning from Anderson, he said, "Do you not agree, Mr. Holmes? That Lester killed him because of the girl?"

Holmes, lost for a moment in thoughts of his own, and having no interest in the ongoing speculations of Anderson and Teague, raised his eyes and said, "What? Lester the murderer? No, not directly, at least. Tell me, Commander, how did these two cousins come to be assigned here together like this? Isn't that somewhat odd?"

"Warren's assignment was purely through the influence of his grandfather, or so I understand. He wanted him to put in several years of service of some type, in order to build his character, so to speak. He probably arranged things so that both cousins would serve together. It's not unusual, when someone of position and influence takes an interest and throws his weight around."

Holmes nodded, and then looked sharply at the door, which had been suddenly thrown open with great violence. Standing there was Mr. Collins, the American. Behind him, looking flustered, was Fellows. "Where is my daughter?" the older man thundered.

We looked at him in shock, but with no answer. He repeated his question, adding, "She left almost as soon as you did, heading down the hill. I couldn't stop her. I've never been able to stop her. She said something about speaking to young Lester. When I finally decided to come find her, I met a man who said that she had gone off toward East Dean with the scoundrel, riding in the back of a wagon-for-hire."

"What?" said Teague. "Lester has gone?" He turned to look toward Holmes.

My friend simply smiled. "She has been provoked, after all," he said cryptically.

"I knew we should have guarded them," muttered Anderson.

"He has well over an hour's head start on us," said Teague. "I guess that answers the question. Lester *was* the murderer."

"There is more to this matter than you know," said Holmes.

"I don't care about any of that," bellowed Collins. "I want my daughter brought back now!" He turned toward Holmes. "You're the famous detective. Find her!"

Holmes made no move to spring upon the girl's trail, simply saying, "She will be back here shortly, I assure you."

That did not satisfy Collins, who turned to Anderson.

"You then. You're the police. Rescue her from that murderer!"

"At once," said Anderson, standing up and moving toward the door. "I will telephone immediately and have every direction watched. If you will come with me, then, Mr. Collins?" He led the fuming man outside, and shut the door behind him. Holmes resumed his contemplations, and did not appear overly concerned.

Anderson returned in a few minutes without Collins, but accompanied by another man, a stranger, who stood by the doorway. Anderson informed us that he had sent Collins home to await word, and that he had arranged things so that a watch would soon be in place for Lieutenant Lester and Miss Collins, in whatever direction they might happen to go. "But I hope that they don't go across the open country," he added. "There are paths every which way out there. But if they reach another town or village after leaving from Eastbourne, they will be spotted."

The man who had returned with Anderson was old, short, and suspicious. Anderson called him forward from where he waited by the door, stating, "This is Goins. Lester hired him to drive them both to Eastbourne in his wagon."

"Oh, yes?" said Holmes, with only mild interest. "And did you deliver them there successfully, Mr. Goins?"

Goins mumbled something that was totally incomprehensible to me, but seemed to make sense to both Anderson and Holmes. The gist of the man's statement, after it had been translated, was that he had deposited both Lester and Miss Collins at the Eastbourne station, and the last he had seen of either of them was when they went inside. Each had been carrying a small bag. Goins was thanked and dismissed.

At that moment, Anderson was called back to the adjacent building to receive another telephone call. He quickly returned, beaming. "They've got them! Caught two stations up the line, they were, standing on the platform, arguing, and calling attention to themselves." He shook his head. "It seemed someone had recognized them and brought them to the notice of a constable on watch."

"Yes," interrupted Holmes, "that someone would have been my agent, Hipkins. I asked him to keep an eye on Miss Collins, should she choose to do anything interesting, such as arrange to meet with one of our suspects, or to depart the local area. I told him that if she left with someone, he was to stay on their track, and then to turn them over to the police as soon as it was feasible."

Anderson gave Holmes a strange look, a mixture of admiration and vexation. I had seen that same look on the faces of many a Yarder for more than two decades now. "I was told," continued Anderson, "Lieutenant Lester had changed his mind about leaving with the girl. He had just purchased two tickets *back* to Eastbourne when he was caught, and was telling the girl that she had to come along with him, although she was very much in disagreement with that idea. Now why would he decide to come back?"

"Perhaps he had learned the truth and knew that it was the right thing to do," said Holmes. His statement made sense to me, but I could tell that the other two men were puzzled. "Let me explain.

"I approached the scene as I have done at so many others before, with no preconceived notions in my mind." He then continued to lay out his reasoning for Anderson and Teague, telling them of his observations that a woman had first handled the poisoned brandy bottle, why he wished to obtain samples of Miss Collins's finger marks, once he learned that she was the girl most likely involved, and how he had determined that she had held the poisoned brandy bottle at some time before the victim, making it probable that she was the killer.

"While this is only a theory, I believe she felt that she could marry one of the lieutenants, thus becoming the wife of the heir to a fortune. It was probably several weeks ago, when she switched her attentions from one cousin to another, that she probably learned that her first interest, Lieutenant Lester, was not as interesting as Lieutenant Warren, since the latter was actually first in line to inherit his grandfather's fortune. No doubt she discovered this fact from conversations with one or the other of them, or from both. She threw over Lester for Warren, as her prospects in this

156

place must have seemed very remote indeed. With the discovery of a couple of heirs to a vast fortune right under her nose, and the opportunity to marry one and escape this dreary life with her father, she was surely and overwhelmingly tempted.

"I had learned from my source in London, as related to me here by telephone, that Warren was the primary heir. For some reason, Edith Collins decided to kill Warren and make Lester the heir. Perhaps she thought that she had a better chance with Lester, and wanted him placed in the more advantageous position. She may not have originally intended to murder Warren so soon, but was possibly provoked into acting quickly, as she had learned that the station was being closed and the two men would soon be transferred beyond her grasp.

"I doubt if she had any true plan, but rather she was clumsily reacting to situations as they presented themselves. I've seen this type of situation before, as has Watson. A rash action is taken, with no thought as to the consequences. Sometimes, even with a clever murderer, the effort to control events leads to additional murders, each easier for the killer than the one before. In this instance, the girl could think of no better plan after her foolish impulse of poisoning the brandy and giving it to Warren than to convince the other heir to flee with her.

"After we all left the Collins's house, I stopped to show Watson the memorandum case with her finger marks. I then looked back to discover that Miss Collins had seen me doing so from her window. Although I'm certain that she could not know *why* this was of interest to me, she probably *did* remember holding the case, and she perceived that I suspected her involvement and guilt.

"She is young and unsophisticated and not very clever, and is not cut from the same cloth as a hardened murderer. Therefore, she reacted without thought, as would be expected, and came down the hill to convince young Lester to flee with her. I do not think that he was actually involved in the murder. He could have arranged for the death of his cousin any number of ways at other times, rather than relying on whatever scheme the Collins girl could devise. I believe that shortly up the line, he realized the entire truth about what she had done, or else she had already told him something about it before they left, and he comprehended the full consequences of escaping with her. He then immediately purchased tickets to come back here and face the music, and was in the process of forcing her to join him, when both were apprehended."

And such proved to be the case. When they both arrived back at the house where we waited, they were brought before us, Lester standing upright, and Miss Collins spitting and struggling like a trapped cat. Her father was kept outside by a suddenly and surprisingly able Fellows.

157

Lester confirmed Holmes's solution of the matter. "You must understand that neither Andrew nor myself," he said, glancing coldly toward Miss Collins, "were completely attached to the lady. However, she was pleasant enough company, while we were stationed here, and it was certainly interesting to meet an American girl. I enjoyed our little flirtations, but when she took up with Andrew a few weeks ago, I did not find myself suffering from any serious disagreements about it."

"You lie!" cried the girl. "You said you loved me!"

"A summer romance," said the young man offhandedly. I had thought he might have been of better character, after learning how he had already chosen to return to the village just before his capture. Now, I felt that I understood his nature more clearly. How sad that this girl had allowed herself to commit murder in order to make this young man the heir and subsequently – she foolishly hoped – her chosen husband.

After we had departed the Collins's house, the lady had realized that she had fallen under suspicion, although she did not know how or why, exactly as Holmes had theorized. She had decided to convince Lester to flee with her before it was too late, and to marry him once they were away.

"If she meant nothing to you," said Holmes, "then why were you convinced to leave with her so easily? Surely you must have understood that such an action would draw attention toward you as the guilty party."

Lester fumbled at that point, and Miss Collins burst in. "Because he knew that he had been hinting to me that he would be better off with his cousin dead. He didn't know yet for sure that I had done it right then, but he was afraid that I might tell someone some of the things that he had said to me, and that would get him in deep. He finally agreed when I said that we should run away together. It was only a little later, when he made me admit everything to him on the train, that he realized that just because he had wished for Andrew to be dead and had put the idea in my head, it didn't make him guilty. He said he had come to know that running away with me was foolish, and that we must go back. He dragged me off the train. I ran out of the station, but he caught me and brought me back. I went easily enough, as I didn't want to attract any attention, and I thought that I could still talk him around to leaving. He bought the return tickets, and that's the spot where we were caught."

"She is correct," said Lester, pulling himself together. "Simply mentioning that my life would be eased considerably with Andrew's *departure*, so to speak, does not make me guilty. I cannot be blamed just because someone else foolishly chose to act upon that statement without my knowledge or consent."

"Ah," said Holmes, "the tired defense of Henry the Young King after the murder of Thomas Becket. 'Will no one rid me of this turbulent priest?'

I fancy your grandfather will not be sympathetic to your position, Lieutenant Lester."

"Alas, I fear that you are correct."

Lester's situation resolved itself as expected. In spite of the fact that no actual or direct instruction could be established from young Lester to the girl regarding the murder of his cousin, the wealthy grandfather, Ebersole Emerson, quickly disinherited Lester, instead favoring his fortune on a great-niece of excellent character who subsequently used the money to assist the poor with great success.

Later, after the Collins girl was officially in custody and Lester held for further questioning, Holmes and I departed. Anderson had seemed rather ill-tempered after the girl's arrest, as if it pained him that a young woman would commit such a crime. He had offered the use of his wagon to drive us to Holmes's villa, but Holmes insisted that we would rather walk. I must have given some sign of dismay, for Holmes himself took my heavy travel bag and carried it. "After all," he said, as we watched Anderson's wagon, along with the prisoner and Lester disappear over the distant hill, "it is my fault that you are bearing such a heavy burden."

"That statement," I replied, "could apply to more of our adventures together than I care to count."

He laughed, and started up the hill along the cliff tops behind the guard houses, choosing to walk that way, rather than along the road below.

The views were incredible, though we both stayed well back from the edge, where every now and then a long crack ran parallel to the cliff-line, indicating where the next collapse would likely occur. There were also numerous pits and holes in the ground as we walked, some hidden by the thick grasses that grew along our way. Occasionally I would see a grouping of dark snail shells, some as big as my thumb joint, clustered here and there around these holes. These allowed the rainwater to run down into the ground, and on into pockets and voids behind the cliff face. As each of these tiny chambers in the ground beneath us grew with each rainfall and winter freeze, the cliffs were further weakened. I saw that Holmes was correct and that, over time, the edge of the country at this point would keep receding, and long past the span of our lives, the entire shape of the coast would become unrecognizable. However, this knowledge could not take away from the beauty of the place that afternoon. The sun, the color of the sky, the birds wheeling in the air, were all nearly indescribable. And then I saw the travel case swinging at the end of Holmes's arm, and I felt a chill. The matter of the kidnapped child quickly put my postcard reverie in perspective.

We were climbing slowly toward one of the higher cliffs, which rose to the south of Holmes's farm, directly between it and the sea. Once I turned and looked back toward Birling Gap behind us. The locals were still standing and talking in groups of various sizes. There was no one at the Collins house, halfway up the far hill.

"I feel sorry for the man," I said. "They came all this way in order to hide, and to protect his daughter, and then she destroyed everything during a moment of stupidity."

"Quite," said Holmes. "Perhaps, if her path had never crossed that of Warren and Lester, her life, and theirs, and even that of Mr. Collins, would have had far different outcomes." He had been looking with me back toward the village. Resuming his walk to the top of the tall cliff, he said, "Hopefully the fact that our path is now converging with that of the kidnappers will provide an outcome for them that they did not anticipate."

We walked silently for a moment, and then I asked about the new arrangements for the delivery of the ransom.

"The exchange is set for tonight," Holmes said, shifting my bag from his right to his left hand. We had reached the top of the cliff, and he stopped, but he did not set the bag down. He looked at the sea, and then down the hill, across the scrub, toward his farm in the distance and across the road. "I sometimes think that I should drag a bench up to this spot, so that I might come up and contemplate life's mysteries in solitude."

"You would be too obvious up here," I said. "Constable Anderson would find you and try to involve you in every petty crime in the district. If you do not make yourself visible up here, then he will have to go to the villa whenever he wants your help, and there attempt to pass Mrs. Hudson, who will never let him know whether you are actually at home or off on one of Mycroft's quests."

"Ah, Mrs. Hudson. My own Cerberus."

"Holmes!"

"Hmm? Perhaps that is too harsh. I do not know what I would do without her."

"Speaking of doing," I said, reminding him of my earlier question about the new arrangements, "what is the plan for tonight?"

"I am to deliver the money to a house north of the road to Eastbourne. From the directions given in the note, it is the very same house that I had previously determined to be Chetwood's current den. I suspect that after he gets the money, he has arrangements in place to immediately flee to the Continent, trusting that even though he has been seen, we will not know who he is or how to trace him. Oh, the arrogance of the stupid criminal. One would hope that, somewhere in the midst of his escape plans, he intends to release the boy, or at least tell me how to find him.

"When the time comes tonight," Holmes continued, "I am to bring the money alone. Your presence here is unexpected, and you were

160

specifically mentioned in the latest letter from Chetwood. He insists that you remain seated in the front parlor of the villa over there during the time of the exchange, in front of a window with a lit lamp beside you. I don't know if it is so that I'll know that you are exposed and can therefore be threatened while I carry out the delivery of the money, thus keeping me in line, or if the kidnappers simply want to make sure that I don't have the use of my good right arm."

I appreciated this compliment, but bristled at the idea that Holmes was required to deliver the money alone, and I said so. "It is surely a trap," I concluded.

"A valid argument, Watson," he said. "But do not forget that we know Chetwood's identity, and that we already knew about the house where the exchange is to take place. I have other assets in place on the chessboard, and this change of plan does not spoil anything."

I knew that one of the assets was Hipkins, but I did not know who else might be involved. Constable Anderson had given no sign that he was privy to anything about the kidnapping, which was in accordance with the instructions originally sent to the Earl, forbidding police involvement.

Holmes took one last look toward the sea, and then with a deep breath, he set off down the hill, leading to right or left as necessary through the undergrowth. We soon reached the road, and crossed to the drive leading toward the house, nestled nearly invisible back in the trees.

We made do for ourselves for the next several hours, discussing old times and Holmes's current activities. Mrs. Hudson had left more than ample supplies in her kitchen, and we had a late luncheon, although I must admit that mine was considerably more substantial than Holmes's. Soon after, I was not surprised to find myself falling asleep into a pleasant afternoon nap. When I awoke, it was clearly getting on toward evening, and Holmes was moving about in another part of the building.

He came in a few minutes later, wearing a rough, worn, and familiar-looking suit. While I tried unsuccessfully to place where I had seen something like it before, he crossed the room, positioning a lamp underneath the large window facing the road. Turning toward me, he said, "I will be leaving soon, Watson. Get what you need to pass an hour or two comfortably here in this chair by the window. Might I suggest some of that tobacco in the tin on that table? It was a recent gift from a vicar in Berwick-upon-Tweed, after I located a particularly bonny emerald that had been secreted two hundred years ago in a hidden cavity in his mantel."

He left the room, and then returned once more, stopping near my chair and leaning down to retrieve my portmanteau, where it had been sitting since our arrival several hours before. "My thanks for bringing this," he said. "When the Earl needed someone to go around to his bank and collect

161

the quarter-of-a-million pounds for transport to Sussex, I could think of no better man."

I grumbled a response, and said, "I wonder how people would have reacted today if they had known I was carrying such a sum with me as we traipsed back and forth across the countryside."

"You might have even turned poor Miss Collins's head, had she but realized the nature of your burden."

I admonished him that such a statement was in poor taste. "Perhaps you are right. In any event, I shall attempt to take care of your case, and to bring it back to you in as good a condition as I have received it."

I laughed, thinking of the many strange places the poor bag had already visited during the course of my adventures with Sherlock Holmes. But my attention was called back as he gave me one final instruction.

"Stay here in the chair until I return if at all possible," he said. "In case someone is truly watching the house. I will finish my arrangements and slip out the back. Hipkins is waiting with the Rover in the barn, and he will drive me from there. I should be back with news soon, and I trust that it will all be good."

And with that, he left the room. I heard him in the rear of the house, and then he walked through and out the back without any further communication. In a few minutes, I heard the low rumble of the automobile as it pulled out of the barn, and then past the front of the house and out to the road. It turned toward the east, and was gone.

I could see nothing from the window except my own reflection. It was unnerving indeed to think that I might be watched at this very minute. Perhaps an assassin was lining up the sights of a rifle, or an air gun perhaps, on my silhouette in the window. How could Holmes have asked me to make such a target of myself, considering the number of enemies that both of us had accumulated over the years?

But no, I said, calming myself. I trusted my instincts, and I felt nothing of the well-honed and long-earned sensation that one has when he is being watched. Sitting there in the comfortable chair, I felt nothing. I was certain that, in spite of the instructions to keep me out of the action and to deprive Holmes of my assistance, no one was out in the darkness that night.

Nearly two hours later to the minute, I heard an automobile pull into the yard in front of the house. It stopped, and then there was the sound of a single door opening and closing. Footsteps crossed the gravels, and the front door flew open. Standing there, with an evil look upon his lean and sallow face, was Hipkins.

I stood up, the book on my lap falling to the floor. "What is the meaning of this?" I cried. "Where is Holmes?"

162

"Do be careful with that volume, Watson," said the voice of Holmes from Hipkins's mouth. "It is nearly a hundred years old, and I paid a pretty penny and even greater effort to track it down." I realized why Holmes's old suit had looked familiar before he left. He had clothed himself in nearly the same clothing that I had seen earlier that day upon Hipkins, although I could not fathom why. He stepped to a mirror, and began to rearrange his face back from Hipkins to Holmes. "That book came from the basement of a shop in Charing Cross Road, and I nearly broke an ankle fleeing up the uneven steps to lead the owner's nephew, who just happened to be Phelps, the Bickleigh murderer, into my trap."

"I trust," said I, as I bent to pick up the book on the floor, "that you can explain everything. But that can wait. The boy?"

"Safe in his father's house," said Holmes, pulling wadding from his mouth that had changed the shape of his face, making his cheekbones more pronounced and adding gaunt shadows underneath. "Most of my time has been spent at the manor, explaining the sequence of events to the Earl. The rescue itself was almost immediate."

He excused himself, and returned in a few minutes, attired in his own clothing and a dressing gown, and wiping the last of the sallow coloring from his face. While he had stepped out, I retrieved my bag from by the door, where Holmes had dropped it when he entered. It was back to its normal condition – that is to say, not filled with a quarter of a million pounds.

Holmes settled into his chair and thanked me for the brandy that I had poured and placed by it. "So Hipkins was involved?" I said.

"I am afraid so," said Holmes, "up to his eyes. I am very disappointed in him, but it seems that his greed, or perhaps simply his loyalty to his stepbrother, outweighed any feelings he might have had for staying on the right side of the law."

"His stepbrother? Chetwood, you mean?"

Holmes nodded. "After I traced Chetwood and learned who he was, I set my agents to finding out details of his background. One thing that was repeated from several sources was his close association with his stepbrother, one Alfred Hipkins. Imagine my surprise at this unexpected connection, as Hipkins had been acting for me for several years now. He was never an Irregular, you understand, as he was recruited more recently by Shinwell Johnson, and I had always found that I could trust him. He had certain skills that sometimes came in handy. You may have noticed his odd voice?"

I nodded, and Holmes continued. "The result of being too close to an explosion a few years ago, when he was trying his hand at safebreaking. He had no difficulty reaching the location of the safe, but he was not so

163

skillful with his use of explosives. It was thought that the experience, for which he was never implicated or arrested, had been enough to scare him onto the straight and narrow.

"At first, the relationship that I discovered between Hipkins and Chetwood was nothing but a curious fact. However, when I asked the Earl for a list of current and former employees at his estate, thinking that the ease in which the boy was taken right under their noses might be explained by the familiarity possessed by a former staffer, I was amazed to see that Hipkins had worked for a time in the Earl's stable, back in the mid-'90's. He had been let go then after being implicated in a theft, although he had vociferously maintained his innocence. Here, then, was a link, although its exact shape and connection would have to be explored. However, I now knew that Chetwood, who was definitely involved in the kidnapping by his action of mailing the ransom letter, had a close stepbrother who had worked on the estate where the child was taken, and also had reason to be angry with the Earl.

"I set some further inquiries in motion in London regarding Hipkins as well, and learned that he had been out of town since approximately the time of the kidnapping. He had not been seen in this area, but he could have been here, possibly acting as the boy's captor, and keeping himself out of sight.

"I arranged for a message to be passed to him, wherever he might be, by one of his trusted associates in London who did not realize my true purpose. I urgently requested his aid on a matter in Sussex. This might not seem unusual to him, as he has helped me numerous times before, especially since my retirement, and of course he knew that I lived here now. Certainly it would be an odd position in which to find himself if he was already here, involved in the kidnapping. In any case, he could not easily refuse to help me. And within a few hours, he presented himself here to offer his services.

"My agent here confirmed that Hipkins did not arrive by train, and further determined that the Rover driven by him was rented in Eastbourne two days before my message was sent asking for his assistance."

"Who is your agent?" I asked. "Siger?"

"Of course," said Holmes, without elaboration. I nodded. This is not the place to explain or discuss the assistance provided to Holmes by young Siger during those early years of the new century, but suffice it to say that Holmes would have been greatly hobbled as he carried out various tasks for his brother Mycroft throughout that time had he been deprived of the aid provided by his young apprentice.*

"So Hipkins arrived on the scene, then?"

164

"Correct. He officially presented himself to me, and we discussed the proposed arrangements for delivering the money to the kidnapper at the Tiger Inn. I did not let on that I knew the kidnapper's identity, and I did not mention Hipkins's connection to Chetwood. And I did not tell him that you were the man who would be bringing the money down from London. He could honestly perceive, from his position on the inside, that I was not involving the police, and was seemingly attempting to faithfully adhere to the kidnapper's demands.

"It must have shocked him to see that you were the man who arrived this morning in Eastbourne with the money. But upon reflection, he would understand that you were the obvious choice. My only worry was that he would knock you on the head and take the bag during that short drive from the station to St. Mary the Virgin. However, he was being watched during that time, and he would not have escaped."

"I suppose that you did not tell me because you felt that I would have shown to him in some way that I was aware of his involvement," I said, having experienced this same type of controlled ignorance many times before. "It would have been nice, however, to know going in that I faced the possibility of having my head knocked."

"Ah, but I did not truly think anything of the sort would happen. They had no reason to believe that the ransom would not be paid, allowing the two villains to slip away into wealthy anonymity – or at least they planned for that. If Hipkins had stolen the money from you directly, then his association with *that* crime would be undeniable, and he would be an identified fugitive. Besides, neither Hipkins nor Chetwood has ever shown any indications of truly violent actions in their past."

"A quarter of a million pounds can make a man alter his behavior fairly quickly. But do go on with your story."

Holmes took a sip of brandy. "As you know, the exchange this morning was interrupted by Teague, and then by our subsequent involvement in the murder investigation. As Chetwood fled the inn, I nodded that Hipkins should follow him. Actually, I wanted Chetwood to know the truth, that the meeting was interrupted for an unexpected and legitimate reason, and that we had not reneged on our agreement to meet at a neutral location and deliver the money.

* Editor's Note: For more information about the true identity of Holmes's apprentice, Siger, see "The Adventure of the Other Brother" in *The Papers of Sherlock Holmes,* Vol. II (2013).

"Later, Hipkins lied to me and reported back that Chetwood had waited and written the note to revise the details of our next meeting. In fact, as Siger let me know later, Hipkins and Chetwood had a close discussion and wrote the note together. It was never left for me at the Tiger Inn, as Hipkins said. Rather, it was simply brought by him to me at the guard houses."

"Where Hipkins then offered to take my bag with the money in it and deliver it here."

"Well, he might not have hit you on the head for it an hour or so earlier, but you can't blame him for trying to get it another way," said Holmes, laughing.

"And your disguise? What did that accomplish?"

"It was something spur of the moment. By then I knew that Siger was waiting there at the house, and I wanted to rattle Chetwood. When I left you here by the window, I completed my transformation into Hipkins. Then I went out to the barn in the darkness. Hipkins paid little attention to me, so I was able to approach him from behind and quickly render him unconscious with chloroform. After binding him and tossing him in the back of the Rover, I drove to Chetwood's house.

"I parked and went to the door. Chetwood answered my knock, no doubt expecting to find Sherlock Holmes standing there with the money. Instead, he discovered Hipkins, back in the shadows, urgently explaining in Hipkins's odd voice that the plan had gone wrong, and that we needed to move the boy as soon as possible.

"With a curse, Chetwood flew past me and around to the back of the house. I followed as he led me into a distant copse of trees, and on through onto a narrow trail down toward a marshy hollow. On the far side of that was another stand of trees, and at its verge was an old building, not much more than a roofed pen, used at some point in the past by a sheep farmer, but now obviously abandoned.

"Chetwood forced his way inside through the nearly collapsed doorway and pulled aside a stack of lumber to reveal the Earl's son behind it, tied and gagged against the back wall, and watching us with large terrified eyes. I later determined that he had not suffered any damage, but it was certainly not clear to me at that moment. As Chetwood leaned toward the boy, I stepped up with my chloroform bottle and pad, making good use of it for the second time tonight. Then I gave two blasts on my cab whistle, which is a sound rarely heard in these parts, I can assure you, and Siger seemed to form out of the very shadows. We freed the boy, bound Chetwood with the same ropes taken from the lad, and got them both back to the house and the car. The two men were left with an

166

astonished Constable Anderson, along with a quick explanation and a promise for more soon, and the boy was returned to his father."

"All in all, a good night's work," I said.

"It is not over yet, I fear," said Holmes, as the sound of a wagon drawing up outside became louder. "I believe that will be Anderson, asking for the promised elaboration upon the capture of the two men that are now in his custody."

And so it was. Holmes spent the next hour or so sociably explaining to Anderson the full nature of the events of the last few days. At first, Anderson was quietly irate that such a matter had not initially been brought to his attention, but he eventually realized that his involvement would have been noticed, and might have led to more danger for the boy.

Finally, Anderson rose to depart, and the house returned to silence as Holmes and I resumed our seats, with one more brandy poured for each of us. We did not speak for some time.

Then, Holmes said to me, "What you said before. About feeling sorry for Mr. Collins, moving here from America to hide from his enemies and protect his daughter, only to see his plan come apart because of her stupidity."

I could see that he was exploring his thoughts as he went, and allowed him to find his way. After another silent moment, he continued. "Is there a pattern to it all, Watson? Does one person cross another's path for a reason? Was Lieutenant Warren destined to die here because of the awkward machinations of an American girl, who was only in this location at this time because of her father's activities? If we could fly over London, like the bees resting in the hives out there, and perceive the paths and wanderings of all the habitants below us, what strange intersections would we see, where each encounter pushes a person off in one direction or another along a dark and unknown path?"

I took a sip of brandy. "Living down here so close to the sea has inflamed your philosophical side," I said. "What is it that brings on these pensive thoughts?"

"Perhaps it is being involved more and more with Mycroft's work," he answered. "For years, Mycroft has been a voice crying in the wilderness, warning of the possibility, nay, even the likely inevitability, of a European war, the likes of which have not been seen before. My involvement in these cases has brought me to an awareness that I have not previously had of his perceptiveness."

"You and I have both been involved in certain matters before this, wherein the possibility of a European conflict has been identified and diverted. You were not completely unaware of this type of thing before your supposed retirement a couple of years ago."

"I was aware, but it did not affect me on a daily basis. Down amongst the trees, taking on this or that case, I did not fly above and see the forest. The bigger picture, you understand. Perhaps I should have assisted Mycroft sooner, or more often, as he kept insisting. As I did during those three years when I was presumed to be dead."

"You have done a great deal of good with those cases 'down amongst the trees' over the years," I said. "You have helped many people."

"But could I have helped more, perhaps, on a greater scale?" He shifted in his seat. "Do you know how a bee leads the members of the hive to a discovery of food?"

"No, I suppose that I never considered it."

"When a likely find is made, say flowers at that critical peak of bloom, with the nectar at its most tempting, the explorer bee returns to the hive and performs a dance of sorts, simply loaded with coded information that will give the direction and distance from the hive to the treasure. I have seen this for myself."

"I fail to understand – "

"Do you recall the hornets that you observed this morning on the path leading down toward the inn?"

"Yes."

"I am afraid that some day, one of those hornets will cross paths with one of my bees. Perhaps it will be part of the plan, or instead it could just be a puff of breeze that makes one or the other go left instead of right, up instead of down. On that day the hornet might not be interested in finding a food source that has been discovered. Instead, he may find it a more useful service to lead his own troops to where my bee's home hive is located. He will return to his own place, and do a dance of death letting them know exactly where to go. Man is not the only creature that goes to war, Watson."

"So you fear that the hornet tribe might attack and destroy your hive?" I said.

"Exactly. And the more that I perform tasks for Mycroft, the more aware I am that at some time in the future, almost certainly, a hornet, by plan or chance is going to find or be given a reason to lead his attackers against our peaceful domestic hives. I am troubled, Watson, because I do not know which seemingly random encounter, which piece of shared information, which riot or insult or even assassination of some unknown pawn will be the spark that touches off the powder keg that all our tangled treaties have wrapped around us, to mix a metaphor. Is it any wonder, then, that I ponder whether there is a plan for us all, or if we simply function in a kind of mindless chaos?"

168

I had never heard my friend sound as worried or resigned as on this night, and I did not know quite what to say. "All of this possibly random entanglement that you perceive around us is not a bad thing," I finally offered. "I have said it many times before: if I had not encountered you following my return to England after Maiwand, I would likely have ended up broken or dead, like so many of the other poor injured soldiers that washed up in the cesspool of the capital. That random encounter certainly turned out to be a good thing, branching out from there in many ways."

Holmes smiled. "Perhaps you are right, Watson. I've become maudlin in my old age."

I shook my head in mock dismay. "Old at fifty-one. How should that make me feel, then, a full year and a half older than you are?"

"Indeed." He stood then, and walked over to the side of the room, where a desk was piled with papers. "I was looking through some old documents from my trunk the other night. Would it surprise you, Watson, to learn that our meeting at Barts was not the first time that our paths had crossed?"

"Not at all," I said. "Over the years I've become aware of several instances when we met unknowingly before that New Year's Day in 1881. London, after all, is not that big a city. Especially in the late 1870's."

Holmes found the sheet that he was looking for and tossed it to me. "Do you remember anything about that?" he asked.

I glanced at the writing. Although faded, it was obviously Holmes's distinctive fist. The date at the top was 19 November, 1879. I scanned the contents of the document, and then a flash of memory washed over me.

"I recall this," I said. "I was on leave from Netley, and I had come up to London for a few days, and had gone to see the race-walking competition in Islington."

"A wobble, they called it," interrupted Holmes.

"Exactly. Those poor fools would walk for a week round and round a track for very poor rewards indeed. One of the men had taken ill, and I was called into the tent where he was resting to examine him."

"And he later died, as you might recall," said Holmes. "From strychnine poisoning."

I nodded. "It initially seemed to be a saline deficiency, and I recommended rest and that he be pulled from the race. Later, his symptoms worsened, and he passed away. I made my report at the time to the policeman in charge, and returned the next day to Netley. I never heard what happened after that."

"The important part, as far as you are concerned, is that you were allowed to return to Netley to complete your training to become a military surgeon, thus making it possible for you to be in Afghanistan, where circumstances caused an injury that forced your return to London, where you met me, and – having tied up your fortunes with mine for so many years – it seemed the logical conclusion that you would be called down here today when I needed your assistance once again, leading us to have this conversation here tonight. More brandy?"

"Certainly, but what about this matter has brought it to your attention now? Obviously you were involved, as this document is a report or diary entry about the case. Perhaps if I read it again more closely – "

"Do not bother. I shall summarize for you. When the competitive walker was taken ill during the *wobble* and you were summoned, there was no indication that he was truly dying. It was only after your visit that it was ascertained that he had been poisoned with a massive overdose of strychnine. The police sergeant in charge of the case, realizing that you had spent some time alone with the patient before his condition became worse, theorized that *you* might have given him the fatal strychnine yourself for some unknown reason during your examination. After all, who would suspect a doctor? The victim was initially only somewhat ill before you examined him. After you were with him, alone, I might add, he became worse and died."

"But . . . but I had no idea of any of this!" I cried, feeling a defensive panic for an event that had happened and then been settled over a quarter-century earlier. "It was ridiculous to think that I might have murdered the man."

"Obviously, but the sergeant did not know anything about you. To him, you were just another young man in his late twenties. You might have had your own hidden association with the dead man, and finding yourself with the means, determined to kill him. You and I have seen something similar in the past. Do you recall the unexpected encounter with Dr. Mells of Templecombe? Or more recently, the sinister plan of Dr. Knox and the Waringstown Tincture?

"It was only after the police sergeant consulted me during the course of his investigation, visiting my rooms in Montague Street, that I was able to nudge him toward the correct solution. You never even knew that you had been under suspicion."

"That is true. I simply went back to Netley and resumed my studies."

"But this is my point," said Holmes. "If the sergeant had not questioned me, then things might have taken a different turn. At that time I was preparing to leave the country for many months, to join the Sassanoff Company in their American tour. What if I had already been gone? The sergeant might have arrested you on suspicion, just to be on the safe side.*

"Most likely your innocence would have been proven, but even so, the simple fact that you were involved could have been enough to be a blot upon your record. Your entire future might have been altered. Might it have been better? Who knows? You could be living in a fine house, winding up an honored career while looking out over your heirs. Or you could have started a decline then and there that ended your story far sooner than it should have.

"So tell me, Watson, was it part of the plan that the police sergeant consulted me, thus freeing you from his suspicions early in the process, or was it random? Are we all simply specks suspended in solution, attracting or repelling one another in some Brownian Motion of humanity until the end?"

This was too deep for me, so late at night with one too many brandies inside me. I tried to divert the subject. "Why were you looking at these papers from your trunk?" I asked.

"Ah," Holmes replied with a smile. "Perhaps it truly was part of the plan that the former police sergeant, and subsequently a respected inspector, sent me a letter a day or so ago, requesting my assistance on a new matter. In a fit of nostalgia, I pulled out the old papers to review various instances of my previous aid to him over the years, and when I saw the details of this case from 1879, including your name and profession as one of the suspects, I realized just how our paths had crossed before. The story suggested itself to me as we were discussing the random versus predetermined nature of existence. Is your wife expecting you back soon?" he asked abruptly.

"Why, no. I told her that I might be here for several days, possibly until the next weekend. Why?"

"The inspector is now retired and settled in the west of England, specifically in Chudleigh Knighton, not so very far from that place that you called *Coombe Tracey* a few years ago in one of your publications."

He reached for an additional document from the mound teetering on the desk and handed it to me. "It relates to this," he said. I glanced down. It appeared to be a monograph of a dozen or so worn pages, entitled, *Some Instances of Sacrifice and Subsequent Hauntings in the Middle Ages in Order to Obfuscate Information Regarding Treasure.*

* Editor's Note: The events of the "wobble" contest and the murder that took place there in November 1879 are obviously those that are recounted in *Wobble to Death* (1970), presented to the public by Peter Lovesey. This is the first published of eight excellent books (and one short story, along with several television episodes from the early 1980's) featuring Sergeant Cribb, the unnamed policeman to whom Holmes refers. Interestingly, *Wobble to Death* does not mention Cribb's consultation with Holmes at all, nor the fact that Watson, who simply appears as an unnamed doctor examining the dying man, was ever under any suspicion.

"He seems to have come across an interesting little case down there," said Holmes, "and if you are so inclined, we will leave for there in the morning. I think that you will find it to be an excellent addition to your chronicles."

And his assessment of the situation turned out to be true, although I did not know why then. Over one more brandy, Holmes told me a few more details, and I agreed that it certainly sounded interesting indeed. When he had revealed all that he was willing to for the moment, I left him there, smoking his pipe, and ascended the stairs to get some rest for the morrow.

The Gower Street Murder

Part I: A Chance Encounter

The sky that morning was as bright a blue as one could hope for, reflecting the crisp bite to the late September air. I remarked on the day's beauty as I dismissed my cab, and the driver agreed with me. I had thought that I would walk back to Baker Street upon the completion of my errand. However, my appointment took quite a bit longer than expected, and by the time I exited the austere and imposing residence, a line of dark clouds had hove in from the south, along with a brisk damp breeze promising rain.

Still, I stubbornly decided that I would walk at least part of the way before the weather overtook me, and I set off on foot, crossing Constitution Hill before entering the tree-shaded protection of Green Park, already unnaturally dark but temporarily protected from the rising wind at my back.

Traversing the wide pathways, I glanced at the occasional man or woman who passed me, each facing straight ahead or looking fixedly at the ground before them, intent on their own personal thoughts. Several times as I crossed the Park, I patted my breast in order to reassure myself, although I had no reason to believe that the official missive tucked into my pocket had managed to work its way loose.

It had been to take delivery of this document that I had journeyed to the Palace that day, representing my friend, Mr. Sherlock Holmes, in a matter that has no relation to the present narrative, and must remain unrecorded until such time as a future Prime Minister deems it prudent. Holmes had felt that it would be better if the final loose ends of the affair were tied up without his participation, and considering the harsh words and vile epithets that had been hurled toward him the night before by the broken and beaten nobleman, Lord D------, in Holmes's sitting room, I tended to agree. Therefore, I had made the excursion and subsequently taken possession of this *second* handwritten confirmatory confession, which – like the first that had been signed the night before by his co-conspirator – would never see the light of day, provided that Holmes's conditions were followed to the letter.

I had no fear that anyone would try to take the document from me, as it was in everyone's best interest, at least for the immediate future, that it be placed into Holmes's safekeeping as soon as possible. And yet, I was beginning to rethink my desire to walk part of the way home, not because

I feared that the document would be taken. Rather, I suspected that it might be damaged by the rapidly approaching rain.

As I reached Piccadilly, I looked in both directions for a hansom, but surprisingly there were none to be seen just then on that busy street. Quickening my pace, I crossed and turned toward the east.

I had passed by Brick Street and White Horse Street when the rising wind from the south increased. As I moved past Cambridge House, a young man appeared in my path, pulling the Out gate closed behind him. He was facing away from me, and did not see my approach, forcing me to shift my stride to avoid a collision. It was then that the first of the rain began.

I reached Half Moon Street, and quickly turned left and ducked into the most accommodating doorway, No. 4, in order to shelter myself while I attempted to open my umbrella. I was not the only person to have this idea, as suddenly the young man who had been departing Cambridge House also dashed into my doorway, instantly placing me on my guard. Our eyes met, and we nodded at one another, with my expression rather more wary than his. He must have followed me.

"Dr. Watson?" he said softly.

As I acknowledged the fact, the wind gusted, pushing several larger drops of rain with it. My new companion, on the uphill side of the doorway, was more exposed than I, and appeared to catch the brunt of the spray. I noticed that he did not have an umbrella. At this time, after knowing Sherlock Holmes for so many years, I could not help but also observe that he appeared to be a clerk in his mid-thirties, right-handed and accustomed to writing often, as shown by his worn sleeve. He was a wiry fellow, about five feet and nine inches, and not much more than twelve stone. His clothing was modest but well-kept, and he looked like half a million other similar fellows that might be seen but not necessarily observed on any day of the week around the Capital. There was nothing unusual about him, save for the mourning band on one sleeve.

He noticed my glances up and down his figure, and he formed a faint smile. He quickly looked at the rain, now falling steadily onto the street, and returned his gaze to meet my own. I started to look away, having been discovered studying him, but the sudden smile lighting his face stopped me.

"You don't recognize me, do you, doctor?" he asked.

"I'm afraid not," I admitted, with wariness rather than any sudden relaxation. Working with Holmes has provided a great deal of excitement over the years, as well as numerous rewards, but unfortunately, it has also caused a number of people, including family members of criminals exposed and brought to justice along the way, to have a certain amount of antipathy towards us.

"I'm Wiggins," he said. "Peter Wiggins. Of the Irregulars."

A flash of recognition passed over me, as I associated this neatly dressed man with the ragged boy from so many years ago. He was the first of many of Holmes's lieutenants, the leaders of his Baker Street Irregulars, who had carried the name "Wiggins."

"Of course," I replied, finally lowering my guard, and holding out my hand, which he shook heartily. "I must admit that I did not recognize you, Wiggins." I turned my head toward the street, where the rain already seemed to be tapering into a steady soaking drizzle. "How have you been? It's been so many years since I last saw you . . . . "

"Nearly twenty, doctor," he agreed. "Then I moved on and my brother took over my duties with the Irregulars. I have been quite happy with my life since then, thanks to the assistance given to me by Mr. Holmes so long ago. I work for a man in King's Bench Walk, near the Temple."

"You're quite a distance away from there to be caught without your umbrella on a day such as this," I said.

"Oh, no sir, I'm not working right now," he declared. He gestured toward the mourning band. "I'm making some final arrangements for the funeral later today. Will you and Mr. Holmes be stopping by? We would all appreciate it so very much."

I confess that I was completely puzzled by his question. Holmes had made no mention of anything of this sort, and I did not have the faintest idea to what Wiggins was referring. I think that I must have shown my confusion, for Wiggins continued, "My mother, sir. She passed away last Thursday."

"I'm so sorry to hear it," I murmured.

"Thank you," Wiggins replied, quietly. "I believe that she was quite ready. She had been ill for several years now, and my sister had been living with her."

I nodded, still trying to catch up, and he continued, "Her last years were quite comfortable, certainly more so than they might have been, had not Mr. Holmes done so much for both her and our whole family."

"Really," I said, unsure of my ground, "I am afraid that I was not aware . . . ."

He smiled knowingly. "I see that Mr. Holmes has not told you the story. I'm not surprised. Well, it's not my place, if he has chosen not to reveal it after all this time, and I must be getting on. However, you are certainly invited to my mother's home, where we will all be gathering early this afternoon, before the funeral this evening. I know that my sister was to send a card to you both, and it will provide you with the address, although I'm certain that Mr. Holmes still recalls it." He glanced out at the street, where the rain was already drawing to a close. "I must dash, but I hope to see you this afternoon!"

And with that, he was gone. While he returned to Piccadilly, I refolded my barely used umbrella, and continued up Half Moon Street to Curzon Street. Turning right, I worked my way into Berkeley Square, and managed to hire a hansom in front of General de Merville's corner home, the site of Holmes's disastrous interview with the general's daughter, just weeks earlier.

The streets were fairly clear at that time of morning, and it wasn't long until I was back in Baker Street. Entering the front door, I let Mrs. Hudson know that I had returned, and hung up my hat and coat. As I climbed the stairs, I could see from the window upon the landing that the day was already clearing again, returning to the bright blue skies that had initially greeted me when I started upon my errand.

As I stepped into the sitting room, I found Holmes reclining in his chair, pondering an unlit pipe. Crossing to the hearth, I removed the document that I had carried to and from the Palace and placed it into his hand.

"Any difficulties?" he asked, barely glancing at it. He had written most of it himself the night before, along with its twin, before forcing the first grudging signature from one of the guilty parties. Today's additional signature had simply been sewing up the final stitch of the complicated tapestry that had taken Holmes two full days to complete.

"Not at all," I replied, turning toward the sideboard. It had been a difficult morning. Holmes responded to my unspoken question by indicating that he did not wish to join me in my early restorative. "And the document's final resting place?"

"With Brother Mycroft, I think," he replied. "Then it will be someone else's problem."

"So all is well," I breathed. "I did not like the idea that you might wish to keep it here, or that you would have me keep it with *my* papers."

"Indeed," Holmes responded. "The political mind that would create such a convoluted scheme as this would not hesitate to burgle these rooms someday, or even the vaults of Cox and Company, should he ever reconsider his confession and come to believe that a vigilant government has stopped keeping track of him and these papers."

Turning toward him, I wanted to ask about the steps that he had taken over the past couple of days, leading from a cryptic reference about a cormorant in the Agony Column, followed by the desperate dash to the Kent lighthouse on a hastily hired Special. But I could see that his thoughts were already on some other matter as he tossed the document carelessly

176

onto the small octagonal table by his chair. I settled into my seat across from him, and sighed as I stretched my feet toward the fire.

"How far did you walk before the rains overtook you?" he asked.

I glanced down at my damp cuffs. "Elementary," I said. "You heard the hansom arrive, but you see that my clothing is wet from the earlier rain."

He nodded and began to scrape inside his pipe. "As you say."

"The deluge, though arriving and departing quickly, caught me in Half Moon Street. And can you deduce with whom I shared a doorway while waiting for the rain to pass?"

He dramatically touched the stem of the pipe to his forehead and closed his eyes. Then, with a smile, he opened them and said, "A Wiggins, of course. But I must confess that I do not know precisely which one."

I snorted, amazed as usual, and totally at a loss to explain how he had reached his conclusion.

I did not need to ask him to confirm his supposition, as he continued, "Upon sitting down, your eyes began to look quickly from here to there, searching for something. You glanced significantly at the mantel, where my correspondence is usually affixed by a jack knife. After several seconds, you looked away, but you continued to glance about, indicating that what you were seeking was some sort of communication that you would have expected to arrive while you were gone, and what you sought was not there.

"Immediately thereafter, you spotted the black-bordered envelope which stands here upon my side table, propped against my morning coffee cup. You then showed a satisfied expression, as if your conclusions had been verified. That led me to understand that you somehow expected that such a letter would be here.

"Since it arrived while you were out this morning, neither of us could have known about it beforehand. Therefore, you had somehow learned of it while you were out on your errand. Knowing as I do that it came from the Wiggins family, and realizing that you could not have learned about it from any other source, since I have ascertained that there was no mention of the lady's death in the morning newspapers, I concluded with near certainty that you had spoken with a member of the family. Since, as far as I know, the only Wiggins's that you have ever met have been members at various times of the Irregulars, the only question that remains is to determine which one it was?"

"Peter," I replied. "From 1881."

"Ah, yes. Wiggins the First. From several years before 1881 as well, however," Holmes explained. "He was my lieutenant for a while, before you had occasion to first encounter him during the Jefferson Hope matter."

"There have certainly been a passel of them over the years," I replied.

"Indeed. Even I sometimes have trouble keeping track of all of them."

I took a sip of my brandy. "How did you meet them?" I asked. "The Wiggins family? When we first met, back in '81, you already had your system of Irregulars firmly in place. At what point did the Wiggins clan become the official and perpetual leaders of the group?"

"My dear Watson, that is a story. And as I hear Mrs. Hudson climbing the stairs with our lunch, which I asked her to prepare early today, perhaps I can relate it before we depart for the Wiggins home to pay our respects."

Part II: The Gower Street Murder

I did not question that he would assume I was going with him, since in fact I had planned to, once I learned about it. I agreed that an early lunch would suit me, and rose to open the door for the long-suffering landlady.

She had provided us with some cold beef left from the night before, and bread for making sandwiches. I thanked her, while Holmes nodded in a distracted way and began to prepare something small for himself. I could see that he was recalling the details of his story. In a moment, he began.

"You may recall," he eventually related, "that when I left Oxford and came up to London following the events relating to the matter of 'The Gloria Scott,' I lived for several years in Montague Street, immediately beside the British Museum."

I nodded. "I lived in Bloomsbury for a time myself, while finishing at the University of London and before joining the army," I reminded him. "South of Great Russell Street, in Southampton Street.* Number 6 it was."

"Quite," Holmes said. "I have no doubt that our paths crossed many times without even knowing it."

"Exactly," I said, warming to memories of my younger days. "For instance, on that occasion when you and I visited the Alpha Inn a few days after Christmas back in '87, I meant to tell you about one of the earlier times that I had been there with Stamford. We had left Barts that evening, only to discover – "

* Editor's Note: Several locations mentioned by Watson in this particular narrative now go under different names in modern London. For instance, Southampton *Street*, located south of Great Russell Street, the British Museum, and Montague Street in Bloomsbury, is now known as Southampton *Place*.

178

"As I was saying," Holmes said, with no rancor while interrupting my reminiscences, "I was living in Montague Street, in a house leased by the widow of one of my father's cousins, a Mrs. Holmes. If I ever knew her first or maiden name, it is completely lost to me now. The lease was initially in her family name, before she renewed it with the Bedford people as Mrs. Holmes. Mycroft had first resided there, when he came up to London after Oxford, and it was to that same house that I went after leaving old Trevor's place in Norfolk in the summer of 1874.

"Over the next few years, while making Montague Street my base of operations, I set about learning my craft. I studied some at Cambridge during this time, but also spent a great deal of my energy in London, finding clients when I could, intruding into police investigations as much as I was able and allowed, and making the acquaintances of various lesser underworld figures, learning whatever skills from them that they were willing to teach. The rest of my time I spent in the British Museum, directly across the street from my meager lodgings in No. 24.

"As I recall, it was in the fall of 1877, when I had established enough of a practice that I could afford my rent, and an occasional bit of bread and cheese besides, when I first made use of the Irregulars. You understand, they didn't have a title then. It was only when you and I moved into these quarters, and you were being introduced to my little methods, that I made some joke or other about utilizing the 'Baker Street division of the detective police force.' Over time, we began to refer to them by the noble *sobriquet* which they now use to identify themselves.

"In those early days, I would simply hire one of them here and there, as needed, and as I could afford it, to watch a house or visit an address to see if a fact could be observed or verified or extracted when I did not have the time to go there myself. Soon the two or three lads that I had initially hired told others, and it became known that a man on Montague Street was doing detective work, and paying real money for assistance.

"And so I began to be pestered quite seriously by the lads, all wanting to participate in something or other in order to earn a coin. I could not step out of No. 24 to go to the Museum or the Alpha 'round the corner without being stopped in the street with questions about 'where are you going?' and 'do you need any help?' And I can assure you that my landlady, the grim Mrs. Holmes of distant relation and dubious memory, was not nearly as tolerant of these fellows as our dear Mrs. Hudson has come to be.

"It was at this point that I turned to young Wiggins to organize these Irregulars, as they came to be known in later years. Already, I had found that he was more intelligent than his fellows, and that often I could entrust him with the complicated tasks that I would not choose to delegate to his comrades. I could usually explain in much greater detail what it was that I

179

was looking for in any given matter, and he would grasp the object of the exercise and go forth with my complete confidence, usually returning with exactly what I needed to complete, or at least further, my case.

"I spoke to Wiggins about better organizing the group, so that he would be the leader, and more importantly, the principle person with whom I would have dealings, so that Montague Street would not be choked with street lads, waiting to catch a glimpse of me whenever I stepped out, rather like a school of South American *piranha* fish, hoping that some sluggish agrarian beast might wander into their river realm to be picked clean."

I laughed at Holmes's simile, picturing exactly what kind of agrarian beast that he would turn out to be, and reached for the makings of another sandwich. "So that was how you met the first Wiggins," I said. "But that in itself does not explain the family's fierce loyalty to you, or the fact that other Wiggins's over the years have taken Peter's place as the leaders of the group. Obviously, there must be more to the story."

"Obviously," said Holmes dryly, pushing back his plate with its half-eaten sandwich. "And it all relates to how Peter's widowed mother was saved from the gallows."

With that statement, he stood up. "Perhaps I am being overly dramatic. It was but the work of a day or so, and the gratitude of *famlias Wiggins* over the years has been far too exaggerated for the small effort that I made."

He stopped for a moment to gather his thoughts, and then moved to the fireplace, where he reached for a pipe. As he began to pack it with shag, he glanced at the clock and pronounced, "We have a little time before we must depart. You will accompany me, of course? Your name, after all, is also on the note."

"Certainly," I said, taking a bite of the second sandwich. "I had planned on it. Pray continue your tale."

Holmes sank into his chair, his back to one of the tall windows looking out onto Baker Street. I, having twisted myself around at the dining table to watch his progress across the room, turned back to face my plate while the story continued behind me.

"It was in August of 1879, just a few months before I would sail to America for a year with the Sassanoff Company, when Wiggins came to see me. I had no investigation taking place at that time, so I was mildly surprised that he would make such a dramatic appearance.

"He seemed quite agitated, very unlike his usual confident young self. I had only managed to get him seated in my small front room on the first floor, overlooking the street, when he bounded up and began to pace,

180

telling me that there was no time to talk, and that I needed to accompany him immediately, because his mother had just been arrested for murder.

"I must confess that up to that time, I had not really given the idea of Wiggins having a mother very much thought. Although I was not quite twenty-six years old at the time, I was still rather insular in my thinking, and had not devoted much concern to how any of the troops in my unofficial force made their way when they were not working for me. I had observed that Wiggins seemed to be better dressed and fed than the others, but I suppose I had ascribed that to the fact that his greater intelligence had simply found a way to live a more prosperous existence.

"I attempted to calm the boy. I again directed him to a seat and began to question him in an organized manner. He explained that he lived with his mother and brothers on the first floor of a small house on George Street, north of Euston.

"I know the place," I said. "I took Wiggins home in a cab once, years ago. Going north on Gower Street, we crossed Euston into George Street*, and it was in a small, drab house on the left side of the street.

Holmes nodded. "Wiggins's father had been dead for several years at that time, and his mother had found work as the cook and housekeeper in the home of an old widower several blocks away to the south. The fellow seemed to have no family, and had been quite accommodating regarding Mrs. Wiggins's need to only work during the daylight hours, in order to be home at night with her family.

"As I began to frame more questions, Wiggins sprang to his feet, having none of it. 'You can ask me on the way!' he cried. "I am sure the inspector is still there. Hurry, Mr. Holmes!'

"He fairly dragged me down the steps and into the street. Although he had indicated that I could question him as we went to the scene of the murder, it was obvious that I would not be able to do so, as he kept running ahead, and then stopping to make sure that I was following, rather as if he were a small dog on a long leash, out for a stroll with his master.

"We did not have far to go at all. Not long after starting north on Montague Street, we turned left into Montague Place, passing behind the Museum and so into Gower Street, where Wiggins dashed unheeding into the foot traffic there before veering right. I followed more carefully, until we had almost reached Keppel Street. There, on the eastern side of Gower Street, and almost at

* Editor's Note: *George Street*, the location of the Wiggins home, is now known as *North Gower Street*.

the corner, was our destination, as shown by the solid and unbreachable presence of a constable standing in front of the door.

"Perhaps you know those houses in that area, Watson. There is a certain sameness to that block, on the southeast corner of Gower and Keppel, all with their grim dark brick and lack of ornamentation. I had passed that way a number of times, but like so many buildings, they were simply part of the background, to be ignored as one goes from here to there."

I had my doubts whether anything was ever part of the background to be ignored for my friend Sherlock Holmes, but I held my tongue, lest I interrupt the flow of his narrative. Pushing back my plate and dropping my napkin, I made my way toward my chair.

"In those days," Holmes continued, "the London constabulary did not know me quite as well as they do now, and in any case, the individuals that did recognize me had no great affection for me. However, I was able to convince the constable that it would be advantageous for me to speak to the inspector in charge of the case, should he still be on the premises. After a long moment of ponderous consideration, the constable turned and went inside. There was a moderate crowd gathered outside the door of the house, as you will have seen at the presence of any London murder, and it spread beyond the width of the building in question, and past the houses on either side as well, all the way to Keppel Street on the north, one house away.

"With the temporary departure of the constable, the crowd behind me surged a step or two closer, pushing Wiggins and myself onto the small square stoop, only three or four inches higher than the adjacent pavement, and surrounded by sturdy iron bars over the area below. When the constable reappeared, he looked suspiciously at us, and glared at the restive assemblage pressing behind us. Then, he stepped aside to let the two of us in before planting himself firmly again, ready to defend the castle at all costs.

"I did not know whom or what to expect. Stepping inside, Wiggins and I followed the sound of voices upstairs, where, on the first floor, we found a small group of three men congregated in the back bedroom, two standing by the window in discussion while looking out over the mews behind the house, as the other was leaning over a still figure on the bed.

" 'Ah, Mr. Holmes," said a voice that I recognized. In some ways I felt fortunate, as I had worked with this man on quite a few previous occasions. However, I also knew that he was still resistant at times to my contributions to a case, and a part of me had hoped that I might find a different inspector in charge with whom I had had no previous dealings.

"The inspector, as you may have determined, was our old friend Lestrade. By that time, he and I had known each other at least five years. We had met not long after I first set up lodgings in Montague Street, but when these events were taking place he was only then starting to realize that I looked upon what I did as a profession, and not as a dilettante seeking distraction from some other less interesting portion of my life. And, as a matter of fact, I had been quite useful to him in the past, so I do not believe that he truly resented my appearance that day in Gower Street.

"As Lestrade spoke to me, his voice was neutral, but then he perceived that Wiggins stood behind me, unable to look away from the grim figure lying on the bed near the window. 'I told you to be gone, boy,' he began, before realization crossed his face, as he understood that I had been brought there by Wiggins.

" 'I see,' he continued gravely. 'The boy has asked you to save his mother from a charge of murder.'

" 'She didn't murder anyone!' cried Wiggins, moving from behind me and up to Lestrade, who was forced to take an awkward step back. The man who was leaning over the bed, obviously a left-handed police surgeon, Crimean veteran, and inveterate low-level laudanum addict, snickered to himself, and continued to make a cursory examination of the dead man. The third man, a stolid constable, made no comment whatsoever.

" 'Hear now,' said Lestrade, righting himself and placing a not unkind hand on the boy's shoulder. 'I'm afraid we can't change what's obvious. I'll be happy to discuss this with you, Mr. Holmes,' he said, turning toward me, 'but the boy must wait downstairs.'

"Wiggins started to protest, but with a glance and a wink from me he was given to understand that I would represent his interests in the matter, even in his absence. With a truculent expression on his face aimed toward Lestrade, he turned to go.

"After his departure, which was signaled by suspiciously heavy steps going down the stairs, I pushed the door partly shut, but not all the way closed. If I knew my Wiggins, he would be listening through the crack in the moment or two that it would take him to silently return up the stairs. Turning back toward Lestrade, I asked him to summarize the events that had led to the arrest of the boy's mother.

" 'The dead man,' he said, gesturing toward the figure on the bed, 'was a reclusive fellow named Silas Raines. Comfortably well off, and not in the best of health. No close family, no demands on his time away from this house.'

" 'And you have ascertained this how?'

" 'Some we learned from questioning the neighbors, and other information we gleaned from Mrs. Wiggins herself. Before she knew that she was under suspicion.'

" 'How was the body discovered?' I asked.

" 'By Mrs. Wiggins. Her story is that it was her duty to arrive here every morning, clean the house as necessary, and prepare the daily meals. She is a widow who lives not far away, up near Euston Station, with her children. The one that brought you, Peter, is the oldest. She indicated that Mr. Raines had no objection to her leaving in mid-afternoons, when she had completed the evening meals, which he would then eat later as the mood struck him.'

"At the bedside, the physician stood and backed away without comment. I took his place, taking several moments to examine the dead man. He had obviously had a weak heart, and the froth at his lips, combined with the sour unnatural odor emanating from his open mouth, made the cause of death all too obvious. The remains of a meal, spread out on both the bedside table and spilled across the man's sheets, further confirmed the conclusion.

"I looked at the doctor and said, 'Poison? A fast-acting alkaloid, perhaps?'

"The man nodded. His predilection for the soothing joys of the poppy did not diminish his medical abilities. 'Probably in the pudding, no doubt,' he replied, indicating the bowl and its half-eaten contents that had dropped onto the bedclothes beside the body, the remains of its contents smeared down the man's nightshirt.

" 'It seems obvious,' said Lestrade, 'that he was in the process of finishing his meal when the poison took effect. He was in poor health to begin with, so it would have been easy for him to be carried off."

" 'The process was accelerated,' interrupted the surgeon.

" 'Perhaps,' continued Lestrade, 'if he had not been elderly and alone, he might have been able to seek help as the symptoms overtook him. Instead, he died alone. I wonder if he realized who killed him.'

"The surgeon nodded. 'At his age, and in his condition, it would have been quick.'

"I must say, Watson, that I was not convinced the poison had been in the pudding. Perhaps it was in a portion of the meal that had been consumed before he started the pudding, and it took longer to take effect than the surgeon estimated. 'Was it usual for him to eat his dinner in bed?' I asked.

" 'According to Mrs. Wiggins, it was,' replied Lestrade. "She would arrive in the mornings, straighten up the house as needed, and usually retrieve the dinner dishes from the night before from this room. Mr. Raines did not like to eat breakfast, but he would eat a small luncheon in the dining room downstairs, looking out onto Gower Street, and then spend the rest of the day researching a book that he was writing. Something about the Lost Tribes or some such drivel. He had an arrangement with the British Library whereby they would send materials to him as needed, relieving him of the necessity of leaving the house.'

" 'And you say that he was comfortably well off, in order to be able to maintain such an arrangement?'

" 'It isn't confirmed yet, but the neighbors who knew him – and none of them knew him very well – indicated that he had made a fortune as a young man, traveling in the Canadian provinces, before returning to London ten or twelve years ago. His health was irretrievably shattered, and he was able to use his accumulated resources to set himself up here, writing his book. Often on warm evenings he would take a turn in the mews behind the house, which are shared commonly with the other houses on this side of the street. He was quite voluble in explaining where he had come from, and what he was currently doing.'

"I gestured toward the remains of the food. 'Will that be analyzed for poison?'

" 'Certainly,' replied Lestrade. 'Although knowing what type of poison it is won't change the fact that he was murdered.'

" 'Nevertheless,' I said, 'I wonder if I might take a sample as well, to perform my own analysis. As you know, I am a student of crime, and every lesson, no matter how small, is valuable to me.'

" 'Of course,' Lestrade agreed tolerantly. 'As long as you share your results with me,' he added. I removed a few of the small glass vials from my coat that I invariably carry with me, even in those early days, and began to retrieve samples of the food.

" 'What do you need that for?' asked the doctor as I placed the top on the vial containing the pudding, and began to take some of the scraps of meat from the plate on the bedside table. 'The poison is in the pudding.'

" 'Hypothesized, but not confirmed,' I replied. I was curious about the remains of the unusual sauce that seemed to be on top of the last of the meat. It was a dark color, and laced with a half-dozen small specks that appeared to be fragments of some type of seed. I made sure to leave an equal amount for the doctor, should he choose to examine it. Finally, for the sake of completeness rather than because I believed that it might be revealing, I placed three of the neglected peas into a vial of their own as well.

"Standing, I said, 'And Mrs. Wiggins found the body this morning, when she came up to retrieve the dishes?'

" 'That is what she says,' replied Lestrade. 'Her story is that she thought Mr. Raines had suffered from a fit during his evening meal. His contorted limbs, as well as the expression on his face and the matter expelled from his mouth, might seem to suggest such a thing. She ran to the neighbor's house for help, and they in turn summoned Constable Henry here.'

" 'And what was her demeanor when you arrived?' I asked the constable.

"He pondered for a moment, and then said, 'She were upset,' he finally said, gruffly.

" 'Unusually so?'

" 'No,' he replied. 'About what you might expect, I suppose. She were crying a bit.'

" 'A very natural reaction,' I said. Turning back to Lestrade, I said, 'So far, there is nothing that points to Mrs. Wiggins as the culprit behind this crime. What is there about any of this to make you specifically think that she is the murderer?'

"Lestrade appeared to become exasperated. 'Mr. Holmes, she was the cook, the food was poisoned, and she is the only other person that the man ever had in his house. According to the neighbors, it was no secret that Mrs. Wiggins had set her cap for Mr. Raines. The neighbors that we spoke to said that it was fairly obvious. In all likelihood, Raines had given her to understand that such a marital alliance was not going to happen, and she killed him because if it in a fit of female rage.'

"I thought that I heard a low growl through the cracked door, and spoke quickly to cover it. 'But why kill him then, Lestrade? That seems a little drastic, don't you think? If she *did* hope to marry him, that would be the way that she could gain access to his money. By killing him, she not only loses any future chance to win him over, but she also loses her comfortable position as well.'

" 'A woman spurned, and all that,' Lestrade replied with a rueful smile. 'They don't think rationally, they simply act. If you'd seen the same thing as this as often as I had, Mr. Holmes, you would have recognized it immediately for the situation that it is. And after all, poison *is* a woman's favored method.' Then his smiled broadened, as if I'd fallen into a trap. "There is one other piece of evidence.'

"I simply waited, until after a long awkward moment he reached into the pocket of his coat and withdrew his leather wallet. Opening it, he pulled out a scrap of paper, originally a quarto-sized sheet that was torn along one edge. He handed it to me, and I observed that it was a very cheap paper, with fibers still obviously visible in the texture. Written on it with a dull wide-leaded pencil were the words *Mrs. Wiggins did it*.

186

"I looked at it for another moment, attempting to determine any other fact of importance. There were one or two that I docketed away for further consideration before handing it back to Lestrade.

" 'Exactly where did you find it?' I asked.

" 'It was lying beside him on the bed, tucked down in the sheets where Mrs. Wiggins wouldn't have noticed it when she discovered him.' He folded it, and replaced it within his wallet. 'I think that you must agree, Mr. Holmes, that this fact, combined with the opportunity and possible motive, indicates that there really is no question about who murdered Mr. Raines.'

"I wanted to argue with him. I wanted to question why a supposedly rejected and irrational woman would take the time and trouble to find and use an alkaloid poison, rather than some other less subtle but more immediately satisfying emotional method, such as clubbing him with a poker or pushing him down the stairs. And as far as his assertion that poison was a woman's weapon, I had already investigated a number of cases in which poison was used by men as well as women. Besides all that, there was one fact that Lestrade was ignoring. However, all I said was, 'It still does not hang together,' to which Lestrade simply replied with a smug smile, similar to the many others that I had seen from him on a number of occasions, and would see again over the years.

"Without asking permission, I stepped to the bed and made a thorough examination of the bedclothes. Then, I extended my search to the floor underneath, and finished with the top and interior of the small bedside table. What I was looking for, what should have been there, was not. And Lestrade had missed it.

"I glanced around the room. 'Have you examined his private papers?'

" 'I have,' he said, misunderstanding me. He pulled a folded sheaf of papers out of his pocket. 'These were on the dead man's desk downstairs, in his study. They are a representative sample of his handwriting. And before you can point it out to me, Mr. Holmes,' he added, 'even I can see that these examples of his fist do not exactly match that which is on the note identifying Mrs. Wiggins as the murderer. However, the man was dying, and it cannot be expected that he would exhibit perfect penmanship under those circumstances.'

"I glanced at the papers, and saw that he was right: The writing did not match. I had to agree with him that under the circumstances that was not unusual. However, that was not why I had asked about his papers.

" 'Does the man have an heir?' I asked.

" 'Not that we could determine, although we have not made a complete examination of his personal effects. All of that type of material

187

appears to be in his study downstairs,' said Lestrade. 'If you would care to follow me.'

"I perceived a faint scrambling sound outside the bedroom door, as if someone had been caught surprised by our intention to leave the room and was quickly creeping down the stairs. Lestrade did not seem to hear it, and when he pulled the door open, the landing outside the bedroom was empty. He led me downstairs, leaving the doctor and the constable with the unfortunate deceased.

"We found Wiggins innocently leaning against the front door frame. Lestrade looked at him and said, in a rather sour tone, 'Could you hear everything all right?' Then he turned toward the back of the house, leading us behind the stairs and into a small study, piled with papers and teetering stacks of books. The room was dim, and had a musty smell to it. Heavy drapes were closed behind the desk, and I stepped around the inspector and pulled them open. It appeared that Mr. Raines had preferred to do his work in near darkness. The disturbed dust set us all to coughing, including Wiggins, who had followed us and was standing in the doorway to the hall.

"I sat down behind the desk and began quickly sorting through the papers. Lestrade watched for a moment, and then, seemingly becoming impatient, said, 'Let me know if you find something useful.' Then he turned and departed the room.

"Taking advantage of the opportunity, I quickly said to Wiggins, 'Do not become angry because I ask, but did your mother truly have any hopes of marrying Mr. Raines? Be honest now. Remember that I need the truth.'

"He seemed reluctant to answer for a moment, and then said, 'She might have. She talked several times about what a nice man he was, and so easy to take care of. But there's no way a man like that would want to take on a family like ours, now is there?'

"I nodded, and thought how perceptive the young man was. I could see just from examining the various piles of handwritten papers on the desk that this fellow had been lost to his own interests, and the idea of tearing himself from that world and becoming a father to a brood of Wiggins chicks would have horrified him. He would not have traded his work to become the husband of his housekeeper. Wiggins had unknowingly confirmed a fragment of Lestrade's theory, as had my own small observations.

"I examined the rest of the victim's papers, finding very little of relevance. He had a bank book for the Oxford Street branch of his bank, showing a substantial sum indeed, but no other meaningful financial documents, if one did not count those relating to the usual household accounts, the baker, the butcher, and so on.

"I did find one small packet of old letters, resting on top of a pile of documents in one of the drawers and tied with a blue ribbon. The ribbon had recently been retied, as evidenced by the new knot in an unmarked section. The letters were all short, never more than a page or two each, and addressed to Raines. Dated from nearly thirty years before, they were written by a barely educated girl named Abigail Tremblay, replying to letters from Raines, and answering his romantic questions in the affirmative.

"While I was reading through the letters and the other material, Wiggins sat quietly in a chair on the other side of the desk. At one point I was aware of the sounds of men entering the house through the front door and going upstairs, only to return a few minutes later, moving much more slowly and carefully. The body was being removed. Soon after, Lestrade returned to the study.

" 'Did you find anything? A will, perhaps?' He glanced at the boy, who scowled back in return. 'Anything that mentions the housekeeper?'

"I shook my head, and held up the packet of letters. 'There is nothing romantically inclined here whatsoever, except for these ill-written and awkward love letters from the last generation, addressed to our Mr. Raines when he was younger and living in Canada. However, they are mere flirtations and promises to wait for him, and there is no conclusion to the unfinished tale of whether he ever went back and found his princess.'

"Lestrade snorted, and indicated that if there was nothing else, he was going to lock up the house and leave it under the care of a constable. As he shepherded us toward the front door, he suddenly stopped and laid a hand on Wiggins's shoulder. 'I am sorry about your mother, lad,' he said. 'I would change things if I could.'

"I could see that Wiggins was tempted to toss his shoulder and throw the hand from him, but instead he bore it, though it must have burned him to do so, and said, 'You're wrong. She didn't murder anyone. You'll see.'

"Lestrade simply shook his head sorrowfully and led us out onto the pavement. The crowds had thinned following the removal of the corpse, but there were still a number of busybodies, standing in clumps and clusters, whispering their ignorant theories to one another and pointing toward us. I distinctly recall one of them pointing a sausage-like finger directly at me and whispering to his neighbor, 'I think that skinny one there did it.'

"After Lestrade departed with a reminder to let him know if I discovered anything of relevance, Wiggins and I spent the next hour or so knocking up the different neighbors in that part of the street, all of whom shared the common mews with the deceased's house. None seemed to question either my right to ask questions, or the fact that I was being

189

accompanied by a young street Arab, even one that was better dressed and behaved than most that roamed the area.

"Each neighbor essentially provided the same information. Raines had been a relatively quiet – but not unfriendly – man who had moved into that street nearly fifteen years before. He had employed a series of housekeepers over the years, with Mrs. Wiggins being the one with the longest tenure. The neighbors knew her from occasional conversations in passing. I asked each neighbor about a possible romantic association between her and Raines, although I was reluctant to do so, as Wiggins was always by my side during these interviews. However, in each case, the neighbors, who did not realize that my companion was the accused woman's son, had no hesitation in answering the questions. They all agreed that there had never been any sign of either romance or impropriety between the employer and Mrs. Wiggins. However, the fact that the poor woman had been arrested seemed to incline them to quickly accept the notion that something must have been going on that had remained undetected.

"Only one neighbor was able to offer any additional information. Mr. Howett, who lived in the corner house situated between the victim's residence and Keppel Street, had noticed that Raines had an occasional visitor during recent weeks. 'I often step out my back door in the evening, especially this time of year, to have a smoke. Don't like to do it in the house, you know. The smell gets in the draperies.'

" 'Starting about a month ago, I noticed on three or four occasions that Raines, who would often take a turn about the mews of a summer evening, was at the back gate, letting in a fellow. They would then sit on that bench over there, where the mews opens into Keppel Street, and talk for fifteen or twenty minutes. Then Raines would let him back out and shut the gate before going inside.

" 'Sometimes I would still be standing here when Raines would return to his own door, and we would speak. But he never elaborated on who his visitor was, and the young man never joined him in the house that I knew of.'

"Answering my next question, Howett said, 'No, no signs of any arguments between them. They would simply talk. Mr. Raines was never in a bad mood after his visitor left, but never in a particularly good one, either.'

"Upon further questioning, Howett said, 'Did I mention that he was a young man? I meant to. I guess that he was. Looked to be in his late twenties, or possibly a little older. Strongly built, dark hair, common clothing. That's really all that I could say about him. I never heard them speak, they kept their voices low. I don't know if they knew that I was out here, but more likely they just didn't want to disturb the peace of the evening or be heard from the street behind them, over the wall."

"Howett confirmed that these visits would always take place near twilight, long after Mrs. Wiggins had departed for the day. And that information about Raines's mysterious visitor, received from his one observant neighbor, was the last data that I received at the Gower Street location.

"The constable keeping the house told me where Mrs. Wiggins was being held, and Wiggins and I set off at a brisk pace. In those days, shekels weren't as plentiful as they are now, and hiring a hansom was a luxury that was not really a consideration.

"Mrs. Wiggins was still being held at the Bow Street station, where I managed to convince Wiggins that he would not be able to accompany me while I questioned his mother. Leaving him in a hard and uncomfortable chair, I was led back to a room where I could meet with the prisoner.

"She was a small woman, careworn and upset, and she had not yet been placed into prisoner's clothing. She knew who I was, and immediately thanked me for the opportunities that I had given to her son, and also for taking an interest in her own problem. I knew that we would not have long to talk, and brushed aside her thanks, anxious to discuss more relevant matters.

" 'The police,' I began, 'believe that you killed Mr. Raines because you wished to marry him and he rejected the idea.'

"I expected an emotional denial, but instead she gave a reasoned nod. 'I know it,' she said. 'And I must admit that the idea had passed through my mind once or twice. And why not? I certainly didn't love the man, but he was kind in his own way, and seemed to be quite well off for someone so alone. I'm a mother, Mr. Holmes, with a great number of mouths to feed. I can't be there for them all the time, and I know that as they get older, they will try to run wild. And they might not all be as lucky as Peter, finding work with you as he has.'

" 'But I realized a long time ago that a man like Mr. Raines would not be a good father to my children. He was so wrapped up with that book he thought that he was writing, and I knew that I was much better off staying on as his housekeeper, instead of taking a chance that it would all be ruined if I chased him to make him a husband.'

" 'You state that he *thought* he was writing a book. Do you mean that he was actually doing something else?'

" 'No,' she said. 'He really believed that he was working on something important. But he'd been at it since I went to work for him, and he never made any progress that I could tell. He would have books sent from the Library, and he'd start in on them as if he had received candy at

191

Christmas. He would make notes, and talk to himself, and send for more books, often the same ones that he had borrowed only a few weeks before. But I never, in all the time that I was there, actually saw him make a start on writing a single thing.'

"This fit with my own observations of the scattered and unorganized notes on the man's desk. I wondered if he would have ever reached the point where he considered his researches complete, and felt that he was ready to begin his opus, or if he would have happily played with his notes for the rest of his life, moving them from old pile to new pile, without accomplishing anything. As it turned out, no doubt to Mr. Raines's most sincere surprise, it was the latter.

" 'If I may change the subject,' I uttered, 'It is obvious to both the police and to me that the man was poisoned by way of last night's dinner, although we may have some minor disagreements as to specific details. The man had no visitors in his house that we can discover, and you were his cook. How do you explain the fact that the poison was most likely introduced into his food?'

" 'I cannot,' she said. 'Yesterday was no different than a thousand other days. I cooked his noon meal, and he ate it as usual in the dining room. Then, it being a Wednesday, I went marketing in the early afternoon, before returning to prepare the evening meal. It was a piece of beef, peas, and a little pudding. Mr. Raines liked things simple, and he was never any trouble. After the food was cooked, I set it on a plate, told Mr. Raines that it was ready, and departed like I did every day.'

" 'I didn't know that anything was amiss until I returned this morning. I entered the house and went upstairs to retrieve the dinner dishes and make up the bedroom. I believed that Mr. Raines was already in his study, as he usually was at that time of the morning. Many was the time that I did not see him until his luncheon was ready. At that point, I would summon him from his work to the dining room. Then, while he ate, he would often like me to stay with him while he chattered about the progress that he thought he was making on his book. After the meal was over, he would return to the study, and I to the kitchen.'

"I thought for a moment, and then something that she had said prompted a question. 'You said that Mr. Raines liked his food simple.'

" 'Oh yes. He was never interested in anything fancy, which worked out well, since I only know how to prepare good, plain food.'

" 'And yet,' I said, 'I noticed that there was some form of sauce on the remains of the beef.'

"She appeared to be genuinely puzzled. 'Sauce?' she asked. 'Not from me, there wasn't. I never made a thing like that, the whole time that I was there. Just the beef."

" 'And you never purchased or prepared anything like that?' I asked.

" 'Never," she stated, emphatically.

"She did not realize that she had provided me with a thin thread. A few other questions gave me to understand that she had nothing else useful to offer. 'It's not my own reputation that I'm worried about,' she said. 'I know that nothing improper ever happened between myself and Mr. Raines. But I need to get back to caring for my boys. Please help me.'

"I assured her that I would do everything possible, both to earn her freedom and restore any stain on her reputation. And then I left her there as she stood to watch me go. The last glimpse that I had of her was when she was being warded deeper into the building by a grim matron.

"Outside, I offered Wiggins the chance to carry on with his own activities, but he made it quite clear that his path was with mine. And mine was to Barts, where I wanted to carry out my own analysis of the food samples from Mr. Raines's last meal. For it takes no great feat of deduction to realize that I had concluded there was something about the sauce that seemed questionable. I disagreed with Lestrade when he asserted that it did not matter what type of poison it was. And in this case, it seemed that discovering whether the poison was actually in the pudding or the sauce might be an important factor in catching the true murderer. I had no doubt that the police would determine as easily as I would wherein the poison had been hidden, but I had no confidence that they would be able to do so anytime quickly, or be able to do anything with the fact once it was established.

"In those days, as you know, I had that curious arrangement with Barts wherein I was able to come and go as I wished, making use of the laboratories as needed, and attending those lectures which I thought might be useful to advancing my unusual education. All of this was due to the gratitude of a certain Mr. Blevins, whom you may recall, after the slight service for him which resulted in his son's fortunate and timely escape to America.

"Finding the laboratory free, I was able to begin my analysis immediately. It is one of my foibles that I tend to lose track of time when involved in a chemical question, and therefore it was approaching mid-afternoon when I had settled to my own satisfaction the issues at hand. I glanced up to find that Wiggins had fallen asleep on the floor, his back against one of the walls. I was fearful that I would require another trip to interview the boy's mother, but fortunately he knew the answer to my question, having accompanied her on several occasions when she did the marketing for Mr. Raines.

"I had expected that we would have to travel a fair distance, but I should have realized that Mrs. Wiggins would do her marketing close to home. We found the shop in question in a busy portion of the Tottenham Court Road. After receiving Wiggins's assurance that he would remain outside, unseen, I went in. Fortunately, it was quite crowded, and I was allowed to wait my turn for several minutes, while other customers before me took care of their business and I made a number of observations.

"By the time the way was clear for me, I had learned all that I needed, and could have departed. However, in order to see things through completely, I stepped to the counter and engaged a certain fellow in conversation, asking his advice and pretending an interest in his answers. After doing so, I was glad indeed, because I saw behind the counter, an additional item that helped me to seal the guilty person's fate.

"Departing the shop with my purchases, I considered throwing some of it away as unwanted, especially as I now had the evidence that I needed. However, I realized that I would have to spend some time considering what I had learned, and would be best served doing so in my own rooms in Montague Street. Wiggins and I returned there, and I gave the unwanted purchase to the landlady, asking her to prepare it for our early dinner. Then we went upstairs, where Wiggins entertained himself with the particularly gruesome and graphic illustrations in one of my anatomy texts, while I sat by the window, smoking, and trying to think of the best way to trap the killer.

"For I knew now who he was, and I could theorize why he had committed the murder, but there were still a great number of gaps in the narrative. And I was not sure how to snare him into an admission of guilt that would subsequently free Mrs. Wiggins.

"An hour or so later, I knew what I had to do. I realized that poor Mrs. Wiggins might have to spend a night behind bars.

"I had written the necessary note and given it to Wiggins, along with his instructions, when the landlady brought up the item that I had purchased, now cooked in her plain way. I could see that Wiggins wished to be gone, but I knew that, in his urgency to aid his imprisoned mother, he might not eat at any time in the foreseeable future. I insisted that he put off his errand for a few minutes and consume the food. As I had no appetite at that point, I did not join him. After Wiggins finished, surprising himself with how hungry he had turned out to be, I sent him on his way. I was quite anxious to see if my deductions were correct. In any case, I had to speak to Lestrade as soon as possible, and I realized that if I could not, my plan would fall apart."

With that, Holmes turned his head toward the clock, and then stood abruptly. "And I see that the time has slipped away from me," he said. "We must prepare for departure."

194

"You should have been a storyteller," I said with a laugh, as Holmes walked toward his room, shedding his dressing gown as he went. "You knew just where to stop to increase your audience's dramatic interest."

"The next chapter," he called, "will be told in a cab, heading toward the Wiggins's home."

"Shall I summon a hansom?"

"It has already been arranged," he replied cryptically.

Part III: The Inspector Joins Us

We stepped outside to find a four-wheeler waiting by the curb. Inside, to my great surprise, was our old friend, Inspector Lestrade.

"Didn't expect to see me, did you, doctor?" he asked with a grin. Then his mirth faded as he seemed to recall our destination. He was dressed in black, and it took no great deductive feat to realize that he, too, was going to the Wiggins's home. My only question was why? I had never noticed any great feeling between Lestrade and any of the Wiggins clan that had been around Baker Street, one way or another, for over twenty years.

We took our seats, and the cab moved away at a stately pace. No instructions were given to the driver as to our destination, and I therefore concluded that Lestrade had already indicated our route before we had joined him. Looking at both my friends in their dark clothing made me wish that I had been able to return home and change as well.

We turned from Baker Street into Marylebone Road, heading east. The streets were quite crowded, thronging with a warm London afternoon multitude, and our progress was slow. I glanced away from the teeming humanity in the streets toward Holmes, who smiled and seemed to read my thoughts.

"I believe that we have a few minutes before reaching our landing place. During that time, Lestrade, you may be willing to add a fresh perspective. I have been recounting for Watson the events of Mrs. Wiggins's arrest, so long ago."

"Twenty-three years ago," said Lestrade. "I was thinking of it myself, earlier today."

"We had reached the point," said Holmes, "where I had approached you and asked if would throw in with my scheme."

Lestrade shook his head. "I didn't know you so well, then, Mr. Holmes," he said. "Doctor, what he wanted seemed ludicrous at best."

"And that was – ?" I prodded.

"To set a trap for the real murderer." He adjusted himself in his seat, turning slightly to face me.

"And who was the murderer?" I asked.

"All in good time, Watson," interrupted Holmes. "He needs to be sewn into the pattern of the story, one stitch at a time. I had to do the same thing then. And I needed to convince Lestrade that I had identified the true killer."

"I didn't want to believe you," added Lestrade. "When young Wiggins brought me your note, Mr. Holmes, I must admit that I was not inclined whatsoever to meet you back at the victim's house. But even then," he said, "you had already been of some help to me in the past."

"Once or twice," murmured Holmes.

Lestrade nodded with a smile. "Once or twice. I owed you some consideration, at the very least. So off I went. When I arrived, doctor, I was led by Mr. Holmes straight through the house and out into the mews, where we sat on a bench, and he explained his theory."

"The same bench," said Holmes, "where Raines had reportedly met with his evening visitor."

"First," continued Lestrade, "Mr. Holmes told me of the results of his research, earlier that day at Barts. Would you believe that the poison was from a lowly cocklebur?"

"Pardon me?" I said. "A cocklebur? Are you referring to the Xanthium plant?"

"Very good, Watson," said Holmes. "Native to North America, and invasive in many other regions as well."

"As I recall from the time I spent in San Francisco, the cocklebur produces symptoms of weakness, vomiting, rapid heart rate with a weak pulse, breathing difficulties, and eventually death."

"Correct," said Holmes. "The entire plant is poisonous, but the seeds are the most toxic part. The particular species of seeds in this instance were quite small, not much different from a fennel seed, and would not have seemed completely out of place in a sauce, especially if the victim were trying something new and unusual, or possibly sampling a reminder of his youth in Canada, and did not know that the sauce was not supposed to have that type of seed in it."

"I take it, then, that the seeds were the poisonous substance present in the unexplained meat sauce, and not in the pudding, as was hypothesized by the police surgeon."

"I fear that you have been around me for too long, my friend. I cannot surprise you any longer. It was indeed the small seed that I had observed in the sauce, of which I took half and left the rest for the police to analyze. My research confirmed that it was a small example of the cocklebur seed."

"I would like to mention," said Lestrade, "that the surgeon also confirmed that the seed was a cocklebur, although it did take him another day or so, by which point the murderer was already in custody."

"So," I said, "a North American seed, and Raines had spent his youth in North America. There was a connection?"

"Quite," said Holmes. "After I had identified the poison, and its probable location of origin, I devised at least seven separate theories which might explain how it ended up in Raines's last meal, always going on the assumption that Mrs. Wiggins was innocent of the crime. As you recall, she had professed to have no knowledge of the sauce, and I went forward from that point. I did not find any indication of the sauce elsewhere in the house. There was not a jar of it in the pantry. In fact, there was not a jar of that type anywhere in the house, or, I might add, in the rubbish. And there was one other clue at the scene that seemed to point to where the sauce might have originated."

"And I missed it," said Lestrade with a rueful grin. With a nod from Holmes, he continued. "I was so interested in the note found by the body, stating that 'Mrs. Wiggins did it', that I neglected to notice that there was no pencil in the bedroom that Raines could have used in order to write the note." He shrugged. "It didn't occur to me that if Raines had been forced to arise and find a pencil in order to write the note, he could have sought help as well. It isn't reasonable to suppose that, upon discovering there was no pencil in the room in which he was expiring, he would go downstairs to find a pencil, write a note naming his killer, leave the pencil where he found it, and then return upstairs – carrying the note – and crawl back into bed to die alone."

"And not only that," said Holmes. "I recognized that the broad soft-leaded strokes comprising the message were unique, and were usually found associated with certain kinds of pencils that are only used in a few professions, one of which was that of butcher. You will have noticed, Watson, butchers using that type of pencil to write on the paper that wraps cuts of meat at the time of purchase. This, coupled with the fact that an unusual sauce was found with the remains of the meat, indicated that I should visit the butcher used by Mrs. Wiggins when shopping for Mr. Raines.

"Upon locating the shop with Wiggins's assistance, I had stood behind several customers while waiting for them to be served. It gave me a chance to observe all of the employees, and particularly the butcher's assistant. He was a young man, in his early thirties, with a marked Canadian accent. Thus, another tie to Raines's past. When it was my turn to receive assistance, I made an excuse to discuss cuts of meat with the

197

man in question before making my purchase, which was the very same piece of beef that I took home and had served to young Wiggins."

"You neglected to mention that you had specifically purchased meat," I said. "Perhaps if that bit of information had been revealed too early, your story might have been less of an interesting tale, possibly too tinged with romanticism, and more like the Fifth Proposition of Euclid."

"I bow to your knowledge and experience as a writer," said Holmes, "without confirming or denying anything. But to continue with my story . . . .

"As I started to leave the shop, I saw for sale, on a shelf behind the counter, several small jars of a reddish sauce. Asking what it was, I was informed by the Canadian gentleman that it was a recipe that he had brought with him from across the sea when he came to England a few months earlier. The preparation was to be placed on meat, providing a New World alternative to horseradish. His employer had allowed him to mix it up in batches and sell it in the shop to their more adventurous patrons. I myself bought a jar, and later found that it matched the color and consistency of the sauce on Raines's plate. But without the cocklebur seeds, I might add.

"Although it seemed certain that this was the man that I was looking for, what was not certain was the exact motive for killing Raines. Possibly it was a revenge killing, for some long-ago crime committed by Raines against the young Canadian's people. Perhaps there was some other motive that I was not even considering. However, in my opinion, the greatest probability was that he had a personal relation to Raines, and it was upon that basis that I decided to proceed."

We were passing Park Crescent, and I knew that in just a few minutes we would arrive at our destination, assuming that the Wiggins family still lived in the same home as before. I quickly reviewed Holmes's reasoning, and could see that, although he had made a few leaps, it generally held together.

"But," I asked, "where was your proof? How could you find a way to connect him to the crime? The meat sauce and the butcher's pencil led you to him, certainly, but those facts alone would not be conclusive. He could simply claim that the pencil might have come from anywhere, and that Mrs. Wiggins had bought the sauce from him at the butcher shop, and added the poisonous seeds to it herself at some later date."

"Yes, that was a problem," said Holmes. "And that was why friend Lestrade was asked, that evening in the mews, to take a leap of faith and go along with my plan."

Lestrade shook his head. "Mr. Holmes had never led me astray, but it was asking a lot at the time, and I was not so senior or secure in my position myself then, either. It was something of a professional risk, but he had convinced me."

I turned my head, indicating that he should continue. After a silent moment, and with a glance toward Holmes to see if he wished to take over, Lestrade spoke.

"As we sat on the bench, and I heard the results of Mr. Holmes's investigations, my first inclination was to make excuses. We've all known each other far too long for me to pretend otherwise now. I had missed the clue about the pencil, but I didn't want to give up my suspicions of Mrs. Wiggins. Then there was the writing on the note in Raines's bed, which matched that on the butcher's wrapping paper Mr. Holmes had obtained earlier in the day. Then the evidence of the sauce and the seeds, tied to the Canadian at the butcher shop, was compelling. But when the list of facts concluded with Mr. Holmes telling me the man's name, which he had inveigled out of him during their conversation, I could no longer deny that he was likely on the right track."

"Ah," I said. "The confirmatory fact."

"The confirmatory fact," said Holmes.

"This Canadian?" I asked. "Would it be revealing too much at this point in your story to now ask his name? Was it perhaps Raines, the same as that of the dead man?"

"Now the fellow is stitched into the pattern, Watson," said Holmes. "You see the way that this path is leading. Should I ever attempt to write up any of my investigations, as you have so often urged me, I will need to do better at hiding the clues. But," he added, "in spite of the fact that the Canadian man did indeed turn out to be Silas Raines's illegitimate son, his name was actually Martin Tremblay, the same last name as that of the girl, Abigail Tremblay, who had sent the small packet of letters that I had found in Raines's study."

"Too many connections to ignore," interrupted Lestrade.

"At the conclusion of our conversation in the shop," continued Holmes, "after I had obtained opinions about cuts of meat and his sauce recipe, I inquired after his name, with many thanks and a promise that I would be back in the future." He smiled as he recalled it, that dangerous smile that has boded ill for so many over the years. "I'm sure he believed at the time that I would be returning as a customer."

"The meat sauce and even the pencil might have been explained away, or blamed on Mrs. Wiggins," said Lestrade. "By itself, the fact that Tremblay was living and working so near to Raines was not damning, since he had ties to the old man, and had in fact visited him in what was observed to be a friendly way. But the poisoned sauce and the old connections together became too significant to ignore."

I nodded. "It all becomes clearer now. The son, abandoned by his father at some early age, tracks him down in England and travels here with murder in his heart, either due to motives of revenge, or perhaps intending to claim an inheritance. But you did not know any of this for sure at that time. You did not know that Raines was the man's father. All you knew was that the sauce with the poisonous seeds had come from the butcher shop, where it had likely been prepared by Tremblay."

"But I was proceeding from the assumption that Mrs. Wiggins was innocent," said Holmes. "Therefore, someone else had to be guilty. Tremblay had been seen visiting Raines on a regular basis, and the poisonous seeds found in his sauce were from North America. Of the various theories that I had constructed, the family relationship seemed most likely, and it was enough to be going on with. And it was also enough to enlist the participation of our friend here."

"First," said Lestrade, "The fact that the man's unusual name, Tremblay, was mentioned prominently in the package of letters was quite convincing. I cabled the Canadian authorities and queried them regarding this butcher's assistant. And then – "

He stopped and looked down at his hands, shaking his head. "I still don't believe that you talked me into it. We just did not do things like that in those days."

"You always were the best of the Yarders," said Holmes quietly. Lestrade looked up quickly. He gazed intently at Holmes, and then swallowed. "Thank you, Mr. Holmes," he said after a moment. Then, clearing his throat, he said more clearly, "Thank you very much for that. It means a lot."

We did not speak for a moment, each lost in our thoughts. Finally, as the cab rattled across Tottenham Court Road, I was moved to state, "Gentlemen? How *did* you catch him?"

Holmes straightened in his seat and said, "I'm afraid Watson, that the explanation must wait a little longer, as we are rapidly approaching our destination, and have still more history than journey left. Perhaps, Lestrade, you would care to join us afterwards, as we raise a glass to Mrs. Wiggins, and recount the trapping of Martin Tremblay in the Keppel Street Mews?"

Part IV: We Pay Our Respects

Lestrade readily agreed to Holmes's proposal, and we spoke no more of the matter then. However, my thoughts continued to dwell on that long-ago case, when these two men had worked together to prove Mrs.

200

Wiggins's innocence. I doubt whether Holmes could have imagined that saving the woman would have led to so many years of devoted service by the various members of the Wiggins family. It had probably been no more than another problem to him, as so many others had been throughout his career. And yet, even as that thought passed across my mind, I remembered all the times that his great heart, which he labored to hide behind that cold and logical veneer, had been moved to action when someone in trouble had needed his help.

The cab swayed as we turned out of the bustle and energy of Euston Road and north into the relative quiet of George Street*. It was only a moment until we stopped before a narrow brick building on our left. As we alighted, Holmes dismissed the cab, tossing a coin to the driver.

---

* Editor's Note: Again, this is now known as *North Gower Street*.

"Many thanks, Mr. Holmes," said the driver, a bluff fellow named Giles who would have died on the gallows in '97 for a murder he didn't commit, if not for the timely intervention of Holmes, who had produced a plaster-of-Paris cast of a *third* left footprint, found at the scene of the brutal crime.

There were several men standing near the door of the house, smoking in grim silence. As we approached, I recognized all of them as Wiggins's that I had known over the years. There was Michael, now a shopkeeper, and young Henry, who had been instrumental in the successful resolution of the incident at Colwyn Bay, and some of the others. I nodded to Warren, now recently returned from the Navy.

There were a half-dozen of them all told, and I knew that they were not all Peter Wiggins's brothers. Rather, there were some cousins of the first and second order mixed in, and to a man, they all pulled themselves a little taller and straighter as Holmes approached them. Holmes nodded as we passed amongst them to reach the door. One said, respectfully, "Mr. Holmes," and reached by him to turn the doorknob.

We stepped inside the dark interior and removed our hats, which we hung on pegs. Removing and hanging our coats as well, we started up the stairs. I was aware that the men who had been loitering outside were following us in.

As we turned at the first floor landing, I could see the large front room overlooking the street. The shades were drawn, and the room was in shadow. Underneath the windows was a coffin, supported by a bier. A number of people were sitting in the dark places around the perimeter of the room.

I identified some of the other faces seated around us. There was Joseph Wiggins, who had led the lads during the search for Mordecai Smith's boat along the Thames back in '88. And there was Sally Peake, *nee* Wiggins, who had been of such vital assistance during the affair of the kidnapped costermonger's daughter. She had been so fearless on that cold night, when she took it upon herself to disobey Holmes's instructions and cut the tarred rope around the frightened child instead of just locating her, while the killers argued with increasing ferocity in the adjacent room. It was hard to believe that this girl, who had shielded the kidnapped child when the shooting began, was the same person, a woman now, singing softly to the tiny baby held in her arms.

There had been the low buzz of conversation as we came in, but it stopped, replaced by the sound of every man and woman in the room rising to their feet to acknowledge the presence of Sherlock Holmes.

Holmes seemed unaware of the great respect directed toward him. He glanced around the darkened room until his eyes rested on Peter Wiggins, my companion this morning in the doorway in Half Moon Street.

Peter took a step forward, saying, "Thank you for coming, Mr. Holmes. I know that your being here would have meant a lot to my mother." He looked toward Lestrade and me as well. "Thank you."

We nodded, and Peter led us to the coffin, where we stood for a moment in silent contemplation. Mrs. Wiggins had been a tiny woman, even before the age-related wasting illness that had eventually claimed her. Her white hair was combed neatly, straight back from her forehead, and her gnarled and veined hands, reflecting a lifetime of hard work, were folded peacefully.

"If you hadn't saved her that day," said Peter, "her life would have turned out much differently. It would have for all of us."

"That's right," said one of the shadowy figures behind us gruffly. Whoever had spoken cleared his throat, but spoke no more. I believed that it was Albert Wiggins, formerly one of Holmes's bravest irregulars, and now a constable on the Surrey Side.

"She never forgot what you did for us," said Peter. "We always toast you at Christmas, Mr. Holmes."

"She was innocent," replied Holmes simply. "I would have done the same for anyone."

"But it was more than that," said Peter, taking a step forward, closer to the coffin, so that he might face Holmes directly. "After you obtained her release, and discovered the real murderer, you found her new employment at Cambridge House. And I cannot even begin to tell you what opportunities you have provided for me, and my brothers and sisters, and my cousins as well. You gave us an income, and more importantly, a purpose, and respect, and when we outgrew our usefulness as Irregulars, you found us professions. Truly, and speaking for my mother in her presence here today, as well as all the rest of us, we thank you."

Behind us, Simon Wiggins, formerly trained by Holmes in the art of pickpocketing, and now a newly ordained minister, said softly, "Amen."

Another voice, one that I did not recognize, muttered, "Hear, hear!" and several others repeated it. I was moved to notice that one of those voices belonged to Lestrade.

Holmes lowered his head for a moment, and then raised it to face Peter Wiggins. And then he turned to the others as well. I wondered what he would say. It had only been a couple of years before that Holmes had been deeply moved after receiving praise from Lestrade, following the masterful recovery of the stolen Borgia Pearl. "We're not jealous of you at Scotland Yard," Lestrade had said then. "No, sir, we are very proud of you, and if you come down tomorrow, there's not a man, from the oldest inspector to the youngest constable, who wouldn't be glad to shake you by the hand."

Holmes had awkwardly thanked him that day, and had then abruptly changed the subject, dismissing Lestrade by requesting that I search his files for a case that had already been completed. Lestrade had understood Holmes's difficulty, and had left with no hard feelings.

And now Holmes was facing a room full of men and women who thought the world of him, in the presence of their departed mother. Would he say something abrupt or awkward? If he did, it would not surprise or offend these people who had known him for so long in so many different circumstances, and it would not diminish their feelings for him in the least.

But Holmes simply said, "Thank you," in a quiet and sincere voice. And, after laying a hand on Peter Wiggins's shoulder, he said, "I am very sorry for your loss." Then, nodding to several of the standing figures around him, he turned to go.

The occupants of the room remained standing as we made our way back to the head of the stairs, and so on down. After retrieving our coats, we found ourselves in the street, and I wondered to myself why we had dismissed our cab, if our intention was to leave so soon after our arrival. My unspoken question was soon answered.

"We are not too far from the Alpha Inn, at the Museum," said Holmes. "Shall we stroll down that way and have some refreshments, and finish telling the rest of our tale?"

Lestrade and I agreed immediately. Some of the Wiggins men had followed us downstairs and had resumed their places by the doorway. Peter was standing with us nearer the edge of the sidewalk, and he nodded as well, realizing that Holmes's invitation had also included him. He

203

turned and spoke to his brothers and cousins for a moment, informing them that he would be back in an hour or so, before the funeral, and then joined us as we began walking to the south.

As we waited to cross Euston Road and on into Gower Street, Holmes told Peter the subject of our earlier discussions, as he and Lestrade had related to me the events of his mother's arrest, years earlier. "We had reached the point in the narrative where I was convincing Lestrade to help trap Martin Tremblay. My plan was to use his greed, plus the surprise of learning that someone knew about his connection to Raines, to trick him into revealing what had happened."

"You make it sound so simple," muttered Lestrade.

"It was," interjected Wiggins. "You see, doctor, Mr. Holmes simply made Tremblay believe that Silas Raines had another son who was set to inherit, possibly ruining all of Tremblay's plans."

"And this other son was . . . ?"

"Why, it was Mr. Holmes, of course."

Part V: The Trap

We walked for several blocks down Gower Street, with Holmes setting a pace that did not encourage conversation. After a very few minutes, we crossed Keppel Street, and he abruptly pulled up in front of the second house on the left, south of the intersection.

"There it is, Watson," he said. "That is the house where Silas Raines was killed."

It was a plain-looking place, with dark-colored bricks and a door set in the right side of the building, under a simple fan light. It was three stories tall, and there was an area-way leading down beneath the walk. The stoop was only a few inches high, and I could almost see Holmes and young Wiggins as they approached it, those many years ago, identifying themselves to the constable before being admitted, where Lestrade waited inside with the body.

"There is not much to see here," said Holmes. "Even if we intruded upon the current residents and made an examination of the interior, I do not believe that it would add anything to your understanding of the matter. However, let us walk around to the next block, behind this one, and I will point out one or two places of interest in the mews."

We went down Keppel Street, along the side of the buildings. In the distance in front of us, I could hear an atonal ringing sound, almost musical, and the voices of children at play. About halfway to the next street, the house ended at an opening into the Mews. There was nothing unusual about it at all.

A little way in front of us, we could see a number of children running up and down the walk, banging the lampposts with sticks. Each rang with a unique tone, and the faster the children ran, the more musical the glissando of tones became.

It was a pleasant sound, encountering the laughter of children on that quiet back street. And then I glanced at Wiggins, who had a look of sadness on his face. I realized that his childhood had been quite different from the one shared by these well-dressed and carefree children. Although he had experienced many unique adventures as a child, before growing into an adult with a secure job, it could not have been an easy life. Again, I understood how grateful the entire Wiggins family was toward Holmes, and for the opportunities that he had provided for so many of them.

Holmes stepped to the entrance to the mews*, and the children, eyeing us with suspicion, retreated to the far end of the block, although they did not leave entirely. Turning into the mews, he glanced around before waving me over as well. "There, Watson," he said. "Do you see that bench?"

I moved to his side. It was a low marble affair, quite stained, and unusually wide from side to side. It would have been able to comfortably seat three or even four people, instead of the usual two-person bench of similar construction. It was placed very near the wall that we had just passed, along Keppel Street.

I indicated that I had spotted the bench, and Holmes said, "And over there, the back of the row of houses? That second door, the red one at the top of the steep steps? That was Raines's house."

He shifted back and brushed his hands. "Now you know where the trap was laid. The rest of the story will make more sense now. On to the Alpha Inn. Faces to the south, then, and quick march!"

Passing through the Mews, we turned left into Montague Place, quickly reaching Russell Square. I realized that we were entering Montague Street. Holmes was feeling sentimental today, although he would never admit it as such, and was revisiting several old points of interest along our way.

* Editor's Note: These mews are now a portion of *Malet Street* and specifically the *Malet Street Gardens*.

It was only a moment before we reached the white front of No. 24, where he had lived when he first came up to London after deciding to pursue his vocation as a Consulting Detective.

I wondered if he would pause there for a moment, or decide to keep walking around the corner to the Alpha Inn. The decision was taken away from him, however, when Lestrade, who happened to be in the lead at that moment, stopped and looked up at the first-floor window, directly over the door.

"It has been a long time," he said, nodding his head toward the building. "Whatever happened to that landlady that was your distant relation?" he asked. "She did not like me."

Holmes shook his head. "I do not know. She was only a Holmes by marriage to some cousin of my father's, and after I moved out in early '81, I lost track of her whereabouts. Several years later, when Watson and I were called here to investigate a murder in my old rooms, there was a new owner who knew nothing about her."

"Gregson's case," said Lestrade. "He never visited here in the old days as often as I did."

"Only a few times," said Holmes. "Inspector Plummer was often here, but he retired soon after I moved away. I liked to think that he had put in a good word for me down at the Yard before he departed."

"He did," said Lestrade. "It made things easier for the rest of us when we started to make use of your abilities more and more often. He paved the way for us at the Yard to consult with you."

"Gentlemen," said Wiggins softly, "we appear to be attracting attention."

I followed his gaze to the Museum which loomed behind us. There were a number of people gathered in one of the tall windows, pointing excitedly toward our party, and more specifically at Holmes. In his unique fore-and-aft and Inverness, which he insisted on wearing both in the city and the country, he had become quite recognizable.

With a final glance up at the window over the door to No. 24, Holmes said, "Let us be off, then. We'll join together to tell Watson how we removed Mrs. Wiggins from under the shadow of suspicion."

Entering Great Russell Street, I glanced over toward the gardens in Bloomsbury Square. I could not see through them, but I knew that Southampton Street was on the other side. I had lived there at No. 6 for a short time in 1878, earning some small fees as a new doctor before deciding to leave England and explore the world. I knew that Holmes and I had frequented this neighborhood at the same time in the late seventies, and was certain that we must have encountered each other before Stamford introduced us in the lab at Barts on New Year's Day in '81, following my return to London after Maiwand. However, for the life of me, I could not recall a single instance when I had taken notice of him.

Reaching the corner entrance of the Alpha, Wiggins held the door while we preceded him inside. It was quiet this time of day, which suited our moods, and there were very few patrons. Holmes walked unerringly down the narrow path between the bar on the left and the tables under the windows on the right, reaching a small table just past the bar at the back. Fortunately, it was empty, and he began to divest himself of his hat and coat.

I noticed that he had intentionally passed several other empty tables, aiming for this one. With sudden perception, I said, "Was this your favorite table in the old days?"

Holmes smiled. "It was. Although I was never a social creature, even in my youth – or perhaps especially in my youth – I did have a certain set of cronies that I would meet on random occasions. And this is where we would sit."

"I remember you!" I cried. "It was winter, and I had come in with some of my friends. This was our favorite table as well, and you and some others had already occupied it. My friends and I sat nearby instead, over there by the window, but I recall that you looked up and noticed my obvious disappointment. You raised a glass of beer to me!"

Holmes nodded. "I recollect that incident. Your dismay when seeing that table was occupied was palpable. I considered offering to move, but my companions, which you may not recall, were too far gone at that time to suggest it. I hope that the evening was not spoiled for you."

"I must admit that I don't remember anything else from that night," I said with a smile, seating myself in a chair.

Holmes motioned to the man behind the bar, holding up four fingers. In a moment, the fellow was placing a glass of beer before each of us. "The beer is excellent here," said Holmes.

"As good as their geese?" asked Lestrade softly. I looked at him with surprise, and he was smiling in my direction. "I read *The Strand*, doctor," he said. "back when you were still publishing the stories. I remember that you stopped here while following along after that jewel thief, nearly fifteen years back." He shook his head. "And I also remember that you let him go because it was Christmas."

"Enough of that," interrupted Holmes. "We are here to conclude the post-mortem examination of the matter of Silas Raines, and *not* to rehash the matter of the Blue Carbuncle."

"Agreed," I said. "Tell me then of this trap, and how it relates to the mews behind Raines's house."

207

Lestrade seemed ready to take up the tale. "First I wired to America for details regarding our Mr. Tremblay. They didn't arrive in time to provide us with any additional facts before his arrest, but we did receive enough information later that helped us know that he was the right man, which we already knew by that time anyway. It was no secret where he came from that Raines was his father. His mother never married, waiting for Raines to come back for her. She lived in her father's house until she died young, and then the old man, her father, had brought Tremblay up the rest of the way. Cruel he was, too, it sounded like.

"In the meantime, I went around and talked to my superior, explaining Mr. Holmes's plan. I also made sure that Mrs. Wiggins was comfortable, and was not treated as a regular prisoner, since it was likely that we would have her there until late that night, after the trap was sprung.

"In the meantime, Mr. Holmes had holed up in Raines's house for over an hour, forging documents after Raines's handwriting."

"Even at that age, I had the gift," murmured Holmes with a smile.

"Lord help us all," Lestrade muttered. Wiggins laughed.

"I required something to show to Tremblay when I approached him that evening – something that would shake him loose from his confidence that his plan was working. I needed a document indicating that Raines had two sons, and that – unknown to Tremblay – I was the second."

"Our plans were in place by early evening," said Lestrade. "It was then that Mr. Holmes waited outside the butcher's shop as it closed for the night."

"I stayed well back," said Holmes, "as Tremblay and the butcher came out together. The butcher locked the door, and Tremblay said good night and started south down Tottenham Court Road. I followed discreetly behind him.

"By this time we had ascertained that he lived not too far away. I let him get almost to his lodgings before I increased my pace and approached him, calling his name.

"He turned, and for a moment I could see him try to place me. Then he recognized me, although he still appeared puzzled, wondering why someone from the butcher's shop earlier that afternoon would now be at his place of residence.

" 'Yes?' he asked good-naturedly, 'Was the cut of meat to your satisfaction? I'm afraid the shop is closed, but I'll be happy to speak with you tomorrow.'

" 'I'm not here about the meat', I said. 'That was an excuse to get a look at you. We have something else to discuss, which will benefit us both.'

" 'And that would be?'

208

" 'Perhaps I should introduce myself. My name is Thomas Raines.'

"He made no connection for a moment, and then I could see that the last name meant something to him. 'Raines?' he said.

" 'That's right,' I said. 'You knew my father. I am Silas Raines's son. And your half-brother as well.'

"That rocked him back right away, and with a shake of his head he backed up against the steps leading to the door. Finally, he muttered, 'Not possible. It's not possible.'

" 'Ah, but it is,' I said, pressing forward. 'Come over here, away from the street, and I'll show you.'

"He followed me to the side of the building. There was still light enough to see the document that I pulled from my pocket, the very one that I had forged not an hour earlier. He read it quickly, and then again, more slowly this time. At times his lips moved as he mouthed the words. I knew the parts that were causing him the greatest consternation. I had written them to do so.

"Essentially, the document, supposedly written by Silas Raines, stated that he had *two* sons, one by Abigail Tremblay in Canada years before, and me, Thomas Raines, from a short marriage after he had arrived in England. Thomas's fictional mother had died soon after giving birth, and Silas had placed me in the care of trusted friends, since he was in no position to raise me himself. However, he did not want to neglect either of his sons, and had written this statement in order to record his acknowledgement of both of us.

" 'He left this with me several months ago. You'll notice,' I added, as he finished re-reading it for a third time, 'that we have to claim the inheritance together, and vouch for one another, or neither one gets anything. I think that he meant to introduce us to one another before he died so suddenly last night. He had told me about you, obviously, and how you found him after coming over from Canada. I'm guessing that he hadn't managed to get around to telling *you* about *me*.'

"I reached out and took the forged sheet back, replacing it in my pocket. He shook his head, trying to get his thoughts in order. Then, he said, 'That paper won't be enough,' he said. 'I have the letter that he wrote to my mother in Canada, after she let him know that I had been born. That will be enough to prove that I'm his son and heir. He acknowledges it, and I know that there is not a will. What other proof do you have?'

" 'How do you know there isn't a will?' I asked.

"He shook his head and asked, 'Where is your proof?'

"I pulled the second forged sheet out of my pocket. 'Here,' I said. 'I'm afraid that it's rather like a treasure map.'

209

"He grabbed it, and I let him take a good look at it. 'It won't do you any good to take it from me and use it by yourself without me,' I said. 'We both have to be present to inherit. It says so in the letter. And there *is* a will, as you can see from that drawing, which tells where to find it. I think that he was trying to be clever, but it isn't too hard to see that he buried it by the bench in the mews.'

"He looked at the sheet, a crude hand-drawn map that made clear in the simplest terms possible that the 'treasure' was indeed buried under a paving stone by the bench in the mews, the same bench where Raines and Tremblay had met on several occasions. Tremblay stared without speaking for the longest time, and then nodded once, and again. Finally, he said, 'What do you suggest?'

" 'Simply that we go and get it,' I replied. 'We may have to hold on to the will for a while, until things calm down, before we can use it. I was in Gower Street today and heard that they had arrested our father's housekeeper for poisoning him. But the crowd outside the house said the poison was in the meat sauce. What with you working for a nearby butcher and all – you can see the connection, I'm sure – that made me curious, and I thought that I'd step around and get a closer look at you.'

" 'The housekeeper killed him,' he asserted. 'Everyone in the shop today was saying so. I heard that the old man wrote a note accusing her before he died.'"

" 'I didn't hear anything about them finding any note,' I said, thinking to make him a little uncertain about the success of his plan. 'All I know is we'll have to time things right to make sure the police are happy with the person that they have arrested, but not so late as to let the estate get away from us. Now, are you with me? Shall we go?'

"He looked over his shoulder uncertainly, as if he wanted to go into his lodgings and shut the door, pretending that I had never accosted him. But I was there now, and he did not know what I might do if he let me get away. I had hinted that I knew of his complicity in the murder, and in spite of the conditions of the forged letter, saying that we had to inherit together or not at all, I might be able to throw him over if it could be proven that *he* had been the killer. He really had no choice but to come with me.

"We walked the few blocks back to Gower Street, as the sun dropped behind the buildings, and the streets fell into shadow. We went past Raines's house, and I noted with satisfaction that there were no lights showing inside, and no sign of a constable keeping watch."

"We had removed him," said Lestrade, "and also warned Howett and the other neighbors to keep inside and to themselves, no matter what they heard outside in the next few hours."

210

Holmes continued, "Turning down Keppel Street, Tremblay said, 'Perhaps we should wait until it's later.'

" 'No,' I replied. 'It would be more suspicious if we came back and were caught out digging in the middle of the night. Right now, people are inside and distracted. The map shows right where it is. We'll just get in and out, and then we'll discuss what happens next over a pint.' Then, I added, 'Surely you can see the sense in that, brother.'

"That startled him, but he nodded, and we turned into the mews. He walked straight to the bench. 'When did you first come over from Canada?' I asked, in a voice a little louder than the situation called for. Tremblay, obviously very nervous by this point, hissed for me to be quiet, and turned on me as if he were going to strike me. It was then that Lestrade, wearing a very suitable set of old clothes, walked up out of the darkness.

" Tremblay nearly jumped back in surprise. 'Who is this?' he whispered.

" 'My friend, Geoffrey,' I replied. 'He doesn't know what's going on exactly, but I wanted him to know that I was here, and to get a good look at you, just in case. I'm sure that you understand. Have you seen him, Geoff?' I asked. Lestrade nodded, but did not speak. 'Good. Go on to the pub then, and we'll meet up later.' "

Lestrade interrupted. "I walked away and out of the mews, and then kept on going slowly, whistling as I went. But as soon as I was out of their hearing, I ran around through the next street, and so on until I was able to sneak back into Keppel Street, where I took up my position with the others, right outside the wall, just alongside the bench where Mr. Holmes and Tremblay were standing inside. When I got back, the two of them were having some kind of argument."

"A very quiet argument, indeed," said Holmes. "I had repeated my question concerning when Tremblay had first come over from Canada. He turned it over in his mind for a moment and did not see any harm in answering. 'Three months ago,' he finally whispered. 'In the spring.'

"He then turned back to the bench, and in two steps was kneeling beside it, scrabbling his fingers in the dirt around the paving stone that had been identified on the map. In just a moment, he had found the small iron box, which I had placed there myself just before starting off to follow him from the butcher shop to his residence.

"He stood up with it, and tried to open it, but it was locked. He shook it in anger, and we could hear something inside, presumably the will. I had known that it would be locked. When I had chosen it from among several similar boxes in Raines's house for just this purpose, I had made sure that it was sturdy, and that it would keep him out until I was ready to let him in. As he groaned in frustration, I gained his attention and held up a key. 'This,' I said, 'was with the map and the letter.'

"He made to reach for it, but I yanked it back. 'First,' I said, 'another question.' He neither agreed nor disagreed, but simply stood there, clutching the box, and beginning to give off the smallest hints of panic. His plan, which must have seemed to have started so well for him, was falling apart, and he was quite off balance. Another son of Silas Raines, who knew so quickly of his connection to the dead man, was not supposed to have appeared.

" 'Earlier you said that you knew there wasn't a will. What made you think so?'

"He frowned, and then said, 'What?'

" 'You said there wasn't a will. How do you know?'

"Because I looked for it, and didn't find it," he said, his stress becoming a little more obvious and pronounced with each passing minute.

" 'When?' I asked. 'When did you look for it? On some night when the old man was asleep in the house? He told me that he always visited with you out here, at this bench, and that you didn't go inside.'

" 'That's right,' snarled Tremblay. 'He wouldn't even invite me in. Oh, he would talk in the mews 'til the sun went down, but I wasn't fit to soil his castle.'

" 'And did he tell you there wasn't a will? Because if he did, then he must have lied, since we just found his treasure box where he said it would be.'

" 'He never said a word about a will, one way or another. I thought, however, from the things he said to me after the first time I met with him, that he wasn't going to give me anything.'

" 'So if he didn't tell you there was no will, how did you know that there wasn't one? When did you look for it?' I asked.

" 'At night.'

" 'When he was asleep?'

" 'No, last night.'

" 'Last night, after he died?'

"That stopped him, as he realized what he was about to admit, and I thought that I had overplayed my hand. To distract him, I handed him the key to the box. With a lurch, he grabbed it and turned toward the dim lights coming from Howett's windows.

"He twisted the key, and with a wrench had the box lid open. He reached in and drew out the false will that I had created, duplicating Raines's handwriting and phrasing as well as I could in the short amount of time that I'd had.

"He dropped the iron box with a clatter, by then seemingly oblivious to the need to stay quiet. He was nearly panting as he unfolded the document, and then turned it this way and that as he tried to read it. In a moment he gave a little cry. I knew what he had just read.

" 'What is it?' I asked. 'Here, let me see.' I made as if to move toward him, but he pivoted and took a step back. There was a new look of madness in his eyes.

" 'It doesn't mention me,' he said. 'It doesn't mention me at all. It simply refers to his *only son*, Thomas Raines. You inherit everything.'

" 'Here, let me see,' I repeated to him.

" 'It was supposed to be *me*,' he said softly. 'It was *my* mother that died of a broken heart, waiting for him to come back. It was *me* that was raised fatherless by that evil old man, while over here *he* was starting a *real* family.' He took a step toward me.

" 'So you poisoned him?' I asked.

" 'All that stands between me and the old man's money,' he replied, 'is this will and that piece of paper in your pocket naming both of us as his heirs.' He took another step, and I fell back to match it. "If I get rid of those, all that will be left will be my letter that he sent to my mother, telling the truth!"

" 'Did you poison him?' I cried.

" 'Yes, damn you, I poisoned him!' He was reaching for me, and I backed toward the gate to the street. 'And when I came in last night to leave the note and take away the jar, he was still alive. He was looking at me when he died, and I cursed him to hell when he drew his last breath. He knew it as he went. I could see that he did.' I stopped retreating, and he closed the distance toward me.

" 'And then I spent all night looking for the will, so very carefully, so that no one would realize that I had ever been there, but I couldn't find it! I thought that there was no will, but I had to make sure before I told anyone about my letter! Sometimes I would go back upstairs and look at him there. I wanted to spit upon him, but I couldn't leave any indication that anyone had been there. Then I looked some more for the will. And all along he'd buried it out here, naming you as the heir!'

"It was then that his hands touched my throat. Before he could squeeze, however, before he could exert any kind of force or pressure at all, a hellish shriek shattered the quiet night. It seemed to echo off the walls of the mews and the backs of the houses, and there was no way to tell where exactly it originated. Even I, who had expected it, was momentarily struck with a kind of paralysis and terror. Tremblay jerked as if he had been shot, stood upright, and would have bolted if Lestrade and his men, who had been hiding behind the wall right outside the gate, had not boiled around us at that instant and taken him into custody."

"We had heard everything," said Lestrade. "His entire confession. He fought like a madman, and it took six big men to bring him down. He nearly bit off Carter's thumb in the process."

"And the scream?" I asked. "The one that stopped Tremblay for just a crucial second?"

"That was me, doctor," said Wiggins. "A talent that – sadly – gets little demand these days in King's Bench Walk."

"The confession was as clear as could be wished for," said Lestrade. "He broke down later that night and told the whole thing. He had been raised by his grandfather, a sinister old man who had whipped him often simply because he was his father's son. Eventually, as we confirmed from information in the cables received from Canada, he had beaten his grandfather to death. Thus, the provinces had become too hot for him, and he fled to England, intending to find his lost father along the way. Even then, he had devised his basic revenge, as he had brought the poisonous seeds with him. Once here, he located Raines, obtained employment nearby, and began to observe and make more detailed plans."

"After living here for some little time, he had finally approached the old man," Holmes continued, "and identified himself as his son, but he was not as warmly received as he had hoped. This only confirmed in his mind the designs that he had made for his father, and he bided his time, waiting to determine the best circumstances in which to carry them out, and also whom he could frame for the crime.

"Finally, he felt that he could wait no longer, and he met with his father for what seemed like just another usual visit in the mews. Tremblay, knowing that Mrs. Wiggins had bought meat that morning at the butcher's, brought along the poisoned sauce, and suggested that his father try it, indicating that it might remind him of the old days in Canada. As we know, Raines *did* try the sauce, that very night. Tremblay made his way into the house, picking the lock without leaving any evidence that I could detect, using skills that he had acquired during his younger days in Canada.

"By the next morning, Tremblay had not found any will, and was convinced that none existed. He retrieved the poisoned jar and left the accusatory note in Raines's bedclothes, stupidly forgetting to leave the pencil with which it was written. Then he made his way out of the house before Mrs. Wiggins's usual arrival time. He went to work as if it were simply another day, intending to bide his time for several weeks, certainly until after Mrs. Wiggins's guilt was firmly established, and then he would make his claim as Raines's heir, using the old letter that acknowledged him as Raines's son as his only proof."

214

"As you may be sure, we released Mrs. Wiggins later that night," said Lestrade. "Tremblay's plan was full of holes, but it was the best that he could come up with."

"And even if the true villain had eventually been unmasked," said Wiggins, "my mother would have had to suffer untold horrors before the truth was discovered, if it ever was." He turned toward Holmes, holding up his nearly empty glass. "A toast to you, Mr. Holmes." Lestrade and I raised our glasses as well.

The tale having been told, we looked at one another. There did not seem to be anything left to say. The fine beer was gone, and we all stood and prepared to depart.

"I'm sure it would not inconvenience Mrs. Hudson too much if you were to all join me for dinner," said Holmes as we walked along the bar toward the door.

"I truly appreciate the offer, but I must return for my mother's service," said Wiggins. "The minister will be arriving soon. But she would have wanted me to spend this time with you, of that I'm certain."

"I must be getting home as well," said Lestrade. "The missus will be expecting me."

"I, too, should be getting back," I agreed. "My wife returns from her visit tonight."

We stepped outside into the twilight, only to be confronted by a tall man, wearing evening clothes, and weaving slightly from side to side as if in the grip of strong drink. In his right hand was an Italian dagger, the blade long and thin.

"You've ruined me, Holmes!" growled Lord D------, looking much worse than he had this morning at the Palace, when he had grudgingly affixed his name to the second confession that I had carried there. "It has all come crashing down! I'm a ruined man! You must make amends!"

Lestrade and I separated ourselves slightly on either side of Holmes, as the three of us tensed to make whatever defense was necessary against the raving criminal. However, before we could make any sort of move whatsoever, a piercing scream shattered the early evening around us. It echoed far to the Museum walls, and back again onto the pub behind us. It was everywhere at once, and terrifying. Lord D------ jerked back to see who or what had made such an ungodly noise. Before he could determine its source, however, Wiggins stepped quickly past us, grabbing the enraged peer's knife arm, and deftly using the man's weight against him, throwing him over and onto the pavement. Holmes stepped forward, stomped a foot onto Lord D------'s arm, and with the other foot kicked away the knife into the street.

As Lestrade blew on his police whistle, bringing constables running from all directions, Wiggins cleared his throat and grinned. "Just like you taught me, Mr. Holmes?"

"Exactly like that, Wiggins," replied Holmes.

"And did he teach you to scream like that?" I asked, astounded that a human throat could make such a noise. Wiggins simply tried to look humble, and then laughed.

Later, after Wiggins had said his goodbyes and started back toward his mother's home, Lestrade stood with us for a moment while Lord D------ was loaded into a growler by two burly constables. "He'll be out by tomorrow," Lestrade said with disgust.

"Nevertheless," said Holmes, "he is a broken man. Look at him. He won't find the fortitude to try anything like this again."

Lestrade nodded to both of us, climbed in the four-wheeler, and departed.

"Well, Watson," said Holmes. "Are you up for a walk?"

We were quiet as we wound our way gradually west, over to Wigmore Street before turning toward Queen Anne Street. Finally, pausing before No. 9, we stopped. The lights were on inside, and I suspected that my wife was already home from her travels.

"Would you care to come in?" I asked, but I knew that Holmes would decline.

"Another time, perhaps." The gaslight threw shadows across his face, hiding his eyes underneath his fore-and-aft cap. "Give Mrs. Watson my regards."

"I shall."

"And do stop by in a day or so. I've received an interesting letter from a man in Exeter with a rather unique problem. He is the verger at St. David's Church. The current building was completed only two years ago, but there are reports of a hooded figure from Anglo-Saxon times rising from the crypts of the former church, threatening the nearby residents, especially the children. It sounds . . . intriguing."

With that, he turned and walked away towards Baker Street. I stood on the pavement for another moment until he vanished from sight, and then turned and went inside.

Chronology Notes

For those Chronologists who are interested in such things – and I am very much in that camp, having spent over twenty years compiling a *Whole Art of Detection* of the lives of Holmes and Watson, consisting of a massive Chronology that includes events from the Canon as well as any information from countless other sources that relate <u>true</u> and <u>correct</u> versions of cases involving Our Heroes – these are the dates (some approximate) when the narratives contained in this volume took place:

- "The Mystery at Kerrett's Rood" – April 7-8, 1883 *and* early to late September 1878
- "The Curious Incident of the Goat-Cart Man" – September 27, 1890
- "The Matter of Boz's Last Letter" – Early to mid-June 1897
- "The Tangled Skein at Birling Gap" – September 23, 1905
- "The Gower Street Murder" – Late September 1902 *and*   August 21, 1879

Sherlock Holmes

and

The Eye of Heka

FROM THE NOTEBOOKS OF
DR. JOHN H. WATSON M.D.

"Marcum could be today's greatest Sherlockian writer,
and Conan Doyle himself would be proud of this story."
LEE CHILD
NY Times Bestselling Author

David Marcum

Editor's Introduction

As related elsewhere, I've been reading and collecting the adventures of Sherlock Holmes and Dr. John H. Watson since I was ten years old in the mid-1970's. During all those years, I've accumulated literally thousands of narratives detailing the activities of Our Heroes, and in 2008, that collection increased when I found one of Watson's "lost" notebooks, consisting of nine previously undiscovered adventures. These were eventually edited and published as *The Papers of Sherlock Holmes* (2011, 2013).

I was obviously thrilled, but that feeling managed to keep growing when I was contacted by an individual who wished to remain anonymous. This person, having seen the first publication, revealed a manuscript that he or she wished to see published, for various personal reasons. It eventually appeared under the title *Sherlock Holmes and A Quantity of Debt* (2013). I was soon to learn that each lost Holmes manuscript leads to the next.

In September 2013, I was in England for my first (of three, and I hope more!) extensive Holmes pilgrimage, wherein my ever-present deerstalker and I spent several weeks visiting Holmes-related sites. (If it wasn't about Holmes, I pretty much didn't do it.) I've told elsewhere, (specifically in the introductions to the three volumes of *Sherlock Holmes in Montague Street* [2014] and *Sherlock Holmes – Tangled Skeins* [2015]) how I was met near Leicester Square and given a package containing additional Holmes-related documents, as penned by Watson. These papers have made up the two aforementioned titles, as well as a number of other stand-alone adventures that have been published in other locations. I cannot express how satisfying it was to come across more of Watson's efforts, but I was also becoming concerned, as the bottom of that box was in sight.

In September and October of 2015, I was back in London for my second Holmes Pilgrimage. Part of that trip was to launch the Holmes collection that I had envisioned and then edited, the massive three-volume *The MX Book of New Sherlock Holmes Stories*. Luckily, during the time that I was there, I had an encounter that gave me access to a massive amount of newly discovered Holmes adventures.

As I did on my first Holmes Pilgrimage, I conducted extensive research of locations to visit, based on more than two-dozen Holmes travel books in my collection. Some locations of importance from the initial trip were obviously revisited, either on purpose or by chance, as many of the sites are very close to one another, and one almost can't go from A to B in

London without running into three other Holmesian places of interest along the way.

One of these sites was Queen Anne Street, where Watson moved in mid-1902 following his third marriage. This isn't a long walk from Baker Street, and Holmes and Watson stayed in regular contact during this time. I had found Watson's old house during my 2013 trip, and hadn't meant specifically to go back there in 2015, but I happened to be walking the route taken by Holmes and Watson during "The Empty House", and as it passes right across Queen Anne Street, I took a slight detour. And I'm glad that I did.

As I was taking an awkward photograph of my deerstalker and me in front of Watson's old doorway, I was embarrassed to hear the door itself open behind me. I turned and started to apologize and explain, surprised that this kind of thing hadn't happened to me before, but the deerstalker on my head apparently told the whole story. Before I knew it, I had been welcomed inside, where I identified myself, and explained my nearly lifelong passion for all things Holmes. Meanwhile, as I talked, I glanced around at the lovely room with its old but very well-kept furniture. I was very conscious that I didn't want to move too rapidly, possibly damaging the chair that held me.

My host noticed, and laughed, saying, "That was one of his, you know."

"*His?*"

"Dr. Watson's. I'm descended from his third wife's sister. The doctor had no heirs, so – except for a number of case-related mementos that he bequeathed to Mr. Holmes – he left everything else to his wife's niece."

I looked around with much more interest. "He died in 1929," I said, rather stupidly, searching for something else to say.

My host nodded. "We've been here ever since, holding on to the lease."

"You said that the case-related mementos were left to Mr. Holmes. Did that mean Watson's notes as well?"

"Oh, no. Many of those are still here."

That raised an eyebrow. Long ago, before I went back to school to be a civil engineer, I was a federal investigator. As part of that profession, we were given training in interview techniques. I tried to recall everything I had known to make sure that I understood what my host was saying. After much tolerant (on both sides) question-and-answering, I determined that there was indeed quite a large cache of Watson's writings still located within the house. And then I tentatively asked if I could see them. I was told that I could.

It was explained to me – a fact that I actually already knew – that Watson spent the last years of his life writing up as many adventures as he could, based upon his old notes. A certain number of manuscripts were placed in his old Tin Dispatch Box at Cox and Company. Others he gave away freely to the participants who had been involved in the old cases. Still more were in the house when he unexpectedly died, as he hadn't had a chance to properly place them.

The upshot of that visit was that I've been given permission to release this trove of lost papers. Luckily, the internet was laid on in that house, and I was able to show my *incognito* host my past work in this field. Some of the manuscripts are complete, while others require a bit more editing. One of the first, as timely today as when it occurred, is the book you hold within your hands. I was interested and pleased to see that it reaffirmed some of the facts relating to Watson's earlier days, as well as the location of his Kensington practice, and specifically facts about his *first* wife, Constance – whose existence was hinted at in The Canon, and who came before Mary Watson *née* Morstan. Other documents, as they are released, will also help to confirm additional details of the lives of our heroes, as well as fill in missing pieces that have been identified by Holmes Scholars over the years.

As always through this process, I wish to thank with all my heart both my wife Rebecca and son Dan, who are so tolerant of my ever-increasing Holmes addiction. You are both everything to me, and the best!

David Marcum
April 5th, 2021
The 127th Anniversary of Sherlock Holmes's
return to London following The Great Hiatus

A Chronological Note:
Watson's *First* Wife

Two of Watson's wives are specifically mentioned in The Canon: Mary Watson, *née* Morstan, Holmes's client in *The Sign of the Four* (which occurs in September 1888), and the unnamed lady to whom Holmes refers (in "The Blanched Soldier", which occurs in January 1903) when he writes: *"The good Watson had at that time deserted me for a wife, the only selfish action which I can recall in our association."*

But in the case of Mary Morstan, there are some troubling chronological questions. If Watson didn't meet Mary until autumn 1888, then how does one explain some curious references that imply a Watsonian marriage *before* this date?

For example, at the beginning of "A Scandal in Bohemia", Watson mentions his recent marriage, and then states:

> *One night – it was on the twentieth of March, 1888 – I was returning from a journey to a patient (for I had now returned to civil practice), when my way led me through Baker Street.*

So he's married in the spring of 1888, but meets his wife in the fall of 1888 . . . ?

And then there's "The Five Orange Pips", which Watson specifically says occurs in '87. Soon after he writes:

> *My wife was on a visit to her mother's, and for a few days I was a dweller once more in my old quarters at Baker Street.*

But Mary Morstan was an orphan – *She had no mother to visit!* – and this case occurred in autumn 1887 – *a full year before Watson would even meet Mary for the first time.*

Clearly, there is a *third* wife.

Dealing with the chronological questions and inconsistencies that regularly occur in The Canon is no easy thing, but some of us thrive on it. And yet, at times much of the heavy lifting for these questions has already been done, if one is willing to let go and accept what others have determined. In 1962, William S. Baring-Gould published his masterpiece biography *Sherlock Holmes of Baker Street*, in which he compiled

Foreword

In my time, like so many others, I have faced losses. As a young man, I lost my father to the evils of drink, and subsequently my mother as well, when her heart was broken because of him. My brother fell to the same demons, but fortunately I avoided that trap. I believed that my own destiny was to serve as a physician in the British Army, only to be grievously and surprisingly wounded and sent home, told that what I had to offer was no longer required.

Later, I carried the burden of the supposed loss of my friend, Sherlock Holmes, when he was believed to have been killed by the villainous Professor Moriarty back in '91. That, along with the death a couple of years later of my beloved wife, Mary, nearly broke me. Like the despair that I felt following my battle wounds in 1880, I think that I might well have eased slowly toward an early grave during that period, having lost both my wife and closest friend, if not for the reappearance of Holmes in 1894, whereupon subsequent involvement with his work saved me, as it had done before in 1881.

Many people are aware of how I first met Mary, occurring as it did during one of Holmes's investigations that I later worked up into a published form, and how she and I later married. A year after that story had appeared publicly, I continued those tentative efforts as a writer by preparing a quantity of Holmes's other adventures for the public, publishing them in a newly-formed and popular periodical. Soon I was faced with a vexatious dilemma, as I realized that quite a few of those events that I had shared with Holmes had taken place before my time with Mary, during my *first* marriage.

Many people are not aware of that first marriage. I was initially hesitant to write up those many cases that occurred then, referring as they occasionally do to my earlier wife, Constance. I did not want to bring any pain to Mary by reliving earlier days too often. However, it was through the urging of my literary agent, Conan Doyle (now Sir Arthur), that I was – shamefully, I see in hindsight – encouraged to gloss over the very fact of Constance's existence. Doyle rationalized at the time that the narratives could be written in such a way that the casual reader would not realize that the marriage that I referred to in some of those earlier tales was *not* to Mary, and I went along with his plan.

Only now, many years later, do I realize that – while I did save Mary some initial melancholy because of reminders about my earlier wedded condition – I also did a grave disservice to Constance, whom I had also loved and lost far too quickly.

Recently, Holmes tried his hand at writing and publishing his own account of one of his past adventures, taking place not long after the turn of the century and carried out without my participation. He admitted how difficult he found writing it, after years of criticizing my own efforts. In that particular narrative, which took place back in '03 and concerned the circumstances relating to an unfortunate veteran of the Second Boer War, Holmes happened to mention that, at the time of that case, I had deserted him for a wife, referring to it as "the only selfish action which I can recall in our association." It is true that Holmes and my third wife did not mix well, at least at first, but there should be no implication or understanding that they were enemies. Yet, it was upon reading this comment of my friend's that my mind was set on a reminiscent path, leading from my third wife, back to the other two.

Holmes and Mary were always friends, although he was admittedly at a loss when she and I married in 1889. It was during this time that certain bad habits threatened to overtake him, and my departure from Baker Street only seemed to exacerbate the stress that he faced. But Mary always thought of him as the brother that she never had, and I know that he felt the same affection as toward a sister for her. Through both our efforts, Mary and I were able to wean him of his addiction, if only for a time, although it was only several years later that he was able to finish the effort completely on his own.

With Constance, my first wife, Holmes had a somewhat different relationship. I had met her during a period when I was not living in Baker Street, so he only became aware of her rather after the fact. Circumstances sadly kept them from having much regular contact with one another during my marriage, but my friend was always supportive throughout those trying months as her condition worsened, and even though he did not know her as he would come to know Mary, he never failed me, proving yet again that he was more of a brother to me than that of my own blood.

As I recently brooded upon those long-ago days, I was reminded by the current events of one of Holmes's long-ago investigations that took place at approximately the same time that my marriage to Constance came to a close. Those were dark days for me, but as usual, the distraction of participating in Holmes's adventures served as the cure for my inner illness.

As I grow older, and attempt to put my papers in some semblance of order, I know that I must not leave this tale untold. Even now, certain aspects and identities must be disguised. And forgive me, reader, if I find that Holmes's monumental efforts cannot be untwisted from the personal concerns that were taking place at the same time in my own life. I would have told this, one of Holmes's most important investigations, without involving my own pain if I could have found a way. And yet, perhaps telling it all as it happened will help to paint a truer picture than if I selectively and subjectively withdrew a thread here and there from the greater tapestry.

As always, I hope that this, like all of my efforts, serves in some additional way to illuminate my friend, Sherlock Holmes.

Dr. John H. Watson
4 June, 1927

"[L]ife is infinitely stranger than anything which the mind of man could invent. We would not dare to conceive the things which are really mere commonplaces of existence. If we could fly out of that window hand in hand, hover over this great city, gently remove the roofs, and peep in at the queer things which are going on, the strange coincidences, the plannings, the cross-purposes, the wonderful chains of events, working through generations, and leading to the most outrè *results, it would make all fiction with its conventionalities and foreseen conclusions most stale and unprofitable."*

– Sherlock Holmes
18 October, 1887

Part I

Chapter I
An Explosive Encounter

The sound of gunshots meant that something had gone very wrong indeed.

I strained to hear whether my name was really being called, as I suddenly thought, or if it was some trick of the fog, twisting the distant echoes and moving shouts into an illusion that resembled actual words. Cries grew both louder and softer, and running footsteps went by in the street, on the other side of the building from where I was concealed, but never approached my hiding spot. I involuntarily flinched when there was a muffled explosion, but quickly reasoned that it posed no danger to me. Then something, perhaps a piece of wood thrown by the blast, slammed into the wall not two feet from where I crouched in darkness.

There was an escalating panic to some of the voices that I could now hear more clearly, and I was reminded of the pleading I had heard on long-ago battlefields, when men alternately begged for their friends, their mothers, or for me, the doctor. The words blurred then in a different way than how I heard them now. Those cries were continually drowned out by the artillery fire and ricochets that spun around my head like bees from an overturned hive.

But I was long years and thousands of miles from that, my last battlefield on the plains of Maiwand. Instead, here in this dark London night, away from the tumult occurring in the next block, I could not be certain about any of the voices that I was hearing. My friend, Sherlock Holmes, had instructed me to maintain my position here, no matter what happened. But he had also been clear that the disruption of the gang's activities would be accomplished peacefully, without violence. Something had gone very wrong indeed.

"Baron Meade is a coward at heart, Watson," Holmes had said confidently as we approached the rendezvous in a hansom cab, not a quarter-of-an-hour before. "The surprise will be enough to force him to surrender." It was hard to believe that things could have turned so suddenly in such a small amount of time.

We had abandoned the cab a couple of blocks away from the nondescript house off the Brixton Road. Inspector Lanner and his men were waiting in the agreed-upon spot, and it was to be a simple matter of surrounding the building and making our way inside. I knew that the fog was an unexpected complication, but Holmes didn't seem to mind.

235

However, he did surprise me when he suddenly insisted that I take a spot behind the narrow old house, in the mews that opened off the alley beside it, running on through to the next street. I had thought to go inside with the rest, but he gave me to understand that possibly he was not as confident as he had first appeared.

"Stay alert, Watson," he had said as he plucked my sleeve. "And don't leave your post, whatever happens."

Then he and the others disappeared into the murk. I, along with a young constable assigned to accompany me, found our assigned spot. We reached a darker region of shadows away from the dim gaslight reflecting out of the adjacent streets, about thirty feet behind the building in question. Finding a hiding place, we settled in to wait. I could hear my companion's breathing, ragged and nervous, and I smiled a bit at my apparent calm. Almost immediately, however, I heard the police whistles and the banging of doors. And then the gunshots began, followed by the unmistakable explosion, and I realized that my breathing had become as that of the young policeman.

Because of the dampening effect of the fog, I couldn't tell from which direction the shots came, but common sense indicated that since they were occurring simultaneously with the raid on the Baron's heinous operation, there must certainly be a connection. I struggled to understand what must have happened.

The gunfire stopped. It had never been close enough to leave me with a ringing in my ears, so I immediately began to hear the other sounds that I might have missed otherwise. Dogs barking, police whistles, more running footsteps. It was all happening on the next street over, while I was still crouched here in the alley behind the house, wondering if I should break my orders and join the fray. Even now, after the battle appeared to be over, I felt the need to step across and see if my assistance as a doctor was required, should the confrontation have produced a casualty or two.

I heard a noise and saw my companion, the constable, rise from his hiding place and trot away without a word or backward glance down the alley toward the front street. I had almost talked myself into stepping out of my own carefully chosen shadow when a curious thing happened.

The back of the house that had been the focus of our attention was a blank-faced thing, looming in the blackness, its high edges a penumbra in the gaslight haloing it from the street beyond. As my eyes had adjusted, I had seen the outline of the sole door, reached by a short flight of wooden steps, and the four shuttered windows looking out toward the back alley. But there had been no indication of the other door, a *secret* door, in the wall along the ground until I glimpsed a deeper darkness begin to widen near the building's foundation.

236

It opened ever so slowly, at first no more than a thin vertical bar of deeper Stygian night, infinitesimally emptier than its surroundings. Initially I thought that my eyes were seeing an illusion. I shifted my gaze to one side of the crack, knowing that peripheral vision is stronger in the absence of light. I found that I was holding my breath, threatening to cause spots to appear in my vision before me, and I released it slowly, forcing myself to breathe in even regularity. I was not mistaken – the crack had widened in a place where I had been certain that no door existed.

Perhaps in daylight it would have been more obvious with an extensive examination. Possibly Holmes had spotted it earlier, and this was why he placed me here. Still, an explanation beforehand as to what to expect would have been useful. But none of that mattered now, as I realized it was only I who stood between whomever was slipping away and his freedom. And I was quite certain as to whom that man was.

I don't know how wide the hidden door was built to open, but after an aperture of only a foot or so was achieved, an arm and shoulder began to slip through. This was quickly followed by the rest of the man as he ducked and wiggled down to pass his head. I could see that the secret door was little more than four feet in height, a fact that had been hidden until then due to the odd lack of perspective in the lightless alley. The man was wearing a dark coat and had a cap pulled low on his head. I couldn't identify him, but I knew that it was certainly he who had visited our rooms that morning, in a futile attempt to decoy Holmes in the wrong direction.

The man paused to pull the door shut, no doubt to prevent any indication from showing inside how he had made his escape, thus keeping pursuers from getting on his trail any sooner than necessary. There was a small click, barely heard in the muffled alley, as he snicked the door shut. Then he stood to his full height and turned my way.

He pulled up short when he saw me standing there, having emerged from my makeshift hunting blind. Holding my faithful service revolver, I said unnecessarily, and feeling slightly foolish, "Stop."

With my left hand, I patted my coat for a moment, before cursing silently to myself as I realized that I had forgotten my police whistle. Possibly I was out of the habit, or more likely the events of recent weeks had distracted me, in spite of Holmes's efforts to help acclimate me to my recent loss. Regardless of all that, I was alone with a desperate criminal, and had to find some way to herd him down the alley toward the street and the authorities.

"Holmes!" I called, although it sounded weak and uselessly muffled in the mist. "Holmes!" Then, without waiting for an answer, I gestured with the pistol toward the passage that led around the side of the house and toward the sounds of the police. "That way," I said, my voice softer now, feeling and sounding unpleasant to me.

He turned, but I should have noticed that there was no sign of defeat about him. It was too easy, and it was my own fault for not spotting it. He had only gone four or five hesitant steps as I carelessly closed the distance between us when he seemed to pivot on one foot, and before I knew it, he was slamming into my left side, forcing the gun in my right hand in the opposite direction. A chop across my forearm, and it spun away into the darkness.

I think that was all he planned to do. He certainly didn't want to stay and fight me. Rather, he only wished to run like a rabbit into the warren of streets stretching away to the south. But I instinctively reached out and grabbed his coat, twisting the fabric around with a grip that surprised me. He tried to shrug out of it, but it was buttoned, and the angle with which I held the fabric didn't give his arms the freedom of movement to work free.

He lurched from side to side, making frustrated mutterings as he attempted to weaken my hold. I was able to right myself somewhat, and – finding that I had both of my feet solidly on the ground – lifted one of them to kick his legs out from under him. He fell heavily with a grunt, pulling me down with him, my fingers still entwined in the cloth. For no special reason, I noticed that it was wool, with a wide herringbone pattern that was visible even in the dark, though just as lighter and darker shades of gray and black.

My knee hit a cobblestone as I landed, bringing tears to my eyes and focusing my thoughts intently on the struggle. The man was attempting to get his arms up to break my grip. Once, twice, he chopped, and one of his arms had gotten between my own as he attempted to reach my face. His fingers were scrabbling about on my chin, working toward my eyes, when I propped and centered myself on the injured knee. With a gasp from my sharp and renewed pain, I pulled up my other leg abruptly, slamming that knee into my opponent. And then, as he twisted beneath me, again.

With a groan, his hands immediately dropped away from their struggles, but he didn't stop trying to get away, twisting weakly from side to side. He began to curse under his breath, wheezing specific words and phrases of the vilest sort. And then he looked up, our eyes locked, and he spat at me.

I think of myself as several things. I am a doctor. I was a soldier. And for little more than a fortnight now, I had been a widower. The feelings that had remained constrained within me since my recent loss, pushed down with medical detachment and military discipline, found their own secret door just then. A thin black crack in an obscure part of my own dark foundation was all that was needed.

And then I went mad.

If Holmes and Inspector Lanner hadn't arrived then, I'm not sure what else would have happened. As it was, I was prevented from causing any permanent harm.

Even as I heard the footsteps running toward us from the front of the old house, I released my right hand from its twisted grip in the man's coat and immediately refolded it into a fist. "That is enough of you," I muttered, and he looked up at me with suddenly widened and fearful eyes, seeing in my expression just what he had awakened, if only for an instant. It was only Holmes's cry of "Watson!" that prevented me from punching the villain's head into the cobbles beneath it, possibly with enough force to fracture his skull and kill him. If I had known then what was to come in the days ahead, perhaps I would have followed through. Instead, I pulled my force at the very last instant, simply hitting him on the intersection of his mandible with his skull. His head whipped around, and the resulting motion, reacting on that delicate mass of brain tissue within, dropped him instantly into a state of unconsciousness.

Releasing my left hand from his coat allowed his now-tensionless upper body to sag to the ground. I painfully rocked back on my knees and pushed myself up to a standing position. Holmes and Lanner were there by then, alternately looking between the unconscious man on the ground and at me. I didn't need to examine my opponent to know from his regular breathing that he was all right and would be awake soon. I had recognized him for certain at the last minute, just before I hit him. "It's Baron Meade," I said, my voice sounding rougher and more winded than I would have liked. "He came out the back." I swallowed. "There was a secret door."

Holmes glanced sharply toward the building, but then back to me as several constables entered our immediate vicinity. Lanner directed them to carry the unconscious man toward the street. "My apologies, Watson," said Holmes quietly, as the others left us. "I should have made sure that the constable assigned to watch with you back here knew to stay put where he was placed. I'm not surprised that you wouldn't let anything past you, but I had no idea how desperate things might become."

"The gunshots? The explosion? Was anyone injured?"

"No. One of the Baron's men panicked and began to fire when we stormed the house. He was subdued quickly, but as you can imagine, the shots escalated the business considerably. And then . . . ." He paused and rubbed his face with uncharacteristic worry, "Then one of the men tried to ignite a barrel of fuel. Inexplicably, there was a flash and bang, but it didn't set off the cache stacked around it." He shook his head. "Thank God. The man who tried to kill us all, however, didn't survive. The rest were much more fortunate."

239

Holmes started to turn away, but I stopped him as I had a moment of clarity. "You sent me back here because you sensed there might be danger up front. You were diverting me out of the way." I gestured toward the house. "You didn't know there was a secret door. You thought no one would come this way." It was a statement, not a question.

He at least had the decency to look embarrassed. "Nonsense," he said, gesturing toward the dark building. "We knew from my reconnaissance earlier today that there was a rear door, and someone had to watch it. The fact that the constable left before the Baron appeared proves that the police could not be trusted to do the job."

"You forget, Holmes. You told me you spiked their guns earlier today when you examined the house by fixing the known rear door so that it couldn't be opened from within. The same for the windows. You believed that no one would be able to escape by this route. You placed me here to keep me out of the action."

"Watson – "

"I do not need any protection," I said, a trace of bitterness in my voice, reawakening the anger that had been in me for weeks. Striking Baron Meade had not drained it away.

"Watson, it has been less than a month since . . . ."

"Holmes, thank you for what you tried to do, but do not do it again."

He was silent for a few seconds, and then said with a nod, "I apologize, my friend. It is fortunate that you were here after all. My efforts to seal the place up appear to have been circumvented, as the rat had a different escape route."

"Not at all," I said, willing to let it go for now. I looked around for a moment, retrieved my revolver, and then took a step toward the house. "Let's see this secret door." I led him to the foundation of the building and, lighting a match, showed him the line demarking the edges.

"Blast!" said Holmes. "If only I'd had time to fully explore the house earlier today, I would have seen this. But the Baron's untimely return mean that I had to get out without finishing the job."

I pushed on the hidden opening, but it refused to yield. However, a kick snapped the weak catch and the passage was visible before us. We found ourselves in the basement of the house. Holmes examined the door from the inside, lamenting again that he hadn't had the time to make further explorations during the day when he had briefly invaded the building while it was unoccupied. We found our way to the stairs and quickly went up to where the last of Baron Meade's men were being led out in handcuffs. In the corner was a body, now covered by newspapers, except for the stump of an arm that was revealed flung out beside it in an already congealing pool of blood.

240

The smell inside the house burned my eyes, matching how Holmes had earlier described it. Lanner was standing nearby alongside a series of many stacked barrels and boxes, his arms akimbo. Hearing our footsteps, he turned. "Are you sure it's safe like this?" he asked.

"Reasonably," replied Holmes, "although we should move it out as soon as possible, separating the materials in the different containers from each other. Where are the explosives men from the Special Branch?"

"I've sent for them now. They were waiting one street over." He lifted one of the lids, and then quickly replaced it when the strong ammonia smell washed over us. "What unholy mess is this?"

"A compound of nitrogen-based materials – fertilizers, actually. When combined with these other barrels of coal oil, they can form an incredibly powerful explosive agent."

"And the crates of machine parts? Screws, and the like?"

"Shrapnel."

"And he intended to blow up Parliament?"

"Possibly. Or Scotland Yard, or perhaps some other target. With the amount of these materials here, all mixed together and ignited, the blast would have been catastrophic. This is not a puny bomb assembled by your typical radical dynamitard, Lanner, to be left in haste by a wall of the Yard or at the base of Nelson's Column. Baron Meade is more ambitious than that, and combined with his superior knowledge and malignant motivation, much more dangerous as well."

"And tell me again, Mr. Holmes, how you got on to him?"

"The Baron's shoes didn't fit correctly," he said, turning away. Lanner glanced toward me in frustration, but with his mouth tight, as if he didn't trust whatever words might come spilling out.

I moved to the stack of materials and looked into a few of the crates. There were nails, and door hinges, and countless other metallic objects. When combined with the explosive force of the nitrogen compounds and the fuel oil, the deadly destruction would have been incomprehensible.

Through the open front door, we could hear the arrival of the heavy dray wagons, brought to evacuate the potential explosives from our presence. Holmes made sure that the different materials were kept separate and loaded onto their own individual wagons.

I stood to one side on the street and watched the progress of the silent and efficient men. I was wool-gathering in the aftermath of the affair, and unaware at first when the Baron was led nearby, in the grasp of two constables, toward a nearby Maria. I only came back to myself when one of the constables muttered in anger as the prisoner forced himself to a stop.

"Dr. Watson," he called with menace.

I turned his way. Even in the gaslight I could see a bruise forming on his jaw beneath his left ear.

"I won't forget this," he hissed. "Remember, sir – you have brought this on yourself."

My eyes narrowed. "Take him away," I said in a low voice, feeling how easy it would have been to reopen that hidden door within myself, seeking the satisfaction of bringing the butt of my gun down on his head.

Holmes joined me, watching the disgraced nobleman being placed in the vehicle while stating that our work was finished for the night. We walked out to the Brixton Road, and turned toward Camberwell New Road, seeking any sign of a cab.

"Lanner would have arranged for transportation," I said.

"Perhaps. However, I believe that he would like to carry on from here without us."

The fog seemed to thicken as we incrementally approached the river. "Why here?" I asked. "Why did he not find a house in which to store the materials closer to his targets?"

"This location is out of the way without really being that far from important targets. Up the Brixton Road, pass near the Oval, and so on across the Vauxhall Bridge. Then he would have been just a few minutes from everything. Who would question a few wagons carrying barrels and boxes openly through the city streets? Once in place, he might even have set off this hellfire in Trafalgar Square at mid-day. Imagine the carnage he could have caused."

"I would prefer not to." I could not force myself to think of it. "All because of the loss of a loved one," I said softly. "He blames the Crown for the death of his son."

"Not just the Crown," said Holmes. "The entire British people who would tolerate a system that, in his opinion, let his son die." We walked on in silence for a few more minutes, before Holmes added, "Grief can cause a man to do strange things."

He was not subtle. "Such as a man giving way to the urge to beat another into a pulp?" I asked. When he didn't answer, I said, "I only hit him the once, you know."

"That is true." Then, "That was enough."

When he didn't speak again, I felt the urge to fill the silence. "I admit the motivation was there to do further damage." I paused. "I'm glad that you and Lanner arrived when you did. Perhaps . . . I'm not ready yet to be accompanying you on these investigations."

"Nonsense!" Holmes cried, coming to a stop and facing me, startling me with his loud call in the oppressive fog. "Work is the best antidote, my friend!" And he clapped me on the shoulder, repeating in a softer tone,

"Nonsense. I will not tolerate it." Then, louder, "Look!" He pointed into the distance. "Finally, a cab."

In spite of our adventures, we actually returned to Baker Street at a comparatively early hour. Mrs. Hudson offered to provide us with some refreshments, but instead we deemed that whisky before the warm fire was exactly what the doctor ordered – with me serving as the doctor. There was no conversation, only companionable silence, and eventually I rose and made my way upstairs to my room, leaving Holmes staring pensively into the flames.

I slept far deeper than I would have anticipated, and awoke rather early, refreshed and surprisingly care-free. My mood was not even spoiled by the fact that rains had moved in, threatening to turn to ice as the temperature experienced a bitter January drop. Holmes, expecting few clients that day, started to shuffle through the mounds and stacks of papers that he was periodically forced to address, and I settled myself before the fire, painfully wincing whenever I was forced to move my sore knee.

And so Inspector Lanner found us when he made his way to Baker Street later that morning, to inform us that Baron James Osborne Russell Meade, former politician and philanthropist turned criminal, had escaped from custody late the previous night, not long after his arrest.

Chapter II
A Seemingly Innocent Matter

We had first tumbled into the seemingly innocent matter of Baron Meade only the day before, as revealed by an apparently innocuous client, one of several seen that morning. It was not unusual for any number of callers to visit our rooms in Baker Street on a daily basis. From nearly the first day that I had started sharing lodgings with Holmes, seven years earlier, he had been consulted by a great many of the residents of London about their little problems. "They are mostly sent on by private inquiry agencies," stated Holmes that day in early March 1881, referring to his many mysterious visitors when first explaining to me his unique position as a *Consulting Detective*. We had been fellow lodgers at that time for only a couple of months, and the mystery of uncovering Holmes's profession had served to fill my empty days as I sought to regain something of the health that I had lost the previous July in Afghanistan. "They are all people who are in trouble about something," he continued, "and want a little enlightening. I listen to their story, they listen to my comments, and then I pocket my fee."

He also explained that his turns for both observation and deduction, which had initially caused me to scoff in derision at what I believed was an exaggeration, were "extremely practical – so practical that I depend upon them for my bread and cheese."

I soon became a believer in my friend's methods, and a frequent participant in his investigations as well. I no longer doubted him – well, hardly ever – and never tired of seeing what he was capable of determining from the trifles that would seem to the rest of us as the merest moonshine.

Holmes, on the other hand, never ceased trying to help me to learn his methods. I must brag that I have had a few successes over the years, as he finally convinced me to look at the knees of a man's trousers, or the writing on an envelope, for instance, before proceeding hurriedly and directly to the contents of the enclosed letter. I believe that I have been of some assistance to Holmes, as he wouldn't have had the patience to tolerate my friendship for this long if I had not. And yet, when our latest visitor departed the previous morning, I'd had no sense that there was anything more serious about the man's problem than an insignificant theft from a warehouse.

I began to perceive that there was something of more concern about our visitor's tale when, after the withdrawal of the fellow, Holmes slipped out of the room to the landing and had a word with the page boy. Then he returned and sank back into his armchair, tapping his lips with the stem of an unlit pipe, and cogitating furiously while staring at the floor past his outstretched legs. Finally, he seemed to return to himself most abruptly and, reaching for the tobacco in the nearby Persian slipper mounted below the mantelpiece, he said, "You saw that he was lying, did you not?"

I cast my mind back. The man, the third to climb the steps that morning, had identified himself as a Mr. Walthrop, manager of a warehouse south of the Thames, not far downriver from the Tower. His clothing was worn, but not overly shabby. His speech was plain and unremarkable. But I had shaken his hand, this supposed manager of a warehouse, and recalled now the smoothness of his palm and fingers. And then, as I cast my mind's eye over him again, I saw it.

"His shoes!" I exclaimed.

"His shoes," Holmes agreed, scratching a light for his pipe.

"They did not seem to fit his feet."

"Clearly," said Holmes, "they were not his shoes at all. They were too short for his feet, and his toes could be observed pushing uncomfortably along the top leathers, and not fitting at all into the stretched and established spaces where the toes of the true owner have previously rested."

"But surely the fact that he's wearing incorrect shoes is not enough to say that he was lying. There must be countless explanations why he would be in the wrong shoes – "

"Yes. Seven immediately come to mind."

" – but that doesn't necessarily negate what he told you."

"Nevertheless. You might also recall that his clothes did not fit either. He was trying to disguise himself. Also, his hair was freshly barbered, and he still had the subtle smell of the scented lather that had left him so clean-shaven, highlighting the lighter skin by his ears and on his lip, where were previously covered by side whiskers and a mustache. No, he was clearly not who he wished us to believe, as the man inside did not match the outside. He is too refined to be the warehouse manager he impersonates, and his entire story becomes suspect." Now, with the pipe well-lit, Holmes asked, "When did Mr. Walthrop state that the barrels first disappeared?"

"Just last night. He said they were catalogued as part of the inventory yesterday afternoon for today's shipment, and that they were missing this morning when the warehouse opened."

"And don't you find it unusual that he immediately high-tailed it to our door to seek our assistance? Do you not believe that barrels of building materials have gone missing at warehouses before, even those supposedly managed by the worthy Mr. Walthrop? Was this a significant enough occurrence for him to specifically seek out my services?"

I agreed, seeing his point.

"So why now? Why make the journey this morning, specifically to arrange for me to be watching at the warehouse *tonight* for the delivery of a similar set of barrels, on the shaky assumption that since the first barrels were taken – somehow – the next set will be as well?"

"When you explain it that way – "

"Did he give any indication that he believed that some supernatural occurrence was responsible for the theft, or perhaps it was caused by the participation of some international gang of barrel thieves?"

"No, he did not."

"He offered nothing unique at all about this random and superficially insignificant warehouse theft. Yet he patently wants to ensure that we will be at a certain place at a certain time tonight, but for no particularly good reason. Therefore, I think that we should be anywhere else *but* at his warehouse. The question now is to determine where else in the world we *should* be."

As Holmes finished speaking, a knock was immediately followed by the entrance of the page boy, whom I had heard slipping up the stairs seconds earlier. He was out of breath, but struggling to speak clearly. "I had to jump on the back of the carriage, since I didn't see any of the other lads at first," he explained. "We were nearly to Portman Square when I gave the sign to Morton, and he managed to take my place. He'll stick with them. Bates was with him too, and was keeping up, last I saw. I came back to report."

"Well done," said Holmes, reaching into his pocket and pulling forth a monetary reward. "We shall await developments."

And they were not long in coming.

Within the hour, the front bell heralded the arrival of Bert Deacon, rampsman-turned-cabbie by way of being cleared by Holmes of a murder he did not commit back in '82. The big man paused upon entry to the sitting room, catching his wheezing breath. I had a chance to examine him, from his large smiling face to his inwardly turned left foot. I was surprised to realize that I had already identified our visitor as he climbed the stairs, before even seeing him, from the sound that foot made as it dragged awkwardly on every other tread. Perhaps Holmes's methods were rubbing off on me after all.

"I have a message from one o' your lads," he began.

"Morton?"

Deacon nodded. "He fetched up at a house on the Surrey side, just off the Brixton Road."

"Not in Rotherhithe?" Holmes glanced meaningfully at me. The warehouse in question had been described as on the river, in the East End, and definitely *not* in Brixton.

"No, sir. Morton had waved a couple o' the other lads to follow the carriage as they went south, and when they caught up with him, he told them to keep watch on the house where the gentleman stopped. Then he saw me on my way back towards the bridge and flagged me down." He paused to pull a wadded tear of paper from his waistcoat pocket. "This would be the address."

Holmes unfolded it, muttered, "Excellent," and flipped a coin toward Deacon. Catching it, the big cabbie muttered, "Thankee," and then, seeing the denomination, repeated more clearly, "Thank you, Mr. Holmes."

"Mmm," said Holmes, deep in thought. Then, rising suddenly, he instructed Deacon to wait for him downstairs. "I'll be with you momentarily." Over his shoulder, he added for my benefit, "Watson, I must reconnoiter the enemy camp." He passed into his bedroom.

"You think of this Mr. Walthrop as an enemy, then?"

"Better to be safe than sorry," he called through the open doorway, "as we have had cause to learn in the past, and sometimes painfully." I could hear drawers opening and closing. "Any man who would disguise himself, more ineffectively than he realized, and take time to try and decoy us elsewhere is certainly up to no good."

He returned to the sitting room, dressed as the common loafer that he so often favored when venturing out as someone else. Crossing to the door, he said, "Please remain available, as I don't know when I shall return. I hope to have the threads in hand before we're expected at Mr. Walthrop's warehouse later tonight." And with that, he was gone.

I spent a dull afternoon watching the skies cloud over through the sitting room windows. I tried to distract myself with a novel, but to no avail. Mrs. Hudson brought tea, and seemed as if she wanted to stay and talk, but apparently something in my visage sent her back down the stairs. I was relieved. After the events of a few weeks earlier, I was very glad for all that she had done to care for me since, but I was not yet ready to discuss it.

Holmes returned a little before six. I could smell the cold air that came in with him. It was a bitter January so far, which was only another factor in my despondent mood. "I took the liberty," Holmes called from his bedroom as he resumed his normal guise, "of having Mrs. Hudson bring up something to eat a bit earlier than usual. We will be going out soon."

"Not to Walthrop's warehouse, I expect."

"Correct. Although I did take the time to outfit a couple of willing acquaintances to fill those roles. They will appear in suitable Holmes and

247

Watson clothing, pulled from stores that I maintain in one of my hidey holes, in order to give them some semblance of appearance to the two of us. As we speak, they are loitering in the shadows, but not *too* shadowed or hidden to be ignored, near the warehouse, giving the impression that both you and I are diligently, though incompetently, on the job, ready to catch the wicked thieves of Mr. Walthrop's next barrel shipment – a thing that I suspect will *not* occur."

I didn't want to dwell on the idea that Holmes had a double of me out on the streets of London. Rather, I asked, "What did you determine?"

Mrs. Hudson, whom I had heard climbing the stairs, chose that moment to enter with a loaded tray. It was only an hour or so since she had served tea, but she brought enough food to nourish me as if I were starving. At least, I assumed that a great deal of it was for me, as she must have known that even a hungry Holmes would eat very little indeed.

I joined my friend at the table, reaching for the makings of a sandwich. He said, "First, I have determined that Mr. Walthrop does not exist." Slathering mustard over folded bread and ham, he continued, "The manager of the warehouse is a certain Oswald Brinker. Our visitor this morning is actually someone else, a completely different man that you may have read about: Baron James Meade."

Enlightenment was sudden. "You will recall that he has been somewhat vocal of late," Holmes continued. "Since the riot."

I nodded. The fellow had been quite vociferous in recent weeks, making numerous public speeches, as well as providing written commentary in the form of pamphlets and letters to the editors, criticizing both the Government and the Crown. Previously a patriotic member of society from a long-standing and wealthy family, he had almost overnight become a bitter opponent of the established order following the death of his only son the previous November, just a couple of months earlier. At the time of the events that came to be known as "Bloody Sunday", this son, a young officer in a famous and noted regiment, had been in London, simply watching the unfolding and escalating events from a location beside one of the buildings facing Trafalgar Square. He wasn't a part of the four-hundred soldiers or the two-thousand police officers who were assigned to break up the protest that day.

Things quickly descended into a tumult, and when the authorities rode into the ten-thousand protesters on horseback, a wall of fleeing people were forced to surge past where the Baron's son was standing, knocking him to the ground. He suffered several seriously broken bones, but appeared to be otherwise unharmed and was expected to make a guarded recovery, until later the next day, when a bit of marrow from his fractured

248

femur dislodged and entered his bloodstream, forming a blockage that resulted in his immediate and untimely death.

"A tragic affair," I said. "But why would Baron Meade be decoying us away from a warehouse?"

"A warehouse where he has no connection at all," reminded Holmes. "But I'm telling things out of order, which is a bad habit indeed."

I allowed that obvious dig at my own small efforts to pass unremarked. "Tell it, then, the way you wish."

He took a bite of the sandwich, swallowed, and said, "Deacon first delivered me to the house off the Brixton Road, whereupon I made myself visible until Morton approached. He explained that the man he had followed had gone into the house for only a few minutes, and then had departed, walking up the street to a nearby pub. He was still there, drinking beer after having previously consumed something for lunch.

"I looked across the street to the house. It was obviously untenanted. The street was deserted, and the chance was too good to miss. Leaving Morton and his compatriots on watch, I made my way to the house and slipped inside. What I found was puzzling at first, but suddenly I realized what I was looking at.

"There were no furnishings, and it had obviously been empty for quite a while. In fact, the only items there whatsoever were countless crates and barrels. I had smelled the strong scent of ammonia when I entered, far too much to simply indicate that tramps had found a way to get in and hide in this empty house. I quickly ascertained that the smell was coming from many of the barrels – but not all of them. Piled nearby were vast amounts of coal oil, also adding their own powerful scent to the mix, and boxes and barrels of metallic objects, such as nails, screws, and even hinges and other metallic hardware.

"I see that you are puzzled, Watson. In spite of being exposed to some of the worst that society has to offer, you have thankfully not seen everything. Certain types of nitrogen-based compounds, such as that contained in the ammonia-smelling barrels, when mixed with fuels, make a terrible and violently powerful explosive."

He let that statement hang in the air between us, and I had a terrible realization. "Guy Fawkes," I breathed. "He intends to fulfill his new hatred for the Crown and blow up Parliament."

"If not Parliament, then some other place, in order to exact his revenge."

"Good Lord!" I breathed. I set down the rest of my sandwich untouched, my appetite gone. "But how do you know it's Baron Meade? I don't believe that his image has been in the newspapers."

"Because afterwards, I followed the man in question back to his home," replied Holmes. "But to continue: While I was in the house, I realized dimly what he was planning. Knowing that a police raid would be needed to take possession of these materials, I set about sealing the back door and windows so that entry and – more importantly – exit can only be effected from the front of the building. But before I could explore further, I heard Morton's unique whistle, indicating that our man was returning from the pub. I slipped out the front door, which was screened by some bushes from the walk, and just made it to a side alley when our man went inside. He was only there for a few minutes before leaving and locking up. Rather than go back in, I chose to follow him, and when he found a hansom, I was in Deacon's right behind him. I trailed him all the way to Bayswater, where he was driven to the front door.

"That in itself was unusual for a man in working garments, but I already knew that they weren't his clothes, and that he was likely to be a gentleman. When the front door opened upon his arrival, and he was greeted by his man, I managed to be nearby, and I knew from the murmured conversation before the door shut that he held a position of authority, and that he was certainly entering his own home. It took no great effort to then determine that the residence was that of Baron Meade, and that the man's description fit that of our visitor.

"I proceeded to Scotland Yard, where I discussed the events with Inspector Lanner, who I think can be trusted to handle things effectively. He then *liaised* with Special Branch, and the upshot is that we will be joining them in a couple of hours for a raid on the house."

That simple statement did not fully encompass all that then occurred. Later, as darkness was falling while we rode in a hansom over the river into Lambeth, Holmes explained that the police would also be helping watch the warehouse where our doubles were stationed, to protect them in case any unlikely attacks were made against their persons.

We arrived at our destination, a dark street a block over from Baron Meade's empty house, and met up with Inspector Lanner. He was in his mid-thirties, trim and capable, and a fast-riser in the Force following his return a few years earlier from military service. He carried himself with pride and a typical good humor, and I knew that he was one of the men of the Yard that Holmes had some use for, although he often despaired for all of them when he was frustrated about how they frequently handled an investigation.

Lanner greeted us warmly and informed us that, as an added complication, the Baron and a few others – "His men," as Lanner put it – currently seemed to be on the premises, and their activities indicated that the materials were to be moved that very night, probably to the location where they would be detonated. "There are several heavy wagons parked in front. Very lucky, indeed, Mr. Holmes, that you were able to direct us here when you did."

"Not at all," said Holmes. "The Baron himself started our countermove in motion when he visited me this morning and attempted to distract me. I must admit that some of my contacts within the government have noticed his revolutionary talk these last weeks, and had already consulted me on the subject. Therefore, I wasn't entirely unaware of the man, and possibly he was aware of my new interest in him as well, causing him to come up with this plan to try and divert my attention in a different direction tonight. But really, I had no suspicion that he was up to something of this nature before today, and if he had simply left me out of it and gone about his nefarious business, he would certainly have gotten away with it."

Lanner nodded. "Be that as it may . . ." he said, and then he turned away and proceeded to give additional instructions regarding the positioning of his men for the raid. I ended up behind the house, as I have previously described, and so the night went, with the plot averted, and Baron Meade in custody. And then the next morning, Lanner had traveled through the winter rains to inform us that the man had escaped.

"I am sorry," said the inspector, sitting in the basket chair and trying to warm himself before our fire. "He was initially taken to one of the smaller stations south of the River, to avoid his being seen at the Yard and possibly causing a public spectacle. As he was being led from the carriage toward the building, he wrested himself away from us and fled down the street, his hands still fixed in the darbies. He was gone into the maze before we could organize ourselves."

There didn't seem to be anything left to discuss, although Lanner seemed to think that Holmes would smoke a bit and then tell him just where to place his hands on the fugitive. However, after several awkward minutes, in which it became obvious that the policeman had already been dismissed, Lanner departed with a promise to keep us informed of further developments.

We spent the rest of the day in our rooms. Holmes sent several wires at different times, as new thoughts would occur to him. There were no callers, but the fact didn't seem to cause my friend any dissatisfaction for a change. He seemed to be considering something, and I could only assume that it related to the difficulty at hand. Finally, I asked if that were true.

"I've been pondering the nature of the Baron's plot and subsequent escape. However, I believe that it can best be handled by the police at this time. I have, of course, put out the word with my various associates to keep

251

an eye out for the man. I expect we'll hear from him again, but for now he will likely try to lay low."

As the day turned toward evening, I ventured to suggest that Holmes might employ the next two or three hours before we ate in making our room a little more habitable. He tried to offer excuses, and insisted that, as he'd now finished pasting cuttings into his scrapbook, he had planned on conducting a chemical experiment. I pointed out that he was likely to asphyxiate us, as we could not adequately ventilate the room on this cold January day, and that he should do something more profitable. He could not deny the sagacity of my request, so with a rather sour and rueful face, which raised an unexpected laugh from me, he went off to his bedroom. I heard him knocking around for a few minutes, and then he returned, pulling his large tin box behind him. Placing it in the middle of the floor, he pulled over a short three-legged stool and squatted down in front of his burden. He threw back the lid, and I could see that it was already partially full of bundles of paper, tied up with red tape.

But, instead of putting things away, he started pulling *out* the packages, stating, "Here's the record of the Tarleton murders, and the case of Vamberry, the wine merchant, and the adventure of the old Russian woman, and the singular affair of the aluminium crutch, as well as a full account of Ricoletti of the club-foot, and his abominable wife." Then he reached deeper into the box and, shaking off a ribbon-tied bundle that tried to stay with it, he pulled out a small wooden box with a sliding lid. "Ah, now, this really is something a little *recherché*."

Inside the box was a crumpled piece of paper, an old-fashioned brass key, a peg of wood with a ball of string attached to it, and three rusty old disks of metal. "Well, my boy," he asked, "what do you make of this lot?" He seemed very pleased with himself, seeing that I was interested.

"It is a curious collection," I remarked wryly, with a long-acquired ease of noncommittal engagement. I realized what he was doing – attempting to distract me from the cleaning and sorting that he had obligated himself to do before our dinner was served. And yet, I allowed myself to be swept into his little game.

"Very curious, and the story that hangs round it will strike you as being more curious still."

"These relics have a history then?"

"So much so that they *are* history."

"What do you mean by that?"

"These," he said, with the sly smile of a fisherman who knows the hook has been set, "are all that I have left to remind me of the adventure of the Musgrave Ritual." And then he proceeded to tell me the tale.

Chapter III
Past Adventures and
Fresh Memories

Sherlock Holmes leaned forward in his chair, taking a sip of cold tea after speaking steadily for the better part of an hour, recalling those events of nearly a decade earlier. He tossed another lump of coal onto the fire, and turned his face back toward me. The light from the flickering flames grew as the weight of the black nugget shifted the hot embers. The flare of ignition caused shadows to dance across the plains and hollows of his lean countenance, giving him a look of ageless knowledge and understanding. And then he spoke, the spell was broken, and he was again simply my friend, a grin forming on his face.

"What did you think, Watson? Was the quest to find the meaning of Musgrave's riddle a fine tale for a cold winter's evening?"

"Absolutely," I responded sincerely. It had indeed been a fine tale. I had heard him casually mention the events connected to this Musgrave Ritual on previous occasions, but never to the depth that it had just been explained. As I have related the story elsewhere, I do not propose to take time, space, and effort to retell it here. Suffice it to say that it serves as a good example of how Holmes's abilities were sharp, even in those earlier days when he was still first establishing himself as a consulting detective.

"Speaking as a former military man," I added, shifting in my chair and glancing at the mess on the floor between us, "both as an active participant in, and also as a student of, certain well-known battles, your story certainly served as a fine diversionary tactic, as you no doubt intended."

With a snort, Holmes slapped his knee and settled back in his chair. "I deny any such charge!" he cried, waving his hand toward the large tin box resting at his feet. "Did I not show every intention of fulfilling my duties as a fellow lodger, taking time from my busy and demanding schedule in order to organize my documents? I was simply following your suggestion to sort through my papers, intent on the task at hand, when you expressed an interest in one of my old cases. It was only polite to stop what I was doing and relate to you the dark details of the Musgrave Affair."

"You knew exactly what you were about," I replied, glancing at the clock to see if there was enough time for a warming brandy before dinner. There was not. "I will admit some responsibility as well, as I allowed you to tell me what happened, but we both know that you really had no real intention of sorting through this . . . this *disjecta membra* of your past." I waved a hand at the shambles spread around us. "You distracted me as if I were a child that was given a watch on a fob as a temporary plaything."

Holmes smiled. "I admit to nothing," he said. Then he glanced ruefully at the floor, where the box was surrounded by items that he had removed from it before discovering the relic that reminded him of the Ritual. "But I must say that things look worse now than before. At the very least, this trunk will need to be repacked tonight. I'm sure that Mrs. Hudson will have something to say about it, and I certainly don't want anything kicked over or disturbed when the fire is lit in the morning."

He was still sitting there and considering the task of replacing the various tied bundles in the trunk from whence they had come when we heard the sound of footsteps on the stairs. Holmes sat up abruptly as if he had been stung by a bee, a look of panic on his face. I will be the first to admit that I am not my friend when it comes to observing and deducing, but I could see the thoughts run across his face as clearly as if he had shouted them. Mrs. Hudson's tread, always steady and even, was slower on those regular occasions when she was bringing our meals. This was one of those moments. I could tell that Holmes was calculating the amount of time he had left before Mrs. Hudson reached the door, opened it, and then entered to discover the unholy mess on the floor.

Three steps had already been climbed, and Holmes leaned forward to grasp a bundle of tied sheets in each hand. He placed them quickly and with purpose into the tin box, not simply tossing or dropping them. But one of them immediately slumped to the side. Obviously, the box would need to be repacked more carefully than this, and there was no time for that. Two more steps climbed. I smiled with a satisfaction that sadly didn't speak well of me as I watched Holmes slide to the front of his chair, obviously considering dropping to his knees in order to speed the process.

Mrs. Hudson had reached the landing in the mid-point of the stairs, with its window looking out on the small back yard where she sometimes grew herbs in the summer, near the lonely plane tree located there. She made the turn and started up the final climb. Holmes looked at me, a fleeting dash of panic in his eyes, perhaps a mute plea for help, before resignation washed over him, and he settled again against the back of his chair, ready to take his medicine. He covered his eyes with his fingers. The door was slowly opened.

Mrs. Hudson made her way into the room, eyes on her goal – the dining table in the corner by one of the tall windows. Then, she saw *and* observed the new stacks of papers stretching across the floor, like a wave frozen in its path along a beach. She stopped, only for the time it would take for the next step, and scowled at Holmes as if he were a boy caught writing something naughty on the wall.

"Mrs. Hudson." He raised his head. "I lost track of the time – "

"I'm sure that you did," she replied coldly. Setting down the tray, she turned and, placing hands on hips, she scolded in her most Scottish tones, "You will have that cleaned up *tonight*, Mr. Holmes. I won't have the tweeny breaking her neck tomorrow morning when she tries to climb over it to light the fire."

Holmes nodded, and then she turned to me with a look on her face that made it perfectly clear that she unfairly considered me to be an accomplice in the business. Rather than uselessly trying to explain that it wasn't *my* disarray, I simply and tacitly accepted responsibility as well, nodding my agreement instead of prolonging the encounter. Often, this is the simplest way. I have stated elsewhere that I have an experience of women stretching over three continents, although this has been somewhat subsequently exaggerated over the years. However, I do know enough to realize when it is the time to say nothing at all. Apparently, in spite of his regular insistence that the fairer sex is *my* department, my friend somehow, on this occasion, had comprehended the truth of this as well.

Mrs. Hudson, having made her point quite well, turned and left the room. We were able to wait until we knew that she had descended the stairs all the way to the bottom before our laughter burst forth.

It was surprising that I could laugh, in that January of 1888. Only weeks before, on the next-to-last day of December, my wife, Constance, had unexpectedly contracted diphtheria. We had only been married at that time a little over a year. As Holmes and I stood from our chairs to move toward the table and the food left there, an unexpected vision of my late wife suddenly appeared in my imagination, and I almost faltered. I found that happening quite often that winter.

Constance and I had met in the spring of 1885, when I had been summoned to San Francisco, working to pay off my brother Henry's debts while nursing him back to health from an illness of his own making. Having gone there, I had set up a practice to earn money, doing what I knew best, and Miss Constance Adams had been my first patient. When I returned to England just a few months later, I could not forget her. After journeying back to the United States the following year to assist Holmes in one of his cases, I asked her to be my wife, and she accepted. We were married in November 1886 and settled into our domestic arrangement, with my days spent in the ground floor medical practice of our Kensington home, the lease newly purchased.

I stepped around the stacks of paper and made my way to the table, already realizing from the smell that Mrs. Hudson had made curried chicken, perfect for such a cold January night as this. My mind turned back to my late wife.

Constance had always suffered from bouts of poor health, and I only came to realize when it was too late that bringing her to the unhealthy climate of London had exacerbated the problem. The sea fogs of San Francisco were much different than the poisonous coal-saturated particulars of the British capital. A series of ever-worsening illnesses left her weak, her condition only improving when she was able to travel away from London with her mother, who – having no ties left in America – had moved to England at the time of our marriage. Of course, these occasions when Constance was traveling allowed me to continue to participate in a great deal of Holmes's adventures and, as always, I made notes of them, with the hope of someday having something published.

Holmes and I ate in companionable silence. Mrs. Hudson had again prepared one of my favorite meals. It had been that way since my return to Baker Street several weeks earlier. Holmes, of course, cared nothing for what was being served. Food to him was only a fuel, and if he was in the middle of a case, he considered it a distraction. Still, he could not be unaware of the effort that Mrs. Hudson was making for me.

I reached for the pepper, moving aside the tall silver goblet that had been resting on the table for the last several days. It had been used in a particularly brutal murder in Chipping Ongar, and after the killer was caught, following an evil night hiding beside the Motte of Ongar Castle, Holmes had kept it as a souvenir. In the days since then, it had stood unmolested on the table, until such future time as it might find its way to a different location in the sitting room.

I smiled to myself. In the time that I had been married and living elsewhere, I had actually forgotten what it was like to reside at 221b Baker Street. I had always wanted to write about the adventures that Holmes and I shared, but how could I ever explain something like this, and how it really was, during those days?

My wish to publish something to honor Holmes had recently been realized, although not as I had first envisioned. It was a narrative about our initial meeting and first investigation together. Working with a friend who acted as my literary agent, and who also contributed a lengthy middle section to the tale detailing the historical background of the case, it had been made public in late 1887. I had stopped by Baker Street to present a copy of the slim volume a couple of days after Christmas, and unexpectedly found myself involved in yet another of Holmes's cases. After a chase around London, stretching from a pub in Bloomsbury and thence to an unlikely vendor of geese in the fruit and vegetable market of Covent Garden, and finally back to Baker Street again, I had returned to my Kensington home to discover my wife suffering from a fever. Three days later, she was dead.

Holmes was a tower of strength during that period, immediately inviting me to stay in my old rooms, as both he and Mrs. Hudson knew that I should not be alone during that time. I quickly realized that I had no interest in returning to the Kensington practice, and within days I had put it up for sale, as it was clear that I was welcome to return to Baker Street permanently, should I so choose. And I did.

Those weeks had not been without interest. Already Holmes and I had traveled down to Birlstone, where the awful events in the room overlooking the moat had played out. And then there was the strange medallion of the gypsy, Pitt, who had apparently known Holmes since both were boys, although when I pressed for details, they only grew quite serious, with Pitt shaking his head, and Holmes declaring that the world was not yet ready for such a tale – an excuse that I had heard before, and would often hear again.

Now, on this cold rainy night, with thoughts of my departed wife never far away, and just a few weeks after her death, I found that I was able to smile and even laugh. I did not know yet what to make of that fact, but I resolved not to think upon it too much.

Later, I was back in my chair before the fire, enjoying the brandy postponed by our meal. Holmes was doing what he should have done hours before, carefully replacing the papers removed from the trunk, and sorting others from around the room to join them. That was when a question occurred to me.

"You said," I opened, "that the Musgrave Ritual was the *third* case that was brought to you through the introduction of old schoolfellows. What about the other two?"

"Hmm?" said Holmes, his attention fixed on a knife lying across his knees, the tang wrapped only in a material that looked like bandages. The blade was either rusty, or covered with dried blood – in the firelight, I could not tell – but it certainly looked ominous.

"You said that when you were first starting out, and living in Montague Street, you sometimes had cases brought to you by former fellow students, and that the third of these was the incident of the Ritual, when you were visited by Reginald Musgrave."

"That's right."

"Then what about the other two?" I asked. "Heaven knows I don't mean in any way to distract you from what you're doing, as happened earlier today, and I certainly don't want to be the cause of Mrs. Hudson's wrath falling about your head, but I would enjoy hearing about these other cases as well."

257

I knew that I was taking a chance asking about Holmes's former investigations, as often he did not feel the need to discuss past events, considering them to be a closed book, unless some aspect of a distant investigation might have some related and comparative association to a current case. And yet, that particular January, Holmes had been more willing than ever before to share with me the stories of some of his old adventures. I believe that, as my friend, he was trying to distract me from the recent death of my wife, and it was much appreciated. Already, he had told me about the Skinless Serpent – not the cold-blooded variety that one might expect! – and the Bigamistic Banker, and the painful matter of the Montague Street Butcher. I had also learned of other bits of his history, such as what happened at Arnsworth Castle, and even the investigation that had convinced him to become a consulting detective, a sordid tale of blackmail and family secrets in Norfolk that had stretched over decades.

To hear of these adventures only now, after all this time, having known Holmes since the first day of January 1881, was still something of a surprise to me, considering how reticent he typically was. It must be recalled that at this point in time, almost exactly seven years after I had first met him, Holmes still hadn't told me of the existence of his brother, Mycroft. That would only happen later in that year of 1888, during the early days of the awful Autumn of Terror. But that was still in the future, and, looking back now from a distance of so many years, we didn't know what we were going to face.

Holmes placed a last tied bundle into the tin trunk, closed and fastened the lid, and stood, stretching like a cat. Then he reached for my glass, walked to the sideboard, and refilled it, pouring another for himself. He returned to the fire, handed me my brandy, and settled into his chair.

"Surely one story was enough for today," he said. "Even the king did not require more than that from *Scheherazade.*"

I laughed. "That is true. However, you are singularly unoccupied at present, as we are allowing the police to search for *Baron Meade*, and before some new client wanders in and you hare off in a new direction, I propose to get another tale from you." I crossed my legs and took a small sip, holding it in my mouth for just a moment and feeling the welcome heat. "Feel free to begin at any time."

"Ha!" he said, pulling his feet into the chair, and twisting them in something of the manner of the fakirs that I had seen in Afghanistan and India. "Another tale you want? Then a tale you shall have. Gather round for the story of The Eye of Heka, and one man's foolish belief that he ought to own it."

The wind picked that moment to rattle the glass in our windows. A glass of brandy, a warm fire, a dark night, and a story. I was going to enjoy this.

Chapter IV
The Adventure of the Museum Theft

"The Eye of Heka?" I asked. "Sounds rather eastern."

Holmes took a sip of the brandy and said, "Don't tempt me into telling a story the wrong way around, as you did with your recently published effort."

He gestured to the small octagonal table beside his chair, where a copy of *Beeton's Christmas Annual* still rested in the same location that he had tossed it when I first gave it to him, just after the holiday. It contained my labors, and those of my friend Conan Doyle as well, to honor and bring to public notice my friend's singular gifts. The story it told, with the admittedly fanciful title of *A Study in Scarlet*, recounted the first time I had seen my friend in action, having just learned that he earned his living as a "Consulting Detective".

Holmes placed his brandy next to the small journal, and I wondered about his comment, which implied that he might actually have read the story, thus giving him enough data to decide that I had told it in a manner not to his liking. The fact that he would certainly disapprove of how I had related the events was no surprise to me at all. The volume certainly looked untouched, but I knew that he treated all documents, books, and so on with such exaggerated care that, even if he had read it as I hoped and was starting to believe, there would be no indication of it, either shown by wear or turned-down pages.

"Do feel free to begin at the beginning, then," I said.

He nodded. "As I only want to tell one more tale tonight, I will refrain from giving you the particulars of the second case brought to me by an old University chum. Suffice it to say that it involved a map, a bottle, a key, a killing, and an excursion into the grates leading down beneath Charterhouse Square to the lost Fleet River and beyond. For now, you will have to make do with a much simpler case that involved a visit to my humble rooms in Montague Street (those same rooms that I earlier described to you at the beginning of the Musgrave affair), this time by Ian Finch, the Earl of Wardlaw.

"I met Ian at University," he continued, "in the early days. We were not friends then, nor at any time thereafter for that matter. Rather, we were thrown together often by a common course of study. He was a second son, and was learning something to serve him in good stead when he took an administrative post in the east, as had been planned for him by his father.

"The fact that we knew each other at school is unimportant to this story, except that he was aware, like many of my compatriots, of those special skills which you have had cause to observe from time to time. When I came up to London to follow my profession, I never gave Ian Finch another thought.

"Sometime after that, his older brother was killed while visiting Africa. This brother had been on a grand tour, seeing the world before returning to his duties at the family estate in northern Essex. Their mother was long dead, and Ian had been somewhere on the Continent when it happened. He had met up with his father, still the Earl then, at some out-of-the-way rendezvous, and then they continued on together to bring back the body. While there, Ian had decided to stay behind while the Earl and his dead older son returned to England.

"Of course, I knew nothing of this at the time. It was only later that I learned what had happened, along with other pieces that Ian shared with me. As I said, I was living in Montague Street, spending my time in a constant trot, attempting to learn all that I might need to prepare me for my profession. I had yet to completely define the parameters of what would be expected, as well as what I would expect for myself, but I knew enough to associate with certain individuals that might be considered questionable by the more law-abiding segments of our community. By gaining their trust to a degree, I was able to begin learning special skills, such as how locks work, or patter from the criminal argot, that I knew would be handy later.

"When not studying the ways of our criminal brethren, I took myself a great deal into the British Museum, across the street from my rooms, reading on a variety of subjects. And occasionally – and truly, not often enough in the early days – a case would come my way, either by referral from someone whom I had previously helped, or from the police, who were already finding their way to my door with increasing regularity.

"The house where I lived, at No. 24, was leased by a woman who had been widowed by one of my father's first cousins. She and I had an uneasy truce at best, and I tended to avoid her as often as possible. This wasn't too difficult, as in those days, my rooms were at the very top of the building, on the third floor. She offered a shabby breakfast each day to her tenants as part of the rent. However, if I was able to earn enough from my own work, I was able to eat elsewhere and avoid her to an even greater degree than normal. Therefore, it was worth it to me to find employment and have a few extra coins in my pocket each month.

"As I recall, it was in the latter part of May, in '78, that I found myself unoccupied with paying work for a period that had lasted a couple of weeks. I had been involved in several cases earlier in the month, but had found nothing to challenge me since then. I planned to spend the day in the Museum, intending to broaden my perspective on some of the archeological explorations that were going on around the world. Does that surprise you, Watson?"

"Hmm?" I said, not expecting that Holmes would interrupt his narrative with the request for an interactive response. "Why should it?"

He gestured toward the *Beeton's* containing my effort on the table beside him. "I gather that you thought that I was serious when I talked about only taking in what knowledge is absolutely necessary." He reached for the small journal and picked it up. Proceeding to turn the pages, he quickly found what he sought and read to me: "*'I consider that a man's brain originally is like a little empty attic, and you have to stock it with such furniture as you choose. A fool takes in all the lumber of every sort that he comes across, so that the knowledge which might be useful to him gets crowded out, or at best is jumbled up with a lot of other things so that he has a difficulty in laying his hands upon it. Now the skillful workman is very careful indeed as to what he takes into his brain-attic. He will have nothing but the tools which may help him in doing his work, but of these he has a large assortment, and all in the most perfect order.*" He looked toward me under his lowered brow, deepening his voice and reading with dramatic emphasis: "*'It is a mistake to think that that little room has elastic walls and can distend to any extent. Depend upon it there comes a time when for every addition of knowledge you forget something that you knew before. It is of the highest importance, therefore, not to have useless facts elbowing out the useful ones.'*"

He closed the volume and held it in his lap. "Apparently you believed me when I said that."

"I know better now. It is an accurate record of what you said at the time, and considering that I had only known you a little over two months then, and that it was the same day you also revealed your perfectly unique profession, it is not surprising that it would make an impression on me."

He nodded and tapped a long finger against the spine of the book. "Your ability to recall and accurately record conversations is really quite a gift, you know. Although I deplore the idea that my investigations should be presented as some sort of penny dreadful," he said, replacing the *Beeton's* on the table, "I cannot fault you for the precision of your reportage."

"At least," I responded, "the question of whether you have read the d---ed thing has been answered!"

262

He smiled, and I prompted, "So you were planning to spend the day in the Museum then, finding appropriate furniture for your brain-attic?"

"Correct. I was attempting to establish in my own mind a general feel for recent archeological discoveries in Greece. As I recall, the day before was spent determining what I could about the previous year's uncovering of 'Hermes and the Infant', as found in the ruined Temple of Hera at Olympia. Certain aspects of my reading had suggested another path to explore. I was considering where to begin my next excavation, so to speak, as I entered the Great Court of the Museum from Great Russell Street. Normally I am the most observant of men, but that day, it completely escaped me that I had been noticed by another fellow, walking quickly away from the Museum and towards me and the street.

"'Holmes!' he cried, coming to a stop in my path. 'Holmes! Is that you?'

I saw that the past few years had not been kind to Ian Finch. He was always a big man, and his clothing looked as prosperous as ever, if not more so. But there was a dissipated look about his face, and his gait seemed the slightest bit forced, as if he suffered from a form of rheumatism that should not have been present in a man of our age. As he reached me, I observed that his eyes were yellow, and that his breath had the sour smell of last night's alcohol. He was clean shaven, but there were a couple of missed patches along his jawline, and his collar was clearly from the previous day.

"'Just the man I need!' he cried.

We had never been close, and I greeted him with a reserved formality. He appeared not to notice, as he planted himself a little too close to me and, in a suddenly quiet tone, began to speak.

"'I've heard that you have set yourself up as some kind of detective.' He glanced back and forth across the courtyard to ascertain that there was no one nearby.

"It was a statement rather than a question, but I acknowledged the fact. 'Just what I need, then. I'm not quite sure what to do, and you can take charge of things.' He turned and looked over his shoulder toward the Museum entrance. 'These fools want to call in the police.'

"'Perhaps,' I said, 'we should discuss the problem further. Shall we step into the Museum?'

"'No!' he erupted, and then he quieted again. 'I told them I'll handle it, and if we go back inside they will be trying to interfere. Besides, there is no privacy in there.'

"I smiled. 'Then I suppose the Alpha Inn across the street would also be unsatisfactory, should they be open this early.'

263

"He simply glared, and I quickly added, 'My rooms are just beside us, in Montague Street. We can talk there.' And turning, I led him out the gate into Great Russell Street, and so on around the corner and back to No. 24.

"He seemed wary when we reached the building, but I held the door and then followed him into the narrow hall. He made toward the large parlor that opened to our left, with its unusual painting above the fireplace. However, that was part of the landlady's territory, and I indicated the narrow, steep, and curving stairs at the rear of the hallway which led up and on up to my room. I listened with a secret smile to his increasingly labored breathing as we ascended to the first and second floors, and when we started up to the third, with the stairs more like a winding ladder, his perturbed grunts became even more amusing.

"My room in those earlier days was on the top floor. In my last year there, before abandoning the place completely to move to Baker Street, I was able to afford something a little bigger and closer to the ground, but in those days I lived nearer the angels. Unlocking my door, I allowed Ian to precede me into the small room, where he immediately took the better of the two chairs, while I sat in the other.

"We each prepared to smoke, he a foul cigar and me with my pipe. Then, with a final sour look at my humble lodgings, the walls close upon him to both the left and right, he began to speak, explaining that an object that had recently been donated by his family to the British Museum had ended up stolen, just that morning. He elaborated that he had brought it back from northern Africa two years earlier, at the time of his brother's death, when both he and his father had gone out to bring the body back home.

"He described the stolen object as a figure of a lesser-known local deity, identified popularly as 'Heka', about a foot in height. It was of a polished and heavy stone – smooth, dark, and with lighter streaks running through it. But what made it unique was a carving of a severe but rather plain face on the front, upon which was placed a large ruby, centered in its forehead above the eyes. It was this jewel which gave the idol its curious *sobriquet*, 'The Eye of Heka'. Ian added vaguely that this stone was meant to represent the focus of the effigy's power. 'It was the very devil getting the thing home,' explained Ian, 'but we finally managed it. Took it on to the family estate, out in Essex, but my father has never been comfortable with it there. Finally, he insisted a month or so ago that it be sent to the Museum.

"'Frankly,' he continued, 'he made the initial overtures to the Director behind my back. I'm the one who brought it back here to England, and I should be able to keep it, but my father holds the purse strings, so I can't protest against him too much – for now. But I made sure that we still retain ownership, and that the arrangement with the Museum is simply a long-term loan. When I'm the Earl, I'll bring it back home.'

"I couldn't resist asking, 'Isn't its home actually where it came from, rather than either your estate *or* the British Museum?'

"He scowled at me, and then spit a piece of tobacco from his tongue onto my rug. 'I can see you're one of those who would give back the Empire, a tiny piece at a time.' He waited for my expected defense, but when I simply continued to watch him, as one waits to see the next response in an inevitable chemical reaction, he settled back in his chair with a shake of his head.

"'Doesn't matter,' he said. 'I still need your help. As I said, the thing has been stolen.'

"'Ah,' I said, finally getting to it. 'From the Museum, you said?'

"He nodded. 'I just found out a few minutes ago. They haven't even had it for a full day. Yesterday morning, the thing was crated at the estate, and I, along with two of my friends, brought it up to London.'

"'Who knew that you would be bringing it?'

"'My father and my two friends, Conner and Malloy. Our old butler, Fisk, knew something about it as well, but he wouldn't share any secrets.'

"'What about these two friends of yours?'

"'Completely trustworthy. They were with me when I brought the thing back to England two years ago.'

"'What about any other servants? Who crated the idol for shipment?'

"'Did it myself. I didn't trust anyone else to do it. After I finished, I put it away for safekeeping, and then yesterday morning we set out early. I'd cabled ahead and had a growler waiting at Liverpool Street Station. We then brought it over through the Holborn to the back of the Museum over there, where an assistant curator named Williams took possession of it. It was supposed to be examined, photographed, catalogued, and so on, before being placed in the collection this morning.'

"'Isn't that somewhat sudden?' I asked. 'To have an exhibit publicly displayed so quickly after its acquisition?'

"He nodded. 'One of the conditions my father arranged. He wanted to make sure that it was clearly known that it was no longer at the estate. We've . . . we've had a few instances of someone breaking into the house over the last couple of years, and we're convinced it was someone trying to retrieve the idol.'

"'What made you think that?'

"'On one occasion, we disturbed an intruder. The man escaped, but it was clear from what he left behind, matches and fuel and such, that he was trying to start a fire and burn us out. In addition to the other materials, a shoe was left behind by the intruder. More of a sandal, really, such as what they wear down there.'

"'Do you still have it?'

"'No. I threw it into the fireplace.'

"'Unfortunate. Can you describe it?'

"'It was just a shoe, Holmes!" he said with impatience. But after I let my question hang, he continued, "It was old and dusty, with a crack from left to right across the center, where a foot would bend it while walking. I couldn't tell if it was a right or left sandal, but that's typical of the kind they wear. And it was odd in that it was lost in the middle of winter, when that attempt took place. My father reasoned that only a foreigner unprepared for the journey would have been wearing that type of shoe in the cold English winter.'

"'And what did you think? Do you believe it was left by someone who followed the idol here?'

"Ian seemed troubled. 'I suppose it could have been. As I said, it took some effort to bring the statue here. There were several attempts to take it from me then, before we even departed, and we had never had any break-ins at the Essex house until after the idol came there.'

"'Why didn't they find it?'

"'Because it was in a vault that defeated them,' he said. 'My father had it built years ago, a big walk-in contrivance, such as one might find in a bank. He never liked the idol from the beginning, and insisted that it be kept locked away, instead of on display. Truth be told, it turned out that he was correct, as I had initially wanted to show it prominently, which would likely have led to its theft on the very first attempt.'

"'And so eventually your father wanted it out of the house completely, and arranged to have it sent to the Museum.'

"'Exactly. After signs that someone was still coming around the house, he wanted it gone. So I brought it up yesterday and left it with that Williams at the Museum, thinking that they knew their business, and then I went on to the Langham with my friends. I didn't want to travel all the way back to Essex just for the night, only to come back today and see how they have the thing set up.

"'I went to the Museum this morning to look at my idol, but when I arrived, there was some embarrassed shuffling, and then the man who met me at the door hemmed and hawed before finally leaving me, only to bring back Williams and the Director himself. Both apologized, telling me that not fifteen minutes before, they had discovered that it was missing from its designated resting place.

"'I insisted on looking around, and quickly saw that they had ignored my concerns and placed the thing in a very insecure glass case, centered right in a public passageway. It was one thing to give in to my father and let the Museum keep it, but another for them to offer it so easily to the first thief that walked by. The glass on the top of the case had been cut, not broken, and whoever had stolen the idol had simply reached in and taken it. I looked for any sign of who could have done it, but I didn't see a thing.'

"'Perhaps I'll see something that you missed,' I said, standing up.

"Ian blinked once or twice, and then said, 'You want to go over there?' When I nodded, he stood as well, following me out and down the twisting steps to the street, his cigar clenched in his teeth.

"Stepping across to the Museum, we entered, and Ian led me, in a roundabout way, to an upstairs gallery. The high windows revealed row after row of artifacts, carefully organized. Cases contained pottery and tools, and in the distance were what seemed to interest the general public most of all, the mummies.

"As we got closer, I saw our goal. There, in the main aisle, stood four men around a glass case. On either side of it were several other cases filled with various bits of ancient detritus.

"Ian stepped up and, without any word of greeting, explained who I was to the men by the case. 'This is Sherlock Holmes. He's my detective, representing me.' He glared at them all with belligerence.

"I repeated my name, and said that I was pleased to see them. I already knew two of the men, and was quickly introduced to the others.

"Williams, the assistant who had initially taken possession of The Eye the day before, was a slight man with thinning sandy hair. The Director, whom I had met on past occasions and seen many times from a distance, was a much more forceful personality than his subordinate, and even though in this instance he was very deferential to Ian, he did find it in himself to initially ask, 'No offense to Mr. Holmes, but is there really a need to bring in an outsider?' However, a glare from Ian instantly silenced him. The third man turned out to be Hayes, the supervisor of the Museum guards, while the fourth was an acquaintance of mine, Inspector Plummer, who was quite supportive of me in those early days as I was finding my footing in my new profession.

"A quick examination of the case revealed that a fair-sized hole had been cut in the top, as Ian had said. The circular piece was resting in the case beside a small satin-covered plinth, which had obviously been the resting place for the idol. Centered in the circular glass cut-out was a mashed knob of plumber's putty, used to grasp and lift the piece when it was freed.

"'They cut the top out instead of the side,' said Plummer, painfully pointing out the obvious.

"I nodded. 'Although it is a little more awkward, the thief was able to cut a much smaller hole and lift the idol straight up. A cut on the side would have required a much bigger area to remove the object.'

"Plummer nodded. 'And whoever it was left the cut-out piece of glass inside, rather than placing it on the floor or propped against the case, where it might have been noticed.'

"'Do you not have guards to walk through at night?' asked Ian. 'How could they not see this?'

"Hayes, the guard supervisor, took a step forward. 'We do walk through here regularly, sir. But as you can see, the suddenness of this exhibit's installation has meant that the lighting has not yet been adjusted to favor this area. Also, to be honest, I must confess that the men were not alerted specifically to be aware of this new exhibit, and if the theft occurred early last night, they may have only seen an empty case, not realizing that there was something already missing, as they might have believed it was empty all along and still being prepared for exhibition.'

"'We'll need to speak to those guards from last night,' I said.

"'They are being fetched now,' replied Plummer. 'Their shifts ended several hours ago.'

"I continued to examine the case, seeing one or two features of interest nearby. Before I could follow up on them, the guards arrived.

"Well, Watson, to keep this story from being any longer than it needs to be, the guards were unable to provide any relevant information, except to confirm what the supervisor had theorized. They had seen the case containing the empty plinth, and that it had been that way from the beginning of their shift. As they had not been notified that the idol was to be located in that case, they had no reason to suspect that it was gone. It was not an unusual thing for empty cases to appear without explanation as new exhibits were constantly being prepared. The men had no other information to give us, but Plummer asked that they stay for a while in case we had further questions.

"Ian began to harangue the Director and Williams, evenly dividing his ire between the loss of the idol and the subsequent summoning of the police. Then he turned to Plummer. 'Since you're here,' he said, 'the milk can't be put back in the cow. What are you going to do?'

"Plummer didn't seem to be fazed by Ian's outburst, stating calmly, 'We will continue our interviews. I intend to put out the word to keep an eye out for your idol. The usual places will be examined – pawn brokers, jewelers, and the like, in case someone tries to sell it or remove and break-up the ruby. And of course, we'll also check with the ships that are leaving soon, in case someone is trying to take it back from whence it came.'

"Ian, listening to this litany of unimaginative but necessary routine, was working himself up to an apoplectic fit. This was especially evident when Plummer mentioned the possibility of cutting up the ruby. However, before my acquaintance could further vent his anger, I said, 'We may be able to take a short cut, Inspector, although I certainly cannot argue with making sure that all other eventualities are covered as well.' Turning to the Director, I said, 'Might I trouble you to examine the files concerning your employees?'

"The Director nodded and led me to the Museum offices, where I looked over several documents. While the others remained puzzled, Plummer smiled as he saw my trail. I wrote down a name and address, handing them to the inspector. With a nod, he turned and said, 'I'll summon a cab.'

"Five minutes later, Plummer, Ian, and I were racing east toward Hackney, our cab followed by another filled with constables. Plummer asked, 'What did you notice?'

"'The floor around the display case had not been mopped recently, although other areas nearby had. The oblique reflections of the light showed the streaks and marks of the water elsewhere on the floor, but not around the case. However, immediately next to the display case, well away from the mopped areas, was a fresh dried ring, most likely left by dampness from the bottom of the mop bucket. Additionally, there were several dried drops across the floor leading to and from the mopped area, showing the path to the display case by which the bucket had been carried.'

"'So you've decided that one of the cleaning people has stolen the idol?' asked Ian.

"'He probably carried it out in the bucket,' said Plummer.

"'A review of who was working last night, compared with the records, provided me with a likely suspect.'

"Plummer glanced at the paper. 'John Goins.' He looked back up, curiously. 'An American. He hasn't been over here for very long.

"'We would have questioned him,' said Plummer to me. 'Calling in the cleaning staff was already being taken care of. This Goins would have been of special interest, being foreign and having recently arrived from outside the country.'

"'Ah,' I said, 'but would he have come to you when called? Would he have answered your summons? How long would you have waited before determining that he was *not* coming? And how long before you have examined his records to determine that he has only been employed at the Museum for less than two weeks?'

"'Two weeks!' said Ian. 'That's around the time that my father first reached out to the Museum about letting them keep The Eye.'

269

"'Someone,' I said, 'has been keeping tabs on your activities, and knew about the statue's transfer. If they couldn't get to it in your house, then it was worth it to them to make a try at this other end.'

"Plummer smiled and shook his head. 'I have to give you credit, Mr. Holmes. You are correct in stating that it might have taken some time before we attached any significance to Goins, and he would likely have been long gone by then. Assuming, of course, that you're right.'

"'We'll soon know,' I said, as our cab turned from Homerton High Street and into a sordid cul-de-sac.

"The inspector's men surrounded the building, and it was Plummer himself who kicked in Goins's door. It was all very anticlimactic. The man himself was still there, although we saw that he was preparing for imminent departure.

"He was a most unusual fellow, Watson. Tall and thin, his great bony head seemed too heavy for his thin neck. His skin was tanned, and his hair thick and black. The area around his eyes looked bruised. His arms were long and thin, like the rest of him, with oversized hands that each seemed to be curled around some invisible object. He looked sickly, and yet as if there were hidden depths of strength within him.

"But it was his eyes that were the most disturbing. As the door was forced open, he straightened where he had been standing, but made no other motion with his body. Those eyes, however sunken, were a startling light blue, and seemed to shine with an inner light. They were compelling and intelligent and enraged, darting from one to the other of us, as if memorizing all of our features for the someday when we would be on the other side of this offense. He gave me my share of attention in those long seconds, but it was at Ian that he peered most intently. I know that it sounds fanciful, but I was glad when this odd scarecrow of a man turned his attention away from me.

"The idol itself was standing on a rough deal table in the center of the room, in front of our prisoner, the ruby glinting from its forehead like some third eye. I must confess, Watson, that the thing seemed to draw the focus of the room in an unusual way, even more than one would expect from such an unusual artifact."

"Holmes," I said, with some amusement. "You almost sound as if you believe the thing had some power."

Surprisingly, he didn't answer immediately, but glanced toward the fire, which was slowly burning itself out for the night. "An object may be simple stone and crystal, Watson, and still have power, if only that which is invested in it by those that believe and are willing to commit acts in the object's name." He looked up then, his face very serious. "As I learned after the fact, the carving was coveted by a group of obscure zealots that refused to stop trying to get it back. John Goins was their agent. It turned out that Ian seemed to have some reverence for the idol as well. He had no intention of returning it to its original home, but he did realize after these events that he had no business keeping it for himself either. He continued the arrangement for it to remain at the Museum, but in a much more secure setting than before. Even after his father died and he became the Earl, I understand that he left it here in London, rather than taking it back to Essex as he'd originally planned."

With a sudden deep breath, he stood up and looked at the tin trunk nearby. "So, two tales in one day. I leave it to you to judge which was the more interesting, this one or that of the Musgrave Ritual."

"I'm not sure," I meditated from my chair. "The second has untold possibilities, and your part seems to have been workmanlike – "

" – but negligible?" he finished for me. "You are correct about that. Inspector Plummer was right in the sense that the foreign cleaner would eventually have been identified, although I did help to make sure that he was caught in time."

"Whatever happened to this John Goins?"

"I don't know. I assume he was jailed, or deported."

"Were there ever any other attempts to steal the idol?"

"I'm not aware of any, although there is no reason that I should be. I've seen Ian, now the present Earl of Wardlaw after the death of his father, in passing over the years, but we've never conversed since that morning when he regained it. He slipped me a very stingy fee that was something of an embarrassment, and I was glad to be shed of him.

"However," he added, bending to reach for the tin trunk, "discussing the episode has reawakened a desire to see The Eye of Heka again, since I was only able to view it just the once. Seeing as how the Museum is under some obligation to me for several other little problems that have been resolved in the years since, I don't think there would be any difficulty in viewing it. What do you say to a little excursion tomorrow to Bloomsbury?"

It seemed to promise a peaceful trip, and I remarked that it seemed a fine idea indeed, little realizing the events that would follow. With my agreement to accompany him the next day, he wished me good night, leaving me there in my chair, watching the fire die while the room cooled around me. Soon my eyes were unfocused as I stared into the cryptic flames, recalling and reliving scenes from a previous life, now gone forever. But I only allowed those visions to go on for a few minutes before, with a sigh, I stood and made my way upstairs to my own room.

Chapter V
Old Haunts

Holmes and I each had separate errands to take care of the following morning, and we agreed to meet at noon in front of the Museum, whereupon we would take a look at the idol, and then have a late lunch.

I stepped out into the bright January sun, grateful for my heavy coat. Although the rains had ceased, a much colder spell had settled over the capital since the day before, and I felt the usual concern for those who were not as fortunate as I. In particular was the constant worry about the lads of the street, the Irregulars as we called them, those that assisted Holmes in his investigations. I knew that some came from meagre homes and would find relative warmth and shelter there. But others were not so fortunate, and I could only hope that they would survive the bitterly cold weather unscathed.

Adjusting the loosely stitched mourning band upon my sleeve, I hailed a hansom and directed the driver to Kensington. We set off to the south at a brisk pace, and I tugged my scarf tighter around my throat. Turning west at Oxford Street, making better time than I would have thought, we passed along the northern rim of Hyde Park, before eventually alighting at the small street where my former home and practice stood.

I was a few minutes early and, having paid the cabbie, found myself standing on the pavement, facing the steps leading up to the front door. I had been back here several times since Constance's death, but it was still too soon, and I was numb. This empty building had been both a home and a future, and was now simply a grim reminder of what had been taken from me.

When Constance had accepted my proposal of marriage, I had only a vague idea in mind for our path. My work in San Francisco had shown me that I could establish and manage a practice, something that I had tried to do only once before. After I had graduated with my medical degree from the University of London in '78, I had set myself up in harness in Southampton Place in Bloomsbury, but my heart wasn't in it, and soon after I had joined the Army. Upon my invalidation back into civilian life, I had spent time working in hospitals, mostly Barts, and also assisting as a *locum tenens* with several willing physicians. But setting up my own shop in the United States had taught me what needed to be done, and that I could do it.

After Constance agreed to be my wife, I had returned to London, ready to transition myself from Baker Street to the life of a married physician. I had carefully scouted until I found a suitable Kensington location, not far off the High Street. Through a combination of a fortunate inheritance, along with careful nurturing of various fees and rewards that I had shared with Holmes by way of assisting him with his work, I had accumulated enough resources to purchase the lease on a building with an existing practice from a retiring doctor, and when Constance and her mother arrived in England, I was already set up, although still living in Baker Street, as I didn't want to take possession of the residential portion of the house before Constance had also claimed it as her own.

Our marriage, in November 1886, was a happy event, with my friend Holmes standing with me as best man. Constance and I settled into our lives in Kensington, as she and her mother went about making the house into a home – not including the parts set aside on the ground floor for my ever burgeoning professional domain. In the meantime, I was fortunate in that I still had free periods here and there to assist Holmes with his investigations.

But Constance's health quickly began to deteriorate, and she and her mother were forced to travel to better climes, while I remained in London, building what I believed to be our future. And then, in a matter of days, she was gone.

The service was well attended, or so I'm told, although I have little memory of it. My mother-in-law left England soon after, her heart broken, and I fear that she held some resentment toward me, the doctor who could not save his own wife, and the man who had dragged her poor daughter so far from her original home to a land that only seemed to make her ill.

Several friends at a few of the hospitals put out the word that I wished to sell, and it didn't take long at all for a prospective buyer to approach me. Apparently I had selected a good area in constant need of a doctor, and had made the place much more successful than I'd realized. The price that I set was met without any disagreement, and soon the whole business would be finalized.

I was pulled back from my reverie by the sound of hoof beats. I hadn't realized that I was daydreaming, and the cold from the pavement had transmitted itself up through my ankles. I was quite stiff as I turned to view the approaching cab.

As expected, the arrival was the man purchasing the practice, Dr. Colin Withers. About ten years older than I, he too had served in the military, although he had voluntarily resigned in order to raise his daughter following his wife's death many years earlier. Never remarrying, he had built a successful Portsmouth practice, but had recently decided to move to London as his daughter became older. We had met twice before, following his initial letter to me expressing interest in buying the result of the labors that had so occupied me during the past fifteen months. On each of the previous two occasions that we had encountered one another, he had been both sympathetic for my loss and understanding regarding my feelings, even though his wife had died over a decade before. He was also quite enthusiastic about setting up in London, envisioning his plans for what he would like to accomplish.

I stepped forward to greet him, and he waved, but then turned back toward the hansom. Reaching up, he paid the driver, and then assisted a young woman down to the ground. I had not realized that his daughter would be joining us.

As when I had met her once before in the company of her father, I was immediately taken aback by her beauty. I knew from conversations with Dr. Withers that she was about twenty years of age, but she radiated the poise of one much older. She was wearing a stylish but heavy coat against the cold, and a warm hat which protected a great deal of her face without hiding that she was very lovely indeed. Taking her arm, Dr. Withers stepped forward. "Dr. Watson. Good to see you again." He nodded to the girl. "You remember my daughter?"

She offered a dainty gloved hand. As I reached for it, she glanced up, murmuring some greeting, and I could see again in her eyes, in just that instant, that she had the bright light of intelligence shining within her. Clearing my throat, I said, "Miss Withers. My pleasure indeed."

She took a step closer, keeping my hand. "Call me Jenny. Thank you for showing us the house once more. I thought of some more questions as I planned how we would arrange it."

"Not at all," I said, dropping my hand from hers. I was grateful that she was so forthright, and didn't try to offer still more comforting words, as so many had done over the past weeks. There was nothing else to say – no need to fill conversations with empty platitudes such as, "She is in a better place," or "It was a blessing, after all."

Dr. Withers cleared his throat. "Perhaps we should go inside and get out of this cold."

I agreed and led them up the steps, pulling out my key as I did so. "I'm afraid that, as before, it will not be much warmer inside. There has been no fire since . . . since . . . ." I found that I couldn't complete the thought, and simply went about the process of unlocking the door.

The place already had that musty smell of an empty building, in spite of the fact that it had been a home just weeks before. As I had foretold, it was nearly as cold inside as out, and we chose to stay in our coats and gloves.

Withers and I were scheduled to settle the purchase the next day, but he had reached out to me a day or so before about taking another look around. "*I have no worries about the soundness of the building,*" he had assured me when writing to make the appointment for this morning, "*but I want to fix in my mind the layout of the place.*" There had been no mention of his daughter.

I led them from room to room on the ground floor, pointing out this or that feature that I might have forgotten before, and answering questions when asked. I mentioned a few of the more interesting and memorable patients, and indicated that I would certainly be available for consultation if the doctor had any further queries in the future. Miss Withers only had minimal interest in the areas that would make up the medical practice, although she did examine with greater scrutiny the kitchens and back rooms of the ground floor. And then we had seen all there was to see down there, and it was time for them to explore upstairs.

I found that I did not want to go up there, to the floor where my wife had recently died. I do not believe in ghosts, and I have been around death more times than I can count – quiet deaths and violent ones, deaths that follow long illnesses as if they are the granting of a prayer, or those that arrive quickly and unexpectedly. I have held men and women dying from old age and sickness, and murder and war, and most importantly my own wife as she departed this world. Death held no mystery or terror for me.

But I did not want to go upstairs.

The doctor and his daughter seemed to understand, and left me there, in the dark and cold ground floor hallway, while they made their way up. I heard them moving around, ascending on to the next floor beyond, mostly silent, but with muted conversations sometimes that still sounded too *normal* for this house of pain. I forced myself not to check my watch, or to wonder too much about what was taking them so long.

Finally, a light creaking from the stairs told me that one of them was returning. I knew that it was the daughter and not the father. The footsteps on the carpeted boards were lighter, and sounded like those made when Constance used to come down the steps. Involuntarily, I shivered.

Miss Withers walked from the base of the stairs toward me, where I waited near the front entrance, and stopped two or three feet away. My back was to the door and I could see her in the glow coming in through the fanlight behind my head, although I doubtless appeared to her as a haloed blackness. She held her hands clasped in front, and her eyes were too shadowed to reveal themselves clearly. "My father told me more," she said, almost whispering. "About how your wife died. Without warning."

"The diphtheria was too much for her," I said, my voice rough from lack of use, and from standing there reliving memories. I cleared my

275

throat. "But she had been ill for quite some time. She was originally from San Francisco. It is similar to London in some ways, quite foggy and damp and cold at times, but the atmosphere was cleaner. The move to the foul air here in the capital did something to her. Perhaps if I had realized it sooner – if I had picked up and moved to a healthier location . . . ."

She stepped forward and placed a hand on my arm, light as a feather, heavy as an anchor. "You mustn't blame yourself," she said quietly. I could see her eyes now. One glistened as a tear formed on the lower lid. "I can see that you do, you know. You're so like my father. He was the same way when Mother died. The illness was different, but he felt that if he had tried harder, or been more aware sooner of her symptoms, or simply been a better doctor, she might have been saved." She dropped her hand then, although I still seemed to feel its weight. "He spent years punishing himself. In some ways he still is. It achieves nothing. It was your wife's time to pass, as it was my mother's when she died, and that is the way it was supposed to be. It accomplishes nothing to keep thinking of it."

She glanced into the dark sitting room with its closed drapes and shutters, untouched by the bright morning sunlight outside. I realized that I had been holding my breath, and took a small step back from her. My wife was dead less than a month, just weeks really, and I found myself hypnotized, like a mouse before a cobra. A wave of guilt washed over me. I felt that I was committing a betrayal. "Was your wife happy here?" she asked. "Were *you* happy here?"

I nodded and swallowed. "Yes." Clearing my throat again, I repeated, "Yes, we were. But there were so many plans. Dreams that will now never come true – "

I stopped, and she seemed to know enough not to prompt me with questions or offers of any further comments. Anything else would have likely devolved into the mere phrases of comfort that I had been so grateful not to receive when we had met earlier in front of the house, those that are offered to the grief-stricken when one doesn't know what else to say. She had no doubt heard too many of those when her mother died.

A sound at the top of the stairs alerted us that her father was returning. As he came down the steps, I saw with some little surprise that he limped, a fact that had previously gone unnoticed. It appeared to relate to some stiffness in bending his knee. When he reached the floor of the hall and left the steps behind him, he walked toward us and the limp went away. That, I realized, was why I hadn't seen it before.

Still, it had been disconcerting to see him limping on the stairs, as I so often do when my old Afghan wound is bothering me. I looked at him more closely, as well as I could in the dim light, and realized how similar we were in other ways. His hair and moustache were more grizzled than my own, but were trimmed in quite the same style. We had similar builds, and even equivalent styles of overcoats. He moved, as he rightly would, like a man in his mid-forties, a decade older than I, but then again, I believed that I was probably moving more that way myself during these last few weeks, as I often found myself at frequent and unexpected moments recalling and feeling pressed down by my wife's death.

I found that Dr. Withers was speaking, expressing pleasure at taking ownership of the house the next day. He asked his daughter if she had any questions, and she responded succinctly that she believed she had seen enough to continue planning how to lay out the house to their mutual satisfaction. She spoke more brightly at the possibility than she had just moments before, when she was offering calm words of comfort to me after finding me lost in thought in the dark.

With nothing left to do, we went outside, and I turned away to lock the door as they went down to the pavement. Joining them, we confirmed our arrangements for completing the transfer of ownership, and they set off toward Kensington Church Street. I let them go on, as I didn't feel like walking with them and making more idle conversation.

It would be easy to let myself fall once again into a brown study as I stood alone by the street, my recent companions making their way to the distant corner. I shivered and stamped my feet a couple of times, forcing myself back into the present.

It was only then that I had, just for the slightest instant of time, the feeling that I was being watched.

It passed instantly, but I did not negate it. I had learned over the last decade, first in the Army, and mostly in the company of Sherlock Holmes, that I should trust my instincts. And I had learned as well never to go unarmed. I patted my hand softly against the bulge of my service revolver, carried under my coat.

I assessed the sensation, and still found it to be valid. But I didn't have that feeling of being a target, another impression with which I have been intimately familiar. So rather than make any obvious motions, such as hiding suddenly or looking in vain for my observer, I forced myself to remain still, cool, and normal.

When Dr. Withers and his daughter were far enough ahead and turning the corner, I casually glanced at my watch, realizing that more of the morning had passed than I had thought. I had just enough time to make my appointment with Holmes in Bloomsbury.

Going a different way to the main road, but not walking in any sort of hurry that would indicate that I believed myself to be observed, I found a cabbie that I knew, with the odd name of Giles Styles, waiting at the usual stop in the High Street. He greeted me with quiet reserve, knowing of my recent bereavement. Nodding back to him, I told him our destination, and we set out at a brisk trot.

The sensation of being watched vanished with every hoof beat.

Chapter VI
We Examine an Artifact

The London streets had become more crowded since I had come this way earlier in the day, but we still made good time, and soon turned up Bloomsbury Street, and then almost immediately into Great Russell Street, which I shall always associate most with the odd investigation of the Three Split Bones, and not necessarily the overwhelming Museum, as one might expect.

Arriving at our destination and stepping down from the cab, I could see that Holmes was having a conversation with one of the guards at the great gates. I paid Styles with a good tip. I knew his regular haunts were in Kensington, and I didn't know how or when or even *if* I would see him very often in the future, but I wanted to honor his service. A veteran of Maiwand like myself, he had been the one to fetch the additional physician I requested when I first returned home just weeks before and found my wife near death. The servant who had run to find Styles and then given him my message had later told me of the man's relentless tracking of the specific doctor that I desired, when the man wasn't immediately available at the most likely place. Styles was a good fellow, and I would miss him.

I joined Holmes, who was explaining, "Nonetheless, Fletcher, you would do well to trust your wife a little more. It is obvious from your boots that she still loves you." Turning my way, he said, "Shall we go inside?"

Unacknowledged – but certainly noticed by my friend, who noticed everything – Fletcher touched a respectful pair of fingers to the bill of his cap in a salute. Holmes and I then navigated across the Great Court, and so on inside, my eyes blinking to adjust from the bright but cold sunlight we had left behind to the sudden darkness. Holmes unerringly led me through several turns to a bank of offices that would always remain unknown to most casual visitors. Almost immediately, we were shown into a vast room with high windows. Stepping from behind a massive desk was the Museum's Director himself, Sir Quinton Havershill, happily reaching for our hands. "Holmes! And Watson as well! To what do we owe the pleasure?"

My welcome, as ebullient as that for Holmes, spilled over from the Director's obvious high regard for my friend. Holmes explained that we had been discussing his old cases the night before, and the circumstances relating to the short and quickly solved theft of The Eye of Heka had come up. "I mentioned to Watson that there was a chance to have a look at it, and he agreed."

"Certainly, certainly. Anything for the man who so quickly resolved the question of the Ptarmigan Egg."

I raised my eyebrows. "Before your time, Watson," said Holmes. "And it was a jewel, not a real egg, as you might have understandably thought. Somewhat bigger than the ruby in The Eye of Heka, but with a much less colorful history."

Sir Quinton had leaned out into his anteroom while Holmes was speaking and issued instructions. Soon, we were joined by a somewhat disheveled man in his late forties, his light and thin sandy hair, combed loosely over his shining crown, doing nothing to disguise the fact that he was going bald – in fact, his journey to that condition was essentially complete. His face was sallow, and there were dark circles under his eyes – not those of illness, but rather a natural feature of his weary countenance.

"Holmes, You remember Clement Williams?" said the Director.

"Ah, yes. You were present that morning when The Eye of Heka went missing."

"Yes, sir. I trust you have been well since then?"

"Quite, thank you. And yourself?"

Williams glanced at the Director. "Still plugging away," he said.

There was an unspoken tension in the answer, which did not pass unnoticed by Sir Quinton. "Williams is a valuable member of our staff," he said after the slightest awkward hesitation. "He's a hard worker, and quite good at his job," he added.

"Thank you, sir," Williams said softly.

"Well, then, Williams," Sir Quinton stated in an overly hearty voice. "History repeats itself."

"Sir?"

"Mr. Holmes has returned regarding The Eye of Heka."

Williams's eyes widened. "I trust there isn't a problem?"

Sir Quinton shook his great head. "No, no. He and Dr. Watson would simply like to have a look at it."

Williams looked from one to the other of us for a moment, and then repeated, "The Eye of Heka, sir?"

"Yes, the Eye." Sir Quinton seemed a trifle vexed. "Just a routine viewing for some friends of the Museum." He turned to Holmes. "As you know, after the last incident, we do not publicly display the item. Originally, the Earl – that is, the Earl at that time – was anxious for it to be publicly visible, so those that had been attempting to steal it from his estate would realize that it was no longer at his home and leave them alone. However, following the attempt here, only hours after we acquired it, we learned more about the . . . umm, shall we simply say 'nature' of The Eye, and it was agreed that a less public area would be best all around for its safe-keeping."

His reference to this "nature" sounded intriguing, as did his mention of a colorful history, and I resolved to question Holmes more thoroughly about it when we had the chance, possibly at lunch following our viewing of the thing.

"Do you receive many requests to see The Eye?" asked Holmes.

Sir Quinton glanced at Williams, who simply shook his head. The Director frowned slightly, possibly expecting a more extensive verbal answer followed by a "Sir". Turning back to Holmes, he said, "There have been one or two representatives of the Foreign Office who have checked on it over the years, I suppose to make sure that it is still locked away, but that is all. Its presence here is not common knowledge, as you know."

"And the current Earl? He was quite . . . attached to the idol, and at one time vowed to bring it back to Essex once his father died. I understand that he decided to leave it here after all, but does he not occasionally want a look at it?"

"I'm not aware of a single instance in all the years since it was left with us that the Earl has asked to see it. Williams?"

"That is correct," said Williams. "I believe that once he realized he couldn't safely bring it home without encouraging the attempts to steal it, he decided simply to let it go."

"Hmm," said Holmes. "I must admit that surprises me. He was quite fond of it."

"It was undoubtedly the wisest course," said Sir Quinton. "This is certainly the safest place for it to be kept." He glanced toward his desk, which was a smooth and completely uncluttered expanse. "If there isn't anything else that I can do for you, gentlemen, I must get back to my duties. I'll leave you in Williams's capable hands."

With that, and a round of handshakes, we were led out of the office and through a maze of exhibits at a brisk pace. Williams wasn't inclined to carry on a conversation, walking several steps in front of us. He seemed tense, and I wondered what about this request had affected him so. Perhaps there was some unknown factor between himself and the Director that contributed to the man's immediate behavior. One certainly had the impression from the brief snippet of conversation that Williams felt he should have advanced to a higher position than he currently held. I would be certain to question Holmes about his thoughts on the matter after we had departed.

We detoured to an office, where Williams retrieved a set of keys from a locked safe. Again taking the lead, he led us onward. Considering what

I had just learned about the security needed for the idol, I wasn't surprised when we left the main halls and entered a much less ostentatious hallway, deep within the building. Then we went down several flights of stairs into a series of confusing interconnected cellars. Not far down a final narrow hallway with a low ceiling, Williams stopped before a heavy iron door, like that of a vault, and pulled the ring of keys from his pocket. Turning the solid-sounding lock, he ushered us inside, reaching past us to activate an electric light, as there was no indication that gas had been laid on here.

I could see that it was necessary in this musty windowless chamber. Any sort of flame in here would have quickly become distinctly unpleasant. However, I knew that before the Museum had been wired for electricity, just such a lantern light would have been used here by necessity on a regular basis.

Williams walked straight to a set of heavy steel drawers on the facing wall, each with its own sturdy individual lock. Selecting another key from his ring, he unlocked one at waist level and pulled it out silently. Inside was a bundle, wrapped in a red velvet cloth.

We stepped closer as Williams lifted it out, still wrapped. Then, carefully cradling it in his arm as if it were a very young child, he pulled back the folds of rich material, as though exposing the infant's face to a group of admirers in the park.

"I'm afraid I cannot let you handle it, gentlemen," he said. "It was cleaned before storage, and I neglected to bring any of the white cotton gloves that we use to routinely handle exhibits. However, I can tilt it this way or that as you require to give you a better view."

I leaned in, eager to have a look at this figure that had led to numerous robbery attempts. I have to admit that at first glance, I was rather disappointed. Having seen quite a few truly magnificent artifacts, both great and small, during my time in India and Afghanistan, this simple stone carving, not much more than a foot in length, seemed rather . . . ordinary at best.

As I had been led to expect by Holmes's description, it was made of something like marble, mostly black, with white or gray streaks running lengthwise. It was polished to a smooth shine, and there was a simple face carved at the top of its foot-long body. And then, of course, there was the ruby, fixed in the forehead and centered above and between the two eyes.

Williams shifted the object slightly, and the light from the electric bulb played about it at different angles. I was able to get a better look at the face. It consisted of a leering mouth, only a couple of inches wide, lips protruding slightly from the smooth outer surface, with something of a twist. There was a raised teardrop of a nose, nubbed outward above the smooth cheeks, and then the two eyes, which were not modeled to actually look like eyes at all. Rather, where they would have been were simply two holes, dark in their emptiness, and very small, about the diameter of a pencil. I couldn't tell from where I stood how deeply they extended into the carving.

And above them was the ruby, blood red in the artificial light of the storage vault. It was roughly oval-cut, and the flat planes of the surfaces showed an unevenness, betraying that it had been prepared by an unskilled craftsman from long ago. It was quite large, perhaps the diameter of a shilling, but it was unclear how deeply it penetrated into the carving, or what held it there. No indication of any sort of fixtures to keep it in place, such as one would find on a pendant, were obvious. The stone would have been valuable on its own if separated from its resting place, and certainly it could have been recut to a finer shape, even if that meant losing some of its size and weight in the process. But removing it from the statue would have somehow diminished it. Like so many historical museum pieces, its greatest value was as a part of the whole.

I recalled what Holmes said about objects having power simply because someone believed in them and invested them with value and importance. But looking at this example of a sculptor's art, I simply did not understand the attraction. It was just cold stone, with a prominently displayed cold gem. I was unimpressed.

I stepped back, but Holmes continued to peer at the effigy, shifting from foot to foot and angle to angle, attempting to avoid blocking the light as he did so. Williams made some minor efforts to accommodate him, but seemed instinctively to move the wrong way every time Holmes tried to get a better view. Finally, after resting his gaze on the thing for another long minute, the dead silence of the vault broken only by the sounds of our breathing and the rasping of the cloth of Holmes's Inverness when he moved, my friend straightened his back, saying, "Thank you for your time, Mr. Williams. Upon recalling the idol yesterday to my friend here, I was suddenly of a mind to see it again, after so many years. It is certainly amazing how much one can forget over so long a time."

Williams, in the act of rewrapping the statue and replacing it in the drawer, said, "Think nothing of it, Mr. Holmes. Simply part of my job."

Before Williams could complete his task, Holmes turned. "We will show ourselves out, then." And he strode to the door, leaving me to follow. Nodding a quick thanks to an obviously surprised Williams, I hurried to catch up.

Outside, Holmes led me back to the main galleries. Then, as I was able to walk side-by-side with him as he strode down through a connecting hallway, and out into the Museum proper, I said, "Holmes! Must you – "

283

"Not here, Watson!" he hissed, and I resigned myself to staying even with him.

Once we had exited the building, although still on the wide terrace behind the tall columns, Holmes turned quickly left, toward the Montague Street side of the great courtyard. I followed, struggling to adjust my coat in the sudden cold. Finding a sheltered spot in the shadows, Holmes paused and turned to face me.

"What is it, Holmes?" I asked. "Why are you suddenly so distressed?"

"Because that was not the real idol, Watson. Someone has substituted a clever fake!"

Chapter VII
Set Into Motion

"**A** fake!" I cried, but softly. "How can you tell?"

He patted his coat, and I knew that he was considering lighting a cigarette. Then he stopped himself. "Because I took the trouble, a decade ago, to examine the true idol when I had the chance. And I assure you that this simulacrum, no matter how well conceived, is *not* the real thing."

"Holmes, surely a plain stone object such as that would not have enough specific identifying features that you could recall them after all these years. It was simply a crude and rather ordinary sculpture, fashioned by some long-dead craftsman."

"Ah, Watson, but it *did* have identifying features. I had a chance to look it over quite carefully long ago, when we first recovered it in John Goins's Hackney rooms. There was a definite white streak on the front, near the base but centered below the face, that looked distinctly like a wavy letter '*H*'. I thought with some fanciful amusement at the time that it looked like the initial from my own last name, as if it were spelled out in smoke. I tell you that the mark was *not* there on the statue we just saw.

"But there is more. If you were to have seen the thing, the *real* thing, you would feel that it had . . . weight. A *presence*, one might say, or a sense of its history."

I looked at him in astonishment. This was not the sort of description that would normally be given about something by Mr. Sherlock Holmes.

"What we just examined was nothing," he continued, "but a stone carving, such as might be found in some curio shop down by the docks. It might as well have been a newel post or a doorstop. Granted, a great deal of effort, and probably expense, has been expended to make this look like the real thing. This is no casual substitution.

"But finally, and most telling of all, was the ruby. Surely you could see that the one we just saw was a reproduction? Oh, it was crafted intentionally to look crude, as if it had been fashioned by a native and not a modern gem cutter, but it was clearly a counterfeit, nonetheless. Even in that poor electric light, the real Eye of Heka would have shone with an inner light. This thing was simply a dead lump."

His description of the stone figure was quite unusual, considering that my friend generally had no respect for what he called "superstitious claptrap". And yet, he seemed completely serious about this business.

"Surely Williams must realize that the idol he showed us is not the real thing?" I said. "The man is a specialist. He has worked at the Museum for years, and the Director said he is very good at his job."

"Exactly! I'm certain that he *does* know it is spurious. And unfortunately, he also realizes now that *I* know it as well. I tried to be circumspect with my inspection, but I'm afraid that I let my surprised reaction show for just for the fraction of an instant, and Williams, who clearly did *not* want to display the idol to us at all, was watching for the slightest twitch that might reveal that I had spotted the fraudulent nature of the object."

"What should we do, then?" I asked. "Do you intend to notify Sir Quinton? Should we send a message to your acquaintance, the Earl, notifying him of the situation?"

Holmes started to answer, and then, with a surprised hiss, he pulled me deeper into the shadows. As I followed him, I pivoted to see what he had observed in the courtyard.

It was Williams, without a doubt, coatless and propelling himself toward the gates at a near trot, looking neither left nor right. Holmes did not hesitate for an instant before deciding on a course of action. Shedding his Inverness and fore-and-aft cap, he dropped into a slouch, immediately taking six inches off his height. Handing me his bundled outer garments with one hand, he used the other to reach up and brush his hair forward into a messy tangle down his high forehead.

"Wait for me at the Alpha," he said, loping off in pursuit of Williams in a manner which would never suggest that he was the well-known detective.

"Holmes," I said, quietly and rather ineffectually since he was already beyond the hearing of my still-conversational voice. "You'll freeze without your coat." But by then he had passed out of the gate and was gone. "You'll make yourself ill," I added.

I followed more slowly through the gate, expecting Fletcher, the guard, to ask me about Holmes's unusual departure. But he simply nodded, having either been unaware that Holmes had gone by, or more likely not surprised at my friend's odd appearance. I walked at a much more leisurely pace than Holmes had just done, and crossed Great Russell Street to the Alpha Inn, that fine old establishment on the corner just across from the Museum. I had been a frequent visitor there in my student days, given its proximity to both the University of London slightly to the north and my later short-lived practice in Southampton Place just a few blocks east. Seeing no one I recognized inside – and not expecting to, as I assumed that some changes had obviously taken place during the ten years that had passed since I was a resident of this neighborhood – I made my way to the

286

bar. Finding the place to be surprisingly well occupied, I asked for a pint of beer and a sandwich before settling myself at a table near the back, my old favorite actually, and looking out through the windows into Museum Street.

I had time to finish my abbreviated meal and most of the beer when I saw Holmes through the window, making his way quickly toward the pub's door at the corner. Downing the last swallow from my glass, I stood as he reached my small table.

He had brushed his hair back into its regular neat arrangement, and he was now standing at his usual lean height, somewhat over six feet. For the most part, his features were pale with the cold, contrasting greatly with both the redness of his nose and the bright look in his eyes. A faint smile played around his lips. "The game is afoot!" he whispered.

Obviously he felt no need to eat anything himself. He reached for his Inverness and hat, slipping into them without a word. I put myself back into my own coat as well and then followed him out into the street. Very quickly we were ensconced in a hansom, rapidly making our way west. "30 Wellington Square, Chelsea," he had called to the driver, who acknowledged with a nod.

Holmes then gave further explicit instructions, telling the driver to avoid the Strand, running to the south of us and parallel to our current route. "I followed Williams down that way," he said, "and the streets there are quite jammed with the mid-day traffic."

"Did you choose to let him go, or did you lose him?"

"Watson, please. Mr. Williams revealed what I needed to know, and I had no further need for him." He reached into a pocket and handed me a blank telegram form, smudged with dirt. Tilting it back and forth in the poor light from the cab's window, I could see that writing was imprinted into the surface of the paper.

"I followed him several blocks straight south, until he neared the Strand. He seemed to know where he was going, and led me straight to a telegraph office," Holmes explained. "He didn't recognize me, and I was able to stand immediately behind him while he filled out the form. After he paid and left, I let him go. Then, approaching the counter, I sent the clerk on some false errand while I obtained the blank sheet directly underneath the form that had been used by Williams.

"Outside, I found that I did not have a pencil to bring out Williams's message. But some dirt from the pavement, rubbed into the surface of the sheet, served the purpose just as well, and revealed the writing."

He pointed to the top of the form. "It is addressed to the Earl's residence in Essex."

287

I glanced up. "If Williams is aware that the idol is a forgery, and has been keeping that knowledge to himself, why would he immediately get in contact with the Earl as soon as he realized that you had perceived the truth?"

"Exactly. Now look at the rest of the message."

It said *"Holmes knows of substitution."*

The implications washed over me. "Then the Earl *is* aware of the substitution. He found a way to take it home with him after all, and he's allowed the Museum to go to the trouble of guarding the fraudulent object for all these years as a decoy."

"Obviously. But this is more serious than you realize."

"In what way? Because Williams is actually in the pay of the Earl, and willing to lie to his employers at the Museum?"

"No, my friend, it is very much worse than that." And then he drifted into that taciturn state that did not invite further conversation.

We eventually worked our way west and south, into and through Sloane Square, and onto the King's Road. Shortly we found ourselves turning into the short *U*-shaped Wellington Crescent, with its elegant white houses lining both sides, all facing a well-kept and tree-filled little park in the center. No. 30 looked like all the rest, four stories rising solidly above us. We mounted the four shallow steps to the small porch, and Holmes rang the bell while I looked down into the areaway, noticing the darkened windows through the iron railings.

"This is Ian's city home," he said. "When in London, he doesn't live in Mayfair or Belgravia, as one might expect. I have never been inside, but I had reason to be aware of it when it was mentioned in a newspaper article about a charity function that took place here." He glanced to the right and left, no doubt seeing more than I ever could. "I expect that he's at his Essex estate, where Williams sent the telegram, but I don't want to overlook the opportunity to speak to him here, on the off-chance that he's in town."

Holmes rang again, and then knocked. I remarked, "I don't believe that anyone is at home."

"And I believe that you're right." He turned. "The postman is making his rounds. Speak to him and determine if the Earl is currently in residence. I'll ask a neighbor."

The postman, a friendly and garrulous sort of chap, confirmed that not only was the Earl away, but his entire staff was as well, and that the house had been closed for over a month. Managing to extricate myself from the enthusiastic civil servant, who had progressed to gossiping about other residents of the Square, I rejoined Holmes in front of No. 30, where we stood near the door while he told me that he had found a neighbor who confirmed the postman's statement.

288

"I had hoped to find Ian here," he said. "We have no choice but to proceed to his country home."

"Could you not send a wire?"

"I would prefer to arrive unannounced. Williams has already notified him that I know of his deception regarding the substitution of the idol at the Museum. Now I need to speak to him in person, rather than engage in an endless series of explanatory telegrams on my part followed by denials on his."

We returned to the hansom. "Liverpool Street Station," Holmes told the cabbie.

"Holmes," I asked. "Why the urgency? Why travel to Essex, without even making the effort to send the Earl a telegram, asking him what's going on?"

"Because we're already playing catch-up," my friend replied tersely. "Williams has informed Ian that I know about the substitution. That, I'm afraid, will set things in motion."

"Things? What things? What is it about this idol that concerns you so?"

"Because of Ian's belief in it. His belief, and many others besides him. And believing in something gives it power. Now, Watson, I beg of you to let me get my thoughts in order. I assure you that I will explain things shortly."

We crossed London slowly, and I could sense my friend's frustration. However, he kept it to himself, and it was only when we were entrained and headed to Chelmsford, where we would change to a northern line and the Earl's home, that he began to speak.

"I told you last night about Ian's visit to my Montague Street rooms, back in '78, about how he described the statue, and that he had faced some difficulties bringing it to England."

"You related that he said he had a devil of a time getting it back."

"That's right. However, in telling the story to you last night, there was no need to elaborate upon some of the details that Ian provided at the time regarding his experiences. Now, that part has become relevant to your understanding more about the idol.

"As I told you, I had brought Ian to my room, as he didn't want to return to the Museum or join me across the street in the Alpha in order to tell his story. As we smoked, and before he shared the details of the recent theft of the idol from the Museum, he also related about how he had first acquired it.

"'You may have heard,' Ian told me, 'that when my brother died a few years ago, my father and I went out to bring him home.' I nodded. 'It was rough on the old man. His elder son, and all of that. I'd never been

289

particularly close to Jimmy, but I went along nonetheless. My duty, you know.

"'Father and I met up halfway, and then proceeded on together. There wasn't a lot of conversation between us, but I knew what he was thinking. I've always been something of a disappointment to him, and now I was the heir. Realizing what he so obviously felt didn't make me any happier, as you might imagine.

"'We arrived and took possession of the body. Simple enough on the surface. But it was a bit odd, in that no one could tell us much about Jimmy's death, except that he'd died in a fire while on a trip into the far desert. However, we simply accepted it as a given that there would never be an adequate investigation.

"'After meeting up with Jimmy's friends, Malloy and Conner, I managed to learn some more. When Jimmy had died, they had all been away from their hotel, having traveled somewhere out into the distant wastelands for several days to look for relics. It was something of a lark. They hadn't gone to any of the usual tourist spots. Instead, they'd headed toward a remote valley far to the south that had no reputation for that sort of thing.

"'Before they arrived at their goal, while camping one night, an accident happened, and Jimmy's tent caught on fire. The officials who spoke to us suspected that he was too drunk to escape, although they didn't come right out and say it that way.

"'The night before my father and I were to return to England with the body, Conner and Malloy visited my room to give me additional information, making it clear that their visit was a secret, and that they didn't want my father to learn of it. They explained that their visit to the remote valley had been more than some drunken distraction. They had previously obtained knowledge of the location of a hidden artifact in the desert, the finding of which might make their fortunes.

"'I could understand their interest in such a thing. Conner and Malloy were both second sons like me, and until Jimmy's death, I was facing the same bleak future that they were, packed off after completing school to work in a dead-end and thankless civil service job in some fly-specked country. In fact, truth be told, these fellows had always been more my friends than Jimmy's, and had only accompanied him on his trip because I myself had no interest in joining him and visiting that part of the world. Quite frankly, I also didn't want to spend that amount of time with my brother, either.

"'It turned out that Jimmy had been the financing partner in their amateur archeological expedition, and now, with him dead, they wondered if I might be willing to take his place and go back into the desert. At first

I was skeptical, as you might expect, but their descriptions of the item were enough to get me interested, at least. Enough so that I told my father the next morning that he would be returning with Jimmy's body alone to England.'"

"Your acquaintance, the Earl," I said, interrupting Holmes's narrative, "continues to sound like a singularly unpleasant individual."

"That is certainly the most accurate way to describe him," replied Holmes.

"And this object they were searching for. The idol?"

"Exactly. And it was at this point I asked Ian more specifically about what they had been searching for.

"'It's a stone carving. They call it "The Eye of Heka",' he replied, looking for a place to stub out the remains of his cigar.

"'Heka?' I asked, attempting to recall some fact or other that I had read. 'Isn't that one of the minor deities? An obscure god of magic?'

"'Right. Magic.'

"'And this 'Eye'? I take it, then, that there is a jewel involved. There is always a jewel.'

"He smiled, a rather unpleasant smile, I must say. 'So I was given to understand at the time. I didn't know much more than that about it then, although I've learned a great deal since. Several days before Jimmy's death, Conner had been in the Bazaar when he was approached by a wizened man, an odd-looking old chap with light blue eyes who looked more European than local. He offered to sell a parchment map that would supposedly lead him to a treasure bestowing great power. Conner had bought the map for nearly nothing, thinking it would make an amusing souvenir and nothing more. Later, at the hotel, he showed it to Jimmy and Malloy. While they were looking it over, a hotel employee delivered some drinks to their room, and Malloy impulsively asked him if he could translate the writing. The fellow couldn't, but directed them to the university, where he had an uncle who would know about such things.

"'The next day, they found their man, a little scholar who became quite excited when examining the document. He told them that it revealed the way a remote valley far out in the desert – he wasn't even sure that it was on any official map – where the tomb of an ancient merchant was buried. This man's most valuable possession, which was buried with him, had been a statue representing this Heka, the God of Magic. The map also contained a warning, stating that the object must remain buried with the dead man, as it was too powerful to be allowed to continue causing harm in the world.

"'My brother and his friends didn't believe anything about the statue having any powers – my brother never much believed in anything – but

291

they talked amongst themselves, and worked themselves up, and were tempted by the fame that might come from unearthing a lost treasure. I gathered that they were already bored, and this would be something new. I could certainly understand that. And it didn't hurt that the old man also said the statue had a great ruby mounted in its forehead, rumored to be as big as a child's fist. This jewel was there to channel – to *focus* – the Magic of Heka, which could tap into the power of *ka* – what some of them call the soul – in order to bestow the *ka* of the gods to its possessor.'

"Ian saw my look of skepticism at this point, and with a sheepish look, began to pat his coat, looking for another of his rotten-smelling cigars, having puffed through the first in unusually swift fashion. 'I know it sounds silly. But when you're sitting in the middle of a foreign country, and hearing something like this whispered to you in nervous confidence, it begins to take on a bit more substance.' He pulled out the cigar, lit it, and continued.

"'Conner and Malloy told me that the old man at the university seemed lost in the books and scrolls that filled his little office, and as exciting as the possibility of finding the statue was to my brother and the others, it was soon forgotten by the old man when he began to look through his documents for something about a similar legend. They left him there as they found him, and set about organizing a small expedition to the remote valley.

"'Conner and Malloy said that they felt as if something were wrong about it from the very beginning. The night before they were to leave, they were set upon in the street, but they managed to fight off their attackers. They returned to their rooms to discover that they had been ransacked. The hotel employee who had first directed them toward the old man was acting suspicious, and seemed to be watching them more than he ought. It was then that they noticed that he had the same light eyes as the old man who had sold them the map. It was almost with relief that the expedition began.

"'By the fifth day, they were part of the way there, and had settled into camp for the evening when a little old man was led into their presence. He also appeared very similar to the fellow who had sold them the map – dark features, and very light eyes. When they asked him his name, he ignored the question, instead entering into a sing-song warning about not opening the tomb, as the evil that had been sealed with such an effort by his ancestors would be unleashed once again.

"'Jimmy, as the leader of the group, tried to question the stranger, but could get nothing useful out of him, except for a vague agreement that the evil being described by the old man referred to the very same idol that the expedition was there to seek. The natives, who hadn't been told why they were hired, seemed somewhat unnerved by the old man's assertions, but they were poor and their loyalty could be bought for pennies. When Jimmy directed that the old man be thrown out of the camp, they complied.

"'When the sun set, everyone separated. And only a few hours later, after the winds had turned and picked up, the cry of fire rang across the camp. Of course, it was from Jimmy's tent, and he was dead when they finally put out the flames and pulled out his body. Conner and Malloy knew that they had to bring him back to civilization, but they were also concerned that, now that the existence of the tomb had been revealed, someone else would find it and take the carving before they could get back. However, they had no choice, and they took some comfort in the fact that the men they had hired seemed to have been unnerved by the old man's story, and after his departure, they had been noticeably reluctant to continue onward to the tomb, as if even discussion of it radiated unpleasant vibrations that only they could sense. Jimmy's death only seemed to make all of this certain to them.

"'After Conner and Malloy finished telling me their story, I spent an hour or so pondering it before deciding that I wanted to find the idol as much as my brother had. I told my father that he would be taking Jimmy back to England alone, and that I would follow in a few days. We had something of a row, but that was nothing new, and after I saw him off, I set about arranging a new expedition to the valley shown on the map.

"'We set out, and after a week, we reached there without incident, traveling with many of the same hired men that had gone out with the first group. They were reluctant, but money overcame any of their fears. No one appeared to warn us away this time. We found the valley, and then the tomb, as shown on the old map: Two knobs of stone, jutting from a short hillside. These marked the hidden door.

"'The native laborers dug down, beneath and between the stone knobs, to find the outline of a wall. Then they chipped out one of the stones, a large one, leaving a tunnel-like hole into a void beyond. I wiggled in first, followed by Conner and Malloy, and then some of the natives. It was a simple tomb, or so I'm told, with something like a plain coffin, stacked on a table of rock, sealed with pitch, and showing none of the characteristic decorations that one expects in that part of the world. And there didn't seem to be any statue or great ruby anywhere either.

"'But I remembered some of the wording that I had been told, where the old man had translated about sealing the evil and powerful statue away, and I had the idea to break into the pitch-covered coffin. Cutting and scraping through the old tar that bound it shut, I finally burst through to reveal a body – not a mummy, but just a desiccated husk – and a smaller item in a plain wooden box.

"'The natives were becoming upset at this point, and it was only through threats by Malloy that a near-riot was prevented. As all this was going on, I took hold of the box and opened it, revealing the object of our quest: The Eye of Heka.'

"At this point," Holmes said, "Ian described the idol's physical characteristics in greater detail, as I related to you last night. But I didn't mention what else he said.

"While he was telling me all of this," Holmes continued, "Ian's eyes took on an odd cast, as if he were looking far beyond the walls of my small Montague Street rooms. He held his cigar in his hand, forgotten, as the smoke twisted lazily toward the ceiling.

"'They say it channels power, Holmes,' he muttered, his voice low and hard to hear. He was speaking more to himself than to me. 'The inner power that all of us have. Call it magic, or, your soul, or whatever you like. It's said to be a connection between the little spark in each of us that is part of something greater, and that same power rests within the gods as well.' Then, he seemed to realize that he was speaking aloud, or sharing too much, because he visibly pulled himself back to my room and straightened in his chair with a laugh. 'It was the very devil getting the thing home,' he added, 'but we finally managed it.' Then, for the rest of the conversation, he simply told how they came back to England, and about the way the idol was subsequently stolen from the Museum, as I've previously related."

We were silent for some minutes while he smoked and I pondered what he had told me. Then I spoke. "It's apparent that the Earl gives weight to the stories about the talisman's supposed powers. It's no surprise that the superstitious folk also believe in it to some greater or lesser degree. But you, Holmes? You uncharacteristically seem to ascribe some importance to the object as well. May I ask why?"

He kept looking out of the window for so long that I thought he hadn't heard me, or was choosing to ignore the question. Then, with a sigh, he shifted and faced back into the compartment.

"When I found the time during the months following the idol's recovery," he said, "I managed to research what I could about it. I didn't pursue the question actively, you understand. But here and there I managed to put together enough puzzle pieces to create a recognizable picture."

"Then first," I asked, "please elaborate on this 'Heka'. This fellow has heretofore passed by me unnoticed."

He nodded. "Heka is a lesser-known deity, mentioned in ancient documents, although that does not make him any less important. Although Ian described him as the 'God of Magic', he is more accurately defined as the *embodiment* of magic, and also the *activator* of magic and its related

294

uses within a person. This magic, known as *ka*, was considered to be an essential and basic part of the make-up of each person. This is somewhat along the same lines of what we call a soul. In ancient beliefs, each person's *ka* is linked to the much greater and more powerful *ka*'s of the other gods, and Heka was the connection that enabled one to access both the magic within one's self, and also to channel the gods' powers. Heka was thought to be the son of the creator god, and because of his ability to draw upon and direct the other god's powers, he was considered very powerful and supremely important. He was known for being very influential and omniscient, and if a mortal could gain control of him, he could use his powers for his own purposes."

"Hence the idol," I said.

"Quite. As I said, I was able to learn some about it, after the fact. Apparently, Ian's discovery and subsequent removal of it from its ancient hiding place stirred ripples that are still washing back toward us. After he and his friends returned to England, word spread, and many people were curious about what he had discovered. What he said about having 'the very devil getting the thing home' wasn't exaggeration. When he and the others took it out of the tomb, several of his workers demanded that it immediately be resealed within the chamber, lest its evil be released into the world, as the old man from the earlier expedition had predicted. When one of the workers became violent, Ian shot and killed him. The other workers backed off, but there was a great deal of grumbling and anger, and Ian's party considered themselves lucky to make it back in one piece.

"There were several instances where one or the other of the party was waylaid, but they always managed to fight their way clear. On the last day, as they rode to the docks, a small mob attacked the wagons carrying them and their luggage. More shots were fired, and two locals were killed. It seems that Ian bribed the police, and he and the others were allowed to board the ship and depart with their prize. It was learned after the fact that the mob and the two dead men were from a village near where the idol had been found. They had lived with the legend of the object and its burial for countless generations, and after Ian departed, they set about spreading the word that the evil was again loose in the world. Most people ignored them, but there is always a contingent that is like an empty bowl, its only purpose to be filled with such a bitter brew. A cult seems to have sprung up in the last few years around the idea of this tool being used to access the power of Heka, and these men and women have been demanding its return to the land of its fathers. It has become obvious that they don't wish to reseal it into the tomb, or to use the power that is supposedly granted by it to a sole possessor. Rather, they wish to use it for more nationalistic purposes."

"Presumably while being wielded by some kind of savior. Like the Mahdi."

He nodded.

"You said that if someone could gain control of the god, Heka, through possession and use of the statue, he could use the god's powers for his own purposes."

"That's the tale that is now being told. Who knows what the idol was originally designed to represent so long ago? It certainly doesn't favor the traditional visage of Heka, usually pictured with entwined arms that might either represent grain or serpents."

"Entwined serpents? Sounds rather like the *caduceus*, or the Rod of Asclepius."

"Fitting in a way, since Heka is also associated with healing. However, the *caduceus*, as you well know, is more closely associated with Hermes Trismegistus, a combination of the Greek god Hermes and the Egyptian god Thoth. The Rod of Asclepius only has a single wound serpent, and is solely associated with the Greek god Asclepius. Despite that, the fetish, as you could see from the fraudulent copy that we examined a few hours ago, has nothing about it suggesting serpents. It is a simple polished stone cylinder, just inches wide and a foot tall.

"I should mention," he added, "that my sources have been unable to find a reference to an idol dedicated to Heka in any of the more important translated texts."

"It sounds to me as if your sources are fairly well placed, even if they haven't been able to obtain definite information about the thing. You're certainly well informed about what happened following its discovery and removal to England."

"I have certain contacts within the government and the Foreign Office who understood the concern I felt after hearing both Ian's explanation, as well as seeing glimpses of his strange obsession with the idol."

From my current vantage, with many years behind me, I know Holmes must have then been referring to his brother. But even upon meeting Mycroft Holmes later that year, I wasn't told immediately that the man, with his incredible ability to take in vast amounts of disparate knowledge and find previously unobserved connections and patterns, was sometimes considered to *be* the British government. Holmes was never one to reveal more than necessary, and I believe that he only informed me of his brother's existence in the first place in order to prove a conversational point that there was someone with even greater powers of observation, deduction, and induction, than he himself had.

"Any object such as this," Holmes continued, "with a fascination powerful enough to the malleable masses to cause them to rumble into motion, must be watched with caution. Hence, the Foreign Office's interest in it, and Williams's statement that the only visitors to check on it have been government representatives.

"Over the years, the story of the talisman and its supposed powers has only grown in the telling in certain regions. There are certain evil men in power to wish to manipulate the faction that would like to regain it, believing that, through its use, wars can be started. To their benefit, the British might be thrown out of Africa.

I nodded in understanding. Since we had defeated the Egyptian Army in '82 and made that country a protectorate, newspapers both there and all over the world had regularly featured stories of the rising resentment throughout the region. The same would be true in all of our colonies. We had seen it before in the Great Indian Rebellion of 1857.

"I think that I understand why you speak of its power. It doesn't matter what the object is. It could be a stone cylinder with a face and a jewel, or a supposed bone from a legendary leader – "

" – or a Holy Grail or a fragment of a 'true' cross," Holmes finished.

"If it is an object that can be rallied around, then it has power."

"And no magic need apply."

"But the British have only been influential in that area since 1882," I said. "That was several years *after* the idol was found and removed. Surely there hasn't been enough time for such resentment to build against us."

"Nevertheless, the story about the statue's powers had started growing from the time it was found by Ian and his friends. Now it has become a symbol of the downtrodden to many in the remote wastelands. They are disorganized and purposeless now, but less so with each day. Suppose knowledge from those who wish for war is released, and it becomes known that the carving has been liberated from the man who had stolen it? Word spreads that it is coming home. The directionless meanderings will suddenly be much more focused. Borders mean nothing, and as the war-mongers become organized, others might join in, swept along by the building momentum. Right now the movement is contained, and the disaffected masses are lying around like dry tinder, full of dangerous possibility, but inert. A match will be all it takes to light it ablaze. You know how quickly the Mutiny took hold in India. This could sweep north, and then into the regions far to either side as well. Like one domino into another, along the Mediterranean, and so into eastern Asia.

"A few victories on their part would just enhance the idea that the idol is responsible – that it deserves the credit for being able to influence events and channel a great power for those who hold it. The movement would build upon itself, and soon the whole region might be involved in conflict. Our interests, and those of our allies as well, would be jeopardized

297

as the whole of the region spiraled into war. And that might only be the beginning. Some in our government, some whom I trust, believe that even then it would not be contained. As the varied European governments found themselves being frustrated regarding their own concerns, tensions would rise, leading to unpleasant escalations that could undermine peace elsewhere in the world. The strangling treaties of Europe would pull in one country after another. Then America. It would be a world war.

"The fact is, Watson," he added, "that there are men in power all over the globe, our enemies *and* our supposed friends, who have no belief in a magical idol, but who will seize any opportunity to cause disruption and chaos. They know that in such circumstances, they will be positioned to obtain incredible wealth and power. It is in their interests to encourage the worst possible outcome. They always look for such chances, with a dozen conflicts maturing at any given time. This one is a perfect opportunity."

I could see it in my mind. The world, with all its dangers and inequities, was essentially a fragile place. All of that could be upset in an instant if one inflamed group was holding an object that they believed was able to give them the magic of the gods, letting them have the divine power to overcome their enemies.

"But," I said, as something occurred to me, "perhaps there is nothing to worry about after all. Just because a decoy idol was in the British Museum, and the actual object is apparently still in Essex at the Earl's estate, as evidenced by Williams's telegram there, does not mean that the real one is likely to fall into the hands of those who would use it to start a war. Surely those who seek it must still think that it's in the Museum's vault."

Holmes worried at a thumbnail with his teeth. "That is all true," he said. "But that is not my only concern."

After he failed to continue, I finally asked with a touch of exasperation, "Then what is it?"

"The men after the object are not the only ones who clearly believe that it has some type of power. It was obvious when he was first telling me about it, in my rooms in Montague Street, that Ian himself gave the story of the thing's potential a great deal of credence. It seems apparent, based on Williams's actions, that Ian had the false idol constructed at some point in the last ten years, and with Williams's help, he swapped it out and regained the original."

"Again, what does it matter? As I said, if they think that it's still locked beyond their reach, deep within the Museum, its power to be a symbol is neutralized."

"Neutralized for them, perhaps." said Holmes. "But Ian believes in it as well. He has had an incredible rise in good fortune and attainment since

298

he was a young man, and from what I've heard, he isn't very discreet about showing it. Of course, the first instance of his advancement was when his brother was killed, elevating him to the position of heir. That occurred before he had even found the idol. Since then, beginning with the untimely death of his father, he has had an incredible run of successes, especially financial. I don't believe that the object has any power. But I do think that Ian's *belief* in it has given him the confidence to make his own luck, sometimes using very questionable, immoral, and even illegal methods."

"But even if he believes in it, and if he's committing crimes to advance his position in life, based on his sense of confidence and entitlement as given by possession of the thing, he wouldn't reveal that he has the effigy, knowing that there are those waiting for its reappearance so they can try to take it back."

"Not under normal circumstances. But now he *does* know that his deception has been uncovered. Today, I mistakenly let Williams see that I knew about the false idol. Williams then immediately notified Ian, as he had apparently been ordered to do if anyone caught on to the ruse. Now Ian may be prompted to act out . . . *somehow*, and do something foolish – I know not what. But if he's careless in the least little bit, now that he has been spooked and flushed, the seekers of the idol, both for its supposed magical powers and its use as a tool to cause global destabilization, will become aware that it is in play once again, and they will make a move. The thing could very well be lost to us before we could stop it. The match might be lit that would lead to a global confrontation." He closed his eyes.

"And all of that, Watson, would be my fault."

Part II

Chapter VIII
The Dead Man

$\mathbf{M}$y friend lapsed into a dark silence, his cold pipe clenched in his teeth. I still had questions, but when he was like this, his mind was somewhere else entirely, constructing and tearing down delicate edifices over and over until he found one that could stand independently, even when shaken from all sides.

My own thoughts examined what he had revealed, and I tried to imagine an entire world at war. Smaller battles and wars are fought every day in every corner of the planet, but I couldn't conceive of something on the scale that Holmes implied. Granted, the Crusades, spanning hundreds of years, had been along the same lines, but they were confined to smaller and focused geographical areas and separated by great distances, and travel to those places had taken inordinate amounts of time. The Mongol invasions of previous centuries, reaching to central Europe before withering, had been more like what Holmes feared, but those long-ago battles had been about conquest for territory, and not whipped to a frenzy by men of great influence with modern motives.

No, what Holmes described was war on a global scale, taken to a level of deadly destruction that would have been unimaginable just a generation of so earlier. Gone were the days when England and Europe had been protected by distance. This would not be like the various local conflicts, earth-spanning as they had been, of the Seven Years War more than a hundred years in the past. The ability to inflict death had achieved entirely new levels. The American Civil War of a quarter-century before had shown the world that warfare was now a completely different type of animal indeed. Modern transportation and communications could move armies in a fraction of a fraction of the time that it had taken just a century before. And if some brilliant general or tactician happened to wrest for himself a position of leadership within the councils of our enemies, by way of a mistaken belief in a supposedly magical rock, then we could indeed be facing a very grim prospect.

Like all knowledgeable Englishmen, I was aware of the scope and breadth of our Empire, and also the resentment – some of it earned – that it caused around the world. Holmes was correct: If the idol were to fall into the wrong hands, it would be as if a lit match had dropped onto an already wide and thin sheet of spilled lamp oil. The resulting conflagration could flash and spread with incredible destruction.

We remained quiet throughout the rest of our journey, each deep within our own imaginings. I was sure that Holmes was playing out variation after variation, while I was sunk into my own memories of the horrors of war.

Upon reaching the quaint station in Chelmsford, we quietly changed trains, only waiting for a few minutes before heading northeast, toward Sudbury. I had no idea where our final destination was to be, but I was following Holmes's lead, as I had done so many times before.

As we took our seats, my coat knocked against the woodwork. Holmes glanced toward it and then smiled, knowing that the noise had come from my ever-present service revolver.

Somewhat before reaching Halstead, my companion, still quietly thinking and smoking, shifted, readying himself to stand. I followed suit, and in a few moments, we had disembarked upon a small platform of something between a real station and a mere halt. Locating an official, we were told that there was only one cab for hire, but that it was currently in use, taken by a passenger from the previous train. "They had to go about five miles out. If Thomas – that's the cabman – is sent back instead of being required to wait, then he should be here soon."

"Tell me," said Holmes, with a gleam in his eye, "was the man on the previous train a balding fellow, tired looking in an ill-fitting suit, no coat, and rather nervous?"

"Ayuh, that would be him," said the official, raising an eyebrow, as if inviting an explanation or further comment. However, he received neither, and Holmes thanked him curtly, turning toward me.

"Williams," he confirmed. "After he left the telegraph office, he must have made his way directly to Liverpool Street Station and set out for here on the earlier train, no doubt following some instructions that he had been given if this situation ever arose. In the meantime, we made the effort to detour by Ian's town house."

Remembering another question, Holmes turned back to the official, who had never really stepped away. "This other man," he said. "Did he go to the great hall, the Earl of Wardlaw's residence, about halfway between here and Steeple Bumpstead?"

"Ayuh, that's right. But it's more like halfway between Toppesfield and Gainsford End." He seemed as if he were willing to stand and debate it with us.

Holmes nodded and handed over a coin, for which he received a routine and mumbled thank you. Then, the man took a better look at what he had received, and said, "Much obliged indeed."

The official left us then and went into an office. Holmes began to pace the platform while I stepped into the station's waiting room, taking a seat on a worn but solid bench by one of the walls near a stove, struggling and ultimately failing to warm me.

It must have been only ten or fifteen minutes before a ragged carriage became visible in the distance, heading our way. I walked out and joined Holmes at the edge of the platform while the single driver drew near. Finally, he stopped within hailing distance and asked, "Are you gentlemen waiting to hire the station fly?"

When we said yes, he glanced longingly toward a low building that seemed to be a pub a few hundred feet away. With a sigh, he stated that he needed to water his horse, and then he would be at our service.

When we were underway, the driver shook his head. "I go for months without driving out in this direction, and then do it a couple of times in the same afternoon."

"The man you took before," said Holmes. "Did he say anything?"

"Not a word after telling me the destination. He did seem anxious, though. He was tense, and sometimes he had to wrap his arms around himself to keep his hands from picking at one another, as he did when he just left them in his lap. Or maybe he was just cold."

The five miles passed without incident, although I would have imagined that the distance was actually somewhat greater as we wound this way and that on the twisting narrow roads. Finally, after a sharp left bend, we topped a small hill and could see our destination immediately before us. "Wardlaw Hall," said the driver, gesturing with his whip. It was the only time he had used it on the entire trip.

I was surprised. I've learned over the course of my life that nothing ever turns out as one first imagines it. This is true for attending social events and meeting strangers, and especially visiting new locations. In spite of that, I had supposed that this house would be somewhat resplendent, given that Holmes had related how Ian Finch, the Earl of Wardlaw, had been quite fortunate in recent years. The town house in Wellington Square had been nice enough, if rather conservative. I had thought that this would be a showplace. Instead, what was revealed as we came over the hill was a massive structure that had been left untended and unloved for so long that it was in danger of becoming a derelict.

The landscape was completely out of control. There were great hedges, some probably hundreds of years old, now so completely ragged that it was unlikely they could be reshaped without killing them. The lawn near the house, which had probably once been green and well-manicured, was now weed-choked, and numerous low spots had sunken and formed, holding ponded rainwater that was now sheeted with ice, pierced by thick stalks of invasive plants like spears through a glass. Of course, it was January, and one would not expect the landscape to have the vibrant life

305

of spring or summer, but this went beyond something that was merely lying fallow due to winter. This had been left to return to the wild, as if the owner had no further interest in cultivating it.

The dead gray grounds were the same color as the pale washed-out stone of the house. Taken together, they appeared to be some massive watercolor, with the lines between sky and building and earth blurred, as though a bucket of mop water had been tossed on the finished painting, softening the drab colors and letting them all run together.

"This cannot be the house of a successful man," I whispered to Holmes.

"I've kept track of Ian over the years, and I know that he has done well for himself. Seeing this, I'm not sure in what way he chooses to express his success, but certainly he doesn't measure it by showing off his estate." A little louder, Holmes spoke to the driver, asking, "How long has the house been in this condition?"

"I can't rightly say. I rarely get out this way. I do know that it was in this shape the last time I was here."

"When was that?" asked Holmes.

"Oh, six months or so ago. It's hard to believe they could let it get to this state. I'm not surprised, though. The Earl let his staff go quite a while back. My cousin used to work here, back when the Earl's father was alive, and it was certainly different then. She, like all the others, were surprised when the new Earl turned them out. He only kept the butler."

"Fisk, I believe was his name?"

"No, he died. This one came later. His name is Dawson."

"Do you know if the Earl is at home now?"

"No idea. They have their own horse and buggy, and so of course I'm never hired by them. When the Earl comes down from London, he wires ahead and Dawson comes out for him." He flicked the reins, with no apparent acknowledgement from the horse, and added, "I'm the one that brings out the telegrams when one arrives – though those are rare enough."

"But you delivered one earlier today?"

"I did," the man said, suspiciously now. "Two, actually."

"Two?" I asked. I turned to Holmes. "The one sent by Williams, certainly, but who could have sent the second?"

The driver just looked at us, probably wondering why it was any of our business. Holmes asked, "Did you make separate trips for each of the telegrams that you delivered?"

"No, I brought them out together at the same time."

"But one arrived before the other?"

"Somewhat, I suppose, but there wasn't a great deal of time between them." He looked as if he wanted to ask why we were concerned. "We don't worry ourselves so very much about these things out here, I suppose. I had intended to deliver the first telegram at some point, and then the second one arrived, so I decided I'd better get to it. I thought two telegrams might mean a tragedy, so I brought them and put them into the butler's hand, and then went back to the station."

"And then you brought out the man who came down on the train?" I queried.

"No, he was with me when I delivered the telegrams."

"That's right. You did say you made 'a couple of trips' – this one, and the one with that man – Williams."

"Three birds with one stone." The man laughed.

By then we had dropped down the low slope and were approaching the front door. From this closer vantage, I could see that long strips of paint were peeling away from the wood. Holmes roused himself. "The man you brought out before us," he asked. "Did he ask you to wait?"

"No, although I would have. He was surprised when I jumped down when we got here, and then irritated when he learned that I was just then delivering the telegrams. But then he calmed himself, and just handed me some coins – more than what he owed. The door had opened before we reached it, as if someone had been watching for us. It was the butler. After handing him the telegrams, and seeing as how I hadn't been instructed any differently by the man from the train – this Williams, I suppose – I turned around and left."

We stopped, but apparently no one was watching for us this time, as the door remained firmly closed. Handing the fare to the driver, Holmes said, "I trust that this will be enough to retain your services for the journey back."

He glanced at his palm and smiled. "Certainly will."

"Excellent."

We climbed down and approached the door. I could see that the peeling paint was matched by the fine sun-damaged cracks that were appearing in the wood. There were streaks of greenish stains along the stonework arching over us. Simply judging from the front door, one could see that if the house weren't rescued and repaired soon, it would reach the point of no return.

However, the bell still worked, for we could hear it from somewhere deep inside. Holmes was in the act of ringing it a second time when the door was suddenly pulled open rather violently by a most curious little man.

He was probably an inch or two under five feet tall, wearing a formal black coat that looked like something styled from fifty years before. Resembling the walls of the entry arch in which we stood, it seemed to

307

have been damaged by the damp and streaked with a greenish sheen. He had on a rusty white shirt, and a filthy white waistcoat was buttoned across his round barrel chest. It was stained with something that looked quite like dried mustard.

His odd trunk was supported by short pipe-stem legs, encased in dull black pants. He had very large hands for such thin arms, and they were swollen with arthritis, the knuckles red and knobby. The thumbs were longer than normal, curving out away from his hands, and they had unusually wide but short nails. The most curious feature of all, however, was his head. It was jammed into his body, so that it seemed as if it was an extension of his ribcage, thus forcing him by its fixation to always look straight ahead, turning neither left nor right, or even up or down, without some great degree of pivoting difficulty. The skin of his face was red, and he was clean-shaven, except for a patch or two along his upper cheeks or jawline where he had missed a few stray white whiskers. His hair was thick, although his forehead was high, and it was white and unbrushed, sticking straight up in an uneven tangle that most resembled the wild hedges surrounding the house. Finally, his features were frozen in a scowling grin, or perhaps it might better be described as a grinning scowl, his lips pulled back in a rictus over his unusually big and strong-looking yellow teeth. He looked for all the world like a cross between the Wee Falorie Man, Humpty Dumpty, and some ghastly illustration out of a Dickens novel – although I would be hard-pressed to decide exactly which one had ascendance over the other.

His voice sounded exactly as I would have expected: Rough, uneducated, and somewhat garbled, as if his mouth had difficulties forming the words.

"Can I help you?" he asked in some semblance of serviced politeness.

"We are here to see the Earl on urgent business," said my friend. "My name is Sherlock Holmes, and this is my associate, Dr. John Watson."

The man may have looked like a caricature, but one could see that he was intelligent, if only in some low crafty way. A flash of recognition at my friend's name caused him to close his eyelids for a just a fraction. Then, his manner seemed to change, and a note of whinging despair came into his voice.

"Are you with the man who came here before?" he said, a noticeable cringe in his tone.

"We have been trying to catch up with him," replied Holmes.

The man nodded. "Sirs, I am so glad that you're here, I am! There has been an *accident*!" His voice lowered dramatically with that declaration, and he looked at me, as best he could, turning and tilting his entire body. "You are a doctor, I believe?"

"I am."

"Come quickly, then. Perhaps you are not too late."

He moved aside, letting us into the house. The strong smell of cool damp and decay assaulted my nose, and I gave an involuntary cough. Clearly the roof was leaking somewhere, perhaps in many spots, to have so let the house get in this condition and to feel this fetid inside.

The door closed solidly behind us, and my eyes struggled to adapt from the weak sunshine we had just left. There was only a single low-burning candle on a side table, and the little man picked it up too quickly, causing the flame to momentarily flicker. "This way," he said, shuffling through a large doorway that led us deeper into the house. "Hurry."

"On your guard, Watson," whispered Holmes as we followed.

We twisted through dark halls and darker passages, moving ever toward the rear of the sprawling building. Finally, the little man threw open a door, causing me to stop in my tracks. I was blinded as my eyes were filled with brightness. We had reached a grand ballroom, lined all along one wall with south-facing windows reaching to the high ceiling. The floor was of white marble, as were various columns around the room. The windows faced into the afternoon sun, now low in the January sky, its light flooding in and reflecting off the countless white surfaces.

The little man had kept walking toward a far wall, and Holmes, who had also stopped beside me, resumed in the same direction. Moving to keep up, I reached them both just as the butler pulled aside a heavy drape, revealing a shallow alcove. He shifted the candle to his left hand and reached out with his right, taking hold of what I could now see was the edge of a door, covered with the same rich plaster-like material as the walls. It would be concealed when closed, and it seemed to be very heavy. It was all that he could do to force it into motion.

"In here," he said, panting. "There has been an *accident!*"

I could see that the door was very thick, and appeared to be made of metal underneath the outer covering. Could this be the vault mentioned by Holmes, where the idol had been kept before being moved to the Museum? Was this where it had been kept again following the substitution?

We stepped inside and, by the sole light of the candle, I could see a body crumpled on the floor. It smelled of death in the close little room. The chamber was barely six feet in height, about five feet from side to side, and eight feet deep. Like the door, the floors, walls, and ceiling also appeared to be made of metal. There was no light, save for the thin candle in the butler's grip.

I pushed my way forward, intent on examining the body. Holmes maneuvered himself behind the butler, allowing the light from the feeble candle to project without being shadowed by his tall thin frame.

"I found him this way," said the little man. "Can you help him?"

I carefully examined the body. The dead man was crumpled, face down upon the floor. His skin was already cool, and I knew that he was beyond my help.

"He's dead, Holmes," I said. "It's Williams."

"Can you tell how he died?"

"There is no great amount of bleeding. While there may be other trauma that I cannot find without a better examination, there is a wound at the top of his neck, a narrow laceration. He appears to have been killed by the direct insertion of a thin blade into the base of the skull, either severing the spinal cord, or more likely entering the *cerebellum* of the brain, depending on the angle. An autopsy can tell for certain."

Holmes took the candle. "You are Dawson, the butler?"

"I am. How did you – ?"

"Where is your master, the Earl?"

"I . . . I will go and fetch him." He turned and scampered out of the vault.

I expected Holmes to join me in examining the body. Instead, he put his finger to his lips, and then said, loudly, "If you will just help me turn him over, Watson, I think we can find one or two other interesting facts."

But he didn't move to the body, where I still crouched. Rather, he gestured for me to join him, nearer to the vault door. I rose, stepping with exaggerated care so that my footsteps remained silent. We had just stopped when a shadow, clearly that of Dawson, appeared on the outer floor, alongside that of the great metal door. And as we watched, the door began to slowly swing shut!

"Quickly, Watson!" Holmes cried, and we both rushed forward, pushing back against the door and reversing its motion. I heard Dawson grunt, and then with a frustrated sob, he gave up. The door moved freely, and we heard the sound of a falling body as we stepped out into the alcove.

Dawson was already picking himself up from the floor, rolling awkwardly to one side with his stiff frame, when I placed myself in front of him, having trained my gun on him in the process.

"Watch him, Watson," said Holmes, returning to the vault, this time to truly examine the body without fear of being trapped. "He is as dangerous as a swamp adder." But Dawson simply lay there, half propped, looking off into space and muttering angrily to himself.

"You are correct – I can see no other wounds," called Holmes before stepping back into the great room. "Of more interest is this vault. No ventilation, no lights, nothing on the inside of the door that can open it. If this creature had succeeded in shutting us inside, we would have remained

310

in there with a candle and the dead man until we, too, were corpses." Looking down at Dawson, he snapped, "Where is the Earl?"

"Gone!" snarled the little man, his attention pulled back from his grumblings, and clearly no longer trying to appear meek or bewildered. "He received the warning."

"Warning? From Williams?"

"Yes. That the truth is known. The idol is no longer safe."

"Where did he go?"

Dawson only grimaced, and did not offer an answer to the question.

Holmes tried again. "If Williams sent the Earl a telegram, then why did he also need to come here?"

"Part of the plan. Always part of the plan. The Earl did not know but that he would need assistance if this should ever happen. Young Williams had worked for him for years, ever since they met when the statue was first taken to the Museum. My master paid him to keep an eye on things after the real idol was brought back home."

"But why kill Williams after he arrived? What did that accomplish?

"The plan!" answered Dawson, looking at the floor, seeing something that we could not. "It all becomes part of the plan. The Master realized that Williams could offer nothing else, so he sacrificed him to tie off a loose end. And he saw it as a way to stop you as well. He knew that you would be coming. He showed me how to trick you into the vault." Then his anger seemed to disappear as his face collapsed into sadness. A tear pooled on one of his rheumy eyes and trickled down his cheek. "I failed. I failed him. I wasn't strong enough to slam the door. I have failed."

Holmes turned away in disgust from the figure on the floor. "Give me a moment to look around, Watson. I suppose that Ian is truly gone now, but I'll just make sure."

For the next few minutes, I heard him moving through the house, and even outside. Then he returned, explaining that the house was truly empty. "I checked the stables. There is evidence of one horse, which has very recently been hitched to a dog-cart and driven away. I asked our driver outside, who would surely have been sent on his way by our friend here after we were sealed away, if there are any other roads back to the station. Unfortunately, there are a variety of different routes, which explains why we didn't pass Ian as we traveled."

"But how did he know for sure that we were coming, Holmes? Just because Williams told him that you had spotted the fake is no reason to assume that we would immediately beat a path here. You said that Williams didn't spot you when you followed him from the Museum, and there was no one at the Wellington Square house to notify him."

311

"Don't forget the second telegram, Watson. I suspect that someone actually *was* in Ian's house in London, perhaps another trusted servant like Dawson here. When we stood near the front door, discussing our plans to travel down here immediately, that person likely overheard us, standing on the other side of the door, and then sent the other wire. Although he only received the telegrams at the same time that Williams arrived, Ian knew for certain to expect us, and soon – although he had time to plan this macabre little trap, baited with Williams's carcass."

He stepped over and pulled Dawson to his feet by the grimy collar of the butler's coat, marching him through the house with us to the front door. Outside, the driver was surprised, but when we explained the situation, he understood, and hurriedly drove away to bring the police.

Dawson didn't speak again during the period that we waited with him in the house. Holmes used the time to further explore the vast premises, but he failed to discover any other clues, except for signs in the Earl's disheveled bedroom of a hurried departure.

When the local constable arrived, brought back by our driver, Holmes identified the both of us, and luckily the policeman had heard of him. Soon other men arrived, clearly locals deputized to follow by the overwhelmed constable. After an hour or so of assisting their fruitless and frankly meandering investigation, we were transported back to the small village where we had initially entrained. Dawson was taken and placed in the sole small cell maintained in the village while we stepped over to the tiny post office to inquire about the telegrams that had been received that day for the Earl. Upon learning of our connection with the investigation, the fat man behind the counter rubbed his hands obsequiously and acknowledged that two wires had indeed arrived that afternoon. He showed copies of them to us, revealing that – as Holmes had predicted – the first was the one from Williams, and the other was from someone named Harbottle, sent from a Chelsea telegraph office, indicating in terse terms that two men referring to each other as Holmes and Watson had been at the Wellington Square house, and were overheard to say that they were proceeding on to the Earl's home in Essex.

"No doubt we'll find that Harbottle is the caretaker at No. 30," said my friend. Turning to the fat man and holding up the copies of the messages, Holmes stated, "I understand that these were not delivered immediately."

"Well," the man drawled, "that's right. It's five miles out and the same back, and I just have Alfred, the boy, here for help around the office." He gestured a thumb at a slack-jawed fellow in his mid-twenties, standing in the shadows behind him. "He delivers the messages to nearby spots here in the village, but we have an arrangement with the station cab for those that are too far for Alf here. When the second wire came in, I sent Alf to give it to Thomas Keller, the cabbie. Turns out, he hadn't taken the first one yet, so he hopped to it, and went away with both of them." He lowered his voice with added gravity. "It's very rare for the Earl to receive wires these days. It's been a long time indeed, and I felt that two so close together must mean something important."

Holmes thanked him flatly for his time without giving any of the additional information that the man so clearly desired. My friend then dispatched a couple of wires of his own, the first to that location where he often sent messages to young Wiggins, one of the many members of that family who had served over the years as leaders of his unofficial Irregulars, asking him to arrange for someone to keep watch on the Earl's house in Wellington Square, in the unlikely event that the Earl should return and go to ground there. The other was to Inspectors Gregson and Lestrade, our long-time associates from Scotland Yard, advising them to put out the word to be on the lookout for Ian Finch upon his likely arrival in London.

While Holmes was writing, the local constable came in, also intending to send a wire of his own, requesting assistance investigating the murder of Williams, whose body had now been brought back from the vault at Wardlaw Hall. He told us that he wanted to make sure that he adequately took care of any unexpected complications, since he admitted with open frankness that he had never been involved in something like this before. Both he and Holmes watched the fat man pointedly until they were certain that their messages were sent immediately, instead of being simply put at the bottom of a pile of things to be accomplished sometime that day.

Outside, Holmes had a few quiet words with the constable, who showed a sudden surprised expression. As he stepped away, he additionally advised the young man to keep Dawson in custody until further notice, charging him with our attempted murder if need be, as the odd dwarf's true part in the events had yet to be entirely explained.

Finally, after shaking hands with the officer, we returned to the small station, where we confirmed that Ian Finch had indeed arrived on a dog-cart and caught the up-train that departed not long after we had set out for the Hall. Holmes shook his head in disgust. "A comedy of errors and lost opportunities, Watson. Surely the gods arrange these little near-misses to break up their eternal monotony."

Finally, the next train arrived and we climbed aboard, to travel back to Chelmsford, and thence ultimately to London and Baker Street.

Chapter IX
Legal Matters

It was getting dark when we opened the door to the sitting room. I was immediately struck by a most unusual and unpleasant aroma.

Holmes noticed it too, as I could hear him decisively sniffing. I concluded that he must have forgotten some chemical experiment that had taken a turn for the worst. It would certainly not be the first time.

Mrs. Hudson had left our mail on the table, as usual, and I was surprised to see a box, about a foot square in both height and width, wrapped in plain brown paper. It was simply addressed to *Dr. Watson, 221 Baker Street, London.*

I picked it up and found that it was heavier than it looked. Returning it to the tabletop, I reached for a knife to cut the twine that bound it.

"Watson," said Holmes in a low voice. "As you value both our lives, do not open that."

"Hmm?" I said, glancing toward him.

"Step away, please. I have a suspicion . . . ." He moved toward the door from where he had been standing in the center of the room. Opening it, he called for Mrs. Hudson, who appeared a moment or two later, having climbed the flight of steps with her usual stately manner, drying her hands with a towel.

"This package," he said. "I see that it has no postage stamps."

I looked and noticed that he was correct. How he had observed that from halfway across the room was amazing, and yet it was the sort of thing that he did every day.

"Did it arrive with the regular post?" Holmes continued.

"Why, no," Mrs. Hudson answered. "There was a ring at the bell, and then I found it propped against the door. It couldn't have been there for more than a minute or so, the time it took me to get to the door from the kitchen, but I saw no signs of whoever might have left it."

"I'm sure that you weren't meant to," said Holmes, dismissing her with thanks.

He crossed to me and leaned down, peering at the package more closely, and sniffing again. "The smell is coming from here," he said. As I bent to confirm it, he added, "It is ammonia, of course."

"Ammonia!" I thought, trying to recall where I had heard that mentioned in the last day or so. And then, I knew.

"Baron Meade," I sighed

"Correct," Holmes replied. "He seems to favor explosives using nitrogen-based compounds. They are easily constructed from commonly acquired materials. And apparently he continues to blame you for his defeat the other night."

"But . . . I was simply one of many."

"Yes, but you have put a face to his anger."

Holmes had the page boy call a constable, who in turn summoned Inspector Gregson. Our old friend had been spending a great deal of his time in recent months seconded to the Special Branch, as there had been renewed concerns since the previous November that a group known as "The Dynamite Gang" might have extended their activities to London, following statements that were made in the press by a radical Irish-American named Cohen. Investigation with Holmes's quiet assistance had led to the arrest of two possible conspirators, Harkins and Cullan, but tensions were still running high. The discovery of Baron Meade's home-grown plot two days earlier would only compound the situation.

Gregson soon arrived, bringing with him several of his men, all experts in explosives. They agreed with Holmes that the package was likely a bomb, and that fact was confirmed later in the evening when they detonated it at the special facility constructed for that purpose near the Shadwell Basin.

"It was the same sort of thing that was found in that house the other night," Gregson told us a few hours later, over brandies by our fireside, "although on a much smaller scale. There was a detonator affixed to the string tied around the carton." He fished in into his coat and pulled out the string itself, along with the folded wrapping paper. "The string went through a small hole in the box, and was attached within to the device. I knew you'd want to see these. We preserved the knot, but I think you'll agree that it's nothing special. No sailor tied it. Just someone who only knew how to produce a regular knot. The string is common. The same with the wrapping paper – exactly what you can find in a thousand places in London. Regular ink and typical pen as well."

While Holmes examined the items, Gregson smiled at me. "Mr. Holmes is slowly rubbing off on us, Doctor. I, for one, unlike some down at the Yard, am happy to take advantage of whatever modern methods he can teach us to give us an edge on these criminals." And he took a sip of brandy, holding it in his mouth with obvious pleasure for a moment before swallowing.

Holmes confirmed Gregson's findings, and the policeman departed soon after, warning me to be careful in the future, as I was apparently being stalked by a madman.

After the inspector left, Holmes and I sat quietly for a few minutes, before he said, "He's right, you know. You're going to have to be on your guard."

"It won't be the first time."

"Nevertheless."

I shifted in my chair, watching the fire. I felt strangely ambivalent. I found that I didn't care whether I was a target or not. A part of my mind knew that it was related to the ever-present hopeless feeling that was always there beneath the surface since Constance's death. And I also realized that some part of me welcomed the fact that I was being hunted, as it might give me a legitimate opportunity to confront someone – anyone – and vent my anger. If that someone turned out to be a lunatic, so much the better.

Finally, to soothe Holmes's apparent worry, I said, "The man is a coward. He won't try anything face-to-face. He has to plant hidden bombs and send packages. I'll simply be more careful to examine my mail before opening it."

With a shake of his head, Holmes stood and wished me good night.

In the morning, I looked out and saw that the sky was clear, but not quite as bright as yesterday. It didn't feel as cold either. I came downstairs to learn that Holmes had already gone, having left a note explaining that he had some things to arrange regarding the search for the fugitive Earl of Wardlaw and the missing idol. He pointedly did not warn me to be careful, but I knew that it was implicit. We both realized that Baron Meade was fully cognizant that his package hadn't detonated, and that I was still alive.

When Mrs. Hudson came up later to clear the dishes, I warned her again regarding our latest enemy. Threats were nothing new for her, I'm afraid, but this latest variation, consisting of the delivery of an explosive device strong enough to raze the house, was. As always, she displayed her strong Scottish sensibility and refused to be terrorized or intimidated. Seeing her example, how could I offer anything less?

I set out in plenty of time to meet Dr. Withers, in order to sign the papers that would exchange my medical practice, and all the hopes that had been appended to it, for a sizeable payment. I would have traded it all and lived in penury for the chance to redeem Constance from her fate, but that was a foolish and unfulfillable wish. Since her death, I couldn't stop imagining what might have been, which only led to a greater sense of suppressed anger. I didn't know how to extricate myself from this cycle, and I felt that it was growing stronger. Holmes had tried to distract me with tales of old cases and adventures, and Mrs. Hudson had overwhelmed me with kindness and favorite foods. But still the feeling persisted.

It was with this on my mind, and my teeth gritted, that I stepped outside, looking from left to right, hoping to see Baron Meade lurking somewhere, so that I might discuss the little episode of yesterday's "gift". My fists curled involuntarily, but uselessly – as he was not there.

I hailed a hansom and set out for the offices of my solicitor, Mr. Marchmont, in Gray's Inn. I looked forward to settling the business quickly, and then perhaps walking to the nearby Ships Tavern and having a pint of the *Old Peculier*, or maybe two, as a solitary toast to my broken plans.

But that plan, too, was destined to fail.

A taciturn secretary ushered me into the large room where Marchmont met with clients. The lawyer, a heavy-set middle-aged fellow, stepped forward, his chubby face wreathed in a smile, to wring my hand in both of his, while past him, I could see Dr. Withers rising in greeting.

Beside him, no surprise I suppose, was seated his daughter, Jenny.

There was no reason why she shouldn't have been there, but again, there was no reason why she should have, either. I ought not to have been surprised. Her plans and future were as bound as those of her father to my old practice. It was to be her home as well, and I had the impression that she would be of some daily assistance in her father's work, to one degree or another. Yet, I found myself somewhat irritated by her presence, and I didn't know why.

Dr. Withers offered a hearty greeting, and Miss Withers nodded with a quieter but no less sincere, "Doctor."

Marchmont settled me on one side of the table, across from the doctor and his daughter. The lawyer and a member of his staff placed themselves at one end, and with the two interested parties on each side, began to explain the several documents that were involved. His assistant kept them in order, passing and retrieving them as necessary to be signed by one or the other of us, or both. I found myself recalling a similar scene, just a bit over a year before, when I had attended the same sort of ceremony, but that time as the eager purchaser. Constance and I were not yet married then. In fact, she was still traveling from the United States with her mother. After the procedure was concluded, I had immediately taken myself off to Kensington and my new home, and had let myself into the empty building to wander about, somewhat in shock at my good fortune. The world had stretched before me, full of promise.

Now, all that I could see before me for certain was that I planned to have a pint at a nearby pub, and that a madman was trying to kill me.

My reveries were far more interesting than what was occurring in the office, and at one point, my attention had to be called back to the present when I was asked to turn over my key to Dr. Withers. "Oh, of course," I said, pulling it from my pocket. The lawyer laughed and rubbed his hands, and then progressed to other legal pronouncements, as I again lost interest.

Then Marchmont was congratulating us, and asking if I wanted his office to take care of depositing so large a check at my bank. "Cox and Company?" he confirmed. I nodded.

As we all stood to leave, Dr. Withers said, "We must celebrate. And I have something I'd like to discuss with you, Doctor. Will you join us for lunch?"

My first reaction was to apologize and excuse myself. But I saw that Miss Withers was looking intently, as if she was as sincere as her father sounded. I thought one last time of my plan to walk to the Ships, and then let it sail away.

"Excellent," said Dr. Withers. And he led us outside to find a cab.

If Miss Withers hadn't been with us, we could certainly have walked, in spite of the cold. We drove south for only a few blocks before angling into Aldwych, and thus into the Strand. There was only time for a bit of polite conversation about the weather before we arrived at our destination, Simpson's.

I knew that women were not allowed to join us, but I felt that my long association with the place would earn a blind eye from the staff – as it did. Long a favorite of both Holmes and myself, I was a regular patron of this historic restaurant. It was often the chosen setting to celebrate the conclusion of a particularly difficult case, or simply the obvious destination if one wanted a good bit of roast beef. I should have felt some relief in that it had never been a favorite of my wife's, as she hadn't ever warmed to British cooking, and thus dining here would hold no memories of her. However, the fact that she had simply expressed an opinion about the place, even a negative one, was still enough of an association that thoughts of her flooded into my mind.

Understanding the doctor's kind offer, I pushed aside my feelings and resolved to devote myself completely to being a gracious guest. Still, I couldn't help but observe the prominent mourning band on my own sleeve as I raised my arm and reached out to assist Miss Withers as she stepped down from the cab.

Inside, we were led up to the first floor dining room that looked out over the busy street. It was comfortably lit, with the high north-facing windows illuminating the room without overwhelming it. I suspected that at certain times of the year, the afternoon sun would painfully reflect off the glass across the street. The same thing happened during summer mornings in Baker Street.

The food, as usual, was excellent, and the company quite companionable. We each opted for the famous roast beef, traditionally cut

318

for us at the table from a distinctive rolling cart. The doctor and I had a Yorkshire Pudding with our beef and vegetables, but Miss Withers opted to avoid it. Conversation ranged from doings in Portsmouth versus London, individuals that we knew in common, and polite questions regarding my association with Holmes. Neither seemed to be either very aware or interested in his investigations, which was something of an unusual relief. There was also a pointed avoidance of my recent bereavement.

Dr. Withers related how he had come to injure his leg, explaining the limp that I had noticed the day before when he descended the stairway. "It was in early September of '72, and my unit was in Honduras. Things had been tense for several years, ever since the Icaiche Mayas, who controlled the jungles in the lower peninsula, had occupied Corozal Town a couple of years earlier. I had only been at my post a little over two weeks when they attacked Orange Walk Town, resulting in a retaliatory raid.

"It should have gone like clock-work. We had incendiary devices that would fire through the air, allowing us to burn the natives out of their houses while staying well back from any return fire. They were thunderstruck, and quickly surrendered. They lost the taste for the fight and overthrew their leader, a surly chap named Canul, who had been in charge for several years by then.

"But there were still a few pockets of resistance, and I was attached with a group making a routine sweep when we encountered one of them. Some unexpected shots wounded one of our commanders, not fatally as it turned out, but as I was treating him, a bullet entered my leg from behind, subsequently exiting from the front with a chip of my knee-cap along with it.

"Miraculously, there was no more serious damage, and I healed rather quickly. Over the years, it hasn't really given me any difficulties, except when descending stairs, or during cold weather, like we've had for the past few days."

"Father was sent home to recuperate," added Miss Withers, "and while he was here, mother passed away."

Dr. Withers nodded. "She came down with a fever, and as I was flat on my back recuperating, I was unable to assist in her treatment." He added, in a softer voice, "I couldn't spend any time with her at all at the end."

Miss Withers laid her hand upon her father's. "She knew how you felt."

Conversation faltered at this point, and nothing more was said until the waiter returned to ask if we needed anything else. The doctor requested pudding and coffee, and in spite of the fact that I felt quite full indeed, I joined him.

As we were finishing the last bites, talk turned to the practice itself, as Dr. Withers picked my brain regarding certain patients, and which of those he might expect to retain following the transfer of ownership. Of course, as part of the purchase process, he had been given access to various documents, including patient records, in order to determine the viability of the operation. He was excited to obtain the lease to the building because of its excellent location, but in acquiring the practice, he was also paying for something much more ephemeral, for there was no guarantee that the clients that I had worked to earn would stay with him.

Some patients would naturally leave for different physicians, while others would remain, either out of habit, or simply to give him a try. Certainly, he would take on new clients who had shown no earlier interest in seeking my advice, and eventually, if he worked hard and proved to be a good doctor, as he seemed to be, the practice would continue successfully, and would even grow. But he still wanted my opinion to help make the transition as smooth as possible.

"It is related to that," he said, "that I wished to discuss something else with you." He cleared his throat and continued. "I – that is to say, *we* – realize that your loss was very recent."

His mention of something that had been approached indirectly but tacitly avoided so far throughout the conversation surprised me a bit. I saw that Miss Withers was watching me intently, and I nodded noncommittally, a reaction that could mean anything.

"We understand your desire to divest yourself of any painful connections to your former home and practice. I must admit that I felt the same way when my wife died. Newly widowed, I chose to leave the Army in order to raise Jenny. I couldn't bear to stay in that house where we had all lived, as every aspect of it reminded me somehow of my wife. The furniture we had picked together – each piece suggested a memory or story to me. The wallpaper, unnoticed by others, reminded me of the decisions she had made to select it. Eventually, I did what you are doing, and sold out and moved to a new location.

"Now obviously, as the purchaser of your old practice, I cannot turn around and tell you that you've made a mistake. I understand what you've done, and why. But I *can* tell you that starting over somewhere else is going to be a lot of work, should that be your plan. From what I've seen, and from the records that I've examined, you are a good doctor. A man of good character as well. And even if you plan on stepping away from a practice altogether, I must urge you not to completely sever your ties from what you've accomplished."

320

I believed I understood the direction he was taking. "Are you asking what I think you are? For me to maintain a connection with the practice?"

He nodded, looking relieved that it was now out in the open. "I am. I know that there is a natural tendency for a man in your situation to withdraw for a time. I felt it myself. But, knowing what I know now, I believe that it is the incorrect path. You should work through it, and keep moving forward, and avoid losing the professional momentum that you have attained. If you allow yourself to roll to a complete stop, every day afterward will be that much more difficult in terms of breaking yourself loose again, and inertia will own you.

"You know this practice," he said, leaning forward intently, "and you know these patients. You will not have to learn anything new by remaining involved in their care, and quite frankly it would be of benefit to me as well, in order to ease the transition. I'm not asking that you continue to be associated on a full-time basis. Rather, you will act as a consultant, assisting part-time as you wish and as needed. You can still work in the hospitals, or as a *locum* for someone else, even fulfilling that function for me as well. You might even have time to assist Mr. Holmes on the occasional investigation, as you have done before."

He leaned back before concluding, "Well, I hope you'll consider the idea. Work is the best antidote to sorrow."

My eyes widened slightly at that. It was what Holmes had told me regularly, beginning right after I had returned to Baker Street.

"I, too, hope you'll be joining us, Dr. Watson," added Miss Withers, touching my arm gently while putting a different emphasis on the word *hope* than her father had done.

I kept myself from looking down at her fingers, resting upon my sleeve. I nodded to move past the conversation, merely meaning that I would consider the offer, and not realizing then that what I was doing might be construed as a tentative agreement of sorts. But even as I was shaken by the idea, I knew that I had no intention of accepting it. In my mind, my life in Kensington was now a closed book. Today's sale of the house and associated medical accoutrements and appurtenances had been absolute. If I had wanted to maintain a connection with the place, I wouldn't have divested myself of it so quickly.

Clearing my throat, I thanked them for both the consideration, and for lunch. "Most appreciated," I added.

We made motions of conclusion, and the waiter approached. Dr. Withers settled up, and we went down to the lobby. Retrieving our overcoats, we helped each other get prepared to return to the cold outside. As we started to walk toward the door, Miss Withers said, "One moment, Doctor," and touched my arm again. She left her hand in place.

321

Her father noticed, smiled almost knowingly, and said, "I'll secure our cab, my dear."

As he passed on through the great revolving door, Miss Withers took a step to the side, placing herself in front of me. "We are quite serious, Dr. Watson," she said. "About wishing for you to join us." She moved her gloved hand upwards to brush the mourning band. "I understand how you feel, and know that it has only been a few weeks since your loss. But you are so much like my father, and watching him come to terms with my own mother's death taught me that pushing past it is the only sure way."

I started to speak, feeling that there were numerous unspoken implications hidden within her words. Before I could frame a response, however, she continued, "Growing up as I have has let me understand that clinging to the past can be like finding oneself trapped in quicksand. Refusing to move on, and also worrying too much about what society requires of us, can be such a terrible thing. Day-to-day conventionality is the same sort of trap." She lowered her eyes, and then said, without looking up, "I'm sure you understand."

I didn't know what to say. I could not speak. I began to suspect what she was implying.

Misunderstanding my confusion, she gave a small knowing smile. "You are so like my father," she repeated. "He told me that this would be your reaction, and he tried to prevent me from broaching the subject too soon. But I have always been strong-willed, as you will come to know, and I do get what I want. I know how to get it, and I'm not afraid to do the things that need to be done." She placed her hand directly onto my mourning band and squeezed. "I know you think it's too soon, and possibly it *is* too soon, but really, that mindset is just another conventional snare. I suspect that – "

But while I thought that I knew, I was not to learn for sure what it was that she suspected, as the unmistakable sound of gunfire erupting in the street interrupted her further declarations.

Chapter X
Field Medicine

I rushed out of Simpson's to discover Dr. Withers, lying in a crumpled heap near the street. Although it had only taken seconds to exit the building and reach him, there was already a pool of blood widening underneath his left shoulder.

I came to an abrupt stop as I saw who was standing just beyond him, a smoking gun hanging from his right hand. The screams of nearby women receded into a dull roar as my eyes met those of Baron Meade.

His gaze had lifted from the wounded doctor, and when he first saw me, he showed no signs of recognition. Then a look of amazed surprise spread across his face as he realized that I was standing before him, and not lying wounded on the pavement. I instinctively understood that he had been waiting for me to leave the restaurant, having known I was there. He must have been following me all morning, as he undoubtedly had the day before, when I had sensed that someone was watching me.

He would have known that his plot to bomb our rooms in Baker Street had failed. Surprisingly, he had decided to try something more direct. But waiting outside in the cold and anticipating his chance to take his vengeance for such a long period while we dawdled over our meal had made him careless. When Dr. Withers stepped out of the restaurant, the Baron had seen someone who had a strong resemblance to myself, and had jumped the gun, firing at the wrong man. Now, his confusion was obvious, as he found himself in the presence of what he must have believed to be *two* Watsons, one wounded or dead on the ground before him, but the other one – the *correct* one – alive, and willing, nay *anxious*, to fight. Even as I wondered to myself if there was a constable anywhere near, I launched myself toward the would-be killer.

He tried to raise the gun, but I swung my stick around as I ran, completing its arc on the Baron's wrist. The strong wood, loaded with extra weight as a precaution learned long ago after aiding Holmes in his investigations, came to a satisfying stop as its momentum was arrested by the bones of Baron Meade's arm, and the gun dropped from his lifeless hand. Before he could utter a cry, or prepare himself further, I slammed into him with my propelled weight, forcing him over backwards.

I grimaced as the impact jarred my teeth, and a shooting pain raced through my long-ago wounded shoulder. It never even occurred to me that my own gun was in my coat pocket, and I doubted that the mere threat of "Stop or I'll shoot!" would have made any difference at all.

I felt my grip loosen on my stick, but rather than try to retrieve it, I let go and then curled my hand into a fist, swinging and catching the Baron on the jaw. There was a roar in my ears as I looked at this criminal, a man willing to indiscriminately take the lives of others as a recompense against his own loss, and at that moment I illogically associated him with the random unfairness that had taken my wife before her time. Just then, he represented everything that had caused me such terrible pain for the last few weeks, and I quite simply wanted to beat him with my fists until the rage that had been building inside me was gone and he was a pulp of shapeless meat, Hippocratic Oath be d----d.

With the prone figure laid out before me, I didn't want to avenge Dr. Withers, or punish Baron Meade for his attempt to set off an explosion that might have killed hundreds. I simply didn't know what else to do with my constant anger. It was always lurking just beneath the surface, and this man's earlier plans to injure so many innocents, and this present attack on another undeserving victim when he stupidly believed he was attacking me, was enough to ignite the flame that I had tried to ignore.

Yet, as I braced myself to strike him once again, my foot slipped in the spreading puddle of blood, jamming backwards into the wounded doctor's side. He didn't make a sound as my foot kicked him, and a part of me was grateful that he was in his heavy coat, which might have just protected him from obtaining several broken ribs – provided that he was still alive.

I regained my footing and lurched forward, attempting to grab the Baron's coat as he also stood. Part of me remembered just a few nights earlier, when I had held on so tightly to this very same coat as he had attempted to escape from the explosive-filled house following the disruption of his terrible plan. On this occasion, however, my fingers could not find a grip.

Baron Meade was torn between his desire to stand and fight me, and a cowardly urge to flee. He took a step back, and my tentative hold on his coat was lost. I reached blindly, and my fingers rasped against his face. I could feel that he had not shaved in days, likely since his earlier escape. He cursed and turned, but I managed to hook my fingers on the collar of his coat, yanking him backwards. I pulled him to me, and with my other hand, I began to piston a fist into the area of his kidneys. However, it wasn't doing any good, as all of my blows were completely negated by the heavy fabric of the garment.

He pivoted on one foot, and my hand, still grasping his collar, was twisted painfully, while my entire arm was curled into a position around his neck, seeming as if we were entering an unholy embrace. I could see his face, very close now, and his teeth were clenched in rage. His breath was foul, and his eyes were bloodshot. He had several old bruises on his skin, no doubt caused by me the other night.

With a cry of rage, he pushed at me twice, and then raised his arms in a whipping motion, breaking free from my grip on his collar. "Don't you understand?" he screamed. "They killed my son, and they have to pay! Why are you helping them against me?" He then lurched backwards for a step or two while I regained my balance, wincing at the fresh pain in my arm. Before I could recover, he turned and dashed down the Strand toward Trafalgar Square.

"*Where is the constable?*" I thought to myself. For a fleeting instant, it crossed my mind that the Baron possibly felt the same helpless anger and pain that I did, with the death of his son haunting him every day, but on a much greater and more destructive scale. I pushed the feeling aside, rationalizing that while I wanted to punish this one man who had just committed a murderous attack, Baron Meade wanted to kill hundreds who had never even heard of him, and who deserved none of his misplaced vengeance.

I remembered the gun in my pocket only then, but even as I reached for it, I knew that the fugitive would be beyond range before I could retrieve it. If I fired in frustration, I would likely hit a pedestrian, or send a stray bullet through one of the many windows looking down on the street. My only choice was to chase after him.

As I moved to pursue, and had only taken a few faltering steps, I heard a voice scream behind me, "Doctor!"

I stopped, watching the Baron dart this way and that through the midday crowds, like a deer cutting between bushes before reaching the safety of the trees. Turning to see who had called for me, and realizing vaguely that the voice sounded familiar, I saw Miss Withers, on her knees beside the wounded man, her own coat now soaking up her father's blood.

"Father needs your help!" she cried urgently. I was frozen. Her words made perfect sense, but they didn't seem to connect. I wanted to run down the Baron. Didn't she understand that he was getting away? I realized my hands were clenched into fists, so tightly that pain was shooting up my arms.

"Doctor Watson!" she said again, this time with an edge to it. Commanding. "Do your duty as a physician!"

That reached me. I *was* a doctor. It was my obligation and covenant to treat the sick and injured. But I wanted nothing more in that moment than to injure rather than to heal. And yet, despite what I felt, my feet began to propel me in uneven steps toward the fallen man.

Dropping to my knees on the other side of the figure from where his daughter rested, I reached out carefully and determined that he still had a strong pulse. I couldn't see the wound, and was considering the best way to turn him, when a voice interrupted.

"Here, now, what's this?" Looking up, I saw the silhouette of a man wearing the distinctive helmet of a bobby, shadowed in the early afternoon sunlight behind him. I didn't recognize him, but he apparently knew me. "Why, Dr. Watson!" he said. "What has happened?"

Rather than try to explain the nuances of the incident, I stated concisely, "This man was shot by a fugitive wanted by the Yard. Baron Meade. I attempted to stop him, but he just ran off toward Charing Cross Station. I'll attend to the wounded man. You try to stop the fugitive."

"How will I know him?"

"Middle aged. Dissipated. Dark thinning hair, heavy tweed coat. Looks as if he's been in a fight, probably out of breath and acting suspicious. Be careful." I noticed Baron Meade's gun, which appeared to be a .22 caliber target pistol, still on the pavement. "He dropped that, but he may still be armed."

"Right," said the constable, leaving the gun and turning to lope off toward the west. Say what he would to criticize the official police, even Holmes was always willing to praise the bravery of the men who served on the Force. This time it was no different. As Constable Rawlins, for I now remembered who he was, turned without question to pursue a man willing to kill, carrying nothing more than his truncheon, his fists, and his number twelve boots, I could only admire him. I knew that it was nearly impossible that he would capture the Baron, or even overtake him, but it was still the best that could be done, an honest effort made by a good man.

As Rawlins' boot-steps faded away, I could hear that he had pulled his whistle from his pocket, using it fiercely while he ran. Perhaps, if others became involved in the chase as well, there might be a chance that Baron Meade would be captured, although I remained doubtful.

Dr. Withers groaned and moved an arm, as if he were trying to gain leverage to turn himself over. Letting him know in a soft but clear voice that we were going to take care of him, I helped him to shift, so that he was lying on his back. Still not knowing how seriously he was wounded, I wanted to make sure that any movements didn't make things worse. As the doctor sighed and settled back with his eyes closed, a man standing nearby stepped forward and placed a folded garment underneath the victim's head. I saw without looking up that it was one of the distinctive coats used by the Simpson's doormen.

Dr. Withers opened his eyes then, but he was clearly not yet entirely conscious. I pulled aside his coat as gently as possible, causing him to vent

326

an involuntary cry. I tried to set aside my queasy recognition that he had been wounded in same general area that I had been at Maiwand. But this was different. The ragged projectile that had damaged my subclavian artery was fired from a Jezail rifle, and very unlike a .22 revolver bullet. It did not seem as if there was nearly much injury to the tissue here as what I had endured.

Dr. Withers' shirt around his left shoulder was soaked in blood, and an initial examination showed that there was a bullet entry wound somewhere below where the trapezius muscle wound up and over his shoulder and the through the arch of the collar bone. Pulling back his coat further, I saw no blood pooling near the shoulder blade, or even staining the back of the shirt, indicating that the bullet was still inside him somewhere. Luckily, this meant that there was no ragged exit wound, with the terrible damage that would have been associated with it.

I feared that the bullet might have been deflected in some way, and thus traveled along a deeper path into his body, but feeling along the top of his shoulder through his shirt soon revealed an unnatural lump, which was almost certainly the bullet resting there, just beneath the skin. Most likely, the impact as the projectile went through the collar bone had been enough to slow its momentum, preventing it from exiting the body. The doctor was most fortunate. An exit wound have been much messier and larger than an entry wound, and even though this meant a painful recovery, especially while dealing with the shattered bone, he would not have to be probed in order to find the bullet in some other part of his body. The threat of infection still existed, but with proper care, he would most likely make a full recovery.

I pulled my handkerchief from my pocket and placed pressure on the wound. I was pleased to see that the bleeding already seemed to be stopping on its own. I realized that Miss Withers had been speaking. At first I had ignored it, thinking she was comforting her father. But then I understood that she was addressing me. "Dr. Watson," she said, with some force to get my attention, "will he be all right?"

"Yes, I believe so." I explained to her about the bullet's path, and how the object would be easily recovered. "It could have been much worse."

Her lips tightened, and she seemed to be trying not to speak. However, what she wanted to say would not be suppressed. "It certainly would have been much worse indeed, if you had persisted in running off after that man."

"But . . . he had just shot your father," I tried to explain defensively.

"You are a *doctor*," she hissed. "Your duty is to the injured."

"You don't understand," I explained. "The Baron intended for *me* to be the victim . . . ." I trailed off, seeing a sudden confusion cross her face.

327

"What do you mean?"

"The man. His name is Baron Meade. Holmes and I stopped him the other night from a plot to blow up half of – well, a plot to use a bomb. He escaped, and now he apparently blames me for what happened. He left another bomb for me last night in Baker Street, and now – "

A look of horror spread from her eyes outward. I thought that it related to what the Baron had done, but instead, she said, "My father was shot because this man thought that *he* was *you*? Because of something that *you* had done, relating to one of those *investigations*?" She said the last word as if it were filthy and unmentionable.

I nodded. "I'm afraid so."

She started to speak again, but pursed her lips when Dr. Withers groaned then and reached up, grasping my forearm. "Dr. Watson," he said. "What happened?"

"You have been shot through the left collar bone," I said, speaking clearly and simply so that he would understand. It was the same as I had done so many times before on the battlefields, and how my own wounds had been explained to me when I had finally reached the Base Hospital at Peshawar. "The bullet is still inside you, lodged underneath the skin, high above your shoulder blade." I eased the pressure on the wound and lifted the handkerchief. Other than minor seepage, the bleeding appeared to have been controlled. I knew, however, that we would need to be careful when shifting him to an ambulance so that the bullet's entry wasn't reopened.

Miss Withers stroked her father's brow, but didn't look up or speak to me. "Miss Withers," I began, not sure of what I wanted to say, but unwilling to end the discussion. I felt the need to explain further, but at that moment, a constable pushed his way through the crowd that had formed around us, stopping beside me. I didn't look up, but noticed the solid stance of his regulation boots as he stated, "Dr. Watson, I've summoned an ambulance. Rawlins sent me back to tell you that Baron Meade got away. He first cut down toward the Embankment, but then circled back and got into Charing Cross, where he made it onto a train. We've sent out word to be on the lookout for him, but he'll have changed trains or gone somewhere else on foot before we can trap him, unless we're just lucky."

I thanked the man, and then helped to load Dr. Withers into the ambulance, which arrived at that moment. I ordered the driver to take us to Charing Cross Hospital, just down the street in the direction of Trafalgar Square. Miss Withers rode with us, but continued to whisper to her father, never deigning to look my way. I felt as if I should apologize, having inadvertently allowed my own difficulties to result in the mistaken attack on her father. But I didn't know quite what to say, and she clearly didn't want to hear it right now.

At the hospital, I succinctly explained the situation to the surgeon on duty, and helped to get Dr. Withers stabilized. The patient was conscious but somewhat confused, and after he was given morphine in preparation for the extraction of the bullet, he quickly fell asleep. I felt that there was nothing else that I could provide.

I walked out into the hallway, where Miss Withers was waiting, sitting alone on a cold chair, her coat pulled tightly around her, her father's blood still staining it and the dress underneath. I related again the basic facts of her father's condition, and what was now being done to remove the bullet. She nodded, stating with a cold expression, "I have assisted my father before, Doctor, in medical procedures. I'm aware of what is involved."

Once more, I felt the need to add something that would elaborate upon all that she did not know or understand, and also to apologize for the way that she and her father had been pulled into my problems. "Miss Withers . . . ." I began.

"Thank you for your help, Doctor Watson," she interrupted, without looking up, her voice flat and cold. "As I'm sure you can understand, I would really prefer to be alone now, until I can see my father."

"Is there anything that I can – ?" She shook her head, decisively.

Clearly she had nothing more to say to me, and I could only envision that any further attempt on my part to elucidate upon the facts of the matter would simply result in fumbling awkwardness. Choosing a different path, I told her that I would check back on her father tomorrow, and that if she needed anything from me to please let me know. Then, bowing my head, I departed.

Chapter XI
A Baker Street Conversation

I returned to Baker Street. Mrs. Hudson sensed my mood and offered to make some tea, but I wanted something stronger. Settling into my chair with a glass of whisky, I allowed myself to relive the events of the day. The visit to Marchmont's offices, the lunch at Simpson's – which was initially more pleasant than I would have expected. The following conversation in which Jenny Withers reemphasized her father's offer, along with the implication of a second more subtle consideration for my future, and then the gunfire from the street and everything that followed.

I was unsettled, wishing to both venture forth and roam the streets looking for Baron Meade, and also to stay inside and while away the day until there was no time left to go anywhere. If I went out, I would have no idea where to search. The only way I might find the man, other than some infinitesimal chance encounter, would be to hope that he was already back on station, watching for me as he had undoubtedly been doing for the few days, waiting for another chance to kill me. I swirled the whisky in my glass, looking at it and considering the afternoon light visible from the windows beyond. It was a foolhardy thought, but part of me wanted to walk outside and attract his attention in order to lure him to me.

That part, the man who had lost his wife just weeks before, did not care about his own safety. But I found that another part still did, although when I asked myself why, I couldn't provide any satisfactory answer.

I was still having these thoughts when I heard the front door open. It was immediately obvious that Holmes had returned. He bounded up the steps in one of his fits of enthusiastic energy, singing something that I recognized from Verdi's *Otelo*, which had premiered in London nearly a year earlier. I was certainly not an opera enthusiast, but Constance and I had attended a London staging at the invitation of friends, and I recalled this theme clearly, as it was repeated several times throughout the performance, before appearing ominously at the end, altered into a darker and maddened jealous heartbeat when Desdemona is strangled. I wasn't aware that Holmes had seen the opera or knew of the song, and I thought it an odd choice to sing when one was in an apparently ebullient state of mind.

He opened the door and, seeing me, threw a greeting my way while placing a heavy black leather case along the wall behind the door. Then he divested himself of his Inverness and matching ear-flapped traveling cap. Hanging them, he poured himself a brandy and joined me by the fire.

He immediately registered my mood, and his enthusiastic mien vanished in an instant. "My dear Watson," he said. "What has happened?"

"How do you know that anything has happened?" I asked peevishly. "Might I just be despondent over recent circumstances? I did, after all, spend the morning divesting myself of a medical practice that I worked for over a year to build, all in the hopes of . . . ." I fell silent.

Holmes cast his eyes down. "Your shoe tips are scuffed and the knees of your trousers are unusually and newly worn, as if you've been recently crouching on pavement. Your knuckles are freshly scuffed, indicating a fist fight. And most telling of all, there is quite a bit of dried blood on the cuff of your right sleeve. It isn't difficult. Something has happened."

I glanced at my arm and saw that he was right, but I felt no need to immediately change my shirt. The stain was like a badge, reminding me of what had happened. "I'm tempted to mention that there was really nothing to those observations at all, as even I would have been able to notice those signs on my own person, if I had bothered to look." I paused to take a swallow, noting that I had barely consumed hardly any of the whisky since pouring it. Rather, I had sat in thought, merely holding and tipping it back and forth in the dying light from the windows. A glance at the clock showed that it was later than I had realized. "Suffice it to say, I had an interesting afternoon," I said, "but I'd rather hear first about what made you so happy while running up the stairs."

He could see that I had no intention of explaining any more before he told his story, so he began. "I have spent the morning and a good part of the afternoon researching aspects of Ian's background. I began by conferring with various specialized individuals within the government who are aware of the idol, and the threat that it represents. I learned that they have kept regular tabs on it at the Museum, as mentioned by Williams. They were not, however, aware that the Earl had made a substitution and was concealing the real thing in the hidden vault in Essex.

"I then had a meeting with Sir Quintin Havershill at the Museum. He wasn't a great deal of help, as he had passed the years between the time the substitution was made and now happily believing that the object in the locked chamber was the real thing. He indicated that the responsibility for it rested with Williams, the murdered man, and no one else, so there isn't another soul that can provide any more useful information. Williams had been with the Museum since the early '70's, obtaining his post straight out of University. He was a quiet man, not given to mixing with his coworkers. He was moderately ambitious, but had refused several upward promotions into other areas, instead remaining at his same level within a sub-department of his discipline, indicating that he would prefer to rise in that area instead of obtaining some easier advancement in another department."

"That isn't necessarily an unusual desire to have," I said. "Perhaps he was more comfortable with his one certain area of expertise."

"Possibly, if that were the only consideration. But I was able, in the company of Inspector Gregson, to examine Williams's lodgings in nearby Coram Street. They were quite modest, but he had a small art collection of his own, with several original pieces that would seem to far outstrip his regular wages."

"Purchased through funds received by a legacy, perhaps?"

"Ah, Watson, you are asking the right questions, but they have already been answered. I cannot impress you enough regarding the concern that the missing idol has caused at the highest levels. When the officials are moved to act, they can accomplish great things very quickly. An examination of Williams's financial dealings, instigated with great urgency and efficiency by these events, revealed no inheritances that might have accounted for this private collection. But we did learn of the dead man's bank account, which currently holds a balance of something over £30,000."

"Good heavens!" I cried, sitting up a little straighter in my seat. "On a Museum employee's salary? Are you certain that such a sum didn't come from a rich relative? How could he possibly have saved that much?"

"Because," replied Holmes, "he was receiving a generous monthly stipend in addition to his modest salary, and had been since 1878. Very soon, in fact, after the statue was first stolen from the Museum by the mysterious John Goins. And who do you think was providing Williams with these funds?"

I began to dimly follow what Holmes was driving at. "Surely it must have been from Ian Finch, the Earl of Wardlaw."

Holmes slapped the arm of his chair. "Exactly. Ian seems to have conceived the plan of substituting the idol soon after his father arranged to have it loaned to the Museum. Knowing that Williams would be in direct charge of it, Ian bought his servitude. This explains Williams's reluctance to take a promotion into a different sub-department. He was ambitious enough, but only wanted to rise in a position where he would still receive the extra money and have control over the storage of the sculpture."

"And to report if or when the substitution was ever discovered," I added. "That explains why he was so quick to leave yesterday, when he realized that you had spotted it. His first action was to notify his secret employer, the Earl, who then killed him."

"Oh, Ian didn't kill Williams, Watson. Did I leave you with that conclusion?"

"What? But surely – "

"No, there is no doubt that Ian is on the run with the idol, but it is more complicated than that. The murder was committed by that odd little butler, Dawson."

"When did you decide on this?"

"Yesterday, when we found the body. The angle of the wound into the base of Williams's skull is clearly from a man much shorter than Ian. In addition, the footprints on the vault floor indicate that it was only Dawson who ever approached the body. Ian wears a much larger shoe, and there were no fresh prints of that size anywhere nearby."

"But surely he must have gone into his own vault at some point in the past?"

"Of course he did, as evidenced by the older larger prints near the door of the vault. Indications are that he entered regularly, no doubt to meditate with his idol. But as it was kept near the front of the vault, he had no reason to venture any deeper. None of the Earl's prints extended into the back where the body lay."

"Then was the Earl even present at the time of the crime?"

"He may or may not have been there at that precise moment, but his footprints were certainly intermingled with those of Dawson at the front of the vault at nearly the same time. They overlap one another quite a bit."

"But why would Dawson kill Williams?"

"Who knows? Orders? An impulse? Protecting his master? Something to do with his own agenda? To be certain, I've made sure that the police will continue to keep him under lock and key, although without letting him know that his true actions have been discovered."

Holmes went on to explain that, after he had made sure that Dawson would be held locally, the government's concern had led to the transfer of the butler to London the previous night from the village jail where he was being incarcerated, pending further investigation into the facts of Williams's murder. "He has been given to understand that we still believe his assertion that Ian committed the crime. The charge right now is simple association with the killing, so that we don't tip our hand about how much we know, to either Dawson or anyone else that might be connected to these events.

"I met with the man myself early this morning, without letting him know that I knew the truth, and he could really offer very little that was any more substantial than what we heard from him yesterday. He did explain in greater detail about how Ian had caused a replica of the statue to be made years ago, even before his father, the Earl at the time, had fully

333

arranged for it to be transferred into the Museum's keeping. He recalled the name of the craftsman hired to create the replica – Hayes, in Church Street in Stepney.

"I made a trip to Hayes' shop earlier this afternoon, but I learned nothing except confirmation that the counterfeit had indeed been made during the period indicated by Dawson, and some specifics about the materials used. Hayes did his best to replicate the marble from the original, but it seems as if Ian was frustrated that he couldn't make it even more precise. Still, it seemed as if Ian realized he couldn't do any better, and in the end he accepted possession of the false idol. Obviously, Hayes was told nothing about what was to be done with it. And knowing all of this really adds nothing to the case, other than verifying the assorted facts."

He gestured toward the black case that he had set by the door upon returning. "If we need a better idea of how it looks, we can examine the copy whenever we want."

"What?" I asked, half-rising. "You have it here?"

"I do. I intend to hide it here for the time being. It was accomplishing nothing, locked as it was in the Museum's vault. Ian knows he has the true idol. The people who seek to find it will either believe it still rests in the Museum – since the vault where it was supposedly kept remains inaccessible, whether or not an idol is actually in it – or they will become alerted somehow that Ian is on the run with it."

"But why bring the false idol here?"

"I have a little idea about a way that it might be useful."

"As a decoy, perhaps?"

"Perhaps – if word gets out that the carving is once again obtainable by those that would use it. Right now I'm not sure that is the wisest path. The search for the real idol must be discreet, and we must play our cards carefully. It was naively suggested to me, for instance, by a youngster at the Foreign Office, that we could take photos of the counterfeit, since it looks enough like the real thing, and make advertisements to help locate the authentic article. He had neglected to consider that, if one hands out flyers to every constable on the beat, word will inevitably get out even faster that the statue is on the move, if it hasn't already, and that is what we are trying to prevent. So far, it's just possible that the watchers who are looking to liberate it – and you can be sure that they have never stopped looking, Watson – may still believe it is locked in the Museum vault. Therefore, we must find Ian before he mistakenly reveals the true idol and starts a war.

"The only other information of value that Dawson could provide was about some of Ian's habits of late. It seems that he lived as one might expect of someone in his situation, an individual with wastrel tendencies, and a second son as well, elevated unexpectedly to a better position in life than he had ever anticipated. Following the death of his father in 1879, he divided his time between Essex and the Wellington Square house in London. He seemed to have a regular and steady series of notable financial successes in whatever he touched, through no great skill of his own, and he was quite forthcoming to Dawson, who held his full confidence, that he privately attributed these achievements to the possession of the idol, which he venerated as an object of power.

"However, several months ago, he seemed to change, becoming upset at the slightest provocation, drinking more and sleeping less, and generally giving all the appearances of someone who was constantly in an agitated state. He saw enemies everywhere, stopped traveling to London, closed the Wellington Square residence, and instead became almost a hermit in the Essex house. Dawson isn't sure why, as he is not aware of any specific occurrence that could have caused the change, but he feels that the lifestyle that Ian was leading was finally catching up to him. He became more and more obsessed with the fetish, fearing to be too far away from it for any length of time, and terrified that it would be discovered and stolen. He stopped attending social functions, and ceased welcoming any visitors as well, with the exception of one man, whom Dawson simply identified as 'Sir Edward'."

"Sir Edward? Did you find out who that is?"

"Yes. After Dawson mentioned his name, he seemed to regret it, and afterwards steered the conversation in a different direction whenever I attempted to learn more. It took me the better part of an hour to track down that he is actually Sir Edward Malloy, recently knighted over his successful trade negotiations with something involving North Africa."

"Malloy. One of the names of the men who were with the Earl when he found the idol."

"Exactly. The same man."

"If he's the only man to have remained in contact with the Earl after other social encounters ceased, he may have some insight as to what is going on."

"More importantly, he might be able to tell us how to find Ian, so that the idol can be returned to safe-keeping before terrible events are set into motion."

"Did you try to speak to Sir Edward?"

"I went to his home in Mayfair early this afternoon, but was told that he is unavailable. I was prepared to depart and obtain the full clout of the government behind me in order to gain entrance, but before I needed to do so, his man further informed me that I would be welcomed at ten o'clock tomorrow morning." Holmes turned up his glass and finished the last sips of his brandy before setting it on the small table beside his chair. "And so the incident stands. The authorities are quietly looking for Ian, and I have also spread the word through less official channels, and also to watch for Baron Meade as well. However, I don't expect much immediate success for them in terms of my old acquaintance, as Ian has no doubt burrowed into some hidey-hole that he has long prepared for just this eventuality.

"By the way," Holmes continued, crossing his legs, "I confirmed that Ian's man Harbottle is staying at the Wellington Square house, and that he was the one who overheard us through the door yesterday before passing on the information to Ian in Essex. He's been at that house for several decades, since it was owned by Ian's father. He has been questioned, and could provide no other information. He was simply following instructions, as he had been told to keep the door closed, make the place appear deserted, and report on anything that seemed important. He has been removed to a place of safekeeping, and replaced by a government man, in case Ian shows up there. I don't foresee him attempting to return to Wellington Square, as that would be too obvious, but if he should, he will be taken.

"And equally obvious is the fact that my efforts to keep an eye out for the Baron have been unsuccessful as well." He gestured toward my damaged clothing, pivoting to a new subject. "I take it that there was another attack."

Briefly, I explained how, following our meal at Simpson's, Dr. Withers was shot by Baron Meade, who believed that he was shooting at me. "The doctor will make a full recovery, provided no infection sets in," I said. "But Holmes . . . ." I looked at the glass of whisky, still essentially untouched, and realized that I didn't want it in the least. I set it down beside me.

"Holmes," I began again, "I understand the need to find the Earl and his idol. No one knows more clearly than I do the destruction that a war such as you describe would cause. I saw something of the sort at Maiwand. The savagery . . . the butchery. And the women . . . they were worse than the men. The soldiers that fell into the paths of those women during the retreat – It was . . . it was simply too awful. Should a spark ignite and spread, across all those unprepared towns and cities, the families who only want to live in peace – it simply cannot be allowed to happen."

He started to speak, but I waved him to silence. "I understand all of that, and will help in any way possible. But my first duty must now be to find and stop the Baron. He has made this personal, for no reason that I can understand. He attacked Dr. Withers, just because the man has a slight resemblance to me, and if things had worked out differently, he might have injured or killed the doctor's daughter as well. Or other bystanders on the street. They didn't deserve any of this. It only fell upon them because of a temporary association with me."

Again, Holmes started to say something, no doubt to logically refute my self-blame, but I cut him off, speaking more quickly now. "It could have been Mrs. Hudson yesterday if that package had detonated. Or you. I couldn't bear that. You are . . . you are both . . . ." I couldn't finish. I couldn't bring myself to say that they were the only family that I had left.

Instead, I cleared my throat and continued, "Or he might decide to do something worse, and some other innocent might become a collateral target as well."

"And certainly if he remains uncaught," agreed Holmes, "he will no doubt quickly attempt to repeat what he nearly accomplished the other night, with that unholy houseful of explosives, injuring countless innocents."

"Perhaps the only reason that he hasn't done so already is that, in his madness, he has shifted his anger to me."

"That," said my friend, "is something else to consider."

I nodded. We were quiet with our thoughts, and the various implications of the attacks on me. "But that isn't the *only* consideration," I finally said. "I also realized it today when he and I were fighting. He . . . he also became the focus of *my own anger*, as I am to him. He put a face onto the emotions that I've felt for the last few weeks, much as I have apparently become the object, at least temporarily, that personifies his own revenge."

I lowered my eyes, ashamed. "Holmes, perhaps you cannot understand the way I've felt. The frustration that has accumulated over the months as I, a doctor, was unable to heal my wife."

"Watson, you know you cannot heal everyone – "

"No, Holmes, it's more than that!" I snapped, my voice rising. "It's the overwhelming regret, knowing in hindsight that she had so little time. That *we* had so little time, and that I was unable to spend it with her. The traveling she did with her mother to better climates – if I had sold out and gone with her, instead of trying to stay here and build up the practice for our future. Did I really think that she would someday acclimate herself to London, and would then be able to live in health here?"

"Watson, you must not – "

"Why did I waste all of that time? Every day was precious, and I plodded along, investing in a future that would never have been tenable."

"You could not have known. No one can ever see how the threads of their lives will be woven."

"But what if I *did* know, secretly, somewhere inside? Was I selfishly choosing to devote all my efforts to staying in London, while realizing deep within that it would end like this?"

"No, Watson, you most definitely were not," my friend said firmly. "You forget that you weren't functioning in a vacuum during all of this. Do you not recall all of the conversations that we had last year, during your visits, when you and I sat in these very chairs? We have wrestled with these questions already. You kept me apprised of your wife's failing health throughout that time, and many various options were discussed, including the possibility of your moving to a location better suited to her health. You had never ruled it out, and if the sudden diphtheria hadn't struck last month, it is very likely that you would have positioned yourself to move away. But you know, in your head – if not yet your heart – that you weren't yet able to set those things into motion. What happened last December is no different than if she had been killed in a railway accident, or struck down by a runaway cab. It was fate, cruel fate, that interrupted your plans. But just because they were interrupted is no reason for you to forget that you *did* have plans. You are not to blame."

"But the *anger*, Holmes! I have never felt like this, not even when I returned to London following my injuries in the war, turned out of the Army that I had believed would be my future, into this cesspool where I had neither kith nor kin."

"Watson, *you* were the wounded party then. You were ill, and you turned inward as you healed and moved slowly toward your recovery. There was no room *then* for the anger that you feel *now*. But if you recall, you were not completely passive at the time, either. You weren't simply complacent when notified for good that you were deemed no longer fit to return to the Army. You were quite upset, and you made it well known to those 'idiots', as you called them, when making your case at their various offices. And you worked past it.

"In the case of Constance, you were observing from the side, able to see with your medical training and full faculties that something, possibly something terrible, was slowly taking place, but unable to do anything immediately effective, except to allow your wife to be removed to healthier locations by her mother, until such time as you were in a position to make the move permanent. But then fate struck unexpectedly, no different for her than the Jezail bullet at Maiwand was to you.

"Is it all random, this unexpected occurrence of our souls knocking around the universe like so many billiard balls, unknowing as to which direction they may be sent next, or by what? Or *was* it predetermined at the beginning of time? I have no clue. We are all too small to see the great pattern of fate, or if there even *is* a pattern. But I do know this, my friend:

You will continue to have anger, and you will have pain for a while, and there is no reason that you shouldn't. It would be abnormal if you didn't. But you also will heal, with each passing day. And as I've told you before, and certainly will again, work is truly the best antidote to sorrow."

Rarely had my friend acknowledged the things of which he just spoke, and I did not know what to say. In spite of his efforts to present himself as simply a perfectly balanced reasoning machine, divested of human emotion, there was a great heart there as well as a great mind. And, as I respected him as the best and wisest man whom I had ever known, I knew that I should listen to, and try to find, the wisdom of his words.

"Never fear, Watson," he added. "We will stop the Baron. How can we not? But we must also work to recover the idol before an unexpected tragedy is aimed toward all of these other unsuspecting people that would be caught up in the resulting war, affecting their lives like Constance's illness did to her, or when the projectile was fired at you by the murderous Ghazis. I promise you, Watson, that we will not neglect Baron Meade."

I had been looking at my hands, twisted in my lap, for most of this conversation. Now I lifted my head, and saw my friend, sitting forward in his chair, his attitude deadly serious, his gaze focused like that of a predator. I nodded my agreement. It was time to turn my anger towards something useful.

339

Chapter XII
The Knight's Tale

Holmes and I continued our discussion long into the evening. Mrs. Hudson once again provided one of my favorite dishes, and afterwards, over a final pipe, it was decided for now to trust in the police and Holmes's agents to keep up the search for both the Earl and the Baron, while he and I would visit Sir Edward Malloy at his home in Mayfair.

We were up early the following day, and I descended from my room to find Holmes already at the table, idly pushing his breakfast around on his plate. Settling in, I reminded him that before our appointment in Mayfair, I wished to stop by Charing Cross Hospital to check on Dr. Withers. He nodded in silent acknowledgement, clearly preoccupied with thoughts of his own.

I knew when we crossed from the front door of 221 to the waiting cab that it was likely that Baron Meade was watching me from somewhere. In spite of the knowledge that Holmes had loaded the surrounding streets with his Irregulars and other lesser-known agents, to hopefully let us know if or when the Baron had entered within our defensive lines, I could not relax. Although I was loathe to credit it, I had to acknowledge to myself that I was unable to sense his location. Still, I had that indefinable feeling that could not be ignored of being watched.

The cabbie, with the unusual name of Cable Hitch, was known to Holmes and myself. He was aware of the situation, having been summoned specifically that morning by Eldridge, one of the more responsible of Holmes's brigade of street Arabs. Hitch took a round-about path to the hospital, through less-traveled streets that were even emptier and still during that very early hour. This was partly to make Baron Meade more obvious if he was following us, and also to avoid the loss of innocent lives should there be some new attack. Because of all our efforts, or perhaps in spite of them, we saw nothing.

At the hospital, I was informed by the surgeon on duty that Dr. Withers was progressing quite well following the successful extraction of the small .22 bullet. "A wonder that Baron Meade hadn't managed to acquire a more effective firearm," Holmes murmured.

"A fortunate wonder," I replied. "And now he's lost that one as well."

I had noticed that there was no sign of the doctor's daughter, but I didn't want to specifically inquire as to her whereabouts. The question was answered in a moment, however, when the surgeon stated, "I'm afraid that you won't be able to speak with the patient right now, as he's sleeping. He had a fitful night. Didn't do well with the morphine, I'm afraid. His daughter sat up with him, and only left a few hours or so ago, when he finally dropped off to sleep."

"Very good," I said, explaining that I would be by later to check again on the patient's condition.

Outside, we regained our cab and set off for Mayfair. "You seemed relieved that Miss Withers was not present. You were looking around for her, and then you visibly relaxed when informed that she had gone home."

I nodded, debating whether to elaborate. Then, deciding to offer something of an explanation, I said, "Our parting yesterday was understandably strained. She was angry that her father had been wounded by someone who thought he was aiming at me."

Holmes thought for a moment, and then said, "But there is more than that."

"Yes," I admitted. "Before the shooting, I had been asked by the doctor to continue to assist him with the practice on a part-time basis. I politely acknowledged it, but have no intention of actually doing so. However, Miss Withers and I had a moment alone inside while her father went to summon a cab, and she reiterated his offer." I thought to stop there, but plunged ahead. "It was rather awkward. I had the feeling that she was intimating that there should be a . . . deeper relationship between the two of us in the future."

"Indeed?" said Holmes, his eyes cutting to my mourning band. "After meeting just a very few times. Most forward thinking on her part."

I nodded. "She spoke of how she doesn't agree with conventional behavior. She seemed to give an indication that my further involvement with the practice was only to be a prelude to my . . . to a future relationship between the two of us. Of course," I added with not a little embarrassment, "I may have simply been incorrectly perceiving the meaning of her words."

"I very much doubt it," countered Holmes. "You have always had a special understanding of the ways of women. You may be somewhat numb after the events of several weeks ago, but I do not think that you could misunderstand something like that."

"Perhaps you're right. The idea certainly seemed obvious as she was speaking, but before she could become more definite, and more importantly before I could tell her that what she implied would not be possible, we were interrupted by the sound of gunshots." I paused for a moment, and then said, "It seems certain that her anger related to her father's wounds will push that idea out of her mind."

Holmes raised an eyebrow. "Now you sound as if that disappoints you."

"What?" I said with surprise. "No, certainly not. She's a lovely girl, and in the little time I've known her father, I've grown to like and respect him. But Holmes, my wife died less than a month ago. What kind of man would I be if I were to completely disrespect her memory and immediately begin to pursue another woman? Or in this case, allow myself to be pursued? In either case, it is completely dishonorable."

"But Watson," said Holmes, "you yourself have railed in the past against some of society's conventional behaviors. Yesterday we were discussing fate, and the unpredictable events that unfold in each life. What if this is your destiny? I'm not advocating it, certainly, or trying to talk you into anything, but if you are supposed to be with this woman, should the circumstance of unfortunate timing, or the fact that you are put off by her forward behavior, be enough to bring it to an end before it begins?"

I shook my head. "No, Holmes. Your Devil's Advocacy aside, it simply isn't right. I can feel it. And I would prefer not to discuss it any further."

With a wave of his arm and a flick of the fingers that looked suspiciously like a Frenchman washing his hands of something in disgust, my friend became lost in his own thoughts. And we remained that way until we arrived at Sir Edward Malloy's very tasteful abode.

Hitch's horse was skittish, and it took a few extra seconds to get the four-wheeler steady before we could step down to the street. Holmes led me to the heavy double door, surrounded by a stone arch with a *faux* keystone carved upon it. Within moments, it was opened by a thin, sour-looking butler who led us inside. Our coats and hats were taken, and we were steered through the house to a dimly lit receiving room. Standing by the fireplace was a man about our age, his hands clasped behind his back. Stepping forward, he nodded, saying, "Mr. Holmes, thank you for returning this morning. I am sorry that I was unable to receive you yesterday. I had other pressing business."

Turning to me, he said, "You must be Dr. Watson. My pleasure, sir."

He offered refreshments, which we declined. The butler was dismissed, and Sir Edward gestured toward a grouping of tall chairs nearby. We sat, and he said, "I understand from the message you left yesterday with Crye that Ian has gone missing?"

"I'm afraid it's a bit more complicated than that," said Holmes. "There has also been a murder."

"So I've since learned. But surely Ian could not be involved in that," the man said softly. "There must be a mistake. Some other explanation."

"The incident occurred at his Essex home, and he fled immediately thereafter. Additionally, his man there, Dawson, has related that the crime was committed by the Earl, so that seems to be well established."

I had known Holmes long enough to keep myself from giving anything away. Not only was he allowing Sir Edward to believe Dawson's assertion that the Earl had committed the murder – he was also relating it as an established fact.

Our host raised an eyebrow. "What? Dawson has implicated Ian as the killer? Impossible." He shifted in his chair, sitting strangely tense for all of the calmness in his measured voice. "Simply impossible. I confess that after your visit yesterday, I instructed my solicitor to find out what Ian had gotten himself into. He spoke to a superintendent that he knows at Scotland Yard, but information from that quarter seems to be singularly restricted."

"That is upon my suggestion," said Holmes. "The murder relates directly to the idol which you, the Earl, and a man named Conner, helped to bring back to England years ago

"The idol? Do you mean The Eye of Heka? But how is that possible? It's been locked in the bowels of the British Museum for years and years. No one knows or cares that it's there, any more than they pay any attention to all of those other dusty stones and trinkets that litter the place. It's been there ever since Ian's father became fearful because of all the attempts to steal it out of their house."

"Then you didn't know, Sir Edward, that the statue at the Museum is a clever fake? You weren't aware of that fact?"

Sir Edward's eyes widened. "That's ridiculous. There is no fake. The idol has been put away in the basement of the Museum for a decade."

"Still, the facts indicate that the Earl had a duplicate made and then swapped it with the assistance of the murdered man, a Museum employee named Williams. He had secretly been in the Earl's employ for quite a while."

"But why would Ian murder him? This simply doesn't make any sense to me, Mr. Holmes."

"After I unfortunately gave away to Williams that I had spotted the false idol, he was prompted to notify the Earl that the deception had been uncovered. He then immediately traveled down to Essex. Dawson later told us that the real idol has been kept there in the same vault that was originally constructed by the Earl's father. Upon Williams's arrival, the Earl, apparently in a paranoid or delusional reaction, killed Williams and fled, taking the real idol with him."

"I see, but I still don't understand. Frankly, this is hard to believe, gentlemen. I cannot imagine any reason why Ian would have behaved in

343

this manner." He glanced down for a moment, and then asked, "May I ask why you've come to see me?"

"There are several reasons," said Holmes. "First, to determine if the Earl has attempted to send you a message you since he fled two days ago."

"No, I haven't seen Ian in months. I understood that he had closed up his London house."

"We have confirmed that, as well as reports that he was acting strangely in the time leading up to his move. Had you heard anything along those lines?"

He shook his head. "I'm afraid that my involvement in other situations has caused me to lose touch with many of my old friends."

"Speaking of which, can you tell me anything about the other man who joined you on the expedition, this man named Conner? I've been unable to find out any real information about him."

"Alas, poor Herbert. I'm afraid that he died years ago, not long after our return to England with the idol, in fact."

"Can you elaborate?" Holmes asked.

Sir Edward seemed nonplussed by the question, as if his statement about the man's death was all that needed to be considered. "Herbert was the son of Mr. Abel Conner, of the banking family, you know. Grew up around the corner from here, actually. Like Ian and myself, he was also a second son, and as such, we all initially had lower expectations for our futures. However, I'm sure you're aware that Ian's brother Jimmy died while traveling. Herbert and I were both already acquainted with Jimmy through Ian, and as Jimmy had never had many friends of his own, we were suggested as companions for him on his great tour. Ian never really could stand his brother, and had refused to go. Herbert and I, however – well, we felt that we couldn't turn down the opportunity.

"While down there, we learned of the location of a lost tomb, and planned an expedition to find it. But on the way, before we reached the location, Jimmy's tent caught fire and he burned to death, elevating Ian unexpectedly to the position of heir.

"Soon after we returned to England, there was a scandal in which Herbert's father and brother were implicated, and it was revealed that they actually had very little money. Furthermore, Herbert's older brother, Raymond Conner, was found to be embezzling from the bank. Both Abel and his son Raymond committed suicide, not long before their arrests."

"I remember something of it now," said Holmes. "The double suicide of both father and son was considered rather unusual, as was the method." He turned to me, stating, "They seated themselves in an upstairs parlor of their home – as you say, Sir Edward, just around the corner – and turned on the gas, filling the room. I recall reading that they were discovered by the unfortunate Herbert Conner."

"Yes, Mr. Holmes. Unfortunate indeed. I did all that I could to help, and Herbert and I even worked together in a few business deals, but without any great success. He wasn't really cut out for business, you see. Not long afterwards, Herbert threw himself into the Thames. It was believed that he decided to end his life because of the shame associated with his father and brother's activities, and also due to his own reduced circumstances." He lowered his voice, adding, "I should have recognized the signs in him, and done more to prevent it. Conner always was rather weak, you see."

"Your own expectations as a second son also improved," said Holmes unexpectedly, and rather improperly as well, I thought.

"Yes," said Sir Edward, sitting back a bit in his tall chair. "My own older brother was killed in a hunting accident a year or so before my father's death. Like Ian, I was elevated to the position of heir to the estate when my father passed." He seemed disinclined to add anything further.

"You have certainly made a success of your situation," said Holmes, waving a hand. "I believe that, like the Earl, you've been able to increase your holdings tremendously in the years since."

Sir Edward shifted straighter in his chair. "I'm not sure that that is any of your business, Mr. Holmes, or what any of this has to do with Ian's disappearance. But, in fact, you are correct. I have been fortunate, and it turned out that I have some skills in these things."

"I simply ask about your situation in relation to the Earl's success, as both you and he seemed to prosper following your return with the idol, whereas Mr. Conner had a much more unfortunate fate."

"Although Ian and I have lost touch with one another for the most part over the years, I understand that he has also done quite well for himself. From what you tell me, however, his path will likely follow a different course from this point forward." He shook his head. "Murder. Dear me."

"Are you aware that he credited his successes to the idol?"

"What?" His eyes cut up from his considerations. "By magic, you mean? That is ridiculous!"

"That is what his man, Dawson, related to us when we spoke to him in Essex two days ago. Apparently the sculpture, always an unhealthy fascination for the Earl, held an ever-increasing amount of his attention, and he believed that it was the source of his steadily improving good fortune. That's why he wanted it with him, instead of leaving it in the Museum, and it also seems to be why he has now taken it with him following the murder of the Museum employee."

345

"I cannot imagine why Ian would think such a thing. When we were sold the map, we all had ideas that we would discover a lost tomb filled with riches, or important archeological discoveries. Even after Jimmy's death and Ian's arrival, it was on that basis that we talked him into going on the search. Instead, what we found was simply a plain chamber containing a single ancient coffin, and all that it held was the curious but rather plain stone figure. We were told at the time of some legend or other, and how the idol related to an obscure local god, this Heka for whom it's named, but it was just so much nonsense and superstition. Those sorts of stories are scratched on every rock out there.

"I did know that there were subsequent attempts by men who had followed it to England to steal it back, but they were certainly just the ignorant and the superstitious with their own agenda. Maybe the conviction that these people felt it was important and gave credence to such a notion was enough to plant the idea in Ian's head, making him believe he'd actually found a magic talisman."

"But the power of belief is an important thing," said my friend, shaking his head. "Dr. Watson here will affirm the importance of the placebo effect when dealing with illness. Making the patient *believe* he is being cured is sometimes enough to actually *cause* the cure. Belief in an object can sometimes be enough to focus hopes and plans in one's self, thereby allowing one's desired outcomes to be achieved."

Sir Edward smiled and shook his head. "Surely you don't believe in this magic rubbish, Mr. Holmes."

"No, but I know that there are people who do, and they can use the power and motivation of that belief to make things happen, or as an excuse to do things that otherwise would be abhorrent to them. Such as murder."

"You feel, then, that Ian believes his idol is being threatened, and that has caused him to take it. That sounds as if he has lost his mind."

"That, too, is a possibility. His behavior was reported as being erratic in the months leading up to these events. As far back as when he closed the London house."

Sir Edward frowned, leaning forward in his chair. "I'm forced to wonder why you came to me to ask these questions."

"We are simply seeking further knowledge regarding the Earl's fixation upon the idol. It is obviously a motivation for his actions. This can possibly be accomplished by determining his history with the object from the beginning – a topic for which you have obviously provided a great deal of information. Also, I wanted to determine if you have had any recent contact with him, especially since he vanished following the murder in Essex."

"Well, I'm afraid I cannot help you any further. It is distressing that my old friend has taken this path, and I hope that you find him quickly, but I don't know what else that I can do to help." He stood and we followed. "However, please feel free to let me know if I can answer any additional questions. In the name of our long-ago friendship, I owe Ian that much."

He rang, and in a moment the butler, presumably the man Crye of whom he had previously spoken, entered, only to lead us back through the house and into the entry hall, where we donned our outerwear. On the street, the cold air passed across my face like a freezing liquid. As the door closed, I said softly, "You didn't mention to him any of the possible ramifications should the idol fall into the hands of those who would abuse it. He might have thought of something to add if he knew just what was at stake."

"Later, Watson," said Holmes, looking sharply at our cab. I followed his gaze, not seeing anything unusual for a moment. And then it hit me – our cabbie, Cable Hitch, was not the man sitting in the driver's seat!

The fellow that had replaced him was bundled up in a coat very similar to that which had previously been worn by Hitch. In fact, it might have been the very same one. But this man, sitting calmly with the reins held loosely in his hands, had nothing of Hitch's plain and stolid British features. The new driver was much smaller by many stones, and his skin was darker. I could see that he had on what was likely Hitch's cap, but it did not hide his thick black hair, the sharp features of his face, or his oddly light-colored eyes.

"Do not worry," the man said with a low but pleasantly accented voice. "Your friend is being well-taken care of. I assure you that he will not be harmed. I must earnestly ask that you accept my invitation."

Holmes took a step forward with a frown. "Invitation?"

"Yes, Mr. Holmes. You and the doctor will meet with my – with *someone* to discuss the events related to a certain idol which has gotten loose from its moorings."

"Indeed. And who is this 'someone'?"

"All in good time, Mr. Holmes. All in good time."

"Then tell me, where is this meeting to take place?"

The man on the box gestured vaguely east. "I can have us there in less than an hour, if you'll just climb into the cab."

Holmes looked at me. I nodded, lightly tapping my overcoat, where my service revolver rested. "I'm game if you are."

"I expect that we'll certainly find out more this way than what we just learned from Sir Edward," he replied. "After you."

I climbed into the cab and Holmes followed. Without another word, and with just a quiet snick to the horse, our new host turned the vehicle sharply with skill and set off toward the north and then east.

Chapter XIII
Beneath Limehouse

We had barely begun before I whispered, "This does not bode well for the plan to keep knowledge of the missing idol a secret."

"I'm not so sure, Watson," Holmes replied, quite softly. "Clearly this driver is somehow connected to John Goins – "

"Not so clear to me, but I'll take your word for it."

"The *eyes*, Watson. They are similar to Goins'. You won't have forgotten that the man who sold the original map had light eyes, as well as the other who tried to stop the expedition. It's very likely," Holmes continued, "that the person at our destination will exhibit the same characteristics. But if that is the case, why would they need to speak with us?"

"What do you mean?"

"All of the events connected to this business over the last few days have started because we went to visit the Museum, and Williams was provoked into sending a pre-arranged warning to Ian. It seems that his plan to swap statues and keep the real one at his country home had gone undetected up until that time. Those who wished to recover it had apparently been deterred or fooled by Ian's substitution and the Museum's security measures, and had made no further efforts over the years to retrieve the thing, willing to play a wait-and-see game. It was only when Ian panicked and went on the run with the idol that we now find ourselves invited to take a cab ride."

"To be fair, Holmes, it's only been two days since the Earl bolted. Regardless, whomever it is that we're going to meet has now involved himself in this mess, when for years there has been no activity. For whatever reason, we are in some way required."

"Too true. There have evidently been watchers in place to see if the sculpture ever became recoverable. The events of the other day, including Williams's dash to Essex and Dawson's subsequent arrest for his possible involvement with the murder, were not completely hidden, and have obviously come to the attention of the watchers. They must also be after Ian and the idol, wherever he is, even as we speak. After our appearance in Essex, our involvement in the problem has been clear as well. We were certainly found quite handily this morning."

"We are being too easily stalked from all directions," I muttered.

Holmes continued, "So why are we being taken to visit this mysterious person? What does he or she expect from us? I have inadvertently flushed it for them. What else do they need from us? Is this meeting to warn us off from additional involvement? Surely it cannot be thought that we will assist in the recovery of the idol for the agitators that wish to make use of it."

He glanced toward the roof of the cab and then lowered his voice further. "Don't give away anything," he said. "Let *them* tell us what they know. And let *them* reveal whether or not they are aware of the false idol in the Museum. If they don't know about it, we might use that to our advantage."

Throughout this conversation, we had steadily headed north out of Mayfair, and then east onto that long latitudinal passage across London, initially known as Oxford Street, and then High Holborn, Holborn, and so on. It was still early enough in the morning that traffic wasn't too entangled. I was aware of various locations and fixtures as we passed them, including Bloomsbury and the Museum to the north, where the carving had supposedly rested for all of these years, adjacent to Holmes's old Montague Street rooms. And then somewhat later, we skirted that area of London around Barts, where I had obtained a great deal of my medical training, and had first been introduced to Holmes. I still pondered where my path might have taken me, had not I met this unique fellow, then not quite twenty-seven years of age. I've long suspected that, returning as I recently had to London as a wounded soldier with few prospects, I might very well have ended a drunkard or worse, if I hadn't had the distraction of Holmes's investigations to pull me out of my despair and pain, along with the nurturing care of Mrs. Hudson, whom I would not have known at all but for meeting Holmes.

Holmes had fallen silent as he considered our situation, leaving me free to continue to observe the surroundings as we traveled. I had never been overwhelmed with too much imagination, and my time in the military had taught me to separate myself from any anxiety that might be manifested before an upcoming battle, so I was able to remain relatively undisturbed during our passage across the great city. But perhaps I would have been better off had I been worrying about what was to come. Instead, I found myself falling into the familiar feelings of despair related to my recent loss. And yet, strangely, I also discovered that I was returning to the conversation of the day before, when Miss Withers had indicated that joining her father in the newly sold practice might be just the first step toward a completely unanticipated future.

I shut my eyes, as if that would keep me from examining these thoughts that were unexpectedly surfacing in my mind, continually drifting into my field of vision like a lifeline that I was determined to ignore. I had no doubts whatsoever that selling the practice had been the correct decision. And likewise, I knew that I didn't feel any genuine attraction toward Dr. Withers' daughter. Granted, she was beautiful, and she radiated intelligence. But I simply wasn't interested in pursuing a future relationship with her. I still loved my wife.

Then I remembered yet again – as I was forced to dozens of times each day – that Constance was gone, and all that stretched before me now seemed empty and unfulfilling. Perhaps –

But no. This was not worthy of me. I made myself recall the tightness of the mourning band on my arm, while being quite careful not to raise my hand and make any move to touch it, lest such an action be noticed and interpreted in some way by my companion, as he certainly would. In any case, after the events of the previous day, it was clear that Miss Withers should have obviously changed her mind about a man such as myself, whose associations placed those around him, and most recently her father, in the gravest of peril.

I checked my watch and saw that we had been traveling for approximately forty minutes. Not knowing our destination, I could only guess that we would be arriving shortly, as based on the estimation of our driver during his invitation. We were now making our way awkwardly around Aldgate, before entering the Commercial Road, and thus into Whitechapel. Here the traffic thickened noticeably, and the view from the windows revealed a slice of a London that many will never see, although it was not unfamiliar to me. There were people of numerous nationalities and races, all jostling together, calling out to one another in so many languages that Babel itself must have seemed as only a dim precursor to all of this. There were stalls set up along the edges of the main street, and the flowing foot traffic was occasionally pushed into the road like water diverted around a rock. And yet, it all seemed to piece itself together without any difficulty.

Although still relatively early in the morning, the merchants and sailors intermingled with dubious women and mothers with their children. There were colorful costumes interspersed with dark winter coats, and the whole of it surged and seethed like a single living organism.

Soon enough, though, we left much of the bustle behind as we continued down Commercial Road, nearing Dockland. We were passing through the northern edge of Shadwell when the driver turned to the right, and so down the Stepney Causeway. A left on Brook Street, and then right into Cranford. Immediately, the noise of the busier thoroughfares was cut off, and all that could be heard were the echoes of the horse's hooves on the cobbles, returning from the dark irregular bricks making up the close buildings beside us.

"We are on the outskirts of Limehouse," Holmes said softly. We took a sharp left into a narrow alley labeled Bere Street. On our right was a building of a lighter-colored brick, broken up with three or four separate doorways.

The cab pulled about halfway down the alley and stopped. The far end narrowed before opening into another cross street. Immediately to the left and just before this intersection was a tall building, four stories, with an odd arched window at its top, overlooking the surrounding neighborhood. I idly wondered if one could see the Thames, only a few blocks to the south, from that high perch.

At the base of this building was a recessed doorway, nothing more than an upright rectangle, deep in shadows cast by the edifice across from it, stretching down the south side of the street. Standing just outside the door, barely visible as he halfway leaned out, was a man wearing a curious mélange of a garment combining styles from several continents. It was finished with loose sandals on his feet. I thought that he must be very cold indeed to be wearing such inappropriate clothing.

Holmes and I climbed down, as it seemed to be implied that we had arrived at our destination. We looked back at the driver, who gestured toward the doorway. Holmes didn't look away from him, instead asking, "What of our cabbie?"

The man looking down at us smiled, and there seemed to be no malice there at all. In fact, the only feeling that he betrayed was one of a great and gentle weariness, overlaying what seemed to be an old and kind soul. "I give you my word, gentlemen, that Mr. Hitch has not been harmed, and that his cab will be returned to him immediately, with more than adequate compensation for his troubles. It was unfortunately necessary to use these means to guarantee your cooperation."

"It was not necessary at all, but you could not have known that," said Holmes. The driver simply smiled again and looked back at him silently, and then nodded, as if an understanding had been reached. Holmes did the same, and then the driver turned the horse's head, pulling him back around to depart with the same gentle skill he had displayed when removing us from Sir Edward's street.

We turned and walked across the short distance to the doorway, where the robed fellow awaited us. When I was closer, I could see that he was older than I had first thought. His skin was weathered, and his black hair was shot with streaks of gray. A most noticeable feature about him was the great scar running down the left side of his face, crossing from forehead to cheek, directly through where his left eye had been. Now, it

352

was just a closed and puckered thing, long healed, but still an angry red in contrast to the brown of his face. His right eye – light-colored, I noticed – glared.

"This way," he said, in a surprisingly rumbling and deep voice with a strong accent. He cocked his head to the side, compensating for his monocular outlook. Gesturing us over the threshold, he pulled the door shut tightly behind us. Inside, there was a single lantern hanging nearby, so that the entryway wasn't in total darkness. The room was very cold, really no different than outside, and it seemed obvious that the building was long abandoned from its original purpose.

Taking the lamp down from the peg upon which it was hanging, our guide began to lead us deeper into the building. It wasn't long before we reached a narrow stairwell that descended into darkness. "Mind the steps," said our leader unnecessarily, and with no apparent malice.

I could see that he was putting a great deal of trust in us as he held the lantern high, so that we might better find our footing. No implication of any weapon or even threat had been produced. Allowing us to be behind him on such a stairway opened him up to attack, should we so choose. However, both Holmes and I were thoroughly interested in following this thread of Theseus on through the Labyrinth toward whatever Minotaur might be awaiting us, and it would have accomplished nothing to force our guide to take us where we were already going.

I was relieved when we reached the bottom of the steps, one level below the ground floor, and started off through the center of a long open room, pitch black beyond the short range of the lantern light. I had feared that we might keep going deeper and deeper into the earth, dropping down through other stairways and even ladders and tunnels, into some pernicious and hidden stronghold. Doing so wouldn't have been the first time that Holmes and I had ventured into such a rat's warren, buried deep beneath Limehouse, but fortunately this time was quite different, and we were soon to speak to someone far different than that evil man whom we had previously encountered on those other subterranean sojourns.

In the shadows, I could see the featureless detritus remaining from whatever commercial function had once been carried out here. I also heard the unmistakable brushings made when loathsome rodents were carrying out their *Muroidean* business in the darkness beyond the lamp's reach. It was with some relief that I saw we were approaching a closed door, with light showing through the crack at the bottom. For good or evil, I thought, we were about to get some answers.

The robed man knocked, opened the door with a prosaic knob – how different from the portals in those underground chambers of that other Limehouse resident! – and motioned for us to precede him. Holmes went

353

first, and I followed. Our personal Diogenes, bringing with him not one but two reasonably honest men, came last and closed the door behind him.

We were in an office, although I couldn't imagine who would have ever wanted to have such an arrangement down here. Unlike the outer rooms, it was well-lit by lanterns, and cleaned up as well as it could be under the circumstances. A chair and desk were pushed against one wall – apparently the outside wall, as there was a high window above them near the ceiling, probably opening into a window well outside on the street. It was heavily curtained, likely so that no light would escape and reveal that the room was now being occupied.

A small fireplace was on one of the inside walls, but no fire was burning, and the room had a damp and cold feel to it. However, on a small iron stand within the fireplace was a spirit lamp, heating a coffee urn. The smell of the strong brew did much to improve the dismal atmosphere.

A half-dozen wooden chairs were grouped in a loose circle in the center of the room, which was no more than twenty feet square. Standing in front of one of these was a small man, well-dressed in English clothes, but clearly of the same group as the others. His light eyes gleamed in the dim light. His hands were behind his back, and he bowed formally.

The incongruity of his presence and his formal welcome, after the subterfuge of coercing us across London and then down into the abandoned building, was somewhat ludicrous. Yet there was a serious formality to the man's greeting that added to the mysterious gravity of the situation. I found myself nodding in something of a return bow, and noticed that Holmes did the same, his wary eyes never leaving the man.

Holmes took a step closer. "You summoned us?" he said.

"I hope you will see it as more of an invitation, and I apologize for the necessity of it," replied our new host, with only a trace of an accent. His voice was soft, yet commanding. "I could not be sure that a mere request would suffice." He glanced to the left and right. "I felt that talking here might be better. We, that is, the group that I represent, sometimes find it easier and rather necessary to make use of this place, so that our activities might not be observed."

"You would make a better job of it," replied Holmes, "if you arranged your approaches better. The way that we were brought into Bere Street up above would have been very obvious if anyone had a mind to look. I noticed one of the residents across the street, for instance, surreptitiously watching us from behind her closed curtains."

"You are correct," said the man. "Normally we are more circumspect, and there are other ways into this building besides the direct entrance through which you arrived. But we did not want to inconvenience you

354

further by some of the trials that those ways would require, and regardless of that fact, it was urgent that I meet with you both as soon as possible."

"I believe that our address in Baker Street is probably not unknown to you. In future, should it be necessary, a message can easily be delivered to arrange an appointment."

"I understand. But today we did not want to go there and so alert anyone watching you. And as you probably know already, you are being watched."

"We are aware of that, but thank you for letting us know. I take it that, while you have been carrying out your own surveillance, you have noticed the man known as the Baron dogging Dr. Watson's steps."

"Yes, the solitary man in the tweed coat with the singularly intent focus on your residence. We saw him two days ago, when he left a package at your front door. He was lurking there when our man arrived. It seemed to us that he might be your enemy, and that his delivery was related to the visit by the police later that day, after you returned home. We saw that they were carefully removing the very package left by this man that you call the Baron."

"That is him," I said. "It was a bomb."

He nodded as if that didn't surprise him and gestured toward the chairs. "I'm sorry. Won't you both have a seat? I apologize for the arrangements. We are not set up here to be one of your St. James clubs."

Holmes and I moved to chairs where we could face the man. He nodded again and said, "May I offer you some coffee?"

I could see no reason why we would be drugged or poisoned at this point, when we could have been attacked as soon as we arrived at the building – or earlier for that matter. Holmes must have agreed, for he, like myself, nodded. The one-eyed man moved to the desk, where he retrieved cups, and then to the fireplace, where he poured.

He distributed them, and then poured another for himself before joining us at the chairs. Clearly, he was not a mere servant. "Thank you, Micah," said our host.

Holmes took a sip, and then, with a look of surprise, took another, savoring the coffee in his mouth for a moment before swallowing it. I followed suit, finding it to be quite dark and rich, and – most importantly in that cold cellar – hot. I had enjoyed thick strong coffee such as that before, and had developed a taste for it in my travels. Usually it could only be found in London in certain specialized locations in the East End.

"The man who drove you here – " began our host.

"Your brother," interrupted Holmes.

Our host seemed surprised. "How do you know this?"

355

"There are a number of telling factors. Most importantly are the eyes, of course. That seems to be a family trait. Then there are the ears, which usually maintain a certain family resemblance. Then, you are also both wearing rings of a certain design, probably a family insignia, as is this man here – " He gestured toward Micah. "Also a brother, I can see."

"That is correct, Mr. Holmes. You do not disappoint."

"And our driver? What is his name?

"Andrew."

"And you are . . . ?"

"My apologies, gentlemen. My name is Daniel Mizer."

Holmes smiled and raised an eyebrow. Daniel appeared to understand, for he replied, "Our true names do not matter. We have chosen to take other names during our sojourns into the wider world."

Holmes nodded an acknowledgement. "Your brother, Andrew, then. When he tendered your 'invitation', he mentioned something about an idol."

"That is correct."

"Might I inquire, what is the idol of which you speak?"

"Come now, Mr. Holmes, we do not have the time to fence around any longer about this. You know about The Eye, and the fact that I am asking about it reveals that I know it as well. I understand your concerns, and why you do not wish to acknowledge it, but I assure you that it is in both of our interests to have frank and open discussion regarding this situation."

"I'm not yet convinced that I have anything to discuss with you. However, this is good coffee, and I will listen if you care to speak."

"Then I shall certainly do so, and you will understand that we are not your enemies.

"The idol," Daniel continued, "as you both undoubtedly know, is referred to as 'The Eye of Heka', representing one of the old gods. Very old. Ancient, long before the borders or even regions that you now recognize even existed. There is no need to waste time describing the physical object to you, but I will mention that it is revered by certain groups as a legendary talisman. They believe that it can be used to access and channel power – Magic, if you will."

"So much nonsense," prodded Holmes.

"I agree. Nonetheless, it cannot be denied that people believe in its power – and a great many more each year. There is a growing interest in and awareness of it both far and wide, both on this side of the world and in America, even if it is only vague and little thought-of in actual day-to-day life. It was believed by most to be lost, and only a distant legend, mentioned mostly in morality tales for children about how a powerful man used it and was subsequently corrupted by it. Upon the death of this man, after a life of wealth and influence that were both used for great evil, the thing was buried with him, sealed up to protect others from its use or its corruption upon the user.

"The man who actually wielded The Eye is known in the tales only as Mustashar, or '*The Counselor*'. Thousands of years ago, he was the advisor of a little-known regional official named Orkahn. It was into that same barren region, far inland from the coasts, that the idol was later found and brought forth by the English visitors, the Earl of Wardlaw and his friends.

"The legend tells that Orkahn was quite wealthy, but he was only a figurehead whose riches and power had come through Mustashar's use of the idol. The legends tell that Mustashar was the man who had made a bargain with the god Heka, to be able to use the god's own powers of channeling magic through his very own soul. It was this soul that Mustashar traded for the idol, which he could then use as a tool to achieve his goals. Preferring to work from the shadows behind Orkahn, he plundered the countryside. The people could not understand the manner in which they were being subjugated. But eventually things changed when someone, just a boy, a poor servant in Mustashar's household, discovered him using the idol, and finally understood the power it was conveying to and through him."

Holmes snorted, and started to speak, but Daniel raised a hand and continued. "This boy was my ancestor. He was a pure-of-heart lad named Ham-El, who found the courage to cast down both Orkahn and Mustashar. According to the legends, the idol had become so tainted from Mustashar's use that it could not stand against the rare goodness of the boy. Orkahn attempted to flee, coward that he was, and was killed in disgust by Mustashar from behind as he ran. Ham-El then faced the evil counselor alone, with only his sling and three stones."

"Rather like David and Goliath," I interjected.

Daniel nodded. "Except for the difference that Goliath was a giant warrior, and Ham-El was instead facing an adept wielder of magic. It was not a fair fight, however, much to Mustashar's shock, as Ham-El was able to throw his stones with the sling through the glamours and illusions and powers cast up by the sorcerer. The first stone knocked the idol from Mustashar's hand. The second hit him in the chest, stopping his heart, and the third hit him between the eyes, for he still lived in that last moment between the second and third stones, long enough to see his defeat overtake him. The evil was overthrown, and his soul was taken by Heka in payment, as per their original agreement, leaving a smoking husk of a corpse, lying on the sand next to the idol.

357

"The people of the land immediately knew that their oppression was at an end, and both Orkahn and Mustashar were entombed in secret. Through the words of my ancestor to the people, it was recognized that Orkahn was partly innocent, having only been used by his master as an unwitting tool, so his remains were treated with dignity, and some of his worldly wealth was hidden with him, as prescribed by tradition. His tomb is thankfully still undisturbed, and he was buried with some jewels that legend says were secreted within his coffin. But Mustashar was buried only with the idol, sealed in the Counselor's coffin with layers of pitch. This was done at Ham-El's insistence in order to prevent it from being taken and used again towards some future evil, and also to keep its corruption from destroying any man who might rediscover it and attempt to use it again."

"Fascinating," said Holmes. "To a collector of legends. Similarly, we have men in this country still seeking Excalibur."

"Ah, Mr. Holmes. Although this is considered just another story from the past, there are some who always knew that the idol itself was real, even if the magic was simply a children's story. In the centuries that followed, my family divided – some of us remained in the lands where we had existed beyond memory, while others traveled, visiting parts of the world hundreds of years before they were 'officially' discovered by European explorers. East and west, north and south, our people have established colonies across the seas. And wherever members of our family settled, secret lines of communication have been kept in place, however tenuous.

"We have never meant any harm, wherever we go. We keep to our ways, never forcing them on others. We have been mistaken for gypsies in some parts of the world, and lost European settlers in others. In fact, it was our people who sheltered the doomed Raleigh settlers of North Carolina in the late sixteen century, guiding them far inland to our own colonies when they were abandoned and then threatened by the natives."

"And these groups can still be found spread throughout the world, even today?"

"Oh yes. If one knows where to look, members of my family are still in enclaves in the isolated mountains of eastern Europe, and the unexplored interiors of Africa. We are known in the high mountains of Asia, and also in the remote areas of America, especially in what became parts of eastern Tennessee, as well as western Virginia and North Carolina."

"Ah," interrupted Holmes. "I should have recognized from the distinctive light-colored eyes, present in many of your family. I have read of this American group, which has come to be known as the Melungeons."

358

"Yes," agreed Daniel. "The Melungeons. From the French word *mélange*. Supposedly a mixture of many races – it is a belief, an explanation, that we allow, and even encourage. It gives us protection, and peace. Although the various groups from around the world have continued down their own paths, pursuing their own destinies and meanings, the ties between those far away and we who remained in our homeland have never entirely diminished, no matter how the years pass. It has been a story of hardship and oppression, as we have faced mistreatment and worse the world over, in spite of our peaceful intentions. But we are strong, and it has not weakened us.

"Through the long centuries, however, two of the groups have held to the secret ways and stories more than most, never forgetting the old legends. Those located in the southeastern United States have never forgotten the tale of The Eye of Heka, while my own family – the house of Ham-El – never forgot our responsibility for protecting it. We have spent the intervening years guarding against the reappearance of the idol. It is dangerous, either as a magical tool, if you believe that, or simply for what it represents. Far in the past, following the overthrow of Orkahn and Mustashar, the entire region, then liberated, wanted to make Ham-El a ruler, but instead he set himself up as a simple rug merchant, having no interest in the temptations of power. He was quite successful, and what he built has been the foundation of my family's fortune, and is still the trade of our house to this day.

"But there are always some of us, from every generation, one to the next, who are tasked to protect against the rediscovery of the idol. For countless years, this meant no more than continuing to make certain that the tomb remained hidden. But then, ten years ago, it was found. An old man, a member of our family, lost himself and betrayed us. He stole a map and sold it. We weren't ready when the idol was found. We examined ourselves and saw that we were woefully unprepared to defend against its removal from our country. We failed to prevent its departure. Guardians had to be appointed – Conscripted, actually. My brothers and I were chosen, and since that time we have been here, in your cold and wet land, keeping watch. We have been unable to retrieve The Eye. We are not thieves, you see, and did not know what to do. Before coming here, I was a scholar. My brothers worked in the family rug business. Thus, our attempts to recover the idol were doomed to failure from the start.

"We finally decided that allowing it to remain in the British Museum would assure its continued safety. After all, even though we were unable to retrieve it to take it home ourselves, it was not being used for evil, as its powers seemed to be ignored and unknown in this country, and it seemed nearly as safe in the Museum as if it were still buried in Mustashar's tomb."

"In the meantime, what did you do during all of these years?" I asked. "Did you simply wait, day after day and year after year, watching the Museum?"

Daniel gave a tired smile. "No, Doctor. We have not been so useless as that. While we are not natives of your country, we have attempted to be good citizens while we have sojourned here. I am a teacher of children, as I was in my home. Andrew and Micah have respectable jobs as well. Being near the idol does not take all of our time. Some days I am sad, thinking of how I wish to return to my own land, rather than wait and wait for nothing. I know my brothers feel the same. But we have been prepared to stay here as long as necessary, fulfilling our family's oath, even if the idol is to be locked away forever." He sat up straighter, as if what he wanted to tell us next had extra importance. "We have waited all this time, to make certain, for it is our duty to be here, near The Eye."

"For it remains a threat," I interjected.

Daniel nodded. "I do not claim that the object has magic, but certainly, when used by someone who *does* believe in its power, it can intimidate the gullible and give great confidence to the user. It might stir the many to actions that are terrible to contemplate. Little is known about what was actually done with it in the days of Orkahn and Mustashar. The legends vary. There are some who think that the object was used to carve out a kingdom, while it may have only been to do something as insignificant as hitting a neighbor over the head before his stealing his donkey. If you are very poor, the idea of what constitutes great wealth and riches is a relative thing.

"Whatever its past history, the fact is that the idol, The Eye of Heka, was rediscovered by the young Englishmen. After knowledge of the statue's disinterment was revealed, the word spread quickly, and the poor of the region began to speak of the powerful talisman that had been returned to the world of men, after having been hidden for centuries, and how it would help to change their lives and ease their burdens.

"You know what happened then. Our family made poor attempts to steal it back from the young Englishmen, both before and after it came here to England. Others with less noble motives tried to steal it as well, being interested in its supposed power. There are men who are only interested in fomenting war, using the idol's symbolic power as a spark, hoping to light a fire that will burn steadily towards a specific goal: To drive out the Europeans, and even possibly extend their own control over European lands here, if such momentum can be achieved. The countless poor would be used and harnessed and directed into the ensuing destruction as if they were mere beasts of no value, their lives to be wasted even as others followed along behind them doing the same, walking over their corpses to replace them. The innocents who would die on both sides would not matter to these rich indifferent men, the igniters of this blaze. They are only interested in power, and what can be accomplished through the turmoil of war. This sculpture is the tool that they intend to use.

"After the idol was put into a safe place, deep inside the Museum, interest in it again waned for a time. Other things appeared to occupy the attention of the war-mongers. But, like my brothers and I, their agents have also been continuously set in place to see if any hint of the idol's reappearance meant that it could be retrieved after all. And then, two days ago, their patience was rewarded, even as my brothers and I felt renewed despair, when the Earl of Wardlaw's actions revealed that he had had the idol and that it was attainable yet again, ready for the taking of those who would use it.

"So you see, gentlemen, I *do* know about the idol. And that is why we should work together."

Chapter XIV
Other Factors

Holmes nodded, apparently accepting the statement at face value. "I see that it does no good to continue denying our knowledge of the idol. And your understanding of what would happen should it light the tinder box is ours as well. The British Government has long been of the same mind, aware of what would happen if it became such a focus, but inexplicably they left things alone, trusting in the care of the Museum, believing that they could guard it there as well as anyone else, and that it would be available in the future, should they decide to use it in some crack-brain diplomatic scheme. Now this complacency has turned back to bite them."

I gathered from this that Holmes was letting me know he had decided to go forward on the assumption that Daniel and the others were unaware of the existence of a substitute idol, and, as I had been warned, we should not give away anything about it at all.

Daniel nodded. "There are many of my people who have no more wish for war than you do. The meaningless deaths of thousands, perhaps millions, for such a misguided and evil purpose, is not a true reflection of our peaceful beliefs."

"It's hard to credit," said Holmes, "that in this day and age, the superstition that gave this object such power in the old stories can still exist."

I nodded. "And yet, I saw much of this type of thing in India and Afghanistan. Many of Ayub Khan's followers attributed to him an almost mystical presence. They were motivated to fight beyond themselves – like men possessed by demons."

"That is true," said Daniel. "If the people believe they are justified by some ancient magic, they will lift themselves to be worthy of it in ways that are almost inconceivable. There is a deep need in many people to attach themselves to something magical. Their passion will feed itself. It truly will be as if a wild fire is sweeping across the lands. Countless innocents will die, both those in front of or caught between the armies, and within the armies themselves. They should be left to live their own lives, instead of being manipulated by the evil men in the shadows around the world who would set this thing into motion."

"What of these men?" I asked. "You mentioned them before. Who are they?"

"They are a loosely connected band of the wealthy and powerful, both in England and across the world," said Holmes. "They never cease laboring to increase their influence and fortunes through the upheaval and destruction that a conflict of this sort would bring." His gaze seemed to focus away over a great distance for just an instant, while he continued to speak, his tone almost hollow. "They are the industrialists and politicians, rich beyond imagining and without compassion, who care nothing for common humanity. Rather, they only see their fellow man as beasts to run their machinery, or economic factors to exploit in any way possible. They are evil beyond imagining, and only interested in increasing their own power and wealth, at whatever cost. And there is one man, a great brain, an abstract thinker, who has repeatedly offered his assistance to their machinations, knowing that he can make great strides toward his own ultimate goals by threading his way through the chaos of war. Should this man ever gain access to the idol, using it to manipulate a conflict that cannot be controlled, we are doomed."

I knew without asking that he was thinking of his great foe, Professor Moriarty, a man who had tried things exactly like this several times in the past. If the Professor were to reach an accord with these rich and powerful men who wanted to use The Eye of Heka, it could well be disastrous.

"It is a little known fact," added Daniel, "that these same men were loosely connected with the Mahdi when he began his revolution in 1881. A nudge here and a nudge there precipitated the conflicts that followed, and they hoped that it would spread. However, the Mahdi's own supporters, who foolishly believed that he would lead the wave to start the war that they desired, were quickly disappointed, for he was more interested in perverting his religion than starting the bloodshed that resulted. He also became embroiled with more local matters, including that which took place upon the arrival of your General Gordon."

"The British were ready to abandon the Sudan when Gordon got there," I said. "The Mahdi's engagements leading to the siege and subsequent slaughter at Khartoum only served to bring forces down on his people that might not otherwise have been engaged or even interested."

"As you know, however, the British government did *not* want Gordon to make a defense," said Holmes. "His mission was to evacuate thousands of civilians in the Sudan, bringing them back to the north. Instead, he dug in on his own and proceeded to defend Khartoum, which led to his eventual death by the Mahdi's forces."

"Thank heavens the maniacal fool died six months after Gordon was murdered," I said.

"But what he started remains in motion, with subtle encouragement by these same evil and manipulative men," said Daniel. "The Mahdi's tomb has become a rallying point for those who would continue the fight, showing again that objects can have power when followers believe in them."

"There are other more current factors as well," said Holmes. "Are you all aware of the meetings currently taking place in Constantinople?"

Daniel nodded, but I shook my head, still amazed at Holmes's awareness of obscure facts. It was a long time indeed since those early months in Baker Street, when he had pretended to be intentionally ignorant of whole areas of knowledge, just to leave spare room, as he explained, in his "brain attic".

Micah, who had been mute up to this point, sat up a little straighter, both hands curved around his empty coffee cup. "I know of it," he rumbled. "Since the British took control of the Suez Canal, there has been concern from other countries about its continued use and associated safe passage."

"Correct," said Holmes. "France, Germany, Russia, Spain, and others, are all in current talks in the 'Gateway to the East' about keeping the Canal open for world trade. One cannot underestimate the Canal's importance since the rise of steam-powered ships. Since they can travel against the constant west-to-east winds that defeat sailing ships there, it has become one of the most important locations in the world in relation to international commerce. I have it on good authority that the governments meeting in Constantinople will be signing a treaty later this year to guarantee free access to the Canal."

"I notice," said Micah, with a trace of bitterness, "that you didn't mention any involvement of the countries physically contiguous to the canal in these talks, even though one would think that its interests would be thoroughly tied up with it."

"As you are certainly aware," Holmes responded, with an ironic tone in his voice, "local concerns are being handled by the British government."

"So if a war were to occur . . . ." began Daniel.

"Then the safety of the Canal, and commercial passage through it, could not be guaranteed, treaty or no treaty."

"And if the European countries that you mentioned," I added, "France, Russia, Spain, and so forth – "

"And certainly the Ottoman Empire as well," added Daniel.

I nodded. "If all of those countries were blocked from using the Canal by a regional uprising, sweeping up along it and then crossing to the Arabian Peninsula on the other side, it could very well increase tensions to such a point that the European countries might also be pressed to go to war with one another to protect their own interests, even as they were facing attacks from the south."

364

"Exactly," said Holmes.

"And all because of the reappearance of this stone idol," said Daniel.

"Not *all* because of it," added Holmes. "Some of this is already in motion. But it certainly complicates matters."

"What have you done to locate this Eye?" I asked the two brothers.

"I'm afraid, following its reappearance two days ago, our plan has been to rely on you, up to this point." The scholar smiled tiredly. "We were rather caught unawares." Daniel gestured toward his brother with his coffee cup, and while Micah refilled his and the others as well, he continued. "Our brother, Andrew, has a job near the Museum, working for a nearby dealer in Scottish fabrics. He was doing something near the front window the other day when, by merest chance, he happened to see one of the men that we regularly keep under observation, the Museum employee named Williams, depart in haste from his place of employment. You will understand that, with the idol residing in the Museum, Mr. Williams has been of great interest to us. He appeared to be quite unnerved. Only moments later, another man followed him, clearly trying to avoid being seen. Andrew, who has an understanding with the owner of the shop, left quickly, trailing both of them to a telegraph office."

"Allow me to compliment his tracking skills," said Holmes. "For I was the man following Williams, and I was completely unaware of Andrew's presence."

Micah looked shocked, resuming his seat and widening his remaining eye, while the skin stretched along the horrible scar covering the other. "Impossible. You look nothing like the man that Andrew described. You do not move as he said that man did. You are too tall." He shook his head. "Impossible. We have been curious as to whom that man could have been, and have wasted much time looking for him."

"Nevertheless," said Holmes, "please continue your tale."

Daniel took a sip. "After Mr. Williams sent his wire, with great urgency I might add, he departed, and the man – that is, you, Mr. Holmes, for I must accept what you say – stepped to the counter as well. At that point, Andrew chose to stay with Mr. Williams, to see what had upset him so.

"He soon obtained a cab, and Andrew followed suit. My brother was fortunate, in that on many occasions cabbies will refuse service to foreigners such as ourselves. But this driver was interested in the coins that Andrew showed to him, and followed his instructions to keep the other cab within sight, a task that was easy, due to the fact that the streets were quite crowded with midday traffic.

"They reached Liverpool Street Station, where Mr. Williams purchased a ticket to Chelmsford. Andrew did so as well, and soon they

365

were traveling east. Andrew was quite careful to avoid the man's glance, but he needn't have bothered, as Mr. Williams was very absorbed in his own thoughts. Andrew said that he knew something was troubling him, as he had left the Museum without his overcoat, and seemed to be quite cold, huddling into the seat as he was.

"In Chelmsford, he bought a ticket for a northbound branch line, and so did Andrew. Again, Mr. Williams should have noticed him, on that nearly deserted train, but he had no awareness for anything except his own thoughts.

"Andrew's luck failed him at the halt where they descended. Mr. Williams hired the station's only wagon and set off, while Andrew was left behind. However, he had an idea that Mr. Williams was going to see the Earl, whose house, he knew, was nearby. About what the meeting was to be, however, he had no knowledge.

"Not knowing what else to do, or if he was even following Mr. Williams for any good reason, Andrew decided to conceal himself nearby to see what he might see. He observed your arrival sometime later, gentlemen, and he recognized you that time, Mr. Holmes, as you had by then returned to your normal appearance. We have been aware of you for quite a while, as you were the man who located the idol when it was recovered from John Goins, so many years ago."

"One of your agents, I presume?" Holmes asked Daniel.

The man narrowed his eyes tellingly and shook his head. "Not so. Even then, as we had followed the idol to England to try to retrieve it, so had certain members of a more fanatical group that would seek to make use of its supposed powers. John Goins, whom you briefly met then, is one of those men."

"Do you know what happened to him after his time in prison?"

"He was released, only to drop from sight soon after. But he has been in this country ever since, coordinating the waiting game on the other side of the chess board from where my brothers and I sit, each patient for something to happen."

"Which it finally did," said Holmes, "when I unfortunately set these events in motion."

Daniel raised his eyebrows. "You, Mr. Holmes? How did you accomplish that?"

Holmes answered vaguely, "I had innocently mentioned the idol to Watson the night before. Realizing that I had a desire to see it again after all these years, he and I had dropped around the Museum to get a look at it." He then chose to obfuscate the portion of the story concerning the existence of the copied idol. "We were told that the idol couldn't be viewed," he lied. "But Williams must have been frightened nonetheless, as he left abruptly to warn his master, the Earl, that I had been there asking questions, which is what alerted Andrew. When we also noticed that Williams was leaving in such a hurry, I immediately suspected that something was afoot, and thus enlightened, we followed him to Essex, only to arrive after he had been killed. The Earl had already fled with the idol."

I was gratified when Daniel nodded, indicating that he had apparently accepted that truncated version of events without digging deeper into the parts that weren't quite there. Micah said, "Andrew said that he saw you when you arrived at the station on the next train, but he did not see your return later from the house."

"And that must be because, instead of waiting to see us come back to the station," Holmes said, "Andrew was already following the Earl after he showed up there sometime later, having passed by us on a different road as we went out to his house."

"How could you know that?" asked Micah with astonishment.

"It is true," agreed Daniel. "We have all come to recognize the Earl, as well as the other different players, quite well over the years. Your arrival there that afternoon, Mr. Holmes, so soon after Mr. Williams's journey, surprised Andrew, and it gave him to understand that perhaps this occurrence was even more serious than he had first thought, as beforehand he had nearly convinced himself that he had followed Mr. Williams for no reason at all."

"So the Earl arrived at the station," I said, "and Andrew, seeing him carrying a mysterious bundle, followed him."

"Yes, the bundle. A cloth bag, not more than a foot long, that the Earl kept desperately clutched to himself. It was his only luggage, and seeing how anxiously the man behaved, Andrew then began to realize what was in it – the idol had been in Essex all along. He thought about making a try for it then, but on the crowded train, there was simply no way to take it and then escape."

"But if Andrew followed the Earl all the way back," I reasoned, "surely he must know where he went to ground, and more importantly, where the idol is now located." Holmes nodded.

Micah lowered his head. "We are ashamed," he said. "All of us. Andrew and the Earl traveled to London by the same route that he had covered with Mr. Williams, just hours earlier. At Liverpool Street Station, the Earl made for the cab rank, and Andrew followed. But several trains had arrived nearly simultaneously, discharging their passengers, and before he could obtain his own cab, most were taken. There was a great confusion as many people tried to depart at the same time. While looking around for an empty conveyance, he realized that he had lost the Earl.

Abandoning his attempt to secure his own transport, he ran down the streets, frantically trying to locate the man, hoping that somehow he would instinctively know which cab was correct. But he saw nothing to tell him which of the many departing and passing vehicles held the Earl, or in what direction he was heading."

Holmes shook his head. "Most unfortunate. And when did you learn what had happened to Mr. Williams?"

"Andrew knew that something serious was taking place," replied Micah, "but not exactly what. Upon arriving in London, he wired to let us know where he was, and then I began to try to find out why Mr. Williams left the Museum so hurriedly, although I was not sure if that knowledge would be of immediate benefit."

"We then decided," interrupted Daniel, "to determine the reason for *your* involvement, Mr. Holmes, since you had been friends with the Earl long ago, when you first recovered the idol for him."

"Not friends," Holmes corrected. "An acquaintance, nothing more."

"Andrew was told to forget about the Earl and instead to watch your home in Baker Street," continued Micah. "Later I went as well. We found a spot to keep watch, and it was there that Daniel joined us sometime later. Andrew explained all that had happened, and then we set about discovering the rest of the story about the death of Williams."

"And it was while hiding there," I said, "that one of you saw Baron Meade leave the bomb at our door."

"It was Andrew who saw this," said Micah, "although he did not know that it was a bomb. We later knew that it was something dangerous, due to the behavior of the police who took it away."

"And you are certain that your opposites in this affair also know of the statue's liberation?" asked Holmes.

Daniel nodded. "We received word that our foes had been motivated into unusual motion on that same day. In some way, we know not how, they had also learned that the idol was obtainable once again. We began to hear enough whispers and reports from our friends, those who know John Goins's men, that they also knew of Mr. Williams's initial departure on the day of his death, and that it was somehow related to your visit to the Museum."

"You learned all of that from your informants?"

"Our family's wealth has been useful in support of our cause. This includes some well spent coins toward purchasing a word or two from those who can listen without being noticed."

"And so your only plan right now for finding the sculpture," continued Holmes, "has been to hope that I would uncover it for you."

Daniel shrugged. "Your reputation is well known. We are few. Myself, my brothers, a limited number of other members of our family, along with some informants who are sometimes paid more by us than our foes, sometimes not."

"Your organization is not as helpless as you would portray. For instance, Watson and I had no idea that we were being followed this morning to Sir Edward's home in Mayfair. In fact, we chose the route so that anyone attempting to do so would be exposed."

Daniel gave one of those shrugs that one sees so often in foreign counties, as if to express, *"What can I say?"* He shifted almost uncomfortably in his chair. "Others may follow as skillfully as you are reputed to do, Mr. Holmes. I do not know if you were aware that this Baron was also following you this morning, but I assure you that he was there. I myself shadowed you yesterday as you visited various government buildings in Whitehall, as well as making a stop in Pall Mall. I was also near Sir Edward's house in Mayfair yesterday when I heard you agree to return this morning. That is how Andrew knew to find you there."

"And Dr. Watson?" Holmes asked. "Was anyone watching him yesterday, when his companion was attacked on the street in the Strand?"

The brothers glanced at each other. Then, Micah said, "I was nearby. I was . . . taken unaware by the attack on Dr. Watson's friend."

"And you stood there," I asked, attempting to control my sudden irritation, "after watching another man shot in cold blood, and made no effort to stop the attacker, or chase him down?"

"I had not been in Baker Street when the bomb package was left," said Micah defensively. "I did not know who this man was, so I had no reason to suspect that anything terrible was about to happen. The man with whom you had arrived at the restaurant stepped out to hail a cab. Almost immediately, this other man stepped forward and shot him. Then you came out, and I chose discretion, waiting to see what might happen. After all, you and Mr. Holmes have many enemies, and this might have been related to some other set of events with which we are not concerned."

"As, in fact, you are not," said Holmes.

Daniel agreed. "I am sorry that my brother did not step forward and subdue this Baron, assuming that he could have, but to do so might have involved him in a business that did not concern us before we had decided how to approach you."

I started to respond with resentment, but Holmes waved his hand.

"It is in the past now. What's of more immediate importance is that none of us have any good ideas as to where the idol might now be located. Am I correct?"

369

The two brothers nodded. "We had hoped that your visit this morning to Sir Edward might give you the information you needed. Both he and the Earl have been quite close over the years."

"But, Holmes," I began. "Sir Edward said that they have – "

Holmes smiled. "What my friend almost said, before trying to shut that barn door after the horse has escaped, is that Sir Edward indicated this morning that he has lost touch with the Earl over the years, and could provide no real helpful information." Holmes's smile vanished. "I didn't believe him."

Daniel nodded. "As you might expect, we have also kept a close eye on the Earl over the last decades, watching both his wealth and influence grow. This has only been matched by his debauched lifestyle. Throughout, he and Sir Edward have been in regular and constant association with one another, visiting each other's homes quite often, although they do not socialize together in public. I had assumed that you knew of this, Mr. Holmes, when you arranged yesterday to visit with the man."

"Not at all. I merely wanted to speak with him in order to get some background information on the original discovery of the idol, and also about a few of the statements by the Earl's man, Dawson, following his arrest, in which he indicated that the Earl actually believes in its magic, and that this was the reason and cause of the Earl's successes."

"Yet another example of men foolishly investing these things with powers," said Daniel.

"Perhaps not so foolish," grumbled Micah. "You know, my brother, that I have long said you should be more open-minded. If a fool such as the Earl can make a success of himself, then there must be something to the idol's influence after all. Now that we know he really has had it for all of these years, using its powers to increase his wealth, much can be explained that puzzled us before – "

"Enough!" snapped Daniel. "I will not tolerate such talk. Magic stones! I will not credit this object as being anything more than a dangerous lens for focusing trouble."

Micah nodded and lowered his head, but just for an instant, in that dark room beneath the level of the street that was lit only by lanterns, I thought I saw another glow, deep within his eye. The Earl was not the only man in London who believed in the power of Heka.

Chapter XV
An Accord

I almost looked to see if Holmes had noticed, but stopped myself. It would not do to give away that I had seen, just for a moment, the naked lust in Micah's eye when he spoke of the supposed power contained within the missing talisman.

Holmes looked at Daniel. "I cannot speak in regard to your family's service over the millennia in keeping watch over the hidden statue, but I'm certainly glad to know that you are here now."

Daniel rose and took a step forward, offering his hand. My friend and I stood as well. We shook hands with both Daniel and Micah. Without the need to speak it, we seemed to have reached an accord to work together. And yet, had we, in making the covenant with Micah, somehow weakened our own forces?

"How many men do you have, then?" asked Holmes. "Besides the three of you."

"Not enough," sighed Daniel.

"Five," added Micah. "We three brothers, and two others."

"It has been difficult to know whom to trust," Daniel said.

"On our side," said Holmes, "we can count on the police and the Foreign Office, but having such a great wind in our sails is useless without a direction in which to steer. It seems as if the Earl has gone to ground, having been willing to abandon everything that he has in order to safeguard his treasure."

"He would have been better off to sit still, rather than fleeing in fear," said Daniel. "He had fooled us all for years into believing that the object was safely tucked away within the Museum."

"We've been told that his behavior changed in the last few months," I said. "Possibly he wasn't thinking in a rational manner any longer, and couldn't reason his way to seeing that the situation might have eventually worked out in his favor."

"His need," interjected Holmes, "to possess the talisman clearly outweighed anything else."

"And drove him to murder in the process," Daniel added.

"As you say." Clearly we weren't sharing every fact with our new allies.

Daniel waved an arm. "So what do we do now, gentlemen? Good men and bad are scouring this great city, looking for some indication of the

Earl's passage. He has abandoned his home and his resources, but he must be somewhere. Our enemies are also searching, even now, and if they find the idol first, you may rest assured it will be removed from this country as fast as it can be carried. They will not wait. Within a week, you will begin to receive reports of uprisings. These will swell and flow together, and soon the sheer volume of it all will overwhelm any resistance."

"Surely," I said, "it will not be as sudden and awful as all of that. As you have said, there are many who want peace, and would not be part of the twisted and violent plan that you have described. They will surely stand against it, or at least not join with them."

"I believe you underestimate the forces at work, Doctor. It will be a tide that cannot be resisted. The return of the statue will be a tipping point, the final raindrop that breaks the dam, and their only path to safety will be to run in front of it. The initial successes of the group will give it confidence, and it will grow and grow as long-held angers are brought out and fed. Many will flock to the cause in countless numbers." He looked at Holmes. "We must find the idol, Mr. Holmes, before that happens."

"That we will do so was never in doubt," said my friend, "and neither is the necessity of the endeavor." But then, he seemed to remember the scope of the task. "We can but try," he said more softly. He glanced toward the doorway. "It is now time to go our separate ways, but we'll stay in touch. As soon as we hear any whisper as to where the Earl might have hidden himself, we'll let you know. Will a message reach you here?"

"Indeed."

Holmes nodded. "In the meantime, then, assign your resources in whatever way you feel is best."

"We shall. And," Daniel added, with a weary smile in my direction, "if we happen to observe this Baron setting another bomb against your front door, we will attempt to take him for you, as well."

"That would be much appreciated. But," I added, "be careful. He is dangerous, without doubt."

Micah led us out of the room. I looked back before the door closed to see Daniel, standing as we had left him, but with his head bowed and his hands folded together, as if he were in prayer. The yellow light from one of the lanterns hanging behind him outlined his figure in a fiery halo, and he looked like a dark angel. Then Micah pulled the door shut, and we were again in darkness, except for the small light again carried by our guide.

He led us upstairs. Holding the outer door, Micah muttered, "We cannot return you as you were brought, as my brother has already taken the cab back to its owner, and then he is to be about other business."

Holmes nodded absently, and we stepped outside. I started to speak, but before I could do so, Micah pulled the door shut without a further word.

"Holmes – " I began, but he narrowed his eyes and shook his head with a small sideways motion, likely not even visible from a few feet away.

We walked down the small alley that made up Bere Street, and so through the narrow winding passages into Commercial Road. I checked my watch, and saw that we had been in conference with the two brothers for less than an hour. It seemed as if much more of the morning should be gone.

When we were some distance up the street, Holmes and I stepped out of the teeming throngs and into a quieter doorway where we could speak. By long habit, we faced so that each could see past the other, scanning the horizon for incoming threats, or perhaps simply to check if there was someone that seemed too interested in hearing what we had to say.

"Did you observe Micah?" I asked. "When Daniel chastised him for a belief in the magical powers of the idol?"

"I did. I cannot help but think that Micah hopes that finding the sculpture will be of some specific use to him or his family in the future. I'm not convinced that, should *he* be in charge, the idol would be returned to its obscure tomb."

"So not only do we have to worry that it will fall into the *wrong* hands, but now we also have to worry about it falling into the *right* hands as well."

"Perhaps it's not as bad as all that. Sufficient unto the day," said Holmes. "We certainly know what John Goins and his associates will do if *they* retrieve the idol, and that must be prevented. That is enough to worry about for now. When we have the cursed rock in hand, we can decide what to do about going forward. You will notice that, while we are working as confederates with Daniel and his band for the recovery of the idol, I did not make any guarantee that it would be returned in the end to the safekeeping of the House of Ham-El, and so on to be reburied in a tomb, only be taken again at some future point. No, the official plan is still to keep it here in England, where it can be guarded and hidden – certainly more effectively than it has been in the past."

"To hide it again means that it must first be found. Do you have a more specific plan that you haven't shared?"

He shook his head. "I'm afraid that we keep doing what we have been doing. Watch out for Ian. Try to find his other friends, if any, to determine if they have seen him or if they're helping him. At least now we have Daniel on our side."

"He will not be happy when he discovers that we intend to keep the statue in England – should we be the ones to find it first."

"I'm not so sure. He sounded as if he were content when he believed that it was in the Museum for over a decade. That's not to say that he and the others wouldn't have tried to take it back if it had become more

373

accessible. However, his overriding concern rightly seems to be that it not fall into the wrong hands, and leaving it here, far from where it might cause the least amount of damage, is an acceptable solution."

"What shall we do now?"

"First, I'll try to pay more attention. We've been observed or followed too easily, in too many recent instances, without ever being aware of it. Additionally, it is inexcusable that I neglected to ask at the time whether anyone else got off the train with Williams when he arrived in Essex. If I had thought of that – if I had known sooner that a foreign-looking man of distinctive appearance had also arrived at such a location that probably only rarely sees visitors – I would have known sooner about this new thread in our skein."

"But it might also have confused the issue. Had you known about an additional factor, it could have distracted you from the bare facts of Williams's murder. You might have believed that Andrew, the mysterious man on the scene, had something to do with it, rather than quickly determining that Dawson killed him."

I coughed at some drifting East End odor and pulled my coat tighter around my throat. "So I ask again, Holmes – what shall we do now?"

"We can only keep shaking the trees," he said. "I'll confer with the Yard so as to see what has been reported in the search for Ian, and also speak with my contacts in the Foreign Office. You must hold yourself in readiness."

I nodded. "But first, I'm going to return to Charing Cross, to check on Dr. Withers."

Holmes raised an eyebrow but didn't comment. I could almost hear the thought jumping across his mind, wondering if I was also interested in seeing the doctor's daughter, and my eyes narrowed, as my response to him crossed mine.

"Be careful, Watson," he said, and before I could counter that any ideas about Miss Withers were incorrect, and that I had nothing in relation to her to be careful about, he added, "Baron Meade is still out there."

I was caught short, surprised for a moment to have forgotten that threat. "Surely, after his last attempt, the man will flee. Why would he keep focusing on me? Killing me will do nothing to further his misguided agenda. There is simply no logic to it."

"Don't make the mistake of assigning logic, as understood by your perfectly normal and rational brain, to the Baron's motivations and actions. He is in a rage, and has crossed the line of sanity. He will not stop his plans to do as much damage as possible, and you are now included in those whom he blames for his pain."

"I will be careful," I promised. With a nod, Holmes stepped away from the door, hailing not the first or even the second, but the third empty cab that rolled our way, heading west.

We shared it as we journeyed across the capital, traveling in silence. Passing along the Strand, I looked over at the pavement before Simpson's, where less than a day before, Dr. Withers had been shot by that man who believed he was killing me. Now, people walked there, both ways, a milling throng, completely oblivious to what had so recently happened on that spot. I tried to see if the doctor's blood still stained the pavement, but we passed too quickly.

I rapped on the roof of the cab across from the passage to William IV Street and Agar Street, which curved up and around the hospital. Agreeing to meet Holmes later that day in Baker Street, I climbed out. Crossing the street, I watched the cab blend in with all the others as Holmes made his way on to Whitehall and Scotland Yard. I wondered what exactly he would be able to accomplish. I had seen him do some amazing things, but I had the feeling that the Earl of Wardlaw would not be found until he was ready to be found. With a sigh, I walked up the slight rise and away from the Strand.

Chapter XVI
Unwanted Advice

Inside the hospital, I was told that the patient had been released that morning and had returned to his hotel. I confirmed that it was still the one where I had initially met him, only days earlier. He and his daughter had chosen to stay in a small private establishment off Portman Square after they had traveled up from Portsmouth. I resolved to make my way there, as it was on the way home to Baker Street.

I was headed toward the hotel when I realized that I hadn't been as careful as Holmes, who had followed his own dictum about not catching the first cab available at the start of our last journey. It was a good rule at any time, and one that had been brought home to me on several occasions over the years, varying from some simply annoying encounters to others that were quite a bit more painful. It was these same types of circumstances, in addition to others with the questionable individuals that one inevitably ended up being associated with during Holmes's investigations, that provided the reason to always carry my service revolver whenever I went out. I knew that I had been distracted over the last few weeks, but I simply couldn't allow myself to drop my vigilance. There were enemies constantly afoot, and more than the most obvious of the lot, Baron Meade.

In spite of having chosen the first cab that presented itself, the ride passed without incident, and my carelessness didn't cause me any difficulties this time. Arriving at the hotel, I sent up my card. In a moment, the boy returned to say that I would be seen upstairs, where the doctor and his daughter had a suite of two bedrooms with a shared sitting room.

I stopped outside the door, pausing before I knocked, suddenly realizing that, while I was there to check on the patient, I would also need to try to apologize to the man's daughter for inadvertently putting her father at risk.

Taking a deep breath, I knocked decisively and was bade to enter. Stepping in, I found Doctor Withers, wrapped snugly in a dressing gown and rising from a settee. He took a step toward me, wincing as he did so.

"Doctor Watson," he said. "Come in."

I approached him, glancing at the bandage extending around his neck and down into his clothing. He held his body stiffly, and his left arm was done up in a sling. I wondered if I had appeared the same when recovering from my own war injuries nearly a decade earlier.

"I wanted to see how you're getting on, and the hospital informed me that you had already been discharged."

"I discharged myself," he said. "I saw much worse than this in combat, and you did as well, I'll wager. No reason to give in to it any more than I have to. And you know yourself that staying in a hospital dramatically increases the chances of infection." He waved me to a chair. "Something to drink?"

I thought of our recent conference in that basement on the edge of Limehouse, drinking the dark thick coffee, and considered that the doctor was likely offering something far stronger and much more tempting. "Please," I said.

As he turned toward the sideboard, I made as if to take care of the duties myself, but he waved me away. In a moment, he had poured one-handed a couple of glasses of whisky, each a substantial portion. Handing the first to me, he returned for his own, and then raised it in my direction. "For the pain."

I smiled, returned the salute, and took a drink. For an instant as I sipped, I suddenly had a vision of my poor father and brother, who had both so loved the taste of this liquid, far too much than was good for them. Their pain was different than mine, and in my opinion not worthy of all the attempts they had made to drown or suppress it. I was of their blood, but I knew without question that, as I dealt with my own losses, it would never be with the contents of a bottle.

Setting down the glass, I took off my coat and laid it across a chair. We sat, and Doctor Withers adjusted his shoulders until he found a position of relative comfort. With a sigh, he said, "That's better."

"How bad is it?"

He shook his head. "You would think that it would be worse, really, but it's no more than a dull throb. Except if I forget and move suddenly. Or when I tried to sleep last night."

I took another small sip. "Jenny is resting," continued my host. I looked up, and he was watching me with a slight smile on his face.

"I imagine she is exhausted," I answered noncommittally.

"Not so much as you might think," he said. "She has gotten used to times when normal schedules are ignored, and has been quite invaluable to me over the years at the Portsmouth practice. As I certainly expect her to be at this one as well."

"She certainly showed no signs of panic yesterday when you . . . when you were wounded."

"I have no real memory of what happened after the shot. I recall stepping out to secure a cab, when a man approached to my left. I was really more aware of his shadow than his presence. He yelled, 'Dr.

377

Watson!', and since you were on my mind, I turned, thinking that you had already joined me and were only a step or two away. Then this man pulled the trigger, two or three times I think, but he was clearly agitated, or at least seemed so in the brief glance I had of him, before one of the shots hit. I went down, and he stepped closer. I believe he would have fired again, but then something stopped him."

"I expect it was my arrival on the scene. He thought that he was shooting me, and was unnerved to see me suddenly appear from the direction of the restaurant."

He gave a wry smile. "It has been remarked that we look somewhat similar."

Without thinking, I started to ask by whom, but then I held my tongue. Instead, I said, "I'm deeply sorry that you were dragged into this problem, Doctor."

He shook his head, and then winced. "That was one of the times I forget my wound and move too quickly."

"Perhaps I could prescribe some medication for the discomfort?" I said foolishly, before remembering that I was speaking to a doctor with a decade's more experience than myself.

"Thank you, no," he said with a grin. "I'm fine. But tell me, who was this man that tried to kill us?"

"His name is Baron Meade. His son, a military man, was accidentally killed late last year during the Bloody Sunday riot, and he has since become fixated on taking revenge against the British government. The other night, Holmes and I foiled his plan, which involved a massive amount of explosives. He had intended to tote all of it to some location in London and then blow it up. During his capture, he and I tangled, and now he has a face upon which to fix his anger. Unfortunately, he escaped from the police that night. Yesterday's attack with a gun was not his only attempt on my life." Dr. Withers raised an eyebrow, and I continued. "Two days ago, he left an explosive device for me. Luckily, Holmes recognized it for what it was, and the bomb specialists with the Yard and the Special Branch were able to take care of it."

He looked a bit amazed. "Does this sort of thing happen to you often?"

I shrugged and gave a small laugh. "More often than you might think."

"What did your wife think about all of this?"

I was surprised at his question. I had already learned that it seemed as if most people danced around mentioning a recently deceased spouse, using instead such supposedly harmless euphemisms as "your loss". I shouldn't have been surprised that a widower and former military surgeon

378

was unafraid to say what he thought in a more direct fashion, and to ask a question with tact but without fear. I would have done the same.

"She didn't mind it," I said. "At least, I believe that to be the case. She was ill for most of the time that we were married, and traveled often with her mother to healthier climes while I maintained the practice." I chose my words. "It seemed as if she were . . . grateful that I had the . . . the distraction of helping Holmes with his cases."

He nodded, and then cut his eyes toward my coat, lying on the chair nearby. "It has not escaped my attention that you always go about armed, at least during the few times that I've encountered you. This indicates the ongoing presence of danger. Was any of that ever directed toward your wife?"

I shook my head. "During my marriage, that part of my life and the times spent on Holmes's investigations were quite separated. He only visited the house in Kensington on a few occasions. More often than not, he would summon me by telegram when needed, or I would become involved in a case only after dropping into my old rooms in Baker Street for a visit."

"You must have visited quite often."

"Moderately, I suppose. I did do quite well at building up the practice, as you've seen. I never neglected it. If I did have to be away, several other excellent doctors located nearby were more than willing to help, and of course I returned the favor. And as I said, my wife traveled a . . . a great deal, I'm afraid, so I had significant spare time on my hands." I glanced at my hands, fingers curled around the whisky glass. I seemed to be doing considerable staring into whisky glasses of late.

Dr. Withers was silent for a moment. Then, "But you chose to sell the practice immediately following your wife's death."

"Yes." I looked up then. He was watching me intently.

"I know it was painful, but did you not consider throwing yourself deeper into your work, rather than abandoning all that you had so recently built?"

"You do not understand," I said softly. "I couldn't face it."

"Is returning to the distractions of Mr. Holmes's cases that enticing, then?"

I felt a defensive flash of anger for just an instant, but I let it pass and thought for a moment, before replying, "How can I explain it to you? When I returned from Afghanistan, wounded out of the Army and living on half-pay, I was living in a private hotel off the Strand, much like this one. It was clearly beyond my means, and I was headed for certain ruin if I didn't get a proper hold on my situation." Raising the whisky to my lips, I took a fiery sip and swallowed, and then continued. "It is not a path that

379

has been untrodden by men in my family before. Deprived of my health, I was without a career or purpose. It was being introduced to Holmes, and being able to see him work and then to join him in his investigations – "

"His 'adventures' – " Was there a hint of a sneer in his voice?

"Yes, adventures, if you will. It was joining in on those that helped to heal me, and to distract me from my pain, and my disappointment, and my situation, and also the fact that the Army no longer had any use or place for me. When Constance died a few weeks ago, I felt as lost as I had when I was invalided back to England. It seemed to be the most natural thing in the world to return to the situation that had restored me in the past. I do not have a daughter like you, or someone for whom to carry on. If I had remained at the practice, I would have no doubt continued to make a go of it, and a successful one at that, but what would it have been for? Doing the same thing every day, the same empty view from within my consulting room, before trodding upstairs at night to the equally empty living quarters. At the end of the day, what would I have accomplished?"

"Well, first of all you would have continued to aid many people who need a good doctor. That is certainly more useful than assisting those that seek out Mr. Holmes's assistance."

"I wouldn't be too sure about that – " I said, but he continued before I could finish.

"And who is to say that you might not ever marry again? Wouldn't it have been better to keep the successful practice going, and have it in place when you do find a new wife, rather than have to begin all over again?"

My nostrils flared, as I thought that he was pressing a little too close. I was certainly not ready to consider a new wife, or to take advice from this man that I barely knew. I doubted, considering how I felt now and with all respect to his daughter, that I should ever marry again. But before I could respond, he went on. "I know what it was that Jenny was going to discuss with you yesterday when I went to locate a cab."

I didn't respond, but glanced toward the door where he'd said that she was resting. "Do not think that I'm somehow trying to talk you out of selling the practice," he continued. "How could I? It's done. I wanted it, I bought it, and I'm glad that I did it. We wanted to move to London, the two of us, and what you were selling was perfect for our needs.

"But," he continued, "I believe that it can be even more of a success than it already is. Certainly it will continue to grow, and there will be room for another doctor. There already is, if the books you've shown me are any indication. I have an idea that I could even maintain a small private hospital there, right in the house, just a few beds for short-term cases. And you would be just the man to help me do that.

"I haven't known you for very long, but I'm a very good judge of character. The patients already know you. You need something to do, and it shouldn't be spending your time following after your friend on his petty criminal investigations."

"I'm not sure you understand," I interrupted, taking offense at this, "just how serious some of Holmes's investigations are. I told you of Baron Meade's plans, for instance – the very series of events which led to you being shot – and there is another even greater situation that we are investigating right now as well."

Dr. Withers waved this aside with his good right hand. "You are a doctor, not a policeman. A *good* doctor. I saw that immediately, and it was only my selfishness at desiring and acquiring your existing practice, and the knowledge that if I didn't buy it you would still sell to someone else, that kept me from trying to tell you these things a week ago when we first met. But just because you've sold it now doesn't mean you can't still be involved in it. You should beware these false distractions. You are a *doctor*, sir! You can't *stop* being a doctor. You know it, I know it, and Jenny knows it too."

My eyes again turned involuntarily toward her door, and then back to him. He had seen what I did, and he smiled. "She is too forward sometimes, I know, too presumptuous, for her own good – or for mine. Conventionalities rarely suit her. From the day she met first you, she decided that you are to be part of her future, and the fact that you momentarily oppose it, and that you tragically lost your wife just weeks ago, will not deter her. And truthfully, how can we disagree with her? Why *should* we? We've both been in the Army, seen things on the edge of civilization that are too much to comprehend. We've seen how cheap life is, and more importantly how short it can be. Is there really any good reason to follow some societal behavior dictating mourning customs and related niceties when what you need is right in front of you?"

I saw that he had been leaning forward slightly while making this speech, and now that it was concluded, he allowed himself to settle back with a tightening of his pained lips.

I cleared my throat, and then replied, in as even a tone as I could manage, "Sir, I see that I must speak plainly. I do *not* wish or intend to remarry." A pause, and then with what I hoped was finality on the subject, "Not to your daughter, or anyone else."

He snorted and shook his head. Then, after taking a sip of the whisky, he sat silently for a bit before finally clearing his throat, saying, "Nonsense. It's just a matter of time. Why do you insist on waiting?"

"Nevertheless," I said simply, feeling a bit like Holmes. Then I was quiet.

He regarded me then, waiting for me to elaborate, and perhaps to fill the awkwardly growing silence. But I had seen that trick used too many times, and nearly always successfully, as Holmes allowed someone to crack, to begin burbling nervously while revealing much more than had ever been intended. I successfully fought against the urge to start explaining myself again, or rephrasing my thoughts in a way that might suddenly be clear where they had not been before, and finally, the tension of the moment built so that Dr. Withers himself gave in and spoke with a weary smile.

Setting down his drink and then turning over his right hand, he said, "Ah, well, don't expect me to give up that easily. You'll agree that I'm right in the end. And Jenny is much more stubborn than I am. You really do not have a choice."

"I don't understand," I said, although I hadn't meant to. "Why me? You both only recently met me."

"As I explained, I can see that you need this, and you are also the best man for the job. Joining the family, so to speak, sooner rather than later, would only make things easier. And then there's Jenny. She knew what she wanted as soon as she saw you."

I had to wonder about all that that implied, seeing as how much I resembled a younger version of her own father in so many ways. All the more reason for me to extricate myself from this situation as soon as I politely could.

There was still a substantial portion of the whisky in my glass, but I found that I was more than ready to leave. I turned it up and finished it quickly, perhaps too quickly, as I had to cough my way clear once or twice while my eyes watered. Then, standing up, I said, "Thank you for that. And thank you for the offer as well. I'm sorry that I cannot accept, but when I decided to sell the practice, I did so for a very good reason. Perhaps someday I will think that doing so was a mistake, but I don't believe so, and for right now, it was exactly the course that I needed to follow."

He struggled to his feet as well. Stepping over, he held out his hand. We shook. "We're not done talking about this," he said, "no matter what you may think." Releasing my hand, he walked to the door while I retrieved my coat. "Jenny will be sorry that she missed you."

"I'm not so sure of that," I said. "She seemed rather abrupt yesterday, after my affairs inadvertently involved you, resulting in an attack that could have been fatal."

He shook his head. "You don't know her. Not yet."

As I finished closing my coat, he unexpectedly said, "Might I ask you for a favor?"

Surprised, I said, "Certainly."

He began to fish awkwardly in his coat pocket. "As the practice was transferred to me yesterday, I had already made arrangements to have some of our possessions delivered to it in Kensington, using the spare key you had provided to me last week. The movers were supposed to drop off the various items yesterday afternoon. That is where Jenny and I would have gone after Simpson's, and before I was . . . shot. Since then, we have obviously been unable to go there and make sure that everything was delivered shipshape as promised, and the house properly relocked. Would you have time to check it for me? If not, I'll understand."

I tried to see if there was some ulterior motive in his asking me to visit my former home. Possibly he was hoping to make the idea of returning easier.

Then I thought of the ongoing search for the Earl of Wardlaw and The Eye of Heka, and how I had said that I would meet Holmes later in Baker Street. But after the conversation of the last few minutes, I only wished to be alone, not wishing to return just yet to that situation of danger and threats of death.

"Of course," I said. "I shall go there immediately, before returning to Baker Street."

"Thank you," he said. "I'm certain that all is well, but it would be good to have someone who knows what's what put a pair of eyes on the place to make sure."

He found what he was seeking in his pocket and removed his hand awkwardly, a grimace of pain crossing his face as he did so. He pulled out a key, the same one that I had given to him yesterday. I had never expected to hold it again.

I took it and nodded and, without further conversation, departed.

I made sure, upon reaching the street, to seek out the third empty cab. I thought about Baker Street, so close to the north that I could easily have walked, but I was simply not ready to return home yet. *Home*, I thought. *How curious that I can already think of it again in that way.*

The journey passed without incident, nearly repeating the route of a couple of days earlier when I had gone to Kensington to meet both doctor and daughter on the day before the sale. Hyde Park to the south looked bleak in the brassy January light, now past the midpoint of the short day. It occurred to me that I hadn't found myself any lunch, but I had just consumed a rather large whisky. Surprisingly, I was neither hungry nor inebriated.

The cabbie deposited me in front of the house, and I should have told him to wait. Instead, I paid him and stood watching as he drove away. I was about to go inside when I heard a small voice call my name.

"Dr. Watson! Dr. Watson!"

383

I looked, surprised to see that I was being approached by a boy at a dead run from his home two doors away and across the street. He pulled himself to a lurching stop in front of me, out of breath from covering the short distance at such high speed.

"You shouldn't be out without your coat, Lyndon," I admonished. "You know that, after your illness at Christmas, you must keep yourself warm."

He nodded, but said, "Is it true? That you are moving away? I've seen strangers there. One man just asked me yesterday where you were. I told him that you're going to live somewhere else. That's what my mother said, and I thought that she was right. But she must be wrong, because here you are."

I nodded my head sadly. The little fellow had shown a great interest in someday being a doctor, and I had let him spend some time in my surgery, with the approval of his parents, teaching a few basic facts about anatomy and chemistry. "I'm afraid it's true," I said. "There will be a new doctor here soon. He has a daughter, although she's grown. They are very nice people, and you'll like them quite a lot."

He scowled in disagreement. Then, he seemed to remember something, and his eyes widened. "Is it . . . is it because Mrs. Watson . . . *died?*" He whispered the last word, as if that would lessen its impact.

I swallowed. "Yes, I'm afraid it is."

"Where will you go?"

"I'm moving to Baker Street, to stay where I lived before my . . . before Mrs. Watson and I were married."

"Baker Street," he said, eyes widening. "With Mr. Holmes?"

"That's right."

That fact seemed to be too momentous to initially afford a comment. Then, he said, "I saw him once. One time when he came to visit you. I was watching out of the window, and saw him drive up in a cab. He looked just like they say. And then the two of you left together in a hurry."

I nodded, recalling the occasions that my friend had come to summon me, eyes shining, and with a cry of, "*The game is afoot!*" Some of those times when I had gone had been easy, as my wife was away from home. But once in a while she had still been there when I had departed, and those were the moments that I would never have again.

Before I let those thoughts overtake me, I looked past my young friend and saw his mother, Mrs. Parker, leaning from her front door, her arms folded against the cold air, and looking our way. "Your mother is waiting," I said. "You'd best be getting home. I'm sure we'll see each other again very soon."

"Probably not," he said, with surprising bitterness for one of only ten. "That's what people always say when they go away."

"I mean it," I said. "You've been very helpful to me, and you have a future as a doctor, if that's the path that you decide to pursue. I want to help with that, if I can."

"Really?"

"Of course."

"Well, then . . . well, then, thank you, Dr. Watson. And . . . and I'll see you soon too, then!"

He nodded his head once, turned, and ran back toward his own house. I raised an arm to wave at his mother. She returned the gesture, with a little reserve it seemed, and then gathered the boy against her before going inside.

I turned again to face the empty house. My feet seemed to root themselves onto the pavement, but I swallowed and decisively went up the steps. Then, taking the key that had once been mine from my pocket, I approached the front door and let myself in.

The door had been locked, just as it was supposed to be. It was cold and dark inside, no different than two days before, although there seemed to me that there was already an odd smell of abandonment. Piled up and down the hall were all of the boxes, recently delivered, that belonged to the new doctor and his daughter. I had verified what I was supposed to. There was no reason to stay. I should go. But instead, I continued to stand there.

It was hard to believe, looking at it in this way, that it had ever been what it had meant to me before Constance's death. Everywhere I looked, I could picture some scene from our lives – Constance coming down the stairs to greet me when I returned from my rounds, Constance leaning out of one of the farther doorways to tell me something inconsequential but precious – but now the memories were already darkening like the rooms around me, and I questioned whether I was remembering them accurately, or revising my recollections into comfortable chapters and vignettes that could be opened and examined like photographic albums with less and less pain through the passage of time.

I wandered through the downstairs, closing doors that I would not open again, the kitchen and the side rooms, and then the cellar, the dark steps yawning before me. And then I reached the base of the stairs in the front hall. I had been unable to make myself go up the other day, but now I felt that I had to. If I didn't, I would always regret it.

At the top, my feet took me, without conscious volition, into the master bedroom where Constance had passed. The furniture was still there, exactly as I'd left it. I had no need of it now, and had sold it all with the

385

house. I stumbled to the overstuffed armchair near a front window and sank into it, facing the bed. I had forced myself go upstairs, but I couldn't approach any closer to the place where she had died.

I sat in the dim light, looking blindly before me, staring so intently that my vision wavered at times, giving the illusion that the bedsheets were moving slightly of their own accord. I had seen this type of phenomena before. I recalled when I was young, and one of my grand-uncles had expired from extreme old age. Sitting with my mother, we passed what seemed to be hours, simply contemplating the man's life and death, while across from us, just feet away, his body lay in its burial clothes.

I knew, even at so young an age, that it was my imagination. But I swore at times that I could see his chest rise and fall, or his eyes shift as if dreaming under the closed lids, or perhaps the twitch of a lip or nostril. I knew it was only my imagination, but still it had seemed so real. And that was now what appeared to happen in that room of death. I seemed to see a movement of the sheets, and I so wanted it to be true. For if something like that could happen, then it might mean that the rules meant nothing – that she was not really gone from me at all. There would be no absolute that said she must be dead. It was all a terrible mistake, or I had been dreaming, and I had a chance to be with her again, and to make different choices this time, not wasting any of what we'd had. I might stand up and walk out of that room to find her, and it would be as if it had never happened at all.

I stared and stared at the bedclothes, until my eyes began to burn. And then the tears coalesced on my eyelids and ran down my cheeks, and more followed, and soon I felt something tearing loose inside me. It pulled me forward, my chest hugging toward my knees, and I cried out. My grief had finally surfaced, and I now wept beyond control for my beautiful lost wife and the life that we had planned together, both now gone forever.

Chapter XVII
Threads Become Knots

I walked home to Baker Street, not caring whether I was someone's prey.

I made my way into Hyde Park, passing south of Kensington Palace, on a more-or-less straight line east until I encountered the Serpentine, near the Long Water. I recalled an incident, just weeks before my marriage, when Holmes had been tasked to find the missing Hatty Doran, presumed at the time to be the new bride of Lord St. Simon. The girl's silk wedding-dress, matching satin shoes, and bride's wreath and veil had been found floating in that body of water, and friend Lestrade had arrived at our doorstep, announcing that he had been having the Serpentine dragged for her body.

Holmes had laughed merrily and commented on the foolishness of the inspector's efforts, as he already had a good idea about what had really happened. "Have you dragged the basin of Trafalgar Square fountain?" he asked the irritated inspector.

"Why? What do you mean?"

"Because you have just as good a chance of finding this lady in the one as in the other."

But here, standing at the Serpentine on that bleak winter afternoon, I stopped and stared at the water, and could understand why Lestrade might have believed that someone's body could have ended up there.

The wind was kicking up a chop across the surface, and it was finding its way underneath my coat. My face felt numb, and I knew that if I had any sense, I'd locate a cab and retreat to my old chair in front of the fire in Baker Street posthaste. But I felt like walking.

Turning southeast, I traversed the lower edge of the lake. I maintained this path, following when the shore turned back and curved in the other direction. Now walking along the northern bank, I stopped again and faced into the wind. From that vantage, I could see several people pressing on in huddled fashion at different locations in the park, all hurrying head-down about their business. None of them seemed to be out for pleasure – it was far too cold for that. I found that I was mildly curious about what their own stories were, and where they were coming from and going to. With a bit of surprise, I even noticed that the sun, to the southwest, was trying feebly to warm my face. In some strange way, after my earlier emotional release, would I be coming back to myself?

I turned and resumed my way to the east, crossing Park Lane and entering Mayfair. I threaded my way through the mostly empty streets, with the strong breeze sometimes rushing at my back, and other times protected from it as I changed directions. I saw that I was but a block from Sir Edward Malloy's house, where Holmes and I had visited, just that morning. Could it have only been a few hours earlier? It seemed so long ago. Our mysterious trip to Limehouse, meeting Daniel and his brothers, my conversation with Dr. Withers, and then my cathartic trip to Kensington. It was no wonder that I was weary.

I thought about altering my path to pass by Sir Edward's house, but realized that it would accomplish nothing. I might spot one of Daniel's watchers, perhaps even his brother Andrew, but that would serve no purpose, and seeing me there might confuse them. Instead, I resolved to continue on to Baker Street.

Turning north near Grosvenor Square, I quickened my step. I had been having less trouble with my old Afghan wound in recent months, and it felt good to be stretching out my pace. Perhaps, I naively hoped, the seven-and-a-half years since I had been injured was long enough for me to be mostly healed. The doctor in me, however, knew better.

I finally reached 221 Baker Street, checking the time as I entered. It was somewhat later than I had thought. Hanging my coat and hat in the hall, I saw that Holmes had returned, and also that we had a visitor.

I climbed the steps and, upon reaching the landing outside the sitting room, heard Holmes call, "Come in, Watson. Your counsel is required."

Entering, I found Inspector Lanner, sitting in the basket chair with his feet stretched toward the fire, and a glass of something amber in his hands. The heat in the room hit my cold face like a slap, and my eyes watered for just a moment. I blinked, sniffed, and made my way to my own chair. "Inspector," I said. He nodded.

"Lanner brings news of Baron Meade."

"Nothing for certain, I'm afraid," said the inspector, pulling his feet back and sitting up straighter. "As you know, we lost him yesterday, after his murderous attack on your friend in front of Simpson's. Nothing has been seen of him since then, but it is our considered opinion that he has fled London."

"And he has convinced you of this how?" asked Holmes.

"Well, the cumulative lack of any sign of him. After all, why would he stay? His plans have been foiled."

I coughed. "Do you mean that, because you have been unable to locate one man in a city of millions, after only looking for a day, you have given up and decided that he is not here to be found at all?"

388

Holmes's eyes flashed at my irritated question. I knew that he agreed with me.

Lanner shifted forward in the chair. "The Baron is not your average criminal," he said doggedly, and with a trace of exasperation. He began to raise fingers to enumerate his points. "He is a rich man, who doesn't have a clue how to hide in the rat's nest that is London. He can't fit in, you see. He has no friends in those places to help him. His own kind won't shield him, not now. And he isn't part of any radical group that will take him in. Rather, he was acting alone – the common materials for the explosives he assembled could have been obtained by anyone, after all – and he didn't need any help for that, other than that of the laborers he hired to move it, and they didn't know what it was about. There was no fancy clock-work mechanism that only some radical would know how to assemble. And after we arrested him the other night, and then he escaped, the Foreign Office stepped in and cut off all of his funds. Gentlemen, he has nowhere to hide, and no resources. He must surely have fled."

"But your argument about why he could not stay in London," said Holmes, "would also explain why he would have nowhere to go if he *left* London. As you say, he has no resources, no radical associates, and no ready funds to go anywhere else. I take it that you've men at both his London residence and his country house?"

Lanner nodded. "We sent them there after the Baron's arrest, to see if there were any additional explosives, or related evidence. Since his escape, our men have remained on duty there. He hasn't put in an appearance."

Holmes shook his head. "I'm sorry, Lanner, but your logic isn't convincing to me. Nor is it to the doctor, I believe. I feel that the man is still here in London, biding his time. He didn't leave after he first escaped, as shown by his appearance in the Strand yesterday. He is too angry, too vindictive, and too clever not to have found some hidey-hole before trying something again."

"If that's true, then what do you suggest, Mr. Holmes? We don't know where to search, and we can't just sit and wait for him to reappear."

"But that's exactly what you will be doing if you make the assumption that he has gone. You say that he can't be here, and he can't be anywhere else either. But he didn't just vanish."

"It seems likely he left the country," insisted Lanner, almost in a truculent mumble.

"You have men watching the ports, do you not?"

"Yes."

"Even so, it's barely possible that he got away by one of those routes, but I believe that he won't go until his work is done. And now, in addition to punishing the country that he feels is responsible for the death of his son last year, he has also irrationally decided to focus his attentions on Watson."

"Exactly," said Lanner. "But we can't just wait and use the doctor as bait in a tiger trap." He looked at me. "Can we?"

I started to answer, and in the mood I was in it would have been in the affirmative, but Holmes cut me off, saying firmly, "No," even as his eyes met mine, understanding what my thoughts had been.

"Then again I ask, Mr. Holmes, what do you suggest? The materials that the man used for his explosives aren't difficult to obtain. Perhaps you're right, and he does have a place to hide. If so, he could already be filling it up with the same types of chemicals and metal parts that we found the other night off the Brixton Road. There's no reason that he couldn't blow up Parliament at any time he gets ready, and *then* come after the doctor. It doesn't have to be the doctor first, you know."

"I'm aware of that," said Holmes, "and I must confess that I'm uncertain what to do. I've put out the word that I wish to know about any new substantial purchases of the same materials that he used earlier." He tapped his finger on the table beside him, with a small stack of notes and telegrams lying on top of the *Beeton's*. "I have my sources looking for him, and also for someone else who is associated with an entirely unconnected but equally serious episode. I'm afraid now that all we can do is wait and – "

He was cut off by a frantic ringing of the front door bell, followed immediately by an urgent pounding. We all stood up, looking at each other. Holmes had already started toward the landing when we heard Mrs. Hudson cry out in shock, calling in an unusually shrill tone, "Dr. Watson! *Dr. Watson!*"

I moved then too, pushing my way past Lanner and wondering what could make her ask for me specifically and with such exigency in her voice. My only idea was that the Baron had just made his latest play against me, and that our dear sweet landlady had now paid the price, even as Dr. Withers had the day before.

Throwing open the sitting room door, I fairly leapt down the stairs. Throwing out a hand at the newel post to anchor me as I rounded at the landing, I could see a couple of figures huddled in the shadows surrounding the front door, both appearing to sag slowly to the ground even as I approached. One was Mrs. Hudson, and I feared what sort of wound could make her behave so.

But then she spoke, with a distressed tone in her voice. "Help me, Doctor!" she cried. "He's in a terrible state! I can't hold him!"

By the light coming in the still-open door, I could see that she had her arms around an unconscious man who seemed to have collapsed, taking her with him. She must have opened the door to discover him, and he fell forward to the ground while she tried to brace him. Stepping awkwardly around the both of them, and incredibly relieved to hear that Mrs. Hudson didn't appear to be in any danger herself, I lifted the man by his clothing away from her and shifted his weight so that I could lower him flat upon the floor. Later, I would marvel at how the adrenaline, produced in that moment, had allowed me to out-race my friend as I flew down the stairs, and then to move the big man as if he were a mere piece of luggage.

I stood up and then bent again to help Mrs. Hudson to her feet. I ascertained that she was uninjured and simply surprised at the unexpected events when she had opened the door. "He took a step forward," she explained breathlessly, "and started to fall. Please help the poor man, Doctor. Oh, is he dead?"

I had resumed my examination of the unconscious man, rolling him onto his back in order to better evaluate his injuries, even as Holmes came to a stop beside me. I noticed that the mysterious victim seemed to be well-dressed in expensive clothes, but there was an odor about him that is associated with garments that have been worn for too long, often to be found in the poor and homeless who only have one set of attire to wear. I was looking at the man's wrists, which appeared to have been recently tied and rubbed to the point that the skin was scraped raw, when Holmes hissed, "His face, Watson! Let me see his face!"

Lowering the man's arms, I reached up and gently turned the casualty's head, taking it by the chin and rolling it until it faced up into the light. He was unshaven, and his lips were cracked. He appeared to have bitten them in several places, as dried blood was crusted in arcs across them in patterns clearly resembling teeth marks. He looked to be in his forties, with graying temples and a day or two's worth of whiskers, but my medical experience told me that he was actually several years younger than that, and had only achieved this appearance through a long participation in a dissipated lifestyle.

I heard Holmes take in a quick breath. I would hesitate to call it a gasp, as that was a reaction that my friend rarely manifested. However, considering the completely uncharacteristic shock in his next utterance, perhaps a gasp is the only way to describe it.

"My God," he breathed. "Ian!"

I turned my head toward him quite sharply. "Ian? Do you mean that *this* is the Earl of Wardlaw?"

"The same indeed," Holmes breathed softly. I remembered Lanner for the first time, now stepping closer behind us. "Doctor?" he asked. "Mr. Holmes? Who is this man?"

"What has happened here?" hissed my friend, softly, so that only I could hear. "How did he arrive on our doorstep? Did he come on his own, or was he brought? And most importantly, *where is the idol?*"

Holmes had said all of this in a rough whisper. I became aware that Inspector Lanner had stepped even closer, now standing slightly behind us and beside Mrs. Hudson. "Who is this?" he demanded. "Do you know this man?"

"Holmes?" croaked the man on the floor in a cracked and dry voice. He opened his eyes and looked up, trying to focus on my friend, who was illuminated above him by the daylight still spilling in from the street. "Holmes?"

"Yes, Ian. I'm here."

"He took it, Holmes! He has it, and he wanted me to tell you that he has it!"

"Who, Ian? Who took it? Do you mean the idol?"

"Yes. The Eye. He has it!"

"Who, Ian? To whom are you referring? Is it John Goins?"

"I don't know him," said the Earl. "I don't know his name. He . . . he has it now, and he wanted you to know. He brought me here to tell you." Then he lapsed into unconsciousness.

"Who is this man?" asked Lanner again. From his almost petulant tone, I wouldn't have been surprised if he followed the question by stamping his foot on the entryway carpet.

"He is connected to another case," said Holmes with almost a sigh. "He is the Earl of Wardlaw."

"The Earl – ? Wait – Is this the man that is being sought in connection with a murder out in Essex?"

"He is," said Holmes.

"And he has been cruelly used," I interrupted. "Let us get him upstairs, where I can better evaluate his injuries." I stepped back. "Lanner, do you get his legs while Holmes and I support his upper body. Mrs. Hudson? Hot water, if you please. If," I added, "you are all right." She smiled and nodded, and then retreated to her own part of the house.

Holmes took a moment to look outside. "Nothing," he muttered. Then, between Holmes, Lanner, and myself, we managed to get the Earl up to the sitting room without causing him too much distress. He remained unconscious the entire time, and in moments he was reclining on our settee while I made my examination. Even as I began, Mrs. Hudson entered with the water. I thanked her for the quick assistance, and apologized for what had happened when she opened the door.

She shook her head. "We were long overdue this week for something of the sort," she said in her understated Scots accent. I smiled, shook my head when she asked if she could help any further, and then turned back to the patient as she departed.

Holmes moved to stand closer beside me, leaning in and noting the lacerations on the patient's wrist. "Rope marks," I said, and he nodded.

"Only recently removed – they're still oozing fluids from the abrasions. And they weren't tied on for very long either, just within the last couple of hours. He certainly hasn't been bound and held captive for the entire time that he's been missing."

"No bruising," I agreed. "The only other apparent wound, other than the damage he has done to himself by biting his lips – and that explains the blood upon his shirt – is on the back of his head. He has a sizeable lump there, probably rendered not long before his arrival at our door, but it should cause him no long-term damage."

"Implying that he was brought here, having been made harmless for easier transport. The knees of his pants are scuffed and dirty, and the overall poor condition of his clothing is very indicative – but I hesitate to connect that with this incident, as they could have been damaged at another time during the last few days, while he was on the run with the idol."

"Idol?" interrupted Lanner, who had been standing behind us, shifting from right to left as he attempted to get a better look at my treatment of the Earl. "What is all this talk? Is there something that I can assist with?"

Holmes shook his head. "It is another problem, concurrent with that of the Baron, but equally – if not more so – serious."

"Hard to believe that something like blowing up Parliament could be equaled," muttered Lanner.

"Nonetheless, the situation regarding the idol that we have mentioned could have consequences far beyond the shores of this country."

"The idol," a weak voice interjected. "He has the idol!"

We turned back toward the Earl. Holmes took a step forward and leaned down into the injured man's field of vision. "Tell us, Ian. We cannot find it until you tell us where to look. Who has taken it?"

The injured man coughed, and I moved to raise him up. Gesturing to Lanner, I indicated that the man needed something to drink. The inspector quickly obtained a respectable brandy from the sideboard.

The Earl swallowed too quickly, coughed again, and then took another larger sip. He motioned for help, and we finished rotating him to a sitting position. Resting his feet on the floor, he leaned forward, arms across his knees, one hand loosely holding the last sip of his restorative.

393

Then he cleared his throat and looked up, first at Holmes, then right and left to me and Lanner, who lingered several feet away.

"I don't know his name, Holmes," he said. He coughed roughly. "He managed to get into the house this morning, after you had been there, and wanted to know the purpose of your visit."

"The house? Ian, what house? The only house we have been to this morning – " He stopped himself abruptly. Glancing my way, he said, "Sir Edward's residence in Mayfair." Back to the Earl, he added, "Ian, have you been hiding at Sir Edward's house?"

The Earl nodded. "After Williams came out to Essex, to tell me you had spotted the false idol in the Museum, I didn't know what to do. It had helped me for so long, and now you would come and take it back. I couldn't lose it. Not now! It's mine! I had paid Williams to keep an eye out in case anyone ever found out, and it had always been understood that he would notify me if someone spotted the substitution, and then come out immediately for further instructions."

"And then what happened? We know that Dawson killed Williams. Why did he do that?"

"I don't know, Holmes!" cried the Earl. "I knew that I had to get away from there, and take it to a place of safety. You would be coming for it, to return it to the Museum, even though it is mine. *Mine*, I tell you! I found it, and I'm the one who knows how to make use of its powers! It has aided me all these years, and I won't give it up!" He had tensed, half rising from the chair even as his voice became increasingly shrill. But then he sagged back, as if a supporting wire inside him had snapped.

"But Dawson, Ian?" continued Holmes. "Why did he kill Williams?"

"I heard what you said," replied the Earl vaguely. "This morning when you were with Edward. I was listening from the next room – when you said that Dawson accused me of the murder. I didn't know that Williams had been killed until after it had already happened."

"Surely Dawson had a reason. Why?"

"I'm uncertain. I was retrieving The Eye from where I kept it in the front of the vault, and I was aware of Dawson and Williams moving around behind me. Then I heard a gasp, followed by the sound of someone collapsing to the floor. I looked around, and Dawson was standing over Williams's body, a thin knife in his hand. There was no blood that I could see, but obviously the man was dead."

"And did you question Dawson? Could he provide no explanation?"

"He simply said that he was protecting me. I don't know why he did it, or what Williams was about to do that made him deserve death. Perhaps he was reaching to take the idol away from me while my back was turned. I only know that Williams and Dawson were talking together while I retrieved it. I couldn't hear what they were saying. Possibly Williams said something that provoked Dawson. Maybe he protected me. Then he told me that I had to leave."

"To go to Sir Edward's house." The Earl nodded. "Did you go straight there?"

"Yes. Edward was angry with me, and worse when I told him about what Dawson had done. But he understood, and he hid me and the idol in an empty bedroom. He keeps very few servants, so only Crye, his butler, knew that I was there."

"But someone found you," said Holmes. "Today, after we left. The man you say now has the sculpture."

"Yes. Edward and I were in his study, discussing your visit. The Eye was sitting on the desk between us. Edward has known about it from the beginning, you see, and knew that I had found a way to keep it. In fact, it was he who came up with the idea of making a substitution. I . . . I've never been good at this sort of thing. Of thinking of plans, and keeping secrets, or even managing my own business after my father died. It's only been more difficult as time has gone on. But Edward has helped me over the years. He taught me how to make use of the idol's powers. And it didn't hurt him, either. We have both benefited from it."

"But the other man, Ian. Who is it that you said now has the idol?"

"I don't know his name, Holmes!" he cried. "As I said, he got into the house after you left, and found us in the study while we were talking. I remember seeing him come in behind me, through the door, and then he hit me over the head. I blacked out, and came to discover that my hands were bound, and that I was lying on the floor. The man didn't notice that I was awake at first. His back was to me, and he was questioning Edward, about why you and your friend had been there, and what you wanted. I couldn't see what he did, but Edward cried out. Several times. It was . . . it was terrible. And so very loud. I don't understand why no one came to see what was the matter. Finally, Edward admitted that your visit was because you were searching for me and . . . and The Eye.

"I must have gasped to hear Edward reveal the truth, because the man noticed me then. Oh, if only Edward had remained strong!" With a groan, he closed his eyes.

Holmes took him by the shoulder and gave it a shake. "Ian, can you describe him?"

The Earl shook his head. "No. It was all a blur."

Holmes groaned. "What happened then, Ian? Tell us!"

The Earl opened his puffy eyes, noticing first the empty glass in his hands. He held it up, and Lanner wordlessly refilled it, this time with considerably more than the amount that had been previously offered.

Taking a healthy swallow, the Earl continued. "The man pulled me up into a chair. My head hurt terribly, and I thought that I might be ill. The chair was turned so that I couldn't see Edward. The . . . the man wanted to know more about the idol from me as well, but I wouldn't tell him. I wouldn't! I would rather have died!

"So he returned to Edward. I couldn't make out what he was saying then, it was very soft and coaxing-like, but Edward was screaming. Then I relapsed into unconsciousness. I only came to in a carriage, just as I was pulled out to the street and pushed toward a building. 'Tell Mr. Holmes and Dr. Watson,' the man said in my ear, pulling me up to the door, pounding on it and ringing the bell. 'Tell them I have the idol.' Then he turned and left me, climbing back onto the carriage and whipping it up, even as the door opened. I remember falling forward, but nothing else until I was here in this room."

Standing up, Holmes took a couple of quick turns around the spaces between the furniture, eyes intensely envisioning some scene playing out before him. Then, "Obviously, we must make our way as quickly as possible to Sir Edward's home. Lanner!" The inspector raised his eyebrows. "Summon a constable and a cab, in that order!"

Lanner, thankfully acting and needing no explanations, turned and ran down the stairs. In a moment, I heard his police whistle frantically blowing, followed nearly immediately by the other used to signal a four-wheeler.

"Watson, get Ian ready to travel."

"Holmes, in his condition, I'm not at all certain that he – "

"We have no time for this, Watson. Don't you see? I fear that we are already too late, but perhaps we might pick up a clue before the trail grows too cold. Surely you understand what has happened?"

I thought that I might, but before I could establish further facts, Mrs. Hudson chose that moment to reenter the room. Holmes brushed past her and out to the stairs, while I helped the Earl to his feet. With our landlady's assistance, we made our way down, step by step, to the entry hall, where I put one of my old coats around the Earl's shoulders. I then followed by putting on one of my own. Thanking Mrs. Hudson, and reminding her to continue to take every precaution, I assisted the injured man to the freezing street.

Holmes was carefully instructing the constable to get word as fast as he could, by way of the closest station, to either Inspectors Gregson or Lestrade. They were to meet us at Sir Edward's house as soon as possible. He made the constable repeat the address, nodded a dismissal, and then turned to the cab, where Lanner and I had loaded the Earl.

"Aldford Street in Mayfair, and drive like the devil!" Holmes cried. The cabbie started to protest, but Lanner showed him his police identification, and the man relented.

The Earl had lapsed into a groggy state, and was unable or unwilling to answer any more of Holmes's questions. I started to question Holmes further, but didn't want to distract him. We were fortunate that the cabbie chose a route uncluttered with traffic, and we quickly traveled south toward our destination. Finally pulling to a stop in front of Sir Edward's address, we exited from the cab and stepped up to the door. Holmes nodded grimly, showing where the front door was pushed to, but not closed all the way. "This isn't good, Watson," Holmes muttered.

Lanner and I helped the Earl under the lintel and so inside, while Holmes cautiously pushed ahead. I slipped out from under the Earl's arm, leaving Lanner to support him. Then I pulled my revolver from my coat pocket and moved forward to join my friend.

Just inside the next room we found the body. It was Andrew, the man with the weary and gentle-seeming smile who had driven us to meet his brothers, hours earlier that very day in Limehouse. The front of his head was caved in, and he was lying in his own blood, pooled and congealing beneath him. He was clearly dead, but I knelt anyway, finding no pulse beneath his already cooling skin.

"No weapon," I said, glancing around.

"I know what killed him," said Holmes. He gestured toward the smooth shape of the massive concavity in the man's skull. "I fancy you can work it out as well."

Holmes then nodded his head toward the floor, where a track of bloody footprints led from Andrew's body to the rear of the house. With a hiss, Holmes nodded for me to follow. I heard Lanner discovering the body for himself, but didn't stop to offer any explanations.

We moved deeper into the house, following the tracks, and on into the room where we had met Sir Edward hours earlier that very day. Unexpectedly, we found another man there, lying flat on his back in the center of the carpet, a stunned expression his face and a bloody lump on his forehead. It was Crye, the butler.

He was unconscious, but breathing regularly. His body was wrapped like a mummy in a cloth that had clearly been pulled from a nearby table, upsetting the various items that had stood upon it. An overturned flower vase had spilled its water, which had pooled on the table and was slowly dripping onto the highly polished wooden floor. The cloth from the table was tucked around the butler's body, immobilizing and swaddling his arms and legs in such a way that he would have been unable to free himself without great difficulty.

I bent to examine Crye, but Holmes impatiently gestured that I continue with him deeper into the house. I stood, feeling that the butler would be all right for a few more minutes, and we moved on, quietly entering another series of rooms, always leading toward the rear of the house. Holmes pointed toward the floor. Continuing in the direction we were exploring was the series of rough bloody footprints. "Prepare yourself, Watson," Holmes whispered.

We reached a half-closed door, which Holmes pushed open. It was only then that I noticed that he, too was armed with a gun.

The fire had been built up in the room, and the trapped heat from the mostly closed door washed out over us like a wave. Cold as I was from the flying trip we had just made, I couldn't suppress a shiver. I like to hope that it was from the sudden change in temperature, and not from what we saw in the room.

For it was Sir Edward, propped in his chair, behind his desk. He was still breathing raggedly, but insensible, and in a terrible condition. His arms were tied, bound by a rope in a peculiar criss-cross pattern, in order to pull the limbs together – even the upper portion. A quick look showed that they were not actually ropes at all, but bell ropes, at least two of them from their differing patterns, twined across and through his arms. As the cords had been tightened, rather like lacing a pair of shoes, the man's upper arms had been pulled closer and closer together, to the point where they had each obviously dislocated from the shoulders. They were now aligned nearly parallel to one another, and the pain must have been agonizing before he blacked out.

There had also been quite a few blows to the head, as shown by bruises and contusions. Some of them had opened, letting rivulets of blood run down his face like tears before curving under the jawbone and collecting upon his collar.

I heard a step behind me and spun, my service revolver at the ready, only to find Lanner and the Earl in the doorway. Lanner's eyes widened, and the Earl raised his head long enough to understand the scene in front of him. With a groan, he collapsed to the floor. The inspector let him fall.

Holmes was taking in everything at once, as was his way, and while I normally knew better than to step further into the room, possibly altering or destroying evidence, I pushed past him – there was a man who desperately needed medical attention.

"Help me cut these ropes," I said. I realized that I might be disturbing Holmes's investigation, but treating this wounded man came first.

When the bonds had been cut, the tension holding Sir Edward's arms, pulled so cruelly out of their sockets, was released. With a moan at the fresh pain, he came to himself for a second, and then lapsed back into a renewed state of unconsciousness. Perhaps it was a mercy. I knew without any further examination that his shoulders and arms were ruined, and that he would never again function normally or without great pain.

I could sense Holmes moving with purpose behind me, seeing *and* observing all that there was. I glanced back, and discovered that his eyes had lit on a single sheet of paper, resting obviously in the center of the otherwise empty desk. The idol, described by the Earl earlier as having been sitting on this same desk when his discussion with Sir Edward was occurring, was no longer present.

I heard a sound from the front of the house. Gregson's voice, calling, "Mr. Holmes! Mr. Holmes!"

Lanner started to speak, and then did not. It appeared that he could not find his voice. "Back here, Gregson!" I called, while Holmes's eyes urgently scanned the sheet in his hand. A terrible look crossed his face.

"What is it, Holmes?" I asked.

He shook his head, his free hand rising to pinch his lower lip. He was deep in thought, and visualizing something in his mind that was far from this terrible room. Just then, both Gregson and Lestrade entered, stepping over the unconscious Earl and stopping behind Lanner. A pair of constables were visible past them. They all quickly surveyed the room.

"Mr. Holmes?" said Gregson.

Holmes looked up. "The idol was here," he said angrily to me. "The Earl brought it here when he left Essex."

"Then where is it?" asked Lestrade, glancing around with an understandable desperation in his voice.

"Gone." Holmes looked from one to the other of us, and gestured with the letter. "It's good that you're here, too, Lanner. It appears that our situation has just grown infinitely more complicated."

"Holmes," I said. "What do you mean?"

He turned his eyes toward the sheet. "It is addressed to me. It says:

My dear Mr. Holmes,

I foolishly believed that your only business right now would be trying to stop me before I can bring about the justice that this country so certainly and richly deserves. Therefore, I followed you here this morning, uncertain as to what anyone in this house could have to do with me. I was quite curious, you see, when I saw, from my vantage across the street, your cabbie being taken prisoner and replaced by a foreigner. But I decided to stay and find out what connection this place had to my business.

Imagine my surprise when I entered after you both departed and learned that the happenings here had nothing to do with me at all. As I crept through the house, I was accosted by the butler, whom I silenced. I explored the house further and locked the few other servants in the cellar, where you will find them unharmed. Then I found this study, where the two men were talking. One, with whom I was slightly acquainted, was Sir Edward. He was explaining to the other that everything would be all right, and that they would continue to be able to use the power of the idol just as they had before.

Now, that mention of an idol, along with the presence of the stranger earlier, made me curious. I entered the room, incapacitated the two men, and proceeded to find out just what I needed to know about this ugly rock. Sir Edward shared with me all that rot about magical powers, which he does not seem to believe, although he stated that many others do. But more importantly, he mentioned that the other believers are the enemies of England. When I questioned him further about this, and seemed to be too interested, he understood my purpose, and he begged me not to let the idol fall into their hands, as it could unleash a war that could destroy us. He had no idea that he was telling that to the very man who was seeking exactly that outcome.

I was on my way out, when whom should I encounter but the stranger from this morning, sneaking in for some reason. Strangely, I almost feel sad for this man whom I was forced to kill, when I can't feel any sadness at all for the people of this country who will rightly suffer as I have. And they will, I assure you. But I cannot simply take the idol and give it to those who will use it to ruin England. First, I must let you, and especially your friend Dr. Watson, know exactly what is going to happen and why, even if it makes things a bit more difficult for me. This country must understand exactly what is about to occur, and the reason. This country destroyed my son. Therefore, this country must be destroyed.

Holmes paused, and then looked at both of us. Softly, he stated the obvious. "The letter is signed '*Baron Meade*'."

Part III

Chapter XVIII
What Sir Edward Revealed

I was stunned as I tried to grasp the implications of what Holmes had just read. Perhaps it was already too late. Baron Meade, from all accounts an intelligent, if misguided and dangerous, man, now had a more powerful weapon to aim at Britain than a simply-constructed though massive-in-scale targeted explosion at the center of our government.

Simply-constructed, I thought to myself. *As if his earlier plan, designed to kill hundreds – if not thousands! – of important men and women, as well as to destroy incredibly important and symbolic landmarks, was nothing. Yet compared with the potential death of a war caused by the rediscovery of an idol, it* was *nothing.*

"Wake him up," said Holmes tightly.

"What?" I asked, my thoughts interrupted.

"Wake Sir Edward up. We must question him immediately." Then, turning to the gathered inspectors, he said, "Do you understand what this means?"

I didn't see their reactions, as I had turned to aid the damaged man, but Lanner said, "Well, I don't. It's obvious that this Baron – "

"Shut up, Lanner," muttered Lestrade. Then, louder, "We do, Mr. Holmes," he continued. "It's hard to believe that this thing which we've heard so much about in the last few days can cause so much pain and destruction, but we understand."

"Then you know what to do," said Holmes.

"Right," said Lestrade. "Come along, Lanner. We need to hear what you've already done to locate the Baron. And then we need to do it the right way this time, or England will be at war in less than a fortnight."

I laid Sir Edward back in the chair, in order to make him as comfortable as possible. I could hear Holmes pacing behind me. Suddenly, a thought occurred to me. "Holmes!"

I looked over my shoulder. My friend had stopped, his thoughts broken. "Get one of the constables in here."

Without questioning me, he nodded and left the room, stepping around the Earl, who was still collapsed upon the floor. I looked around for a decanter of brandy, found it, and poured a generous amount. Sir Edward was going to need it for the pain. It was times like this that I regretted not carrying my medical bag. I shook my head – a doctor without his supplies, but armed with a gun.

I heard Holmes return with the policeman, who was saying, "We found the servants, what there are of them, locked in the cellar. They don't know anything, except that a man was suddenly among them, a stranger, and he herded them in and locked the door."

"Watson," said Holmes.

I stood and turned. "Lest anyone forget in the confusion," I said, "I wanted to make sure that Crye the butler is checked, and also that an ambulance is called. Several in fact, enough to transport all three of the injured men. I assume that none of the servants locked in the cellar need medical attention?"

"That's correct, Doctor," said the officer. I recognized him now as Hewlitt, a solid man who had been to see me a year or so earlier for a broken thumb, obtained when a miscreant had fought back with enthusiasm, bending the constable's grasped truncheon the wrong way.

"Excellent."

He touched a couple of fingers to his hat and departed. At that moment, Sir Edward gave a great groan, and I placed the glass to his cracked lips. He sensed it was there, even though his eyes were closed, and started to raise an arm to take hold of it. The pain was immediate and intense, and his eyes flew open, even as he shrieked.

"Do not move," I said softly but firmly. "Your arms have been dislocated from your shoulders, and there is a great deal of nerve and muscle damage there as well." I didn't tell him that it was unlikely that the greatest surgeon alive would ever be able to repair what had been done, and that the pain he felt now would never entirely abate. I had seen men with less wreckage than this quickly turn into alcoholics or morphine addicts in an effort to escape it, an effort that was inevitably doomed to failure – and often led to suicide.

Sir Edward nodded and closed his eyes. Tears ran freely down his cheeks. I helped him take a sip, and then another.

Holmes stepped closer. "Sir Edward," he said. "This is Sherlock Holmes. Do you recall meeting with us this morning?"

The man swallowed and nodded again. He tried to speak, but nothing came out. He licked his lips and tried again.

"Yes," he said. "Before Baron Meade came into the house."

"You know him?"

"We've met."

"He has taken the idol," said Holmes.

"I know. Ian had brought it down with him – he needed to be with it constantly. Ever since he arrived here, he's carried it around from room to room like a child with a doll. It was here when the Baron came in, sitting upon the desk. He didn't know what it was, and didn't care at first, but when he forced me to tell him why you'd been here, he became more interested. I warned him about it, and he became very excited." He gasped, and gave a little cry, sliding down in the seat. I helped to reposition him. Beads of sweat were popping out on the man's forehead.

"You helped Ian hide the carving for all of these years," Holmes stated. "You were the one who came up with the plan to let the Museum keep the imitation, while Ian had the real idol."

He nodded with a grimace. "It was my idea to go after it as well, all those years ago. Jimmy didn't care anything about it at first. I talked him into buying the map, and then financing the expedition. Then, after the fire killed Jimmy, and Ian arrived, I was able to convince him to continue what Jimmy had started."

"But why?" asked Holmes. "What purpose did it serve?"

Sir Edward shook his head. "Nothing then. Just a distraction. I had nothing of my own. It amused me to manipulate them into situations of my choosing. Knowing that I had gotten them to fund an expedition into the desert was . . . entertaining." He winced.

"And later?" asked Holmes. "When you realized you'd discovered something of importance?"

"At first it was nothing to me. But then I saw what it meant to Ian, and I pressed him to see how far he would go."

"And when the Earl's father wanted to place it in the Museum's keeping . . . ?"

"I knew by then how much it was already preying on Ian's mind. He believed in its power, you see. I thought it was all nonsense, but through the use of it, I found that I could influence Ian." He gasped, and I gave him another sip of brandy. Half of the glass was now gone. I wanted to ease his pain, but I didn't want him to become too intoxicated to answer Holmes's questions. Still, I believed that a combination of sharp intense pain and a long tolerance to the fiery liquid would leave him unaffected for quite a bit longer.

"Influence him? How?"

"After the idol was stolen from the Museum, and I knew how much it haunted Ian's thoughts, I convinced him to have the counterfeit made and substituted. I had no money of my own then – that was before my father died – but I was able to convince Ian what to do. He's always listened to me. Ian paid Williams at the Museum to accept the false idol as the real thing after you recovered it, and then Ian kept the real one. He was never very smart, and was glad of my advice."

"And you stole from him without his knowledge along the way, no doubt."

A tear rolled down Sir Edward's cheek, from the pain I was sure, and not from any guilt. "It was my skills that increased his wealth. He believed it was due to the magic of the idol – but it wasn't. He was very happy with the arrangement. Later, when my father died and I came into my own fortune, I was able to do even more with our combined funds, benefitting the both of us." He grimaced and coughed, and then continued. "By letting him think we were *both* tapping its magic."

"And Dawson," said Holmes. "I take it that he was really in your employ all along, and not the Earl's."

Sir Edward tried to nod, nearly retched, and then gasped. "He was originally my own servant. He was with us in the desert when we found the idol. Afterwards, it seemed best to put him put in a place where he could keep an eye on Ian." He licked his lips, and I gave him another sip. "Dawson understood. Ian was never very strong, and not very intelligent either. He needed a minder. Dawson helped to keep him on track."

"Then why did Dawson kill Williams?" asked Holmes.

"I don't know." His eyes widened. "But wait! You said this morning that *Ian* killed him."

"I wanted you to think that was my conclusion. However, I already knew the truth from the evidence, which indicated that Dawson stabbed him while Ian was retrieving the idol. Ian confirmed that to me a few minutes ago."

"How . . . how did he tell you that? Where is he?"

"Here. In this room, unconscious on the floor over there. He was hit on the head by your attacker, the Baron, and then dumped at my doorstep, to lead me back here so that I would know what had happened, and that it has been taken."

"The man seemed excited when he discovered what it was. Is he another one of those fools that believes in its magic?"

"Not at all. But he intends to give it to those that do, hoping to unleash a conflict that will somehow grow until it embroils England within its coils."

"A war? But . . . why?"

"It would take too long to explain. Did he give any indication where he was going?"

"No, not at all. But then, I . . . I passed out, and don't know what happened after that."

There was a noise from the doorway. It was Lestrade. "We've sounded the alarm," he said. "The entire force will be looking for the Baron, even though we already were. The military will be involved. The train stations and all the ports were already being watched as well by policemen now, to be augmented by soldiers. He can't get away."

406

"Ah, Lestrade, if only it were that easy. Baron Meade is a clever man, and has avoided capture for several days now."

"But the effort directed toward finding him has multiplied," insisted the inspector. "And before he was only in hiding, probably staying close and biding his time in order to do more mischief. Now he will be on the run, trying to get the idol out of the country and back to where it can do the most damage. We will find him."

Holmes looked doubtful. "He won't need to leave the country at all. There are agents here already that have been seeking the statue for their own purposes, and they will happily take receipt of the thing and easily carry it away on their own."

At that moment, the Earl, still resting on the floor near the doorway, began to stir, and there were footsteps in the corridor leading to the study. It was another constable, this time one that I didn't know. "Ambulances are here, Doctor," he said.

I nodded as I walked over and knelt beside the Earl. I examined him, believing that he would eventually make a full recovery, unlike his friend behind me, breathing raggedly in the chair.

I watched as Holmes's eyes cut down to the floor and the bloody footprints there. Then he walked out of the room, disappearing for a few moments, and apparently following the trail of those same prints that had led us here from the front door, and then deeper into the house.

"The butler has awakened," added the constable, and I realized with a terrible feeling that I hadn't yet fully examined that injured man after the dreadful discovery we had made here in the study. I stood and made my way toward the front of the house.

Crye was now seated in a chair, holding a handkerchief to his head. I briefly examined him and found that, except for a headache, he was going to be all right. Still, I believed that further examination at the hospital wouldn't hurt, and told him to go with the ambulances.

While I directed the attendants toward the back of the house, Holmes returned and leaned in to speak with Crye. By the time I had supervised the loading of both Sir Edward and the Earl onto stretchers, Holmes seemed to have finished with the butler. The man was led out by an attendant.

"He knows nothing," he said. "He was surprised by a stranger, obviously the Baron, who struck him. After that, all is a blank until he was awakened a few moments ago."

He turned and began walking to the front of the house, careful to avoid the bloody footprints on the floor, even though they had clearly been stepped in by the other men – inspectors, constables, and ambulance attendants – that had been going back and forth in the house.

He stopped by the body of Andrew, being watched over by a constable. "We haven't touched him yet," said the man. "Inspector Lestrade said you'd want to look at him first."

Holmes nodded and dropped to his knees. He passed his hands over the corpse. "Watson?"

I leaned in to examine the unfortunate dead man. The left side of his head was massively caved in, obviously by a single blow of some curved object long enough to stretch from the front to the back of the skull.

"The idol?" I asked, although I already knew that to be the right answer.

"Undoubtedly. The footprints tell the story. As his letter informed us, after the Baron entered the house, to see what it was that had brought us here and how it related to him, he encountered Crye, whom he disabled. Then he locked up the other servants, without any great difficulty, as there are so few of them. He discovered Sir Edward and Ian in the study, overheard enough of their conversation to become interested, and took them prisoner before torturing out the story of the idol.

"He was leaving this way when he encountered Andrew, who had returned to watch the house. There must have been a suspicion among Daniel and his brothers, not shared with us, that either Ian or the statue were here, given both our interest and Sir Edward's past associations with the Earl. Andrew, watching outside, saw Baron Meade enter suspiciously, and then decided to come inside in order to discover what was going on. They encountered one another unexpectedly here in the hall. He was then killed before he could defend himself.

"It seems that it was only at this point that the Baron decided to write the letter. Perhaps seeing Andrew recalled to his mind that he had observed him earlier this morning, when we were driven away for our meeting with Daniel, and realizing a connection between us, he decided to taunt us with the knowledge that he now has the object. He tracked Andrew's blood back to the study, where he wrote the note. The footprints, much fainter by that time, depart the study and move on through the house and out of the rear door, where they fade while heading toward the stables. Ian's footprints are intermingled with those of Baron Meade's after they departed from the study, as he was a prisoner by then, taken to be deposited in Baker Street."

"And after that errand was accomplished, the Baron could have gone in any direction. He could now be anywhere."

"Exactly, Watson. And God help us."

Chapter XIX
Dawson's Story

Holmes rose and indicated to the constable that he was finished examining the body of the unfortunate Andrew. He and I then stepped outside, where he peered up and down the street. "What are you looking for?" I asked.

"To see if Daniel has anyone else on duty." He continued to turn his head this way and that, before exclaiming, "There!"

But he did not point. Instead, he moved away from the house with purpose, headed directly for an alley-way that seemed to lead to a mews several houses up the street. I glanced back to see that Lestrade, Gregson, and Lanner were carrying on a discussion nearby while watching Holmes's actions. I followed my friend.

He walked directly to the alley entrance, where a boy, probably about ten years of age, was standing, having shifted out of the shadows upon Holmes's approach. He was dressed in rough and worn English clothing, but he was clearly foreign. And he had the family's characteristic light eyes.

"Are you waiting to hear word from Andrew?" Holmes asked gently. As I had seen before when he had dealings with those Irregulars who were his eyes and ears around London, and to whom he humorously referred at times as the Baker Street Division of the detective police force, he had a way of talking with them that was quite remarkable in both the respect that was offered and given.

The boy nodded, nervous, but making an effort to stand up straight. "What is your name?" asked Holmes.

"Luke. Andrew is my cousin."

Holmes nodded. "Luke, I have some bad news, and I need you to relay a message to Daniel. Tell him that Andrew has been killed."

The young man's eyes dropped. "I feared as much," he said softly. "Earlier, we saw a man enter the house, acting in a very strange manner. Andrew said he was the same evil man who left a bomb at your door. After a few moments, he told me to stay here, and then he crossed the street and went into the house as well. He did not return. I waited, and argued with myself as to whether or not I should follow. Sometime later, I saw a carriage coming out of the mews. It was driven by that man, the evil one. There was another man slumped inside who looked to be asleep. He was clearly *not* my cousin. I did not know what to do, and did not know where

Andrew was, so I waited. Then I saw all of you arrive, including what seemed to be the same man again who had been a passenger in the carriage. Then the police came. I still did not know enough to report to Cousin Daniel what had happened. And I waited."

I could see that he wanted to ask questions, to find out more. But he simply watched us, confident Holmes would make the next move.

"Take the message to Daniel," said my friend, his voice quiet. "Tell him that Andrew has been killed by the man that you saw, known as the Baron, and that I will have more to share with him if he will make his way to Baker Street. He will know where. We will be there in two hours."

Clearly, Holmes had nothing left to add, although the boy wanted to know more. The news had shaken him, but other than to repeat his earlier comment in a whisper, "I feared as much," he gave no other reaction. He solemnly nodded to each of us and departed, making his way down the street in the opposite direction, so as not to pass Sir Edward's house or the police congregated in front of it.

We crossed and joined the inspectors. Lanner clearly looked shaken, as he had now been initiated into a terrible club, educated by the others about what the Baron's actions and intentions meant. I was struck with the curious and incongruous thought just then that, although we got along well enough, I doubted that Lanner and I would ever be friends. It was odd, as there was no reason that we shouldn't be. We were both about the same age, and had some of the same background. He was intelligent and competent, and had certainly shown none of the disrespect toward Holmes that was apparent at times from some of his peers. And yet, there was just something about him, his current reactions towards the news about Baron Meade being the most recent instance, that I simply could not warm to.

Lestrade spoke. "Lanner has been telling us what has been done so far to locate the Baron. I must say that he seems to have left no stone unturned, so to speak, even if he was wrong to think that the man had fled the capital."

Gregson nodded. "As you and I discussed this morning, Mr. Holmes, all eyes are on the lookout for the man. The full resources of both the Yard and the Foreign Office are pulling together in harness on this."

"And yet," said Holmes, "it has been of no avail so far." Lanner started to speak, and then stopped himself. Gregson's lips tightened, and Lestrade simply narrowed his eyes. "I imply no criticism," Holmes added charitably. "I don't believe the lack of success reflects negatively in any way upon any of your efforts. Baron Meade is a different sort from what we have faced before."

"God's truth," muttered Lestrade, fishing out a cigarette.

"What next, then?" asked Gregson, glancing at the smaller man beside him. In the early days, Gregson and Lestrade had been friendly rivals, with the emphasis more on the rivalry. There was no sign of that now. There was no place for that now.

"Keep a weather eye. In the meantime, Watson and I will interview Dawson, something that I should have done sooner. I don't believe it will advance the search for the Baron one iota, but it will fill in some of the blanks in the meantime. I suspect that he can confirm some of my suppositions. Where is he being kept?"

"At the Yard," said Gregson.

"Has anyone attempted to visit him?"

Gregson merely shook his head.

"Very good. I would advise that you keep the injured men, both Sir Edward and the Earl, as well as the butler Crye, under guard and in isolation after they have been treated for their injuries."

The inspectors nodded as one, and Holmes continued. "We then plan to return to Baker Street after that. If you would be so good as to keep us informed regularly of your progress, or even the lack thereof . . . ."

With that final parting instruction, we set off on foot to find a cab.

"The Baron has been cleverer than I would have thought," said Holmes. "In spite of our efforts to the contrary, I never saw him follow us this morning to Sir Edward's residence."

"It is a pity that he has allowed his bitterness to overwhelm him."

"Quite. Until the death of his son, the man led an honorable and useful life. He was involved in many behind-the-scenes negotiations and transactions that have been of great benefit both to England and other countries within the Empire. For instance, he was vitally important in the secret give-and-take that went on in '86 concerning the Ireland Bill."

"Holmes, that was generally considered to be a fractious disaster."

"But it could have been much worse. It was Baron Meade's influence and mediation that salvaged what could be saved from the situation." He pulled out his pipe and worked on lighting it. "Of course," he continued, "the fact that he has been so involved within the workings of government has given him a level of knowledge that is dangerous to us now. For instance, he will probably have no trouble finding a way to get the idol to the very people that should not receive it."

I pondered that thought while we walked in silence, before I was prompted to comment, "Holmes, this knowledge of the Ireland Bill is yet another example of you knowing far more about something than you should, considering that you've stated in the past that you ignore facts that might crowd out something else from your brain attic."

411

"I assure you that, except for noticing it in passing in the newspapers of the time, I knew nothing specific about the Government of Ireland Bill until I was researching the particulars of the Baron's background. It was just one of a full list of valuable accomplishments in his *vitae*, a long chain that began during his university days, right up to the death of his son late last year. In fact, having identified his plot for what it was, it took a great deal of effort on my part to overcome the disbelief and outright hostility in certain quarters that came my way when I first revealed his plan."

I glanced at Holmes as we walked, finally nearing Berkeley Square, where several cabs could be seen. "And *can* he be stopped?" I finally asked.

My friend turned his head my way, his expression blank. "You know the motto of the firm, Watson. *We can but try.*"

He had said the same thing, earlier in the day following our trip to Limehouse. But now Andrew was dead, and the Baron had the idol. We would have to try harder.

Taking the second of two cabs, to the irritation of the driver of the first, we set off for Whitehall and Scotland Yard.

"Surely there is something more useful we might accomplish right now than questioning Dawson," I said, sitting back tiredly.

"What would you suggest?" asked Holmes peevishly. "For it is now up to the Yard, and the Foreign Office. Perhaps in a few hours, after we've had a chance to speak to Daniel, and begin to receive reports on the search for Baron Meade, I might see something that will be useful. It will be maddening to sit in Baker Street like a spider in the center of a web, waiting and hoping to feel the vibrations upon one of the strands, but to rush around without purpose would accomplish nothing. In the meantime, we have a free hour or so, and speaking with Dawson may help fill in a few of the unpainted corners."

We wended our way down to Piccadilly. Seeing how crowded it was, Holmes knocked and told the driver to turn down by way of St. James and so on a parallel route. We did so, immediately leaving the throngs behind us. Moving along the much quieter Pall Mall, I had no idea, not yet having met Mycroft Holmes, that we were passing the Diogenes Club at No. 78, about halfway between Marlborough Road and St. James Square, and across the street from Mycroft's lodgings. I would visit it for the first time later that year, in September, during the curious doings related to Mycroft's neighbor, Mr. Melas, and the bizarre incidents related to the Greek visitors to our shores.

It is only now that I realize Holmes must have been working closely with his brother during the search for the idol. I heard references throughout the events to meetings between Holmes, the police, and representatives of the Foreign Office, to which I was not invited. Due to his importance within the government, the older brother's connection to the events must have been certain. But during all the years since, I have never thought to ask Mycroft about it, as my subsequent and numerous meetings with the man have always been of immediate urgency relating to this or that other difficulty on hand at the time. Too, we have never had the level of friendship between us to simply sit and reminisce. And yet, on that day when Holmes and I traveled Pall Mall on the way to the Yard, I am certain that I did not observe any indication that my friend's eyes gave a single glance toward the Diogenes Club on the right as we passed. Knowing Holmes as I do, I doubt that he gave the Club a second thought just then, as it wasn't important in that moment to what we were doing.

The cabbie dropped us in front of the main door to the Yard, that rabbit's warren of buildings then occupied by the Metropolitan Police. This was a year or so before their move to their digs in the curiously handsome-looking buildings overlooking the Embankment and the Westminster Dock. Holmes strode toward the entrance, and it was a mark of his ever-growing stature within the organization that his presence was not questioned. Nor was mine as his associate. In fact, a constable held the door while respectfully touching his helmet with the other hand.

Inside, we quickly ascertained where Dawson was being held and dropped down into the dim bowels of the building. It was cold inside, and I was reminded how my former home in Kensington had felt earlier, when I stopped to inspect it and make certain that Dr. Withers' possessions had been safely delivered. Could that have only been a few hours earlier?

Holmes and I waited in a low-ceilinged gas-lit room for several long and silent moments before Dawson was led in. During that time, Holmes paced, his thoughts apparently racing, only interrupted when the prisoner arrived. The small man was unshackled, but held firmly around the arm by a burly policeman who guided him to a chair. Dawson sat and his guard left, pulling the door shut behind him.

"Cigarette?" asked Holmes, pulling one of the other empty chairs toward himself with a screech, the legs dragging over the raw stone floor, the noise echoing painfully around the brick chamber. The old man eagerly nodded, and Holmes retrieved his cigarette case from his pocket. Both he and I were still in our overcoats, although we had removed our hats. Dawson was in the same shabby clothes that he had been wearing when we discovered him in the Essex house, although his braces appeared to have been taken from him, as his pants did not seem to fit exactly right. In spite of the frigid conditions of the room, wherein our breath fogged before our faces, the little and ill-tempered man didn't appear to be discomfited. He still looked like a fairy-tale figure, a burly Rumpelstiltskin.

Holmes held out a match to the prisoner who then gratefully inhaled, consuming half the cigarette in one steady draw. He would likely need another very soon.

Dawson kept his eyes on Holmes, focusing them keenly from underneath his shaggy brows. Sometimes he would glance my way, off to the side, turning his whole body to shift his curiously fixed head, but he knew who the important one was. He had a slight foxy grin on his face, and seemed much more confident and intelligent than he had at the Earl's house, where he had then appeared to be a scattered and slightly mad eccentric. Now, he was nothing if not crafty.

"What can I do for you, gents?" he asked, dropping the very short stub of the spent cigarette to the floor with a swaggering attitude. Holmes glanced at it, still smoking, and reached out with his foot to extinguish it with a twist of his shoe.

"We've come to get some more information about what happened the day before yesterday, when Williams came to the Earl's house."

"You know all that I do," Dawson replied. "This Williams brought word that the counterfeit in the Museum had been discovered, and the Earl panicked. He had been afraid of such a thing for a long time, you know."

"The idol has surely preyed on his mind."

"That's right. For longer than you know."

"Really?"

"It's the truth. It may interest you to find out that I was with those gents that found it, back in the seventies when they went on their tour." I started to mention that Sir Edward had told us that very fact not long before, but held my tongue. It was clearly in our best interest to let the butler think that he was providing a version of the story to his benefit that we would believe.

"Right from the start," Dawson continued, "the Earl – only he wasn't the Earl then – was taken with the thing. He believes that it's magic, you see, right from when he first heard of it, and that it helps him, poor fool. When his father wanted to give it to the Museum, he nearly couldn't stand it. So it wasn't too long before he found a way to keep it."

"By having a duplicate made and swapped?"

Dawson nodded. "Exactly. A bloody copy." He glanced away from Holmes's eyes, which he had met with remarkable forthrightness up to that point, considering he wasn't telling the whole story. But he didn't know that we knew that. "What about another smoke, Guv?"

Holmes produced his cigarette case, and the process of lighting and quickly inhaling it was repeated.

"So all these years," said Holmes, "the Earl kept the real idol, believing it gave him good luck."

414

"Oh, more than that," said Dawson. "He would take it out and pray to it, or rub its belly or some such, whenever he thought he needed something. You never saw the like of it. Whether it was a business decision, or a reversal of something or other that would favor him over an enemy. It would have been silly to watch, if he didn't believe in it so much."

"And that went on, year after year?"

"It did. I was with him, even before his father died. And I must admit that there was something odd about that. The death, I mean. The old man was in the best of health. Should have lived for years and years. But the old Earl fell into a pit while walking one evening on the estate. It was a foggy night – no reason to be out. And it wasn't even where he normally walked – no reason to go there at all. Broke his neck, he did. The new Earl was broke up about it, he were. I don't think he wished any harm on his old dad, but there you go. He inherited what would have gone to his brother, if the brother had lived, and much earlier than he might have expected it."

"And did he credit the idol with that bit of good fortune as well?"

Dawson laughed, dropping the second scrap of cigarette to the floor, deliberately on the opposite side, away from Holmes's foot. He looked slyly to see if we'd noticed. "He did. He talked himself into thinking that it was doing things on its own to take care of him – doing what it thought best, whether he wanted it that way or not."

"If he believed so devoutly in the magic of the thing," asked Holmes, "then why were you allowed to know about it as well? It seems that if a man had such a magical talisman in his possession, he would do everything to protect it, including keeping it a secret from his servants."

Dawson shook his head, trying to think of an answer. "I suppose I don't know," he finally said. "I would guess because I've been around since it was found. The other servants, what few there were, certainly didn't know about it. Only me. All the time I knew him, he was never very strong, if you know of what I speak. And he was always looking for someone to give him an answer, about anything. He couldn't decide where to go or what to do, or even what to eat, and it was only getting worse. He thought that the idol was guiding him, most times. *Go left, go right. Up, down, stop, go.* It made it easier for him, somehow."

"He was doing something right. He certainly had some financial successes, did he not?"

"That he did," agreed the prisoner.

"But he wasn't the only one."

"The only one what?"

"To have financial successes along the way."

415

Dawson looked suspicious now, in a sly animal way. And rightly so. He sensed that Holmes was advancing toward a goal, but indirectly.

"I've heard that the Earl's good friend, Sir Edward Malloy, has also been quite fortunate over the years."

"Lucky, you mean. That's true enough."

"If you were with them when the idol was found, you must have known Sir Edward from long ago too."

"That's right."

"Then perhaps you'll be interested to learn about his injuries earlier today."

Dawson cocked an interested eyebrow. "Injuries? How?"

"He was attacked today by a man who broke into his home."

Dawson's eyes widened slightly for just a second before returning to their normal state. "Is he all right?"

Holmes cut his eyes toward me. "Doctor?"

"He was tortured," I said. "His arms were violently dislocated from his shoulders. There is severe damage to the tendons and ligaments. The structure of his arms will likely not be reparable. In addition, the numerous nerves in that area were likely extensively damaged." I shook my head. "I wouldn't wish it on any man. He'll be a cripple for the rest of his life, unable to make much – if any – use of his arms. And the pain will be constant and terrible."

Holmes nodded, looking back at Dawson. "Unfortunate indeed. I suppose, Dawson, that under different circumstances, you might have had to make a choice."

"What? A choice? What do you mean?"

"I neglected to mention that when Sir Edward was attacked, he was in the company of your current master, the Earl. At the Earl's house in Mayfair."

"What? You've found him then?"

"We did." Holmes toyed with the cigarette case, but made no offers.

"He's crazy, you know. The Earl. Like I told you. Any man that talks to a stone like that isn't right."

"So far he hasn't done much talking at all."

"Was he injured too?"

"He was only hit on the head. But he'll recover. Aren't you curious as to why he was there?"

"Umm, I reckon that's where he would have run when he left the house after killing Williams."

"You reckon that? Interesting, as I believe that you knew exactly where he was going. You probably gave him the idea yourself, when you sent him on his way after Williams's death."

416

"Well, then, what of it? He needed to flee. I would have taken care of things at the house, only you showed up too early. I wasn't expecting anyone. No one ever comes out to the house. It's too far, and we're long past the days when the Earl receives any visitors."

"No doubt. But as I was saying, you might have had to make a choice. Between rejoining the Earl, or switching your allegiance back to Sir Edward, following his grievous injuries."

"Switching my allegiance? Back? What are you talking about?"

"Yes, switching back. You see, we had a chance to question Sir Edward. He told us about how you were originally *his* servant, and not the Earl's. And about how he arranged for you to become associated with the Earl as his keeper, letting the Earl play at holding the 'magical' idol while he was being manipulated by Sir Edward."

"Oh, he told you that, did he?" Dawson snapped. "And what else did he share with you?" He looked again toward Holmes's hands, as if he would dearly love another cigarette, but still no presentation of one was forthcoming. Holmes had put the case away. He could keep an adversary unbalanced with the smallest of efforts.

"There has also been some mention along the way that the Earl was not the killer of Williams in that vault after all."

Dawson's eyes widened, and then a look of anger flew across his face. "What? He would accuse me? After all that I've done? Oh, he knows better than that! Let me tell you this, Mr. Detective, he'd better not be telling *that* tale, for there are a few that I could tell myself! About *them*!"

"Really," said Holmes, in a disinterested and rather non-believing voice. "I'm sure."

Holmes's apparent indifference provoked the small man. "If he's trying to sway you into putting this on me, and away from his idol-worshiping idiot friend, then he's not going to get away with it! I can tell you what really happened. All along, up and down the line, I can tell you. I was there. I saw it all."

"Really?" said Holmes again, now almost goadingly offensive, with contempt for a liar almost oozing out of that one word.

"I can. You're right. About me being there when they found it, when they were all just young men on holiday. None of them had inherited anything yet. I was there with young Sir Edward, when they all went out with the Earl's older brother. Now there was a true wastrel for you! If he had lived, he would have been a failure ten times over before he was ever thirty. He would have lost everything, and probably died a drunkard as well."

"Go on."

"At least in those days the older brother still had a bit of sense. When that old man showed up with the map, Master Jimmy didn't even care. He just laughed and ignored him. But Sir Edward – he was just Edward then – seemed interested, and he thought it would be a lark to buy it and see where it led. He's always been that way, with a sneakiness to him, getting others to waste their money and working his ways to get them to do something for his own fun. He talked Jimmy into paying the old man something, just a fraction of what was asked. Even after they had the map, Jimmy didn't care. But Edward was bored, and he had a way about him, you see. He didn't believe there was any treasure. I heard him saying so to that poor fool that had come along with them, Herbert Conner. But he wanted to do something to break up the same old day-after-day, and he managed to get Jimmy to pay for it.

"So we all set off into the desert, and we hadn't gone far before Jimmy got tired and wanted to go back. He was hot and thirsty, and he was going to call it all off. And here's the part you need to know, Mr. Detective – This is what you have to understand: The man that is trying to blame *me* for this new crime committed one of his own then, the first of all of them maybe, and I heard and saw all of it.

"It was night, and Jimmy had decided to turn everyone around and start back the next day. But my master, Edward, had, for some reason, gotten the fever by then. I don't know why. He's never believed in the magic of the idol, but he wanted to find it nonetheless. He and Jimmy began to argue quietly. Jimmy didn't want any part of it. To him it was decided – it was his money paying for the trip, and he was done. He told Edward to get out. He just wanted to drink and fall asleep, like he did every night. I heard him say so. But something he did – and I couldn't see, only hear, as I was outside the tent – something he did set my master off. I heard the sound of a blow, a heavy smack, a faint cry, and then – nothing.

"I stepped around and into the tent, where I found Edward leaning over Jimmy's body, a terrible wound on his head. My master looked up and saw me, and in that moment, he understood what I had seen and what I knew, and that from then on we had an *arrangement*, the two of us. A *connection*.

"So to cover up what he had done, he set a fire that looked accidental, and Jimmy's death was blamed on it. And I kept my silence.

"Afterwards, he wanted to keep looking, following the map, but it wasn't practical. We had to do something about the body, so we returned, and then Jimmy's father, who was still the Earl then, and his son came out. And my master Edward knew of something in young Ian that he knew he could control. He's always been like that. If he can use you, he will, and if you're dangerous to him, he'll find a way to destroy you."

418

Dawson shook his head then, with a laugh. "You probably know the rest, or can figure it out. My master managed to talk the brother, Ian, into staying and going again on the search for the idol. And then they found it! I couldn't believe it. The d---ed thing really existed!

"We managed to get it back, but by then, it was becoming obvious that Ian was fascinated with it. Too fascinated, in an odd sort of way. And so were a lot of other people as well, the locals and the ones that also believed in the thing's magic and that didn't like it that we'd looted the tomb. When it became known that we had found it, there were offers to buy it, and visits from officials trying to take possession of it. There were break-ins, and a few times we were attacked in the streets. It finally became a running battle, but we made it back to England.

"And along the way, my master Edward realized that he could now truly control Ian."

"By influencing him through the idol?" asked Holmes.

"Right."

"How did he do it?"

"Oh, simple things. Saying at first that he thought it might be suggesting some investment or other. Eventually Ian began to rely on my master, now *Sir* Edward, more and more, until such time as Sir Edward really had control over everything belonging to Ian. His money, his estate, all of it. Sir Edward used to make something of a joke about it. Often when he would give me instructions, about this or that to do with the Earl, he would refer to himself by some strange foreign word. It was *Musta . . . Musta –* "

"*Mustashar?*" asked Holmes.

Dawson looked up sharply. "That's it. Sir Edward told me that it meant 'counselor'. He would laugh and say that he was the Earl's counselor.'

Holmes nodded. "And you had been put in place to watch over the Earl, who was in fact the Earl by that time."

Dawson nodded. Holmes continued casually, "And of course this was arranged by Sir Edward when he killed Ian's father to advance him into the title."

Dawson's mouth flew open. "How – ?" he asked. "How did you know that?"

"I surmised it," said Holmes, "the same way I expect that Sir Edward killed his *own* father for much the same reasons."

Dawson inadvertently nodded, before angrily realizing what he had done. Then, deciding to acknowledge it, he said, "Well, it's all true. He did the same thing to that Conner lad and his people as well, fixing things so that he could take over what was theirs without anyone spotting it. I'll swear to it all from my own knowledge. I was there, and he had no secrets that he could keep from me. I may look old and decrepit now, but I've always been able to take care of myself. I was safe, you see. I knew what I knew, and had made arrangements for it all to come out if anything happened to me. Now, if he's going to try to throw me over and make me swing for Williams's death, then he'll pay as well."

"Oh, it won't be Sir Edward who makes you swing," said Holmes. "You've done that by your own actions. You see, I already knew that *you* were Williams's killer before we ever met with Sir Edward, and certainly before he was injured. Sir Edward never told us a thing about it. It was already apparent from the moment I inspected the vault at the Earl's Essex house."

Dawson jumped to his feet while Holmes was still speaking. As I had never sat down, I was able to take a step forward, my hand significantly at my overcoat pocket, where my pistol still rested. Holmes didn't turn a hair. He continued to sit, his head only slightly more inclined than before as he looked into the wild eyes of the small man standing before him, fists clenched and chest heaving.

"You lie!" hissed Dawson.

"Not at all. Your footprints gave you away. The Earl never approached the back of the vault where Williams was killed. You did. Later, the Earl himself confirmed my supposition, believing that you must have killed Williams because he was going to return to the Museum and inform them of the switch." Holmes leaned a bit closer to the angry man. "Is that actually why you killed him, then? Or was there another reason? Perhaps you thought that you had time to arrange things so that *both* men would be in your power."

With a roar, the butler raised his misshapen arms, intending to club them down upon my seated friend. But I had by now removed my pistol, and it was but a small effort to bring the weight of the thing down upon a specifically chosen target upon the man's misshapen head. He gave a groan and collapsed to the floor.

Only then did Holmes stand, looking down at him as if he were a pile of empty and filthy clothing. There was no need to question if I had overly injured the murderer – Holmes knew that I was quite careful. "As I said before we came here," said Holmes, "this doesn't advance us a single step toward our goal of locating the Baron or the idol. But it certainly gives us a new perspective upon Sir Edward. I wonder if he will mount a vigorous defense before his hanging, or if the grievous and relentless pain from his injuries will take all the fight out of him and make his execution a mercy?"

"Then this turned out to be a constructive accomplishment after all, while your message makes its way to Daniel in Limehouse," I added.

He nodded and stepped around the crumpled man. I leaned down and determined that his pulse was firm and strong. He would live long enough to be hanged as well.

Holmes pounded on the door, which was opened immediately. The guard looked curiously at the unconscious figure behind us, but wordlessly and without concern let us out. Holmes nodded his head back into the interrogation cell. "After he is seen to," he explained to the guard, "he can be treated as any common prisoner. He, and not the Earl, killed the man in Essex." Holmes patted his coat for his cigarette case. "He is more important, however, because he can testify as to who committed several other murders in the past. Guard him well. His testimony will be quite useful."

He found the case as he started to walk away. I nodded to the man at the cell door and followed. As we reached the corner, I heard the call, tinged with irritation rather than concern, for the prison doctor.

Chapter XX
Betrayal

Outside in the street, Holmes stopped. "Interesting," he muttered.

"What is it?"

"How one thing leads to another. We had him on shaky ground, thus manipulating him into also revealing that Sir Edward additionally murdered Herbert Conner and his family. That would have been a long shot to connect, although I suspected it."

"Indeed."

"Dawson will need to be treated carefully to tease more information out of him. Many specific details must be established. I wonder how many other deaths from the last decade or longer that he'll lay at Sir Edward's feet before all is said and done."

Holmes let two cabs go by before stepping into the street and snaring the next. Inside, we began that steady meander that would bring us back to Baker Street. We were silent the entire way, each pondering our own thoughts. As to what Holmes was thinking I cannot say, but my own mind wandered between affairs of global importance and imminent danger, and issues of more personal concern.

As we stepped up to our front door, and so on in, Holmes checked his watch. "Still a few minutes before Daniel and Micah should be arriving. They will be punctual."

"You expect both of them, then?"

"It seems likely."

And so it proved. In a bit, Mrs. Hudson led the two men into our room. Daniel was composing himself well, I thought, having just learned of the death of his brother. However, Micah seemed to be in much worse shape. His remaining eye was red, and he opened and closed his fists regularly, as if seeking an identifiable target upon which to inflict his strangling anger.

After an offer of tea was made and refused, I directed the men toward chairs by the fire. "We are sorry about the loss of your brother," I said as the two men were seated, Daniel in the basket chair, and Micah in another drawn up beside him.

"Luke told us a little about it. What can you add?"

Holmes explained his reconstruction of events – how we had learned two days earlier the Earl had fled to Mayfair with the idol, returning to stay with the man who had directed his actions for so long. He related some about Baron Meade and the man's vendetta against the British government, and how we had unfortunately led him, through our visit that morning, to Sir Edward's house. Then he told how the Baron had broken in, curious to find out our purpose, an action which had allowed him to lay his hands upon a potential weapon of much greater use to him, more valuable to his own cause than the explosives that he had forfeited several nights earlier during his arrest. Finally, he shared how Andrew had followed the Baron inside, as told to us by Luke, and had then been killed by the Baron with the stone carving when the two encountered one another.

Daniel shook his head. "Monstrous."

"This man," said Micah in a choked voice. "This *Baron*. He had nothing to do with any of this, until he involved himself? Because of *you*? And he used the idol to kill my brother?"

"That is what he said," snapped Daniel. Then, controlling himself, he asked Holmes in a softer voice, "And now what will you do?"

"The police and the Foreign Office are doing all that they can to seal the borders, in order to capture the Baron and prevent him from escaping. But we all know that he doesn't need to go anywhere to accomplish his purpose. He simply has to establish contact with John Goins."

Holmes then leaned forward, taking on that predatory expression that he had when in the middle of a case. When he was like that, he looked more like a hawk than a man, his eyes sharp and dark, and staring with hot predatory focus at his quarry. "In our previous discussion, Mr. Goins was barely mentioned. You said that he is still in this country, keeping his eyes open for just such an opportunity. Do you know where to find him?"

Daniel dropped his gaze, obviously prevaricating. "He might be anywhere. Why would I know?"

"London is not that big of a place. One might argue that your knowing is a logical conclusion. It is either him or someone else. Occam's Razor suggests that you should be able to locate him." Holmes sat back, crossing his legs and steepling his fingers before his face. "After we met this morning, and when Dr. Watson went about his own business, I asked a few questions in the right places, and found that Goins is still very much a factor in all of this. It wasn't difficult to track him down. After ten years, both his presence and purpose are no more of a secret than yours, if one just knows where and whom to ask."

"How did you know that I hadn't told you everything?"

"Why should you have told me? I wouldn't have expected it. Our paths had only just crossed, yours and mine, and then only because you brought us to your lair this morning to find out what we knew. I'm glad that you did so, as I might have remained ignorant that both you and Goins are involved. In any case, it was to our mutual advantage to agree to work together, but I certainly never believed that you didn't also have your own separate agenda, as do we. Even before I confirmed Goins's involvement, I could have listed seven different reasons, possibly even eight, that made me suspect that you knew far more than you were telling.

Daniel nodded. "As I said, he is of our family, but from a branch that traveled far long ago. His band settled in the northeastern corner of Tennessee."

"The Melungeons," said Holmes, repeating the name that he had mentioned only that morning.

"Yes. The Melungeons. Long misunderstood by those who live around them, they have guarded the secrets of our people for generations beyond counting – and there are more secrets in our past than just the idol of Heka. Our brethren in America have been the most faithful at keeping those secrets, and honoring the old ways – and also the most tenacious at defending them.

"When the idol was initially returned to England, and we tried to find a strategy to retrieve it, we sent word to various members of our family in different parts of the world, asking for help to fulfil our pledge to guard it forever. As I mentioned this morning, the group that settled in the American wilderness has long had a fascination with the Eye, and when our request for help arrived, one of their members, John Goins, responded, offering to travel to England in order to attempt the idol's rescue. He had it in his hands, but then you stopped him. We, my brothers and I, then realized that it was our responsibility. We came to England not long after, without realizing at first that John Goins and his own band had never left.

"For he had decided to find the idol for his own reasons – to use its supposed power to elevate our people to a position of power, little understanding or caring what might be done with it instead. He has never stopped looking for a way to get at it, for over a decade, even as we have kept watch as well in opposition. He has waited for the idol's reappearance at any time when it might be more easily accessible. Our paths in London have often crossed over the years, but there has always been an uneasy truce between us. Just yesterday, however, it was reported to me that he is now active again, somehow as aware as I am that there is a chance to recover the object."

"But you intend to *protect* it when it is found," said Holmes, "whereas Goins will attempt to remove it from the country as fast as he can arrange transport, in order to put it into the hands of those that will use it to incite a war."

"As you say, Mr. Holmes." Daniel cleared his throat. "This Baron, then? Is he the kind of man who can find Goins?"

"He can, especially if Goins is as accessible as I have heard. Baron Meade is not stupid. He intentionally alerted us that he has the idol. He will know that we are watching for him to make a move. Even before he began his own personal vendetta, he was quite well connected within certain circles. It has given him knowledge of how things work. Although he has forfeited those associations, there is no doubt from what I've learned of his past that he probably knows whom to seek already."

"Then we must be prepared that he will be able to approach Goins. It will not be difficult at all, as you know from your own questions. Among the right places, his location is common knowledge. A word dropped here or there will put them in touch with one another."

"You must provide to me any additional information that you hold about the man. His habits, his associates. I must know where Goins is – specifically so that I can set a watch, in addition to whatever measures you've already taken. Or instead of simply watching, I may have him arrested preemptively."

"That will do no good, Mr. Holmes. Goins is the head of the snake, and he will certainly want to carry out this thing himself, but any of his lieutenants will be able to accomplish the task if he is removed from the board. This Baron of whom you speak only has to find any one of them, and the deed is as good as done."

Holmes glanced at the man's brother, Micah, who had remained staring into the fire, tightening and loosening his fists as if he were repeatedly choking someone. "Do you agree with your brother's assessment of the situation, Micah?" asked Holmes.

Micah's eyes jerked toward Holmes. "What?"

"Do you agree that it is useless to attempt to arrest John Goins, as one way or another the Baron will find him or his men and start the idol on its journey to those who would use it?"

"What? I do not know. Why do you ask me this?"

"But surely, in the years in which you've been here, helping your brothers in this cause, you have gathered enough information to form your own opinion." His tone sharpened. "Do you or do you not think that it is worth the effort to try to stop Goins or his men from meeting up with the Baron?"

Micah set his jaw stubbornly, as if the question irritated him to the point that he would refuse to answer. He was obviously deeply upset by the death of his brother, and I wondered why Holmes kept pushing him. Soon I understood.

"The fact," Holmes continued softly, "that the idol was used to kill your brother disturbs you."

"What? What nonsense is this? Of course it disturbs me!"

425

"But possibly you are also torn?"

"What do you mean?"

"Possibly," pressed Holmes, leaning forward again, "you are of two minds on the subject."

"Eh?" said Micah, while Daniel glanced between his brother and my friend, uncertain as to where this was going.

"Two minds. You want to take vengeance against Baron Meade, the man who, just hours ago, took the idol for which you have lusted from afar for years, and used it to cruelly smash in the head of your brother, Andrew."

Micah growled softly in anger at this brutal description, but Holmes continued. "On the other hand, there is also your other task – your *secret* task."

"Mr. Holmes?" said Daniel softly, but Holmes ignored him.

"Your *other* quest, Micah," he pressed. "Why don't you tell us more about that."

"Mr. Holmes? Please. What are you saying?" Daniel was looking with growing puzzlement from Holmes to an increasingly agitated Micah.

"You know of what I speak, Micah. You really haven't hidden it very well, you know. After our meeting this morning, when you inadvertently let your feelings show about the idol, for just an instant, I was suspicious. So was Dr. Watson, for he saw it too. After we parted, when I took the time to send word to a few old acquaintances about Goins, I also asked about *you*. They confirmed what I suspected. You have been playing both sides of the fence." His voice became more dangerous. "It was easy to do while the idol was in a place where it couldn't be taken, and both camps spent years entrenched in proximity to one another, in a state of uneasy truce.

"But when word came, by way of your brother Andrew, regarding Williams's suspicious actions the day before yesterday, you suspected that something was finally happening, and you managed to notify your secret leader, thereby causing him to put his own pieces into play.

"So that is what I'm asking about, Micah. How you can accommodate your divided responsibilities? Do you choose to seek vengeance against the Baron, who killed your brother with the idol – a life for a life – or do you let him go about his business, allowing him to roam free before placing the murderous thing into the hands of John Goins, and doing whatever you can to assist so that Goins can then deliver it to those that would use it? Is the belief in the foolish and imaginary magic of a stone, and the very real war and death it will cause, worth allowing your brother to go unavenged?"

426

Daniel looked then in horror at Micah, who did not reply at all. He simply scowled at Holmes, his hands – which had been working regularly, opening and closing – now firmly pulled into dangerous fists, the flesh tight and white and bloodless, resting lightly upon his thighs. His light-colored eye blazed

"I see that my speculation isn't wrong," said Holmes. "Just how long *have* you believed in the ridiculous notion that the idol is some type of magical talisman?"

"*It is not foolish!*" the man roared, now erupting to his feet. "It has *power*! None of you can understand! The old ones knew it, and used it, and then *feared* it to the point that they finally had to hide it away. They *knew*! They knew of the secrets of old that have been lost. In those days, they channeled the energies *of the gods themselves*, as revealed to them by Heka. It was he who made the idol, to give the power to men, in defiance of the other gods. And just because it was later hidden by the weak mortals who feared it does not mean that it should not be used again!"

"Micah . . . ." said his brother faintly, his voice filled with anguish, only to be ignored.

"But it *is* tainted, you know," sneered Holmes. "This cold bloody rock, described for the gullible as a tool for using and channeling the gods' magic, was used *to kill your own brother*. The very stone is now probably still streaked with his gore and blood, the blood of your own family. How can you countenance letting it be used by Baron Meade, when Andrew died to protect it from his dark purpose?"

"The Eye is greater than this weak Englishman who now holds it. After he delivers it, my brother will be avenged, this I swear. But until then, he has his own part to play, and must fulfill his purpose. Later, when The Eye of Heka is returned, it will be purified, cleansed by the power that its possessor wields, burning through it and purging our land!" He raged like a man in a fit. "The power of *the very gods* will pour through it like lightning! Man after man will rise up with a fire inside them such as they have never known. One will inspire the next, and then dozens, and hundreds will march, and then thousands and millions! Our revenge will come!"

Micah's breathing was ragged, and there were flecks of foam bracketing his lips. He was exalted in that moment, and quite mad, and whatever veneer that had covered this had been stripped away as the emotions connected with the loss of his brother, along with the goading of Holmes, had forced him to acknowledge his perfidy. He backed up a step, knocking his chair aside. Daniel looked at him, unspeaking, his face stricken and aghast. Holmes and I were frozen as well, seeing now, raw and unmasked, the crazed passion and hatred that infected the man, and

427

imagining how it might be when multiplied and spread by and through a million other souls. Could the simple *belief* in a dead stone's mythical power, coupled with the accumulated resentment and anger of suppression and opposing viewpoints, be enough to cause such a reaction? Apparently so.

Micah's hot gaze slowly cooled into something much more dangerous, and he dropped the focus of his remaining eye toward Daniel, while the empty socket, bisected by the hideous scar, was now red and throbbing with his rapid pulse. There was no hiding the passion within him now, and neither could he cover the contempt he so obviously felt for his brother.

"How long?" asked Daniel, still seated stiffly in the basket chair. He swallowed and tried again, "How long have you betrayed us?"

"If you mean how long have I known *the truth*, for only a few months," replied Micah, his voice roughened with emotion. "Since the riots."

"Last November?" I asked. "Bloody Sunday?"

Micah turned his attention my way, his expression curling with disgust. "I saw the truth then for the first time. Ten years we've been here, my brothers and I, living amongst you. Trying to fit in and be *good citizens.*" This with a sneer and a bitter hiss. "I have watched each of those days as all of you follow the worst of the ways of men. Your women are temptresses and harlots. Your religions are ignored. Your people commit the vilest of sins, and your greed destroys you as your rich grow ever richer upon the backs of the poor."

"As one would find the same across the width and breadth of the world as well," said Holmes with a sardonic tone. "People are the same everywhere, my judgmental friend, and it has been ever thus. Those great and ancient works and structures that dot the planet were not built by happy volunteers, you know."

Micah grimaced, a look of hatred across his face. "You will not mock me, Detective. Here, with your false values, you wallow in your licentiousness, your greed, and now you defile the rest of the world that does not want you. The true ways, the *old ways*, will lead those who believe to a paradise on earth, and then to the one beyond. The Eye of Heka will let us root out what pollutes us, with fire and with blood. It simply takes one who is strong enough to wield the power, and willing to do what must be done. You, my *brother*," he continue, as if it were a barbed jibe, shooting a dark and contemptuous look at Daniel, "have been happy to wait, year after year, letting the idol of Heka *die* in an *English Museum* – " Here, his voice twisted with contempt. " – rather than make an effort to retrieve it and return it to where it belongs."

428

"The riots," interrupted Holmes, causing Micah to suddenly return to the present, from whatever hellish vision he had been seeing play out behind his eyes. "You were speaking of the events of last November. It is interesting that the Baron's rage grew out of the same event. I wonder what other ripples will return from that single day. Apparently, you and our own homegrown criminal have that much in common. What happened then that gave you your sudden change of heart?"

"I was there," said Micah, suddenly and dangerously lowering his voice. "I saw the way that your soldiers and policemen rode down their own people."

"That woman," Daniel whispered with a look of understanding flashing across his face. "It was that woman that you cared for. Something happened then. You would not say, but I could tell that she had been injured somehow – "

"You lie!" Micah cried. "It had nothing to do with her! I did not care for her, any more than this corrupt society cared for her. To let her be trampled in the panic. To let her be crippled for the rest of her life, when it had nothing to do with her. Just because she was in the wrong place – " He seemed to be watching a scene play out that none of the rest of us could visualize. Then, he refocused on Daniel. "Is this, then, my brother, the society that you would trust to keep watch over The Eye? Where you would let it remain, in their cold and dead Museum, with so many of our other stolen treasures, rather than returning it to where it can accomplish so much that is great and necessary?"

"Your John Goins did no better," said Holmes.

"He did!" countered Micah. "He has never relaxed. He has been ever vigilant!"

"Micah," said Daniel sadly, "I remember when you returned from the riot, and you were so deeply affected. But I had no idea how much. You kept it hidden from me. Still, you must see that allowing the idol to be used by evil men to ignite a war would be infinitely worse than what happened last November. Not just a square full of people, but whole countries, all swept up in the advancing flames of these devils. They have no regard for the innocent, or those who, while not actively opposing them, are yet in the way as weeds to be trampled. You know that the people in the path you are advocating want nothing more than to feed their families and raise their children in peace. Why enable those who would destroy that, thus ruining the lives of so many??

"You speak of lives ruined and destroyed? What I see are lands now ruled by others, treated as *colonies* by those who would be happy to have us abandon our past and our gods and our culture, and remain cast down forever, while they reap the benefits and wealth that is being produced from the labors of our backs – wealth that could be used for our own people.

"Yes!" he hissed angrily. "The evil shall be cast out. The Eye of Heka will give us both the power and the motivation and the reason!"

Daniel stood then, after having been sitting stiffly in his chair throughout the entire confrontation with his brother. He rose painfully, as if he had aged half-a-century in just the past few minutes. Turning and planting himself firmly before the much larger Micah, he spoke. "You are a fool, my brother. This object is neither magical in and of itself, nor will it convey any power upon a person. I had thought that you knew this truth all along, as did Andrew, and as do I, but was mistaken.

"However, set that aside. It *is* dangerous, in that it can set in motion events which will lead to misery for countless men, women, and children. And in spite of the sacred trust placed upon our family for millennia, you have chosen to turn traitor simply because your head was turned by a *madman*."

Micah started to protest, but Daniel spoke louder, his voice overriding the sputtering and beginning to ring with passion. "John Goins is an evil man to pursue this. *Evil.*

"But what saddens me most is how he provided the opportunity for you to betray your family, your duty, and your trust. What he will do, should he get the idol, will be monstrous. But what he has done to our own brother is unforgiveable. How you can assist in his cause, knowing that even now the blood of Andrew stains his purpose, is incomprehensible to me. I beg you, Micah, before it is too late. Return to yourself and your promise. Find yourself! You will do a greater service to us all by helping to *suppress* the evil influence of this thing, rather than *encouraging* its reappearance into the world." And he drew silent then, his arms hanging and hands before him, looking to see if his words had made a difference.

For a moment, I actually believed that Daniel might have influenced his brother. Micah stood there, as if considering all that Daniel said. But then, his face settled into its customary scowl, and his remaining eye seemed to slowly flame all over again with angered passion. He looked as if he wanted to speak once more, either to continue with his tirade, or perhaps loose additional words of rage personally directed at his brother, whom he had pretended to aid and serve for so long. Instead, with a wordless cry of rage that began with a small moan and grew to nearly a tearing, ripping scream, he turned upon his heel and made a dash for the door. Throwing it open, he ran down the stairs. In seconds, I heard the front door open, and then slam shut behind him.

I stood up only then, wondering why I had not done so earlier, and looked for my coat, wherein still resided my gun. Holmes held up a hand.

"Let him go, Watson," he said quietly. "At this point he can make things no worse than they already are."

And yet, having said that, Holmes himself seemed to think better of his own advice, setting himself into motion toward the door. I heard him rush downstairs, and then came the sound of the front door again being thrown open. I looked over at Daniel, but he was lost in his own thoughts, and understandably so. I assumed that Holmes was following Micah, but in a moment, I heard the front door close more quietly, and then Holmes climbed back to rejoin us.

He shook his head. "He was already gone." He walked back to where we stood by our chairs. "I had thought to follow him myself, or have one of the Irregulars do so."

I sank into my seat, while Daniel also sat and dropped his head into his hands with a groan. Then he gave a sob. My initial medical instinct was to rise again and see to his condition, but I was simply too stunned.

"Luke was waiting downstairs," Holmes added. "He saw Micah run down Baker Street to the south, but he didn't know what was taking place, so he let him go." My friend then turned toward our remaining visitor. "Sir!" he said sharply, in order to get the man's attention.

Daniel looked up at us, his eyes red and rimmed with tears. "Yes?"

"Can you tell us how to locate your brother? So that he may be followed. Will he now go to John Goins?"

The words didn't seem to have any impact for a moment, but then, an almost imperceptible nod was followed by another, and Daniel replied, "I believe so. If I make haste, I can perhaps head him off. I do not think that he will leave our home without . . . retrieving certain possessions of his own that are important to him, that are still located there, under my control. I will stop him."

"That," said Holmes, "may not be the best course. Do you know where Goins is located?"

"Only vaguely. He has maintained several lairs from where he directs his men. You think my brother will lead you to him?"

Holmes nodded. "With these new developments, Goins may well drop from sight. If we can track Micah to Goins, we may be able to monitor any upcoming meeting with Baron Meade, when the idol would be delivered."

Daniel nodded. "I understand." Holmes handed him a pad, instructing him to write down the addresses. He did so, and then climbed wearily to his feet. "I must hurry, if I am to outmaneuver him." He looked down again, and then, lifting a hand to wipe his eyes, he said, "Today, I have lost two brothers. I will do all that I can to help you find John Goins."

Holmes nodded and flipped to a new sheet, where he wrote something on a piece of paper. Then he tore it loose. "After you have located your brother, and are having him followed, do not let him know it. Send word to us here, and also to this address. It is a place with connections to the government. They will know what to do with the information, and will make good use of it, I promise you."

Daniel took the paper and, without looking at it, pressed it into a pocket. "I will do as you say, Mr. Holmes." He nodded then, almost a bow, and turned and did the same toward me. He shuffled toward the door, looking decades older than the already careworn scholar who had entered the room just a few minutes earlier. Turning once before he stepped out, he said in a low voice, "I curse the day that these Englishmen came and found the idol. It has been a threat ever since. I have given the better part of my life to prevent what my own brother is now trying to accomplish." He shook his head. "And I also curse the fools who believed in such a thing in the days of old, and those who continue to believe now and encourage others to do so."

He sighed. "Such a waste." It was so soft that I could barely hear it. Then, reaching for the door, he gently took hold of the knob, turned it as if it pained him, and then stepped through before pulling it silently shut behind him as he departed.

Chapter XXI
The Raid

Following Daniel's departure, Holmes sat for quite some time, curled into his chair, pulling on his cherry-wood pipe and gradually filling the room with a low-hanging bluish fog. Finally able to stand it no longer, alternately coughing and blinking tearfully, I stood and made my way to the tall windows overlooking Baker Street, whereupon I opened one as far as I dared, balancing the cold rush of outside air against the asphyxiating cloud.

Down below, the usual throngs made their way here and there along the pavement, some looking around alertly, others so heavily defined by their own cares and worries that they never could face up and engage the world through which they passed. Some of them made their way on their chosen directions straight and true, while others had to constantly and tiringly dance and weave either to the right or left to avoid obstacles, human or otherwise, in their paths.

They had no idea that I watched them, from my vantage just one floor above. I could have been one of the gods of old, peering down at the never-ending, and yet never-new, unfolding story of humanity. But unlike those gods, I had no way to know the specifics of each person's story, and how the separate threads of each of their lives tangled and knotted and strangled. I didn't know their names, and never would. Back before my marriage, Holmes had once told me that "life is infinitely stranger than anything which the mind of man could invent. We would not dare to conceive the things which are really mere commonplaces of existence." He and I had been sitting before the fire when he said that, in this same room we now occupied, but without any concerns before us, just two young men with bright futures having a friendly conversation. "If we could fly out of that window hand in hand," he had said, gesturing over his shoulder to this very spot upon which I stood, "hover over this great city, gently remove the roofs, and peep in at the queer things which are going on, the strange coincidences, the plannings, the cross-purposes, the wonderful chains of events, working through generations, and leading to the most *outrè* results, it would make all fiction with its conventionalities and foreseen conclusions most stale and unprofitable."

I had known he was right then, and nothing I had learned since had caused me to change my mind. But I was burdened at that moment with dread, cursed with the understanding that events were conspiring beyond

433

our control, and beyond the awareness of the people on the street below me – events that could indeed change their lives in ways that they did not yet imagine. Perhaps the old gods were standing somewhere higher still, certainly higher than that first-floor window above Baker Street with a broken-hearted doctor in it, nudging the lumbering structure that was our reality onto a jittery new course, watching this latest complication in the story, wherein the idol would be placed into the hands of those who would start an entertaining war for their jolly enjoyment. It would certainly make for some interesting events for their jaded diversion, should it come to pass.

Behind me, Holmes continued his cogitations. I had seen this before. His nets were cast, the players in this game were making their unknown moves, and there was nothing left for him to do but wait.

Yet I still wondered what we should do next. Scotland Yard and the Foreign Office were following their typically unimaginative but dogged procedures. Daniel was on his way to see about locating his brother, hoping that would provide a trail to John Goins, and he might or might not be successful. And us? Apparently we who sat and waited would also serve.

I suppose that I expected something to happen immediately, but that night, we had no word from anyone. Holmes was like a tightly strung wire, with an almost audible pitch emanating from him as he did his best to wait patiently. Finally, as I knew would happen, he began to throw on his Inverness. I offered to go with him, but he demurred. "I need you here to act as a clearinghouse for whatever information should arrive."

"And what shall I do with it?"

"Whatever you think best. If it requires action, notify someone at the Yard. They will know how to proceed. I'll make sure as I leave that several runners are downstairs, should you need them." Then he pulled on the fore-and-aft, tugging it low over his eyes, and with a grim nod departed.

I saw him intermittently over the next two days. He would stop in to curtly report that no progress had been made toward locating the Baron. On more than one occasion, Daniel came to hold a council of war, attended also by one or the other inspectors from the Yard. As I had feared, he had unfortunately been unable to find where his brother had gone – the man had apparently abandoned his treasured possessions still in Daniel's control after all – but Daniel had some of Goins's known agents under clandestine observation. So far, they were following their normal routines. "It is indicative, Mr. Holmes," he said, "that the idol hasn't yet been delivered by Baron Meade. If it had been, and if it had already left the country, there would be no reason for these men to remain here. Their

434

mission complete, they would either be packing to leave, or already be gone."

"So it is your opinion, then, that there is still hope?"

Daniel shrugged. He looked weary and bitter, but with a determined tightness to his lips that had been absent on his scholarly face just days earlier. "Who can say? But one should never lose hope, even when all is hopeless."

Lestrade, present at that particular meeting, cleared his throat, and I wasn't sure if it was due to a real need, or if he was doing so to avoid rolling his eyes at Daniel's sentiment. He is a practical man, our friend Lestrade, and talk of hope and the lack thereof sometimes rolls off him like water from his pea-jacket.

At one point, I received a note from Miss Withers, asking me to join her and her father for tea at their hotel. I considered ignoring the note altogether, but in the end sent a polite response refusing the offer.

On the second day after the events that led to Baron Meade's acquisition of the idol, Holmes was back for a while in Baker Street, and he and I were finishing lunch. Rather, I was finishing, while my friend was winding up his time in front of a still-full plate where the food had been pushed from side to side, the boundaries between items blurred and combined, but not in any way consumed or made more appetizing. I knew that Mrs. Hudson would have a judgmental sigh when she came to collect the dishes.

I was wiping my lips, anticipating perhaps a cup of hot coffee on such a cold day, when there was a frantic peal at the front bell, followed by a steady and regular ascension of someone on the stairs.

"Gregson," muttered Holmes, feeling no need to mention the thought that he hoped the man brought news.

And he did, of sorts. "That Daniel," he began. "One of his people has given us word that he tracked an associate of Goins's to someplace that none of them have ever been known to visit before. It's possible it has something to do with the idol, or perhaps a meeting is being arranged between Goins and the Baron. We're on the way there now. It isn't far. I assumed that you would both want to come with me."

He was correct, and within seconds, Holmes and I were donning protection against the bitter weather and making our way downstairs, my anticipated cup of coffee forgotten.

As we drove away in a growler, Gregson explained that we were going to Park Crescent Mews, just blocks away on the south side of Marylebone Road and Crescent Gardens. "Some of the old stables there have been converted and rented out to different people in recent years – a few for storage by merchants, when not used by nearby residents, with others taken by costermongers and such as a place to keep their wares."

"I believe that I know the location," said Holmes. "One of them was where Landers' head was found, back in '79."

Gregson looked at him with both respect and a raised eyebrow. "That's right." He gave a chuckle. "The things you know, Mr. Holmes."

My friend waved a hand. "Irrelevant. It isn't likely to have any bearing on today's business – although Goins *was* certainly in London when Landers was killed."

Gregson now raised both eyebrows. "You don't think that he – "

Holmes smiled and shook his head. "No, Gregson. Landers was undoubtedly murdered by both his brother and wife, who were obviously having an affair. It was only through the carelessness of the official force – that is to say, through unfortunate circumstances in the way that the evidence was handled – that they were able to get away with it at all. I was more than satisfied at the time that they were the guilty parties, but it was never my case. In any event, I believe that justice was served in the end."

Gregson formed a speculative expression. "It was. An anonymous letter detailing some of the brother's other unsavory activities was delivered to the murdered man's employer, Everett, himself a killer many times over, throwing them all into such an argument that Everett ended up killing the wife and brother, only to be later hanged himself, after an anonymous tip led to *his* arrest – a neatly constructed anonymous letter, as I recall."

"And thus justice was served," said Holmes. "But I shall be surprised indeed if the vault where Landers' head was found turns out to be the same as that possibly being used by Goins."

And such was the case. After mention of the old murder, we had ridden in silence until arriving at our destination, each with our own thoughts. I saw Gregson glance covertly at Holmes several times throughout the remaining minutes of the journey, as if preventing himself from asking a question, while the consulting detective simply leaned forward, his chin resting upon his folded hands that were themselves supported by his stick.

I was surprised when we did not continue to the passage in question, but rather turned into Brunswick Place, a block north and west of our goal. The reason was soon revealed, as we were met there by a constable, standing with a youth, luckily for his sake better dressed for the cold than I was.

"What's the story?" asked Gregson as we all huddled in a doorway out of the wind.

The constable jerked a thumb toward the lad. "This is Benjamin. He's one of these lads what works for Daniel." The boy was about twelve, and had a very intelligent look about him. Incidentally, he seemed to be constantly laughing at some joke known only to himself. As we talked, I understood that this was his normal attitude when meeting the world.

"He's been helping with us these last few days," said the constable. "He found me this morning to let us know that one of Goins's associates was seen going to this location twice last night, one trip right after the other, and each visit with a loaded cart. He originated at the rooming house that some of this Goins's men have been using in Stepney.

"We've been keeping an eye on that house as well, but no sign of Goins, or anything strange from the other men who live there. Benjamin here was watching the Stepney house last night when he saw one of those men come out and begin loading the cart, carrying out boxes. Both times the man came here, and Benjamin followed him, watching while he unlocked the door to one of the old stables in the mews and carried in the items. He had no help at either place, so each trip took an hour or so to load and then unload. It started about nine o'clock and took a good portion of the night. After he finished carrying the last of it inside, he locked up and returned to Stepney, where he appears to have settled in."

Gregson frowned. "The lad could have told us all that himself." Looking at the boy, he said, "Are you mute?"

With a grin, Benjamin, just shook his head.

"Then why are we just now hearing about it this morning?"

The constable started to answer for him, but stopped himself, nodding toward Benjamin, who then responded in most excellent English. "I waited to find out what was happening before I went looking for one of the policemen. I did not want to summon him for no reason. I saw that the man was finished, after he had returned to Stepney and put away the cart and horse. He went inside, lit a lamp in the upstairs bedroom, and then put it out again in a few minutes. That is when I told someone." He nodded to the constable beside him, a mischievous light in his eyes.

"Quite right," rumbled the constable.

"You could have found someone sooner," Gregson grumbled. "What if the man had done something more suspicious?"

"That was not my task," said Benjamin. He didn't seem to be intimidated by the inspector in the least. "I was supposed to keep watch on these men to see if there was any sign that they were arranging a meeting with the Englishman who has the idol. I saw no meeting. While I did realize that his behavior was strange, I felt that I could learn more if I stayed with him. On both trips, I watched him carefully, and he traveled so slowly, perhaps to avoid attention, that I was able to keep up with him each time.

"It did not seem worthy of finding and telling the policeman then. We do not have a great quantity of our own people here to help us, and just then there was no one else that I could call upon to assist me."

"Do I take it," interrupted Holmes, "that you are the last of the five people who are here to keep watch over The Eye? That group being Daniel, Andrew who is dead, Micah who has betrayed you, the other boy Luke, and yourself?"

The smile was wiped from Benjamin's face. "That is true."

Gregson snorted. "We were led to believe that Daniel had a true organization in place here. Do you mean to tell me that he has been carrying out his part with the aid of just two children, both of whom are definitely known to the brother who went over to the other side, and probably to all the rest of John Goins's people as well?"

"It would seem so," said Holmes.

"Are there not any others that Daniel could have called upon?" asked the inspector.

"There are other brothers and cousins," answered the boy. "But not here. They are involved in the family rug business. I am ashamed to admit that it was never truly believed, at least not by some of them, that guarding the idol was ever really necessary, or would require more than the few who had been in England these last years to fulfill our duty.

"And you and Luke?" I asked. "You were a baby when it was brought here. Luke probably wasn't even born yet."

"Sometimes one or the other family member sends a young man such as myself to assist cousin Daniel, as a part of our greater education." There seemed to be no irony in Benjamin's assertion that he was already a young man.

"Heavens preserve us," muttered Gregson. "How much has been missed because we were relying on Daniel's help, and the only foot soldiers that he commanded were kiddies?"

The constable interjected. "The lad has proven to be a rather sharp individual – "

"There has been nothing to see," interrupted Benjamin patiently, not angry, but not smiling now either. "I have made no errors in judgment. The man that I was following did not seem to be doing anything illegal, and nothing that appeared to be related to either meeting the Englishman or obtaining the idol. It was simply strange. However, it may only appear that way because we do not know his true purpose. Possibly he has simply been moving boxes of laundry."

Gregson's eyes narrowed. "You would joke about it?"

438

The young fellow shook his head earnestly, but his eyes now had regained their impish flicker. "Oh, no, sir. Not at all."

"Then what made you think that it might be laundry?" Gregson was clearly trying to balance his impatience at the idea that we might be on a wild goose chase with the knowledge that something atypical had indeed happened.

"I did not really mean that," said the boy quietly, only now seeming to realize that the inspector did not have a sense of humor.

"Did you try to get a look at them? At the parcels the man was moving?"

"Not at all. I did not want to reveal myself, or to be caught looking into one of them when the man returned from inside for another to carry."

Gregson nodded. "And you didn't try to see inside the building, either?"

"No. I do not think that would have been wise."

The inspector shook his head and looked addressed the constable. "Are the men ready?"

"They are."

"Well, I've got the warrant. You," he said to Benjamin. "I suppose you'll stay to report on what we find to Daniel. But keep out of the way."

"Most assuredly, sir," was the reply.

Gregson turned away with a disgusted snort, walking in front of us and back into Marylebone Road. He raised a hand, and almost magically a plethora of officers seemed to appear out of the shadows. He assigned positions to them, some to circle around and come up the mews from the south. Confirming from one that there was no sign of anyone around our destination, he set a time five minutes hence when all would move forward.

Then, nodding to Holmes and me, we waited in silence until it was time to begin. It passed quickly, although I found my mind wandering as I glanced at the early afternoon passers-by, especially the occasional married couples. I wrenched my thoughts back to our purpose as Gregson looked at his watch, put it away, and waved us into motion.

We set off, rounding the corner and walking quickly up to the third door on the right, painted black like all the rest. "Not the Landers vault," whispered Holmes as one of the constables paced up with a pair of long-handled bolt cutters, snipping through the strengthened steel of the padlock as if it were a rotten vegetable marrow. The hasp was thrown back, and the inspector and one of the constables cautiously entered the chamber.

As I stepped forward, I looked right and left, seeing that the doors to each vault along the row were all double wide, but with some wider than others. Our destination was one of the more narrow doorways. The buildings themselves were low, only two stories, and all of dissimilar styles that stretched side-by-side down the west side of the lane. They had clearly been built to service the adjacent houses behind them in Harley Street, or perhaps the larger and more auspicious homes in Park Crescent to the east.

Just after the inspector and the constable had entered without fanfare, Holmes and I joined them. Although the structure had been converted for storage, it still had the musty reminder that it had once been a stable. It was quite dark after stepping in from the cold sunshine outside, and I was thankful that someone had had the sense to bring lanterns. There were nearly a dozen of us all told, and the chamber quickly had a crowded feeling. "Open up those cartons," said Gregson, gesturing left and right.

One of the constables had found another pair of lanterns hanging on the wall, and soon the room was well lit indeed. I could see now the plain brick floors and walls. All around us, stacked in some places higher than our heads, were boxes of varying sizes, but most two or three feet to each side.

Several were being opened by different men simultaneously, and we moved up to see into the closest one. Gregson reached in before I could tell what was inside and took hold of something. There was a metallic clink.

Withdrawing his arm, he pulled out a great silver serving tray. As the light reflected from it, I could distinguish something engraved on the surface, but I couldn't make out any details. Setting it on a nearby pile of cartons, Gregson reached in again and grasped a large silver pitcher by the spout. It was somewhat tarnished, but one could detect that it was very heavy from the effort that he made to support it.

"It's the same in these boxes, Inspector," said one of the constables, holding up a handful of silver forks, their handles edged in what appeared to be gold.

"What is all this?" asked Gregson, frankly puzzled. He looked around until he found Holmes. "There's far too many boxes here to have just been brought in last night's three loads."

"That is correct, Inspector," piped up Benjamin from the doorway.

"If they're all full of silver and plate, there must be a fortune in here."

"I think you'll find," said Holmes, opening yet another box to reveal many silver cups, "that this is the accumulated loot from all of the burglaries over the past year or so that have focused only on silver items." He placed the cup he was holding back in the box, where it made a muffled ringing sound. Then he shifted that box aside and was preparing to open the one underneath it when Benjamin suddenly cried from outside, "Inspector! It's him! It's the man from last night!"

440

We seemed to be frozen for just a moment before we all managed to make ourselves move. There was a confused pushing amongst the men inside before Gregson and I broke free and made it out to where the boy was waiting. We were immediately joined by Holmes. We looked left and right before seeing a man, sitting on a cart and holding the reins of a tired looking beast hitched to it, farther down the mews to the south. Even as we saw him, he sat up abruptly and flicked the reins before seeming to realize with the same breath that it would do him no good – should the weary old horse be goaded into the motion that he so urgently needed to effect his escape, the only direction that he had to go would be toward us. There was no easy way in the narrow mews to turn around. Therefore his only choice was to jump down from the cart and flee by foot. And that is precisely what he did.

The mews curved to the right and out of sight, and he was instantly beyond our view. Even as Gregson was yelling, "After him!" young Benjamin was already springing into motion. I was reminded of the sudden burst of speed shown by a rabbit when one comes upon it unawares, disappearing in the distance with its ears laid back flat in what seems to be only three or four powerful kicks from its back feet before it's gone.

We followed as quickly as we could, and thankfully didn't have to go far. Rounding the curve, we found that somehow Benjamin had caught the man, tripped him up, and was now sitting astride his legs, contriving to keep him from either rising or rolling over. Our quarry, not a very big fellow, was thrashing from side to side, but his face was solidly pushed in the accumulated detritus at the side of the lane, where it remained until he was hauled to his feet effortlessly by two of Gregson's biggest officers.

Benjamin hopped up with a nimble bounce, a big grin on his face. Gregson clapped him on the shoulder while catching his breath – something that I was trying to do as well. Holmes seemed to have already recovered, as he was stepping around us to get a look at our prisoner in the face.

"Good job, lad!" puffed Gregson, his big fat hand steadying itself on Benjamin's slender frame. Meanwhile, I was watching the captive as he glared at Holmes, eyes narrowed, He would dearly have loved to try and make another attempt at escape, but with his arms solidly gripped, he was going nowhere.

He was short and wiry, and as near as I could tell, somewhere around thirty years of age. He was wearing very conventional clothing, and except for his features, particularly a pair of notably light-colored eyes, he would have looked like any working-class Englishman.

"Well?" wheezed Gregson. "What do you have to say for yourself?"

441

The man shook his head. "I have done nothing. I was simply waiting for you to move out of my way so that I could drive on through to Marylebone Road."

Gregson smiled and shook his head. "No good, my friend. If that's all it was, then why did you run? That won't do. This lad – " and he nodded toward Benjamin, while squeezing his shoulder " – saw you bringing some of those boxes here last night. Isn't that right?"

Now the merriment that had always seemed to be uppermost in the boy's expression was gone, replaced by something quite serious indeed. "That is so, Inspector. Both trips."

The man scowled. "You would betray us to *them*?" he hissed.

"You are betraying all of us to an evil purpose," replied Benjamin without hesitation.

"Bah, you know nothing! You are but a child."

"Are you going to tell us?" asked Gregson.

"I have nothing to say to you."

"Perhaps not," drawled Holmes, crossing his arms, "but I fancy we can infer a bit. Clearly the items you have been collecting here are the accumulated loot from the silver robberies. A little sideline, perhaps, while you and your brethren passed the time here in England, waiting for something to happen in relation to The Eye of Heka?"

At the mention of the idol, the man's expression went rapidly from surprise to anger to a complete blank. "I know nothing of what you say," he replied.

"Oh, of course you do. It would be a waste of time to pretend otherwise. My only question is whether John Goins is aware of this activity and approves of it, or if you are carrying this out without his knowledge."

That was what it took to make a fleeting look of fear pulse across the man's face, before he attempted to return to that state of neutrality he had shown just seconds earlier.

"Ah, then Goins is *not* aware of your treasure hoard. Interesting. Perhaps he favors a severe approach along the lines of that espoused by the Mahdi a few years ago. Let me see now – what is the punishment for a thief? Why yes, I believe it involves the cutting off of your hands. That should make things a bit difficult for you while breaking rocks in Her Majesty's Prison on Dartmoor."

The man swallowed then, clearly trying to catch up on just how things could have gone so badly for him in such a short space of time. "Stealing from such as you is not stealing," he rationalized, with almost a whine in his voice.

"Are you trying to convince *us*? Well, that is one interpretation, I suppose," said Holmes. "Perhaps Goins would have even agreed with you

442

and approved. That is, if he had known about it to begin with, and if you had intended to cut him in for a share. As it is, I suspect that he may not be so understanding, as I have the impression that he doesn't know about your extracurricular enterprise. What do you think, Gregson? Shall we send a message to Goins and ask him?"

"No!" cried the prisoner, wrenching from side to side and surprising the constables who grasped his arms, this new fear breaking past his control. "Please! You mustn't!"

"Indeed? And why not?"

"He will . . . you don't understand. He will be . . . *displeased!* He always insists that the reason for our being here in this awful place is the idol, and that we should be completely devoted to its rescue, and that there should be no distractions."

"Is that so?" asked Gregson. "Well, I'm thinking more and more that we should get in touch with this Mr. Goins. It's the least that we can do, seeing as how he might want to arrange for your defense when the case comes to trial."

"No, please!" the man cried. "He must not know!" He seemed to be collapsing in front of us. How quickly he had been reduced.

"I think that he will know, one way or the other. What is your name?"

"Abraham."

Gregson said nothing for a while. Then, "Well, Abraham, perhaps we can work out an arrangement. That is, if you're forthcoming with us about Goins's plans for the idol."

"What?" A suspicious look came into his eyes. "I know nothing of his plans." He wasn't a very skilled liar.

Gregson snorted. "I'm not going to waste my time, Mr. Abraham. Take him to the Yard. And keep hold of him – he'll definitely be trying to get away."

The man seemed divided, as if he wanted to stay there and tell more, and yet would not – or *could* not. One of the constables produced his darbies and shackled the prisoner, who was led back up the street toward his cart and the cache of stolen silver. Gregson pounded Benjamin on the shoulder with enthusiasm, now completely won over now by the enthusiastic lad. "Not exactly the break we were looking for, Mr. Holmes, but not too bad of a haul. Not too bad at all."

Holmes nodded, but he worried at a fingernail, clearly disappointed that this encounter hadn't advanced us any further toward locating Baron Meade and the sculpture. I stood to one side, with very little to do, as Holmes went back inside and puttered around amongst the boxes while the police organized their removal. Soon, several wagons were arranged to carry the loot back to the Yard, while Gregson and a couple of constables departed for the same location in a growler.

As I watched the cartons and boxes being systematically loaded with a military-like efficiency, as ants divide a morsel of food and transport it back to their lair, Holmes walked up to me, clearly not happy. "Benjamin has gone to report to Daniel," he said. I realized that I hadn't seen the boy leave. "While this is certainly a coup for Gregson, and will close the books on a long list of robberies, I had certainly hoped for more. But perhaps this will be a wedge that we can use to pry out some detail of Goins's plan. I'm going to follow Gregson to the Yard for the interrogation. Do you wish to join me?"

I had already decided that I would rather return to Baker Street. I didn't see anything that I could add to the situation.

"Very well," said Holmes. "I should be back in a few hours." And with that, he rejoined the group that was loading the final boxes from the shed. In a few moments, everyone would be gone, and there would be no signs that anything amiss had taken place here.

I meandered slowly back along Marylebone Road, craving the time alone, even while feeling the cold working up from the ground. The wind was out of the west, and although I was facing it, there was a distinct feeling of the promise of warmth to it. Suddenly, for no reason, I was reminded of a few days earlier, when I had made my way along the Serpentine into a much stronger breeze. Why did that suddenly feel as if it were so long ago, as if it were already an ancient memory, packed away in a tin box and not to be entirely or objectively trusted?

I reached the Baker Street corner, and turned toward 221. Thoughts of my late wife were yet again dancing in the periphery of my awareness, but I pushed them back. It would be too easy to return to my chair and spend the rest of the afternoon in despondency. Instead, as I put my key into the door, I resolved to do something more useful.

In passing, I asked Mrs. Hudson for tea, and then settled in upstairs with my journal, attempting to list the facts of the case while they were still fresh in my mind, and hoping that doing so would reveal something that had been missed. However, while I was successful in recalling what had happened point-by-point over the past week, I didn't gain any new insight.

I was just setting aside my labors when I heard Holmes return. He climbed the stairs slowly, and was clearly in a pensive mood as he sat down across from me, reaching for his pipe.

Before I could ask, he said, "Abraham was convinced of the very real threat that his betrayal of Goins's ideals would be made known, one way or the other, if he didn't cooperate. He gave us several details regarding

444

the silver thefts, which he has been carrying out with a small gang that he organized on his own, completely separate from the other half-dozen men here with Goins.

"He provided names, and the police will be picking them up as quickly as they can. It was really well done – Abraham found skilled cracksmen from very separate walks of life, and brought them together for specific jobs. One is a sailor, who is not even in London at any certain time, and therefore would not necessarily be associated with the crimes. Enough of the lot, the common stuff, was fenced from the older robberies, after the initial efforts to locate it had died down, in order to pay the members of the gang for participating, but Abraham was hoarding the greater part of it to sell later – and what a hoard it was! – believing that the wait for the idol would go on for a long time, possibly years. Suddenly he was out of time, as Goins now seems to believe that he will soon have it.

"When it was confirmed to him by his master that the talisman is in motion, Abraham was prompted to start consolidating the silver from his various rat holes, caching it in one place, while he desperately tried to figure out how to sell it quickly. He is expecting to be leaving England at any time, once Goins has The Eye and gives the order to depart. Goins has in fact been contacted by the Baron, as we feared, but there is a great deal of distrust between the two parties, especially on Goins's side. He has said, according to Abraham, that the actions of a traitor to his country, as Baron Meade is correctly understood to be, cannot be accepted at face value. Goins therefore believes that the Baron's offer must be studied before an agreement between them can be reached."

"Still, it must be just a matter of time," I said. "Until Goins receives the idol. I'm surprised that he would have waited so long already before taking it."

"Apparently he suspects a trap, and he also wants to verify the Baron's incredible assertions that he really wishes to bring destruction upon England. It shouldn't take long, and as Goins *is* desperate to finally get it, he'll certainly accept the Baron's offer soon."

"I don't suppose Baron Meade is trying to sell it. I expect that he's simply offering it to him, *gratis.*"

"Quite. That is doubtless part of what Goins cannot understand, and thus can't bring himself to trust. He doesn't realize yet that the Baron really wants is to do as much damage to this country as possible."

"And so what can we do?"

Holmes sighed. "What we're already doing. Wait. Hope. Try. The police and agents of the government are looking everywhere. I have my own force on the lookout – the Irregulars, and others. What is left of

445

Daniel's group may be small, but it must not be discounted – look at what Benjamin was able to accomplish today."

He became withdrawn. I thought that he might say something else, and I tried to think of a question to continue the conversation, but there was nothing else to say or do. We would have to wait for word to come, one way or the other. We could only hope that it wouldn't be a notification that the idol was on a ship bound beyond our reach.

Chapter XXII
An Opportunity

I considered other times like this, when Holmes had set himself to wait, as there was nothing else to accomplish until some way forward presented itself. Sometimes he would approach such a situation patiently. Others would cause ever-increasing frustration, with sudden bursts of energy and impatience and pacing. Occasionally he would distract himself with chemical experiments, treating the current problem and its awaited solution as just another observable reaction that must percolate and conclude in its own time.

Once in a while, when a case had a long period of waiting that involved setting it on the back burner, he would take on additional unrelated investigations. These were never hard to come by. Most days, there were numerous rings of our front bell as people brought him their problems. Often these visits weren't worth mentioning, reporting or recording for posterity, as my friend would simply listen to the caller's problem, offer his suggestions, and then pocket his fee. Only occasionally would he have to get up and move about and see things for himself. As his fame grew, and the puzzles brought before him became more complex, there was more moving around, but that didn't stop the regular callers who came seeking help from that man in Baker Street who was even then becoming something of a living legend.

Holmes always had some ten or twelve cases on hand at any given time, overlapping and twisting like threads in a tangled knot. I wondered what he would do now if, while he was deep in contemplating the various what's and where's of the current crisis, a new case were to present itself for his consideration.

I thought for a moment that I might have a chance to find that out, as late that afternoon I noticed a hansom turn out of the flow of traffic and stop before our door. The flash of a woman's dress was visible as she extricated herself from within, and I pondered, if only for a brief second, what her business might be. And then, the woman turned, looked up, saw me, and I recognized her. It was Miss Withers, calling here at Baker Street. She gave a half smile, but no other acknowledgement, turning instead to the door. Seconds later, the bell rang, and I heard Holmes harrumph in his chair behind me.

Without turning, my mind working furiously, I said flatly, "It is Miss Withers," as if that explained it all. And I suppose that it did.

Out of the corner of my I eye, I observed that Holmes turned his head, but the angle was wrong for me to see him well, or to discover his expression. Then he uncurled from the chair and stood, turning to face me directly, showing as much surprise as he ever did. The beginnings of a smile started to form at my discomfort, in spite of the fact that just a moment before, he had been furiously pondering those events that might lead to a global war.

"Holmes," I said, a low note of warning in my voice. I was not in the mood for his pawky teasing. He had long realized that Miss Withers had set her cap for me, and it amused his odd sense of humor to think of my discomfort. A man with his disregard for the social niceties could never understand the impropriety or unpleasantness of her suggestions that she and I ought to consider a future together. It seemed to do no good to further explain to Holmes, who worked so hard to conceal the fact that he had emotions like the rest of us, that I was still too heartbroken over my loss to even consider such a thing?

It was all for naught as two sets of footsteps, one light, and the other solid and steady, reached the top of the stairs, and there was a knock on the door. "Come!" called Holmes firmly, and Mrs. Hudson allowed Miss Withers to enter.

As our landlady pulled the door shut, she gave me a curious look. Was she also aware of the awkwardness of this visit? Had Holmes been gossiping with her about my situation? No answers were forthcoming as Mrs. Hudson vanished from sight.

Miss Withers looked curiously at Holmes, as did he toward her. I suddenly remembered that this was their first meeting, although each had heard something of the other. Holmes was frankly watchful, almost to the point of rudeness. She, on the other hand, had a neutral look toward him, although there were unconcealed flashes of what must certainly be disdain in her slightly narrowed eyes.

Holmes politely identified himself, and she likewise. I realized that I should have made the introductions, but I had forgotten to speak. To make up for my lapse, I stepped forward and offered Miss Withers a path to the basket chair before our fire.

Behind her as she passed, Holmes offered the barest of an impish grin, which vanished instantly once he knew that I had seen it. "If you'll excuse me," he said, "I will retire so that you can visit." He stepped over and started to reach for his violin, but as I imparted a questioning, "Holmes?" This encounter would not go easier while trying to talk over his violin practice. He turned, saw my expression, and instead resumed his original course to depart. He crossed the few steps to his own room and closed the door, *sans* musical accompaniment.

448

She watched him go impassively, and then turned back to me. "Shall we sit?" she asked, taking control.

In our chairs, I asked if she would care for any tea, but she stated that she had introduced herself downstairs to Mrs. Hudson, who had made the same offer, which she had refused. I nodded, and then we fell into a momentary and increasingly awkward silence, which gradually coalesced into a knowing smile upon her face.

"You didn't accept my invitation to tea."

"My apologies. Holmes and I are involved in a rather complicated investigation at the moment."

She glanced at his door, and then around the room. "I see. I am sorry," she continued, "that I missed your visit the other day at the hotel. Father should have let me know that you were there."

"That's quite all right," I said, recalling the quiet conversation that seemed to have occurred so long ago now. "You were no doubt weary from the events the previous day, when your father was – "

"When he was *shot!*" she finished. Her mouth tightened. "Still, I would have liked to have joined you both, as I believe that I would have had something constructive to offer." I speculated as to her meaning, but she quickly answered my unspoken question. "I know, you see," she related, "what it was that you and my father discussed. It is really no different than what I had broached to you earlier."

I nodded, uncertain as to what else to do.

She glanced again around the room, her eyes narrowing further at the tables and shelves so full of odd curios and stacks of documents. I, who knew the tales behind many of the unusual items there, but nothing about some of the others, could only imagine how it must look to someone who was seeing it for the very first time. Still, I was quite used to it, and thought nothing of it any longer.

"Your own home in Kensington had none of this clutter," she said. "Is all of this Mr. Holmes's, or is some of it yours?"

"A portion of it belongs to me," I said. "Some of the books. The portraits of General Gordon and Reverend Beecher." I gestured with my head. "That is my desk there, and most of what is upon it is mine."

"Most? Does Mr. Holmes even make use of your own desk?"

"You must remember that I've only been back here for a few weeks," I said. "When I . . . when I married, I left some things behind, and now that I've returned, I assume that I will resume ownership of them, although truth be told, I can take or leave much of it. Some of my other personal possessions, things that are more important to me, are upstairs in my own bedroom."

449

She nodded. "You left behind a great deal in Kensington. Abandoned it, really. But I did notice that nothing of a truly personal nature was forgotten there." She looked more intently then, her eyes boring in. "You took items related to your late wife, I suppose."

I nodded, my throat suddenly tight. I wanted to respond *Of course*, but could not. She went on. "It isn't unusual, you know. For you to feel this way. That is the kind of man you are. I know that you loved her. You still do. I can see it in your face. Some marriages are just for convenience – on both sides of a bargain. But others are true partnerships. It's obvious that yours was that way."

"Miss Withers – " I started – she really had no business addressing me on this subject – but she interrupted me.

"I understand." She began to speak more hurriedly, and for the first time, I noticed a desperate tone in her voice, as if she had finally begun to realize she might lose this argument, and was attempting to overwhelm my objections with one overwhelming plea that would drown them. "I truly do, John. But as you've just learned from going through the death of your wife, life is short and precious. It shouldn't be wasted. Not even a bit of it because of some meaningless rule or custom that says propriety must be satisfied."

"Miss Withers – " I tried again, but to no avail.

She leaned forward, her voice lowering with greater intensity. "I know how *I* feel about *you*! You will also come to feel that way about me, if you don't already. You *will!* I believe that you already do, although you cannot make yourself admit it to me yet."

"Miss Withers," I interrupted, rather harshly. "Miss Withers. You simply do not understand!"

She stood up suddenly then, surprising me, her face suddenly flooded with anger. "Don't call me '*Miss Withers*'," she snapped, "as if it can be placed as a barrier of formality that you suddenly throw up between us!" Her fists were tight, the knuckles white and her arms were pressed flat against her sides. "I know what I want, John! There is no need to waste more time!"

I saw something there that I hadn't witnessed before. I had seen her beauty, and her obvious intelligence. But did I detect, perhaps, just a spark of mania? Or worse. "*Miss Withers*," I said again pointedly, and then softened my voice. I considered standing to face her eye to eye, but chose to remain seated. I willed myself to relax. Taking a deep breath, I said, "Miss Withers. It's not about propriety, as you said. It's not that at all, I assure you. You are a wonderful girl . . . ."

She gave a little involuntary sob in her throat then, and realizing that I had heard it, clenched her jaw. I continued. "You are strong.

Independent," I continued. "A worthy partner for some man with whom you can face life together. But, Miss Withers." I paused to make certain she was listening. "You simply have to understand. I don't know any other way to tell you. I loved my wife. I *still* love her. Painfully so. So much that it threatens to . . . to *twist* me apart inside." I threw up my hands then, and finally I had to stand too. "I simply don't feel that way about you. I simply don't."

She started to object, but I continued, now almost harshly. "And I won't." As a doctor, I recognized that sometimes the treatment must be harsh and swift, and regretted that I had played the gentleman for too long, avoiding doing something any sooner to prevent or entirely avoid this confrontation now. "I'm not sure what you see in me. Perhaps I remind you of your father in some way. He's a good man. You may be recalling when you saw *his* pain when he lost your mother, and believe that the quickest remedy for me will do the most good. But that is not what I want.

"You are a lovely girl," I said gently, "but I doubt that I shall ever marry again. That's it then, really. I've come to that realization, and it's not fair to let you think for a minute that there is a chance otherwise. Someday I may regret it." I lifted my arm and turned over a hand. "But that . . . but that is how I feel. I can't tell you any more plainly than that. You have to listen. You simply must."

I had nothing left to add, but kept my gaze locked with hers, trying to make her accept it. Then she finally seemed to let her face change just a bit, going from a terrible intensity to something more puzzled, as if this place, this ending, was truly something she had never contemplated. She began to look like a lost child.

"Father told me that he spoke to you at the hotel, and what he said," she whispered softly. "He thought that you were coming around."

"I'm sorry."

"And then today, when I went to the Kensington house to check on the deliveries, a boy from a neighboring house introduced himself – "

"Lyndon Parker, perhaps."

"I believe so. He said that you had been back for a visit the other day. I thought . . . I thought that you were having second thoughts. That you were feeling sentimental, perhaps. That you finally understood the opportunity, and that you might be considering . . . ."

"Did your father not tell you that part?" I interrupted. "That he had simply asked me to check the house and make sure that all was well after your possessions had been delivered?"

"No. No, he didn't tell me." She dropped back into her chair. "I thought that you were changing your mind." She looked back up at me then, and a single tear was pooling in the corner of an eye. "The house

451

seems so empty. I sat in the front parlor before I came here, thinking how it could be a home for all of us – father as well," she said. "So many plans." The tear chose that moment to break free and roll down her cheek.

I was trying to imagine how she could have thought that she and I would live there as a family with her father, but before the idea had progressed very far, she spoke again, this time her voice taking on a ragged edge. "I should have known," she said, sinking back into her chair. "You only went back there because you were *asked* to go. You wouldn't have wanted to go on you own, would you? Any more than father wanted to keep our home when mother died – the only home I had ever known, where mother and I had lived when he was away in the Army. After she died, he was too weak to be able to stay there, and you're too weak now!

"It is just a place of death now to you," she continued, almost talking to herself, rocking slightly. "That's all. It has even taken on the smell of death, you know. It hangs in the air there. I noticed it as I sat there today. A foul, creeping odor that I hadn't ever noticed before. From *her!* The one you're still tied to, even after she's gone. It seemed to waft up from the very floorboards underneath me! It – "

At that moment, when she seemed to be building toward some sort of crisis or fit, she was abruptly interrupted, when we were both shocked by Holmes's door, which flew open as he stepped through, brusquely stating, "Miss Withers! About that odor . . . ."

She looked at him in complete surprise, while I turned on my heel. "Holmes!" I cried. "This is intolerable. Have you been listening to our private conversation?"

"Watson," he said, waving me aside, "would you have me sit in there with my fingers in my ears whilst mumbling nursery rhymes?" He stepped briskly toward us until he was directly in front of Miss Withers, planting his feet on the bear-skin hearth rug. "The *odor*, Miss Withers. I give you credit for not imagining it. Describe it, please."

"What? Are you mad?" She glanced toward me, as if for guidance, and then looked back at him with what could only be expressed at best as dislike.

"Not at all. What you tell me now may be the confirmation of a long-shot of an idea that suddenly coalesced and expressed itself within my mind. Please describe the odor. And be quite clinical. I assure you that your choice of words will not shock either the Doctor or myself."

She rose to her feet, moving to stand beside me, facing Holmes squarely while looking up at his greater height with an antagonistic bend to her back. "Describe it, Mr. Holmes?" She turned her head quickly toward me, and her eyes flashed with a bitter anger. "Then I can only say it strongly reminded me of a horse paddock. A filthy one, long uncleaned."

She then pivoted completely in my direction, with anger throbbing in her voice. "That is your house of death, *Doctor*, with its smell of filth!"

I dropped my gaze while Holmes smiled and nodded, seeming to be oblivious to her tone. "Exactly. Would you say, perhaps, that it was an odor reminiscent of *ammonia*?"

My eyes widened at this statement. Surely Holmes couldn't think that – It wasn't possible. Baron Meade could never be so bold, or so foolish, as to hide in that least likely of places. And yet . . . something about it seemed to hold a glimmer of truth.

Miss Withers turned to look back at him, her anger now chased away for the moment as he seemed to know what she meant, as if he had been there and smelled it along with her. She nodded, and said with an almost puzzled tone, "Yes. Yes, I believe that it was."

Holmes nodded. "I thought so. With your extensive medical background, you would certainly have recognized that. The strong uric content of ammonia would, without doubt, remind you of certain aspects of a horse enclosure." Turning, he moved toward the door to the landing. Opening it, he called, "Mrs. Hudson! Mrs. Hudson!"

Then, without waiting for a reply, he turned to his own desk and hurriedly began to write on several telegram forms, one after the other.

Our long-suffering landlady arrived, well past being surprised or offended by any of my friend's abrupt behaviors. He turned to her, holding out the forms. "Please have the boy dispatch these immediately!"

Then, facing back to our visitor as if she had been there all along to consult with him and not me, he proceeded to take her arm and show her out of the sitting room. "I shouldn't go back to that house right away, Miss Withers. It might not be safe. Perhaps what you smelled is a gas leak. And thank you for coming by. It was truly a pleasure to finally meet you, and you may have the satisfaction of knowing that, even as your errand ended in unpleasantness and disappointment for yourself, you may have helped to provide the link that saves us all from a disastrous chain of events. Good day!"

And with a confused look over her shoulder toward me, and a soft questioning "John?" when she reached the doorway, she was nearly pushed out and onto the landing, whereupon the door was firmly shut in her face. As Holmes walked back toward me, rubbing his hands and with an intense concentrated look upon his face, I could hear nothing on the landing, and I wondered if I ought to go after her. But it was certainly best this way. Finally, her light footsteps descended, and in a moment, the front door opened and closed. I stepped to a window overlooking the street and saw her on the pavement, looking neither right nor left, but facing away

453

from our building. I believe she might have turned then, perhaps to look up toward me, but I stepped back.

I did not know how long the unpleasant conversation would have continued, as I tried to convince her of the firmness of my resolve, but somehow Holmes had cut through the Gordian Knot that she was trying to use to ensnare me, and I didn't want a meeting of our eyes between window and street to start the reattachment of even one new thread.

"Holmes," I said, "that was really too much. Even for you."

"What?" he said, pulling his eyes back to the present from whatever variables and eventualities that he had been considering. "Did you want her to stay, then, so you could keep fencing with one another, trying to convince her 'round to your position, while she did the same from the opposing side?"

I shook my head. "No. No, I suppose I should thank you, although it truly was abominable behavior on your part. Even as she seemed to be bitterly accepting my viewpoint, I knew that she would simply retreat and then talk herself into again thinking that we should be together. And perhaps she still will. But this was a welcome break from an unexpected contest of wills that I wasn't prepared to face at this time. I need to prepare my arguments better for next time, should she try again – and I'm afraid that she will. I must convince her truly that I shall never marry again."

Holmes looked at me then for a long moment. I was about to speak, and fall victim to his old trick of letting the uncomfortable party try to fill the awkward silence, when he said softly, "Don't be too sure, old friend. Don't be too sure. I know how you feel right now, and I agree with you. Miss Withers is not the right girl for you. You need someone more stable. But someday . . . ." He waved his hand toward the door. "Someday someone is going to walk in when you least expect it, and she *will* be the right girl." He smiled then. "You *will* marry again, my friend. And it will be as unexpected and life-changing as if you've had been hit by a Jezail bullet on the battlefield. But this time you won't have a friend like Murray who will throw you on a pack horse and carry you away. No, when it's right, *this* friend will happily let you fall to your fate."

I swallowed, not sure what to say. It was certainly an interesting way of putting it, as only Sherlock Holmes could. But before I could acknowledge Holmes's sentiment, such as it was, one of the times that he had revealed that great heart he strove to hide under his giant intellect, he turned away, heading toward the mantel and his pipe.

"Surely you know what she revealed to us, Watson," he said. "What an opportunity this might mean."

I joined him, sinking into my chair, suddenly weary, as if I had just run a long race. I nodded.

454

"The Baron, Watson," he said, the old light glinting in his eyes. "There is a good chance we know exactly where he has gone to earth!"

Chapter XXIII
"So it's to be tonight, then?"

As I reflected upon Holmes's assertion, I realized that he could possibly be right, but I had to remark, "That is one of the longest shots I have ever heard you make. You believe that Baron Meade has hidden himself at my house in Kensington."

"*Former* house," Holmes corrected. "And yes I do. Why not? Consider. The man has identified you as his enemy, and he would certainly go to lengths to learn more about you. It would be easy to determine that, until just weeks ago, you resided at your practice. He could quickly discover that you are no longer there, and in the process realize that the building was now uninhabited. He was in dire need of a place to hide. It fits, considering his new obsession with you."

He saw a thought flash across my face. "What is it?"

"The other day, when I was there – "

"Yes?"

"Dr. Withers asked me make sure that the delivery of some of his possessions was carried out satisfactorily. He was unable to do so himself following the attack. I went to the house. Before I went in, I was stopped on the street by a boy from the neighborhood, asking me if it was true that I was moving away. He happened to mention that a man had asked him only the day before where I was. Now, it may be that the man was simply a patient who didn't realize that I had moved, but – "

"But that man could have been Baron Meade, reconnoitering your haunts, and finding a bolt-hole for himself in the process."

Another thing surfaced in my mind. "When I was there, I walked a bit around the downstairs, shutting several doors as I went, including the cellar door. As far as I know, there was no reason for it to have been open. It is normally kept locked – it was locked when I was previously there with the Doctor and Miss Withers. They didn't go down there then, or even open that door. And there would have been no reason for the movers to open it up. In fact, they wouldn't have been able to do so. They wouldn't have had that key. And yet it was open."

Holmes was silent for a moment. Then, "My dear Watson, it is a long shot, as you said, but I begin to believe that you have had the most narrow of escapes. If, as I seriously believe, the Baron has in fact set up camp in your old house, you were very fortunate indeed, as your visit there was at a time when he was not in residence. Rather, while you were doing a favor

456

for Dr. Withers and verifying that his deliveries had been made, the Baron was likely in Mayfair, possibly already torturing Sir Edward."

"Holmes," I said, "after I left the house, I walked back through Mayfair. I even considered adjusting my route so as to pass Sir Edward's house – for no particular reason. It simply crossed my mind, though we had only been there a few hours earlier."

"Thank heavens you did not, my friend," said Holmes earnestly. "I hesitate to imagine what might have happened if your path had intersected Baron Meade's while he was either approaching or departing."

"But I might have managed to intercept him as he took the idol."

"Unlikely. And the connection between the Baron and The Eye had not yet been made in your mind. The unlikeliness of seeing him there might have paralyzed you long enough for him to inflict an injury."

We each sat and pondered this for a moment, before I said, "Miss Withers mentioned the 'smell of death' coming from within the house when she was there. You narrowed it down to ammonia. Is Baron Meade again up to his old tricks?"

"I'm certain of it," he replied. "That is, if he is truly there at all. One of the wires that I just sent was to a supplier of coal oil and fertilizers, the same one that the Baron used before. We need to determine if the man has started to rebuild his stock, but this time in a location where he thinks he'll be safe and undisturbed."

"That smell, Holmes? Why then did I not notice it?"

"Undoubtedly because he had only begun to accumulate the materials needed for his next attempt at blowing something up."

"Good Lord," I said, another thing occurring to me. "Do you think that Miss Withers was in danger when she was there? Could the Baron have been in the house at that moment?"

"It's very likely. He would do well to stay out of sight, and if he has established a hidey-hole there, then he was possibly on the premises during her visit. But it's more likely that he was out and about, trying to establish a further contact with John Goins and his people. Miss Withers was probably in no danger even if he *was* hiding there – how would harming her, or even taking her hostage, further his cause at this point? No, if he *is* there, he'll want to draw as little attention to the place as possible, and accosting her in any way would have been very counterproductive."

We examined the implications of the idea that the Baron was hiding in Kensington. Eventually our ruminations were interrupted when the front bell rang forcefully, and Holmes nodded. "The police, I suspect. Another of the wires I sent was to request their presence, in order to catch them up."

457

Holmes was correct. Lestrade and Gregson tramped wearily into the sitting room. When they came in and shut the door behind them, I asked, "Where is Lanner?"

"At the Yard," said Gregson. He glanced toward the sideboard, and Holmes gestured for him to go ahead. The big blonde man stepped over and began to pour. "Doctor? Mr. Holmes?" We both nodded. "I know what Lestrade's answer is."

"After this day, of course you do," said the smaller man, sinking into his accustomed place before the fire. Gregson, carefully maneuvering across the room with the four glasses in his thick hands, joined us.

Taking a sip, Lestrade licked his lips and said, "What's this, then, Mr. Holmes, about Baron Meade being found at the Doctor's old house? That was faster work than I would have thought, even for you."

"I indicated that I *may* know," corrected Holmes. He went on to explain his reasoning concerning the Baron's possible awareness of the empty Kensington house.

Gregson nodded. "It could be. His other options are closed to him. This location presented itself, and he does have this new fascination with the Doctor."

"Have you placed the house under observation?"

"It's happening now," said Lestrade. "With some of our best men." My friend started to speak, but Lestrade raised a hand. "I know what you're going say, Mr. Holmes. But these *are* good men, and they will not be seen."

"You mistake me, Lestrade," responded Holmes. "I was simply going to add that, if we are in agreement, then we too shall have to quickly get into position for whatever may come. I may be wrong. We may already be too late. But I would hate to be caught here in Baker Street, waiting to get word from one source or the other, and then arrive only to find that the bird has flown." Turning to me, he said, "Watson? Is there any place nearby that we can use in order to watch for the Baron or a meeting with John Goins?"

I answered without hesitation. "Two doors to the east and across the street. The Parker house. Mrs. Parker was a good friend to Constance, and that house extends a bit closer to the street than the others, allowing a view from a side window."

"Perfect," said Holmes. "I suggest we make our way there, with haste and discretion. I'm taking a toothbrush and a fresh collar. I suggest you do the same. We may be there for a day or so."

All of us were subdued as we crossed London. Holmes suggested that we leave the growler several blocks from my old address in Vicarage Gate, and that he and I approach the Parker residence cautiously from the rear.

458

Lestrade and Gregson agreed, and we decided on a shadowed part of Uxbridge Road, not far from Notting Hill Gate. The inspectors settled into the corners of the cab to try and stay warm as best they could until one of us returned with the all clear.

I led Holmes south through a short maze of streets and mews while he kept an eye out, on the chance that we might accidentally cross Baron Meade's path. I have no doubt that, if his attention wasn't taken up with that task, Holmes could have used his encyclopedic knowledge of London to find a better path than I did.

"Why," I asked, as we paused in a shadowed doorway before crossing an unavoidable open space, "do we not simply have the police raid the house, as took place days ago in the Brixton Road?"

"This has become about more than just retrieving the idol, or preventing a bombing."

"It seems to me as if that's what it has *always* been about. Why has it changed?"

"Because I have a different plan."

I looked at him silently, and then repeated, "A different plan."

"Yes. This cycle needs to be broken." And in a few terse words, he explained how he proposed to do so.

"It's a great risk, Holmes. Are you certain?"

"Absolutely. If Baron Meade is holed up here in Kensington with The Eye, then he likely won't be going anywhere with it until such time as he tries to pass it to John Goins. We'll make sure of that. But if we can also put a stop once and for all to Goins's ongoing efforts to retrieve the object in question, and the threat that it represents, should we not try?" He tensed, and I sensed he was ready to move again. "I assure you that my plan has already been discussed and approved by those in the highest authority. All that was needed was to locate Baron Meade. If he is truly within your former house, then just a few revisions as to the details are necessary, and all should be concluded quite satisfactorily."

And then he was walking quickly to the next corner, and I followed, with no chance to question him further.

We found our way to the rear door of our destination, where we were admitted by a rather confused cook. In moments, we were in the presence of the lady of the house, Florence Parker. I hadn't spoken to her since Constance's service, and then she had only been one of many faces who passed before my grief-stricken figure. Yet I knew that she had been of substantial comfort to my wife during the times of her illness, and that she had helped with some of the final arrangements.

She was a few years older than I, but still a handsome woman. She did well managing the house, which sheltered three rambunctious boys,

Lyndon being the youngest. Her husband, Charles, was a civil engineer, associated with a firm nominally located in London, but carrying out most of their projects in the north, requiring him to travel a great deal of the time.

"John?" she said, glancing curiously between me and my companion. "What is the matter? Why did you arrive at the back door?"

"Let me explain," said Holmes, whereupon I interrupted him, effecting introductions between them.

"We need your help," I added, deferring back to my friend.

"Yes?" said Florence, waving us to chairs.

Holmes proceeded to lay out some of the isolated details of the past week, revealing enough of what was going on, without confusing the issue. He explained who the Baron was, his earlier attempt to gather explosive materials and the subsequent disruption of the plan, followed by the man's irrational fixation upon me.

Without complicating things further by tossing in mentions of either the idol or the various opposing factions, Holmes related how we believed Baron Meade might be hiding within my old house. It is a credit to Florence that she accepted this statement without wasting time demanding proofs or explanations. "What can I do?" she asked.

"In a moment, we wish to speak to your son, Lyndon."

"Lyndon? But why?"

"Based on something he told me the other day," I said, "he may have seen this man."

"Oh. Are we in danger?"

"Not immediately," said Holmes. "But if Baron Meade is gathering more explosives, as I believe, then every house on this street is in peril." He leaned forward, his gaze intent. "Have you seen any indication of a stranger at that house?"

"Yes," she said. "I believe that I have. A few days ago, there was a man waiting on your front steps, Dr. Watson, when a wagon arrived. I happened to glance at the clock, and it was ten sharp. I assumed it was the new doctor, or perhaps someone who worked for him, moving more items into the house, as they did several days ago."

"That delivery contained the new doctor's possessions," I explained. "I came by the day after that to make sure they had been settled properly. It was at that time that I talked to Lyndon."

"And I recall that we waved to one another," Florence added. "Then there were men there yesterday weren't the same as the first group, and instead of delivering boxes and furniture, they brought barrels and large cartons."

460

Holmes nodded. "I expect that would be components of Baron Meade's explosives, as we thought."

"Then there were a great many of them," she said. "And there were other deliveries of the same sort throughout the morning."

"How many?"

"Two others besides the first."

"That you saw."

"I saw them all, Mr. Holmes. They were acting suspicious, and I kept my eye on them."

"Did they see you?"

"No. Our house has a side window which allows a view of the street in that direction. I watched from behind the curtains."

"Excellent. May we see that room?"

"Certainly." She led us through the house to a front parlor, where the small window that I had earlier described was located. Holmes peeped through the lace, and then moved aside for me to do the same. The street was empty, and my old house appeared to be closed up tight.

"Now may we speak to your son?"

Back in the front room, Lyndon stood before us, looking nervous. His two older brothers had attempted to join us, but were sent on their way, with instructions by their mother to remain upstairs. Having once been part of a pair of young brothers myself, I doubted that they would be satisfied to follow her instructions.

"Master Lyndon," said Holmes to the wide-eyed boy, "what can you tell us about the man you spoke to the other day, the one asking about Dr. Watson."

He looked at me, and then said, "He asked where you were, Doctor, and I said that you had gone to live somewhere else. Just as I told you."

"Very good," said Holmes. "And there was nothing else?"

"No . . . ." he said, with a bit of uncertainty. Then, "He did ask if anyone else was living there in your house right now, since you had gone to Baker Street."

"And what did you tell him?"

"Just that a new doctor was going to be moving in, but not yet."

Holmes looked at me, and then back at Lyndon. "Describe this man."

Lyndon closed his eyes for a moment, and then began to relate what he could remember. As a ten-year-old, he couldn't be expected to notice certain things, but his general description of the man's height, hair, and face all matched Baron Meade. Holmes's further questioning brought out details about the man's clothing corresponding with what the fugitive had been wearing since going into hiding. And finally, Lyndon was able to add

461

other bits, such as the man's musty odor, his obviously fragile emotional state, and his barely suppressed impatience.

"Thank you, Lyndon," said Holmes. "You've been very helpful indeed." With a grateful look toward Holmes, and a similar glance my way, the boy scampered out, leaving the door open. His mother smiled, hearing Lyndon's footsteps joined by several others in the hallway as they all ascended the stairs. She rose and shut the door.

"Does that help, Mr. Holmes?"

"It does. The description matches the Baron, and confirms his interest in the place, as well as his knowledge that Dr. Watson is no longer there. Your observations of what is likely the same man supervising the delivery of suspicious materials makes it even more certain." He thought for a moment, pulling at his lip, and then said, "I'm afraid that we need more of your help, madam. A great deal more."

"What can I do?"

Holmes explained that not only would we need to set up camp within her house, along with a gathering of policemen, but that she and her family would need to be evacuated for their own safety. "The same will be done for all the nearby houses. The chance, though unlikely, that the explosives might be set off accidentally cannot be ignored."

"How," she asked, "will you be able to get all those people out without alerting this Baron?"

"Very carefully," said Holmes, with a wry smile. Turning to me, he said, "While you help the Parkers get ready, I'll go back and inform Lestrade and Gregson." Then, with a nod to our hostess, he was gone.

It is a credit to Florence Parker, her sons, and her staff how quickly they efficiently prepared for departure, and by the time the inspectors had returned with Holmes, all were ready to leave. Lestrade awkwardly explained that they would take care of her house, to which she replied with a smile, "I have no doubts of that, sir."

I turned to Lyndon, the youngest of the three brothers, but just then the man of the hour. Leaning down a bit, I said, "Thank you for your help. It was invaluable. Now take care of your mother." I stuck out my hand, which he shook gravely.

"I will, Dr. Watson."

Over the next few hours, the secret evacuation of the neighborhood took place with military precision. Watching from behind the lace curtains in the front room, I never saw anything suspicious in the empty street. Yet the police, as well as augmented forces from the Foreign Office, approached all the neighboring houses surreptitiously from behind, explained the situation, and spirited away both residents and staff through side streets and various mews to quite comfortable temporary lodgings, provided for them by a benevolent and grateful government. Men were placed out of sight at either end of the short thoroughfare to observe approaching visitors, of which there were thankfully none. The postman was replaced by a government agent, and he made his rounds throughout the day without giving anything away. By late afternoon, all the surrounding houses on that street and the one behind were completely empty, except for the Parker house, and possibly the one that had formerly been my own. For despite all of this effort, it was still uncertain as to whether the man responsible for all of this was even really there.

Holmes had not been idle. After thoroughly briefing the inspectors, he had departed to obtain a certain necessary item from Baker Street. Then he had proceeded to visit his contacts within the Foreign Office, as well as to confer with both Daniel and Dr. Withers. I had half-heartedly offered to slip away to meet with the doctor, in order to explain exactly what was occurring within and around his newly purchased property, but Holmes decided it would be better if he carried out that function, and I agreed with no little relief.

Holmes returned as the sun was setting, relating to me the substance of that meeting. "A very solid man," said Holmes. "Very likeable indeed. He welcomed me graciously, although his daughter did not seem quite so glad to see me, and she quickly left the room."

"You did send her packing quite abruptly this morning," I said.

"She has had hours to recover," he replied with a twinkle in his eye. "It reveals something dark in her character that she is willing to hold a grudge."

I waved that away. "What are Dr. Withers' thoughts on these doings?"

"He was somewhat skeptical, but willing in the end to assume that I might know of what I spoke. He is rightly concerned that we prevent his new investment from detonating, and I assured him that we will do our best. Like you, he wondered why we don't simply raid the place and be done with it. I left him with the impression that doing so is our plan."

"As there was no need to explain what you're *really* intending to accomplish with your rather more complicated scheme."

"Precisely."

"And Daniel? Did he contribute any facts or opinions?"

"Simply that there appears to be no sign of increased activity within John Goins's camp, as might be expected. They do not seem to have realized yet that one of their own, Abraham, has been arrested."

"So now we wait."

"Not exactly. When it is fully dark, I shall reconnoiter."

463

And he did. No one was more capable than he for what he proposed, and there was no argument from Lestrade or Gregson, or Lanner either, who had joined us late in the afternoon.

Before he slipped out, Holmes, already in dark clothing, covered his face in lampblack. Satisfied that he would be invisible, he paused in front of me, and I fished in my pocket for the key to the house, given to me the other day by Dr. Withers when he wanted me to check on his deliveries. "I may need it," he said

"Don't take any chances."

"Of course not." And then, after picking up the heavy dark bag that he had brought back with him from Baker Street, he was gone.

The various men hidden in the Parker house waited in silence. At least we didn't have to sit in the dark. Although the shades were all drawn, Holmes had insisted that lights be lit, both in that house and the others nearby, to give the impression that life continued as normal up and down the street. Constables made trips to the neighboring structures to do so, finding their way in by rear entrances, but otherwise the street was kept clear. However, there were many men in hiding in all directions, ready to take notice if a visitor arrived for Baron Meade, or conversely if our prey decided to leave.

Holmes was barely gone fifteen minutes before returning. In fact, he was amongst us before we even knew he was back, so silent was his arrival. Gregson smiled, and Lestrade shook his head, while Lanner seemed somehow offended that he had been caught unaware.

"He is there," said Holmes, before we could ask. "I observed him by looking through the dining room window, which has been blocked, but not successfully." He set down the dark bag that he had taken with him, now noticeably lighter, and began to wipe the lampblack from his face with a handkerchief. "He is sitting alone, staring straight ahead at nothing."

"Did you find the idol?" asked Lestrade.

Holmes nodded. "It was standing on a table, down in the cellar."

"Did you also see that through a window?"

"No, I discovered it when I entered the building."

The inspectors looked mildly surprised, although I had known that this was his intent.

"Holmes," I said, "the key that I gave you only works for the main doors. How did you get into the cellar?"

"I shinned in through the coal chute."

"And you weren't worried that Baron Meade might detect your presence? Going into the house like that?" asked Lanner. Holmes simply gave him a look of disdain.

464

Lestrade rubbed his chin. "So you didn't bring it back with you, then? Even though you were right there?"

"That's right. I had it in my hand – "

"What?" exclaimed Lanner.

" – and before I escaped back through the coal chute, I left it where it can be found when we return."

"And the explosives?" queried Gregson. "If you saw The Eye, I'm betting you found them too."

"They are also in the cellar, which is why I wanted to get in there as well. I knew they would be, since Miss Withers didn't actually see them, but she *smelled* them. The raw smell of ammonia coming from his cache is almost overpowering. I don't know how he can stand to be in the building. It's no wonder that Miss Withers noticed it so strongly when she visited this morning."

"I still don't understand," said Lanner. "If we know he's there, why don't we just go in and get him? Or lure him out, so he can't set off the explosives."

Lestrade had a vexed look upon his pinched features. "We've told you, there's more to this now than just securing the idol. We're going to try to nip this weed once and for all."

"But . . . what about this, then? Why couldn't we go ahead and arrest the Baron, and then let someone else take his place? Mr. Holmes could do it! With one of his disguises."

"We don't know enough," answered Holmes. "What previous messages have passed between John Goins and Baron Meade – if any? We might say or do something that would spoil everything. We have to let them meet for the transfer of the statue."

"What now, then?" I said. "It seems as if both sides are simply waiting. We can't hide here forever, while they decide whether to trust one another."

"We must somehow take control of events, but we cannot rush things," said the consulting detective. "An opportunity will present itself. We must be patient."

And so we were. Nothing happened for the rest of that night, and morning found all of us gathering back in the front room, having slept to better or worse degrees throughout the house. Holmes, I knew, had been the exception to that, smoking long into the night as he considered the different options, variations, and risks within his plan.

We had all made do with a cold breakfast when word came that a telegram had been intercepted, intended for my former address, no name given. As all communications that might be relevant were being

465

monitored, the document was soon within our hands: *Agreed. Bring object to Giles Street 8pm tonight. JG*

"No way to track back and see who handed the message in at the other end," said Lestrade.

"Or to find out exactly where in Giles Street that Baron Meade is supposed to go," added Gregson.

"Hmm," Holmes muttered. "They must have discussed it previously. Giles Street is a short passage, only a few blocks from Daniel's hide-out in Bere Street."

"Is that surprising, Holmes?" I asked. "They've been in an uneasy truce for over ten years. Having nearby quarters is not so unusual in that rat's nest."

"True, Watson. Just an interesting association."

"Is this what you were waiting for, then?" Lestrade questioned.

"I believe it will do to let us take the reins. We just need to alter the message a bit and get the revision into the Baron's hands, and then do the same with his reply when it's sent."

And thus it was done. A new message for Baron Meade was fixed up at the local telegraph office, saying instead: *Agreed. Will arrive 8pm tonight your location to retrieve the object. JG*

One of Holmes's agents was carefully briefed, and sent on by a roundabout way to approach from the front and then deliver it into the Baron's hands. In moments, he had gone and returned to rejoin us, by way of the back door.

"Any problems, Walters?" asked Holmes.

"Not a bit of it, sir. He took the message like he'd been expecting it. He didn't like what he read, but he wrote out a reply and sent it with me." He handed Holmes a form, which we crowded to see: *Why change of plan? Will expect you 8pm.* It was addressed to No. 6, Giles Street.

"So we now send John Goins a message, telling him to be in *this* street tonight at the appointed time, and hopefully they'll both trust one another just enough to agree without sending more messages, and let matters take their natural course."

"I only hope it goes that easily," murmured Lestrade.

The reply was prepared and sent on to Limehouse. We waited, and before long, notification that another telegram for Baron Meade was intercepted, simply saying: *Agreed. JG.* It was decided that this one needed no revision, and was delivered to Baron Meade post-haste by a disguised Walters without further delay. When reporting back to us, Walters said, "Same as before. I knocked, and after a few minutes he came to the door. He looks to be in terrible shape, Mr. Holmes. His clothes are wrinkled, he hasn't shaved, and if you hadn't warned me about that terrible smell in the

466

house, I might have thought that it was coming from him. It fair rolls out the door."

"But he didn't seem suspicious?"

"Not at all."

"Excellent. Satisfactory."

"So it's to be tonight, then?" prompted Gregson.

"Yes, and high time."

Chapter XXIV
The Curtain Rises

Darkness had well fallen as the appointed hour approached. Throughout the day, there had been no other signs of activity at my former home. I had taken more than my share of the watches from the front parlor window, with its view of the steps leading to my old front door. I had never seen the place from this perspective before, and I wondered at how viewing something by moving off to the side can make it look completely foreign. The more I studied the house, the more it seemed as if it were a place that I had never ever been.

Holmes often said that circumstantial evidence might look a certain absolute way when viewed from the front, with only one absolute interpretation, but simply shifting one's viewpoint would reveal it in a completely new manner. I was seeing the same thing as I watched that building. While I would always have my memories there, all from the inside looking out, I was now a step removed, in a different direction, and encapsulating the experience in a covering of scar tissue, even as I was realizing a bit more than I had at any time up to that moment that I would truly be able to move on.

Holmes was in and out, tightening his plans, confirming facts. He left at one point, bringing back Daniel, as well as Luke and Benjamin. My initial reaction was to chastise Holmes for involving the boys in what could be something dangerous, but they had already been a part of it for quite a while, and Holmes himself was no stranger to using lads of similar ages for equivalent purposes.

"I found and spoke with the delivery men that were seen by Mrs. Parker," said Holmes. "Baron Mcade is stubbornly consistent. Coal oil, fertilizers, and metallic machine parts, just as before."

"So delivering the idol, with the hell that it might unleash, isn't enough," I said. "He still wants to blow something up." I waved my hand. "A substantial part of Kensington?"

"No. These same men were hired to return, two nights from now, to move the materials elsewhere, although they weren't told where."

"And they weren't suspicious about the nature of these deliveries, or the location?"

"It was just another job for them, probably no more unusual or eccentric than others that they have had. And bear in mind that, besides not knowing what the combination of these materials would accomplish if

468

detonated, they were all delivered by separate crews from different vendors. The coal oil men had no knowledge of the other deliveries, and so on."

"Well, I suppose it's a comfort that this plan, like the last one, will fail before it even begins."

"True. Baron Meade is already finished – he just doesn't know it yet." And then he gave that peculiar silent laugh of his that I have seen occasionally, always signifying that an evil day was coming for some foul miscreant.

That was one of the very few conversations that I had with Holmes, or anyone really, on that day. My companions mostly left me to myself during those introspective hours. I was vaguely aware of whispers passing at times in the hallway outside the front parlor where I kept my vigil. There seemed to be a constant tension, as would be expected when a group of men are crowded together in such a situation, waiting for a trap to be sprung, but forced to while away the long hours until something happens, and aware that some unexpected factor might still make itself known at any time and spoil everything.

And yet, the hours finally crept by, and the sun started to drop in the southwest. The window which gave the best view upon the Baron's bolt hole faced roughly that way, and for a while there was nothing to be seen in that direction but the blinding sunset. I left the room then, and no one replaced me, as it was thought that somehow, with that side of the Parker house so illuminated, there might be the slightest chance that Baron Meade could see someone there, watching.

There were still men stationed in hiding at the different approaches to the neighborhood, and Holmes had arranged for his Irregulars, along with Daniel's two remaining assistants, to be placed with them, in order to act as runners – the idea being that, when John Goins and his men arrived, no matter from which direction, we would be notified. And that was what happened.

A few minutes before eight, when the winter sun had finally left the sky completely, one of the younger Irregulars, Fred Peake, appeared among us to say that a carriage had parked around the corner where Vicarage Gate curved to the north, and two men had exited. By the time Fred had left, they were simply standing there beside the carriage, waiting. Before that information could be fully assimilated, another Irregular, young Levi, came in as well, reporting that five other men had appeared from different directions out of the shadows, taking stations up and down the street. Luckily our men were hidden even better, thanks to Holmes's excellent planning. In another life, I have no doubt he would have been an excellent military campaigner and tactician.

Just before the hour of eight, Holmes, Daniel, and I slipped out the back and around the house toward the street, where we remained hidden, waiting for John Goins to make his approach. It wasn't exactly a trap, at least not for him, as it was part of Holmes's carefully crafted plan that Goins be allowed to go free in the end. But Baron Meade would not escape from us, one way or the other.

We didn't have long to wait. From down the street, we saw two men stealthily approach, no doubt those who had first arrived in the carriage. I wondered who the second man with Goins might be, but I wasn't surprised that he would bring someone, if only to function as a bodyguard. He seemingly and understandably had trouble believing the Baron's motives, offering to simply give the idol, sought by him for so many years, away free and clear with no strings. No doubt in their previous communications, those to which we had no access, Baron Meade had intimated to some greater or lesser degree why he wished to provide the object to one who would use it to harm England, but someone of Goins's background would not take that at face value, even with Micah's counsel, and could likely only believe the Baron's motives when he truly had the idol in his hands.

The two men mounted the short steps and rang the front bell. Almost immediately, it was opened, and they stepped inside.

"The curtain rises," whispered Holmes, and we began to move, keeping to the shadows as we approached my former front door.

Not wanting to alert any of Goins's men in the street, those that were doubtless watching to detect or prevent a trap, we were careful not to show ourselves. Luckily, the night was dark with building clouds, and Holmes and I were experienced at this sort of hunting. Daniel seemed a little more awkward, but did nothing to give away the game. We reached our goal without any indication from the surrounding street that we had been seen, and even as we took to the steps, Holmes was pulling my old key from his pocket while shifting his stick to the other hand. He slid the key into the door, which had in fact been locked by the Baron after the entry of his visitors. Turning the works silently, he eased the door open, and we crept inside.

I fished my gun out of my coat pocket. The smell of ammonia was almost overpowering, making my eyes water, and giving me the barely controlled urge to cough. Holmes gently closed the door behind us, cutting off the last of the fresh air. He didn't lock it, and then he paused beside us as we each listened to the sound of voices coming from the room on our immediate right – my old consulting room.

"What is so hard to understand?" asked someone in a low and cultured tone. I knew that it was Baron Meade, but it surprised me, as this was the first time that I had heard him speak when he wasn't venting anger.

"I don't require any payment at all. It is a gift. You could have had it yesterday, or the day before, if only you weren't so suspicious."

"You must admit," said a second voice, with a slight cough, as the fumes trapped inside the house apparently affected him, "that what you offer is . . . surprising. I have never heard of you, and to then receive word that you have managed to obtain that which I have sought for so many years, having been forced to remain in this terrible country while hoping for some sort of mistake on the part of my enemies that would give me this chance."

His voice was also low and deep, but with a sly and sibilant pulse winding through it, like the sound of a serpent's scales rasping as it pushes its way through dead leaves. It held intelligence and bitterness and contempt all at once, and I knew that this must be John Goins.

"The other day was like all the rest that we've spent here in this prison," Goins continued. "Just another of many in this land of cold and rain and fog, where you consider it to be excessively hot when the temperature climbs to something barely tolerable. I foresaw no immediate cessation of our ongoing exile, when suddenly I received a note, explaining that not only is the object of my quest is now in the hands of an Englishman, rather than locked and buried in the British Museum, but that you wish to give it to me without condition. How could I *not* be suspicious of a trap?"

"But there *is* a condition," replied Baron Meade. "I've made that clear. You must take it to those who will use it to ignite the fuse against this country."

"Of course I will take it. But why do you hate your own land so much? I find it hard to trust someone who could be such a traitor. I could much better understand if someone like you had found yourself in possession of the idol and were willing to sell it to the highest bidder."

"All that you need to know is that this country needs to be punished for what it has become, and for what it allows to happen to the poor souls who believed in it, and served it, and are then crushed underfoot as if they were valueless insects."

"Life is cheap all over. You still haven't convinced me, Englishman."

"What else is there to say? There is no trap. Here is The Eye. Take it!"

There was the sound of movement, and then the reptilian voice gave a satisfied and surprised "Ah!" sending a chill up my spine. I looked to Daniel, standing beside us in the dark, and intentionally ignorant of the greater part of Holmes's plan, wherein the idol must be given to Goins, or at least be seen by him. Our companion appeared stricken at the thought of his old enemy taking possession of that which his family had guarded

471

for so long. Holmes noticed Daniel's expression as well, and nodded, as if to indicate that everything was still well under control.

"I would have paid *you* a fortune to take and use it," continued the Baron, "if I still had access to my funds. Unfortunately, I am now considered a criminal by these people, and only have the limited money that I'd already hidden elsewhere, and that must be used for other important work – *cleansing work* – here in England."

There was a silence for a long minute, and I strained to determine if Goins and his unknown companion, now having the object of their quest, would simply turn and leave. But in a moment, the sibilant voice resumed.

"Strange," he said. "This is something that has been a legend for generations, and the purpose of my own life for so many years, and yet I only saw it once before, when I took it from the Museum, long ago. To have it here, now, seems almost – anticlimactic."

"When you return with it," said Baron Meade, "you will see its importance. You will see when you reveal it, and set in motion the war that the leaders of this country so fear. And I will be working from this end to destroy their complacency, while you will attack from the other side. It will be *glorious*!"

"The *other side*?" said Goins, with a sneer. "And what gave you the idea that there will be another side to your little war?"

The resulting lack of response from Baron Meade was overwhelming for just a few stretched seconds, and I could hear Daniel beside me as he swallowed. Then, the Baron said, "That is what you have wanted. That is what I was *told* that you wanted when I obtained the idol. To whip up a burgeoning army to destroy the British. That is what I was told. It is why the Government has been so afraid for so long that it might fall into your hands."

Goins laughed. Chills ran up and down my spine. "Why should I want to start a war? How would that benefit *me*? To have destruction burn across the world, destroying it for the sake of *saving* it? No, my naïve but generous new friend, my plan is a bit more conservative that. I have no interest in saving anything. Maybe I once did. But now I am older. I have realized that there is no need to use the idol for cleansing. I'm much more interested in what I can do for *me*."

"But," said a new voice, much rougher in tone, but with a wounded sound, as if a child had been told that there is no Father Christmas, "that is why we are here: To take The Eye of Heka home, and use it to free our people from the foreign filth!"

Daniel, having been concentrating on the conversation while staring intently at the floor, looked up with a start. Holmes noticed it as well. Then, before we could stop him, Daniel had charged forward toward the sound of his brother Micah's voice in the next room. This was not part of the plan. Holmes and I went after him.

Micah was saying, almost plaintively as we entered, "You must use The Eye's power!" Then our arrival was realized. Daniel stopped awkwardly in front of his brother, standing as he was to our right in the group of three. Holmes and I placed ourselves before them, guns drawn. At our far left was Baron Meade, looking even more disheveled than when I had seen him last, running down the Strand after his failed attempt to kill me. The surprise on his face was only matched by that on the tall man in the center of the group, clutching the idol to his chest with both long bony hands.

He was extremely thin. His bald head was oddly shaped, with protruding knobs of bone in unexpected places. His supra-orbital ridges were greatly pronounced, leaving his strangely light eyes, especially in that dim room that was lit only by one lantern on a table behind the Baron, glowing with sinister light. His thin dark lips, in an expression of shock as we ran in, pulled back in a snarl over his twisted teeth – he clearly recognized both Daniel and my friend. I could see that his lower jaw jutted out to a point in front of his long flat nose. The lower mandible was atypically narrow from side to side, the sides of the U-shaped bone running too close together, causing each side of the arc of his lower teeth to be especially tapered, leaving very little room in between for his tongue. Perhaps this explained his hissing manner of speech, which was much more apparent to us, here in front of him, as an impediment. He glared at the Baron, saying, "It *was* a trap, then!"

Baron Meade shook his head, confused. "No. No, it wasn't. I didn't know . . . I don't know how they found me . . . ." His face hardened from uncertainty to rage.

Daniel spoke, his voice accusatory. "Here, then, is my traitorous brother! Here I've found you. Are you satisfied? You, who betrayed your family, who abandoned your birthright, to stand beside the man who killed your own brother, and this other who has been our enemy for so long. And now you don't even have that to grasp any longer. This man for whom you abandoned everything has no plans to liberate our lands with the dark magic that you crave. He is simply a greedy villain, nothing more than a common criminal, intending to fool and control the gullible while he lines his own pockets!"

At first, Micah had seemed to collapse a little with each of Daniel's bitter words, turning his head from side to side as though he was being repeatedly slapped. But then, his expression darkened as he found his resolve, his one eye tightening until it was barely a slit, while his lips pulled back to reveal his clenched teeth. Then, as if he were himself an

473

explosive reaction that had been held and compressed in a vessel for just that much too long, he erupted.

Without warning, he turned to Goins, standing at his right, and before the tall man could react, Micah had wrested the idol from his grasp. He lifted it above his head, holding it so tightly in his shaking hands that his knuckles turned to ivory. By chance, he had taken it in such a way that the empty and ancient countenance on the thing was facing forward, looking down at Holmes, Daniel, and me. Daniel took a step back, an almost fearful look on his face, in spite of his earlier statements that he did not believe its power.

A scream tore from Micah's throat as he shook the carving toward the sky. He didn't know how to control it – did not know how to activate it. But he was awash in his rage, and he shrieked some unknown word that made Goins beside him flinch and take a cringing step away.

We all looked at the stone object, raised before us, dark except for the reflected lantern light. And then – *nothing happened*. There was no fire from above, no explosions or waves of force, or shaking of the earth to knock us from our feet and crack the walls and foundations of the house. The empty expression of the thing never varied in the least, and the jewel in the middle of the forehead remained cold and dark and dead.

Micah waited, and then, when he realized the emptiness of his gesture, he screamed and shook the thing again and again, with the same result. Goins, who had been bent into something of a fearful crouch, stood back up with a look of surprise. Daniel, on the other hand, slowly smiled, as if his long belief that the thing was nothing more than a stone had finally been proven true.

"False," he said, taking a step toward his brother. "False. A lie. You destroyed yourself for *nothing!*" And he made as if to reach and take hold of the idol, still held above Micah's head.

Micah, who had been looking up as if still expecting something to happen, saw the motion and reacted without apparent thought. With no sound or warning at all, he whipped both arms down, bringing the stone carving onto the center of Daniel's unprotected head with a terrifying and terrible wet crack.

My gun, which had never left my grip, seemed to fire on its own. It was far too late to save Daniel, and Micah, already looking in horror at what he had done, was certainly no threat, but my reflexes disobeyed me, and I put a bullet into his shoulder, spinning him around before he collapsed into the puddle of blood already pooling around his fallen brother's crushed skull, his own flowing to join it.

Goins screamed a wordless cry. I looked away from the men on the floor to see him with bared teeth, hissing, "*Sherlock Holmes!* For this you

474

will *die!*" And he made a dive for the idol, still buried in dead Daniel's head. I was closer, hesitant to shoot yet again while knowing that we wanted him alive. I tried to kick out at him but missed. He wrenched the carved stone loose, and then rolled back into an awkward sitting position, pushing himself away from us with his legs in a desperate crab-like crawl. Reaching the wall behind him, he pushed himself up, keeping an eye fixed upon my gun while beginning to smile. "The fool did not know how to use it," he explained, his breath coming in wheezes. "He was nothing but a foolish amateur. The Eye of Heka must be wielded by one who *knows*, one who *believes!*"

Then he lifted it before his face, not quite so high as Micah had done, as if he were trying to see through it, and gave it a great shake. There was no need to cry special words to try to activate it. No need, because – whatever Goins thought that he was doing – nothing whatsoever happened for him as well.

He tried again, giving another wave of the inert block, this time with a frustrated whimper, and then looked up for just an instant like an old man, his odd face turning gray while he slumped against the wall, realizing his purpose had failed. In that moment, Holmes took two decisive steps forward, swinging his weighted stick as he did so and bringing it down precisely upon the knotted skull. With a crack, the stick shattered and Goins was instantly unconscious, dropping to the floor like a sack of grain, the idol rolling out of his limp hands. Holmes kicked it away from him, where it came to rest against the two fallen brothers.

Holmes stepped toward Goins. I glanced to the side and thought that just perhaps I saw the movement of labored breathing in Micah's chest. I squatted to check on him, and it was then that Holmes cried, with a note of panic in his voice, "Watson!"

I rounded to see that Baron Meade, momentarily ignored, had grabbed the lantern, the only light in the room, and was already at the door, running toward the back of the house, skidding as he changed direction in the hallway. Holmes was following, and I rose to join him. I knew where the Baron was headed.

By the time I reached the hall, the Baron was already gone, and Holmes was turning to barrel down the stairs to the cellar. I could see the light bobbing as the lantern jerked up and down with the Baron's movements. I wished that I had asked Holmes where the explosives were placed in the cellar in relation to the stairs, in order to know how much distance the Baron had to cover before he and the lantern reached the barrels of fuel. In seconds, the answer to that question wouldn't matter.

I regretted the impending deaths of the policemen outside, told to wait for our signal that hadn't come. I knew with a sinking feeling that they had probably heard my gunshot, and would just be entering the house when the explosion occurred. I could only take comfort in the fact that the families in the immediate vicinity had been evacuated and would survive, even though their dwellings and possessions would soon be destroyed. But what about those still in the other neighboring streets, I wondered, those who had not been moved? The fire following this explosion – and who knew how big it might be? – would immediately spread. Surely other innocents would be lost as well.

But at least, one way or another, the idol would be destroyed, for I could not imagine that it would survive the explosion. It might be worth it if the thing became part of the debris following the destruction, prevented from continuing its destiny of heartache and grief.

Even as these thoughts were crossing my mind, my body had continued to hurl itself down the steps. Upon reaching the uneven cement floor, I looked madly back and forth before realizing that the light was coming from my right. That was the section partitioned off for coal, where Holmes had entered last night through the chute. I thought of his stealthy mission then, and what he had discovered, and how it did not matter now, with Baron Meade seconds away from setting off his conflagration.

The lantern light waved and bobbed as I found them, struggling. The Baron was attempting to get closer to the barrels of coal oil, whereupon he would toss the lantern in. In less time than could be comprehended, the highly flammable fuel would be set ablaze, and with that much of it radiating out in an explosion, it would set off the nitrogen compounds in a sympathetic detonation. The resulting force would expand outward faster than the human mind could follow, pushing the bits of metal with it, destroying the house around us, and also the others.

But it hadn't happened yet. Holmes, the strongest man that I have ever known, for all of his wiry frame, had so far prevented Baron Meade from releasing his lantern. They were locked together, one of Holmes's hands gripping the Baron's arm like an iron band, while the other twisted in the madman's coat, keeping him from approaching the fuel or swinging the lantern. But even as Holmes matched strength against strength, the sheer maniacal power of his opponent was slowly overcoming him. In the space of the heartbeat or two that passed after I raced into their presence, Holmes was forced back a step towards the pile of coal. And when he reached it, as he could not see behind him, his foot rolled on several of the loose pieces and he began to fall.

With a wordless howl, our foe wrenched himself free then, and started to turn toward the fuel barrels. I screamed at him to stop, my voice in that low-ceilinged cellar sounding muffled in my own ears compared with the pounding drum of my pulse, and he paused, just for that instant, to look over at me with an expression of dawning realization, and then complete hatred. It was when he started to laugh, as he realized that I would die here with him, that he cocked back his arm with deliberation to hurl the lantern, and so I pulled the trigger of my gun one more time, avoiding the ambiguity of firing into the man's body, so charged with adrenaline that he might not be stopped, even if I squarely hit his heart, and instead aiming with long practiced precision between his tormented eyes.

He spasmodically kept hold of the lantern, even as he sank to the ground. I hadn't the time to consider that he might have simply dropped it to shatter on the floor, throwing blazing kerosene in every direction, onto both the coal where Holmes was picking himself up, and into the explosive barrels. Somehow, of all the possibilities that could have gone wrong, in this one instance things worked out for the best.

But not for Baron Meade, who died there, his soul full of overwhelming malignant hate in the instant that he passed beyond. Would he be met by his wife and son – the lad he had sought to avenge? Would he be forgiven, and his terrible pain taken into account? He had, after all, been prevented each time from carrying out his greater plan. But he had tried, over and over again, in a misguided attempt to punish a whole nation for an event whose blame could not be accurately fixed. And he had murdered gentle Andrew.

And what about blame for me? Had I had a choice? Was there anything that I could have done, other than to kill him, there at the last? I like to think that I did what had to be done in the split second when given the opportunity, but I still recall to this day, so many years later, how I felt when pulling the trigger, at the same time purging the very last of my anger and despair from those past weeks. But not my grief. I shed one particular darkness, but the rest of the pain would stay with me for quite a while longer. I could only hope that my poor Constance, who had herself died in a bed two floors above where I then stood over the body of my latest victim, could see fit to understand and forgive me.

Chapter XXV
Ancient God

I slowly became aware that Holmes had joined me. He didn't say anything. We simply stood there, looking at the dead man while our breathing slowed. Then the sound of many heavy footsteps on the floor above became obvious. Holmes looked over at me. "We still have work to do." I nodded.

We were on our way back upstairs, Holmes having retrieved an item propped against a side wall, as Lestrade began to call, "Mr. Holmes! Dr. Watson!"

We met them in the hall, the inspectors and a bevy of constables who were fanning out in all directions. Two went to the cellar, where Baron Meade was waiting for his official discovery. "We ran when we heard the shots. You never gave your signal," said Lestrade, while Gregson moved up behind him. I felt comforted knowing they were there, even after the immediate danger had passed. The best of the Yarders, Holmes often called them, and he was right.

Holmes pulled a police whistle from his pocket with a rueful smile. "We never had time," he answered. "Not long after we entered, Daniel heard his brother speaking and charged in, setting things in motion."

"His brother?" asked Lanner.

"No matter," said Gregson. "We were here quickly, regardless."

"Quickly?" I said. "It feels as if an hour has passed."

"No, Doctor. It has only been about ten minutes since you both slipped out of the Parker house."

I nodded. "I've felt the same thing in battle, the same skewed passage of time. It distorts itself."

A constable leaned out of the consulting room. "Two of them are still alive in here."

"Two?" I said. "Then that means . . . ."

Realizing that I had forgotten the indications that Micah might not have died – that I might not have killed him after all – I rushed into that room where I had spent so much time over the last year, building up a business before suddenly deciding never to return. I had been unable to bear the idea of treating patients there while knowing Constance was gone from the rest of the house. And yet, here I was, kneeling over a wounded man who had been rolled back from his brother's dead body.

I had feared that I might have killed him, and as I had fired at Baron Meade downstairs, I had believed that I would have two souls on my conscience this night. I was more thankful than I could express that one of them would live after all. He had my bullet in his shoulder, in a spot not very different from where Dr. Withers, and myself for that matter, had once been injured. But he was strong, and the injury was not serious.

As I finished applying pressure to the wound, Micah started to regain consciousness. Behind me, Holmes said, "Watson."

I stood and turned, seeing that John Goins was propping himself up, while Holmes was kneeling and pressing his own handkerchief against the blood flowing from the man's scalp wound. When Goins was alert enough to snarl and take the cloth and apply pressure on his own, Holmes stood, making sure that constables were watching both of the injured men, and gestured toward the hallway. Lestrade, Gregson, Lanner, and I joined him.

He explained to them what had happened after we entered the house. The conversation, Daniel's interruption, and Micah's attempt to use the idol. His murder of his brother, Goins's actions, and then the Baron's desperate attempt to set off the explosives and how he was stopped. "For the plan to work, we will have to let them all go. Including Micah."

"But he killed his own brother!" said Lanner. "We can charge him with that, at least."

"We've discussed this already," said Gregson wearily. "We didn't know then that he would kill someone, but for this to work, they all have to go back. We didn't lure them in and go through all of this mummery to start arresting them now and then keep them in an English prison."

"They all have to return home and tell what happens here," Holmes added in a low voice. "Certainly Micah committed murder, but punishing him will be nothing compared to what we will gain by releasing him. And as you know, Lanner, I have been given the authority to speak for the Government in this problem."

Lanner looked as if he wanted to say something else, but stopped himself. "Lestrade," Holmes continued, "have all the other men that arrived with Goins been rounded up?"

"They have. As soon as you all went inside, we brought them in."

"And is that every one of them?"

"It is. We compared the names with the list that we have from Abraham, the one who was arrested. And he's been brought here as well."

"Excellent. Gather them outside for the performance, and we will be with you momentarily." He started to turn, and then added, "And don't forget to bring Luke and Benjamin. They must be told about Daniel's death, and how it happened – but I will do it."

"Very good, Mr. Holmes."

I went with him back into the consulting room, where he gestured toward the prisoners. "Get them up."

I started to protest that Micah's wound might begin to bleed again if he were forced to participate in what Holmes had planned, but I bit my tongue. This had gone too far to stop now, and the man had brought it upon himself.

Goins was jerked to his feet by his free arm, the other still holding the sodden handkerchief to his unusual skull. He glared at Holmes with something beyond hate, but it seemed to wash off my friend unnoticed while he stepped past the wounded men and leaned down, grabbing and lifting with one hand the idol resting against Daniel's corpse. His other hand still held the heavy object that he had retrieved before we ascended from the cellar.

"No, you can't – " hissed Goins as he started to comprehend, but a shake of his arm stopped him.

"Outside," Holmes said to the constables.

We followed them out. Both of the wounded men were led to the center of the empty street, where they were placed with the other conspirators that had arrived with them not that long ago. The houses surrounding us were all empty, their families removed for their own safety, and the windows, most dark but some lit to give the impression of occupancy, all stared down on our strange little drama.

By the foot of the steps were the two boys, Daniel's nephews, along with a constable. I saw that it was the same solid man who had introduced us to Benjamin the other day in Brunswick Place. His hands were resting paternally on both boys' shoulders.

Holmes briefly retold what had happened inside. The two lads, far older in experience than their actual years, took the news of the death of Daniel at Micah's hands in stoic silence. One way or the other, they had tragically lost all of them: Daniel, Andrew, and Micah, the only adult members of their band.

"In spite of his crime," Holmes said, "we are releasing Micah, as soon as he has had medical attention. Will you go with him?"

Both nodded, and Benjamin spoke. "We must see to the burial of our Uncle Daniel, in the same cemetery where Andrew was placed the other day. Then Micah will take us home. It is his duty. He knows this. After that, his fate will be up to our family."

I glanced over at Micah, surrounded by constables. One of them was helping Micah to stand, but the man seemed alert, with a haunted expression on his face.

Holmes nodded and dismissed the boys with his thanks. They were led into the street, near – but not part of – the group of prisoners.

Holmes, still carrying the idol in his right hand and the tool he had brought from the cellar in his left, took a deep breath and walked to an open space on the pavement in front of the gathering. The streetlights illuminated him as if he were on a stage. Clearing his throat, he raised the malign effigy, still covered in Daniel's blood and gore, high above his head and spoke in a commanding tone.

"*The Eye of Heka.* You've all been looking for it, one way or the other, for a long time. Here it is!"

Some directed their gazes toward it, straining to get a good look in the dim light, a combination of streetlights and what spilled from the house behind Holmes, as well as that coming from those neighboring windows that happened to be illuminated. The stone in his hand was dark, and Holmes rotated to display it from several angles.

While many of the men were looking up, others were looking with curiosity and growing consternation at the object held in Holmes's other hand – a heavy hammer, fastened to the end of a long oak handle. It had once been mine, left behind when I walked away from the house. Goins had seen it inside, and knew what the detective intended.

"This idol has been spoken of in legend for generations. It has been guarded by one group, to prevent its supposed evil from being released back into the world by another. It was buried and hidden to protect those who would try to use it from themselves." He paused and looked pointedly at Goins, who grimaced with rage. Micah watched impassively, while the other men and boys began to realize with certainty what was going to happen.

Holmes bent, setting the idol on the ground in front of him, laying it on its side, as if it were asleep or dead. "After it was brought here a decade ago, it was possessed by a man who gave it the credit for his successes. He was a fool. He was being lied to by another who made him believe in its false magic. Owning it obsessed him. It has destroyed him. But he wasn't the only one. You, John Goins – " And here Holmes raised the long hammer and pointed toward the primary prisoner. " – followed it here and waited for years, wasting a part of your life, trying to obtain it in order to selfishly advance your own wealth and power. Without ever having it in your possession, except for the few hours when you originally stole it, you have allowed it to control you, a loss which you will never get back." At this, Goins growled in rage. The constable beside him shook his arm.

"And on the other side," said Holmes, turning toward the two boys, "was the noble family that guarded the thing, also spending years of cumulative service. And for what? An empty satisfaction? Pride? In the end, it comes to this. I will free them, and all of us – all of *you* – from its threat." He turned back to the larger grouping. "Freed from the temptation

481

of using such a thing for wealth or power at the expense of the innocent who would be fooled by it, or the ones who would have their lives destroyed by following after it, or by being victimized by those who believe in it."

He took a step back, raising the long-handled heavy iron hammer in his hands as he did so. His voice rang and echoed from the nearby houses. "*Let this end!*" He swung the hammer high, as if it were an axe poised to split a log, and then started it on a downward trajectory with all his might. A sound between a sigh and a moan rose from the witnesses.

The prisoners tried to surge forward then, even if they already knew it was too late, realizing that what they had feared Holmes would do was true. But the policemen, and there were many of them there indeed, had all been briefed, and they held the captives in check.

I hoped that the stone was not too strong. That the impression that it gave of an impenetrable solidity was indeed only an illusion. I knew that it did not have any power, other than what men were willing to invest in it, but for this to work, it had to be destroyed. The hammer could not glance off, leaving it unbroken, with no disfiguring mark at all. The idol's undoing had to be *seen*.

I need not have worried. At the first blow, the thing shattered into three large pieces, and countless smaller ones as well. Several chips flew off into the darkness. A unified cry went up behind me, but I didn't turn to look, watching as Holmes again raised the hammer. Down it swung, and one of the larger pieces was pulverized. And again. And again. Finally there only remained the segment with part of the face still remaining, and the ruby. Holmes rolled this into position with the toe of his boot, the gem on top, and he attacked it one more time, one hand fixed at the base of the hammer handle as a pivot point, the other sliding from the metal end down toward the base as it rotated around him and full into its target.

Holmes had obviously put an extra effort into that blow, and the hammer bounced back, leaving nothing on the ground but black gravel. Almost unbelievably, the ruby was literally gone, the force striking it in just the right place to completely disintegrate it, its dust joining that of the more common rock in the street around it. Holmes straightened, kicking back and forth with his foot, dispersing the remnants. Just then, the wind, which had been picking up for the last few minutes, no doubt a result of the rain clouds that had slowly been accumulating overhead all afternoon, gusted down the street, assisting his efforts by scattering and carrying away a great portion of the smallest pieces. He couldn't have planned it better for dramatic effect if he'd tried.

He looked up then at all the men in front of him, some watching with disbelief, others with anger, and all realizing that there was nothing else for them to do. Their talisman was gone, out of their reach forever.

Holmes's gaze found Lestrade and Gregson, standing to the side with Lanner, and said quietly, "Get them out of here."

Although that was the plan, it wasn't quite that easy, as a Black Maria had to be called from the side streets, where it had been waiting for quite a while – in fact, since some point following Goins and Micah's initial arrival. The conveyance pulled into the street, followed by several other wagons, all there to carry away the explosives in the cellar.

Holmes watched as Goins's men were loaded, to be taken to a ship that would immediately remove them to their homeland, as was part of the plan. No charges would be filed, as it was felt that getting them out of the country and back home, where they could spread the story of the idol's ultimate destruction, was the best solution to the problem.

Holmes, leaning on the hammer, watched without expression as Goins was led away with the others. The man turned often to look at Holmes, his face filled with hatred. He stumbled several times as he kept his eyes fixed toward my friend instead of where he was going, but the constable's firm grip on his arm kept him upright and moving in the right direction. He was the last to be loaded, and as the door slammed shut, Holmes murmured to me, "We will have trouble with him again."

I wanted to say, "Surely not," but I knew better. And Holmes was right, but that is another tale.

As the Maria left, we could hear Goins intoning, over and over again like a mantra, my friend's name in that sinister hissing rasp, the sound of it floating on the wind. *"Sherlock Holmes! Sherlock Holmes!"*

Micah, looking like a broken man, was not loaded with the other prisoners, but rather helped into a growler, along with his two nephews. They would also be departing immediately after seeing to the injured man's bullet wound, but not on the same ship as the others.

"Daniel's death was unfortunate," said Holmes to me. "But perhaps that was his destiny."

"Like that of his brother, Andrew," I added.

"Both good men, indeed. Their part of the world needs such as them. As does ours. I hope there are others to take their place."

"There are, Holmes, there are."

Holmes glanced toward the wagons, now pulling up in front of the door in the space vacated by the Maria. "I don't know what happened in ancient times, the times of legend. About how much evil was truly associated with this idol. But the fact that its existence led to the deaths of those two men is unforgiveable."

483

I started to reply with some vague metaphysical insight when I was interrupted. "Dr. Watson?" called a constable from the perimeter of the activity.

I looked that way and saw the man. Standing beside him, being prevented from approaching closer, was Jenny Withers. She was waving an arm, calling, "John! John!"

"Oh, dear Lord," I muttered.

Holmes's eyes narrowed. "This is no longer amusing."

"I agree. It ends now." Louder, I said, "Let her through, Constable!"

Hearing that, she ran toward me while Holmes went inside the house. Her arms spread as she got closer, as if she intended to throw herself into my embrace. My own arms came up as well, not to fold around her, but pushed out in front, to grip her by the shoulders and stop her.

She looked surprised, and the expectant look on her face became peevish.

"Miss Withers, what are you doing here?"

"Father told me about the man who was in the house. About why he was so obsessed with you, and the plan to stop him. I slipped out to make sure you were all right."

"You should not be here."

My hands were still gripping her upper arms, as several times she had made small motions, as if to wiggle free and approach me. She looked from side to side with irritation at her trap. I released my hands, taking a step back from her as I did so. She started forward, and I took another. She finally seemed to realize that I did not want to be clasped to her. She looked confused.

"Is everything well?" she asked.

"Yes, the man has been captured, and the explosives are being removed as we speak. The house will need airing out, but it should be ready for you to move in within days."

"No, is everything well between us? Why do you push me away?"

It was then that I truly began to fear that she was mad. Not in the sense that Baron Meade had been, allowing his obsession and hatred to run rampant to unimaginable degrees. But she was obsessed in her own way, and convinced that when she wanted something, it would be hers, no matter what.

"Miss Withers," I sighed, and then I began to grow more irritated. Could I have made it any clearer? "Miss Withers." This time it came out sharply, and her eyes widened. "There is no *us*. What do I need to do to make you understand?"

"But John, you are not thinking. You are trapped by conventional thinking – "

484

"Miss Withers! That's enough of that! You say that over and over, but it has nothing to do with any worry that I might have about what society would think if I were to remarry again too quickly! I know that she's gone, but I still love my wife. I can't end that as if I've finished a book and put it on the shelf, pulling out the very next one. I still love her, and *I do not love you!*"

I thought about saying something else. Rephrasing it to make it easier, or in words that might make sense to her. I could tell her that she was beautiful, and that it was my fault and not hers, and that she would find someone else. That she didn't know me enough to love me. I might try to shock her by pointing out that my similarity to her father was possibly a disturbing factor and a cause of her obsession. I might have done any of that, but that would simply keep intact this tangled web of back-and-forth that I had somehow found strangling me, continuing to perpetuate a cycle of emotions that I simply did not want or need. God help me, I still loved my wife, my dear departed sweet wife, and that was the end of it.

And maybe this time she finally saw all of this in my eyes. Certainly her expression changed as she let out her breath and settled back on her heels. The wide hopeful expression that she had arrived with faded to a neutral – if still calculating – look. Before she could rally and come up with yet another new argument, I shook my head with finality. "Goodbye, Miss Withers." And I walked into the house.

I didn't stop to see when she left, and I was glad that she didn't follow. I hoped that this was over. It's true that many men wouldn't have looked at it that way at all. To them, a wife was an essential part of the machine that makes up a household, and if that part was broken, it was to be quickly replaced, in order to get the machine up and running again. I've never viewed a marriage that way, and while Jenny Withers would no doubt make a fine, intelligent, and beautiful wife for someone, she would not for me.

Inside, the house was quiet, except for noises from downstairs. I noticed various and sundry wheel tracks running along the floor from the front to the cellar door, where dollies had been pushed, carrying out barrels and boxes and cartons while I had been talking to Miss Withers. I wondered if we would ever know what his final target would have been. Parliament, repeating the failed efforts of Guy Fawkes and his band? Trafalgar Square, where his son had been injured, later to die? The Palace, and the Royal family he had once so ably served? Possibly he had written it all down somewhere, but more likely it was contained within his head. Perhaps he wouldn't have decided until the day that the materials were to be moved. It was likely that we would never know.

485

Down in the cellar, I was relieved to see that the Baron's body had been removed, although his blood still stained the floor. Would the new tenants realize what it was? Or would they think it was just another of the patches that darkened and blemished the ground here and there?

I noticed that there were two barrels left, both with the last of the flammable oil. Men were loading one of them onto a dolly, while the other barrel stood to the side. Another worker with a second dolly broke away from the group and started toward it, but Holmes said, "Leave that one for a few minutes." The man nodded and went back to help the men with the first.

As they rolled it to the steps, Holmes said, "This is the last of it."

"Where will it go? Woolwich Arsenal?"

Holmes laughed. "For what purpose? Separated, there is nothing more deadly here than nitrogen, oil, and machine parts. It will all be dispersed where it can be best used, as a donation from Baron Meade. The nitrogen compounds will doubtless be used to fertilize flower gardens in one of the parks, the fuel to heat Scotland Yard, and I arranged for the machine parts to be sent to the warehouse in Rotherhithe, where the Baron, while pretending to be Mr. Walthrop, first told us that such things were being stolen when trying to decoy us away from his last cache."

"That seems so long ago. It's difficult to believe that it is finished."

Holmes looked speculatively at the workmen, who had pulled the loaded dolly up one step at a time. Their feet were disappearing as they reached the floor above. "Not quite finished," he replied softly.

He stepped to a side table, which I noticed had some clean towels placed upon it, obviously cadged from upstairs. "Those are Dr. Withers' property now," I said. "You're going to ruin them."

"I'll send him some more." He looked toward me as he started to remove his coat. "That is, unless it would be a bad idea to reopen communications with the two of them."

I nodded. "Perhaps you're right. I have no doubt that Miss Withers will want to buy her own towels, and not use the ones that I've left behind."

"Miss Withers?" Holmes was rolling up his right shirt sleeve, pushing it as high on his arm as it would go. "Not Jenny?"

"Definitely not."

He nodded with a smile, and then moved to the last remaining barrel. It had a fresh-looking scratch on the side. I pointed toward it. "Is that how you knew which one?"

"Yes. I made the mark last night. I only had a moment to act, after I swapped the idols."

I reached for a towel, as he would soon need it. "And the real one really was too heavy or awkward for you to bring back with you?"

He nodded, contemplating what he was preparing to do. "After I found the real idol here in the cellar, I opened the bag and pulled out the fake that has rested in the Museum for so long. I had hoped when I retrieved it and brought it back with me to Baker Street that I might find some use for it, and luckily a plan presented itself, as you just witnessed.

"Last night, I quickly exchanged the false object for the real thing standing upon the table, and then planned to bring the true Eye back with me to the Parker's house. But it was too heavy, and I feared that I wouldn't be able to climb back up the coal chute – especially as I heard the Baron begin to move about upstairs. I thought this barrel would be as safe a place to leave the real one as any. After all, who would think to look here?"

He removed the lid from the barrel and then bent over it, plunging his lean arm into the oil. He grimaced, either from the unpleasant sensation or from the cold, and moved his arm back and forth for a moment before his expression changed to one of success. Straightening up, he lifted out an object in his firm grasp, shiny and dripping with oil. It was The Eye of Heka.

Even in the light of a single lantern, I could see the difference between this one and the ersatz object that Holmes had just destroyed in the street, for the benefit of his audience. That one, having acted for years as the Earl of Wardlaw's decoy in the British Museum, before being brought to Baker Street by Holmes and then on to the Parker house the previous day, had been a cold and dead rock. This . . . this seemed to have some sort of glimmer, as if it were only partly here, while translating back and again instantaneously from some other place.

And then there was the ruby, the Eye itself, in the center of its forehead. It had a fire of its own that glowed and shifted in a way that was more, in some curious way, than could be simply caused by the motion given to it by Holmes's grip. This, then, was what had undoubtedly fascinated Ian Finch for so long. Was it possible that only some people could see what I now detected? Was its power, in fact, *real*?

Realizing this, I wondered how anyone could have ever been fooled by the spurious figure. Daniel and Micah hadn't known any better, I suppose, having never seen it, and the same was true for the others. But Goins had held the real thing in his hands a decade ago, when he had managed to steal it while working in the Museum as a janitor. Surely he had seen then what I saw now. How could he *not* have seen it? He had earlier given every indication upstairs that he believed that one to be the true idol, both when Micah had attempted to use it, and again when he himself had made the attempt. He had believed it then. But then again, *had he really?*

When he had first received it from the Baron, and had held it, we had heard him say that there was something almost anticlimactic about it. Did he somehow realize the truth then without knowing it? And would his brooding ruminations through the endless hours and days while returning to his homeland allow him to arrive at the realization that he had been tricked? Manipulated into believing that he had seen the true idol destroyed, in order that he would return home and quash for all time the legends of The Eye?

Even as I questioned whether Holmes's elaborate scheme would succeed or fail, my friend was turning the thing from side to side, having lowered it down to his eye level. Was it my imagination, or did Holmes himself appear to take on the same glimmer I thought I had seen? It seemed to pass down his arm, and so on to the rest of him. Did my friend's eyes start to glow with the same power that emanated from The Eye? Did the best and wisest man I have ever known begin to grow while the room darkened and diminished around him?

But then the spell was broken as Holmes gave a merry laugh and shook some of the dripping oil away. A drop hit the lantern's glass chimney and sizzled and smoked. I gave a start. Looking my way, Holmes said powerfully, "No ancient gods need apply, eh, Watson?"

I took a deep breath, feeling as if I had become a statue myself for a moment and was only coming back to life with a great effort. I walked the few steps awkwardly toward him, as if from a faraway place, handing over the towel that I held so tightly in my hand. "As you say, Holmes. As you say."

Chapter XXVI
Manageable Pieces

Morning found us in Baker Street. The clouds of the previous night had continued to build, and sometime late the rains had started. Although the temperature was noticeably warmer, it was obviously miserable outside, and both of us were glad to be in for the moment.

After Holmes had dried himself and The Eye the night before, he had rolled down his sleeve, put on his coat, and then wrapped the thing in some more of the towels, carrying it discreetly up and out of the house. He let the men outside know that the last barrel in the cellar was ready to be removed. When they had done so, he handed me my old key, and I locked the house behind me and walked away without looking back.

The last wagon departed, and Holmes and I found ourselves standing in the empty street. I knew that the inspectors were busy carrying out final details elsewhere, getting the witnesses to Holmes's charade from both camps to the ships that would carry them away – Micah and the boys in one, Goins and his people in the other – notifying the residents of the neighborhood that they could return, and making reports to their superiors. There were criminal cases to build and prosecute against Sir Edward Malloy and his ally, Dawson. Perhaps charges would also be filed against Ian Finch, the Earl of Wardlaw, but I knew that, whether or not he was found guilty of any crime, he was as finished as if he had been pulled down in a maelstrom.

There was no doubt that the inspectors would be visiting Baker Street later on to confer, so this would be a late night. I checked my watch, and found that it was still actually rather early, and we would arrive home really no later than if we had spent a night at a theatre performance. I knew that Mrs. Hudson would be willing to provide us with something tasty with a great deal of hot coffee.

And so it proved. Lestrade, Gregson, and Lanner arrived, explaining that everything had taken place without a hitch. Although some in the government wanted to question them, it was felt best that the all the men rounded up the previous night should be taken to the docks and sent on their way as soon as possible for the ruse to succeed. A formal arrest had been made of the hospitalized Sir Edward, with the unraveling of the strands of his web only beginning. Charges against Dawson were revised, and the Earl of Wardlaw's involvement was being considered. Gregson and Lestrade were both in an expansive and celebratory humor, but Lanner seemed especially subdued, as if he was a bit ashamed of any inner doubts that he might have had about the plan. Holmes seemed to understand, and went out of his way to be gracious.

And now it was the next morning, he and I were in our chairs before the cheery fire, and all was right. Yet I still felt a sense of dissatisfaction. Some of it was related to that sense of loss associated with the reason that I was living back in Baker Street in the first place. A part of it could not be separated from how I had been forced to treat Jenny Withers. And even now I was uncertain as to whether she actually understood what I had told her the previous night. With the first morning's post had come yet another invitation to tea, this time from Dr. Withers himself. I located a heavy envelope and placed the key to the Doctor's new residence inside, along with the invitation. I rooted around in my desk until I found one of my old cards. I boldly underlined in ink the address shown on the front, *221b Baker Street*, shoved it into the envelope and sealed it up with no other response. Dispatching it by way of the page boy, I settled back in my chair and hoped that this would finish it.

Yet the dissatisfaction remained, and it seemed as if the largest part of my dour mood was related to how some of the events of the previous evening had turned out, with the death of Daniel and the ruin of Micah. I had been forced to kill a man, in spite of the fact that I knew he had left me no choice.

And then, as I looked up above my chair at The Eye of Heka, sitting and staring into eternity on our scarred mantel, I wondered again if Goins and the others had truly been fooled by Holmes's elaborate plan.

Of course, my friend saw me glance up and knew exactly what I was thinking. "Even if he doesn't really believe it," said Holmes, "he will never find a way to confirm it for sure. Later today, I will deliver The Eye into the hands of the Foreign Office, and it will be hidden away for good, never to see the light of day again."

"That sounds as if something much more secure than a vault at the British Museum has been planned."

"This time, it has." After a pause, he added, "Or so I'm told."

I thought about that. Then, "Would we have tried so hard – ? No, that's not what I want to ask. Would it have *mattered* as much if we had known that Goins never really intended to start a war? That he only cared about influencing the people for his own greedy advancement?"

"I believe so. Just because Goins's personal intention over the years had become a quest for his own wealth and power didn't diminish the overall power of the legend in others' eyes. And Goins would eventually been tempted to use the idol's influence and reputation for bigger things. Just the knowledge that it existed would have inflamed those who *had* wanted to use it all along for what we feared. If Goins himself hadn't used it to achieve those purposes, someone else would have taken it from him and done so instead."

I stood up and looked at the thing more closely. I knew for certain that I would never ask Holmes about what I had seen – or *imagined* that I had seen – last night, as I supposed now in the light of day must have been the case. Then, it had seemed . . . well, I'm not sure how it had seemed, but today it was only a crude carving, nothing more. Although it *looked* better-crafted than the substitute commissioned long ago by the Earl, and the ruby was undoubtedly real, it was only cold and lifeless, a stub of polished rock.

In spite of how we had wiped it down the previous night, it had left a ring of oil on our much-damaged mantelpiece. But that was nothing worse than many of the other indignities that the poor woodwork had faced, pierced on a daily basis by Holmes's jackknife to hold correspondence, and a constant repository for all sorts of criminal relics, each with its own dark history. Soon the idol would be taken down from there and gone, locked away, and this adventure would just be another series of connected links in a long chain, to be recalled, and perhaps written about, boiled down to manageable pieces that could be organized and examined from a distance while the sharp details faded smooth. And every day that progressed, the same thing would happen with the pieces of my former married life as well.

But that is how one moves on. It is a terrible feeling to know that the little things, the everyday smiles and words of comfort and even the irritations and vexations, will eventually be forgotten. But it happens, every day, as the mind prunes old growth, and to stay sane one must accept it and travel forward. If one does not, if one broods and picks at it and spirals around and around, then all can become madness. It had happened to Baron Meade, that poor tortured man. I would mourn for him, in spite of his crimes, and not let it happen to me.

The rain seemed to blow harder at that moment, hitting the window like shot. "I don't envy your trip to the Foreign Office."

"*My* trip?" said Holmes with a smile. "Certainly you mean *our* trip. I expected you to accompany me as my bodyguard."

"I plan to sit here with my feet up and have a sip or two of something warm."

"I'm afraid I must insist."

"And *I* insist that when you return, you clean up some of these papers." I gestured toward his desk – and mine as well – where the piles and stacks, leaning precariously on and across one another, still threatened to topple onto the carpet. "Your precious filing system will be worthless if those fall and the dust that lies atop it is scattered."

He glanced that way. "I suppose I do have just enough room for some of it." He stood abruptly and crossed to his bedroom. I heard the familiar sliding and tugging, and then he was back with the old tin trunk, that repository of the records relating to so many of his old cases. Opening it, he sighed. Then, with a sudden interested expression on his face, he reached in and withdrew a folded woolen cloth. Inside was a small test-tube, closed with a stopper. A reddish liquid inside it flowed back and forth as he upended it several times, bottom over top.

"What is that?"

"This, Watson, is a vial of blood from Eldridge, the Brighton Fiend."

"A vial of a man's blood? Why on earth did you save that?"

"It is a curiosity, and the clue that solved the case. I obtained this sample myself. It is more than nine years old, and yet, as you can see, it has refused to clot or dry up."

"What? Impossible."

"Clearly not, as you can easily observe. I assure you this is the same blood that I took from the man himself." He held it up to the light, pouring it again back and forth, and then suddenly directed a sly gaze toward me. "Would you like to hear the story?"

I snorted. "I see what you're doing, Holmes. You're trying to distract me again. Well, I won't put up with it. Not this time. I – "

I was interrupted from further remonstrations when the front bell rang, rather frantically. Holmes and I both looked at each other, and he quietly replaced the vial in the trunk before shutting the lid. He then set about taking it into his room.

By the time he had returned, having changed out of his dressing gown to something more suitable, Mrs. Hudson had shown a lovely young woman of about twenty into the sitting room. She was veiled and soaked and chattering with the cold, but I could see that she was terrified as well. Clutched in her hand was a thin red ribbon, to which was tied a bone that I recognized as a human distal phalange – undoubtedly the tip of a thumb.

I directed her to the basket chair, where she could avail herself of the fire's warmth, while Holmes sat and took the bone from her grasp. As she raised her veil and I took a position nearby, he said, "Hmm, a butcher's thumb. Not very old. The signs are obvious. It arrived by this morning's post." He glanced at the girl. "Dorset, undoubtedly. This ribbon is faded, but only in spots, where it has been long creased. Most surprising is your unspoken conviction that you know the man who owned this thumb." He waited for some acknowledgement, but the poor girl remained quiet. Then, warily, she nodded.

492

Leaning forward with his fingertips pressed together before his chin, the grave expression of a bird of prey was noticeably etched upon his lean features, contradicting the excitement dancing in his eyes.

"Now, Miss – how can we help?"

About the Author

David Marcum plays *The Game* with deadly seriousness. He first discovered Sherlock Holmes in 1975 at the age of ten, and since that time, he has collected, read, and chronologicized literally thousands of traditional Holmes pastiches in the form of novels, short stories, radio and television episodes, movies and scripts, comics, fan-fiction, and unpublished manuscripts. He is the author of over eighty Sherlockian pastiches, some published in anthologies and magazines such as *The Strand*, and others collected in his own books, *The Papers of Sherlock Holmes*, *Sherlock Holmes and A Quantity of Debt*, and *Sherlock Holmes – Tangled Skeins*. He has edited almost sixty books, including several dozen traditional Sherlockian anthologies, such as the ongoing series *The MX Book of New Sherlock Holmes Stories*, which he created in 2015. This collection is now up to 27 volumes, with more in preparation.

He was responsible for bringing back August Derleth's Solar Pons for a new generation, first with his collection of authorized Pons stories, *The Papers of Solar Pons*, and then by editing the reissued authorized versions of the original Pons books, and then volumes of new Pons adventures. He has done the same for the adventures of Dr. Thorndyke, and has plans for similar projects in the future. He has contributed numerous essays to various publications, and is a member of a number of Sherlockian groups and Scions. His irregular Sherlockian blog, *A Seventeen Step Program*, addresses various topics related to his favorite book friends (as his son used to call them when he was small), and can be found at *http://17stepprogram.blogspot.com/*

He is a licensed Civil Engineer, living in Tennessee with his wife and son. Since the age of nineteen, he has worn a deerstalker as his regular-and-only hat. In 2013, he and his deerstalker were finally able make his first trip-of-a-lifetime Holmes Pilgrimage to England, with return Pilgrimages in 2015 and 2016, where you may have spotted him. If you ever run into him and his deerstalker out and about, feel free to say hello!

497

498

Edited by David Marcum
from MX Publishing
The MX Book of New Sherlock Holmes Stories
(MX Publishing, 2015-   )

"This is the finest volume of Sherlockian fiction I have ever read, and I have read, literally, thousands." – Philip K. Jones

"Beyond Impressive . . . This is a splendid venture for a great cause!"
– Roger Johnson, Editor, *The Sherlock Holmes Journal,*
The Sherlock Holmes Society of London

Part I: 1881-1889
Part II: 1890-1895
Part III: 1896-1929
Part IV: 2016 Annual
Part V: Christmas Adventures
Part VI: 2017 Annual
Part VII: Eliminate the Impossible (1880-1891)
Part VIII – Eliminate the Impossible (1892-1905)
Part IX – 2018 Annual (1879-1895)
Part X – 2018 Annual (1896-1916)
Part XI – Some Untold Cases (1880-1891)
Part XII – Some Untold Cases (1894-1902)
Part XIII – 2019 Annual (1881-1890)
Part XIV – 2019 Annual (1891-1897)
Part XV – 2019 Annual (1898-1917)
Part XVI – Whatever Remains . . . Must be the Truth (1881-1890)
Part XVII – Whatever Remains . . . Must be the Truth (1891-1898)
Part XVIII – Whatever Remains . . . Must be the Truth (1898-1925)
Part XIX – 2020 Annual (1882-1890)
Part XX – 2020 Annual (1891-1897)
Part XXI – 2020 Annual (1898-1923)
Part XXII – Some More Untold Cases (1877-1887)
Part XXIII – Some More Untold Cases (1888-1894)
Part XXIV – Some More Untold Cases (1895-1903)
Part XXV – 2021 Annual (1881-1888)
Part XXVI – 2021 Annual (1889-1897)
Part XXVII – 2021 Annual (1898-1928)
Part XXVIII – More Christmas Adventures (1869-1888)
Part XXIX – More Christmas Adventures (1889-1896)
Part XXX – More Christmas Adventures (1897-1928)
In Preparation
Part XXXI (and XXXII and XXXIII?) – 2022 Annual

. . . and more to come!

Edited by David Marcum
from MX Publishing
The MX Book of New Sherlock Holmes Stories
(MX Publishing, 2015-   )

<u>*Publishers Weekly*</u> says:

Part VI: *The traditional pastiche is alive and well . . . .*

Part VII: *Sherlockians eager for faithful-to-the-canon plots
and characters will be delighted.*

Part VIII: *The imagination of the contributors in coming up with variations on the
volume's theme is matched by their ingenious resolutions.*

Part IX: *The 18 stories . . . will satisfy fans of Conan Doyle's originals. Sherlockians will
rejoice that more volumes are on the way.*

Part X: *. . . new Sherlock Holmes adventures of consistently high quality.*

Part XI: *. . . an essential volume for Sherlock Holmes fans.*

Part XII: *. . . continues to amaze with the number of high-quality pastiches.*

Part XIII: *. . . Amazingly, Marcum has found 22 superb pastiches . . . This is more catnip
for fans of stories faithful to Conan Doyle's original*

Part XIV: *. . . this standout anthology of 21 short stories written in the spirit of Conan
Doyle's originals.*

Part XV: *Stories pitting Sherlock Holmes against seemingly supernatural phenomena
highlight Marcum's 15th anthology of superior short pastiches.*

Part XVI: *Marcum has once again done fans of Conan Doyle's originals a service.*

Part XVII: *This is yet another impressive array of new but traditional Holmes stories.*

Part XVIII: *Sherlockians will again be grateful to Marcum and MX for high-quality new
Holmes tales.*

Part XIX: *Inventive plots and intriguing explorations of aspects of Dr. Watson's life and
beliefs lift the 24 pastiches in Marcum's impressive 19th Sherlock Holmes anthology*

Part XX: *Marcum's reserve of high-quality new Holmes exploits seems endless.*

Part XXI: *This is another must-have for Sherlockians.*

Part XXII: *Marcum's superlative 22nd Sherlock Holmes pastiche anthology features 21
short stories that successfully emulate the spirit of Conan Doyle's originals while
expanding on the canon's tantalizing references to mysteries Dr. Watson never got
around to chronicling.*

Part XXIII: *Marcum's well of talented authors able to mimic the
feel of The Canon seems bottomless.*

Part XXIV: *Marcum's expertise at selecting high-quality
pastiches remains impressive.*

Part XXV: *The variety of plots is matched by the contributors' skills.
Once again, those who relish traditional Holmes stories will be delighted.*

Edited by David Marcum
from MX Publishing
The MX Book of New Sherlock Holmes Stories
(MX Publishing, 2015-   )

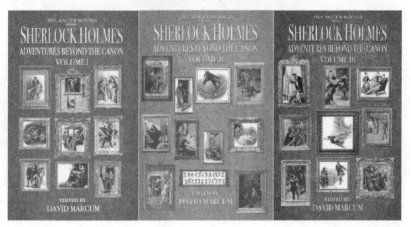
503

Edited by David Marcum
from Belanger Books

Sherlock Holmes: Before Baker Street

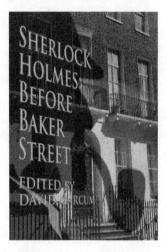

Sherlock Holmes and Doctor Watson:
The Early Adventures
Volumes I, II, and III

Edited by David Marcum
from MX Publishing

Imagination Theatre's Sherlock Holmes

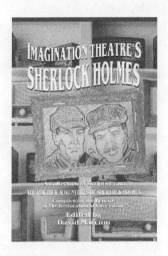

The Further Adventures of Sherlock Holmes:
The Complete Jim French Imagination Theatre Scripts

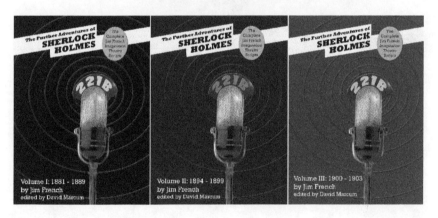

Edited by David Marcum
from MX Publishing

Sherlock Holmes in Montague Street
by Arthur Morrison
Sherlock Holmes's Early Investigations
Originally published as Martin Hewitt Adventures

Complete Hardcover Edition and Three-volume Paperback Edition

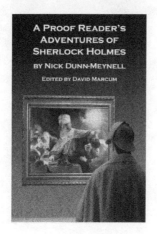

Edited by David Marcum
from Belanger Books

The Complete Solar Pons
by August Derleth

8-volume Paperback Edition

4-volume Hardcover Edition

Edited by David Marcum
from Belanger Books

The New Adventures of Solar Pons

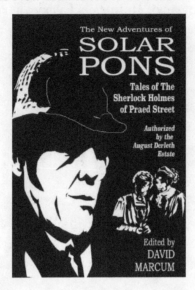

**The Meeting of the Minds:
The Cases of Sherlock Holmes and Solar Pons**

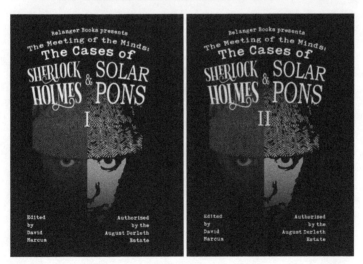

*Edited by David Marcum,
Derrick Belanger, and Sonia Fetherston*
from Belanger Books

Sherlock Holmes is Everywhere!

MX Publishing

MX Publishing is the world's largest specialist Sherlock Holmes publisher, with over five-hundred titles and over two-hundred authors creating the latest in Sherlock Holmes fiction and non-fiction

The catalogue includes several award winning books, and over two-hundred-and-fifty have been converted into audio.

MX Publishing also has one of the largest communities of Holmes fans on Facebook, with regular contributions from dozens of authors.

www.mxpublishing.com

@mxpublishing on Facebook, Twitter and Instagram

CPSIA information can be obtained
at www.ICGtesting.com
Printed in the USA
BVHW032021211021
619240BV00001B/1

9 781787 059047